Painful

S.C. STEPHENS

Painful

S.C. STEPHENS

PAINFUL

S.C. STEPHENS

Copyright © 2022 by S.C. Stephens

All rights reserved. This is a work of fiction. Names, characters, places, brands, media, and incidents are either the product of the author's imagination or are used fictitiously. The author acknowledges the trademarked status and trademark owners of various products referenced in this work of fiction, which have been used without permission. The publication/use of these trademarks is not authorized, associated with, or sponsored by the trademark owners.

Without limiting the rights under copyright reserved above, no part of this publication may be reproduced, stored in or introduced into a retrieval system, or transmitted, in any form, or by any means (electronic, mechanical, photocopying, recording, or otherwise) without the prior written permission of the above copyright owner of this book.

Cover design © Hang Le byhangle.com

Editing by Madison Seidler Editing Services madisonseidler.com

Formatting by HMG Formatting *(hmgformatting@gmail.com)*

First Edition: 2022

Library of Congress Cataloging-in-Publication Data

Painful – 1st *edition*

ISBN: *979-8-41728-152-5*

BOOKS BY S.C. STEPHENS

THOUGHTLESS SERIES

Thoughtless
Effortless (Book 2)
Reckless (Book 3)
Thoughtful (Thoughtless alternate POV)
Painful (Effortless alternate POV)
Untamed (Book 4)

RUSH SERIES

Furious Rush
Dangerous Rush (Book 2)
Undeniable Rush (Book 3)

CONVERSION SERIES

Conversion
Bloodlines (Book 2)
'Til Death (Book 3)
The Next Generation (Book 4)
The Beast Within (Book 5)
Family is Forever (Book 6)

STANDALONE BOOKS

Collision Course
It's All Relative
Under the Northern Lights
Something Like Perfect

For everyone at Pete's Bar. Thank you for keeping Kellan alive.

Chapter 1
EVERYTHING I'VE ALWAYS WANTED

The summer sun pounded on me as I waited in the backstage area with my bandmates, Evan, Matt, and Griffin. The merciless rays made sweat form in every nook and cranny on my body, but I didn't care. It could have been twenty degrees hotter, and I wouldn't have cared. I was about to perform at the largest venue the D-Bags had ever played at—Bumbershoot. And while that fact filled me with adrenaline, it wasn't what was giving me an almost giddy sense of euphoria. My girlfriend was going to be in the crowd. *Girlfriend*. Just the word made me feel like I was floating. Kiera Allen was now mine, wholly and completely. She *loved* me, a fact that was still hard to grasp sometimes. I'd gotten so used to no one giving a shit. But Kiera did, and my band did, and that was more than enough for me. More than I ever thought I'd get out of this life.

"Fucking hell...I'm so nervous."

I turned to see Matt clutching his guitar case, looking for all the world like he wished he could hide inside it. Matt was the brains behind the band. He handled our schedule, made sure we were all where we were supposed to be, basically kept us on track. While Matt pushed for our success, he had always been a little apprehensive about performing. Not because of the music—he loved that part—but because the stress of being in the spotlight was something he struggled with every time he went on stage. It made me appreciate him doing this for us even more. But for him, the D-Bags playing at Bumbershoot never would have happened; we'd probably still be playing out of a garage or something.

"You'll be fine," I said, clapping the thin blond on the back. "It's just like Pete's." Matt smiled, but there wasn't any humor in his pale eyes.

Matt's almost identical lookalike, his cousin, Griffin, slung an arm over Matt's shoulders. "Yeah, do what I do, cuz...picture 'em all naked. And screwing. Hot and heavy, all getting it on with each other...Yeah..."

Griffin closed his light blue eyes as he imagined the orgy, then he started gyrating his hips, like he was joining in on the fun. Griffin was the...comic relief of the band. Or the annoyance that we put up with. Depended on the day.

Matt cringed away from Griffin's antics and knocked his arm off him. "Dude, go have pretend sex with the audience somewhere else, please." Thinking of something, he fisted Griffin's shirt before he started walking away. "Griffin, I swear, if you include my girlfriend in that fantasy, it will be the last fantasy you ever have." Matt had never been one to date before, since the band kept him so busy, but he'd started seeing Rachel a few months ago, and they were still going strong. Kiera constantly told me they were adorable together. I supposed they were. All I really cared was that my friend finally seemed happy with someone.

A slow smile crept over Griffin's face. "Too late, man." He tapped his skull. "Rachel has already satisfied me several times. For being so shy, she's damn feisty. You're a lucky guy."

Matt's face went bright red, and he immediately lunged for Griffin. Luckily, Evan and I had been prepared for that reaction—keeping Matt and Griffin from killing each other was kind of our job in the band. We both grabbed one of Matt's arms right before he could assault his cousin.

Griffin laughed as we held Matt tight. "Dude, lighten up...I was joking. I'm fucking Anna on a near-daily basis. I don't need to fantasize about your little gal pal."

I could tell Matt was still annoyed, but he rolled his eyes and relaxed in our arms. "Not funny, Griffin. At all."

Not agreeing with his assessment, Griffin laughed even harder. "You should have seen your face, man. Oh God, classic."

Releasing Matt, I smacked Griffin across the chest. "Don't be an ass right before a show," I told him. If he'd said that about Kiera, I probably would have attacked him too. And I'd have nailed the fucker.

Griffin rubbed his chest, an offended look on his face. "Dude, I was helping him get over his anxiety. You still nervous, cuz?"

Matt frowned as he shook his head. "No, now I want to go out there just to get away from you."

Griffin's face shifted into a satisfied smile. "See...helping."

Closing my eyes, I inhaled a calming breath. "Griff, do me favor..." I cracked an eye open. "Never try to help me."

Griffin winked and gave me finger guns, and I knew, without a doubt, he'd be "helping" me in the future, in his own special, Griffin-like way. I barely contained my sigh.

One of the crew let us know it was time, and Matt and Griffin disappeared onto the stage. Screams from the boisterous crowd pierced the air, and pulsing energy radiated through my body, gathering strength like a coiled spring waiting to be released.

Evan clapped me on the back. "See you up there, Kell." He had a warm, easy smile on his face, and his dark eyes were eager but untroubled. Evan was probably the most laidback person I knew. Nothing much seemed to rile him, a fact I appreciated since I wasn't always the nicest guy. Especially when I was mad. Or in pain. Hopefully, those days were behind me.

Evan turned to follow Matt and Griffin onto the stage, and my eyes drifted to the colorful mosaic covering Evan's arms. All of my bandmates were littered with tattoos. I only had one, and it was all I would ever need in this lifetime—Kiera's name, right over my heart. Closing my eyes, I put my hand over the tattoo, bathing myself in her warmth, even though she wasn't physically near me. *Let's do this.*

When I reopened my eyes, I couldn't hold back my grin. It was showtime, and aside from being with Kiera, being onstage was my favorite place to be. I felt different the moment I stepped onto a stage—calm, in control, more at peace, less...moody, as Kiera would put it. Even when my life had been falling apart, performing had given me comfort. They probably didn't realize it, but I owed my fans everything.

When I stepped onto the stage, the screams went from ear-piercing to brain-liquifying. I smiled at the fans' never-ending devotion, then raised my hand in a wave. Damn. There were so many people here...Matt must be freaking out. I secreted a glance his way, but he seemed fine...if fine meant ignoring the crowd and remaining steadfastly focused on his instrument. He'd be truly fine once he started playing. Griffin was being his typical self, flirting with the crowd in such an obscene way that we might not be invited back next year. Evan was settling down at the drum set, getting comfortable for the upcoming workout. While performing was relaxing for me, it was the complete opposite for him. He was often drenched when we were done.

Getting to my appointed spot at the front of the stage, I looked around for my girl—she was out there in the clamoring crowd...somewhere...and even though I hadn't spotted her yet, I could feel her eyes on me. Knowing she was drinking me in electrified me more than the buzzing energy emanating from the crowd.

Shifting my eyes, I spotted Kiera instantly. She was standing with Jenny, a few rows back. Tuning out everyone and everything else, I focused on my girl. God, she was beautiful. Even in this heat, she'd left her long, brown hair down around her shoulders, and her hazel eyes sparkled with joy as she smiled at me. Her cheeks flushed red as our eyes locked, and I reveled in the fact that I could still do that to her. I hoped she never stopped blushing around me.

I love you, I mouthed to her. Some of the girls behind Kiera went crazy, like they thought I was speaking to them. Ignoring the women, even though she had to have heard them, Kiera mouthed that she loved me too. I never thought that simple phrase would mean so much to me, but now that I had someone who genuinely cared for me, it meant the absolute world.

Kiera gave me two thumbs up after her statement, like she was wishing me luck, and a laugh escaped me. She was so freaking adorable—that had been a major part of my undoing in the beginning. I just hadn't been able to resist her innocence. Maybe that was because I'd left mine behind so very long ago.

Slipping my guitar over my shoulder, I wrapped my hand around the microphone and leaned in to address the crowd. I swear the screams grew ten times louder when they realized I was about to speak. If they didn't quiet down, they'd never hear me. "Hello, Seattle!" I said, a little louder than necessary. "We're the D-Bags...in case you didn't know." The shriek that followed told me they knew *exactly* who we were. Good. I loved playing for diehard fans. "And we've got something for you...if you want it."

Focusing on some women in the front row, I gave them a seductive *I'm yours if you want me* expression. Aside from singing, this was my job in the band—engaging the audience, making them feel as included in the performance as possible. At a D-Bags show, everyone was my best friend, my potential lover...an integral member of the band. No one here would leave feeling they were just observers, watching a group of guys on a stage. Not if I could help it anyway.

I knew the flirting bothered Kiera, but I also hoped she understood that it was all an act now that we were together. While before my seductive stares had been an open invitation to anyone who wanted to approach me, now they were just a ploy, a ruse to make the women in the crowd feel something. And as much as Kiera probably hated to admit it...it worked. I had the rapt attention of every female in the crowd.

I held up a finger to quiet the group before me, and like I had them all entranced, they obeyed. "Do you want it?" I asked, oozing as much sex appeal into the question as I could. They answered in a chorus of high-pitched screams. Smiling, I brought a hand to my ear. "Well, if you want it, I'm gonna have to hear you ask for it."

As the corresponding screams surely tore a hole through the fabric of the universe, I shot a smile at Kiera. She beamed at me, hooting and hollering along with everyone else. I loved seeing her like that—carefree, overjoyed...in love. It made this moment even better. And it was already pretty fucking awesome.

Flicking my wrist at Evan, I gave him the signal to start the song. He began it instantly. Since this was a once in a lifetime show for us, we packed the lineup with every hit we had—all the songs that got the crowd at Pete's on their feet. There were quite a few to choose from, and Matt and I had had some minor disagreements about the list, but in the end, we'd come up with an amazing concert.

Adrenaline surged through me as I strummed my guitar and sang my heart out. The fans were going nuts—screaming, jumping up and down, singing along. It made me soar with joy. God, I loved this. As we moved into the next song, I set my guitar back on its stand. I wouldn't need it for a while, which meant I'd be able to engage the crowd more. I started getting more and more into it as the set progressed, picking fans at random and singing directly to them. Thankfully, no one passed out at the personal attention—it had happened before, and it always freaked me out whenever it did. I'd feel horrible if someone got hurt because of me; enough people had been hurt because of me.

When we were finally playing our last song, I could barely believe it was over. It had gone by so fast. I put everything I had into that last song—poured every fiber of my being into the words. Performing was one of the few times I felt completely truthful, and some of my songs were more personal than fans realized. Real events, real pain, and in some cases, real abuse. It was kind of a miracle that I could sing about topics that I had trouble talking about, even to my closest friends. Maybe that was because I could brush off songs as just being reflections on humanity—*I'm just singing about life, not necessarily about* my *life.* There was a fair amount of anonymity in the artform.

I bowed to the fans after the final piece was over. "Thank you for listening, Seattle! It's been a pleasure..." As I backed away from the microphone, the crowd screamed, applauded, and in a few cases, cried. Seeing the tears made me happy. In my line of work, waterworks were typically a good thing.

The crowd began breaking apart, some staying to listen to the next act, some going on to find another band at the music festival, some moving closer to the stage to get our attention. The guys began unplugging their stuff, and I grabbed my guitar. Giving Kiera a quick *see you soon* smile, I slipped off the stage. I was on cloud nine—high on life—and I couldn't wait to share the moment with Kiera. No matter how great I was feeling, being around her amplified the emotion tenfold.

Quickly giving my guitar to the crew member who would make sure it was safe and sound in the staging area until I was ready to pick it up, I headed to the "backstage" area, where Kiera and the other girls were most likely waiting for us. When I spotted my girl, I couldn't help but rush to her as quickly as possible. Leaping over the short fence separating us, I scooped her into my arms and lifted her into the air. She giggled as she laced her fingers around my neck, and I was nearly overcome with her intoxicating presence. I never wanted to let her go, but I had to know what she'd thought of the show.

Setting her down, I said, "That was so much fun! I'm so glad you were here. Did you like it?"

Pushing her back by her shoulders, I squatted down so I could look her in the eye. Her eyes were more green than brown in the sunlight, and they were beaming with pride...for me. She laughed at my question, like she thought I was adorable—or absurd—for asking it. Her warm hands cupped my cheeks, focusing her gaze, her love, her joy. "I loved it. You guys were amazing! I'm so proud of you, Kellan."

Her words made me feel like my chest was cracking open—it hurt, but in a good way. *I'm so proud of you.* God, had anyone ever said those words to me before? Before I could dwell on that too much, something about Kiera caught my attention. Pushing her slightly farther away from me, I raked my eyes down her shirt. She was wearing one of the original T-shirts Griffin had made for us, a solid black shirt bearing the full name of the band —*Douchebags*. She must have gotten hot out there in the crowd, she had the sleeves rolled up her arms, but the kicker, the part that had stolen my thoughts and knocked my focus completely on its ass, was the bottom of the shirt. It was tied into a knot high up her waist, exposing her stomach. And now all I could think about was undoing the knot, stripping the shirt off her, and running my tongue up her salty skin...

Peering up at the tease, I seductively told her, "I like your shirt."

She flushed all over in that adorable way that I just couldn't get enough of. I felt my blood surging in response. I couldn't wait to get her home. Or go home with her. Wherever. It didn't matter as long as we were alone. And we could be alone all night, since the D-Bags weren't performing later, and Kiera had the night off from Pete's. For the next several hours, she was mine and mine alone. As soon as we got out of here, of course.

Almost as soon as I thought that, I was bombarded by fans. Hands grabbed my arms, physically begging for my time. Since I owed the fans ten times over for all they'd given me, I tore my attention from Kiera and turned to face them. "Ladies...how's it going?"

A busty brunette started fanning her face. "Oh my God, Kellan Kyle...I love you so much." Her face flushed brighter than

Kiera's after she said that. "Can I have your autograph?" she squeaked.

"Sure thing," I said with a smile. As I grabbed her pen and signed a Bumbershoot flyer, I asked the group, "Did everyone enjoy the show?"

There was a lot of tittering, followed by gushing praise that almost embarrassed me. Laughing at their passionate display, I signed more flyers and posed for photos. Then a girl in a tank top pulled down her shirt, exposing her ample cleavage. "Sign me here? Please, please, please!"

All her friends giggled as they stared at me with eager faces. I flashed a glance at Kiera, who was standing back, respectfully giving me space. What would she think if I did this? She probably wouldn't like it, but really, it was just skin, the important part of the girl's breasts was still completely covered. Kiera would be okay in the end, and it would make the fan's day if I granted her request.

It seemed innocent enough to me since there wasn't any real nakedness, so I grabbed the fan's Sharpie and got to work signing her chest. The girl turned aggressive with me being that close and grabbed my ass while I was signing. I almost pushed her away, but...it was all in good fun. As long as she didn't try to cup my junk, it was fine.

Playing along, I tapped her on the nose with the end of the pen when I handed it back to her. "Be good," I playfully warned.

"Oh sugar, I'm *always* good," was her sultry response. Then she erupted into squeals and giggles and twisted around to show the signature to her friends. Shaking my head, I turned to the next person seeking my attention.

Just as I was finishing up with the group, I heard someone exclaim, "Kiera, my future lover! I'm thrilled you came to check me out. Did you like what you saw?"

Glancing over my shoulder, I saw Griffin cupping himself, making a beeline for my girlfriend. When he got to her, he grabbed her hand. *Oh...I don't think so.* While the look on Kiera's face was priceless—fear mixed with revulsion—I wasn't about to let Griffin finish whatever torment he had planned for her. Excusing myself from the fans, I hurried over and snatched Kiera's hand away from my bassist. Stepping between them, I shoved Griffin's shoulder. "Fuck off, Griffin."

Quickly getting over it, Griffin shrugged and found someone else to pester. Good. Kiera leaned into my side, and I could almost feel the gratitude radiating from her. Griffin was probably Kiera's least favorite person in all the world. "Thanks," she murmured.

Absorbing her comfort, I kissed her head. "No problem. I know how much you love conversing with Griffin."

Waving goodbye to the remaining fans, I led Kiera away from the stage and back to the main part of the park. The guys, with their respective gals, except Anna who was busy today, fell into step behind me. Once we were away from the fans and the stage, no one paid too much attention to us, and we were able to disappear into the masses. That was fine with me. I'd given my fans my all, and now I wanted to relax with Kiera.

Kiera looked lost in thought as we walked along the paths, and I wondered if she was thinking about our first time here at the festival, back when she'd been with Denny, and I'd merely been...keeping her occupied. Of course, it had been a lot more than that. I'd already been in love with her, although, I hadn't admitted it to myself yet. I'd just known she was...special to me. And Kiera...I think she'd been falling for me too, during that time. Denny's sudden departure when he'd left for work had crushed her spirit, and right or wrong, I'd helped her pick up the pieces, and in the process, wormed my way into her heart.

Griffin came up behind me and slapped me on the back, jolting me from my thoughts. Nodding back at Matt and his tiny, Latin-Asian girlfriend, Rachel, he said, "We're gonna go check out some of the other bands. Comin'?"

I looked back at Evan and Jenny, but they were in their own little world, and clearly didn't care about listening to bands at the moment. Kiera might though. While she always told me the D-Bags were better than anyone else, I think she liked hearing what other groups could do. Shifting my focus to her, I started to ask her if she wanted to go with Matt and Griffin, but her stomach answered before I could finish, rumbling with a growl loud enough for all of us to hear. Kiera closed her eyes, embarrassed, and I couldn't help but laugh at her. She gave me a glare that was more cute than intimidating, and I laughed even harder.

Twisting back to Griffin, I told him, "I think we'll get something to eat first. We'll catch up with you later."

Rachel, Matt, and Griffin took off to find entertainment, and I looked over at Kiera nestled in my side. "Should we get some food in you, Noisy?"

She looked so annoyed, I couldn't help but lower my lips to hers. Then she didn't look so annoyed anymore. Her passionate nature kicked in the second my tongue brushed against hers, and her hands reached up to fist my hair. I could feel her fast breath, could imagine her racing heart... The way she reacted to me ignited me, and I knew, if I didn't put the brakes on this quick, we might end up in a very compromising position in a very public place. Not that I would mind if that happened. Kiera would though.

Not able to resist teasing her a little, I pulled away from her with a laugh; her hooded eyes almost drew me right back to her lips, but somehow, I managed to stop myself from caving into the temptation. "Do you need a minute?" I asked, enacting our old code for *Let's slow down*.

Like an agitated cat, Kiera smacked me on the chest and stormed off. Unfortunately, she was heading in the opposite direction of the food. Laughing a little harder, I grabbed her elbow and turned her around. "Food's that way. Unless you had something else in mind?" Her eyes simmered, and I could almost see all the erotic possibilities that had just flooded her brain. I couldn't wait to explore some of them with her later.

God, how did my life go from complete crap to complete

bliss? And why couldn't I shake the feeling that all of this...was temporary.

After Bumbershoot, Kiera and I went to the apartment that she shared with her sister, Anna. She'd moved in with Anna after I'd kicked her out last December, a dark time I hated thinking about. The apartment was tiny, but thankfully it had two bedrooms, so the girls didn't have to bunk up. I kind of hated that Kiera still lived here—I was ready for her to return to me. My place was so cold without her. It felt huge with her light gone, and very, very empty.

Throwing open her apartment door with a dramatic flourish, I led Kiera into her place with a wide smile on my face. This afternoon had been incredible, and I was still buzzing with energy. Energy I now wanted to release...

The second Kiera set her purse on a nearby table, I grabbed her. Before she could truly comprehend what was going on, I had her pinned to the closed door. Like she was a magnet, drawing me in, my mouth instantly lowered to hers. We connected, and I swear physical sparks erupted in the air. Being with Kiera had always been like that—electric, powerful...undeniable. She was my greatest blessing and my biggest weakness.

Memories tumbled through my brain as the heat between us escalated. Memories of meeting her for the first time, watching her from a distance...wanting her. Memories of having her, memories of losing her. Pain tightened around my chest just as surely as love warmed my soul. Would I ever be able to let the past go? The betrayal, the heartache...the agony.

Yes, I had to. Kiera was everything to me, and I wouldn't lose her to my insecurities. We would keep moving forward, and eventually, the past would be so far behind us, the pain would lose its hold on us. *Right...like how the pain your parents inflicted on you is gone? That's the past too, idiot.*

Shoving aside that bitter thought, I refocused on Kiera. Being with her was all I wanted to think about—every second of every day. Her breath was as fast as mine, her fingers firmly tangled in my hair. Every inch of my body was pressed against her, but I still wasn't close enough. Running my hand along her backside, I pulled her leg around my hip, so I could press my body where it longed to be. Kiera groaned, and I pulsed with need. God, what this woman did to me.

Thankfully, I did the same thing to her. She broke apart from me, impatient lust clear on her face. "Kellan...bedroom..."

She wanted me. Just as much as I wanted her. Was she ready then? To amp this up, just a little bit? To somewhat return to where we'd been...before. No. Not return to *that*. But move forward to something much better. Something equal. Curiosity and a different kind of need ate through my desire, poking holes in my physical cravings. I had to ask her, had to find out where she was...emotionally.

But because I couldn't resist playing with her, I didn't pull away just yet. Instead, I lowered my lips to her neck, tasting and teasing every sensitive nerve cluster. Kiera groaned again, rubbing against me in a vain attempt to find relief. And damn, it felt good having her grind on me. Knowing I was close to having her in a frenzy made a small laugh escape me as I ran my tongue along her collarbone. It almost made me want to put my question on the back burner for another day, just so I could tease her longer. Riling her up was definitely one of my favorite hobbies.

Annoyed that I was having a good time tormenting her, Kiera pushed my shoulders back, an adorable frown on her lips. It made me want to suck on them, but I resisted. As much as I wanted to fulfil her request and explore every inch of her, the question I wanted to ask still burned throughout my body, and for this answer...sex could wait. For a little bit.

Kiera stared at me through hooded eyes, her breath still fast with desire. Seeing the physical manifestation of her need sent fire through every nerve ending in my body. I didn't let her see that though. Hiding my own response to her, I shifted my expression to a playful smile and dropped her leg. Cocking my head to the side, I took a step away from her. "Are you ever going to move back in with me?" I casually asked. It didn't feel like a casual question to my stomach, and while I didn't let it show on my face, my heart surged in my chest. I wanted this. Desperately. *Please say yes, Kiera. I'm tired of being apart from you.*

Kiera blinked, clearly disoriented by my odd change in direction. She was having trouble disengaging her sex drive, and I could tell she wanted to ignore my question, throw me down somewhere, and have her way with me. Maybe the hideous orange couch in the living room? Or right here in the entryway? I was open to whatever she wanted, wherever she wanted it. With curiosity and confusion on her face, she took a sidestep away from me, toward the hallway leading to her room. Ah...so it was to be her uncomfortable bed then.

Seeing a way to make my question seem indifferent and not at all lifechanging, even though my heart was still trying to bruise the inside of my chest, I nodded my head toward her bedroom and said, "Because I really hate having sex on a futon. Not that I won't, though," I added with a wink. I'd have sex anywhere she wanted.

My comment worked to disarm her, and she smirked. Grabbing my hand, she said, "You're the one that kicked me out."

Her voice was light and airy, but I heard the pain in her simple statement. *Yes, I did this. I separated us.* It had been for the right reasons, but still, I'd made the cut. Remembering why I'd torn us made acid fill my chest, smothering my rapidly beating heart. Maybe it was too soon, if just mentioning that time still hurt so much. Banishing the anguish from my expression, I forced a laugh. "Well, it sounded like a good idea at the time." Maybe not a good idea, but definitely a necessary one. We wouldn't be the same now if we hadn't...paused.

Stopping at her bedroom door, Kiera put a hand on my chest. "No, it was a good idea." Reaching up, she cupped my cheek. "You and I needed space. We needed to get our heads on straight."

Her words matched my thoughts, but still...I hated hearing her say them. I tried to smile, but a sigh ruined it. "Well, now that they are...why don't you come back?" Feeling painful hope wrap around my chest, I cinched my arms around her waist. When I spoke again, my voice came out more seriously than I intended. "I know we've taken things slow, but I still want to move forward... with you." *All the way forward...'til death do us part forward.*

Kiera's eyes glistened as she stared at me. There was so much love and warmth in her gaze, I could feel it glowing upon my skin. But there was reservation there too...and fear. She smiled in a way that clearly said, *don't take what I'm about to say the wrong way,* and I felt my heart sinking. She was going to tell me no. Like she understood she was about to hurt me, she began running her fingers through my hair in a soothing pattern, and combined with the love emanating from her, I felt myself relaxing. It was okay if she wasn't ready. No matter what she said, it would be fine. We were in this together, and if she needed more time, then she would get it. I wasn't going anywhere.

In a voice oozing reassurance, she told me, "I think it's better if we keep waiting. I've sort of come into my own, being with my sister. I don't want to fall right back into needing a man to feel...complete."

Her words were difficult to hear, mainly because I knew she was right. Denny had been such an integral part of her, and she hadn't known how to be apart from him. That dependence had bitten our relationship in the ass more than once...and theirs too...if I was being completely honest. Hell, if she'd overcome that feeling while she'd been with Denny, then we probably wouldn't have gotten together in the first place...even though I liked to believe we were fated to be together, no matter what. But since being separated from Denny, and from me—since she'd been forced into isolation—she *had* become a stronger person. Every day she was becoming stronger, more confident. She wanted to embrace that growth. I *wanted* her to embrace that growth. I just...wanted her to do it with me. Kiera wasn't the only one with dependency issues.

Even though I partially agreed with her—it wasn't the right time for us—I poured my heart out in a profoundly honest question. "What if I'm the one that needs you?" The truth of that sentence seeped into my pores, stinging me. "I hate sleeping alone." *I hate being alone. You're stronger without me. How do I become stronger without you when you're all I need?*

Something silent passed between us. Understanding. Kiera knew what I was truly saying, heard the words buried underneath my spoken words, and she got it, she got me. Because, while in some ways we were wildly different, in others, we were mirror images. Soulmates. She gave me a bright smile, one that burned away the sudden melancholy, made me feel like I could do anything, as long as she was by my side. Even live apart from her, as ironic as that was. "You'll be all right," she said. I believed her, but I frowned at her anyway. She laughed, then told me, "Besides, we almost always end up sleeping together anyway."

She flushed such a bright red after she said it, that I knew she'd just realized how suggestive that sounded. Always a split-second too late. That was what made teasing her so much fun. Grinning, feeling lighthearted again and confident that my girl loved me, I reached behind her to open her bedroom door. "Exactly. Think of the gas money we'd save." I walked her backward into her room, as I continued trying to win her over with logic. "And rent...you wouldn't have to pay that, living with me. You could work less, concentrate on school more."

With a sigh, she flicked on her light. "I like my life, Kellan. I finally feel...well-rounded."

There wasn't a single part of me that could let that sentence go. Kicking the door closed, I cupped her ass. "Yes, I know, very well-rounded." A peeved curve to her lip, she smacked me on the shoulder. I laughed, then pulled her tight as I let out a dramatic sigh. With a soft kiss, I told her, "Fine." I'd drop it...for now.

After a few soft kisses that got my blood pumping, I pulled back. Kicking off my shoes, I pointed at her ridiculous excuse for a bed. "But that seriously sucks. Can I at least buy you a decent bed?" Something without a hard bar running through it. Something big enough to...stretch out in. Would a California King fit in this room?

Kiera smiled, relief evident on her face. Stepping out of her own shoes, she grabbed my hand and pulled me over to the dreaded contraption. "Of course. You can even help me break it in."

Her slim fingers began removing my shirt, and as I helped her, my grin was unstoppable. "Hmmm...you may have sold me on this idea."

She tossed my shirt on the ground, then ran her hands down my chest. Her finger traced the swirled letters of her name upon my skin, and my breath caught. It was like a jolt of lightning up my spine whenever she touched my tattoo. "Anything that ends with sex sells you," she laughed.

Sex with you, yes. Playfully pushing her back onto the awful bed, I leaned over and murmured, "True."

Her breath picked up pace as I crawled over her, like I mesmerized her, like just the thought of being with me had her on the brink. Did she know I felt the same way? That just being able to touch her amazed me? That all she had to do was touch my cheek, and I flamed with need? That she was the only person on Earth who could undo me?

She had so much power over me, and she didn't even realize it. Sometimes, I was sure Kiera had no idea why I was with her. Why I'd chosen her. Why my heart was utterly hers. And right then and there, I decided, she *would* understand. Before we moved in together, before we took that next step, she would get it, just like she intrinsically got everything else about me. And then she wouldn't wonder why we were together anymore. She'd just...know.

Chapter 2
GHOSTS

I woke up with a start, and the darkness of the room instantly pressed in on me. Where was I? A warm body resting beside me rekindled my memory. I'd fallen asleep with Kiera. I was in her bedroom. I was safe. My heart raced as I let out a long exhale, and I knew I'd awoken from something...intense. Thankfully, not a trace of my dream remained with me. Those were my favorite dreams—the ones I couldn't remember.

Sitting up, I scrubbed my eyes. Nightmares were nothing new to me. My subconscious frequently tormented me with my past. The worst dreams were the ones that mixed my childhood with the present, providing a dire commentary on my current life. I'd do anything to shut off the dreams. Things were good now. I could let it go.

Careful to not disturb Kiera, I climbed out of bed and started my daily exercise routine. Pushups, crunches, pushups, crunches. Whatever it took to clear my mind. When I was done, I got dressed and headed to the kitchen to start the coffee brewing. Kiera would want some when she woke up, which wouldn't be long after I started the pot. My girl could sleep through just about anything, but the aroma of freshly brewed beans almost always roused her.

One of the best sounds in the world met my ear a couple minutes later—warm liquid dribbling into an oversized carafe. The smell reminded me of Kiera, of our stolen moments together in the mornings. The color reminded me of the darker sections of her eyes, and I smiled like an idiot as the pot began to fill. Song in my heart, I started humming as I grabbed some mugs. That was when I heard the apartment door being unlocked. Anna must finally be home.

I set two mugs on the counter right as Anna stepped into the apartment. "Hey, Kellan, good morning."

"Mornin', Anna. You're out late...or early."

Walking into the small kitchen, Anna dumped her mammoth bag onto the floor with a sigh. She was wearing tight pants and an even tighter top, and even though it was early, she looked like she'd just come from a salon. Anna was gorgeous, there was no denying that, but with her it seemed...manufactured. Everything she did, everything she wore, every swipe of her makeup was intentional and direct. While that wasn't necessarily a bad thing, I preferred Kiera's form of relaxed, natural beauty. She didn't need to accent anything—she was already perfect.

"Yeah," she said. "Went to Pete's. Ran into the guys."

From the smile on her face, I knew what that meant—she'd spent the night entertaining Griffin. Having had to listen to Anna and Griffin before, I could only imagine that they'd both had quite a night. I was glad I'd missed the verbal play-by-play.

Anna and I shared a knowing laugh, then she told me, "I heard you guys did great at your big show." She paused to sigh. "I'm sorry I had to miss it."

Thinking about the performance energized me. That had been...truly incredible. I loved being on stage. So much that sometimes it kind of freaked me out. It was the one place I felt completely...free. Aside from being in Kiera's arms, of course. But at times both things seemed so tenuous—a slippery slope that I could easily fall from. What would I do if I lost music? What would I do if I lost Kiera? Squelching the sudden burst of panic, I nonchalantly told her, "It was just a show, nothing you haven't seen before. Don't worry about it."

Leaning back on the counter, I asked about her Hooters calendar photoshoot, the reason she'd missed the concert. Anna grinned, then told me all about the process. Kiera entered as I was, once again, congratulating Anna on being chosen for the 12-month honor. Kiera was dressed for comfort in lounge pants and a worn T-shirt. Her ever-changing eyes were a deep shade of green this morning, and her smile was radiant as she stared at me. She was stunning. Absolutely stunning.

My grin was wide and happy when she slung her arms around my waist—I loved being held by her. "Mornin', Sleepy," I said, kissing her head.

With a sigh of contentment, she buried her head in my neck. "Good morning."

Anna let out a soft sigh. "God, you two are adorable." She smacked Kiera's arm and rolled her eyes. "It's annoying." From the look on her face, it was clear she didn't actually feel that way.

Kiera laughed. "Good morning, Anna. Late night?"

Anna's lips twisted into a devious smile. Biting her lip, she cocked an eyebrow. "Oh, yes. And I can guarantee you it wasn't as cutesy as your night."

Kiera looked away from her, embarrassed, and Anna let out a throaty laugh. Squeezing my girl tighter, I laughed and said, "I wouldn't say our night was cute, Anna."

The second the words were out of my mouth, Kiera flashed me a warning glare and smacked my chest; her face was a ridiculously cute shade of red now. Kiera wasn't one to discuss our sex life in detail, even to her sister. I was generally pretty tight-lipped too, so I completely understood. And even though Anna would probably love an in-depth description, I wasn't about to give it to her.

When it became clear I wasn't going to expand on that, Kiera relaxed. Anna snorted. "I know," she said. She paused to poke Kiera's shoulder. "I know how hot you guys can get." Kiera's mouth dropped open, and I had to refrain from laughing. Anna didn't. Jerking her thumb toward the hallway, she said, "My bedroom is only one room away from yours, Kiera. Maybe the two of you could remember that in the future?"

Mortified, Kiera hid her face and turned into my body. I couldn't hold the laughter after that, and a soft chuckle escaped me as I rubbed her back. "We'll try and keep that in mind, Anna. Thanks."

Anna laughed good-naturedly and rubbed Kiera's shoulder. "I'm just teasing you, Kiera. Go ahead and scream away, I don't mind." Her gaze swept over me appreciatively. "Lord knows I would." I had to shake my head at her ceaseless innuendo. She and Griffin really were a match made in heaven. If only they'd smarten up and realize it instead of using each other as on-call sex buddies. Of course, the fact that they were both into that was one of the things that made them so compatible. Not everyone needed what Kiera and I had.

While I gave Kiera a reassuring kiss on the head, Anna winked at me, then patted Kiera's arm. "Well, I'm off to bed. I'm beat." She turned away from us, heading to her bedroom at the end of the hall. Over her shoulder she tossed out, "I'll be out like a light if you guys want to go at it again."

I couldn't help but laugh at Anna's suggestion. That was probably about the last thing in the world Kiera wanted to hear. She was probably hot tamale red now. So adorable.

When Anna was out of sight, Kiera sighed and looked up at me. She wasn't half as red as I'd expected her to be. Good. Sex shouldn't embarrass her as much as it did. Smacking my chest, she told me, "Would you stop encouraging her?" I smiled in response, and she sighed again, a little more forlornly this time. "I wish the two of you had a better hobby than trying to embarrass me."

I placed a tender kiss on her forehead. I knew I shouldn't say what was in my head, since we'd already gone over this last night, but I couldn't resist pointing out a simple solution to her problem. "Well, you wouldn't have to worry about it at my place. Maybe I'll just embarrass you back to my home."

In case she was annoyed I'd brought it up again, I gave her the sexiest smile in my arsenal. I was pleasantly rewarded with Kiera's lips on mine, but even as our mouths connected, my chest tightened with need. And loneliness. And pain. I really couldn't wait until the day she finally said yes to my request. The day we were finally ready to move forward. But that wasn't today. And that was okay.

Kiera and I spent the entire day getting her ready for school. It was starting soon, and as expected, Kiera was nervous. I really wasn't sure why she let new situations bother her so much. She was smart, beautiful, sweet...she could own every single room she walked into, if she'd just believe in herself more. Her personal insecurity probably fueled a lot of her negative feelings about me, about us. She seemed to think our fire would die and I'd lose interest in her one day. Impossible. On my end, at least. If she saw herself in a more positive light, she'd feel more secure in a crowd, feel more secure about me.

In a way, I was Kiera's opposite when it came to insecurity. Knowing I was physically attractive made me feel very comfortable in groups, or one-on-one, when it was the nonpersonal type of one-on-one—like random sex with a stranger. But true intimacy...opening myself up to someone...that, I struggled with. Daily.

But if I could help Kiera be more comfortable in her own skin, then maybe she could help me be more comfortable knocking down my walls. We were good together in that regard. In *every* regard.

When it was time for her shift at Pete's, Kiera and I headed out to the parking lot. With an adorably cute smile on her face... she tried to swipe the keys to my baby. "Can I drive?" she innocently asked, attempting to jiggle the keys free from my ironclad grip.

When hell freezes over. Okay, maybe that was a bit harsh, but I was still a little miffed at her for stealing my car. Even if she'd been hurt over my...extracurricular activities, her retaliation had been uncalled for. And cruel. The Chevelle was a classic piece of art. Practically priceless.

Giving her a firm expression, I jerked the keys away. "No, you cannot."

She stopped where she was, hands on her hips and an adorable pout on her face, but I forced myself to walk right past her. It was difficult. What I really wanted to do was sweep her into my arms. "Why not?" she asked.

That was too much for me to resist. Turning around, I stepped in front of her and claimed her mouth with mine. "Because...that is my baby, and I don't share her."

"I thought I was your baby?" she squeaked out, breathless.

Grabbing her hips, I pulled her into me. "You are." I kissed her hard, deep, sealing my words with my body. "And I don't share you either," I said, drawing back. Never again. My heart couldn't take it.

The look on Kiera's face was so warm, so loving...so turned on. So darn cute. Even as I laughed at her expression, I felt that connected, loved feeling that I only used to feel—briefly—during sex. Kiera had changed everything for me, and I felt those moments all the time now, for the oddest reasons. And knowing I could feel complete bliss at the strangest, most unexpected times, made every second of life enjoyable. She made me feel so...alive.

We arrived at Pete's Bar not too much later, and I pulled into "my" spot. Getting out, I hurriedly walked around to Kiera's side, but she'd already opened her door. How was I supposed to be the chivalrous boyfriend when she wouldn't wait for me? With a frown, I held my hand out for her. The frown slipped off my face the instant her fingers were safely tucked inside mine.

Walking into the bar filled me with serenity. If ever I let my guard down, even just a little, it was here. This place was home to me, more of a home than my *actual* home had ever been. I led Kiera through one of the double doors and kissed her hand as she extended away from me. I couldn't seem to enter Pete's without broadcasting to the room that she was mine. Probably because I'd spent so long hiding how I felt about her. I was never hiding again.

The bartender, Rita, was eyeing me like a hungry wolf stalking its prey. She typically looked at me that way. Kiera didn't know about my history with Rita, that I'd caved into the older woman's carnal desires and slept with her once. Or at least, I didn't think Kiera knew. I hoped she didn't. That was not my proudest moment, especially since Rita had been married at the time. It hadn't fazed me back then, but now that I was in a happy, healthy relationship, I knew I shouldn't have gone there. Of course, I shouldn't have gone there with Denny's girl either.

I inclined my head in polite greeting to Rita, and she leaned over the counter, showing me her goods. "Hey there, Kellan...Kiera."

Kiera smirked at Rita, then turned to me. "I have to go put my stuff away. Usual?"

Biting my lip, I tucked a lock of hair behind her ear. "Yeah, thanks, Kiera."

She leaned up and kissed my cheek, and I immediately twisted to find her lips. A peck just wouldn't do. Kiera indulged me in my public affections, until my hand drifted down to her ass. Then she pushed me away and pointed at me in a clear warning to be good. I gave her an innocent smile, and she rolled her eyes and laughed before walking away.

While Kiera headed for the back room, I headed for my regular table, up by the stage. None of my bandmates had arrived yet, so I leaned back in a chair and began people watching. A lot of the customers were watching me too, though, so I supposed it wasn't truly people watching. More like having multiple silent conversations.

You're Kellan Kyle, aren't you?
Yeah.
You're amazing!
Thank you.
Can I come sit by you?
No, sorry...girlfriend. I'm sure you saw me kissing her thirty seconds ago.

I hastily broke eye contact from a group of college girls who hadn't correctly interpreted our nonverbal conversation and looked like they were about to pay me a visit. That was when a giant, hulk of a man stepped up to me. "Hey, Kellan. How was the show?" At seeing the behemoth beside me, the girls sat back down.

Smiling, I looked up at an intimidating man with a shaved head and arms the size of tree trunks. Sam was a bouncer here and a friend. He'd been there for me a time or two, sometimes grudgingly, but still, he'd been there. And he'd been there for Denny when he had needed him. And regardless of what had gone down between Denny and me, that meant a lot.

"Hey, Sam...it was good."

He gave me an incredulous look. "Good? You just played friggin' Bumbershoot. Don't hold back, tell me all about it."

With a laugh, I nodded and started recounting the experience for him. Talking about it freshened the memory in my mind, and once again, familiar adrenaline rushed through me. I had a feeling that particular high was going to take a while to fade.

As the night progressed, more of the regulars approached me. They all wanted to congratulate me on the show, hound me for details. I didn't mind. I loved talking about it, even if some of them had a hard time accepting my answers.

"What do you mean you weren't nervous?" Kate asked for about the fifth time. Tall and lean, Kate had the body and grace of a dancer. She also had a deep reddish tint to her brown hair, a fact that had piqued Griffin's curiosity on more than one occasion. Kate had been a fixture at Pete's for almost as long as Jenny, and she'd always thought it was weird that I never got stage fright.

I gave her a nonchalant shrug. "I mean just that...it didn't make me nervous. Excited, sure, but nervous...no. Matt on the other hand, I think he emptied his stomach at some point."

The image of my pale-faced guitarist heaving into a bucket made me laugh. Kate shook her head in disbelief. "It's like you're not human...like you're an alien, rock god sent to Earth to—"

"Please you?" I interjected. My eyes roved the bar, searching for Kiera. Hopefully I'd be able to please her after her shift.

Kate snorted, and when I returned my eyes to her, her cheeks were flushed, and she looked flustered. "Uh, yeah...exactly." Shaking her head, she said, "But no, seriously...you didn't feel the slightest ounce of nerves? If it were me, I'd probably pee my pants."

I laughed, then sighed. "I can keep saying it, Kate, but eventually, you're just going to have to believe me. Performing doesn't scare me." No...pouring my heart out to the woman I loved, that was what had scared me. Everything else was simple, easy.

Kate looked like she was about to question me again, but the front doors opened, and the rest of my band walked in. I was grateful they were here. Kate could turn her endless questions on them. Matt would probably give her much more satisfying answers.

Once the four of us were reunited, the patrons of Pete's broke into thunderous applause. All of the attention was a little bewildering. We played at Pete's all the time, so most of the people here had heard us on multiple occasions. But I supposed the festival *was* a step up from the bar.

While Matt looked like he wanted to walk right back out of the bar, I lifted my hand in a friendly acknowledgement of their praise. Evan looked baffled but honored as he looked around. Griffin looked like the adoration was nothing short of expected. After throwing kisses to the crowd, he started making deep, dramatic bows, like he'd just conducted a symphony orchestra.

Wanting him to show a little decorum, I slapped him on the back to get him to stop. He did, but his grin said he was still reveling in the moment.

Once the crowd quieted down, I told them, "Thank you. Your support means a lot to us." My eyes drifted to Kiera as I spoke; she was beaming with pride just as brightly as everyone else in the bar, maybe more. It was so strange to feel so much...acceptance. A part of me would never get used to that feeling.

Matt took the brief silence to slip away to our table, while Evan found Jenny and wrapped her in a mammoth bear hug. Griffin, though, wasn't about to let his captive audience go so easily. Before I could successfully push him to the table, he told the group, "My johnson is gladly accepting all forms of praise...if anyone wants to congratulate me privately."

After rapping his empty skull, I forcibly moved him to the table to sit down. A little while later, I was again surprised and humbled when Pete, the owner of the bar, came out to congratulate us. It was a little surreal to hear him say he was proud of us as he shook my hand. It was even more surreal to see the weary defeat on his face, like he believed he'd soon have to look for our replacements—a prospect I knew he wasn't looking forward to, since he hated booking bands. Fat chance of that happening though. One show at a major venue, while cool, wasn't going to massively change our lives or anything. That just wasn't the way the world worked. We'd probably never leave this bar; whoever owned Pete's in the future would have to chase us out when we were old and gray and too feeble to play. Or much sooner than that in Griffin's case. But being here, playing this bar every weekend for the rest of my natural life, that was a fate I was completely comfortable with, assuming Kiera was by my side for all of it, of course.

The remainder of the night was pretty damn perfect. The guys and I chatted amicably until Matt took off to hang out with Rachel. That earned him some ribbing from Griffin, but Griff didn't stick around much longer, and left the bar with some blonde. Kiera rolled her eyes and turned her back on the sight of Griffin leaving the bar with someone other than Anna, but from everything I'd seen, those two were far from exclusive, and Anna brought home just as many toys as he did. As long as they were both happy with the arrangement, there was no harm in it, from what I could see.

Evan and I stuck around, since both of our girls were closing. It seemed to take forever, but eventually we were parting ways, and I was able to do something I'd been wanting to do all evening—take Kiera home, to *my* home. It gave me a profound sense of peace whenever Kiera was inside my walls, and a small smile was stuck on my face when I pulled onto my street.

When Kiera and I stepped into the entryway, her eyes floated around the space, taking in everything. She always did that, like she was bracing herself for the ghosts that lived here. I understood. I battled those ghosts daily. *Everything* had started here. Our love affair, betraying Denny, mutually hurting someone we both cared about. Sometimes the past was so thick in my house, it was hard to breathe. It was thickest in Kiera and Denny's old room—I never went in there. I couldn't. But I'd never rent it out again either, wouldn't cleanse it by inviting someone else inside. Even though it was painful for both of us, it was Kiera's—and only Kiera's—and it would be until the day I died.

Kiera sat on my bed while I propped my guitar case in the corner of my room. She seemed a little...melancholy as she sat there, like the ghosts were getting to her. Another reason why she was resistant to move back here, I was sure—the walls were painted in pain. "You all right?" I asked, flicking a glance over at the bedroom she'd once shared with my best friend. Well...my ex-best friend, I supposed, although he'd never truly be an ex-friend to me. Even if I'd stabbed him in the back...I still loved him. He was family.

She threw on a smile that was bright and beautiful, one clearly meant to show me that she was okay, that she was happy.

Leaning back on her elbows, emphasizing her chest, she told me, "Of course, I'm fine."

I smiled at the vision of her on my bed and did my best to let the past slide off me. Sitting beside her, I placed my hand on her thigh. "I'm glad you're here," I whispered. *I'm glad you're mine, and there's nothing I wouldn't do for you.*

Sitting up, she tossed her arms around my neck. "I had no choice," she joked. "You wouldn't let me drive your car, remember?" I laughed, then leaned in to find her lips. Whatever the reason she was here with me, I was grateful for it.

I fell asleep with Kiera safely wrapped in my arms, and my last thought before darkness consumed me was *this is the way things are supposed to be. This is my forever.*

"Your forever? You think someone like you will get a happily ever after? You think you won? I always knew you were a fool."

My heart dropped into my stomach as I opened my eyes. I was in the kitchen, my old, childhood kitchen, staring at my father sitting at the table reading the newspaper—my dead father. "You shouldn't be here," I told him, but even as I said it, I knew I was wrong. Of course, he should be here. This was *his* house. I was the one out of place here, always out of place.

Dad smirked and shook his head. Setting his newspaper down on the table, he gave me a hard stare. I shivered, my heart racing; I knew that look, knew it very well. "I shouldn't be here? And tell me...*son*...who should be here? How about Denny? That hardworking, good-hearted boy who we took into our care, took into our home. The boy you callously stabbed in the back. Because you wanted something that was never yours." His gaze scanned me, contempt and disgust evident in his cold, gray eyes. "You're so selfish...just looking at you sickens me."

"I'm sorry." The words instantly slipped from my mouth, unbidden. Like I was freezing, my shivers increased to visible shaking. How could he still do this to me, after all this time?

As I stood there, waiting for my father to approach me—to reprimand me—I was suddenly smacked in the back of the head with a hard, wooden spoon. A burst of pain shot down my spine, making me gasp. I snapped my eyes to the side, where my mother stood, glaring at me. How stupid of me to forget that my father wasn't the only threat here.

"I can't believe what you did to that boy. Your best friend...I always knew you never really cared about him."

My eyes watered as the venom in her words seeped into my bones. I almost wished she'd hit me again instead of talk. Physical pain didn't cut as deeply as words. "No...I do care. I didn't mean for any of that to happen. Denny meant everything to me...he still does."

A tear rolled down my cheek, and my mother's pale blue eyes grew colder as she tracked its movement. "He means nothing to you. You used him to take what you wanted, because you're a monster...just like the beast who created you."

I violently shook my head. "That's not true..." Or maybe it was. Maybe it was the only truth I had. Maybe she was right... maybe I was a monster. Denny would probably agree.

While my denial died on my lips, I heard Dad's chair screeching in protest against the floor. "Are you talking back to your mother? Do I need to remind you whose house this is?"

My eyes wide and fearful, I looked back at my father. "No, I'm sorry...I wasn't...I'm sorry."

I backed up a step, and even as I did it, I knew it was the absolute wrong thing to do. Dad's face turned a fearsome shade of red as he watched my pathetic attempt to escape. "Where the hell do you think you're going?"

He started undoing his belt, and my heart hammered in my chest. No. This wasn't real. This was a dream, a horrible, horrible dream. My parents were dead. Gone. Buried. They couldn't hurt me anymore.

My dad's lip curved in a cruel smile. "You're wrong about that, son. There's so much more we can do to you now. Because now...we know *everything* you've ever done. You can't hide from us anymore. You'll never be free."

Having Dad inside my head was too much to handle. Twisting around, I bolted for the door. If there was one thing I was good at now, it was running. I was younger than him, faster, had more endurance—he'd never catch me, and unlike when I was a child, I didn't have to let this happen, didn't have to let him beat me. I never had to come back to this hellhole. Ever.

I managed to slip away from Mom, but when I got to the entryway of my massive childhood home, I instantly knew it didn't matter. There were no doors, no windows, no stairs to the upper floors. There was absolutely nowhere for me to go. Dad strolled into the room, smacking his belt against his hand. I twisted and turned, looking for an exit, but even the hallway to the kitchen was gone now. I was trapped. And alone.

"You finally get it, don't you? You can't escape who you are, Kellan. You can't escape your history. There's no point even trying."

He shrugged, like condemning me to a lifetime of pain was a simple thing. Then he brought the belt down. I raised my arms to protect my face, and the thick leather ripped into my exposed forearms. As pain, humiliation, and defeat coursed through me, I realized he was right. He could do so much more to me now... now that he was forever locked inside my head. I'd never truly be free.

Chapter 3
THE NEXT STEP

My nightmare left me shaken. More shaken than I cared to admit, even to Kiera. She noticed this particular dream, woke me up from it. I must have been thrashing in my sleep. Kiera wanted to talk about the dream when I was fully back in reality, but talking wasn't what I wanted. Talking didn't end the pain, only amplified it, and I needed it to stop. To *finally* stop. So, I distracted myself with sex, and Kiera let me. By the time I was lying in her arms, blissful and content, my nightmare had faded into oblivion. Hopefully, never to return.

Kiera watched me like a hawk for the next few days, but the bad dreams never truly shifted into nightmares, so she didn't have to wake me up again. I could see the concern in her eyes every morning, though, so I did my best to convince her that I was fine. Because I was. Even with the occasional nightly terrors, I was great. Kiera was my girlfriend. How could I be anything but freaking fantastic?

It took her a couple weeks, but eventually Kiera seemed to stop worrying about my dreams, especially as school got closer and closer. One lazy Thursday afternoon, we were lying in my bed, enjoying the fading freedom of summer, when I accidentally looked over at the clock, and realized I needed to go. "Shit. Matt's gonna start calling soon if I don't head out." With a sigh, I looked over at her lying next to me. "I wish we could stop rehearsing while school's out. We're good enough, we really don't need to practice so much."

She raised an eyebrow. "Good enough? Is that what you want to be?"

Smiling, I gave her a kiss. "With you is what I want to be."

She giggled as I kissed her, then pushed me back. "You know you can't shirk your responsibilities because of me, Kellan. We should be making each other better, not...lazier."

Climbing on top of her, I pinned her down. "Lazy? Is that what we are? Because that felt pretty aerobic to me."

She laughed again, her cheeks flushing a soft pink. "You know what I mean."

I did, and it filled me with warmth. She wanted me to be my absolute best, just like I wanted her to be her absolute best. We wanted to bring out each other's most positive attributes. And that meant...I had to leave. Damn it.

Even still, I waited as long as I possibly could before I got up and got dressed. Kiera was still stretched out on my bed when I reluctantly grabbed my guitar. She seemed like she was too comfortable to move. Unfortunately, she had to—I had to lock up. Staring at her beautiful, lean, sheet-covered body, I let out a long, sad sigh.

"What?" she asked, examining the covers around her with an adorable frown on her face.

Her expression made me grin, but then I remembered why I felt sullen. I pointed at her relaxed body. "You're so comfortable, I hate to ask you to leave." My mouth twisted into a frown. "You should be able to stay as long as you want. You should be able to come and go as you want. Even if we're not living together, my place is your place..." That thought firmly in my head, I nodded and pointed at her. "I've got an idea. Don't move."

Her mouth dropped open, but before she could ask anything, I dashed out the door and hopped down the stairs. Grabbing my keys off the half-moon table in the entryway, I worked to disconnect the house key from the ring.

I could hear Kiera getting dressed upstairs as I wrestled with the key. *Damn it, I told her not to move.* She came down the stairs a few moments later wearing shorts and a tank top, and I stopped unthreading the metal to stare at her. Damn. She was so beautiful. Did I have time to undress her again?

Stepping up to my side, she tilted her head as she glanced at my fingers. "What are you doing?"

Successfully removing the square key, I held it up to her. "Here, take my house key. Then you can stay and relax before work. I'll be at Pete's later. I'll pick it up from you then. Or...you can just keep it..." My heart started thudding harder in my chest. Kiera having my key was one step closer to her living with me. Where she belonged.

Kiera's lips twisted into a half-smile as she took the cool metal. I had trouble containing my grin—*she took it.* "Keep your key?" she said. "But how will you get into your house if I have your key?"

With a smile, I shrugged. "Why do I need to be here when you're not?" *You're all I need in this world anyway.*

Her lips pursed in amusement, but then she frowned. "You don't have to give me *your* key, Kellan. What about your other keys? My...old key?"

That dark day immediately flooded my mind. Once Kiera had recovered from...her injury...the one she'd only sustained because of me...and she'd moved in with her sister, she'd given me back my house key. Not directly, of course, since we'd been avoiding each other at the time. No, she'd given it to Anna, and Anna had given it to me. At the bar. The night she'd placed that key in my palm had been a bad one for me. I couldn't remember much of what had happened after Anna left, but I did remember that Sam had taken me home.

"I...uh, tossed them. Yours and Denny's." I'd even tossed my spare key, the hidden one only Evan knew about. I wasn't sure why, I'd just...needed it all to be gone. I was alone, so why would I need multiples of...anything. My gaze dropped to the floor as darkness swirled in my mind. "There was just something about having them in my home that I couldn't...I couldn't stomach." With a hard swallow, I let the past go and looked up at her. "But I can get some more made. Get you your own key...if you're comfortable with that?" *Please say yes.*

"I'm..." Pausing, she bit her lip. "Do you think we're ready for that, Kellan?"

I nodded before she even finished her question. "Yes, absolutely. It's...it's the next step, Kiera. The next step forward. You want that, right?" Not wanting her to think I was revisiting our conversation about living together, I quickly added, "'Cause it's not moving in together, it's just...opening our homes to each other. We're still separate, still going slow, but still...moving forward."

I felt jittery as I waited for her answer. Saying yes to taking the key for one afternoon was great, but saying yes to always keeping one on her...that was big for us. My nerves didn't evaporate until a wide smile graced her lips. "Okay, Kellan."

Before I could stop the reaction, my mouth dropped open in surprise. "You're saying yes?"

Laughing, she laced her arms around my neck. "Yes, I'm saying yes. You're right, this is an important step, one that we should definitely take. And I'll make a copy of my key too, then you can come over whenever you want," she added with a shrug.

Wrapping my arms around her waist, I pulled her tighter. "Like late at night, after my shows?" Slipping into her bed was one of my favorite things, and with a key it was going to be so much easier. Not able to resist teasing her, I added, "When you're in bed, all warm and naked, thinking of me...touching yourself..."

Pulling back, she lightly smacked my shoulder. "Kellan! I don't sleep naked...you know that." She flushed a little after saying it, and I had to smile that *that* was the comment she objected to.

"And what about the...other thing?" I asked, lifting my eyebrows. Just the thought of Kiera touching herself, thinking about me, made my blood surge, my body harden. Now, I was *definitely* undressing her before I left.

Kiera's flush deepened, and instead of answering my question—or denying it—she said, "You should go...you're going to be late meeting the guys."

That was true, but staying and tucking her back into my bed sounded like a lot more fun than practicing a bunch of songs I already knew inside and out. "They won't miss me," I said, leaning in for a kiss.

Showing a supreme amount of willpower, Kiera pushed me back. "Yes, they will, Kellan. As much as I would love to spend the rest of the day lounging in bed with you, the band can't do anything until you get there."

Even though I knew she was right, I frowned. "Okay, fine, I'll go. But we're discussing the touchy-touchy stuff later."

Looking adorably embarrassed, she rolled her eyes. "You're incorrigible."

"I'm curious...totally different." I gave her a short kiss that turned into a long kiss, then Kiera scooted my ass out the door before Matt started calling.

As I drove to Evan's loft, I couldn't stop grinning. *We're exchanging keys.* She'd shot me down on moving in together—which I completely understood—but she'd said yes to this, and that meant we were still heading down the right path. The forever path. I was beaming with bliss when I parked at Evan's.

Getting out of my car, I waved at Roxie and the guys at the auto body shop below Evan's place, then I headed up the stairs to the loft. Everyone else was there when I opened the door. Matt greeted me with a frown. "There you are. Did you forget?"

Still grinning, I shook my head. "Nope, just running late. Busy with Kiera."

Griffin nodded, a devious smile on his face like he knew exactly what I'd been doing. Evan smiled and shook his head, while Matt frowned deeper. "Look, I know you're happy, Kell, but things are in the works. Now's not the time to slack off."

Shutting the door, I walked all the way inside. "I know, Matt. I'm not slacking off, just trying to have a life too." Clapping my hands, I looked around the room. "Kiera and I agreed to exchange keys."

They all gave me blank stares. Griffin scratched his head. "And were you naked when this happened?"

Pursing my lips, I shook my head as I set down my guitar case. "No, we were dressed." Shrugging, I added, "I don't know, it's just...it's a big step for us."

Evan smiled, and Matt nodded like he understood. Griffin still seemed confused. Tucking his dirty-blond hair behind his ears, he said, "But you guys used to live together. Isn't that like congratulating you for copping a feel when you've already hit a home run?"

Inhaling a deep breath, I practiced restraint and patience. Then I ignored Griffin and focused on Matt. Stepping up to him, I said, "Hey, I was thinking...U-Dub is starting up again soon. Kiera's going to be a wreck...girl gets nervous about everything. But anyway, I'd really like to be available the night before her first day, so don't schedule anything, okay?"

Matt gave me an amused smile. "I know, Kell. You already told me not to book that night. I didn't."

I sighed in relief. "I know, I just wasn't sure if you remembered. I don't want to mess this up, you know? It's important to Kiera."

Shaking his head, Matt smiled at me. "You're way too high-strung about all this, Kell. Relax. She loves you, man."

My stomach tightened. *I know. But it wasn't all that long ago that she loved someone else. I need to be everything to her, so I can show her that she's everything to me.* Not able to say any of that to him, I instead smacked his shoulder and said, "Just wait until you and Rachel get serious."

He seemed annoyed by that. "We are serious. I mean...we're exclusive. Same thing, right?"

I just raised my eyebrow in answer. *Wait until she's the number one priority in your life, then you'll understand.*

Evan walked over and clapped me on the back. "Congrats, Kell." Looking over at Matt, he said, "Speaking of things in the works, the soundproofing stuff was backordered again. They're telling me it will still be a few more weeks."

Matt's mouth dropped open. "Seriously? What the hell. It's taking forever..."

Evan cringed, then shrugged. "Sorry, Matt. I know you're eager to get going." He snapped his fingers. "And that reminds me...before it gets here, I should probably talk to my landlord. He might not be cool with our plans, you know?"

Matt frowned but nodded. "Yeah...make sure you ask him right away, dude, don't keep putting it off. The sooner we get it set up, the sooner we can record a demo." He smiled, excitement in his eyes. "And the sooner we have a demo, the sooner we can get our name out there."

Griffin had stopped paying attention, but those words got him reinvested in the conversation. "Yeah, let's do this shit! I need groupies on a global scale." He mimed playing the guitar, sticking his tongue out and thrusting his hips. Matt grimaced.

Once Griff was done being a...rock star, he turned to me. "Hey, Kell, since you're passing out house keys, can I get one too?"

Giving him a warm smile, I calmly said, "Not a chance in hell, Griff."

We got down to business after that, and as I'd predicted, everything went smoothly. When it felt like we'd done enough for one day, we hopped in our cars and made our way to Pete's.

Even though it hadn't been all that long since I'd parted ways with my girl, I was excited to see Kiera. I had a feeling I would always be excited to see her. She was my world after all. When I walked through the double doors of the bar, I could feel her eyes on me, waiting. It gave me an unparalleled thrill to know she was just as eager to see me.

There was a mile-wide smile on her face as she walked my way, and if she wasn't the type to be embarrassed about it, I had a feeling she'd skip to me. What had her in such a cheery mood? Me? I hoped so.

"Hey," I said when she was close enough. "You're beaming. I know I satisfied you this morning, but I thought that would have worn off by now."

Rita, behind the bar, was close enough to hear me say that. Under her breath, I heard her murmur, "Sweetheart, it never wears off..."

Thankfully, Kiera hadn't heard Rita. Her cheeks reddened at hearing me though. Ignoring my comment, she held out her palm. Inside it was two keys—the one I'd given her this morning, and one that I could only assume was hers. "I made copies before work," she said, her grin infectious.

Staring at the silver metal in her hand made a rush of love and longing surge through me. I'd wanted this for so long. Wanted *her* for so long. Reaching down, I scooped her up in a hug that left her feet dangling off the floor. Kiera laughed as she wrapped her arms around my neck. "I love you so much, Kiera. I'm so glad we're doing this."

She gazed at me with such affection on her face, that it made my chest ache—in the best possible way. "I love you too, Kellan."

Setting her down, I grabbed the keys from her hand and shoved them both in my pocket, then I grabbed her face and gave her the kiss I'd been dying to give her ever since I'd stepped through the doors. As our mouths moved together, I heard pissing and moaning in the bar. Someone, most likely Griffin, complained that we should get a room. Kiera let out a soft sigh, a sound that nearly undid me, so I ignored them all and continued kissing her. They'd have to pry me away with a crowbar if she kept making *that* sound.

Unfortunately, Kiera pushed me away. I was happy to see she was breathless when she did. "I've got to get back to work," she said, biting her lip and studying my face. From her expression, it was clear she wanted to say fuck it just as much as I wanted her to say fuck it. But she was right, and she did need to get back to work. Sometimes, being responsible really sucked.

She started to pull away from me, but I grabbed her hand to keep her close by. The look she gave me was adoring, but adamant. "I've got to go, Kellan."

Nodding at her, I said, "I know, I just wanted to tell you that we've got plans tomorrow."

"Do we?" she said with a smile. "And what plans are those?"

Giving her a crooked grin, I said, "Bed shopping. I'm done with that futon. In fact, I might burn it when I come over tonight."

Laughing, she gave me a kiss on the cheek. "Don't do that. Then we'd have nowhere to sleep."

"And who said we were sleeping?" I asked, lifting an eyebrow.

Her smile both amused and intrigued, Kiera rolled her eyes at me before she walked away. From behind me, Rita said, "I've got a bed I can sell you, Kellan." The sultriness in her voice left no question to what she was really offering.

Turning to look at her, I tossed a smirk her way. "I'm sure you do, Rita." Not that I would ever go there again.

The night went by slowly. I was too eager to test out my key, too eager to get Kiera a new bed in the morning, too eager to start moving forward. I ended up leaving Pete's before Kiera's shift was over—only because Anna was home, and Kiera had driven Denny's old piece of shit Honda to work. If she hadn't taken it, I would have stuck by her side until closing time. My girl didn't have to scrounge for a ride, not unless I was out late playing a gig somewhere. Unfortunately, on those nights, she usually got off work before me. Not always though. Picking her up was a priority to me and the guys knew that.

After leaving Pete's, I made my way to a 24-hour grocery store. Kiera needed flowers. She would say she didn't, of course, but I disagreed. She did. Whatever it took to make her day a little brighter. I picked up some wine too. I didn't usually drink the stuff, but...it felt romantic, and I wanted a little romance tonight.

When I got to Kiera's, I was giddy when I slid the key into the lock—*my key*. This was the first time in my life that I'd ever had unrestricted access to a woman's place. It was the only time I'd ever been invited into a girl's home when she wasn't there—welcomed into her sanctuary, encouraged to belong. It was a little mind-boggling to me and a touch surreal. A part of me didn't expect the key to work, but the bolt smoothly slid free, and the heavy door easily pushed open. My grin was enormous. Until I stepped inside.

"Oh God, Griffin! Fuck! Yes!"

Once I heard that, I knew I should step back out of the apartment, relock the door, and walk away, but damn if I didn't instinctually look up. I instantly regretted it. Anna and Kiera's place was small, and the living room was right there in full view of the front door. And right there, in full view of *me*, were Anna and my bassist, going at it on the world's ugliest orange couch.

Clothes were strewn everywhere in the living room, and the two...lovebirds were sprawled haphazardly over the sofa. Anna was a little preoccupied, but oddly enough, Griffin heard me enter. He looked up at me, then raised a hand in greeting, like I was meeting him for rehearsal, not interrupting a moment with his...whatever Anna was to him. "Hey, Kell...with you in a minute. I'm so...fucking...close..." His voice was strained, and I did not want to think about why.

"Don't, uh...I'm...Fuck this..." Closing my eyes, I backed out of the room. Goddamn it. That image was going to stick with me for the next hundred years. I really hated walking in on Griffin screwing. And it happened far too frequently. How Matt stayed sane living with him was beyond me. Oh well, better me walking in on him than Kiera. While I could handle the erotic visual, Kiera would probably vomit. Repeatedly.

Speed-walking down the hall, I made my way back to my car. I'd have to let Kiera know to come to my place instead. There was no way Kiera and I were going to have a magical, romantic night at her place with those two around. Anna and Griffin were both insatiable, and it was impossible to gauge how long they might go at it—they could be like that for the rest of the night. It was a sight Kiera didn't need to see. Me neither, for that matter. Damn, I really wish I'd noticed Griffin's Vanagon in the parking lot.

I called the bar once I was safe at my empty, quiet home. The phone rang several times, until finally, Pete answered it in his office. He seemed less than pleased once he realized it was me. "Hey, Pete. It's your favorite rock star."

"Rod Stewart?"

I smirked at his answer. "Funny. No, it's Kellan. I need to talk to Kiera real quick, can you grab her for me?"

"Kellan...? Aren't you in the bar with her?" It was a reasonable question. Unless I was practicing or playing, I was usually at Pete's with Kiera. "If this is some kind of practical joke, I'm not in the mood."

"It's not," I assured him. "I left a while ago." A fact I was now regretting.

Pete let out a long sigh. "Can't you come back if you want to talk to her? I have things to do, other than run errands for you."

I'd considered going back to the bar to tell her, but I had a feeling I wouldn't leave again if I did that, and I really wanted to surprise Kiera. I had romantic plans for the two of us, if only life would stop trying to get in the way of them. "Pete...you know I wouldn't ask if it wasn't an emergency." And it was. Kiera wouldn't want to run the risk of walking in on what I'd just walked in on.

Pete grunted in annoyance. "All right, fine. But it better be an emergency, Kellan."

"I swear on Griffin's testicles, it is."

Pete snorted, then I heard the phone being set down. Kiera's voice was on the line a few moments later. It was music to my ears. "Hello?" God, she sounded sexy on the phone. I should call her more often.

Smiling into the receiver, I leaned against the kitchen counter. "Hi...I was hoping you could help me. I'm looking for the sexiest woman in the world. She's around five-five, with gorgeous wavy, brown hair, sultry hazel eyes that you can get lost in for days, and a body that's downright lethal."

"Hmmm, no...doesn't sound familiar."

Containing a laugh, I asked her, "Are you sure? Because I have it on good authority that she works there at the bar. In fact, I saw her there just today, wearing one of those tight Pete's T-shirts and these small shorts that were practically molded onto her perfect ass. God, when she bent over, all I wanted to do was—"

"Kellan! Oh my God...stop..."

I could hear the blush in her voice, and I couldn't help but laugh. "Ah, so you have seen her."

She giggled into the phone, and my heart damn near skipped a beat. She could argue with me all she wanted, but every single word I'd just said was true. She was perfection. "Why are you harassing me on the phone at work?" she asked. "Did you get bored waiting for me at my place?"

"Ah...if only that were the case. No, I accidentally ran into... well, let's just say Anna and Griffin are on a date, and it's going *really* well. It could be over by now, or it could be one of those marathon things that never seems to end. Either way, you're gonna want to come to my place tonight."

"Ugh, yeah, okay. Thanks for the heads up."

"Not a problem. Whatever I can do to spare you from witnessing what I was...too unfortunate to not miss." Griffin's face flashed in my head. Yep, definitely stuck there for a long time.

Kiera laughed, then slowly said, "Wait, you *witnessed* stuff? Where were they?"

Chewing on my lip, I took a moment to answer her. "It's best if you don't know. Trust me."

She let out a long sigh but didn't press me for details. I was happy she didn't. She'd never sit on the couch again if she knew.

Kiera and I said our goodbyes, then I got to work on my romantic preparations. When I was done, I waited for Kiera to arrive with an almost impatient sense of expectation. It felt like it took forever for the clock to move forward. Why did time have to move so slowly when you were waiting for something amazing to happen? And move so quickly once you were enjoying that amazing thing? That just wasn't fair.

When I finally heard Denny's clunky car pull into the driveway, I could barely contain my excitement. As Kiera shut off the engine, I started lighting my strategically placed candles—there were several of them, all over my room. I was just finishing up when I heard her knock on the front door. Smiling, I ignored the soft sound and poured Kiera a glass of wine. There was one more quiet knock, and then Kiera seemed to remember that she had a key now. My grin was huge as I listened to her turning the lock. Such a beautiful sound.

"Kellan? Did you fall asleep?" Kiera asked as she shut the front door.

Staying still and silent, I didn't answer her. I felt like my jaw was going to crack I was smiling so hard. Inhaling a deep breath, I calmed my features. I could hear Kiera coming up the steps now, and I turned to face my closed bedroom door. "Kellan?" she was saying. "You're not going to jump out and scare me, are you? Because I really hate that."

I bit my lip to stop myself from either laughing or answering her. Every single light was off inside the house, so I could easily see how she'd think I was sleeping or hiding. That wasn't my surprise though. When she finally cracked open the door to my bedroom, I stayed perfectly still and perfectly calm. Fear wasn't my goal tonight.

Kiera's mouth dropped open as she entered my candlelit

sanctuary. The softly glowing lights caressed her face, making her appear to radiate from within—she was breathtaking. After examining the room, her hazel eyes drifted to me, and the objects in my hands: a bouquet of flowers and a glass of wine.

"Kellan?" she said, her voice shaky. "What is all this? Is tonight some special occasion that I'm not aware of?" She chewed on her lip like she was worried she'd forgotten something. Adorable.

Smiling brightly, I told her, "Yes. The most beautiful girl in the world walked through my door...with her own key. That is most definitely something to celebrate."

Her eyes drifted to the floor, and even though I couldn't see it in the candlelight, I knew she was blushing. "Kellan, I'm not—"

Setting the flowers on my bed, I stepped up to her. "I know what you're going to say, and yes, you are." Cupping her face, I gently caressed her cheek. "You are the most extraordinary thing in the world to me, Kiera."

"Because I love you..." The way she said it was laced with sadness, like my adoration was a temporary thing. Like anyone could love me, and the second someone else did, my feelings would somehow change. Like her love wasn't enough. Like it wasn't *everything*.

"No, because you're perfect...and you love me. The best of both worlds."

Her smile was genuine as she leaned forward to kiss me. When we separated, I handed her the glass of wine. She took a sip, her full lips curling over the rim in an intriguing way that made me wish I was her wine glass. Her eyes glanced around our romantic haven again, then she said, "This is very sweet, thank you." I was just about to tell her that I should be thanking her when she suddenly bit her lip and her eyes turned concerned. "Kellan...you know I'm yours, right?"

"Yes." *By some miracle, some incomprehensible twist of fate, you* are *mine. For now.* God, I did *not* want to think about losing her again. But maybe that wouldn't happen. Maybe I'd get to keep her. Maybe.

Kiera looked at me funny, like she'd heard all of my silent additions. Strange, how we were pouring our hearts out with love and devotion, yet, at the same time, confessing all of our doubts and fears. "Okay," she said, setting her wine down on my nightstand. Wrapping her arms around my neck, she added, "I just...I don't want you to feel like you have to be this extravagant all the time. I'm not going anywhere."

"I know that."

"Do you?"

No, not really. But I hoped it every day. Not wanting to outright speak my fears, I sighed. "I'm trying, Kiera. This is all... very new to me."

"Me too."

I couldn't stop the frown from forming. That wasn't entirely true. "No, it's not...you had...you've had this before, Kiera." Admitting that darkened my heart and tightened my chest. We'd never completely be on equal footing, because unlike me, this wasn't her first time. It wasn't as...special.

Maybe sensing that my mood had changed, Kiera ducked down to search my eyes. "Not like this, Kellan. Not like *you*."

The look on her face was full of truth and meaning. She truly felt that whatever magic she and I had, our relationship, our love, was different than what she and Denny had shared together. *Ours* was new to her and in that way, it was special. Maybe not first-love special, but special nonetheless, and hearing that was comforting. It gave me some hope, lightened my heart.

"That is...really good to hear," I said with a smile. And just like that, I was lighter than air again. How she could bend my mood so easily was mystifying to me.

Kiera relaxed in my arms when she saw my untroubled expression. "Can we be done talking now?" she asked, a playful gleam in her eye.

"I thought you'd never ask..." I murmured, lowering my lips to hers.

She giggled as our mouths connected, and I was overcome by a rush of warmth and longing. I loved her so much, and nothing was ever going to change that fact. It was just about the only thing in my life that I was unwaveringly certain of—I was going to be in love with Kiera until the day I died.

Chapter 4
UNCOMFORTABLE/COMFORTABLE

I awoke before Kiera the next morning—not too surprising. After my morning routine, I went downstairs to make some coffee. I was pouring water into the back of the machine when Kiera stepped into the kitchen with me. I did a double take when I saw her. She was yawning and stretching, exposing a good portion of her stomach.

That delicious sight distracted me for a moment, but I recovered when she looped her arms around my neck. "You're up," I said. "I thought I'd have to wake you with the aroma of Arabica beans."

Giving me a soft smile, she kissed my neck—it instantly ignited me. "As much as I love coffee, you smell infinitely better. And the bed was cold without you." She pouted for a half-second, then smiled and kissed me.

Reveling in the feeling of her skin on my lips, I murmured, "How about we go warm it back up?"

She averted her eyes in an expression of demureness that I found absolutely irresistible. Laughing, I pulled her tight and kissed her head. "How about we have coffee, then go search out a new bed. Something large that we can roll around in."

A coy smile was on her lips when she peeked up at me. "Not too large. My room is only so big."

"I'm nothing if not sensible," I answered with a smirk.

She rewarded me with a musical laugh, then placed her soft lips to mine. Heaven. I savored the sweetness a moment, then told her, "I was serious about rewarming my bed though...we've got plenty of time."

Smacking my chest, she moved away from me. "No, we don't. You know as well as I do that if we go back upstairs, we won't come down again until it's time for me to go to work."

I gave her a look of mock indignation. "Are you saying you would hold me hostage in my own bedroom? Make me have sex with you over and over again?" Changing my face, I gave her a wicked grin. "Because I'm completely fine with that." I held my wrists together in front of me, ready for her to capture my body... since she had already captured my heart.

Kiera sputtered, her cheeks flaming bright red. "I...no, Kellan...I...I'm gonna finish the coffee."

Her awkward embarrassment was so cute, so sweet. Half the fun of riling her up was seeing her reaction. But even with how much that amused me, I'd love to see her feel confident and secure enough to throw my sex-filled remarks right back at me. God, that would turn me on. Which might be one of the reasons why she didn't do it. I was already in a perpetual state of semi-arousal around her. If she started talking like me, well, we'd be just as bad as Anna and Griffin. But was that really a bad thing?

While the coffee brewed, Kiera told me about the art class she was taking with Jenny and Kate. "They're both really good. Me? Well, I'm...learning." She frowned after she said it, like she didn't believe she could be taught.

I smiled, both at her expression and her newfound hobby. "Well, I think it's great, and I'm proud of you for trying something a little out of your comfort zone. Although...it kind of sucks that it takes you away from me twice a week." Her class had her bailing from bed Monday and Wednesday mornings.

"I know," she said. "But it's important for us to have interests outside of...each other." I raised an eyebrow at that, and she rolled her eyes. "You know I mean that in the best possible way."

"Mmmm-hmm."

She pursed her lips at me, and I pinched her ass until she giggled. Aside from the noise she made when she hit her climax, that was my most favorite sound. Well, after her saying my name. I guess I had multiple favorite sounds.

Once coffee was done and Kiera and I were dressed for the day—without warming up my bed, unfortunately—we headed out to find her a comfortable place to rest. The minute we entered the mattress store and I saw all those beds waiting...invitingly...I started having multiple inappropriate visions, all of them including Kiera spread out on those perfect, white, pillow-topped—

"Oh my God, Kellan Kyle...walking into my store after all this time..."

Snapping out of my fantasy, I looked over to the salesperson who'd said my name. Our eyes met, and a low swear escaped my lips. I knew her. Well, I knew *of* her, in an intimate way, but I didn't actually know her. I understood the difference now. But even worse than the fact that I'd slept with her before, this girl was one of the nameless faces I'd used to ease the pain when Kiera and I had decided to put an end to the not-so-innocent flirting. That made her a relatively recent fling...an in-between in the grand scheme of Kiera and me. That shouldn't make a difference, but somehow...it did. I felt ill.

Not wanting Kiera to instantly know about my connection with this girl—although she'd probably already figured it out—I slapped on a casual smile and clasped Kiera's hand tighter. "Hey... how's it going?"

The girl eyed Kiera, me, and our interlaced fingers. *Please be cool*, I silently begged. *I was nothing to you, otherwise I would have heard from you again. Don't act all possessive now...now that it could actually do some damage.*

Thankfully, the woman's face shifted into a professional smile. She understood. Hopefully. "Things are good, I can't complain. I'm getting married next spring." She lifted her hand and I saw a sizeable rock on her finger. "And I'm assuming you two are looking for a new bed?"

Oh, thank God...she's engaged. "Yes, thank you...Paige." And thank God for nametags.

Paige's smile brightened. "Well, come on in, I'll show you the very best we have."

I relaxed my hold on Kiera as we started following Paige, but Kiera didn't relax her hold on me. Knowing I owed her...something...I glanced down at her inquisitive eyes. I opened my mouth, but no good explanation came to mind. Lying was something I was very comfortable with, but Kiera and I were trying to be honest with each other. Smoothing this over with a half-truth wouldn't help anything. And besides, Kiera knew all my lines, when it came to this particular matter, at least. I couldn't say she was a friend, couldn't say we used to hang out, couldn't say anything except the truth. Being a former manwhore had consequences.

With a sigh, I gave up trying to think of something nonconfrontational to say. "We can go somewhere else," I told her instead.

Kiera's lips pressed together as I confirmed what she'd probably suspected. I couldn't tell what she was thinking, and that made me a little nervous. She glanced at me, back to the girl, then at me again. Finally, when the curiosity was almost too much for me to bear, she shook her head. "Here is fine. And honestly, she'll probably give us an outstanding deal because you...know her."

Her voice was sullen, unhappy that we were running into yet another one of my dalliances. Hoping she wasn't too upset, I made myself smile. This couldn't be easy for her. I only had to deal with one man in her past, although sometimes, just that one was way too many.

Trying to lighten the mood, I asked her, "How do you know she'll give us a deal? She could charge us more."

Kiera rolled her eyes and shook her head again. "I've slept with you, Kellan. We're getting a deal."

It shouldn't have amused me, but yeah, her comment made me grin. Because of the tender age I'd started, and my proclivity for finding companionship, I had a lot of...experience. Whether it was a good thing or a bad thing, I knew exactly what I was doing when it came to the female form, and *everyone* left my bed satisfied.

Kiera laughed when she noticed my expression, and I took that as a good sign that she was letting this go. It probably helped that Paige was clearly invested in someone else, and that she wasn't eye-fucking me at every opportunity. I think those were the girls who really bothered Kiera—the ones who made it obvious that they wanted another taste and would do just about anything to get it. But truly, those girls were few and far between. Most women used me up and moved on, never to think about me again. I just don't think Kiera realized that.

The new bed arrived late Sunday afternoon, on Kiera's night off. It was large, comfortable, springy, and Kiera had been right—Paige gave us a spectacular deal on it. I couldn't wait to test it out. But unfortunately, I had a gig in Pioneer Square, so breaking it in was going to have to wait until much later. A fact that made me sad, until I remembered that I had a key to Kiera's apartment now. Usually when I wanted to pop in on her after a show, I had to tell her beforehand that I was going to drop by, so she could leave the door unlocked for me. It took a lot of the spontaneity out of it, not to mention, it really wasn't a good idea for her to leave her apartment door unsecured, even if it was just for a couple of hours. I usually ended up asking Anna to stay up and let me in, since I *really* enjoyed crawling into bed with Kiera when she was already asleep. Anna was cool with that...she was a night owl anyway. But now...now I could just come over without all the prep work. I could slip into Kiera's bed without her ever knowing I was planning on being there. I had a feeling she'd like that kind of surprise...I knew I was excited.

"Dude, why are you bouncing off the walls? You're practically vibrating...it's giving me a headache."

I looked over at Griffin, sullenly sitting on a piece of equipment, equipment he should be helping us move. He did look a little ill, like he was hungover or something. At *night*? "Just in a good mood. What's wrong with you? Past your bedtime?"

He gave me a smug look, then flipped me off. "Matt and I stopped by a sorority this afternoon. They were drinking mimosas...so I had some."

Matt laughed as he set down a piece of Evan's drums. "Some? You polished off their gallon jug, then started drinking the champagne straight from the bottle. I think it might be time for you to self-evaluate. You might need help."

Evan laughed while Griffin shot Matt a nasty glare. Lifting his middle finger to him, he said, "Self-evaluate that, fucker. I was just trying to be polite, maybe get a little action."

Shaking his head, Matt said, "We weren't there for action. We were there booking a show." He turned to Evan and me. "They want a band to play at their annual party in the spring. No, let me rephrase that...they want *us* to play at their annual party in the spring."

His grin was a mile wide, until Griffin threw a piece of trash at him. Frowning, Griffin said, "*You* were there to book a show, Mr. Responsibility. I was there to convince the girls that hiring us would be an automatic good time. That's called networking, fuckhead."

Matt's smile faded as he shifted his gaze back to Griffin. "You almost threw up on yourself, and you pushed about three girls out of your way to get to the bathroom. That's not networking. That's...Griffin-ing."

Griffin smiled and raised his hand in a fist bump. No one

connected with him. Lowering his hand, he cringed in pain. "I fucking hate champagne. Does anybody have Tylenol? Or a sledgehammer?"

He laid down after that, closing his eyes. Frowning, I turned to Matt. "Is he even going to be able to play?"

Matt scowled as he examined his comatose cousin. "He has to, we don't have anybody else." Walking over to him, he kicked his feet. "Come on, get up, Griffin."

Griffin groaned and looked up at him. "Why?"

Matt tossed his hands at the equipment we were still trying to unload. "We've gotta get our shit in there." Reaching down, he made him stand. Voice softer, he said, "Come on, moving around will help. I promise."

Griffin grimaced, looking for all the world like every movement he made was killing him. Frowning at Matt, he told him, "Why'd you let me drink so much, dude? I thought you had my back?"

With a sigh, Matt shook his head. "Like I keep telling you, I'm not your keeper. And I did try to stop you. You gave me the bird and told me to fuck off. Repeatedly."

A strange look crossed Griffin's face, like he was trying to remember that. "Oh, well...you shouldn't have listened to me."

Passing by the pair on his way to the van, Evan clapped Griffin's shoulder. "We never do, Griff. We never do."

I laughed with Evan as I helped him carry stuff into the bar. Looking my way, Evan said, "He's right, you know. You *are* practically vibrating. Something going on?" He raised an eyebrow and studied my face.

Grinning, I shook my head. "No, nothing major. Things are just going really well with Kiera. I'm just...happy." For once in my life, every aspect of my life was great. I was *exactly* where I wanted to be.

We got to the back of the stage and set down our stuff. Smiling, Evan clapped me on the shoulder. "I'm glad to hear it, man. And just so you know, yes...I will totally be your best man."

I felt heat in my cheeks. Fuck, was I blushing? I didn't blush. Well...rarely. It took a lot to embarrass me. And what I felt wasn't really embarrassment, it was more like...longing. Kiera as my wife... God, I almost couldn't even picture it.

"We're so not there yet, but thanks...it's nice to know you've got my back. And I won't be stuck with Griffin." As we headed to the van for more stuff, I asked Evan, "What about you and Jenny? Have you guys talked about...future stuff?"

Evan's answering smile was enormous. "Oh yeah, we're totally getting hitched one day. Then we'll get a place, start spitting out kids. It's gonna be awesome."

The way he said it was so casual, like he'd just told me he was getting groceries after the show or something. A part of me was envious over their laidback relationship. Kiera and I, well, we weren't volatile, but we certainly had our moments. "Any idea when?" I asked.

Evan shrugged. "Whenever." I laughed at his answer. Typical go-with-the-flow response.

Twenty minutes later, all our stuff—and Griffin—was in place on stage, and we were ready to go. The bar we were in was just about the same size as Pete's. Truly, it was more of a nightclub, and the crowd in front of us danced their hearts out to every song. Because we played this place often, and we knew what to expect, we only played our fast, upbeat songs, since that was what the crowd here preferred. It was fun, but it didn't allow for any breaks, and we were all exhausted by the end of the night. Griffin especially. He didn't even try to help put stuff away, just shuffled to the van and fell asleep in the passenger's seat. I almost felt bad for him...but then I remembered walking in on him and Anna. *With you in a minute*. Asshole.

Matt drove Griffin's van back to Evan's place, then the three of us unloaded the equipment while Griffin snored. Once we were done, I said goodnight to Matt and Evan and climbed back into my Chevelle. To crawl into bed with my girl. It made me insanely happy to know that I wasn't going to be crawling into a cold, empty bed tonight. Even if Kiera remained unconscious, she'd be with me, and that was all that mattered.

Once I parked my car, I practically bounded to Kiera's door. My smile was huge when I slipped my key in the lock and turned it—I didn't think I'd ever get used to this feeling of belonging. I closed the door behind me, careful to be as quiet as possible so I didn't wake anyone, then I tiptoed down the hall to Kiera's room. The first thing I noticed was her brand-new bed. It was gigantic, almost too big for the room, but man, it looked comfortable. Kiera was sprawled out on top of it, sound asleep. Considering how uncomfortable her futon had been, I had to imagine this was the best sleep she'd had in a while...when she wasn't at my place, of course.

I quietly closed her bedroom door, then undressed. When I was down to my boxers, I pulled back the covers and slipped inside. I instantly sought Kiera's warm, soft body, and like her skin was magic, every worry evaporated from my mind. Wrapping my arms and legs around her, I pulled her in tight. "God, you feel good," I murmured, kissing her neck.

She hummed a pleased noise and angled her face away to give me better access. "Kellan...?" she said, her voice thick with sleep. "I didn't know you were coming over tonight."

"Where else would I go?" I grinned, so happy I could finally truly surprise her with my late-night visits.

A small laugh escaped her. It ignited me. "Your house?"

My tongue reached out to taste her skin, and I heard her gasp. "Like I've told you before, I prefer hot beds that have been warmed up by your naked body."

"But I'm not naked..." she muttered.

"Yes...that is a problem," I told her, sliding my lips up her neck to her ear. Her breath picked up in the quiet room, and her hand clenched and unclenched mine. "I don't know why you insist on wearing pajamas to bed. I know I've told you before... they're just going to get ripped off of you. Why bother?" I whispered, nibbling on her lobe.

"But I didn't know you were coming over," she panted, turning her head my way.

Staring at her, loving the way the darkness amplified her beauty, I smiled and said, "Best to always be prepared then."

Releasing my hand, she reached up for my face and brought my mouth down to hers. I ran my free hand up her chest, around the curve of her breast, teasing without touching. Kiera made an erotic noise in my mouth, then her fingers threaded into my hair. God, I loved that. I swirled my thumb over her nipple, and she moaned. That was the beginning of the end for me.

My lips left her mouth, traveling across her jaw, down her throat; her salty skin was heaven. Her chest was noticeably rising faster when I reached it, and her fingers clenched in my hair. Pushing up her shirt, I found her breast, then lightly ran my tongue over the sensitive peak. A louder moan left her lips, and she pulled down on my head wanting more. My breath picked up as desire pounded through me. This woman before me was a goddess, and I wanted to explore all of her.

After removing her shirt, I enclosed her nipple in my mouth, stroking, swirling, then I moved on to the other one. Once she was squirming beneath me, I moved my mouth down her abdomen. "Oh God," left her lips, and I smiled. I hadn't even gotten to the good part yet. How much she wanted me made me ache, and I was straining against my boxers, eager to be one with her. Soon.

When I got to her pants, I slipped them and her underwear down her hips, then off her legs. She was truly restless now, wanting so much more from me. I gently ran my hands down her legs, calming her, then I leaned forward, and ran my tongue up her core. "Oh...God...Kellan..." That was much louder than before—she was awake in every sense of the word now.

She pulled my head, wanting my mouth back on her, and I went eagerly. A groan left me as I tasted her desire for me. She was so ready, panting in an escalating rhythm that I knew meant she was close. I pulled back, and she clutched my shoulder, hard. Her gaze snapped down to mine, and our eyes locked in the darkness. Hers were nearly wild with desire, and I had to imagine mine looked the same.

"I want you so much, Kiera." Every. Single. Day.

"Take me," she breathed, opening her arms in a welcoming gesture.

I tore off my boxers, then worked my way back up her chest to her lips. Once we were flush together, I pressed inside her. A groan escaped me when I did. I'd never realized how incredible skin-to-skin contact was until Kiera, and I didn't think I could go back to condoms now. Not that I ever wanted to—this was the woman I was going to make love to for the rest of my life. Hopefully.

Her arms wrapped around me as we moved together, drawing me in, drawing me closer. Kiera had a way of making sex so much more intimate than it had ever been before. It was like our souls were connecting, not our bodies. "Oh God, Kellan, you feel... so..." Her voice trailed off as emotion overtook her.

"God, Kiera...I love you..." The words escaped me unconsciously. They did almost every time we made love.

A shudder passed through Kiera, and she worked against me harder, needing more. We were both warm now, breathless. As I moved with her, I felt my climax approaching, and then it was like I was floating, riding a wave of bliss that I never wanted to end. Kiera's cries grew more intense, and I felt her stiffen beneath me as she hit the wall. Her body constricting pushed mine over the edge, and an explosion of euphoria burst through me, intensifying as I came. Oh...God...

It felt like it took an eternity for the wave of ecstasy to subside, and even then, I felt tiny residual shivers of it, like aftershocks. Trying to collect my breath, I clutched Kiera tight. She was having similar difficulty calming down. Every time with her was so intense, it always took my breath away.

When I was more or less put back together, I pulled back to look at her. "I really love this bed," I said with a grin.

Kiera laughed, then gave me a kiss. "And I really love you."

Moving to her side, I pulled her into me, keeping her close. "Now *this* is how you should go to bed every night," I said, the lull of sleep starting to pull me under. Kiera let out a tired laugh, then nestled her back against my chest.

I kissed her shoulder, and Kiera twisted her head to look toward me. "Before I forget...I emptied a drawer for you."

Moving back, I pulled on her shoulder, so I could see her face better. "Emptied a drawer...is that code for something? Because I'm drawing a blank."

She grinned, then shook her head. "No code. I mean that literally." My brows were still bunched in confusion, until she pointed over to her dresser. "I removed all of my things from the top drawer of the dresser...so you could put your things in there. So you don't have to make a special trip to your house, every time you spend the night here."

My gaze went from the dresser to her face to the dresser. "You...you made room for me?" Even though we'd exchanged keys, even though we'd talked about living together down the road, there was something about this unasked for, unexpected gesture of openness that tore at me.

Her warm fingers touched my cheek, returning my eyes to hers. "I'll always make room for you."

A strange feeling ripped through my chest, burning me with its intensity. "No one's ever made room for me. No one's ever..." I couldn't finish that thought and had to swallow back the sudden lump in my throat.

Kiera's thumb brushed over my cheek, and her eyes shifted to concern. "Kellan, why are you—?"

I cut off her question with a quick kiss. "I'm fine, Kiera, I just didn't expect...That was very kind. Thank you." I tried to keep my expression warm and loving, only appropriately emotional, but I could tell from the crystalline glossiness in her eyes, that she could see my pain, my loneliness...my grief.

"I hate what they did to you," she murmured under her

breath, below what she thought I could hear. I knew exactly what she meant, exactly who she was talking about...I hated what they did to me too.

The pain amplified, like a punch to the gut, but still, I kept my expression neutral. "I'm fine, Kiera," I reiterated, trying to soothe the sudden anger in her eyes. I think if my parents were still alive, Kiera would scream at them every day for how they'd treated me. Not that I'd let her near them—I wouldn't allow those bastards to turn their vitriol on her.

Kiera shook her head as she stared at me. "You always tell me you're fine...but there's still so much pain." Her voice hitched, and the wetness in her eyes grew heavier. "Have you ever thought about talking to someone? A professional?"

Rolling onto my back, I stared at the ceiling. "You want me to see a shrink? You think I'm...broken?" My voice had a harsh edge to it. I didn't want it to come out that way, but I couldn't keep the heat out. I really didn't like the idea of Kiera seeing me as damaged goods. Even if that was exactly what I was.

She instantly popped up on her elbow and hovered over me. "No, I don't. You've endured so much, but you're still such a good man..." I had to cringe away from that comment. There were many people on this earth—my ex-best friend among them—who thought I was anything but a good person.

Seeing me flinch, Kiera continued her thought. "You're a survivor, Kellan. But being a survivor doesn't mean you have to keep everything to yourself. Talking to someone might ease the pain. Don't you want that?"

An instant objection on my lips, I looked over at her. The words died as I stared at her perfect face, at the depth of love and caring etched in every line, every curve. She was trying to help me, I knew that. But my parents were gone, and as far as I was concerned, all the horrible things they'd done to me had died with them. There was no need to refresh the memories by talking about them. Whenever I accidentally did, it only made everything hurt again. Nothing eased that pain, and nothing ever would. Except her.

"What I want...is you," I told her. Then I reached up and pulled her mouth to mine.

She sighed before our lips connected. A resigned sigh, like she understood I was closing the door on the conversation. Kissing me softly, she murmured, "You have me, Kellan. Heart and soul."

I smiled, grateful for that fact, then I pushed her onto her back and moved over the top of her. Our kiss grew heated, and a few moments later, I pressed inside her again, showing her that the feeling was mutual—she had my heart and soul too. Hopefully she was kind to it, because whether she realized it or not, she could hurt me a thousand times worse than my parents ever had. And knowing that terrified me.

Chapter 5
GAMES

As the days stretched on, things between Kiera and me just got better and better. We alternated where we met up, swapping out her place for mine. My drawer in her dresser was full of anything I might need whenever I stayed at her apartment, and the drawer I'd emptied for her at my house was equally full of her things. I had to admit, I loved having a part of her in my room with me when she wasn't there physically. It was comforting. Plus, her clothes smelled like her...it turned me on.

I was alone for the time being, working on lyrics in my kitchen. I was just about done with a new song for the guys, something Matt should be thrilled about. Ever since Kiera and I had started dating, my knack for spitting out songs had...slowed. Who knew that being absurdly happy could squelch the creative process? But thankfully, I'd finally come up with something for the guys, and shockingly enough, it wasn't a sappy, all-is-right-with-the-world song. No, it was still about pain and regret. Thanks to the tortured history Kiera and I shared, I still had pockets of remorse to sing about.

Writing about that time always brought Kiera forefront to my mind. She was at her art class with Jenny and Kate. I'd seen some of Jenny's pieces hung up at Evan's place—the girl had crazy talent—but I'd never seen anything from Kiera. She never brought home any of her work, or if she did, it immediately went into the garbage can, like she was embarrassed or something. It left me curious and clueless about how she was doing in the class —how she was *actually* doing in the class. She was all too quick to tell me she had the talent of a two-year-old, but I didn't buy that for a second. I had no doubt that her art wasn't nearly as bad as she thought it was. Kiera was too hard on herself. And she was way too stressed out about school starting tomorrow.

I swear she hadn't slept at all last night, just stared at the ceiling thinking, planning...agonizing. Since this wasn't her first time at the school, I was a little mystified why she was worrying about it. She didn't get nervous going into Pete's anymore, so what was the difference? And it didn't seem to be the upcoming workload that was freaking her out either. It was literally the idea of walking into a new class, not knowing what to expect. It was strange to me, since I didn't get nervous about stuff like that, but it was a real concern for her, so I was doing my best to think of ways to help her through it.

Walking her to class was a given—she liked it, and I liked it too. Honestly, it was one of my favorite things about Kiera being in school. That and helping her study. I was a firm believer that sex before, during, or after studying helped you retain things. A belief I was willing to help Kiera put to the test over and over again this fall. For science's sake, of course.

Laughing at that thought, I set my notebook aside for the day. I wanted to get in a run before Kiera was done with her art class. Maybe exercise would help me think of a way to get her to relax tonight, forget about the needless fears awaiting her in the morning. Something unexpected and fun, something she could think about when she was nervous, something she'd never forget. Yeah, I would do that for her tonight. Help her make a memory, freeze a moment in time. With me.

Eager for the memory to start, even though I had no idea what the memory was going to entail, I quickly changed into my workout gear—a T-shirt and track pants. Grabbing my running shoes, I headed out the door and locked up my house. It was such a relief to know that I didn't have to worry about beating Kiera back to my home—she could let herself in whenever she got there.

My house rested on a steep hill, about halfway down the incline. That meant I could either start my workout with a bang or end it with one. It was still kind of strange to me, living on one of the many extreme hills that dotted the city. My childhood home in West Seattle had been in a relatively flat spot, considering the area, and I hadn't had the truly rugged hill experience until moving here.

I'd started running as a teenager. It had given me an excuse to get out of the house, get away from my parents, and every time I'd gone out, I'd fantasized about never coming back, about picking a straight line and sticking to it, until I was somewhere far away from them. I'd always come back though. Out of fear, I think, fear of what they'd do if they ever found me. Then the moment I'd graduated, I'd run away for real, only to find that my parents hadn't done a damn thing. Maybe I should have run away ages ago.

Not wanting to think about my parents on a day that could potentially be amazing, I forced my thoughts back to my girlfriend. God, she was so incredible. She filled me with light, filled me with hope, and I wanted to do the same thing for her. Tonight needed to be special.

About halfway through my run, I reached the park where I liked to work my muscles. My park...and Kiera's. Sweat poured off me as I did some pushups against a park bench, and pausing a moment, I took off my shirt. As I was doing so, I heard giggling off to my left. I didn't turn to look, but I couldn't help but smile. Kiera had appreciated my form at this park on more than one occasion, and now whenever I heard the titter of intrigued girls, I thought of her...checking me out, back when she wasn't supposed to be checking me out. Sometimes, during dark moments, I wondered if Kiera would have fallen for me if I looked differently...more average, more unremarkable. Sometimes I worried that once my looks failed, or if something happened to make them fail prematurely, Kiera wouldn't want me like she did now. But I knew Kiera loved me for me, the person behind the face, so I had to believe that wouldn't be the case. Hopefully.

Finished for the day, I shoved myself away from the bench and stood up. I accidentally faced the group of girls and caught them openly staring at me; one of them even had their jaw dropped. It was flattering, amusing, but it was also a reminder. My looks were what most people noticed, what they instantly craved. But my looks had nothing to do with me. The real me. Kiera was the only woman who'd ever delved deep enough to find the well-buried core of me. I loved her so much for that.

I gave the girls a charming smile, because I hated being rude without reason, then I grabbed my shirt off the bench and started my way back home. Kiera might be close to getting there, and I really wanted to see her. The group of girls watched me the entire time I passed by them. One of them whistled when my ass was their only view. I shook my head, amused. Girls liked to pretend that they were different than guys when it came to sex—more mature, less primal—but in my experience...they weren't. They were just better at being subtle. Sometimes.

I'd decided to end my workout with a bang, so I was breathing pretty hard when I finally got back to my house. My heart pounded against my ribcage, and I was slick with sweat, but the rush of adrenaline made me feel great. Or maybe that feeling was due to the fact that my front door was unlocked—Kiera was home. That definitely made me feel amazing.

She was in the entryway when I opened the door, a small frown on her perfect face as she studied the mammoth bag she'd brought with her—everything she'd need for school tomorrow. She seemed worried as she stared at it, like she was sure she'd forgotten something. I could almost see anxiety hovering around her like a noxious cloud. Clearly, I had my work cut out for me.

Kiera noticed me a split-second later, then she did a double take. She drank in my half-bare body like she'd never seen it before. It amused me that she still acted that way, and even with my occasional "what if" worries, I wouldn't change the way she looked at me. I loved it when she devoured me with her eyes.

"You're obsessed, you know?" I said, scrubbing my hair dry with my shirt.

Her cheeks suddenly flushed with color, and I instantly realized she thought I meant she was obsessed with my body. While that was certainly true, it wasn't what I meant. I pointed at her school bag. "You're going to be just fine."

She visibly relaxed when I didn't call her out for ogling me. Rolling her eyes at herself, she said, "I know. I honestly don't know why it twists my stomach so much."

With a smile, I turned and shut my door. "I know just how to get your mind off of it." I'd just thought of it on the way up the hill.

I turned back around just in time to see Kiera's eyes readjust to my face. She'd totally checked me out when I'd been turned around. She really was obsessed. At least it was me she couldn't get enough of. I hoped that was always the case.

As she stared at me, my idea sprang into my mind, making me smile. If she said yes, this was going to be so much fun. Kiera tilted her head as I slipped my arms around her waist. "Oh?" she asked, her face amused and intrigued as she rested her fingers on my damp chest.

I gave her body a suggestive once-over. "Yep," I said, offering no further explanation. Kiera bunched her brows in question, and I laughed at her curiosity. Releasing her, I kissed her cheek. "Just let me clean up first."

Moving around her, I could see the questions in her eyes, but she only nodded at me with her lips pursed in contemplation. I laughed at the look on her face, then lightly smacked her butt and hopped up the stairs two at a time. Once upstairs, I took the quickest shower known to man. I half expected Kiera to join me, but she didn't. When I stepped out of the bathroom, it became pretty clear why she hadn't...she was watching TV. Was that because she'd truly wanted to watch a little TV, or was she doing that to distract herself from me? I hoped it was me.

Smiling to myself, I threw on some clothes so I could go back downstairs with her. She was sitting on the couch when I got there, completely absorbed in an educational show about marine life. She was so into the program, she didn't even seem to realize I was in the living room with her. In fact, if she got up, grabbed a notebook from her bag and started taking notes, I wouldn't have been surprised. My girl could be very studious. She was so cute.

But cute or not, I kind of wanted her attention now. She still hadn't looked over at me, so I let out a grunt of frustration, then leaned over to make my presence more obvious. My lips touched her neck, and she startled in surprise, but as my mouth moved against her, my tongue flicking her skin, she sighed and angled her head for me, giving me better access.

"Is this how you're going to distract me?" she asked, her voice low and seductive. If she kept talking like that, maybe...

With a deep laugh, I tossed away that thought, grabbed her by the waist, and pulled her from the couch. "Nope," I said when she was on her feet. A wide smile on my face, I flicked her nose. "I have a better idea."

Kiera's lips pursed into an adorable frown that made me want to kiss her. "You're not interested in...playing with me?" Her question made me want to do a lot more than kiss her, but...all in due time.

Giving her a devilish grin, I shook my head and said, "Oh, I intend to play with you." Her eyes widened, and I couldn't help but laugh. Grabbing her hand, I pulled her into the kitchen. "Just not in the way that you're thinking." I helped her sit down, then kissed her cheek. "At least, not yet anyway," I whispered in her ear.

Curiosity was clear on her face as she shook her head at me. Leaving her there to wonder, I began searching my kitchen for what we needed: cards. Unfortunately, I had no idea where they were, so I started searching every drawer. A surprising amount of crap had accumulated over the years, but I didn't let that deter me. This was happening. I hummed as I worked, and snuck glances at Kiera, intently watching me. Just when I could tell that she was about to ask me what I was looking for, I spotted the familiar white and blue box in the very back of a drawer. "Ah-ha!" I knew I'd had some.

Twisting to Kiera, I showed her what I had in my hand. "Playing cards?" she asked. Her surprised expression morphed into an amused smile. "Are we playing pinochle all afternoon?"

Her question amused me, but I had to tease her a little bit for her game choice. "Pinochle? Are we sixty?" Opening the cards, I started shuffling them as I sat down across from her. "No, we're playing poker."

Kiera's face compressed into a frown. "I'm really not that good at poker."

My grin grew as I watched her study the cards in my hands. "Well, that is actually perfect, because we're playing strip poker."

Her eyes flashed to mine, and the green in them seemed to radiate terror. She shot to her feet, clearly not on board with my little idea. I grabbed her hand before she could completely escape. "Come on, it will be fun." I gave her a suggestive wriggle of my eyebrows. "I promise."

Her cheeks were flushed with color—an appealing shade that reminded me of how she looked right after we had sex. It kind of made me want to skip this part and just get right to it, but this wasn't just about sex. This was about her being comfortable, with me, with her sexuality, with her own skin. And also, it was about us having fun together outside of the bedroom. And then it was about sex, because I definitely wanted to make love to her tonight.

She sat down slowly, reluctantly. "Kellan...I don't know..."

Leaning back in my chair, I studied her body. Why couldn't she see what I saw? The curves of her hips and thighs showcased by her jeans, her flat stomach highlighted by her tight layers of shirts, the swell of her breasts, the long stretch of skin of her neck, begging to be kissed, her full, soft lips, her sultry hazel eyes... whether she was dressed or not, she was seducing me just by sitting there, staring at me. She was utter perfection, clothed or naked, and she didn't need to be embarrassed by this.

"Have you ever played?" I asked, feeling like I already knew her answer.

With a sigh, she shrugged. "No."

I resumed shuffling the cards with a grin on my face. "Good. Then it will be a new experience for you. And I like giving you new experiences." I fully intended to be the one she was with as she filled her bucket list.

The pink tone in her cheeks swept down her neck as her eyes suddenly focused on my lips. It was suddenly very difficult to keep shuffling the cards...to not pull her into my arms and sweep her upstairs. But no, this would be good for her. She should know how breathtaking she was, how insatiable she made me.

She tucked her hair behind her ears, then nervously pointed at my windows. "What about...your neighbors?"

"What about them?" I asked with a shrug. I didn't care if they saw me, and if they saw Kiera, well, it would probably be the best night of their lives. On second thought...

Pulling her gaze from me, she quietly said, "I don't want them looking...at me."

Happy that she was actually considering this, and agreeing with her about the neighbors, I got up and pulled down the blinds on all of the windows. When I sat back down, I raised an eyebrow at her. "Better?" I asked.

She nodded, but she still looked like she might bolt at any moment. She also looked mystified as to why she hadn't yet. With a laugh, I told her, "Would it make you feel any better if I told you that I'm not very good at this either? I'm generally the first one naked." I laughed even more as I thought about all the times I'd ended up in my birthday suit with a group of nearly fully-dressed people. I wasn't sure if that was because I was extraordinarily bad, or because people liked to gang up on me.

Kiera seemed shocked by my admission. "You've played?" From the grimace on her face the second after she asked, she'd instantly realized it was kind of a dumb question. She knew my past; she knew I didn't used to say no very often—if a girl had wanted to play with me...all she'd had to do was ask. And Kiera also knew that I frequently hung out with Griffin. And let's just say, thanks to Griff, none of the D-Bags were strangers to strip poker. And yes, the guys were all aware that I couldn't play for shit. They thought it was hilarious to get me naked. Assholes.

I didn't think Kiera would want to hear about that, though, so I only nodded and smiled. I explained the modified rules I wanted to play with as I dealt the cards. "This is old-fashioned, no frills, no wilds, 5-card draw strip poker. The bet is always one piece of clothing, but it's your choice what you take off. You can fold if you've got crap, but only during the first round. Once you agree to the next round by taking more cards or sticking with what you've got, well, then you're stuck 'til the end, and you're either getting lucky, or you're getting naked." I winked at her, and she sighed.

"Okay...let's do this," she muttered, her voice a little sullen as she picked up her cards.

I picked up my stack then looked over at her. "How many cards do you want? Or are you folding?"

She chewed on her lip in a distracting way as she thought, and one hand idly stroked the guitar necklace I'd given her. I was so glad she still wore it. Even though the night I'd given it to her had been...torturous, it meant the world to me when I saw it around her neck. Like somehow, *I* was around her neck, hanging over her heart. "No, I'm in...I'll take two," she said, setting down a couple of her cards.

Glee made me smile. *She was playing.* "Two, huh? Interesting..." I gave her two more cards from the deck, and she scooped them up with a frown. Resisting a laugh, I glanced at my own cards. *Jack shit. Figures.* Half the reason why I sucked at this game was the fact that I had absolutely zero luck when it came to getting the cards I needed.

I knew I should fold, since Kiera probably had three of a kind, but I felt...lucky. And besides, I wanted Kiera to have a good time, and I had a feeling she'd appreciate the game more if I was the one quickly losing clothes. I set down three cards, then picked up three more. Still jack shit. Goddamn it. This game hated me. Not showing my disappointment, I smiled at Kiera. "Whatcha got, beautiful?"

A brief smile touched her lips as she set down her cards. "Three sixes. You?"

Giving her a seductive grin, I laid down my cards one at a time. "Abso...lutely...nothing."

Kiera laughed, and her eyes sparkled with amusement. Good. I wanted her to enjoy this, and because I wanted her to enjoy this, I took off my shirt first, instead of something small, like one of my socks. Her eyes widened when my abs came into view. Then she giggled. "Okay, maybe this game isn't so bad."

As the afternoon shifted into evening, Kiera relaxed even more. Of course, it helped that she had been wearing a ridiculous amount of clothes to begin with and was still mostly dressed—layering was the bane of my existence in this game. I was down to just my boxers, but she still had on her bra, underwear, and a short-sleeved T-shirt. Getting rid of that T-shirt was my newfound mission in life.

Kiera fidgeted with her necklace while she frowned at her cards. She either had nothing, or she wasn't sure what to do with what she had. Once again, I had crap. But at least this time it was a pair of crap, and I might be able to do something with that. If I was reading her nerves correctly, then she had an even worse hand than I did. But even if I lost, I'd win—with no clothes left, we could quit the game and move this distraction-party upstairs. God, I loved win-win situations.

Like she could feel me watching her, Kiera glanced up at me.

The uncertainty on her face was adorable, and I couldn't resist teasing her. "Nervous?" I asked, pointedly looking at the necklace she was sliding back and forth across the chain.

She instantly dropped it. Then, with a smooth smile that stole my breath, she told me, "No. You?"

The way her eyes ran over my body, subtlety highlighting the fact that this was an all-or-nothing moment for me, made me want to reach over and pull her into my arms. Did we really need to play this game all the way to its conclusion? Or had I distracted her enough? But God...I was so close to that T-shirt. If I could get her to play whatever she had right now...it was mine, I was sure of it.

Biting my lip, I shook my head. "Nope. In fact, I don't even need any more cards. How about you?" *Come on, Kiera...let's see what bra you're wearing today...*

I could see her struggling to not react to my confident comment, could see her trying to figure out what I had, or if I even had anything. I had to wonder if she'd gamble with what she had—like I wanted her to—or if she'd play smart and ask for more cards...even if that would hint at what was in her hand. Either response was fine with me, I just liked to watch her squirm. I even gave her a smug smile, goading her to set down her cards right now.

Surprisingly, it worked. Voice confident, she told me, "Nope, I'm good."

I wet my bottom lip with my tongue, then dragged my teeth over it. For some reason, that move seemed to turn girls on, and Kiera was no exception. Her eyes were glued to my mouth as I started laying down my cards. "Yeah, I know," I told her, responding to her statement. She was definitely good...in all the right ways.

Kiera laid down her cards without looking at my hand. Her eyes remained fixed on my lips. I briefly considered leaning over and kissing her, but curiosity compelled me to look at her cards.

When I saw that she had a pair too, but it was *slightly* lower than mine, I couldn't contain a quiet laugh. *Yes...victory.*

My laughter snapped Kiera out of her daze, and her cheeks flushed as she looked at her undeniable defeat. "Crap," she muttered. Then she looked up at me with pleading, puppy dog eyes. "Really?" she asked.

If she thought being adorable was going to get her out of this, she was dead wrong. I'd been waiting all day for a little bra action. Laughing at the look on her face, I leaned back and crossed my arms over my chest. I wasn't budging on this. "Deal's a deal, Kiera."

"How did you ever talk me into this?" she murmured, sounding for all the world like she regretted every decision she'd made tonight. I just kept staring at her chest, waiting for the goods.

Her fingers slowly, reluctantly, lifted the fabric over her head. She was breathing heavier, and her chest lifted and lowered in an erotic way. I just wanted to touch her. It was exquisite torture to sit there, still, while more and more of her skin was revealed. I'd seen a lot of women strip before, but there was something about the way Kiera did it—the innocence, how oblivious she was to her beauty—she was by far more seductive to me than a trained professional. I could watch Kiera undress all day.

Once her shirt was gone, her pretty, little white bra on display, I couldn't help but imagine the flesh hiding behind it. Images of her body flashed through my mind, and I could practically feel her soft skin, could nearly taste it. Lifting my eyes to her face, I playfully told her, "I love this game."

She laughed, so hopefully she was more amused than embarrassed. Getting her uncomfortable wasn't my goal. Kiera playfully tossed her shirt at me, being a good sport. I immediately inhaled it, flooding my mind with her scent. And that was when something I'd been expecting happened—the doorbell rang.

Kiera instantly lunged for her shirt, like she was going to put it back on. *No way, this is my trophy.* Standing up, I took a step away from her. I set it on the counter with a bright smile. "Oh, good—food's here," I told her.

She seemed mystified by that. And mortified. She crossed her arms and legs like the person at the door could somehow see her. "What food? What are you talking about?"

I understood her confusion—I'd called in an order when she'd been occupied—but her reaction was interesting. And unnecessary. She was heating up with embarrassment even though nothing had changed; it was still just the two of us in here. She didn't need to feel any differently than she did five seconds ago. I didn't. Of course, I didn't really care if someone saw me naked. It was just skin.

Shrugging, I told her, "I thought you might be getting hungry, so I ordered some pizza on your last bathroom break."

I twisted to leave the kitchen, and she shouted my name. When I looked back at her, she flung her hands at my body. My nearly naked body. I figured she wanted me to put some clothes on, but the pizza guy was probably gonna leave if I took much longer. Plus, I loved the way she'd been looking at me tonight... and I couldn't resist playing with her.

"Oh...right," I said, then I headed for my jeans. Picking my wallet out of the pocket, I told her, "I should probably pay them, huh?"

She sputtered incoherently, still gesturing wildly at my body. It was really hard not to laugh. Leaning down, I gave her a kiss, then I jauntily made my way to the front door. The laugh I'd been holding escaped me when I opened it.

A bored looking woman with dark spikey hair was idly playing with a piece of gum in her mouth. She froze when she saw me, a long strand of the gum extended from her lips. Her wide eyes slowly scanned my body.

"Hey," I said. "Sorry about the wait. Thanks for not leaving."

She giggled as she shoved the gum back in her mouth. "Uh, no problem. You just get up or something?"

Grinning, I shook my head. "No. Playing a game."

"Oh..." She chewed on her lip, and her thoughts were clear as day on her face. *Can I play too?* Another time, another place, I would have invited her in, and we would have done...all sorts of things together. But now, all I wanted from her was pizza. *Sorry, not tonight. Not anymore.*

She was still just staring at me, so I opened my wallet and pointed at the box in her hands. "How much do I owe you?"

Shaking her head, she laughed again, then rambled off a number. I doubled it. It never hurt to be generous, and thanks to my parents, I had enough money to be very nice to people. Odd that I actually had something to thank them for.

Her eyes got even wider as she took the cash, then her gaze drifted to my stomach, and she giggled again. "Thank you, and... uh, hold on a minute..." She dashed to her car, then came back with a rectangular box.

"What's this?" I asked her.

She laughed, then sighed, then bit her lip. "Just...I had some... extra breadsticks. You can have them if you want."

"Oh...well, thank you."

"Yeah," she said in a long exhale. Then she pointed to the tattoo on my chest. "That Kiera is a lucky girl."

A secretive smile crept onto my face as I glanced at the wall hiding the kitchen. I wondered if Kiera was still sitting there, almost naked. I had a feeling she wasn't, and that made me want to laugh. So cute. "No...*I'm* the lucky one. She's...a gift."

The girl's face did this weird combination of a smile and a frown. Then she waved. "Enjoy your...game."

My smile turned devilish. "Trust me, I will."

She was still standing there when I started closing the door, and I heard one final sigh of longing, followed by a giggle, followed by the words, "Oh my God..."

Laughing to myself, I firmly shut and locked the door—I didn't want her thinking she could sneak her way into the game. Then I walked back to the kitchen...where I discovered that my girl had indeed covered herself with my T-shirt. "Uh-

uh, that's cheating. You have to stay as naked as you were when I left."

Rolling her eyes, she dropped my shirt. "Even when you're flirting with the delivery girl?"

I set down the pizza box. "I wasn't flirting."

Kiera stood up from the table, not hiding her body from me at all. God, she looked good. If only she realized just how fucking sexy she was, no one would make her jealous. "You weren't?" Coming up to me, she sat back on her hip and pointed at the rectangular box in my hand. "Then what's that?"

Knowing it looked bad, I shrugged. "She had some extra breadsticks. She said we could have them if we wanted."

She shook her head, her expression clearly saying, "*I knew it.*" But whatever she thought she knew was wrong. The flirting was one way, I was just being nice. There was a difference—one Kiera was going to have to get comfortable with, since I did, on occasion, need to be nice.

Laughing at the frustrated, resigned look on her face, I set down the box and wrapped my arms around Kiera's waist. I pulled her tight, then brought my lips to her throat. Tasting her skin, I worked my way up to her ear. Her body stiffened in my arms, and I could feel her breathing pick up. I loved how much I affected her...how much she wanted me.

Shifting my focus, I brought my mouth over hers, a hairsbreadth from touching them. "I can't help what women find appealing." I ducked my hand into her underwear and cupped her ass. "But I only find you appealing." *You're my everything.*

My words, combined with my actions, pushed her over the edge, and she leaned forward to press her lips to mine. I indulged in the contact for a long moment, then I stepped away from her. She looked confused at first, until I grabbed her hand and twirled her away, then back to me. She laughed when she reconnected with my chest, and she had a huge grin on her face when I twirled her away again.

There was a time when I'd thought dancing with Kiera was

better than sex. While I wasn't sure if that was true—nothing could really top sex with Kiera—it didn't diminish the fact that dancing with her was extremely enjoyable. For both of us. And as we danced and ate our pizza, Kiera seemed to forget that we were in our underwear. Or she stopped caring as I twirled her around, one of the two. And when she laughed and shook her ass in front of me, a move that almost got her swiftly carried upstairs, it became clear that she wasn't nervous about school anymore. For one moment in time, she wasn't nervous about anything, and being able to do that for her—give her that kind of peace—opened my heart to the point of pain. There was nothing I wouldn't do for this girl.

Chapter 6
THE PAST STRIKES AGAIN

I woke up the next morning feeling great. I'd done it. I'd successfully given Kiera a night to remember, and hopefully the calm, peace I'd seen on her while we'd danced in my kitchen would continue throughout the day.

It was hours before Kiera needed to be up, so I tried to be as quiet as possible as I made coffee. I should have known that wouldn't matter though—Kiera strolled into the kitchen before the pot was even done brewing. She was wearing one of my T-shirts...and nothing else. Her long, lean legs were all too distracting for this early in the morning.

She walked over to me with a tired smile on her face. "Mornin'," I said.

Wrapping her arms around my waist, she snuggled into my chest. "Good morning." Proving just how sleepy she was, she yawned.

A small laugh escaped me as I rubbed her back. "You don't have to wake up with me. You can sleep in until school starts."

Placing her chin on my chest, she looked up at me. "If you're up, I want to be up," she said with a smile full of warmth. Then she scrunched her brows, like she was suddenly confused by something. "Why do you get up so early, when you've got nowhere to go?"

With a small sigh, I looked away from her. Right, my oddly accurate internal alarm clock. One that was permanently set for early A.M. "Well, let's just say that my childhood trained me to wake up at the crack of dawn." I had several memories of my dad "encouraging" me to get up. In fact, the last time I was treated to his help with waking, he'd bruised my thigh so badly, I'd had trouble walking. Which also got me in trouble.

Looking back at Kiera, I told her, "Waking up on my own was preferable to being woken up. I guess the habit stuck. Now I can't seem to stop waking up early."

Her hazel eyes glistened, and my mood darkened. I didn't really want to talk about my parents again. Kiera seemed to understand that, and she forced herself to smile. "Well, I'm glad you do. Quiet mornings with you are some of the best memories that I have."

Peace swept through me as I recalled some of our sweet, stolen moments, moments that had happened right here in this kitchen. It seemed a lifetime ago, and yet, at the same time, it seemed like only yesterday. "Me too," I whispered, running my fingers back through her dark hair. "I always looked forward to you coming down to see me. Even if it was just for a little while, it still made me feel like we were…together." Even if we weren't, even if it was just an illusion. A painful, wonderful illusion.

Like she could sense the path my thoughts had taken, Kiera cupped my cheeks, forcing our eyes to lock. "We were, Kellan. We were together…even if it was just for a little while."

I couldn't stop staring at her, couldn't help but be absorbed by her intoxicating green eyes. For good or bad, so much had begun here. And ended here. My kitchen was a conflux of pleasure and pain, a swirling storm of emotional highs and lows. But the tempest was over, and our love had prevailed.

Kiera seemed to be just as lost in me as I was in her. So much so, that when the phone in the kitchen rang, she jumped. Even though the sound had surprised me too, I had to laugh at her reaction. It was so nice to know I could affect her that deeply, almost as deeply as she affected me.

She thumped my chest in response to my laugh. "Hello?" I said, picking up the corded phone and smiling at Kiera.

A voice I hadn't expected to hear met my ear, and my smile widened. "Kellan, hey, good morning, mate."

"Hey, Denny, long time, no hear." When Kiera and I had split...and Kiera and Denny, too, I guess, I'd talked to Denny quite a bit. He hadn't wanted to speak to me at first, but eventually my persistence had worn him down. Then we'd talked all the time—mainly me bugging him. But now that Kiera and I were together, and he was happy with Abby, well, our conversations had become a lot less frequent.

"Yeah, sorry about that. Things have been crazy here...work and stuff. And I want to catch up, but uh...I was actually looking for Kiera. Is she with you?"

The feeling that washed through me then was strange. It was heat mixed with ice, comfort mixed with confusion, contentment mixed with jealousy. I knew Denny and Kiera were still friends, and I knew they talked on occasion, but Denny had never called *me*...looking for *her*.

Kiera was turning away, like she was giving Denny and me privacy. Little did she know, we didn't need it. *They* needed it. But I didn't think I could give it to them. I just wasn't at that level of comfort yet.

Doing my best to push aside every ounce of insecurity, I told Denny, "Yeah...She's right here...Hold on."

Kiera froze when she realized the phone was for her, not me. Holding the phone out to her, I said, "He called here for you."

Her eyes widened as she studied my face. I had to imagine she felt strange too, maybe guilty. She shouldn't...but then, I shouldn't feel jealous. And I did. I couldn't deny that. But I didn't have to admit it. I could seem completely fine. Because I should be fine. *They broke up. She's with me now.*

Kiera gave me a sweet, *nothing to worry about* smile. She grabbed the phone from me, and I leaned against the counter. It might be rude, but I wasn't leaving the room while my girl talked to her ex-lover. From the small smile she gave me, it seemed she understood that I wasn't leaving.

Focusing on the phone, Kiera inhaled a deep breath like she was nervous. Was that because of me...or him? Letting the breath go, she brightly said, "Good morning, Denny." He responded with something, and she laughed, then told him, "No, Kellan and I are up."

Hearing another man make her laugh made a flash of something dark wash through me, but her comment about us being together—being a team—instantly dissolved it, and a devilish grin lifted my lips. By telling him we'd woken up together, she'd basically confirmed that we'd slept together. That shouldn't have made me happy, but it did. She wasn't hiding our relationship from him anymore, and while I would always feel guilty about her around Denny, at the moment, I was thrilled. Maybe him calling her wasn't such a bad thing after all.

Denny said something that made her furrow her brow. "Miss what?" I mimicked her gesture and she shrugged. Whatever it was he'd asked her, she was mystified. He must have answered her, for her mouth fell open in surprise. "Did you call just to wish me good luck on my first day of school?"

Her eyes filled with tears, and my stomach clenched. I narrowed my eyes at Kiera. I knew I probably looked angry, but I couldn't stop the reaction. He called to wish her good luck at school? Why would he do that? I mean, I knew they were friends, but this seemed like...more. And she was tearing up, like she was touched. They were bonding over the phone, and I was just standing there like an idiot, letting it happen.

It doesn't mean anything. Calm down. Don't overreact. Don't say something stupid. Don't do something stupid. Don't fuck this up. It doesn't matter if they're bonding...he's thousands of miles away. He can't do...what you did.

That thought made me calm down some, but then Kiera swallowed a couple times, like she was too choked up to speak, and a sliver of anger and jealousy sliced through me. It was quickly followed by guilt, and then sadness. He still had a corner of her heart, and he probably always would.

"No, no, I'm sorry," she said, shaking her head. "Yes, of course you should call me. And no, you didn't miss it, and yes, I'm a little nervous."

My emotions swirled and surged as I listened to her ramble nervously to Denny. Maybe I should have fought through the discomfort and left them alone to talk, because hearing the emotion, seeing the connection...it was too much. But still, I couldn't leave...I had to know what she said. Folding my arms over my chest, I wondered how long I could put up with this torture.

Kiera blinked back tears, killing me with her emotional response. "Thank you, Denny...for remembering. That was incredibly sweet of you." She flushed with color, and I had to avert my eyes. Jesus, this hurt. My throat tightened with pain. Would she forgive me if I reached over and hung up the phone? Maybe I could make it look like an accident. It wouldn't change anything, but it would be extremely satisfying.

She softly repeated, "Thank you, Denny," and I reached my breaking point. I couldn't stay anymore, couldn't listen to this fucking shit anymore. It was like we were back *there* again, like it was happening all over again. My chest felt like it was cracking open, pain seeping around the edges. I'd been so sure I'd never have to feel this way again. How fucking stupid of me.

I took a step away from Kiera, and she grabbed my arm. I stopped, but I still couldn't bring myself to look at her. It felt like invisible claws were ripping apart my insides, like I was bleeding internally. Would this pain ever truly go away?

Kiera laughed, the sound like a dagger to my heart, then she told Denny, "Yeah, I'll be certain to do that." My entire body went taut with tension. I wanted to flee, wanted to run. Kiera's hand on me was the only thing keeping me in place, but even still, a part of me wanted to shrug her off and get out of there—get out of the house, possibly out of the city. If Denny hadn't broken up with her, would they still be together?

Needing to redirect my thoughts, I stared at the coffeepot on the counter. Coffee. The only thing left in the world was coffee. As I let nothing but the black liquid in the carafe touch my mind, my heart, I felt Kiera's fingers stroke my skin in a soothing pattern. It relaxed me. Somewhat. The what ifs didn't matter. He *had* given her up, and she was mine now. We weren't back there again. Things were different.

"All right," she told Denny. "Tell Abby hi for me, and have fun." Hearing Kiera mention Denny's girlfriend made me feel even better. They'd both moved on...so this wasn't a big deal. But then Kiera minutely turned away from me and said, "Hey, thank you so much for remembering, Denny. That means a lot to me." Ice chilled my veins, and it was hard to remain focused on the coffee. Her voice lowering even more, she killed me by adding, "I'm so sorry, Denny, about everything." She softly exhaled, then said, "Bye," and hung up the phone.

She twisted back around to me, but I still couldn't look at her and kept my eyes glued to the coffeepot. *Coffee. Nothing exists but coffee.* But...was that regret in her voice? Regret that he left, that he'd ended things and fled? Regret for losing the first love of her life? *Does a part of her wish she was still with him?*

When I felt like I couldn't ignore her anymore, I slowly turned to look at her. Sympathy and concern were all over her face. It conflicted me even more. Was she truly happy with me? Or did she still long for him? A lifetime of feeling unwanted made it so easy to slip back into feeling that way. Somewhere, buried deep, I knew I shouldn't feel uncertain about Kiera being with me—not anymore—we'd had multiple conversations about this. But still, one emotional phone call with her ex brought it all rushing back. The doubt. The pain. The rejection. *Am I who she really* wants?

Stop. Just let it go.

Brushing a strand of hair off my forehead, she gave me an encouraging smile. "Hey, you okay?"

Not wanting to rehash our past and my fears, I slapped on a carefree smile. A completely fake carefree smile. "Of course, I'm fine. Denny called to wish you luck. That was nice of him." I was pretty proud of myself for saying that in a calm, friendly voice. There was nothing in that sentence that should have given away the fact that I was a whirlwind of emotion, but regardless, Kiera knew.

Letting out a sad sigh, she laced her arms around my neck and said, "You know that doesn't mean anything, right? You know that I love you, and Denny is nothing more than a friend now, don't you?" She searched my eyes, and my smile failed, dropping as quickly as my mood. "Don't you?" she repeated.

Yes, I *did* know she loved me, and I *did* know Denny was just a friend. Deep in my heart, I knew that. But the affection that remained between them, the history they shared, good and bad, the past that would never truly go away...it burned; the pain felt fresh again.

And I couldn't help but think...they were friends because *he* had made that choice.

I tried to turn my eyes from her, center myself by staring at the pot of coffee again, but she grabbed my cheek and made me keep eye contact. She wanted an answer.

Practicing every trick of hiding my feelings that I knew, I smiled like nothing was wrong. "Yes, I know, Kiera. I know exactly what you and Denny are." *You and Denny are friends because he forced you to be friends. He is the love you lost, the one who got away. You love me, but a part of you will always mourn him. And I just...have to be fine with that.*

Kiera gave me a sideways look, like she was judging what I meant, but then she shrugged it off and smiled. Reaching up, she gave me a kiss. "Good, because while he's important to me, you're more important, and I don't want my talking with him to hurt you."

That warmed me, but because the past had pulled me into such a dark place, it also surprised me. And confused me. I was more important? I mattered more to her? Than *Denny*? God, I wanted that to be true, but the insecurity in the far corner of my soul rebelled against the idea. Denny was the one person I just couldn't compete with; I would always fall short of him. *We're only together because he left.* How could I be more important than the one who got away? By its very definition that made me runner-up.

Kiera pursed her lips, then kissed me again. "I know what you're thinking, and you're wrong. You're not second best. I could have fled to him, but I went to you. I couldn't live without you. I chose you. I love you."

It kind of surprised me that she knew just what path my dark thoughts had traveled down, but what she was saying struck deep into my cracked soul. She was basically telling me that *I* was the one who'd gotten away, I was the one who had stuck in her brain, whose absence had made her miserable. The one she couldn't get over. The one who had haunted her. The one she'd begged to take her back. I'd never truly considered it like that before. The fact that she could have chased after Denny, but she didn't. In the end, she'd let Denny go and she'd come to me. Yes, maybe Denny had forced her hand, maybe we both had, but when she'd looked inside herself—*deeply* looked inside herself—I was the one she'd found. She wanted me. Not him.

And God that felt good. Good, but...surreal. I wanted to believe it though, so badly it hurt. I needed to be number one in her eyes, needed it more than anything. She was my entire world... I wanted to be hers too.

I had to swallow back the painful hope in my throat before I could speak. "It still feels...unreal, I guess. I'm not used to being... loved by someone. I keep waiting to wake up." *Please don't let this be a dream.*

Compassion in her eyes, Kiera shook her head. "Well, get used to it. I'm not going anywhere, Kellan."

Please let that be true. I won't survive losing you twice.

My mood lightened over the course of the morning. With Denny far, far away, it was easier to let the past go, let the pain go...let the fear go. Instead of being forefront in my mind, it was once again just an annoying gnat, flying around in the back of my brain, and I could ignore gnats. I'd been doing it my entire life.

In opposition, Kiera's mood began to sink as school drew closer. She was frowning when she came back into my bedroom after taking a shower, and it was either because she'd forbid me from joining her and she'd missed me, or because she was worrying. About nothing. She was going to be just fine. I was just about to tell her that when she pointed at me to stay put on the pillows. An amused smile lifted my lips as I watched her. It was like she thought I would paw her at every possible instant if I were left to my own devices. And that was kind of true. I'd love to strip that towel off her, lie her down, and taste every inch of her. But...she had somewhere to be. Damn shame.

Disbelief surged through me when she started putting on her bra...under her towel. Seriously? I did have some self-control. "I've seen you naked, you know."

Her skin flushed with color as she turned her back to me. "I know, but you just staring at me like that is...different."

A snort escaped me. Did she realize how hypocritical that sentence was? She feasted on me at every opportunity. Not that I minded. I liked her eyes on me. Always had.

Kiera peeked over her shoulder to look at me, then proceeded to slip on her underwear...still hiding her body from me under the towel. Raising an eyebrow, I told her, "It's just skin, Kiera." Scooting to the edge of the bed, I leaned over and grabbed her leg. Sliding my hand up her smooth skin, I added, "And it's far too beautiful to keep covered up."

My breath got shaky the farther up my hand went, and I instantly wondered if she'd be okay with being fashionably late. How much did they actually teach on the first day anyway? But before I could convince Kiera to play with me a little before we left, she stepped away from my touch. Face firm, she pointed at the bed again, commanding me to stay back in an adorable way. "I don't need to get you any more riled up than you constantly are by giving you a peep show."

She began sliding on her jeans, and with a laugh, I relaxed back on the mattress. I supposed she did have a point. After all, I'd already imagined making her very, very late. But still, fair was fair, and she constantly gawked at me. If she was going to deny me eye-candy, then it was only right if I did the same. Wouldn't want her...riled up. "Fine. I'll just remember that the next time you're staring at my body."

Kiera had been digging through her bag for her shirt when I said that. Pausing, she twisted to look at me. Curious what she would do, I kept my expression completely blank. She stared at me a moment longer, then sighed and dropped the towel. Most of her was covered up, but I didn't care—that wasn't really the point. She'd caved because she didn't want me to take my body away from her. Well, and maybe I'd guilted her into it...but I preferred to think that she didn't want me becoming all shy and modest around her. Just like I didn't want her shy and modest around me. She was perfect, and there was nothing that she needed to hide from me.

Looking away, Kiera let me leer at her for quite a while. During those long seconds, I pictured removing her cream-colored bra, sucking her nipple into my mouth. I could almost hear the groan she would make as she begged me to make love to her. Desire surged through me, and I instantly began to harden.

And that was when Kiera decided the show was over, and hastily pulled on her shirt and buttoned it up. Not able to get the image of her pristine skin out of my head, I was still staring at her chest when she finished. She had to clear her throat to break my concentration.

Lifting my eyes to hers, I gave her a mischievous grin. "Well, now I'm turned on, and you can't go. You're just going to have to stay here with me today."

She laughed, then leaned over the bed to kiss me. That was all the encouragement I needed. Wrapping my arms around her, I pulled her on top of me. She giggled in my mouth as we kissed, and euphoria flooded me. *I did that. I made her laugh, made her feel better about today. Made her want me.* She was lightly rubbing against me, quickly turning up the fire inside me, and our kiss intensified. I knew we needed to get going, but as seconds passed, reason started diminishing. *She could start tomorrow, right?*

Like she could hear my thoughts, or sense my growing desire, Kiera pulled away. "I wish I could stay with you," she said, her voice reluctant. "I'm not really looking forward to today."

Hearing her admission made me sigh, and I cupped her cheeks as I searched her eyes. "Someday I'll get you to feel like the confident woman who was prancing around in her underwear last night all the time." I paused to run my fingers through her damp hair. "You are a beautiful, intelligent woman with a boyfriend who adores you. You have nothing to fear...ever."

As she averted her eyes, warmth filled her cheeks. "Easy for you to say, rock star."

Climbing off the bed, she started brushing her hair with a comb. I laughed at her comment as I sat up. "I get nervous."

She paused to give me a *yeah, right* expression. I understood why. I was very good at pretending to be fine; I'd had to be. But the things that I was very comfortable with now—sex, being on stage, telling Kiera I loved her—none of those things had come without some discomfort. Not nearly on the scale of what Kiera was experiencing now...but some. Especially that last one.

Picking the one aspect that was the most similar to her

current situation, I told her, "No, it's true. In the beginning, I used to get nervous onstage."

That was a slight exaggeration, making it sound like I'd been anxious before multiple events, when in truth there had only been *one* time I could think of when I'd gotten a case of nerves. It was right before my first major performance at junior prom with my band at the time, the Washington Wildcats...God, that name. I'd tried to be fine, but I'd been antsy, chewing on my fingernails, bouncing on my toes, swallowing about ten thousand times in a row. My stomach had been doing a really weird churning thing; before that night it was something I'd only ever experienced when I'd known my dad was mad at me. I'd hated feeling that way right before doing something I loved, but I hadn't known how to turn it off. Denny was the one who'd helped me through it. Hand on my shoulder, he'd told me, "Relax, mate. You have a gift. The only thing you should be worrying about right now is whether or not the rest of your band can keep up with you. But your voice... that's golden. You have nothing to fear about being on a stage. Ever."

I'd instantly felt better, and after that show, I'd never again been nervous to perform. Denny's words had just...stuck. I kind of felt bad about that moment now. I'd blown off Denny's concern at the time, telling him I was fine, just excited, but...after everything that had happened between us recently, I kind of wished I'd told him just how much I'd needed to hear that, how much it meant that he'd said it.

How strange that the comfort I'd just given Kiera had, in a way, come from Denny. *Good or bad, he's forever linked to both of us.*

As Kiera bunched her brows together, I let that memory fade into the background of my brain. "Let me guess," she said with a smirk. "You picture the crowd naked now?"

I laughed as I stood up. Amused by her comment, and not wanting to talk about Denny again, I didn't bother telling her the real story. "Nah, I had to stop doing that...Turned me on," I teased. Her answer was more entertaining than the truth anyway, and picturing everyone naked might actually help her.

"You're impossible," she laughed, pushing against my chest as I approached her.

My grin grew as she rolled her eyes. "We all have our weaknesses." Slipping around behind her, I pulled her tight. "You will be great, and I'll drive you every day if you want. Maybe I'll sit in on a class or two."

"I doubt the professor would like you snoring during class," she laughed, amused at the idea. Happy that I'd lifted her spirits, I kissed her neck and closed my eyes, savoring the feel of her, the smell of her, the very presence of her. I'd had no idea just how satisfying being in love could be. Nothing could top this feeling; I was 100 percent sure of that.

When it was time, Kiera gathered all her stuff and grudgingly trudged to my car. I rolled my eyes at the look of defeat on her face, then relaxed back into one of my favorite pastimes—driving Kiera to school. Kiera looked lost in her thoughts as we traveled the familiar path to the university. A smile crept over my lips as I remembered all the times I'd done this with her. Back in the beginning of our...friendship, it had been almost innocent. And then, like us, it had grown to be so much more. It was a way for me to show Kiera that I was here for her. That I had her back—forever.

The prestigious buildings of the university came into view, but Kiera didn't seem to notice that we were almost at our destination. In fact, she was so lost in her mind that she didn't react until I turned off the car. Blinking out of her stupor, she looked around the parking lot in surprise. I almost asked her what she'd been thinking about, but instead, I smiled and said, "Ready?"

Kiera sucked her bottom lip into her mouth, an erotic move that instantly made me think of sex. "Yeah...I'm good. Let's go."

Smiling at her answer, I cracked open my door. I tried to hurry around to her side before she got out of the car, but I didn't make it; she stepped out right as I got there. Brushing it off, I reached out for her hand. Her warm fingers wrapped around mine, and pure peace washed through me. I'd missed this.

As we walked through the familiar campus, my arm around Kiera's waist, my thumb tucked in the waistband of her jeans, several sets of feminine eyes shifted to stare at me. Ignoring the attention I was attracting from the clumps of girls scattered around the lawn, I focused on Kiera. She was the only one whose attention I really wanted. Her nervous eyes took in the girls watching us, and she subconsciously pushed into my side. Most of the girls weren't looking at her though. I think Kiera liked the fact that I generally funneled the attention away from her. Part of me was happy that I made her more comfortable by stealing her spotlight. Another part of me hated her being in my shadow. She should be shining brightly *with* me.

When we got to the building housing her first class of the day, I gallantly held the door open for her. She gave me a charming smile as she stretched out in front of me. "So, I had an interesting phone call with my dad last week," she said when we were side-by-side again.

"Oh yeah," I responded with a smile. I hadn't met her father yet, but from all I'd heard, he seemed to be the protective type. I could only imagine what he'd said to her.

She rolled her eyes, confirming my suspicions. "Yeah. He said he hoped you came to your senses soon and found a real job. Apparently being in a band isn't a viable career choice for the person dating his daughter." With a sigh, she shook her head. "I'm pretty sure my dad won't be happy until you become an accountant."

The image made me laugh. I really couldn't picture myself at a desk all day, staring at a computer. I think I'd go crazy. Kiera laughed along with me, like she couldn't picture it either. We were still laughing over the idea when I noticed a small cluster of guys blocking the hallway. Kiera hadn't spotted them yet, and she was about five seconds away from stepping into a giant of a man. The dude towered over me, and I was six-two.

I pulled Kiera back, stopping her before she collided with the could-be basketball player. A small, startled gasp left her lips, and the imposing man looked our way. Surprising me, a huge smile stretched across his face as he pointed at me. "Hey, aren't you that guy? The singer of that band? The D-Bags?"

Meeting men who knew me wasn't always a...pleasant experience. Once upon a time, other people's relationships hadn't mattered that much to me. I'd been too lonely and desperate for affection to care, a fact that had led to more than one tense confrontation. Surprisingly, I hadn't been in too many fights though; I had a knack for talking myself out of trouble, usually by pointing out that I had no way of knowing what girls were taken and what girls weren't. I only had their word to go on, after all, and it wasn't like a girl about to cheat on her boyfriend was going to tell me the truth. In theory. I had never actually asked a girl what her relationship status was, but I wasn't about to mention that to their furious boyfriends. I wasn't stupid.

I hadn't been sure what this big guy wanted at first glance, and I really hadn't wanted to talk myself out of a beating in front of Kiera. She didn't need to hear that crap. She'd seen and heard enough already. But this guy was just a fan, and I was more than happy to talk to fans.

"Kellan, yeah...I'm a D-Bag," I said with a laugh. *In more ways than one.*

The guys circled me then; they were all huge, and for the first time in a long time, I felt tiny. They were cool though, just wanting to tell me how much they loved my work. For the next several minutes, I shook hands, thanked them for their praise and politely answered all their questions. I could tell Kiera was getting restless, probably nervous about being late to class. Walking in late, with everyone's eyes on her, would be absolute hell for her.

"We've got a class to get to, but you guys should come to Pete's sometime and catch a show," I said with a wave.

As I led Kiera away from the group, they all started saying they would be there. Then they started inviting me to different frat parties. I raised my hand, not accepting, not declining. Leaving things open-ended was usually best. And besides, some of the other D-Bags might want to go. Like Griff.

Kiera laughed when we neared her classroom. "What?" I asked, bumping her shoulder.

Her crooked smile was adorable. "Look at you, finally getting some male fans."

A laugh escaped me as I held open the door to her room. "We've always had male fans, Kiera. You just choose to fixate on the female ones."

She brushed my body as she walked toward the doorway, then she paused and leaned into me. Her nearness instantly electrified me, and I wanted to pull her into me...then take her back to my car. "Well, that's because they fixate on you," she whispered, her mouth teasingly close to touching mine.

My heart surged with the near-contact, and my body immediately began to harden. Fuck, I wanted her. Biting my lip, I let out a soft groan. "Look at you...becoming a seductress," I whispered. *You can take me, right now...right here.*

With a sudden flush to her cheeks, she quickly stepped away from me. Had she seriously not meant to do that? I had to laugh at the embarrassed look on her face. If she only realized how successful her seduction had been, she wouldn't be so mortified. My jeans were still a bit uncomfortable.

Trying to think of anything but Kiera's legs wrapped around me, I gave her a kiss on the cheek and told her to have fun. She told me she would and gave me a quick peck before making a beeline to her seat in the middle of the room. I watched her for a moment, amazed and overwhelmed that a woman as beautiful and wonderful as her was truly mine. With a huge smile on my face, I turned and left her to her studious life. *See you soon, Kiera.*

Chapter 7

A PAINFUL OPPORTUNITY

I ran errands while Kiera was at school. Got some groceries, filled up the Chevelle, and had the local barber give my mop a trim. Like always, the older man shook his head when I told him I only wanted a little bit taken off.

"Are you sure, Kellan? I could give you a really nice, respectable haircut. It would look great on you, trust me."

Smiling, I told him, "Thanks, George, but I'm a bit partial to this haircut and so's my girlfriend. I think she'd leave me if I had respectable hair." Not really, but she'd definitely be disappointed, and the last thing I wanted to do was disappoint Kiera; she stared at my hair almost as much as she stared at my body.

George sighed, shook his head, then reluctantly went about only slightly snipping my hair. Once he was done, it was just about time to get Kiera from school. I thanked him—gave him a huge tip for the inconvenience of putting up with a hairstyle he hated—then climbed in my baby to go get my other baby.

Pulling into my usual spot here at the college, I shut off my car and climbed out. Before I could take a step, I was approached by a group of girls who clearly knew me. "Oh my gosh, you're Kellan Kyle, right? Of the D-Bags?" one of them asked.

Containing a sigh, I smiled and said, "Yeah, that's me."

They all giggled in response, and I knew I wouldn't be meeting Kiera outside her classroom today. Not unless I wanted to be rude to this group, and it was clear they were fans. I hated being rude to fans if I could help it. Leaning against my car, I made peace with the fact that I was missing walking Kiera from class. But she would find me out here, so ultimately, it was fine. I was still picking her up.

"Your band is just...just amazing. And you..." The girl's eyes briefly flicked down my body, and I couldn't help but smile in amusement. "Your...voice...is just...out of this world."

Considering how she was drinking me in, I wondered if she really meant that. "Thank you, that's always nice to hear."

"Are you...putting out an album soon?" another one of the girls asked. "I'd love to...listen to you at home." She bit her lip, and the girls around her giggled. I was pretty sure they would all love to do a lot more than *listen* to me at home. Unfortunately, they wouldn't be able to do *anything* with me at home.

"Matt's working on getting us a demo CD, but I don't know when...or if...they'll be available for fans to purchase. You'll have to come to Pete's to listen to us."

They all giggled again at that. "Oh, we will. We go there all the time."

I nodded, like I knew that, but if they had been at a show, their faces weren't registering with me. I saw a lot of people though, so that wasn't too surprising. "Good," I told them. "We appreciate the support."

A tall, leggy brunette raised an eyebrow. "We don't mean to be forward, but could you settle a debate for us?"

My lips quirked into a half-smile. "What sort of debate?"

She chewed on her lip before answering me. "Well...we've been wondering if you were single or not."

Before I could answer, one of her friends chimed in with, "And if you *aren't* single, how do we convince you to become single...for a night or two at least?"

They all started tittering. Laughing at the nature of their

debate, I turned my head and spotted the answer to their question walking our way. *Sorry, girls, I have no intention of becoming single anytime soon. Or ever again.* My smile grew as I watched Kiera getting closer, but the good feelings faded as I noticed the look on her face. It was contained fury, like she was restraining herself from punching something. Or someone.

The girls around me were still giggling over their question, and Kiera had to elbow her way through them to get to me. That got her a few heated looks, but she wasn't paying attention to them—her fiery eyes were on me. Shit. Was she mad at *me*? I was pretty sure I hadn't done anything to incur her wrath. Recently.

But she was definitely mad. "Let's go," she snapped.

Nodding, still confused, I opened the passenger's door for her. Shutting it, I turned back to the girls; some of them were glaring at Kiera. I didn't know if that was because she had bullied her way through them, or because she was sitting in my car. Wanting to smooth things over, I told them, "I'm sorry, but I have to go. It was nice meeting you all."

They moaned and groaned, but nobody seemed overly angry anymore. Walking around to my side of the car, I opened the door and climbed in. The air seemed chilly inside as Kiera sat there, silent. With one eye on her, one eye on the girls still hovering close to my car, I pulled out of the parking spot.

When we were on our way, I finally asked her what was wrong. "You want to tell me what happened that's got you all ticked off?"

Her eyes narrowed as she watched the girls who were watching us leave. "Not really," she muttered.

With a sigh, I put a hand on her thigh. "Will you anyway?" Her expression was blank when she looked over at me, but it was a tense blank. Forced. Frowning, I added, "You're the one that said we should talk things out...and you look like you need to talk something out."

Grunting in annoyance, she crossed her arms over her chest.

"I have another class with Candy this year. She made sure to say hello afterward."

While I studied the road, I tried to place the name with a face. Clearly, Kiera expected me to know this person. "Candy...?" Kiera sighed at the exact same moment I remembered who Candy was. "Oh, right. Candy." The eager, slightly possessive redhead I'd taken to my bed, just to get a rise out of Kiera. That seemed like a lifetime ago. "What did she say?" I asked, a little scared to hear the answer. Candy wasn't spiteful enough to go into details with her...was she?

Kiera glared at me, heat in her eyes. Her hands tightened, like she was stopping herself from hitting me. Shit. She must have told her...everything. But Kiera's response wasn't what I'd been expecting her to say. "She just mentioned a show that you had last week. You played in Pioneer Square, right?"

A show? That seemed...anticlimactic. Why was she mad about that? Looking up, I thought over my schedule last week. "Yeah, yeah we did." I flicked a glance at her. "Was she there? She didn't say hello." *I swear I haven't seen her in ages...if that's what you're mad about.*

Her eyes narrowed at me in suspicion. "No, a friend of hers saw you there...in the back."

Now I was really confused. By her tone of voice, it was clear that what she'd said was horrible...I just had no idea why. Shrugging, I said, "Huh, well, okay." I raised an eyebrow as I peeked at her. "Why is one of her friends seeing me making you look like you sucked on a lemon?"

I knew I shouldn't have said that the minute it was out of my mouth, but the mystery of why she was angry was starting to annoy me. The next thing she said clarified *everything* though. Voice tight, she told me, "Because she said she saw you doing things...with someone who was not me."

My eyes widened as icy understanding filled me. Oh God, she thought I'd cheated on her. No, it was worse than that. She thought she had a *witness* who'd seen me cheating on her. But that was impossible because I hadn't. I wouldn't. Just the thought of being with someone else made me sick. Knowing I couldn't convince her I was faithful while I was driving, I jerked the car over to the curb. Slamming it into park, I turned to face her.

Her eyes started filling with pain as I stared at her. It cracked my heart to see the doubt on her face, but at the same time, I didn't blame her for her fears. Wasn't I a wreck, just this morning? "I am not doing anything with anyone who is not you. Whatever she said was a lie, Kiera."

A tear swelled in her eye and rolled down her cheek. "She knew about the tattoo, Kellan."

Fuck. That was what had sold her on the lie. The tattoo was something not many people knew about, and the ones who did know, wouldn't go spreading that knowledge around to random fans. It was private. So private, that I rarely took my shirt off at shows anymore. In fact, I couldn't even remember the last time I'd done that. It was probably pre-tattoo.

Cupping her cheek, I brushed off the tear. "Then she saw it somewhere else, or someone told her about it, because I'm not fooling around with anyone." Unbuckling my seatbelt, I scooted closer to her, resting my head against hers. "I'm only fooling around with you. I'm only getting naked with you. I'm only having sex with you, Kiera." I pulled back to look her in the eye, praying she believed me. Pouring my soul into my words, I reflected her earlier sentiment back to her, "I chose you. I love you. I'm not interested in anyone else, okay?" *You're choosing me, and I'm choosing you. We're in this together, 100 percent.*

She nodded, but more tears rolled down her cheek. I hated this, hated the uncertainty that one stupid girl had shoved between us. Wanting to physically reassure her, I leaned forward and gave her a gentle kiss. Kiera seemed to relax under my tender administrations, and I hoped her doubt was dissolving. She had my heart, every piece of it—surely she knew that.

As our kiss intensified, I felt more confident that she was

releasing her fears. Especially when she whispered in my ear, "Show me that you want me, Kellan. Take me home."

She didn't need to ask twice. Putting the car in drive, I had us flying down the road mere seconds later. When we got to her empty apartment, we didn't waste any time getting to her room and getting undressed. It was almost like Kiera needed to be reminded just how much she meant to me. Candy must have really gotten to her. I hated that she had, hated that Kiera would ever doubt my loyalty. But...the way we'd come together...it wasn't all that shocking. I had similar fears at times.

Afterwards, when I had ravished her with as much physical attention as I possibly could, Kiera got ready for work. She seemed better, completely at peace again, but the image of her pain-filled eyes wouldn't leave me. Would we ever truly get past what we'd done to each other? Or would there always be tender scars, waiting to rip open at a moment's notice?

Considering the multiple scars I carried on a daily basis, I was pretty sure I already knew the answer to that question.

When it was time, I drove Kiera to Pete's. Kate was working tonight and greeted us at the door. "Hi, guys!"

Kiera greeted her coworker, then started pulling away from me, like she was leaving me. At the last possible second, I grabbed her waist, pulling her back to my side. "I'll have my usual," I murmured in her ear.

She shuddered under my touch but gave me an annoyed look. "I know what you like, Kellan."

Our recent lovemaking flashed through my mind, and I couldn't contain my smile. Wishing we had time to explore each other again, I slipped my hand into her back pocket. "Yes...you certainly do."

She flushed with color when she realized how suggestive her comment was. Then she pushed me away. "You're so adorable," I said, after kissing her cheek. "Have I mentioned how much that turns me on?"

With a laugh, she responded, "What doesn't, Kellan?" That

was certainly true. With Kiera, at least. Everything about her ignited my blood, my soul.

Knowing Kiera needed to get ready for work, I shrugged at her question, then headed to my usual table near the stage. A group of girls from a nearby table watched me sit down, but they didn't seem inclined to try and join me. I was grateful that they were content watching from a distance. Kiera seemed much happier now than when I'd picked her up from school, but I had to believe she was still a little uneasy. I didn't want her to have to deal with forward woman fawning over me right now. Not after Candy's...accusation.

When Kiera came back from putting away her stuff in the back room, she unwrapped a lollipop and stuck it in her mouth. Seeing her lips wrapped around the sucker put all sorts of wonderful images in my head, and I had to adjust how I was sitting. My eyes never left her as she grabbed my beer from Rita and started heading my way.

She pulled the sucker out of her mouth when she got close to me. Handing me my beer, she said, "Here you go. Your usual."

Giving her a seductive smile, I grabbed the beer with one hand, her hand holding the sucker with the other. Keeping my eyes firmly on Kiera, I brought the sucker to my lips, then closed my mouth around it. The apple flavor was pretty tasty, but it was the look on Kiera's face that I was savoring. Her lips were parted, and she was breathing just slightly heavier. I was sure she was getting turned on watching me...the girls at the nearby table sure seemed to be. A couple low groans drifted my way as I pulled the sucker out of my mouth.

Kiera's eyes darted to my lips, and she looked like she desperately wanted to taste the apple on my tongue. She didn't though. Surprising me, she pushed me back and said, "Ew, Kellan. That's mine."

Her objection was extremely amusing. Especially since I knew it was complete crap. There was no place on her body where my lips wouldn't be welcome. Calling her out, I said, "What? I can put my mouth on your—"

Her hand instantly covered my mouth, and she looked over at the table of eavesdropping girls like she actually cared what they thought about our relationship. "Kellan!" she hissed, embarrassed.

Removing her hand from my lips, I finished my question. Leaving out the crucial part she didn't want me to say, of course. "But I can't enjoy your sucker?"

An amused smile slipped onto her lips as she shook her head at me. To further accentuate my point, and hopefully get her to relinquish her treat, I pouted and gave her puppy dog eyes. It totally worked. With a sigh, she shoved the sucker back into my mouth. As I smiled in victory, she sighed. "You could at least ask first."

Removing the treat slowly, so my lips curled over the edge, I seductively told her, "I didn't think I had to ask to suck on your...candy."

I thought she'd find that sexy, but her expression instantly clouded with pain. "Don't say candy."

The playfulness fell off my face as I instantly realized my error. I'd stupidly reminded her of something she was doing her best to forget. "Sorry," I quietly said. I kind of wanted to smack myself in the face for saying her name.

She shook her head like she was shaking away the memory, then she leaned down and gave me a tender kiss. "It's all right." She kissed me again. "Just ask next time, Sucker Thief."

Happy that she was letting my mistake go, and loving her playful nickname, I gave her a huge grin as I returned the sucker to its rightful place—my mouth. She was smiling and laughing as she walked away from me, and I was grateful for the opportunity to amuse her. Anything I could do to make her happy, to make her forget the...darker parts of our relationship.

A little later, I was watching Kiera chatting with Kate, probably telling her about her first day back at school, when a sudden noise got my attention. The front doors had burst open. Matt strode through them, a look of pure excitement on his face as he immediately looked my way. When he spotted me, the look on his face grew even more exuberant. In all the years I'd known him, I'd never seen him look so excited. I had no idea what could possibly make him so...buoyant.

He sped-walked his way to the table, zipping around chairs in his way. As he rapidly approached, Griffin and Evan entered the bar. They also looked like they were bursting at the seams as they hurried my way. They all looked so thrilled, but for some reason, my chest clenched with dread. What was going on?

"Kell...you're never going to believe what just happened," Matt said, when he got close enough. Frowning, I looked from him to Evan and Griffin. Shit...what happened? Matt sat down beside me, and Evan and Griffin quickly joined him. They all leaned into me, crowding my personal space, and all of them started talking at once in their excitement.

"That band I've been talking to—Avoiding Redemption—I just got off the phone with their lead singer, Justin..."

"He saw us play at Bumbershoot, dude—"

"He wants us on his tour!"

"Yeah, he invited us along! Our first real tour!"

My eyes drifted between the guys, as their words started sinking in. "Tour? Like a concert tour? Seriously?"

"Yeah!" Matt said. "Justin said they're heading out with a half-dozen other bands soon, and they want us to go with them. *Us*, man! We'd be at the bottom of the lineup, 'cause it's a last-minute thing, but who the fuck cares. We're going on tour!"

My heart thudded inside my chest, and I felt ill. Tour...away from here...away from Kiera... "How long?" The words were practically a whisper as they left my lips.

"Six months! Can you believe that shit! This is it, Kell! Our shot to make it!" Griffin exclaimed.

Matt nodded. "It's a coast-to-coast tour. I already told Justin yes. First part of November, dude, then we're gone!"

"Coast to fucking coast!" Griffin said, grinning wide. "D-Bags are about to take over the world, man!"

Matt laughed. "More like the continent, cuz."

Bile rose up my throat as their joy bounced off my skin. Six months. We'd be gone six fucking months...if I agreed to go. But if I said no...fuck, they were all so excited. Saying no would crush them. But saying yes...shit. November? Six months? What would that much time do to Kiera and me? Unfortunately, I already knew the answer to that.

I looked over and saw Kiera curiously approaching the table. Leaning back, I ran a hand over my mouth as fear and indecision battled inside me. Kiera froze when our eyes met, and she suddenly looked terrified. I understood why she looked that way—I felt that way. Six months...away from her. A lot could happen in that amount of time. Just look at how much had happened with her and Denny, and that had been a fraction of the time. There was no way I could say yes to this. Fuck. How could I say no?

Matt patted one of my shoulders, while Evan touched the other one. "Come on, man, this is good news," Matt said. "This is what we've been waiting for. Why do you look like you're gonna be sick? This is our once-in-a-lifetime shot! Why aren't you stoked?"

Shaking my head, my eyes still locked on Kiera, I quietly burst their bubble. "I can't...I can't go." Kiera's eyes shifted to the people around me, and whatever she saw from my bandmates made her back up a step. Knowing they'd figured out exactly why I couldn't go on tour with them—and knowing they were silently blaming Kiera for it—I refocused on Matt and the guys. Voice low and intense, I tried to convince them that it was purely because we weren't ready, that it had nothing to do with my girlfriend. "Call Justin back, Matt. Tell him we can't go on tour right now, that it's not the right time. We're just not ready for that type of performance, not yet. I say we tell him no. I say we stay here."

The guys were angry. Matt shook his head while Griffin

tossed his hands in the air and Evan leaned back with a sigh. "We *are* ready, Kell," Matt said, an edge to his voice. "And we're never gonna get an offer like this again. This is *legit*. We *can't* say no."

"I can't go, Matt. I just can't. Please understand," I pleaded.

"Is this because of Kiera?" he asked, narrowing his eyes. "Are you ditching us for a girl?"

I closed my eyes. *Yes.* "It's just not the right time." *It will be the end of us. She'll find someone else. She'll leave me.* I reopened my eyes to see Matt glaring at me, unconvinced by my statement. "Okay...yeah. It's partly because of Kiera. She and I...we went through so much to get where we are...And we're finally in a good place, and I can't...I can't leave her right now. I'm sorry, but my answer is no. I'm staying here."

Griffin instantly exploded. "Oh, come on, Kellan! Fuck!"

I lifted a hand to him, trying to squelch his anger, but it didn't appear to help. "Griff, I'm not saying we'll never go on tour, I'm just saying not right now." Shaking his head, still pissed, he crossed his arms over his chest and glared at me like I was personally tearing his dream into tiny pieces. And in a way, I was.

Matt hung his head, looking utterly defeated. "I can't believe our chance to make it big is finally here...and you're saying no."

Guilt flooded me. The guys had sacrificed so much for me—given up their entire life in L.A. to follow me to Seattle, and right when we'd been on the brink. They'd never once asked to go back, never once pushed me to leave here. But there was no way I could say yes to this. I'd lose her. But if I said no...I might lose *them*. Fuck. "Guys, please..."

Evan clapped me on the shoulder, like he understood my torment. Leaning in, he said, "We're all leaving people behind, Kellan. We know it's hard, but this...this could be important for our future. For us *and* for them. Why don't you talk to Kiera before you decide anything? She might be more okay with it than you think."

He extended his hand to point at Kiera, and my eyes followed the gesture. Kiera was pale as she stood there frozen, watching us.

She was obviously curious about why we were arguing, but she was nervous too. As she should be. How could she possibly be okay with me leaving for six months? She'd fallen apart when Denny had left for two months. Fallen apart and fallen into my arms. Whose arms would she seek if *I* left her?

With a sigh, I scrubbed my face with my hands. I felt like I was trapped in a cage. No matter what I did, no matter what decision I made, someone was going to get hurt. One of my relationships—either mine with Kiera, or mine with the guys—was going to be forever altered after this moment. It made me want to slug something. Or start sobbing. Everything had been going so well... why did this have to happen now? Now, when I *wanted* time to freeze.

But still, at the very least, I owed the guys a conversation with my girlfriend. Slumping in my chair, I shook my head in defeat. Then I weakly looked up at them and nodded. "Okay, I'll talk to her, then I'll let you know."

I felt like I weighed a thousand pounds as I stood up and faced Kiera. Another weary sigh escaped me when our eyes met. I told the guys I'd be right back, then I began slowly trudging toward her. There was no way she was going to be okay with this. No way on Earth.

Kiera kind of looked like she wanted to run as I approached her, and the bar was deathly quiet. Everyone was aware something major was happening, they just didn't know what. I couldn't look Kiera in the eye when I finally reached her. Keeping my head down, I woodenly asked, "Can I talk to you..." I forced my eyes to her face, my entire body was rigid with tension, "...outside?"

She looked like she wanted to say no, but she nodded. I grabbed her hand, then led her out of the silent bar to the parking lot. Fear and anxiety made me drop her fingers the moment we were outside. It was dark now, just on the verge of being chilly. It matched my mood. As my eyes ceaselessly scanned the lot, I tried to think of what to say to her. How could I knowingly break her heart? Watching her fall apart when Denny left was suddenly fresh in my mind. I couldn't hurt her like that. I just...couldn't. And how could I possibly leave her anyway? Leave her to fall for someone else. She was my entire fucking world. I wouldn't survive if she...replaced me.

"Kellan?" she asked, her voice trembling with worry.

Realizing I was already hurting her by my silence, I turned to face her. I cupped her cheek with a sigh. "I need to tell you something, and I don't know where to start," I confessed.

Her eyes searched mine, the fear in them evident. "Just tell me, because you're really starting to scare me."

Swallowing a lump in my throat, I looked down. My fingers fell to her arm as I began to tell her the "good" news. "Matt has been doing a lot over the summer for the band." Glancing up at her, I shrugged. "Lining up more gigs, scoring that equipment so we can work on soundproofing Evan's place, getting us that spot at Bumbershoot..."

None of this was news to her, so she nodded for me to continue. Stepping close to her, I started stroking her arm. This was the part she didn't know, the part that was going to kill her... and maybe us. "A band that he's been trying to get in with saw us at Bumbershoot. They were impressed and..." With a sigh, I grabbed her fingers and prayed for strength. "They want us to join them on their tour."

I braced for her tears, braced for her outpouring of pain. It didn't come, though. Instead, she blinked in surprise and pulled back to look at me. "You got invited to join a tour? An actual band tour?"

With a nod, I shrugged. "It's a pretty decently sized one, about six other bands are already on it, from what Matt says. We'll be a last-minute addition, bottom of the lineup, but on it, at least." If I could even leave her, of course.

Kiera tossed her arms around my neck...like she was happy I was talking about leaving her. "Oh my God, Kellan! That's amazing!"

She squeezed me tight, and a sad sigh escaped me. Why was

she okay with this? I thought she'd be...devastated. Sensing my mood, Kiera pulled back to look at me. I couldn't meet her eyes, and she cupped my cheek, stroked my skin with her thumb. "You're not excited about this...because of me, right?"

I lifted my eyes to hers and shrugged. "It's a six-month tour, Kiera...coast to coast." She bit her lip, and her eyes started to water with the pain I'd been expecting. My stomach clenched at seeing it. I didn't want to hurt her. I didn't want to hurt *us*.

She smiled, but it was clearly forced. "It's okay," she said, her voice oozing encouragement. "Six months isn't so long. And you'll have breaks, right? I'll still get to see you?"

Even though I wasn't sure what the schedule looked like, I nodded. My gaze drifted to our feet. "I don't have to go, Kiera." Looking up, I shook my head. "I can tell the guys no."

Her mouth dropped open as she suddenly comprehended that I'd already told them no in the bar—that was why they were mad at me. I kept my expression even. *I'd rather have them mad at me than lose you.*

"This is your dream, Kellan," she said, disbelief on her face. "And this could be it for you. This could be your moment, your chance. Isn't this what you want?"

My eyes drifted to the doors of the bar. I shrugged, like it didn't matter, but even as I did, a ball of ice collected in my chest. "I'm fine with my life the way it is. Playing at Pete's..." my eyes returned to hers, "...being with you." I really didn't want to choose between those two dreams, but push come to shove, Kiera would always win that battle. Always.

Kiera pressed her body close to mine and ran her hand through my hair. "But you know you're too talented to keep doing that forever, Kellan. Even though I'd like to keep you to myself, I know that I can't hide you away from the world."

My eyes sank to the ground, an objection on my lips, but she ducked down to look at me and said something I couldn't deny. "And it's not just your dream, Kellan." Her eyes drifted to the bar. I looked with her, and the disappointment on Matt's face flooded my vision. "You know how much this means to them," she said, returning her eyes to mine. "You can't say no because of me."

A sigh of defeat left me. "I know. They're the only reason I'm even talking to you about this right now." I shook my head. "But, Kiera, you have another year of school, you can't come with me. I don't want to leave you—"

She cut me off with a rough shake of her head. "Not because of me, Kellan." Emotion knotted her throat; tears glistened in her eyes. "I won't keep another man from his dream," she whispered.

Understanding pricked my skin as I clutched her tight to me. She wasn't going to say no, wasn't going to demand that I stay behind with her. No matter how much it hurt her, she was going to let me go...which meant...the choice was entirely up to me. A part of me wanted to take a chance on this opportunity and leave. She was right about this being a dream of mine. I might play it off as being unimportant but being on a stage was all I'd ever wanted since Denny had shown me my true path. And the guys...I couldn't take this away from them. But fuck...if I left...what would happen to us? Could we survive that kind of separation? Would she...wait for me?

I was so terrified to leave her, I was shivering in her arms. Kiera felt the vibrations. Her voice in my ear was soft with concern. "You're scared, Kellan. Why? You never get scared."

"That's not true," I murmured, shaking my head. "I'm scared all the time." Terrified as fuck to lose her, twenty-four-seven. Kiera pulled back to look at me, confusion on her face. I swallowed the tight knot in my throat. She wasn't going to like this... but it was the truth. "I remember, Kiera. I remember when Denny left you...what it did to you." My eyes searching hers, I whispered, "I remember how we got together."

Anger burned in her eyes; anger mixed with understanding. She knew why I felt the way I did, but even still, it bothered her. She pushed me back. "You won't leave me because when Denny left—"

"I know you don't like being alone." I remembered all the innocent flirting...that had never actually been innocent.

Her jaw clenched as heat filled her voice. "I'm not going to freak out because you're gone and cheat on you. I'm not...I wouldn't...Why would you think I would do that to you?"

You know why. "Because I was there...when Denny thought the exact same thing, when he thought you'd never cheat on him either." Guilt flooded me with shame. I couldn't solely blame her for that; I'd been an active participant in her betrayal. But still...it had happened, and it was on my mind. I tried to hug her, to take away the sting of my truthful, painful words, but she kept me away.

Her chin quivered with barely contained emotion. "That's not fair. I've grown, Kellan. And you and I were a completely different situation. You can't throw that in my face."

"I know, I do know that. And I know you've grown, Kiera, but still..." Closing my eyes, I looked away from her. How could I squelch the fear? How could I believe, without a doubt, that I completely had her heart, when I knew—I *knew*—Denny had felt the same way, once upon a time.

She was silent for a long moment. "Are you always going to wonder about me?" she asked.

A dark humor filled me. Raising my eyebrows, I said, "Just like you wonder about me? Just earlier today you thought I was cheating on you. You won't worry when I'm gone? I mean, if I go on the road for months...with Griffin...it won't cross your mind?"

"Well, now it will," she said, venom in her eyes. Crossing her arms, she glared at me like I'd already committed a dozen atrocious acts. With a sigh, I turned away from her. We were already mad and suspicious...and I hadn't even left yet. Was I leaving?

I heard Kiera sigh, the resigned sound matching mine. Then she quietly said, "I guess we'll just have to try and trust each other."

With a slow nod, I stared at her feet. That was all we could do...try.

Kiera suddenly cupped my cheek, lifting my gaze to hers. "Did you tell me this out here because you thought I would break down?"

My voice was quiet as I nodded. "I remember that night that Denny told you he was leaving. I remember holding you while you cried...for him. I saw you when his plane left. You were devastated, like a part of you had left with him. I don't want to hurt you like that, Kiera." But I hadn't hurt her at all. She was fine...*I* was the one in pain.

Giving me a soft kiss, she rested her forehead against mine. "Are you upset that I'm not more upset? Was this a test?"

I shook my head. "I wouldn't test you, Kiera, but I did think you'd at least cry, maybe beg a little." But aside from getting angry at me for my comment, she hadn't had a single negative reaction. Not one. She wasn't devastated. She wasn't even sad. I didn't know what to think about that.

Confused and hurt, I tried to move away from her. She held me close. "I will," she said. "Trust me, when you actually leave, I will be a blubbering wreck. But I meant what I said, Kellan. I've grown. A lot has happened since Denny left me that first time. I've done some maturing." She shook her head, almost angry at herself. "I was so scared to be alone. I still don't like it, but I'm more secure now, I think. Mistakes in the past have aged me some."

That made me crack a small smile. "Ah, the wizened twenty-two-year-old."

She smiled with me, and I felt the tension in the air dissipating. "Kellan, you may have a lot more experience, but don't act like you're not the same age I am. I've seen your driver's license."

Raising an eyebrow, I grinned and asked, "The real one?" I did actually have a fake one. Evan and I had gotten some in L.A., just to make performing and hanging out in bars all night a little easier.

But to be honest, I'd barely ever needed mine; my face had opened a lot of doors for me. Of course, my face was also the reason both my parents hated me, so sometimes a blessing was actually a curse... and that was exactly what this tour felt like—a cursed blessing.

Amused at my comment, Kiera smirked and shook her head. Then she grabbed my cheeks, holding me in her gaze. "Do you think I loved Denny more, because it bothered me so much when he first told me he was leaving?" she asked, seriousness in her voice.

My heart cracked as I stared at her, fear slipping inside. *To be honest, yes.* "Can you blame me for thinking that?"

Her arms wrapped around me, and her head rested on her shoulder. "No, I guess not," she murmured. Pure peace enveloped me, and I closed my eyes, savoring it. Even if our love wasn't quite as strong as theirs had been...this was pretty amazing. I'd take it.

She was silent for a moment, as we held each other, then she said, "I didn't love him more than I love you, Kellan." She pulled back to look me in the eye. "I love *you* more. I love you enough to let you go and live your dream." She shrugged. "Don't you see...? I love you more."

I didn't entirely understand what she meant, but the sentiment eased the hole in my heart, and made me smile. She tenderly brushed some hair off my forehead, then stroked my cheek and whispered, "And, yes, I will miss you, more than you can possibly imagine, but I know that you have to do this, Kellan. And you know it too."

Shaking my head in disagreement, I told her, "No, I know that I have to be with you. Everything else is just details." Everything else paled in comparison. *Everything.*

She smiled as she kissed me. "This isn't just your dream, though, remember." With a sigh, she pointed back at the bar. "There's Evan and Griffin and Matt. He's worked so hard for this."

I studied her finger, pointing toward the bandmates I was screwing over by being selfish. Again. "I know..."

Kiera laced her arms around my neck. "And that's why you'll do this. It's their dream too, and you can't take it away from them...for me, for us."

She was right, and I knew that, but God...the thought of leaving her hurt so fucking bad. If only she could come with me. If only we could live out this dream together...then it wouldn't feel so life-altering. So terrifying. "I know," I whispered, wishing I could take the words back.

I held her for as long as I felt I could, then I pulled back. My voice morose, I told her, "I guess I should go tell Matt the good news."

Her eyes moistened as she bit her lip; seeing the tears build up actually brightened my spirits a little. She was genuinely going to miss me. "When does the tour start?" she asked.

My gaze dropped to the ground, along with my heart. *It starts too soon*. "First part of November."

"Oh." The ache of grief in her voice made me glance up at her. She was staring at the ground too, pain clear on her face as she calculated the very limited time we had left. It was close to the end of September. We had just over a month together, then...who knows when we'd see each other again.

The torture of our impending separation swirled around us for a moment, and we both silently absorbed it. Then, needing her reassurance, I grabbed her hand and gave her a soft kiss. I indicated the doors, wondering if she was ready for this. Even though the decision had been made, once we stepped into that bar, it would be official—no turning back. For a moment, Kiera looked like she wanted to do anything other than step inside, like we could avoid reality if she never went back to work. We couldn't though. Reality would find us if we tried to avoid it.

She inhaled a deep breath, then she nodded—she was ready. I led her through the doors. Everyone was watching us. And sadly, there were inspecting us, like they thought we'd gotten physical with each other. It had happened before. In this bar. But that wasn't what had gone down, and once that was clear, the curiosity faded, and people went back to their own lives.

Everyone except my band, of course. They were relentlessly staring at Kiera and me, like they were trying to judge the outcome of our conversation by our body language. I let out a long exhale as I walked us back there. Might as well get this over with. If nothing else, at least the guys would be thrilled.

As Kiera and I approached the table, I studied my friends—they were all watching Kiera, probably wondering what side of this decision she'd landed on. Matt looked melancholy, like he was sure nothing had changed, and I was going to say no again. Evan looked unsure, like he didn't know what he wanted me to say. He had his own reasons to stay in Seattle, after all, and I had a feeling he'd actually be okay if I still said no. Disappointed, for sure, but he'd happily wait for me to come around. Matt, though...he'd be crushed if my answer didn't change. Crushed enough to leave the band, I really wasn't sure. Maybe. But Griffin...there was no doubt how he would react. He would be ticked beyond measure for the rest of our friendship if I shot down this opportunity. As it was, he had his arms crossed over his chest and was glaring at Kiera like it was entirely her fault. If he didn't stop that soon, he just might get a swift kick in the ass.

Clenching Kiera's hand, I stopped directly in front of the trio. I cleared my throat and ran a hand through my hair. They all shifted their gazes to me, their faces expectant. Exhaling slowly, I felt change in the air. And I felt powerless to stop it from coming. Knowing I couldn't put this off any longer, I locked eyes with Matt. "I'm in," I told him.

All of the guys instantly reacted to my words. Evan's grin was wide and proud—he was happy I'd taken a chance on this. Griffin smacked the table, letting out a loud yell of excitement. And Matt was instantly on his feet. He gleefully wrapped an arm around my shoulders—his face was the happiest I'd ever seen it. "This is gonna be great, Kell. You'll see."

God...I hoped so. Because I was risking *everything* for this.

The guys surrounded me after that, flooding me with their sheer joy, then later, people around the bar started figuring out what was going on and began congratulating us. The good-natured energy at our table was contagious, and after a while, I finally started relaxing, finally started getting excited. Everything else aside, this was an epic moment for us. A tour...a freaking tour. Just saying the word in my head seemed surreal. The thought of actually being out there doing it was kind of mind-blowing.

By the time we had to leave Pete's for a show at another bar, I was brimming with endorphins, and actually starting to look forward to our upcoming adventure. I would have loved to finish the night out at Pete's celebrating with my friends, but unfortunately, it was time for us to go.

Leaving took longer than usual; we were all a little reluctant to take off, even Matt. And especially Griffin, who was loving the adoration. Evan and Matt finally wrangled him to the door, but not before he told the bar, "Thank you all, my loyal subjects. And don't worry, I won't ever forget you when I'm famous—I'll only refuse to acknowledge your existence!"

Jackass. Rolling my eyes at him, I headed over to Kiera, to say goodbye properly...and to make sure she was still okay. She had an adorable scowl of annoyance on her face; it was a look she almost constantly had around Griffin. It morphed into something warm and loving when she shifted to look up at me. God, I loved watching that transformation.

Crooking a grin, I tilted my head back at where the tool had disappeared. "What do you think will do him in first? Drugs, money, or women?"

Smiling, she slipped her arms around my waist. "I'm pretty sure it will be a combination of all three."

I had to laugh at her assessment. Yes, left to his own devices, she was probably right. But with Matt, Evan, and me watching over him...well, hopefully we could keep Griffin from fucking up his life too badly. Not that we were actually going to have the grand life I'd insinuated. Realistically, we would probably never be much more than we were now—a small band playing local bars. With maybe the occasional tour. Maybe.

Slinging my arms around Kiera's waist, I started leaning in for our goodbye kiss. I was nearly to her lips when she suddenly blurted out, "And what about you? What will be your downfall?"

Her question caught me off guard. *My* downfall? To have a downfall you had to have a weak spot, and since the only thing that weakened me was her...well, one could say I'd already fallen. Curious about what she thought my doom would be, I answered her question with a question. "You think I'll have one?" *With you by my side, Kiera, the only direction left for me is up.*

Kiera seemed embarrassed for even asking, but then she shrugged and confessed. "It has occurred to me that you're on the path to fame and fame brings certain...hazards with it. You'll be surrounded by so much...temptation." She paused to worry her lip. "And I've seen *Behind the Music*. I know what gets offered to rock stars."

A sliver of annoyance ran up my spine. Getting called out on future bad behavior when I had no intention of doing anything wrong was frustrating. But I understood her comment, and I really couldn't be mad at her for saying it. There was a pretty huge stereotype around rock stars—partying, women, drugs...all-around general mayhem. It was part of the appeal for some musicians, like Griffin, but not for me. All I wanted from this life was to play our music, have fun with my friends, and have Kiera next to me. And in all honesty, two of those things I could get by without.

Not wanting her to worry about future me, since I was going to be just fine, I shut off my irritation and decided to make light of the ridiculous comment she'd just made instead. "Wait, *Behind the Music*?" Wow...just how famous was I in her version of my future? Entertained by how she saw me, I jokingly said, "You've already mapped out my career, haven't you?" I ducked down and playfully looked her in the eye. "So, what is it? Booze? Gambling? Buying too many yachts?"

Couldn't she see how absurd this conversation was? I'd probably come right back here after the tour, and that would be the end of my fifteen minutes. Somewhere deep inside, she had to know that I wasn't going anywhere. The kind of fame she was talking about was exceedingly rare...and not really what I was looking for. But it really didn't matter either way, because even if that crazy situation somehow *did* happen to me, it wouldn't change me. I wasn't going to go nuts or anything. I liked my simple life, especially now that Kiera was sharing it with me.

Kiera lightly tapped my chest, amused at my outlandish suggestion, but then she said, "No, for you, it's women." Her face fell as she shook her head. "Always women."

I could hear the trace of pain in her voice, the sadness, and I knew I hadn't successfully lightened her worries. She truly was scared about my future, about our future. I understood that too; her fear mirrored my own. Kiera still didn't think she was enough for me, and as happy as she was for me, she was worried about me replacing her down the road...just as worried as I was about her replacing me one day. It was that same dark cloud that always seemed to hover over us. How could we possibly survive with all of this doubt between us? Was this *our* downfall? Endlessly worrying about the other person's fidelity until we drove each other insane.

We wouldn't last long that way...even I knew that. We needed to shift our thinking. We needed to start doing what we'd said we would do—try to trust each other. Otherwise...there really would be nothing left for me to come home to. And I *needed* to come home to her. I couldn't picture my life without her.

Sadness overtook me as I searched her face. "You have to trust me, Kiera." I tried to crack a hopeful smile, but I knew I wasn't succeeding. "Just like I have to trust you." That was the *only* way we were going to have the lasting future I desperately wanted.

Needing to lighten the mood, I immediately grinned and

made a crack about her getting tired of me one day, maybe leaving me for a Jonas Brother once I'd sold out and hit the bottle. Amused by the picture I'd painted, her mood finally brightened. She rapped me on the chest again before leaning up to kiss me. "Never. You're mine, washed-up or not."

Exactly, Kiera. Exactly.

"Good," I murmured against her lips. "Because none of that is going to happen." I pulled back to look at her. I wanted her to absorb what I was about to say, believe it with all of her heart. "It's just a six-month tour with a bunch of other bands, most of which are small and unsigned, just like us. And when we're all crammed together on a smelly bus, I'll be wishing that I was back at home with you." *This isn't the beginning of our end. It's just a brief intermission...not a big deal.*

Feeling her warmth filling me, I pressed my head against hers. "And when the six months are up, that's exactly where you'll find me...in bed with you." *Never to leave again.*

"I hope so," she breathed.

Not wanting her to feel anything but wonderful and secure in my love for her, I whispered, "I know so." But even still, my brain couldn't help but reverberate in agreement with her statement. *I hope so too, Kiera.*

Chapter 8
ALMOST TIME

The guys were so excited to leave, they started a countdown on Evan's whiteboard. Forty days until we left for a six-month tour. Then thirty-five days...then thirty...twenty. Each time they changed the number, they talked about how great it was going to be when we headed out. Each time I saw them change the number, I started to freak out a little more inside. What if this was a mistake? What if Kiera and I couldn't handle this? What if the physical separation created an emotional one? What if she couldn't deal with being alone? What if she found comfort from someone else?

But no. *She's not going to do that to me, I'm not going to do that to her.* We were choosing to trust each other, that was our agreement. One that seemed so simple on the surface, so easy to say, but goddamn, actually *doing* it was really fucking hard. Every day the what ifs were slowly killing me, poisoning me with their darkness, and I hadn't even left yet.

"I still can't tell if you're excited about this."

I looked over to see Evan studying me as I drove. Pushing aside my worry, I forced a carefree smile to my face. "Going to see Poetic Bliss? To ask Rain if she and the girls will take over our spot at Pete's while we're gone? I don't know. I'm not excited, but I'm not...un-excited either. More ambivalent than anything," I said with a shrug.

Pete loved having a band play at his bar, but he hated finding talent. To ease his stress, we'd agreed to find him a temporary replacement before we left. Rain and the rest of her band—Meadow, Sunshine, Tuesday, and Blessing—was our most promising option. They were a fun group of girls. We'd hung out on occasion before, and Rain and I...well, she was very forward, and at the time, I'd been up for anything with anyone. We'd had a little fun in my car once, but that was all it had been—a bit of fun.

Returning my eyes to the road, I finished with, "I *am* glad that we won't be leaving Pete in a bind, and I think Poetic Bliss will be a good fit for the bar. They're fairly similar to our sound." And as an added bonus, they were an all-female band, so I wouldn't have to worry about some punk-ass rock star wannabe trying to get into Kiera's pants. That was my job, and mine alone.

From the corner of my eye, I noticed Evan cocking an eyebrow at my answer. "While I agree with that assessment, which is why I suggested them, Poetic Bliss wasn't what I was talking about, and you know it."

A long sigh left my lips. "You meant the tour. Yeah...of course, I'm totally pumped about it."

"It shows," he said with a laugh. "What with you missing almost every rehearsal lately, rarely leaving Kiera's side, looking preoccupied whenever you're away from her...Yeah, it's easy to see just how pumped you are."

I gave him an annoyed sidelong glance. "I *am* looking forward to it, I swear. It's just...things with Kiera are so fragile right now. The thought of being gone for so long...it's really freaking me out."

"Fragile? I don't think that's true, Kell. You guys seem pretty solid to me," he responded with a shrug.

"Yeah..." *That's what Denny thought too and look what happened to him*. God, I wished I could stop thinking about that.

Would I feel differently about this if I'd never known about her separation anxiety with him? Yeah. Probably.

Like Evan could sense my unspoken words, he gently patted my shoulder. "It will be okay, Kellan. She'll still be here when you get back. That girl is crazy about you."

Glancing over at him, I smiled. "Yeah, I know." We were good, really good. Everything was right as rain...when we were together. It was being apart from her that made doubt-filled acid burn my chest. I constantly prayed Kiera and I were strong enough to be apart for this long because we *should* be able to be apart without so much...fear. In a weird way, this tour could actually be a huge step forward in our relationship. *If* it went well. Which meant, I needed to make *sure* it went well. She had to be absolutely positive that I loved her. Every single second of every single day.

Thinking that made my mood shift again. "Even still, I need to make sure she doesn't forget about me while I'm gone." Things between Kiera and Denny had really started fizzling when he'd stopped trying...that meant I couldn't ever stop trying, not even for a second. But what could I do for her while I was gone? That was the real question.

Evan laughed and shook his head, like he thought I was crazy. "What do you have in mind?" he asked.

Multiple romantic gestures had been swimming in my head for weeks now, ever since I'd agreed to leave. I wanted to do every single one of the ideas that had sprung into my brain, but even I knew that might be over the top. I wanted to show her I cared without looking...desperate. "I'm not sure yet. Something simple, something fun." *Something that ensures I'm constantly on her mind. She can't forget about what we have if she's always thinking about me. Right?*

I knew Evan would say I was being ridiculous, so I didn't bother asking him that question, but as we continued on to Rain's house, it was all I could think about. How could I possibly make sure Kiera wasn't so lonely that she found another...me?

How could I possibly keep me at the top of her thoughts twenty-four-seven? And what if that wasn't enough?

I was frowning when we arrived at Rain's house, drowning in darkening thoughts. Evan was still watching me when I shut off the car. "This is gonna be fine, Kell. I promise."

Knowing he was talking about the tour and not our errand, I gave him a halfhearted smile. *It's nice of you to say that, but that's not a promise you can make. Or keep.* "Shall we go brighten someone's day?" I asked, trying to make my voice light.

Evan grinned, clapped my shoulder, and nodded. "Let's go be heroes."

The door to Rain's house opened as we approached it, and Rain stood there, staring at us with a huge grin on her face. Rain was a tiny little thing, with dark eyes, pixie-like dark hair, a great voice, a fearless attitude, and boundless energy. She was going to do very well at Pete's. "Kellan Kyle and Evan Wilder. What brings you two to my neighborhood?" She frowned a little as she looked behind us. "You didn't bring the jackass, did you?"

Knowing she meant Griffin, I smiled and shook my head. "No, we left him with the babysitter."

She snorted, then opened the door wider. "Then you can come in."

"Thanks."

Her smoky eyes watched me the entire time I walked past her into the house. There was a familiar eagerness on her face, an open invitation that said she would do whatever I wanted to do, I only had to ask. Rain reminded me of myself sometimes. At least, the old version of me. Up for anything, no questions asked. While I'd never really thought about it before, now I kind of wondered...had her childhood sucked as much as mine? Was that why she was so...open with herself? Maybe I should ask her, but then again, it wasn't my style to pry.

As Evan and I stepped into the house, we nodded at the rest of the band, lounging around, relaxing on their day off. This group hung out together almost as much as the D-Bags hung out together. Maybe we all had dependency issues.

Rain closed the door then walked around us to join her friends. "So...just bored, or was there something specific on your mind?" Her gaze washed over my body, and one of the other girls sniggered.

A small laugh escaped me. "Something specific." Her eyebrows raised and her smile grew wider. Before the wrong idea could dig itself too far into her head, I quickly added, "A job, actually."

Rain pursed her lips, momentarily disappointed. But then her grin returned. "What job? Playing with you guys?"

I shook my head. "No, not with us...kind of, in place of us." Her frown started to return, and another laugh left me. "We need someone to fill in for us at Pete's." I looked over at Evan. "We got asked to go on tour...and we're gonna be gone for a while." A long while. A fucking long while. An endless fucking long while. God...could I really do this?

Evan frowned at me, and I knew my face had changed again. Darkened with my ever-shifting mood. Inhaling, I forced a smile and looked back at Rain. Her mouth was dropped open in shock.

"Are you fucking with us right now?" she asked, her eyes flicking between Evan, me, and her band. "You want us...to take your spot at Pete's Bar? *The* Pete's Bar?"

"Just until we get back," I told her with a smile.

She hopped up and down in her chunky combat boots. "Fuck, yes!" She looked back at her bandmates—they were all nodding in agreement, sheer joy on their faces. I'd been fairly certain that would be their reaction. It was a really good gig. One I didn't want to give up...even if it was just for a few months. Rain returned her eyes to me. "Absolutely, yes. We'll do it. Thank you, Kellan. Evan."

She let out another squeal of excitement, then shook her head. "I can't believe you guys are going on an actual, professional tour. I'd kill for that opportunity," she said, lightly smacking my arm.

"I'm sure you'll get your chance," I told her. "You guys are awesome."

Rain gave me a seductive smile as she chewed on her lip. "You're pretty awesome too, Kellan." I could tell from her face and her voice that she really wanted to celebrate the good news by having another romp in my car. *Sorry, Rain. My backseat is permanently reserved for my girlfriend.*

Smirking at her suggestive tone, I told the girls, "We'll let Pete know what's going on. He'll have some paperwork for you to fill out, so make sure you stop in soon. You'll start playing...the second weekend of November." We were leaving on the first Saturday of the month. While that was still about two weeks away, it sounded way too close, and my stomach started churning with fear and anxiety. This was going to be the longest two weeks of my life. Followed by the longest six months of my life.

Meadow jumped off the couch and wrapped her arms around Rain. After the girls hopped up and down for a minute, squealing and laughing, Meadow turned to me; her dark brown eyes glowed as brightly as her smile. "Thanks, Kellan! We owe you guys, big time!"

With a small laugh, Evan ran a hand over his dark, buzz-cut hair. "Nah, you're the one doing us a favor. We don't want to leave Pete with a band that sucks. So, thank you...for not sucking."

The girls all laughed at his comment. Clearing my throat, I motioned toward the door. "We've got a bunch of stuff to take care of today, so, we should go. If you have any questions, just call Pete. He'll give you guys whatever you need."

Without looking my way, Rain waved her hand at me and started group-hugging her friends. And just like that, her interest in me was gone. I was forgotten, dismissed, disregarded. Because it was Rain, and I wasn't interested in rekindling anything with her, I really didn't care, but it drove home all my fears about

Kiera. What if she moved on from me while I was gone? *That* reaction could be how she treated me when I got back from this... adventure. A dismissive wave as she went about her life without me.

No...not if I could help it. She wasn't going to forget me; I wouldn't let her.

When the door shut behind us after we left, we could still hear the girls squealing in excitement. Evan laughed at their exuberance. "They remind me of us, back when we got our first big break."

A soft chuckle left me as I thought back to when we'd booked our first major show, back in L.A. Griffin had nearly peed himself he'd been so excited. God, that seemed so long ago. We'd all been so carefree back then, not a single fucking worry in the world. But the world hadn't let us stay that way for long. Or at least, it hadn't let *me* stay that way for long. No, fate had wiped out my parents, then sent me on a collision course with my best friend's girlfriend. And now...now I didn't know what the hell was going to happen.

"Yeah..." I muttered. "Different time..."

Evan sighed, then smacked me on the back. Hard. "Ow! What the hell?" I snipped, glaring at him.

Frowning, he pointed at the sky. "It's a beautiful day. You *got* the girl of your dreams. You're about to have the experience of a lifetime. Quit fucking moping."

I blinked at hearing him drop an f-bomb. He didn't swear all that often since he'd started dating Jenny. She was always getting after us for our language, and it had rubbed off on Evan. Guess my mood was rubbing off on him too. He was staring at me with such an exasperated look on his face that I couldn't stop the laugh I felt bubbling inside me. When he noticed my mood shifting, he started laughing too.

"Okay...Jesus, I'll lighten up," I told him. Reaching around, I rubbed the sore spot on my back. "Why is everyone always smacking me?"

Evan grinned. "Because you're really fucking frustrating." He let out a long exhale. "Goddamn, it feels good to swear." Closing his eyes, he let out a long stream of obscenities. I raised an eyebrow as I patiently waited for him to finish. When he was done, he cracked an eye open. "Got to get it all out now, while Jenny's not around."

Shaking my head at him, I opened the door to my car. "And people say I'm whipped," I muttered.

Evan laughed as he opened the other door. "That's 'cause you are, Kell. We all are," he sighed. Then he frowned. "Well, except for Jackass. He's gonna be a problem on the road. You know that, right?"

I frowned as I leaned over the car. "Yeah...Matt still has that 12 pack of duct tape, right?"

Evan grinned. "Oh yeah. He's already got it packed."

"Thank God," I laughed. At least there was a hint of some fun in our future. Maybe this wouldn't be the nightmare I thought it was going to be. Maybe, like Evan said, everything really would be okay. Maybe.

Thinking about all the good times coming my way with my band genuinely brightened my mood as I drove us back to Evan's loft. If it were possible to take my worry about Kiera out of the equation, this upcoming tour really was what Evan had said—an experience of a lifetime. A dream come true. Traveling around the country with my best friends, playing shows almost every night, singing my heart out to the fans, watching them fall apart. Laughing, drinking, playing...it was almost *all* of the stuff that I loved to do, rolled up in one. I'd just have to do all of it without the single most important person in my life. I'd have to leave her behind, doing God knows what without me.

But I needed to stop thinking about that. *Focus on the good stuff, Kellan. Not the shit you're afraid of.*

Forcing the disturbing thoughts out of my head, I focused instead on something positive. *Anything* positive. We were about to have a great time. I could picture it—the four of us, clowning around on the bus, driving each other crazy, picking on each other, dying laughing... It really was going to be fun. Just...not for all of us. Our girls were going to be miserable while we were gone. At least...I thought they would be sad.

While Kiera told me all the time that she was going to miss me, and she did have brief moments of melancholy, she never seemed truly heartbroken, not like how she'd been when Denny had left her. Sometimes I felt like I was struggling with this more than she was, but then I remembered what she'd said to me the night I'd told her about the tour. I remembered her telling me that she'd grown, matured, and that she felt more secure about being alone. She'd told me that she loved me *more* than Denny. She loved me enough to not make a scene, to not put a stop to this...to let me go. She had already decided that she wasn't going to stand in the way of this dream. Maybe that was why she seemed fine. She was fine because she truly believed *we* were going to be fine. I needed to remember that and stop letting the "what ifs" kick my ass. *Hope for the best, and maybe it will happen.*

But even still, I had to imagine the actual goodbye was going to be really hard on her. Seeing her pain was going to undo me. I wasn't even sure if I could do it—I'd never been good at saying goodbye to her.

I tried not to think about it too much, but every day it got harder to do. I didn't want to think about the moment we left—that actual minute in time when we had to say goodbye to each other. When *I* had to say goodbye to her—that was going to kill me, I was sure. It felt too huge to think about...too devastating. If only there was some way to make our last moments fun, for everyone. But how could we possibly make leaving...enjoyable?

And that was when it hit me. Grinning, I looked over at Evan. He was smiling as he absentmindedly stared out the window, lost in a daydream, and it took him a second to notice my attention. "What?" he asked.

Since we were at a stop sign and no one was around, I twisted in my seat to face him. "We should have a party after our last show. Invite the whole bar." Just saying it started easing the tension around my heart. If I could give Kiera an epic, fun-filled night, maybe the sting of separation wouldn't be so bad. For her...and for me. For a minute at least.

Evan's smile grew. "Like a going-away party? Yeah, that would be awesome. We could have it at Matt's, since his place is a bit bigger than yours, and his street is pretty quiet." He paused, then nodded. "Yeah, I think that would help make it...easier to leave."

I had a feeling he was specifically talking about Kiera and me when he said that. Since I whole-heartedly agreed, I didn't ask him to clarify. Mind made up, I pulled away from the stop sign and made a U-turn. Evan glanced around the area, his grin shifting into a frown. "Where are you going?"

Smiling wider, I nodded my head in the direction of Matt and Griffin's place. "Matt's. Might as well ask him now."

Evan glanced at the sun. "It's still kind of early. Why don't we just wait and ask him at rehearsal?"

I bit my lip, not wanting to answer him. With my departure looming like a thunderstorm in the distance, Kiera and I had been spending as much time together as possible, which meant, I'd been slacking off on my duties as much as possible. I hadn't missed a show, but rehearsals... Like Evan had mentioned, I'd been hit-or-miss on those. Okay, I'd been *miss*-or-miss on those.

Evan sighed after studying my face. "Kell...if you keep missing rehearsal, Matt's gonna lose it. Like seriously lose it."

Picturing my angry, control-freak of a guitarist, I nodded. "Yeah, I know. I won't miss it," I said, glancing over at him. "I'll be there."

An amused sound left him as he shook his head. "Yeah...I've heard that before."

Smiling, I slightly changed my answer. "I'll *try* to be there?" An attempt was better than nothing, right?

Evan laughed a little more. "Uh-huh, sure."

We drove along in silence for a minute, and I tried very hard not to picture Matt's head exploding from the stress I was about to cause him in a few hours. But I knew, without a doubt, he was going to be pissed at me. Again. Because after Evan and I were done with errands, I was picking Kiera up from school and staying glued to her side all night long. Matt be damned. And I was pretty sure Evan knew that.

After another moment of silence, I glanced at him again. "You know I'm not actually going to be there, right?"

Head laid back on the seat, Evan smiled over at me. "Yep, I know."

I let out a laugh. "Okay, just checking."

When we pulled into Matt's driveway, I was damn-near giddy. Doing something to make Kiera happy always put a grin on me, and I was going to make sure she liked this party. Every last second with her was going to be memorable, and I felt the fog of despair lifting from me.

Evan shook his head at me as we got out of my car. "Where was this guy twenty minutes ago? *He* might not have gotten smacked."

Frowning at him, I started walking to the front door. "The other guy can come back any second, you know."

Evan let out a dramatic sigh. "Yeah, I know." He grinned. "That's one of the most entertaining things about hanging out with you. We never know who we're gonna get."

My frown deepened at his comment, but then, proving him right about my mood swings, I shifted it to a grin. Kiera often said the same thing. *Moody artist*, she called me. I'd take it. Being moody was a hell of a lot better than being numb. I knew that for a fact.

Wondering if Matt would even be awake, I did a couple of quick taps on his door with my knuckle. It cracked open a moment later, then Matt's pale eyes were looking at me in disbelief. "Holy shit. Are you showing up for rehearsal? This early?" His jaw dropped, like he really couldn't believe it, but I knew he was just being a smartass. We didn't rehearse here.

I smirked at him as he stepped back to let me into the house. Looking around, I instantly started planning the party. Beer there, games there, dancing there…sex there…this was going to be great. "No, I'm not here for that, I just uh…I had a question."

Matt nodded a greeting at Evan then closed the door. Lifting an eyebrow, he grinned as he shook his head at me. "You know they make these things called phones, right?"

I narrowed my eyes at Matt while Evan tried to contain a laugh. They liked teasing me about my technology issues almost as much as they liked teasing Griffin for being…well, Griffin. "Evan and I were wondering…you cool with having a party at your house?" I asked.

Matt shrugged. "Sure. Tonight?"

I shook my head. "No…after our last show. Right before we leave."

He tilted his spikey blond head at me. "You want to trash my house the night before we leave for six months? Do you have any idea how bad that's gonna smell when we get back?"

I pursed my lips. He had a point. And none of us were going to want to spend any time the next morning cleaning up. I was about to suggest we could hire someone to do it, when Evan said, "I'll talk to Jenny. I'm sure she won't mind cleaning up after us." He paused to raise an eyebrow. "This *one* time."

Grinning at Evan's solution, I looked back at Matt. "So? What do you think?"

He shrugged. "Sure, sounds like fun."

Excited, I slapped my hands together, making a loud clap. From the bedrooms, I heard Griffin yell, "Shut the hell up! People are sleeping!"

Matt shook his head and yelled back, "Person. *One* person is sleeping. Alone. Because he struck out last night." He looked back at me. "It was priceless, man. You should have seen it."

I smiled at his comment, but honestly, I'd seen Griffin strikeout enough for one lifetime. And I'd seen him hit a home run enough for one lifetime. Just thinking about it made a shudder go through me. It was kind of baffling that Griffin was still hitting on random girls when Anna, for some reason, was a guaranteed yes for him—and probably a thousand times hotter than any other girl he might otherwise have a chance with. But maybe Anna had been working, and he'd gotten impatient. Griffin wasn't very good at waiting. For anything.

Griffin's door opened and angry footsteps started thudding down the hall. Matt was already laughing. I sighed. Maybe he was right, maybe I should have just called.

"Fuck you, dude," Griffin spouted at Matt. His hair was a disheveled mess from just waking up, his face was wrinkled from his pillow, and he was only wearing boxer-briefs. Sure, it was early, but it wasn't *that* early.

Griffin's pale, tired eyes acknowledged Evan, then shifted to me. "Hey, Kell. What are you doing here? Shouldn't you be out screwing Kiera somewhere. Isn't that your *thing* now?"

My eyes widened at hearing him say that. Wow. Griffin was being pissy because I was missing *rehearsals*? He was the one always telling us that rehearsals were a waste of time. But then I saw Griffin glare at Matt, and I knew the truth. *Matt* was being pissy. And when Matt was being pissy, he usually took it out on Griffin. I was getting transferal pissiness.

Not wanting Matt to remember my many absences and start in on me, I told Griffin the good news. "Just planning a party at your house."

His face instantly lit up. "Oh, yeah! When? Right now?" He looked around like he expected women to come out of the walls or something.

I shook my head. "No, for later. Matt will fill you in."

Griffin rubbed his hands together. "Party at the Hancocks'! Ain't no party like a Hancock party, 'cause a Hancock party don't stop..." He kept singing to himself as he gyrated to music only he could hear.

Grimacing, I looked over at Evan. "We should go."

Evan had the exact same look on his face as he watched Griffin air-smacking an invisible girl's ass. "Yeah…"

Matt shook his head. "Hold up, I want to show you something."

Evan and I shared a look, then we both looked back at Griffin. He was still singing to himself…and dirty dancing by himself. Basically, entertaining himself while we looked on in a mixture of disgust and amusement. Typical Griffin.

"Yeah, sure…what?" I asked.

Matt nodded to his kitchen. "In here." He glanced at Griffin, grimaced, then hurried away. We gratefully followed him as Griffin started humping the back of a chair. "God, he's got issues," Matt groaned when we were safely out of eyesight.

Evan laughed, then asked Matt, "What's up?"

Matt walked over to a pile of papers on the counter. "I was going to show you this at rehearsal, but…" he paused to glare at me. "Maybe it's better to show you now."

I gave him an innocent *I have no idea why you might be mad at me* smile. Matt rolled his eyes, but thankfully didn't start yelling at me. I think he understood that this was hard for me. Well, hopefully he understood. "As you know, the soundproofing material finally arrived, so I made some plans on how we could set it up. I know it doesn't really matter now…since we're leaving soon…but it would be nice to have it ready when we get back."

Loving the sound of those words—*get back*—I nodded. "Sounds good, let's see 'em."

He started going into the specifics, showing us his multiple drawings, but I kept noticing things around the room, distracting things… entertaining things. Too curious to not say anything, I interrupted Matt. "Okay, I have to ask…what's up with all the sticky notes?"

Matt sighed as he looked around the room. There were neon-colored bits of paper scattered everywhere. There had to be at least a hundred of them, and they were stuck on *everything*. "Griffin. I left him *one* note in the bathroom, asking him to…

clean up if he missed...and his response was...well, this," he said, his finger circling the room.

I snorted, then moved closer to read some of them. A lot of them were gross, having to do with every single fluid that came out of the human body: Don't come on this, don't pee here, etc. Reading the one on the coffeepot almost ruined coffee for me. I even gagged a little after reading it. A lot of the notes had to do with Matt's cock, and where he shouldn't put it: the toaster, the oven...the freezer. But the majority of the notes said the same thing: *Don't be a dick today.*

Looking back at Matt, I smirked. "There appears to be a theme."

He rolled his eyes, then smiled. "Just wait until he sees what I'm gonna do to his bed later."

I almost warned him that whatever his plan was, he might not like the way Griffin retaliated to his bed being messed with, but... I was too damn curious to see what happened, so I kept my mouth shut.

As I stepped back, taking in the room—plastered with all of Griffin's nasty little messages—as a whole, an idea began to form. A wonderful, fabulous, inspiring idea...an idea I almost couldn't believe was born from Griffin's grotesqueness. I knew exactly how I was going to make Kiera think about me while I was gone. It was perfect—fun, lighthearted, but with a chance to be a little serious too. And romantic as hell. I couldn't wait to get started.

Chapter 9
PREPARATIONS

The next several days flew by, and not just because I was dreading my upcoming separation from Kiera. No, instead of dwelling, I'd found something fun and productive to occupy my free time. Operation *Keep Kiera in Love with Me* was in full effect.

I already had a drawer full of little notes that I was going to leave for her to find. A scavenger hunt seemed a lot more entertaining than just leaving them out in the open like Griffin had. Some of the notes were funny, some sweet, some downright naughty—a little bit of everything...just like me. Now I was starting in on the bigger projects: letters. There were a few things I wanted to say to her that couldn't be said on a small piece of paper. Okay, there were a *lot* of things I wanted to say to her, but I was making myself stop at just a handful of letters. Any more than a couple and she might realize just how desperate I really was.

I'd just finished the one I wanted to leave for her the night we left. It was sweet, playful...sexy as hell. I had high hopes she'd be turned on after reading it—that would definitely assure I was in her thoughts all night long. The one I was currently writing was anything but lighthearted. It was my soul, laid bare and bleeding.

I planned on hiding this one really well, so it was the last thing she found. The idea for the letter had started out as a romantic one, but it was quickly becoming...painful.

> *I hid this one in the hopes that you would find it long after I'm gone. I hope you find this, months from now, when I'm still out there, on the road, away from you. I can't imagine what the time apart has done to us. I'm hoping we're closer. I'm hoping we're more in love than ever. I'm hoping that when I come back, you'll move in with me. In all honesty, I'm hoping that when I come back, you'll agree to marry me someday. Because that's what I want, what I dream about. You, mine, for the rest of my life. I hope you feel the same...because I don't know what I would do without you. I love you so much. But, if for some reason we're not closer, if something has come between us, please, I'm begging you... don't give up on me. Stay. Stay with me. Work it out with me. Just don't leave me...please.*
>
> *I love you, always,*
> *Kellan*

Agony filled my chest as I stared at the words that had just poured out of me. Agony, hope...and uncertainty. I couldn't say this to her, it was too much...too needy...too overwhelming. Dropping the pen, I considered crumpling it up and throwing it away. Maybe burning it. It was going too far, even I knew that. And I was basically asking her to marry me in a letter, and I shouldn't do that. We weren't there yet, and...I wasn't sure if that was even what she wanted from me. Just moving back in together sometimes felt like it was...unobtainable.

But what if...what if my fears about us were right. What if we *had* drifted apart by the time she found this? Maybe...maybe this outpouring of hope and pain could start to pull us back together. Maybe if she knew what *my* vision of our future looked like, she'd feel more connected to me. Or maybe I'd just look like a gigantic idiot.

Grunting in frustration, I put my fingers over the paper, ready to destroy it. But still...I couldn't. I *did* want to marry her someday...and I wanted her to know that. I wanted her to know everything about me, even if it made me seem weak. I was weak after all. Barely stitched together.

With my heart beating harder, and my stomach churning like I was going to be sick, I added the letter to the stack of completed notes on my bed. Fuck it. Holding back my feelings from her had only ever hurt us. What harm could oversharing really do?

God, I felt raw though, like when I'd told her I loved her for the first time. I needed to switch gears, do something...fun for her. Standing from my bed, I flexed my fingers and rolled my shoulders, trying to ease the tension that had suddenly coiled around every nerve ending in my body. *It's fine...she'll feel the same. She'll love it. She loves you.*

Shaking my head in a vain attempt to purge the demons, I looked around the room for something else I could do for her. All I could focus on was my bed though, and there was nothing really romantic about it. But...maybe sexy. Hmmm...

Feeling better already, I shoved my notes in the bottom dresser drawer and left my bedroom. *I know I have a camera around here somewhere...*

Twenty minutes later, I found an old digital camera that Griffin had left here a long time ago. I made sure there was nothing already on it, and then I returned to my bedroom to get down to business. A steamy visual of me to keep Kiera entertained while I was gone sounded perfect. Stripping down to my birthday suit, I laid on the bed and tried to take some sexy pics for Kiera. I'd have to hide this surprise well too...definitely wouldn't want her finding it too soon.

Taking my own picture this way was much harder than I thought it would be. Everything was coming out wrong...blurry, bad angle, too much of one thing, not enough of another. Damn it. Apparently, this was not one of my skills. I could easily just turn myself on and take a picture of my hard cock for her, but that wasn't the image I wanted to leave behind. Contrary to what a lot of guys thought, that really wasn't the part of the male body that got women going. It was everything...leading up to that.

Annoyed that this wasn't working out, I hopped off the bed and walked to my bathroom. Maybe water would make it classier...kind of artistic. Kiera would like that. Plus, I think she liked it when I was wet. Turning on the shower, I looked over at my open bathroom door. I couldn't help but wonder what Kiera would think if she happened to come over right now...maybe leave class early to surprise me. Yeah, me about to take a shower with a camera would certainly be a surprise.

Laughing, I shook my head and walked into the warm water. Careful to not get the camera wet, I again tried to take some sexy shots. Still, nothing was turning out the way I wanted, and the constant stream of water in my face was really getting on my nerves. Damn it. I wasn't going to be able to do this on my own. I needed help, but who could I possibly ask to do this for me...

An idea immediately popped into my brain, making me grin. Oh yeah...she'd be perfect.

Turning off the shower, I quickly dried off. Then I erased all of the photos I'd just taken. If I was going to do this—and I was—then I was going to do it right. Kiera was going to love this.

Fifteen minutes later, I knocked on my future photographer's door. God, I hoped she was home. Thankfully she was, and a moment later the door opened to expose the cute little perky blonde who was about to make my fantasy for Kiera a reality.

Jenny tilted her head as she stared at me "Kellan? What are you doing here?" It wasn't very often that I just showed up on Jenny's doorstep. In fact...I don't think I'd ever done it before.

Grinning, I said, "Hey, Jenny. I was wondering...do you think you could...do something for me?"

"Of course," she said, opening her door wide so I could come in. "What do you need?"

I crinkled my nose as she shut her door behind me. I wasn't sure if she'd agree to this, but she was by far my best choice. None of the guys would do it, Rachel was too shy to do it, and Anna would say she'd do it, but then she'd just spend the entire time ogling me. But more than any of that, Jenny had the style I was looking for—she was probably the most artistic person I knew. The classiest, for sure. "I need your help taking a picture."

That surprised her, but she instantly offered her help. "Sure. What kind of picture?"

Biting my lip, I dropped my head and peeked up at her. She might actually have a problem with this.

Jenny was instantly suspicious of my request. Crossing her arms over her chest, she raised an eyebrow at me. "Kellan...what kind of picture?"

I raised my hands. "Nothing too bad, I promise. I just...I want to leave something sexy for Kiera, and I can't seem to do it myself." Remembering my failures made me frown. Everything I'd tried so far had just come out...weird.

Smiling at me, Jenny shook her head in amusement. Then she frowned. "I don't think Evan would be okay with me taking naked pictures of you, even if it is for a good cause."

"I won't be naked, I swear." I made an X over my heart, just so she'd know I was serious. Sure, I'd been naked at home, but I could get the shot I wanted while wearing boxers. I was pretty sure I could at least. I'd try, for her sake. And Evan's. 'Cause she was right...he'd kill me.

Jenny studied me for a second, then she shrugged. "Sure, why not."

My grin was huge as excitement flooded me. "Thanks, I have to pick up Kiera soon, but maybe we could do it tomorrow?" Jenny nodded, and I clapped my hands. "Awesome. Just let me know when you're ready, and I'll come over." While it was fun imagining Kiera catching me with a camera in the shower, it would be a completely different scenario if she caught Jenny with a camera while I was in the shower. I was sure Kiera would be okay with my methods, though, once she saw the result...if she ever even asked. I doubted she'd care about the process once she had the photo in her hands.

Jenny agreed to my suggestion, and I thanked her again. As I was leaving, I told her, "Oh, and don't say anything to Kiera, okay. I want it to be a surprise."

"I'm certain it will be," she said with a laugh.

When Jenny called the next day, telling me she was ready, I explained my concept about being wet...and then I told her how much Kiera loved me being wet. Jenny laughed in response, murmuring, "God, you two..." but I think she liked the idea. Water had an appeal all its own.

I was eager for my photoshoot when I arrived at Jenny's place. I almost wanted to skip the surprise and show Kiera the picture when I picked her up from school...but then I remembered why I was doing this. *I'm leaving. She's going to be alone. What if...?*

Before I could get swept too far away by my dark thoughts, I was distracted by Jenny's door opening. "Hey, Kellan. You okay?"

Fixing my face, I stepped inside. "Yeah, of course."

Jenny led me into the kitchen, where surprisingly, Rachel was standing like she was waiting for us. I knew Rachel lived here with Jenny, but it hadn't occurred to me that she'd be here for this. Like she heard my unasked question, Jenny tilted her head at her roommate. "Rachel is going to be my assistant today."

That surprised me even more. This might be a little more than the shy girl could take. In fact, she was already bright red, and I was still wearing all of my clothes. "Okay," I said with a shrug. I didn't really care how many witnesses were here for this, as long as none of them spilled the beans. "No telling Kiera though," I said, pointing at Rachel. "And no letting the guys tell Kiera. I want this to be a surprise."

Rachel couldn't even speak, and she was having trouble

looking me in the eye as she nodded in agreement. "Okay," I said, clapping my hands. "Guess I'll strip."

I started unbuttoning my jeans, and Jenny snapped her fingers, stopping me. "Nuh-uh. Go to my bedroom, there is a towel waiting for you."

I raised an eyebrow at her. Did it really matter where I undressed? The end result was the same. Jenny sighed at me, then pointed at her room. I laughed but did as she asked. As I walked down the hall, I heard her call out, "And remember, the underwear stays on, Kellan." I held my thumb up in answer and heard Rachel start to giggle.

Once I was in Jenny's room, I quickly undressed. I spotted the towel she'd left on the bed for me, but I didn't bother wrapping it around me. The boxers I was wearing were basically shorts. Certainly, the girls could handle shorts.

But when I walked into the bathroom and saw Rachel's eyes widen and her cheeks redden, I reconsidered. Okay, maybe they were a little more revealing than shorts. Way better than briefs though.

Ignoring Rachel's discomfort, I glanced around the room. Jenny had set up lights and weird filters everywhere, and had a huge, complicated-looking camera hanging around her neck. She pursed her lips at the lack of a towel around me, then shook her head and motioned to where there were about two dozen towels on the floor in front of the shower...I had no idea why. "Stand there please," she said, her voice very professional.

I stepped where she indicated, then turned around and pointed at the shower behind me. "Okay, do you want me to hop in, or should I—"

Camera ready, Jenny interrupted me. "Nope, we got it." And then, before I could do or say anything, Rachel tossed a bucket of water on me.

"Holy fucking shit!" I yelled. The water was ice fucking cold. I stood there shaking, water dripping everywhere, my mouth open in shock as Jenny snapped pictures and Rachel giggled, her cheeks flaming red now. "What the fuck, Jenny! You could have used warm water," I grumbled, finally realizing what all the towels were for. "Jesus."

Jenny lowered the camera for a second. "Language, Kellan." I scowled at her, and she gave me a bright fucking grin. "If we used warm water, that awesome thing going on with your chest right now wouldn't be happening."

I glanced down at my chest. I had no idea what she was talking about. "What? Because my nipples are really hard?"

Rachel made a choking, snortle of a sound. She was clearly *extremely* uncomfortable. I glanced over at her with a huge grin on my face. This was too good of an opportunity to get a little payback. She *was* the one who'd thrown the water at me after all. "What? That word bother you? Nipple..." I wriggled my eyebrows as I elongated the word. Rachel was almost easier to tease than Kiera was.

Rachel closed her eyes in embarrassment as Jenny chucked her toothbrush at me, smacking me in the chest. "Kellan, knock it off. You asked for this favor, so stop...killing Rachel."

I laughed, then nodded. "Okay, fine. What do you want me to do?"

She bit her lip as she studied me. "We need more water..." I groaned, not excited about another dousing. But then Jenny shocked me by adding, "And you need to pull your shorts down."

Rachel and I both snapped our eyes to her, and Rachel finally said something. "Jenny, you said he wouldn't be naked. Matt won't like this..."

Jenny shook her head. "Not *that* far, just...there needs to be a little more. It's not sexy enough."

With a shrug, I started pulling down my boxers, inch by inch. I watched her face as I did it, so I'd know when to stop...'cause she was letting me go pretty low. In fact, I didn't think I could get any lower without this becoming a completely different kind of project.

Jenny's lips pursed as she watched me. "Not too far, Kellan," she warned.

Knowing I was where I needed to be, I paused my hands. I couldn't help but laugh at the look on her face though. "Relax, I'm not going to flash you. Not even if you wanted me to," I added with a smirk. No, everything under here was Kiera's and Kiera's alone.

Jenny rolled her eyes at me, then grinned. "Okay, Rach. Hit him again."

My eyes widened. "Wait, can't we do the—"

They didn't even give me a chance to finish my protest before Rachel threw a second bucket of water on me. And I swear to God it was colder than the first one. *Did* they put fucking ice in that thing?

After a few clicks of the camera, Jenny stopped and frowned. "It's still not quite right." She looked behind her at Rachel. "Can you refill one of the buckets and grab the tallest stepstool you can find. I want to try slowly pouring the water over the top of him."

My jaw dropped at hearing that. Cold water being drizzled over me sounded more like torture than art. "Are you fucking serious?"

Jenny looked back at me with a small scowl on her face. "Stop swearing. And yes, trust me, it's going to look great. This is going to be tricky though." She eyed her small bathroom, working out the logistics. "You're going to have to be in the shower. It's going to be messy."

I stepped into the shower with a sigh. "Couldn't I just take a shower?" I asked her. A warm one.

She shook her head. "No, we'll never get the flow right. This will be easier. Trust me."

Easier for her, sure. It was going to suck for me. But Jenny had an eye for stuff like this, and if she thought it was going to be good...then I could stop complaining and trust her judgement.

We were done in about ten minutes, but it was the coldest ten minutes of my life. Rachel hadn't given me any leniency on the water temperature. While Jenny flicked through the shots she'd taken, I stepped out of the shower, turned the water on as hot as it would go, then stepped back inside. It was heaven when it finally heated up, and the groan that escaped me was downright indecent. Even though I still had my boxers on, Rachel instantly disappeared. I thought Jenny might too, but she was too busy hopping up and down, almost squealing she was so happy. "Oh my God, Kellan, these are awesome!"

Reveling in the heat, I slicked my hair back and looked over at her. "Yeah? Will you print me out some?"

She looked up at me and nodded. "Yeah, I've got a great printer for this. I'll do it right now." Tilting her head, she pursed her lips. "You know...there are a ton of shots here that would look amazing in a gallery..." She closed her eyes, and a dreamy look came over her. "A gallery..." Opening her eyes, she shook her head. "This tour is Evan's dream, but a gallery...I think that's mine."

The bliss on her face made me grin. "I've seen your stuff, I'm sure you'll get there one day." I pointed at her camera. "Just not with my body, okay?" Kiera would not want my chest on display like that. "In fact, can you delete those after you print one for me?"

Jenny looked disheartened, but she nodded. "Yeah, sure, not a problem."

I shut off the water as she left the bathroom. Grabbing a nearby towel, I scuffed up my hair, then dried off my body. That was when I remembered something I'd forgotten to do, something kind of important. I stopped moving and swore. "Goddamn it."

"What's wrong?" I heard Jenny say from the hallway.

"I forgot to bring extra underwear."

Jenny snorted as I sighed. Guess I was going commando for a while. Maybe we should have done this at my place after all. Still laughing, Jenny tossed out, "Evan's got some here. Want to borrow one of his?"

I crinkled my nose as I stared out the open bathroom door. Evan was certainly a better choice than Griffin, but still... "No... I'm good, thanks."

Jenny laughed even harder. Girls.

Wet underwear in my hand, I met up with Jenny when I was fully dressed. She handed me a black-and-white photo, and all the earlier discomfort vanished from my mind as I stared at what she'd managed to capture. This was *exactly* what I'd been hoping for. It was from my jawline to just about a centimeter above my boxers, and with how low my boxers had been, it definitely created the illusion that I was naked. My abs were clenched, thanks to how fucking frigid the water was, and every line popped out. And then there was the water, rivulets running across my skin mixed with still droplets. The overall effect made the photo look...alive. It was perfect.

"Damn, you're good." My grin was unstoppable as I peeked up at her. "Thank you. This is exactly what I wanted."

She sighed as she shook her head. "You're welcome, Kellan. That was probably the best photo I've ever taken...and I can't believe I just deleted it."

I laughed at her comment. "I appreciate your sacrifice."

She rolled her eyes at me, then laughed. I was just about to leave when a thought struck me, and I paused. "Hey, Jenny... we're friends, right?"

Jenny's brow furrowed, like she couldn't believe I was asking her that—especially after what she'd just done for me. "Of course, Kellan. You know we are."

I nodded. I'd really hoped that, but I knew I could be...difficult at times. I was sure I hadn't always been a good friend to Jenny, or at least, that was how it felt to me. And I really didn't know if my friendship with her extended past our circle of mutual friends, if it extended past her loyalty to specific people in those circles...like Kiera. I didn't know exactly where I fit in Jenny's life, how important I was to her, or if I even mattered at all.

"Well, as a friend, would it be okay if...? Can I ask you to...?" I didn't know how to ask for what I wanted without sounding like a controlling asshole. Or pathetically insecure. "Never mind," I told her.

I started to walk away, but she grabbed my arm. "Kellan, what is it?"

Staring at the floor, I let out a long sigh. "Watch Kiera for me?" I swallowed a lump in my throat as I looked up at her. "Just make sure she doesn't miss me too much. Make sure she doesn't..." *Don't let her get lonely. Don't let her cheat on me. Don't let her hurt me. Please...protect me.*

Jenny's mouth popped open as she studied my expression. I knew what I wanted to ask for was horrible, inappropriate... desperate. I shouldn't ask Kiera's friends to shield her from temptation for me, to be her...keeper. And I definitely shouldn't ask them to betray that trust with Kiera if something awful did happen, but it was so hard not to ask for it. I just needed to know that someone staying behind was on *my* side.

"Kellan..." she said, her voice soft. Rachel stepped into the room then, and I could tell from the look on her face, that she'd heard all that, and she'd understood what I was really asking, and she was feeling sorry for me now, just like Jenny.

The sympathy oozing from them was too much to bear, and I quickly changed my mind. *They don't need to know how terrified I am...how much this is killing me.* And besides, Kiera wasn't going to hurt me. She loved me.

Tossing on a casual smile, I indicated both of them and said, "I just mean, you know how mopey she can get. Just make sure you guys take her out, make her have fun. Don't let her be sad about me being gone. Especially right after we leave. She's gonna be...well, you know." I said it with a nonchalant shrug, but thinking about that moment instinctually made my insides constrict with pain and fear. Holding her after Denny had announced he was leaving...that had been our starting point. I didn't want someone else putting her back together when *I* was the one shattering her. "I just want her to be happy," I said, trying to keep my voice light.

Jenny frowned, like she knew that wasn't really what I'd wanted to ask. Then she sighed. "Yeah, of course, Kellan. We'll make sure she's fine," she said, squeezing my arm. Leaning in, she softly added, "But it's going to be okay. Kiera loves you. Have a little faith."

Faith. Right.

Chapter 10
THE FINAL DAYS

It was late when I woke up, later than usual. Guess I'd been tired after my last few busy days of either spending time with Kiera or preparing for my departure from her. I had to admit though, the preparations were going really well. All my notes were done, I just needed to start planting them. And I'd decided, after having that near-embarrassing conversation with Jenny and Rachel, that I was going to say something to Anna and Kate—the more people keeping Kiera busy, the better. I also needed to give someone the steamy letter that I had for Kiera...either Jenny or Kate, since they were going to be working late with Kiera on the night we left. Maybe Kate, since Jenny was going to be dealing with her own stuff; she was going to miss Evan when he left, maybe not as desperately as I was going to be missing Kiera, but still.

Kate would probably end up reading the letter before she gave it to Kiera though, but whatever, I didn't really care. All I cared was that the note got to Kiera *exactly* at midnight. I wanted to be mentally reading the note with her, like I was saying it to her, even though we would be miles apart by then. God, I hated that thought.

Needing her comfort, I instinctively searched for Kiera in my bed, but she wasn't there. *That's right...I slept alone last night.*

Kiera was waiting for me at her apartment. I should get my lazy ass up so I could take her to school.

Yawning, I flung the covers off me and got up. Weirdly, I was completely dressed. *Huh. Well, guess that means I can get to Kiera's even faster.* With a smile on my face, I opened the door... and that was when all the blood drained from my body. The shower was on in my bathroom, but even over the noise of the water, I could hear the sound of people screwing. *I've heard this before. I've done this before.*

Bile rose up my throat, and I knew I was about to lose it. Kiera was in my bathroom...having sex with Denny. He was touching her, kissing her...inside of her. Jesus, I didn't want to live through this moment again. I couldn't. I squeezed my eyes shut. *You're dreaming, Kellan. Wake the fuck up.*

"Interesting moment you decided to replay."

Dread washed through me, momentarily obliviating the nausea. I opened my eyes to see my father standing in front of Denny and Kiera's door, staring at me. Fuck, no...I couldn't handle this. One of my worst memories *and* my dad? *Please wake up.*

But I didn't. Instead, the noises in the bathroom got louder, much louder than they'd been in real life. I felt like I was in the room with them. My dad smiled as revulsion flooded my stomach. "I don't want to do this again..." I murmured, acid crawling its way up my throat.

Dad tilted his head. "No? What about this instead?" He snapped his fingers and the walls around us...dissolved. I was grateful, until the world reformed into something that was almost worse. Dad and I were in the parking lot...*the* parking lot, and Denny was there, screaming at me. "I trusted you! You said you were my brother!"

Denny started hitting me, the blows coming over and over, hard and fast, and all I could do was stand there and take it as pain exploded over me in an endless loop of torture. Feeling broken everywhere, I finally fell to my knees, gasping, and then all of a sudden, Denny wasn't there anymore. No, instead of Denny, it was my father staring down at me. I wanted to fight back, I wanted to do *something*, but like I was a kid again, I was frozen in place, terrified.

"I'm sorry," I muttered. I wasn't even sure what I was sorry for, but I knew that was all my dad would want to hear.

He looked down at me with a sneer on his face. "I can't believe how stupid you are. Leaving her here so you can go off and...what...be a *rock star*?" He said it with a haughty laugh, and I suddenly felt like all my dreams were a foolish waste of time. "You know you're going to lose her, right? The minute you leave, the very second you stop screwing her...she's going to realize she doesn't need you."

Even though he hadn't touched me yet, I felt like he'd just kicked me full force in the gut. All the air left me; I felt sick. I leaned forward to throw up, but there was nothing but pain in my stomach. Dad smiled, satisfied by my reaction. "The only reason you got her in the first place was because you were always around, following her everywhere like some pathetic, broken puppy dog. The minute you're not here, she's going to see just how worthless you really are. She's going to want a real man once she's free of you...and you know that."

Jesus Christ. How could he cause me so much pain without even touching me? *Quit telling me my own fears—I already know them.* But no, that was all it was...fear. It wasn't reality. Kiera and I...we loved each other...we were going to make it, have a life together. A good one. I defiantly shook my head as I kneeled on the ground before him. "No, she loves me," I bit out.

Dad only smirked at my bravado. "Yeah, my wife loved me once too." And then he kneed me in the jaw.

I woke up with a start, my chest heaving, my body covered in a light sheen of sweat, my tousled sheets tight and constricting. I looked around my room, searching for my dad...searching for Kiera, but I was alone. Completely alone. Closing my eyes, I tried to calm my breaths, tried to control my emotions. What the fuck...? Why couldn't I keep him out of my head? Why did all of my worries have to shift into absolute terror while I was sleeping? It really made me never want to sleep again.

Stumbling out of bed, I groggily looked at my clock. Much like in my dream, it actually was getting late, and I really did need to pick up Kiera soon...but I couldn't like this. I didn't want her to see me so...broken. I needed to put my game face back on.

Deciding a nice long shower would distract me, I headed to the bathroom. The freshness of my dream stopped me cold as I stared at the cracked bathroom door. Denny and Kiera... My gaze shifted to their old bedroom door—a door I never opened anymore. *Don't go there. Let it go, or you'll never move forward.* Inhaling a deep breath, I stepped into the bathroom and faced my demons. Again.

The steaming water pouring over my body relaxed me. I didn't need to worry so much. Evan was right, Jenny was right... everything was going to be fine. I was going on tour with my friends. It was going to be fun. It was going to be great. Dad was wrong. When I got back from touring, Kiera and I were going to be better than ever. Stronger. Because this separation was going to test us in a way we'd never really been tested before, and we were going to pass that test. We'd been through too much for this to not work out.

Those words washing over me calmed me, brightened me, and my dream finally faded from my memory...I could barely even remember the details anymore.

I felt bright and peppy when I knocked on Kiera's apartment door a little later. I felt even better when I saw her face. God, she was gorgeous. How could she not see what I saw? The sensualness, the perfection...every time I looked at her, she took my breath away.

"Mornin'," I told her, stepping into her home. I was immediately wrapped in the smell of her, it was like a physical thing cocooning me, comforting me. I was really going to miss that.

Not wasting any of our precious time, I pulled her into me

and began tasting her neck. I was going to miss this too. "Good morning, yourself," she quietly laughed, closing her door.

Loving all of this—our perfect daily routine—made me sigh with longing. *Why can't I freeze time? Stay in this moment forever?* "I'm going to miss taking you to school every day." Just the thought made another wistful sound escape me. I was going to miss almost all of the rest of her time there. "You'll nearly be graduating by the time I'm back."

Kiera gave me a reassuring smile as she began stroking my cheek. "At least you'll be back in time for the ceremony. You can watch me walk down the aisle."

There were so many things about that sentence that I loved: the thought of returning to her, the thought of her being there waiting for me, the thought of her walking down an aisle...*the* aisle. Maybe. One day. That blissful vision filling my head, I confessed my future want, my future hope. "I'd love to watch you walk down the aisle."

Her mouth popped open, like she wasn't entirely sure what I'd meant by that, and I instantly regretted saying it. I didn't want to push her, didn't want to freak her out by moving too fast. And besides, she'd figure out exactly what I meant—what I wanted—on the day she found my letter. God, that letter...*I should burn it when I get home.*

Before Kiera could comment on my innuendo, maybe spoiling my fantasy by reminding me that we weren't there yet—or just flat-out telling me no, she'd never consider marrying me—I looked over at something I'd noticed when I'd first walked in. A gift bag was sitting on her rickety card table. The perfect distraction.

Genuinely curious, I looked back at her. "What's that?"

She giggled as she let go of me. "It's for you. Sort of a going-away present."

While her thoughtfulness was sweet, I didn't need anything from her. I just needed *her*. And honestly, having people buy things for me was sort of...weird. It was something I'd never really gotten used to over the years. "I know money is tight for you. You didn't have to get me anything."

She wasn't in the same boat as me, financially speaking, and she didn't need to waste her money, not on me. She should save it for something...important. Like Kiera sensed my reluctance, she shoved me toward the table. "I got a good deal. It didn't cost me much and it's sort of a present for the both of us."

Thinking of multiple things that we could use *together* instantly cheered me up, and I couldn't hold back my devious grin. "Is it handcuffs?" I asked her. Because I still couldn't resist teasing her, I added, "Did you get the furry kind? Because those feel really nice against your—"

She didn't even let me finish. Smacking my back, she blurted out, "No!" and physically turned my head away from her, like that would stop me from knowing she was turning bright red. I couldn't help but laugh as I picked up the present. God, I was going to miss making her turn that intoxicating shade of embarrassed. So cute.

I was still amused by her reaction as I pulled the tissues out of the bag. When I saw a cell phone resting on the bottom of the bag, I pulled it out and looked back at her. "What's this?" I'd been expecting something a little more...sensuous, I guess. Not handcuffs, for sure, but maybe something a *little* naughty. Plus, a cell phone? Matt had been trying to get me to own one for years, insisting that he should be able to get ahold of me any time he wanted...which was probably why I'd resisted so much. I just didn't see the point. I got along fine with the phone in my kitchen.

Kiera laughed at my comment, then she said something that sounded just like my bandmates. "Well, I know you're a little behind on the times, but they call that a cell phone. It works just like your corded one, but you can walk around with it. You can even use it outside," she said, merriment in her eyes.

Smartass. It was entirely possible she was spending *too* much time around the guys. "I know what it is. What's it for?" Did she want me to be Matt's bitch?

A beautiful grin on her face, she walked over to her jacket and pulled out a matching phone...and that was when the true opportunity she was presenting me flashed into my head. I kind of felt dumb for not seeing it instantly. True, Matt bugging me twenty-four-seven sounded like hell on Earth, but Kiera having unlimited access to me...that would almost be like having her with me everywhere I went. And if she had one too...I could talk to *her* whenever I wanted, and that made all of this seem almost bearable.

Kiera confirmed what I was thinking by saying, "It's so we can keep in touch while you're gone. So you can always get ahold of me, and I can get ahold of you." She shrugged, and her voice was full of emotion when she spoke again. "So, we can try to stay close...even though we'll be really far apart."

So many emotions tumbled over me so fast, I could barely sort through them all—pain, hope, love, desolation, joy. Seeing similar emotions shimmer in Kiera's eyes made me have to swallow through the discomfort of my throat clenching. *I don't want to be far apart from you.* Finally, after what felt like an eternity of struggling, I nodded and told her, "I love it, thank you."

I kissed her then, softly, sweetly, trying to hold our connection while at the same time, trying to break the agony that sometimes came along with it. And as our mouths moved together, her skin igniting me, her scent making me delirious, the pain did shift...right into desire. Did we have time for me to thank her properly? To show her just what this future connection meant to me?

Pulling back, I stared at her mouth, warm, luscious, inviting, and I contemplated it. I could take her to her room right now, make her feel nothing but bliss for hours...but fuck, I couldn't. She had responsibilities she needed to take care of, and I had some things to take care of too. Later. Definitely.

I snapped my eyes up to hers. I could see heat in them, like she'd been sharing my contemplation. That made it really hard to commit to taking her to class. Being an adult sucked sometimes.

Throwing on a smile, I decided to say something playful, something that I knew would get us moving in the right direction. Well, the responsible direction at any rate. "Can I sext you on it?" Even though I was joking, just saying it made a bunch of brand-new possibilities float through my brain. *Oh yeah. No matter what her answer is, this is definitely happening.* Matt was right. I should have gotten a cell phone years ago.

Kiera was appropriately mortified by my question. She didn't even answer me, just started grabbing her stuff. As I tucked my new Kiera torturing device into my jacket pocket, I heard Anna's bedroom door open. I opened my mouth to say hi to Anna...but she wasn't the person who walked out.

Griffin stepped into the hallway, and he was completely fucking naked. Damn it. I saw *all* of my bassist way too often. Griffin yawned as he stared at me. "Dude, what are you doing here so early?"

Even though his lack of clothes was annoying, his comment amused me. Griffin really hated being woken up before noon. At least he hadn't woken up swearing this time. "It's ten thirty, Griffin."

"I know, man, it's fucking earlier than shit," he complained.

Oops. *Guess I spoke too soon about the swearing*. Looking down at Kiera, I rolled my eyes at what my bandmate considered 'earlier than shit.' Kiera barely held my gaze; she was doing everything in her power to make sure she didn't take in even an inch of Griffin's bare skin. Her discomfort with his nakedness was adorable, but...I really should put an end to this. Especially since I could hear Griffin starting to move our way.

I was about to tell him to go put some fucking clothes on, when he interrupted my thoughts by saying, "Hey, Matt wanted me to tell you that if you miss another rehearsal, he's tossing you from the band."

Looking back up at Griffin, I raised an eyebrow. "Really?"

Toss me from the band? That was a new threat. Guess I'd finally pushed Matt to the breaking point with my multiple absences. I wasn't worried in the slightest about Matt actually evicting me—not for a handful of rehearsals—but I supposed it *was* time to start putting in more of an effort.

Lightly laughing, still amused by the idea of Matt kicking me out, I shook my head. "Tell him I'll be there." I looked back down at Kiera, absorbing her absorbing me. Warmth filled me as I remembered our many carefree afternoons together. Those memories were worth the harassment. "I guess my head has been other places lately," I murmured.

Griff took that in the dirtiest way possible. Close enough now to shove my shoulder back, he said, "Well, zip your head back in your pants and get back in the game. We need you on board."

Damn. Griffin scolding me for being flakey—and *meaning* it this time—was eye opening. I guess I really did need to start being a professional again. We *did* have a new song that we were trying to get just right so we could include it on the tour after all. I supposed that was important. Kiera was still handling her responsibilities, going to school...most days, and I wanted her to keep doing that, which meant, I shouldn't be shirking my responsibilities to the band. Kiera wasn't the only important thing in my life, and she wasn't the only person counting on me either. I needed to remember that.

With a heavy sigh, I told him, "I'm on board, Griff. I'll be there, okay?" *For real this time.*

He gave me a sniff, his face actually looking annoyed. "You better."

He turned to leave, but I couldn't let him go without a tiny reprimand. Yes, he was right about my lack of dedication lately, but that didn't give him a free pass to be a nudist in Kiera's apartment. I really didn't care if it was half Anna's place too, that shit needed to stop. Knowing Kiera was going to hate me for calling attention to her while Griffin was naked, I gently said, "Hey, Griff? You mind not walking around my girlfriend's place buck naked? I'd really prefer her only staring at my junk, if you don't mind."

Griffin being Griffin, he, of course, immediately started fondling himself. With a smirk, he said, "Dude, if she's peeking at another man's schlong, then that's between the two of you. The Hulk needs to breathe."

The Hulk? Oh God...no, he did not just say that. I was gonna lose it. Kiera did. She had to slap her hand over her mouth to stop the giggles. Griffin glared at both of us, then retreated back to Anna's room.

We had a pretty good laugh about that once Griffin was out of sight. Then, in the parking lot, Kiera asked me what my nickname was. I'd never named a body part, but not wanting to miss an opportunity to make her face change color, I spouted something ridiculous and dirty to her—The Oh-God-Yes-Harder-Faster-Don't-You-Dare-Stop-Yes-Fuck-Me-Now-You're-Freaking-Amazing Machine. Her reaction was priceless—the perfect mix of annoyance, amusement, and embarrassment.

The levity was much needed, and I was smiling the entire time I took her to class.

After dropping Kiera off, I sat in my car in the parking lot and pulled out my new cell phone. Might as well start learning how to use it. Browsing through the contacts, I saw that Kiera had already programmed some numbers into it for me. I wasn't sure if that was out of thoughtfulness, or if she was just sure I wouldn't bother doing it on my own. Either way, it amused me.

Stopping on her number, I debated texting her. Surely it wasn't too early to start the sexy talk. I was just about to do it when another name caught my eye. Denny. She'd programmed her ex's number for me. That was a little surreal. But not in a bad way—Denny was someone I still wanted to keep in contact with. Even after...everything.

I hit an icon that I was pretty sure would connect the call, and sure enough, the screen told me it was dialing. *See Kiera, I can do this.* As I brought the phone to my ear, I wondered what time it was in Denny's world. Hopefully it wasn't too early. Or too late? Fuck if I knew.

A couple of rings later, a confused voice met my ear. "Hello?"

"Hey Denny, it's Kellan. Kiera got us cell phones, and I wanted to make sure you had my new number." Right after I said it, I realized I should have just texted him since I really wasn't sure about the time difference. This phone was going to take some getting used to.

Denny was quiet for a moment, then I could tell he was yawning. I sighed. "Shit. I woke you up, didn't I? What time is it over there?"

"Don't worry about it, it's fine," he said, his tone forgiving. "Cell phone, huh? I never thought I'd see the day when you got one." He laughed after he said it, amused.

"Yeah, well, it will come in handy soon." Biting my lip, I felt a surge of adrenaline fill me. "The band got asked to go on a tour. An actual freaking tour. Crazy, huh?" Denny had always been one of my biggest supporters, by my side from the very beginning of this journey. I'd been holding onto this piece of information for way too long now. I *had* to share it with him.

His response wasn't what I expected. Instead of an exclamation of surprise, or a heartfelt congratulations, he was absolutely silent. I was about to ask him if he was still there, when I finally heard him say, "That's not too surprising, Kellan. I always knew you'd make it."

I had to scoff at that. While this tour was cool, it wasn't exactly "making it." "Yeah, well, I just wanted to let you know. You've always...been there...for me." *And I repaid you by screwing you over.* Swallowing the lump of betrayal in my throat, I quickly told him, "We're leaving this weekend. We'll be on the road for six months..." God, every time I said it, it sounded longer and longer.

"Six months?" Denny murmured. "Wow, that's...wow." He was silent again, and a strange sort of awkwardness stretched over the line. Somehow, I knew his reaction wasn't really about me and this upcoming opportunity. It was about Kiera. He had to be wondering just what I'd wondered—would she wait for me?

I really didn't want him to comment on it. Hearing him voice my fears would be worse than anyone else speaking them. Denny had the weight of experience to back up his comments, and if he unleashed them on me, that weight would crush me. Dead. "Hey, man, I'm sorry for calling so early. I'll...I'll let you go."

I heard him inhale a deep breath, like he was trying to purge his own demons—demons I'd just reminded him about. God, would there ever be a time when I didn't selfishly hurt him? "Yeah, okay. I'll talk to you later. Congratulations, mate."

Him calling me that made me smile. Despite it all, he was still talking to me, still calling me a friend. Maybe there was still hope for us. Awkward, tension-filled hope...but still hope.

Disconnecting the call, I put my phone back in my pocket and grinned. Kiera was momentarily occupied, and now it was time for me to get to work. I had a lot to do during the brief time she was at school. I still needed to talk to Anna about entertaining Kiera while I was gone, and I was seriously considering paying off Matt's neighbors, so they didn't break up our after-hours party Friday night. I also had a ton of notes to begin planting. Thank God I had a key to Kiera's apartment—that was going to make this so much simpler. I wasn't going to decorate that one until right before we left though. I didn't want Kiera to find the notes too early...and I really didn't want to do it while Griffin was...visiting.

The Hulk. Jackass.

Chapter 11
KIERA'S SHADOW

Time began blurring, everything went by so fast. My preparations kept most of the gnawing dread at bay, as did my recommitment to the band. Matt had chided me pretty good once I'd shown up to rehearsal, and after making me look like an idiot for not knowing all the random little changes they'd made to our newest song in my absence, I hadn't missed another practice. Matt was very proud of me.

But even with all my obligations, I still managed to squeeze in plenty of time for Kiera. I savored every second we had together, wishing I could stretch every moment into its own separate eternity. If I ever developed a superpower, that was what I'd want it to be—the ability to hold onto fragments of time and live them over and over again. But only fragments of my choosing, of course. I'd really love to be able to forever block the bad memories. In fact, maybe I'd chose *that* to be my superpower instead.

Before I knew it, it was Friday...a day full of farewells. The last time I'd be able to take Kiera to school. The last show at the bar. The last night I'd get to spend with Kiera... At least it was going to be a fun one. I couldn't wait for the party at Matt's. Something positive before the potential soul-crushing pain of saying goodbye.

Temporarily. I *was* coming back, and she *would* be here waiting for me. She would be...

I woke up well before Kiera. We were in the same position we'd fallen asleep in, and she had her head on my chest, using me as her pillow. God, I loved that. Careful to not wake her, I gently squeezed her body, pulling her even closer to me. It had been such a struggle to get here, where holding her like this only filled me with joy and not regret. I didn't want life to change, but it was changing on me anyway.

Kiera's room began to lighten as the sun rose higher, the darkness muting, fading. This was usually when I slipped out of bed to exercise a little before making some coffee, but today...I just couldn't. I didn't want to miss a single second with her. And I knew I wouldn't. Today I was her shadow, whether she wanted me to be or not.

I began stroking her hair, tucking it behind her ear, wishing she would wake up so I could feel the warmth of her love in her eyes, but also not wanting to wake her, because once she woke, the countdown would truly begin. And when it ran out, I'd be gone.

Heart aching with the sting of goodbye, I felt her stir and stretch. *Here we go.* I abolished any trace of sadness on my face as she lifted her head and looked up at me. "Mornin'," I whispered, running the back of my finger down her cheek.

The love I felt in her hazel eyes almost undid me. How could I leave this behind? This feeling, this warmth, this tenderness. This was all I'd ever wanted. More than music. More than friendship. And way more than fame. *You're not losing it, Kellan, you'll just be a little farther away from her for a time. Don't freak out. She wants this for you. She believes in you. So do it for her. Make her proud.*

Well, damn. That tiny shift in the way I thought about this actually made me feel about a million times better. Okay. That was what I'd do, how I'd endure leaving her. Everything I did from here on out was *for her*. I was going to do this to the best of my ability. I was going to make her proud of me.

Kiera and I spent the next hour just holding each other, savoring the moment. She looked so forlorn when she finally had to pull away from me to get ready for school. She wasn't yet aware that she wasn't getting rid of me today. I think she sort of began to figure that out when I followed her into the shower.

Holding her while the warm water streamed around us started cementing a memory that I knew I'd return to on the road. The peace, the warmth, the connection. I stared into her beautiful, ever-shifting eyes as I drank it all in, reveled in the feeling of her soft hands on my skin, her trim body in my arms. Heaven. The moment could have easily become a sexual one, but I refrained. Our connection was already so strong right now, I didn't need anything more, and for once, my hands sliding over her skin weren't an attempt to rile her up. I just wanted to help her get ready; fully experience the moment with her.

But sadly, with time running out and the warm water fading, we had to leave our damp love nest and make our way out into the real world. I wanted to have coffee ready for her and thought she might like to ogle me for a little longer, so I wrapped a towel around my waist and headed to the kitchen while she got dressed.

Humming a song to myself as I prepped the coffee, I thought over all the notes I'd hidden around Kiera's apartment. There were a bunch, and they were everywhere. But there were still some I couldn't hide myself—the more obvious ones were going to need an accomplice to successfully pull off the surprise. Good thing Kiera lived with an amiable cohort. I had no doubt Anna would help me.

I leaned against the counter when I was done preparing the coffee, waiting for it to brew and my angel to rejoin me. When she finally appeared, she was carrying a bundle of my clothes. She wanted me to get dressed in the kitchen? I was about to ask her why, but the look on her face as she blatantly stared at my body stopped me cold. Her hungry gaze honed in on my chest, then lazily made its way down to my towel. It made me smile that my body pleased her so much—she was going to love Jenny's photo when she discovered it taped to the bottom of her dresser drawer—but I did find it humorous that there was a definite double standard in our relationship. While Kiera could practically lick me with her eyes, whenever I did the same thing, I got reprimanded. I wasn't going to complain too much, of course. I really liked it when she licked me with her eyes...and she did have a point about her body turning me on.

"Kiera?" I asked, loving her rapt attention.

Her eyes finally snapped to mine, and she almost looked surprised, like she hadn't realized her inspection of me had gone on for so long. "See something you like?" I teased. *Because I sure do.* Even covered up with jeans and layered tees she looked amazing.

Cheeks flushing adorably, she tossed my clothes at me. My hands had been behind me as I'd lounged against the counter and surprise flashed over me as she caught me off guard. I struggled to catch the mess while Kiera said, "Anna's awake and getting ready to come out here. Can you get dressed please?"

That last part had oozed longing, and so did her expression as she eyed my back while I set my clothes on the counter. When she bit her lip, clearly distracted by me, I couldn't *not* tease her. "You sure?"

She glanced back at the bedrooms, maybe gauging how much time we had. "Yes," she said, still sounding reluctant.

With how much Kiera was enjoying inspecting me, I really didn't care if Anna *did* come out here. Somehow, our sweet, tender moment of nakedness in the shower hadn't been enough for Kiera. Maybe it was because she was dressed now, or maybe it was because the bathroom had a certain private feel to it, like her bedroom, or maybe it was simply because she really did have a thing for me being wet and she just couldn't take it anymore. Whatever the reason, my body was doing more for her now than it had all morning. I didn't want to hasten her eye-fucking me, but I supposed I did need to get dressed at some point.

Loving what this was going to do to her, I unhooked my towel and let it fall to the floor. Her eyes instantly widened, like she'd never seen me naked before. It was enough to turn me on a little, especially when her cheeks started blazing with color. I had to shake my head at her reaction; we'd literally spent all morning naked together.

I lengthened the tease by getting dressed as slowly as possible. The look on her face shifted between annoyance that I was taking so long, sadness that I was getting dressed at all, and genuine appreciation for all the genes I'd been blessed with. I was going to have to remind her about this moment the next time she tried to get dressed underneath a towel. *I don't think so, Kiera.*

When I was finished, she gave me a sad smile as she wrapped her arms around my neck. "I'm gonna miss you," she murmured.

Her words squeezed my chest, bringing that familiar ache back to the surface. "I'm gonna miss you too." *So much.*

She leaned up to kiss me, and I lost myself in the tenderness. An amused voice snapped me out of it. "Damn it, was he in a towel?"

I looked up to see Anna pointing at the towel I'd discarded. I smirked at her comment while Kiera laid her head on my chest. "Yes, sorry, you missed the peep show."

Anna dramatized her disappointment with a long sigh. "I always do," she muttered, handing us mugs for coffee.

I had to laugh at the pair of very different sisters. Sometimes it seemed like Kiera thought I'd made the wrong choice falling for her and not her sister, but Anna and I...in some ways we were too much alike. If I'd ever gotten together with her pre-Kiera, it never would have led to something deeper. It only would have been surface-sex, never delving any further, and I'd had that way too many times in my life. But Kiera...she had bored into me, opening me, sometimes against my will, and now, she was all I saw. My light, my future...my *wife*. Maybe.

Even as I poured cups of coffee for everyone, my eyes kept flicking to the living room. That was where I'd hidden *the* letter. It was buried in a small random hole in Kiera's ugly orange couch. I knew the moment I'd placed it that it was hidden *too* well; the odds of her ever finding it were a million to one. But at least I'd done it. 'Cause I still kind of felt like burning it. Crap. What would she think when she saw that? I was almost glad I wouldn't physically be with her when she read it. If she reacted poorly to my plea...it would destroy me.

Anna snapped me out of my darkening thoughts by wishing me good luck on our final pre-tour show at Pete's, and saying she'd be there after her shift at Hooters. I thanked her, nonchalantly telling her that the show should be a good one. Even as I said it, I wondered. Saying goodbye to Pete's was almost as hard as saying goodbye to Kiera. That bar was home to me, it had been for a while now, and it was entirely possible that I might just lose it on stage. I'd shed a few melancholy tears while singing before—usually thanks to some Kiera-fueled emotional torment—but I had yet to have a meltdown. God, I really hoped I didn't break that streak tonight. I'd never hear the end of it.

Anna left Kiera and I to finish our coffee together, and I savored every second as I stared at her over the rim of my mug. Maybe *this* had been our true beginning—quiet mornings bonding over coffee. I knew I thought of Kiera every time I took a sip of my favorite morning beverage; I really hoped she thought about me too.

While Kiera went through her school stuff, checking and rechecking that she had everything, I grabbed my jacket and stepped into Anna's room. She was lounging on her bed, listening to music. When she spotted me standing in her doorway, she pulled out an earbud. "You look like you need a favor. What is it?"

I glanced down the hallway to make sure Kiera wasn't around. She was still sorting through her stuff, so I twisted back to Anna. "I just wanted to remind you about keeping an eye on

Kiera. Especially tomorrow. I just don't want her to..." I had to pause to clear the lump in my throat. "Make sure she's okay."

Anna softly sighed as she sat up. "Of course, Kellan. I remember...take her out a lot, make sure she has fun, don't let her wallow. I'll make sure she's fine, I promise."

Relieved, I let out a long breath. Then I smiled. Reaching into my jacket pocket, I pulled out the last few notes I had, the ones I wouldn't be able to place without giving away my plan. "And, once we're gone, could you stick these around the apartment for her?" I was grinning like an idiot as I handed them to Anna. I couldn't help it. Prepping this escapade for Kiera was one of the few things that had made leaving almost fun.

I started explaining where they should go, and Anna smirked at me the entire time she listened. When I was finished with my instructions, she smiled and shook her head at me. "God, you two are so fucking cute...it's a little nauseating being around you."

She winked after she said it, and I laughed. "That's fine by me," I told her. Being too cute to be around was a major step up from being too depressed to be around. I didn't ever want to be *that* guy again. "Thank you, Anna." I started to leave, then turned back to her. "And don't tell Kiera, okay? I want it to be a surprise for her...once I'm gone."

Anna searched my face, then nodded. "See you tonight, Kellan." And like she knew I was silently freaking out, she added, "And have *fun*."

Fun. Yes, that was my plan. Tonight was going to be a night to remember.

After driving Kiera to school, I walked her to class with my arm slung over her shoulders. I knew it was kind of a possessive posture, but I didn't want any of the frat-boy mini-D-Bags around doubting that she was mine. And besides, I liked cocooning her into my side. It just felt right. Always had.

When we got to her door, I immediately stepped inside the classroom with her; we usually said our goodbyes in the doorway, but not today. No goodbyes were happening today. Kiera gave me a droll look when I started leading us to a row with some empty seats. "I can handle this part. You can go...nap or something."

Amused at her suggestion, I shook my head, grabbed her hand, and walked backward down a row. "I'm not walking you to your seat." Finding the perfect place for us, I sat down and made myself comfortable. "I'm joining you."

I couldn't help but grin as she stared at me with her mouth popped open. She seemed genuinely surprised that I would want to sit through a lecture with her, like it was a sacrifice or something. But spending time with her was never a chore, and even if we weren't doing anything or talking about anything, I was never bored when she was beside me. Hell, I could spend hours just staring at her, imagining all of the things that we *could* be doing together. But this was her ethics class, and I actually was kind of interested in hearing what the professor had to say. This was going to be fun.

Still looking mystified, Kiera agreed to my suggestion as she sat down beside me. "All right."

Wanting to hold her some more, I wrapped my arm around her shoulders. She warned me not to fall asleep, and not to try any "funny business." I assured her I'd be the perfect student. And then, because I loved the way it sounded, I told her, "And if I'm not, you can punish me later." That thought *almost* made me want to try something. But I could control myself. I wasn't Griffin.

And I did control myself, but mainly because the class was actually really interesting. Stimulating in a way that I wasn't used to. I loved hearing the other students' opinions on things, and, not really caring if I sank miserably, I tried my hand at rebutting a few of their ideas. And that was when I discovered that it was unexpectedly satisfying to win an argument I'd been debating. Maybe when the whole music career fizzled out, I'd give college a try. I'd never truly considered that path before; music had always been my focus. Well, music followed very closely by women.

At the end of the class, Kiera seemed impressed by how I'd done. Seeing pride on her face made blissful lightness burst inside of me. It brought to mind the pledge I'd made this morning, about making her proud with this tour. And remembering that made the feeling swell even more. I was walking on air as we left the classroom. *I want to feel this way all the time.*

I was so high on life, I almost failed to notice the group of giggling girls watching us pass by them. In fact, they were barely a blip on my radar until they stepped out and blocked our path. I was almost annoyed, until I recognized the excited glow of eager fans. Knowing what they wanted, I gave them an easy smile. "Ladies?" I asked, giving them an opening.

They tittered even more, all of them seeming too uneasy to talk directly to me. *One of you needs to be bold, girls.* And it really shouldn't have been that hard. I wasn't that scary. Finally, one of them stepped forward. "You're Kellan, right? We just love your band."

I was nodding at her assessment when I spotted something odd. There was a girl in the back who was tugging at something in my brain. *I swear to God, I've seen her before.* From a show? Maybe with this group, since they had clearly heard me before? But, no, that didn't seem quite right. Did she date Evan a while back? Maybe that was it.

Deciding not to worry about it, I tossed on a smile and told the group, "I'm glad to hear you enjoy us. Our last show is tonight at Pete's." Knowing this was their last shot at hearing me for a while, I decided to make my invitation a little more... arousing than I usually did. Leaning forward, I lowered my voice and told them, "I hope you guys can make it." They were clearly hard cores...I'd hate for them to miss this last show, and if my tone sold them on showing up, well, so be it. The more people I could get to come into the bar tonight, the better.

The way the girls responded to that almost made me laugh. But then...that damn girl in the back grabbed my attention again. She wasn't responding to that like the others. No, they were nervously giggling but she looked like she'd heard an unspoken promise in that statement. She was practically undressing me with her eyes, like she wanted to throw me up against the wall and have her way with me. But it wasn't just that...I was kind of used to that. No, there was something else on her face. Something that said, *Come on, Kellan...you know me. Remember...that one night...?*

Probably not one of Evan's exes then. Shit. I must have slept with her at some point, that was the only thing that explained the familiarity on her face. The more I thought about it that way, the more it felt right, but even still, the memory of being with her wasn't leaping out at me. There were vague flashes of kissing, undressing...but that was it. And not being able to fully remember her made me feel pretty damn crappy. *Sorry, Eager-eyes...I don't remember that night.*

I felt Kiera pulling away from me, and I followed her lead. Yes, it was definitely time to go. Thank God Kiera hadn't noticed *that* particular fan. She really didn't like it when my ex-flings mentally screwed me right in front of her. But it wasn't something I could do anything about, especially when it happened around fans. I had an obligation to them, and I really hated being impolite in front of them. They were the entire reason we were going on tour after all.

Maintaining my professionalism, I ignored the girl I should have known better and excused myself to the group. "It was nice to meet you all. I'll see you at the show."

Kiera made an oddly annoyed sound at hearing me say that. I knew she had a jealous streak, but she was usually okay with me interacting with the fans. Why was she irritated? Had she spotted Eager-eyes after all? Damn it. Well, it wasn't like I'd acknowledged her or anything, and she hadn't said anything to me. Maybe it was something else. Or maybe Kiera was fine, and I was reading her mood wrong.

But when we got outside, I knew I wasn't reading her wrong. She was scowling as she huffed down the steps, irritation practically wavered in the air. I desperately wanted to skip whatever this was and return to the amazing mood we'd both been in just a few minutes ago, but I knew if I ignored this, it would only fester inside her, and be about a thousand times worse when we did talk about it.

"Hey, what's wrong?" I asked, ripping off the Band-Aid.

Kiera's response wasn't what I expected. In that snide tone of voice that crawled right under my skin, she childishly mimicked my earlier courtesy. "I hope you all can make it. See you there, ladies."

Stunned, I stopped and stared at her as she walked by me. *That* was what had upset her? My harmless flirting? "I was just being friendly with some fans, Kiera. It doesn't mean what you think it means." I wasn't hitting on them. I was just trying to pack the bar so tonight would be even better. In a way, it was for her. And the band. And Pete. *I'm just doing my job.*

Before I could say any of that, she stopped and spun around, hands on her hips and fire in her eyes. Pointing at the building we'd just left, she bit out, "You've had sex with that girl!"

So, she *had* noticed her, and that was what this was truly about. I knew I should be sympathetic. I knew I should be understanding, but her snotty tone was really starting to piss me off. "And?" I bit back.

It wasn't like this was a new experience for us. We'd run into my ex...whatevers on multiple occasions. And this one...I hadn't even acknowledged her. I could understand Kiera feeling frustration, but the level of anger and just plain bitchiness coming from her right now was mystifying. She had to know I wasn't doing anything with them now. Why was it so hard for her to believe I was capable of being faithful? And what did that mean for us...

"And...and..." The heat in her face dissipated as her argument fell apart. She hung her head, defeated. "And I'm tired of running into girls who know what making love to you feels like."

The weariness in her voice cooled my temper, and I couldn't help but think of all the times Kiera had been approached by women when I wasn't around. She'd been harassed before, and she'd probably heard a shit-ton of gossip. It wasn't just the girls we ran into together that were wearing her down; it was a relentless onslaught of my whoring past crashing into her time and time again, everywhere she went. I could understand how that would be tiring. But what she'd just said wasn't true.

Stepping up to her, I cupped her face. "No one but you knows what making love to me feels like. *I* didn't even know what making love was like until you." I motioned to the building behind us. "What happened with that girl was just sex. A mindless, physical act that had no meaning or feeling behind it. It was just pleasure, and I don't even really remember it."

I squatted down so I could hold her gaze. "I remember every single time with you. Even before we were together, being with you haunted my dreams. I couldn't forget, even when I wanted to..." She was starting to cry, and as I brushed the tears from her cheeks, my heart constricted with the painful memories of needing her when she wasn't mine. It *still* hurt. "You seared me. That's making love. That is something that none of them have over you. You are...unforgettable...and I love you."

She sniffed, swallowed, then finally said, "I love you too."

I wanted that to be the end of it, to leave the past firmly in the past, but when we got to my place, I could tell the conversation wasn't over. Looking glum as she sat on my couch, Kiera confessed that she was curious about the women I'd been with... specifically about how *many* women I'd been with. It was such a loaded question for me, one I couldn't possibly answer without looking bad, and I desperately didn't want to talk about it with her. More uncomfortable than I'd been in a long time, I begged her to let it go, begged her to ignore it, told her it was ancient history, I'd changed, and it didn't matter anymore...but she wouldn't cave.

Her voice sympathetic but firm, she told me that we couldn't have a solid relationship if we ignored things. She wanted us to talk about *everything*, and while I agreed...it was really fucking hard to talk to her about this. I tried one last time to sweep it under the rug, but it didn't work. She wanted more from me, she wanted me to expose all my dark sides to her, for the sake of our relationship. I was a little proud of her for wanting to face this head on, but more than that...I was ashamed. Because I didn't know how many girls I'd been with. I'd never kept track. Getting a high number had never been my goal when it came to women, it was just a side effect of my...desperation. My overwhelming need to connect with someone.

"I don't know how many, Kiera. I'm sorry." I hated myself for admitting that, for confessing how reckless I'd been, how sad, how lonely. I absolutely hated painting myself in such a bad light in front of her.

But knowing I should at least give her *something*, I started mapping out some rough estimates. "I suppose if you did the math...I've been having sex for about a decade, with two or three different girls a week..." Shame washing over me again, I peeked up at her. "On average." I focused on my hands as I mentally added that up. "So that's..." When the number came together for me, I was stunned...and sickened. "Crap," I said, looking up at Kiera. "That's over fifteen hundred girls. That can't be right," I muttered, letting my gaze fall to my hands again.

But even as I redid the math, I knew my estimate probably wasn't too far from the truth. Some weeks were less, some were more, but because I'd started so young, and because I'd given myself to *anyone* who'd wanted me...the numbers had added up on me. Fifteen-fucking-hundred.

God. Now I knew why I hadn't thought about it much. "Jesus...I really am a whore."

Kiera put a hand on my knee in support, maybe even in sympathy. "Well, I can see why you don't remember them all," she whispered.

I felt like I was going to be sick when I met eyes with her. "I'm so sorry, Kiera, I didn't realize..." How could she not hate me after hearing that? How could she not think of me differently, look at me differently? I kind of did. Jesus...what was wrong with me? I obviously hadn't known at the time that Kiera was waiting for me in my future, but still, I should have restrained myself for her. For us. Fuck—for *me*.

I half expected Kiera's face to match how my stomach felt, but that wasn't what I saw as I looked at her. She seemed a little paler, sure, but still warm, loving...accepting. She knew the *why*... and maybe that was enough for her to overlook the massive quantity. Hopefully.

She gave me a reassuring smile as she shook her head. "I wasn't trying to make you feel guilty, Kellan. I just...We should talk about this openly, honestly."

Relief that she wasn't going to reject me flooded through me. Having her support and understanding made talking about my past a lot easier, and Kiera switched the conversation to topics that, in hindsight, we probably *should* have talked about before— like, if I'd been safe with all of those girls. That was the only bright point of the whole conversation for me, because that one was a firm yes, I *had* been safe. Condoms were my number one rule, and I was a stickler about using them. If girls didn't accept that, they didn't get me. I supposed if my upbringing had taught me anything, it was that I didn't wish an accidental child on anyone...or that kind of childhood on any child.

I think Kiera understood that, and mostly believed my answer, but she couldn't help but point out my one and only exception. "You weren't with me. You never even thought about it with me."

Very true. And very wrong of me. Hoping she would understand just how profound she was to me, I told her the simplest version of the truth. "That's because...it was you." But her brows furrowed in confusion. No...she just didn't see herself like I saw her. "I wanted you so much...and in a way I'd never wanted any girl. I loved you...even that first time. I didn't want anything between us. I wanted..."

I had to stop, had to look away from her. I didn't know how

to make what I'd been feeling at the time sound good. It just sounded caveman-ish to me. But Kiera wasn't about to let me run away from the conversation now. "You wanted what?" she asked, gently forcing my gaze back to hers.

Knowing I couldn't get out of this, I confessed my last sin. "I wanted...to own you. I wanted a part of me in you. I wanted to mark you, make you mine." A wistful sigh escaped me. "Because I knew you really weren't, but it made me feel...closer to you, to think that way."

Pain washed over me as the memory consumed me. Any barrier between us just hadn't felt right. But still. It was selfish of me. Of course, having sex with her in the first place had been selfish of me. "I'm sorry. I shouldn't have done that." *Any of it.*

In answer, Kiera led my mouth to hers, and between a tender kiss she murmured, "I love you too." Thank God she did because I was kind of a train wreck.

Kiera pulled me down on top of her after that, and our mouths never disconnecting, we slowly let the weight of the conversation dissolve in our love for each other. She was right, I supposed—it was an important thing to talk about, and we should be able to talk about that kind of stuff—but still, the conversation had affected me; I still felt a little nauseated. When our tender kisses began shifting toward something more intense, I pulled away from her. "Don't take this the wrong way, but can we not have sex right now? Can we just...cuddle...until you have to go in to work? I just want to be close to you for a while."

Her eyes full of love, sympathy, and compassion she said, "Yeah, of course."

Lying down with her, wrapped in her arms, and tangled in her warmth, I slowly let the mistakes of my past slip away. I might have reached a sickeningly high number of conquests...but I had no intention of going any farther. No, my bed-count stopped with Kiera.

Chapter 12
HOME OF THE D-BAGS

Having Kiera's love and acceptance calmed and comforted me, and I felt oddly refreshed when it was time to head out to the bar. Guess we *had* needed that conversation after all. Kiera and I were surprisingly upbeat as I packed a bag for the tour; I wasn't sure if we'd be coming back here after Matt's party or not, so I wanted to be prepared. Kiera didn't notice, but I tucked one of her shirts into the bag before I zipped it closed. I wanted something that smelled like her to bring with me. I had a feeling I'd be needing that comfort on the road.

Once I was packed, I took one last look around my home. I had a complicated relationship with this place, between my parents and the ghost of Denny and Kiera, every square inch seemed to hold a trace amount of pain for me. Sometimes I debated selling it and moving somewhere new, somewhere fresh, but now...now that I wasn't going to see it for a while, I felt the dull ache of attachment. Not all of my memories here were bad ones. I'd met Kiera here, fallen for her here, heard her say she loved me here. *She* was here, buried in the walls, the floors, the bed...and I was going to miss that connection. But I would be back, for my home and for Kiera.

Walking to my car brought my second love to mind. What

was I going to do with the Chevelle for six months? Let her rot in my driveway? No, she needed to be driven, maintained...cherished. And there was only one person I trusted to cherish her like I did. A smile was on my face as I pictured Kiera behind the wheel of my baby. I might not like sharing my car, but if I wasn't here to drive her, then she should belong to Kiera. Temporarily. *Don't worry. I'm coming back for you too.*

Pulling into Pete's parking lot brought another sting of goodbye. My home away from home. I started to feel a little melancholy as I looked over the long, rectangular building lit with various beer signs in the dark windows. Although we'd started in L.A., this was where the D-Bags had truly begun.

My wistfulness grew as I opened one of the double doors. I really wasn't sure if I could handle the compounding goodbyes in the air. It was too much, and a part of me just wanted to scoop up Kiera, turn around, and drive us back to my house. Maybe a quiet night at home with Kiera was a better way to get through this.

But then Sam shoved a shot in my face. Pride in his eyes, he smacked my shoulder. "Here, man, it's your night, drink up!"

He didn't have to tell me twice. Grabbing the little cup, I immediately swished it back. Whiskey. Interesting choice. The burn eased my mood. As did the gesture. "Thanks, Sam. I never thought you, of all people, would hand me alcohol," I added with a laugh.

Sam rolled his eyes as he took my glass. "Well, since you're not going to end up on my doorstep tonight, I'll allow it."

His words shoved that painful night right back into my memory—drowning my sorrow in whiskey, throwing up on his flowers, almost passing out on his porch—but I immediately shoved it back down, because, as Evan often reminded me: I got the girl.

Shaking his head at me, Sam clapped my shoulder again. "We're gonna miss you, Kell." He looked a little melancholy after he said it, which kind of surprised me; I really wasn't used to the idea of people missing me. He started walking away, but not before muttering, "Drunken idiot."

Smiling at his comment, I tossed out, "Thanks!"

I tried walking with Kiera to my table, but progress was slow since it seemed like everyone in the bar wanted to shove alcohol in my face. I happily took every shot handed to me and made sure I thanked each person for their thoughtfulness. Being a little buzzed would make getting through this night a lot easier.

After I was handed my fourth shot, Kiera kissed my cheek and said, "I've got to get to work." I nodded an acknowledgment at her as I threw back the drink.

"Thanks, Jake," I said, handing the glass back to the regular who'd approached me.

I watched Kiera heading to the back room, and momentarily debated following her. Hadn't I promised to be her shadow today? Before I'd gotten distracted by the generosity of my peers...and this weird feeling of...belonging that was happening. My head was already a little lightheaded from the fairly quick intake of multiple shots. I should probably have some water if I wanted to be standing by the time we played. Especially since I could see more people edging their way over to me, alcohol in hand.

Since I knew I'd never make it to the back room before Kiera returned to me, I decided for water instead. Looking back at the bar, I made eye contact with Rita. It wasn't hard. Her eyes had already been glued on me. I made a drinking motion with my hand, and she winked...then set my favorite beer on the counter. *Well, okay, I'll take that too, but I'm going to need something to dilute all this.*

I was shaking my head at her when I spotted Jenny walking into the bar. I shouted her name and her blue eyes snapped to where I was standing, still only about halfway to my table. I pointed at the bar and made a drinking motion. She glanced over, saw my beer waiting and grabbed it. She was already heading my way before I could stop her.

"Hey, Kellan," she said, handing me the beer. "Are you excited?"

Containing a sigh, I smiled at her. "Yeah, I guess." Squatting down, I met her eye. "While I've got you here...you remember everything we talked about?"

With a grin, she nodded. "Yep."

"About the neighbors? And the second payment?" I'd decided to go ahead with the "bribe." I'd delivered the first payment to Matt's neighbors earlier this week, and as long as none of them called the cops and busted the party tonight, Jenny had agreed to make the second payment for me tomorrow. God, tomorrow...I didn't want to think about that. Maybe water could wait after all. I had some aches I wanted to keep on the back burner.

Her face not changing, she nodded again. "Yep."

"About our equipment? About bringing it back for us?" I nodded my head at the stage. We couldn't just leave our setup for six months, not with Poetic Bliss taking our place; they'd have their own instruments to set up. That meant we needed someone to pack it all up and get it back to Evan's place for us. Fuck. I shouldn't be talking about all of this...it was dampening my burgeoning buzz.

Jenny pursed her lips, before smiling again. "That was Evan who asked me to do that, but yes, I remember."

My smile fell as I thought about my most important request. "And...about Kiera?" I flashed a glance at the entrance to the back hallway...she still wasn't back yet, and I suddenly had the need to see her. Like I needed to reassure myself that she was still here.

Jenny studied my expression then nodded. "Don't let her be sad, make her have fun. Check and check." Raising her eyebrows, she put a comforting hand on my arm. "Relax, Kellan, Rachel and I have everything under control, and we'll drag Kiera along when we run your errands...make sure she's too busy cleaning up after you to miss you." With a laugh, she shook her head. "She'll probably be too annoyed by all the menial stuff you boys have left behind to be sad."

That made me grin. "I'm okay with her being annoyed. She's sexy when she's mad." Or happy. Or nervous. Or bored. Or...*anything*.

Jenny let out a hearty laugh as she rolled her eyes. I wanted to go over the list again, but a shot suddenly appeared at my side. "Hey, Kellan. Here, congratulations, man!"

I twisted to face Rob, another regular, and Jenny slipped away to get ready for work. As I took Rob's drink, I tossed out, "Thank you, Jenny!" She stuck her thumb up, and I had to laugh at her.

I was swarmed after that, barely making it to my table so I could set down my stuff. The attention was still a little mystifying, but also...really amazing. And really intoxicating since a lot of them wished me well with booze. I was feeling pretty damn good when I spotted someone else I needed to talk to tonight: Kate.

Kiera had reentered the room several minutes ago, and while I loved having her in my sight again, I needed to make sure she didn't see this exchange. Making sure she wasn't watching me, I opened my guitar case and grabbed my steamy, do-you-miss-me-yet letter. As I picked up the folded note, I paused to smile at the photo of Kiera and me that I always left tucked inside with my guitar. Jenny had taken this one too. It was Kiera and me, outside, caught in a laugh as we looked at each other. That photo was definitely going on the road with me. Looking at it made me wish I had tons of photos to take with me, but this would satisfy the ache of missing her. I hoped.

I took a second to gently touch Kiera's face in the photo, then shut the case, and started threading my way through well-wishers to get to the last Pete's waitress I needed to make plans with. "Kate...Kate-Kate-Kate."

Kate's expression showed her amusement when she looked up from a table of customers to grin at me. "Kellan...Kellan-Kellan-Kellan," she teasingly mimicked. Stepping away from the table, she hugged her notepad to her chest and sighed. "I can't believe this is the last D-Bags show for...a while. It's not going to be the same without you guys here, you know?"

I had to swallow the sudden lump in my throat. "Yeah..." Shaking my head, my vision hazing as I did, I pushed back that pain and focused on what I wanted to say. "Hey, I was wondering...could you do me a *huge* favor?"

Kate's brows bunched in curiosity. "Sure. What is it?"

I glanced around the room, looking for Kiera; she was busy helping someone several tables away from us. Hurriedly twisting back to Kate, I handed her my note. "Could you give this to Kiera at exactly midnight tomorrow? *Exactly* midnight. Tomorrow."

Kate's expression softened, like she thought I was adorable. "Of course...what is it?"

Leaning in close, I told her, "It's a secret."

She smirked as she looked up at me. "I see..." Biting her lip, she paused only a second before asking, "Can I read it?"

I gave her a playful frown. "But then it wouldn't be a secret."

"I'm really good at keeping secrets," she said, her golden-brown eyes hopeful.

I gave her a firm face for a second, then laughed. "I don't care. Just please, don't let her see it before midnight tomorrow. I want it to be a surprise."

"Sure thing," she said, safely tucking it into her apron pocket.

"Thank you so much," I said with a grin. After secreting a glance back at Kiera, I held up my fist for Kate. She giggled as she bumped mine with hers. Phase one was now complete. *Everything* was in place.

I was ear-to-ear smiles with a light heart—and a light head—as I turned to walk back to my table. Before I could leave, Kate touched my elbow and I looked back at her. "Hey, congratulations, Kellan. This really is...very cool."

I nodded at Kate, grateful for her words...and for her accepting my favor. Kiera was going to love that steamy letter and who knows, Kate might like it too. She did share Kiera's love of romance novels after all.

When I got back to my table, Kiera was waiting for me...with a large glass of water in her hand. I almost looked back at Kate, but Kiera didn't seem curious so she must have missed the exchange. I didn't want to spoil the surprise by clueing her in to the fact that something was being planned behind her back, so I ignored my partner-in-crime and reserved all my focus for my beautiful girlfriend.

"Drink this," she said, handing the water to me.

I took a sip, grateful, then I set it on the table and pulled her into me. "Can I drink you instead?" I asked. That sounded by far more appealing than water or alcohol.

Kiera laughed, her eyes a calm shade of brown rimmed with green. She shook her head, then softly kissed my cheek, and I marveled at the fact that my skin still warmed with longing whenever her lips touched me. I hoped that never went away. I hoped *she* never went away.

But she did go away. For the moment, at least; she got called over by hungry customers at a nearby table while I got approached by even more people wanting to congratulate me. And I tried really hard to not let that split feel symbolic.

As more alcohol was handed to me, I became even more grateful for Kiera's water, and for the fact that every time I turned around, it seemed to have somehow been refilled. It was so nice having someone take care of me. So foreign. So...welcome. I was really going to miss that.

Eventually, the rest of my band arrived at the bar. I knew the instant they did—the whole place went nuts. And it was packed, so the noise was substantial. I didn't think I'd ever seen the bar this full this long before a show. It was heartwarming, and surreal, and it drilled through the numb of my buzz, making my chest ache. Especially when Pete came out of his office.

Pete had always looked a little worn to me, but tonight he seemed extra weary. He quieted the bar with raised hands while I made my way over to my friends. Pete's eyes locked on me as he softly smiled. "Kellan...boys...you've done wonders for my little pub, and I'll never forget that. If and when you return, you will always have a place here."

The ache in my chest squeezed into an almost painful wrenching sensation, and my gaze drifted to the floor. Leaving... sucked. But man, I loved what he'd just said, because this place would always be important to me. Having that feeling reciprocated was surprisingly wonderful. *I'm so glad I didn't run from here.*

Pete made an oddly emotional noise, and I peeked up at him. God, if he lost it...I would not be able to keep it together. But thankfully, Pete didn't test my emotional resilience. He shook off his sentiment and indicated the entire bar. "Anyway...a round for everybody, on the house!"

I had to widen my eyes at hearing that. Pete wasn't one to throw around free booze. I'd have to make sure I sent him some money after I was gone, make sure tonight didn't hurt his bank account too much. I owed him that much. Honestly, I owed him way more than I could ever repay. I'd never really felt *home* until I'd come here. Damn, I was going to miss this place. *Keep it together, Kellan. Jesus.*

As Pete began walking over to us, I peeked over at Kiera. Her face was pale as she took in the massive number of thirsty patrons around her who were now expecting free alcohol. Damn. She was going to be busy for a while. Maybe I should throw on an apron and help her. That could be fun. I was just about to do it when Pete stepped in front of us and clapped me on the arm.

"The bar won't be the same without you boys," he muttered. "But I do appreciate you lining up another act for me. They're good...right?"

Smiling, I nodded. "Yeah, you'll like 'em. Give them time, they'll draw a crowd."

Pete nodded, then, out of the blue, he smiled brightly at me. "Hey, once you are all huge stars...I want to put your name on the door. *Pete's Bar, Home of the D-Bags*," he said with a flourish of his hands. "Would that be all right with all of you?"

My mouth popped open in disbelief. *Really?* I glanced around at Matt, Griffin, and Evan. They looked just as stunned as me. Well, except Griffin. He was smirking and nodding, like he'd expected as much. I couldn't even comprehend a world where we were big enough to warrant that kind of honor, but Pete looked so much happier now just thinking about it, that I couldn't deny him his request. Seeing approval on my bandmates' faces, I told him, "Yeah, that would be...Yes, thank you."

Pete beamed at us, thanking us each in turn and shaking our hands. It was all so out there...I suddenly needed more alcohol. And Kiera. I needed things to start feeling real again.

Pete left us with a genuine bounce in his step. I could only shake my head at him. Home of the D-Bags...I had to admit, I loved the sound of it. Not *former* home of the D-Bags, not *birthplace* of the D-Bags, no, just...*home*. As in now and forever it was our place, and that was a really comforting thought.

"Can you believe that shit?" I asked, twisting to face the guys.

Matt was bouncing on his toes he was so excited. Rachel giggled at his side, loving his glee. "Oh my God, Kellan...dude! Home of the D-Bags..." He sighed as he wrapped an arm around Rachel. "I love it."

Evan nodded. "It's perfect."

Griffin frowned. "You know what's gonna happen though, right? Fucking place is gonna become a goddamn tourist trap—with our pictures everywhere, and D-Bags merch everywhere, and horny fans coming in from all over the world..." He paused, then grinned. "I fucking love it."

I shook my head at Griffin's assessment of our future fame. He was even more ridiculous than Kiera.

Once the band was all together, the drinks coming our way were fast and furious. I felt too bad to reject anyone's goodbye gift, so it didn't take long for me to get completely, totally soused. Feeling like my head was detached from my body, I pulled Matt aside. Or yanked him aside. "Dude...you're ready for the party, right?"

Matt nodded. He started to move away, but I stepped in front of him. It took me a second to catch my balance. "Music? Food? Those fruity drinks girls like?"

Matt laughed as he helped steady me. "Yeah, Kell...it's not my first party. We're good to go."

A dopey grin spread over my face. "Good. I want this night to be fun for Kiera. Fun for everyone."

He nodded as he sipped on a beer. "It will be." Raising an eyebrow, he looked me over. "Are you drinking *everything* they hand you?"

My words felt slow in my head, thick coming out of my mouth. "Yeah...what else would I do with it?"

Matt pursed his lips and pointed at our table. My slow gaze followed his finger to see about two dozen shots just sitting there, hanging out. Looking at all the alcohol heaped together like that made me a little nauseous. God...I hoped no one expected me to drink all that.

Matt smacked me on the back. "You're gonna die if you drink it all, man. Tell them thanks, then set it down, okay?"

I looked back up at him; his face was blurry. Damn. I should have started doing that a while ago. "Uh-huh, yeah...I'm-a find... Kiera." Food. That was what I needed. And my girlfriend...I really fucking missed her.

Matt laughed at me, then handed me a glass of water. "You better be able to play, man."

I gave him a thumbs up as I chugged the water. I had time. I could sober up. And if not...I was pretty good at faking it. Matt sighed. "And here I thought I was gonna have to babysit Griffin." He jerked his thumb over at his cousin; he didn't seem nearly as drunk as me. Probably because he was too busy being fawned over by a handful of girls. I smirked at Matt's comment, then flipped him off.

I looked around for Kiera, but I didn't see her anywhere.

Weird, since it was a zoo in here. Jenny and Kate were both around, hustling to satisfy everybody. Rita was busy at the bar; even with Troy pulling a double shift to stay and help her, it was pretty chaotic up there. So, where the hell was my girlfriend?

My sloppy head twisted toward the direction of the back hallway. Was she waiting somewhere private for me? Did she miss me too? Grinning, I started weaving my way through the crowd for her. I felt some aggressively friendly fingers stroke my body as I walked by, heard murmurs of sexual promises in my ears, and even noticed a few things being shoved into my pockets, but I ignored it all as I continued to the back hallway. I was on a mission, and I was not going to be stopped.

Although, I did pause once I reached a garbage can and emptied my pockets. Even drunk, I knew Kiera finding strange phone numbers in my jeans wouldn't end well. And I wanted tonight to end...amazing.

Curious if she was in the back room, I slowly opened the door. Ah-ha...she *was* in here. Seeing her rummaging through a box of condiments made me smile. She hadn't noticed me, or if she had, she was ignoring me. I wasn't about to let her ignore me, not tonight, but there was something about secretly watching her work that was seriously turning me on. The loose ponytail, the tight jeans, the way her shirt was just begging for me to untuck it from her pants...it was all working for me. Or maybe it was just this room. A lot had happened in here, some of it painful, some of it...un-fucking-believable. I'd told her I loved her in here. Turning back to the door, I locked it.

Wondering if she'd roleplay a little with me, I strode right up behind her; if she really hadn't been aware I was here before, she was now. Trapping her against the shelves with my body, I lowered my voice and murmured in her ear, "Don't turn around."

She startled, then started turning. *Didn't I just tell you not to do that, Kiera?* Grinning, I made her head stay forward, then pressed myself harder into her back. She knew it was me, right? "I said, don't turn around."

Her body was still stiff, tight, vibrating with nervous energy. Did she really not recognize my voice? Not able to stomach tormenting her any longer, I started laughing. She instantly relaxed in my arms and spun to face me. "Kellan! You scared the shit out of me!"

She started smacking my chest, and I stumbled back with a laugh. I hadn't meant to scare her, but God, she was cute when she swore. Whatever fear had been there a second ago definitely wasn't there now; there was heat in her eyes, desire. It made an undeniable ache head straight to my groin. *I want you.*

I pulled her into my body, where she belonged. "You're disobeying me..." I playfully said, then I backed her against the shelves, pressing my body flush against hers, where *it* belonged. "I may just have to punish you tonight," I whispered. *Fuck, now I really want you.*

That familiar passion flared between us, and before I knew it, we were both breathing heavy, her shirt was free of her jeans, and my hand was down her thankfully stretchy jeans. *Yes...this is happening.*

But then she told me no and grabbed my hand before I could touch her. "Why'd you stop me?" I asked, reluctantly removing my lips from her skin.

She sighed at me as she tried to remove my hand from her pants. Then her gaze turned inquisitive. "Are you drunk?"

Yep, sure am. But even with me being drunk, Kiera couldn't budge my hand, not even with two of hers. Just a little further and I was pretty sure I could stop her from talking... "Probably," I laughed. "And I want that sex now." *Before I explode.*

But Kiera was firm in her refusal. She was *not* going to have sex with me in the back room. Not even after I let her know that I'd had Pete fix the lock. *We're completely alone. No one will bother us this time.* I did my best to rile her up enough to change her mind, and with how fast her breath was, how much heat I felt when she kissed me, and with how wet I could tell she was when my hand finally rested over her, I think I nearly changed her mind.

But damn if she still pushed me away. "You have to go play, Kellan. Can you even do that?"

With a laugh, I nodded. "There's a lot I can do when I'm drunk." *Like make love to you over and over again. Doesn't that sound nice?* I still hadn't actually touched her yet, hadn't slid my finger into that wetness, and with how hard I was right now, I knew I couldn't wait much longer. But I was really kind of hoping she'd beg me to touch her...

But instead of changing her mind and begging me...she frowned. "Yeah, I hear you make out with Pete's waitresses on New Year's Eve when you're wasted."

Her words were slow to filter through my brain. What I'd been waiting for her to say was, *Oh God, please, Kellan, yes...take me*. Then all bets were off, all clothes were off. But instead, she wanted to talk about New Year's Eve and Pete's waitresses? Did she mean herself? Because we'd never kissed on New Year's. And fuck, we still wouldn't. I'd be gone.

"What?" I asked, wishing I hadn't remembered that.

She struggled with my hand again. "Kate, you ass. You never told me you almost had sex with her...Jenny too."

Kate? I never...oh wait...yeah, I think I did. Huh. But like she said, I hadn't been successful. With either of them. I rolled my eyes at her comment. "I never got anywhere near sex with Jenny. She said no. And Kate...doesn't count."

Her face came right into mine; it took me a moment to refocus on her. God, she was beautiful. Why were we talking about other women again? When I had my hand on her privates and all she had to do was ask me to lift my finger and satisfy her? "What do you mean she doesn't count?" she asked.

"Almost doesn't count," I told her. If we were going to add *that* number to my list, well, fuck, I wasn't sure I could count that high. Especially now.

Annoyed by my answer, Kiera finally successfully pulled my hand out of her pants. I ached with the loss. So close...and yet so far. And now I was going to have a stomachache. My own damn fault, I supposed. Trying to take Kiera in the back room had never worked out well for me. But, still hoping she'd change her mind, I gave her sad, pity-me eyes and a pathetic, I-need-you pout. She just smiled and shook her head. "What am I going to do with you?"

My grin returned as I stared at her pants. "I could think of a few things." *Just how annoyed would she be if I put my hand back?*

Maybe sensing that I might try to seduce her again if she didn't get me out of here, she turned me around and pushed me toward the door. *Guess it's not happening after all.* I let out a disappointed sigh, and Kiera started laughing. "What's so funny?" I asked, frowning. Blue balls were no joking matter.

The look on my face amused her even more. "Well, Casanova...since you are obviously living it up on your night, guess what I get to do later?"

That was an invitation in my book. Twisting around, I pressed into her again. "Me?"

She reacted, fluttering her eyes closed like she wanted me, but then she pushed me away. Again. And even raised a finger, telling me to back off. "No..." As she reached behind me to open the door, she spoke some of the worst words I'd ever heard. "I finally get to drive the Chevelle again."

That almost immediately shut off my sex drive. "What? No way." Amusement on her face, she shoved me out the door. "I'm fine, or I will be fine. I've got hours to..."

My thought trailed off as a part of me started...ringing. *What the fuck?* Did I swallow an alarm clock or something? I started patting my body, searching for the annoying noise so I could shut it off. *Where the fuck is that coming from?* Because it seemed to be coming from my groin. Was my dick so upset with me for failing with Kiera that it was audibly complaining? *Sorry...I tried.*

Lightly laughing, Kiera grabbed one of my hands and put it on my front pocket...where I felt my cell phone. Oh yeah...

Laughing to myself, I told her, "Oh, thank God, it's the phone. For a minute, I thought my cock was ringing." Kiera had to slap a hand over her mouth to stop herself from laughing. It was adorable. So was the bright-red color of her cheeks. God, she was cute when she was embarrassed. It made me want to say the word cock about five thousand more times.

But instead, I pulled out my phone and brightly answered whoever the fuck was calling me. "Yo, talk to me."

Kiera shook her head at me, while the voice in my ear let out a laugh. "Kellan? Hey, it's Denny."

Surprise and delight shot through me. "Dude! Denny, man! You have, like, fuck-tastic timing. Tonight's my last show and Kiera and I were just—"

Kiera's hand shot out and she instantly tried to snatch my phone from me. *What the hell?* I took a step back from her, staying out of reach. "Relax, Kiera, I wasn't going to tell him that you just blew me off."

The look of horror on Kiera's face spoke volumes. What? What did I say? Oh, right...that probably sounded bad. "Oh, Denny, not that she actually blew me or anything, she didn't, she doesn't really hang out down there, if you know what I mean." A dark humor filled me, and before I could stop myself, I laughed out, "And I guess you do, huh?" If there was one guy in the world who knew Kiera's sexual likes and dislikes as well as me, it was Denny...which was exactly why I shouldn't have said that to him. Oops.

Kiera again tried to take the phone away from me. I batted her away so I could apologize for my inappropriate comment. "Sorry, man, you probably don't want to hear shit like that."

"Yeah...I *really* could do without those kinds of visuals, Kellan," he muttered.

Guilt instantly tried to flood through me, but the massive amount of alcohol flowing through my veins shifted it back to humor. "Yeah, well, at least I didn't say you caught us in the middle of doing it...That would have been awkward."

The line went absolutely drop-dead silent. Oops. Maybe I shouldn't have said that either. "Denny? You still there?"

"Yeah, I'm just..." He paused to sigh. "I just called to wish you good luck on your tour. Are you leaving after your show?"

"No, the tour starts tomorrow. We're livin' it up for our last night in Seattle." And my head was already floating...

Denny laughed a little. "Yeah, I can tell. But still, all of this is really impressive, Kellan. I'm not surprised, but at the same time...I almost can't believe it. You're *actually* going on tour."

Hearing the pride in his voice made me beam. Holding Kiera back, since she was still trying to nab my phone, I told him, "Yeah, I know. Six months, Denny. On a bus, man! An actual tour bus, can you believe that shit?"

He laughed again. "You're really drunk, aren't you?"

Why did everyone keep asking me that? "Yeah, I'm seriously buzzin'...why?"

Before Denny could respond with anything besides more laughter, Kiera successfully snatched the phone from me. "Hey, Denny, it's me. Sorry about that. He's been...celebrating."

I crossed my arms over my chest as I patiently waited for Kiera to hand me back my phone. Thief. Kiera didn't give it back though. She ignored my annoyance and kept on going with her stolen conversation. Then she closed her eyes, and I saw something familiar pass over her face...pain. What were they talking about? Me? Was I causing her pain? Or was Denny?

Kiera said something along the lines of "I'm fine," then she opened her eyes and smiled at me. I smiled back, drinking her in as she told Denny, "This is a big moment for him. I'm not going to ruin it by..." She suddenly bit her lip, then she sighed...and turned away from me. "Denny..."

The guilt in her voice cut straight through my buzz. Her turning away from me went straight to my stomach. I wasn't sure exactly what they were talking about, but I felt like it was somehow about our fucked-up little threesome. I didn't want to think about that again. I didn't want to worry. I didn't want to be scared. I didn't want anything but for Kiera to be mine. *Truly* mine.

Don't think. Don't stress. Don't get mad. And don't get sick.

In an attempt to purge my brain from overanalyzing anything my girlfriend was saying, or *hearing*, I leaned against the far wall and distracted myself by only focusing on the exit sign at the end of the hall. White background, a perfect little rectangle, bright-green neon letters. I began mentally tracing them, forcing my head to stop spinning...E...X...I...T. That sign was the only thing left in the world to me. My lifeline.

When I could tell Kiera was getting off the phone, I slowly, methodically, brought my attention back to her. She was looking at me warily as she handed me my phone. *What did he say to you?*

No, don't ask her what that was about, don't think about what she's feeling. She loves you, not him. Don't ruin your last night with her by getting into a fight. Just do what you came back here to do... fix your damn stomach.

I grimaced as I remembered why I'd come back here in the first place. "I'm hungry. Do you want to split some fries with me?" I asked, shoving my phone back in my pocket.

She exhaled, and there was a lot of relief in that exhale. "Sounds great. I'll get some cooked up for you."

The promise of food made me feel better. So did kissing Kiera's cheek and walking out of the hallway with her. I didn't need to worry about Denny...that was over, and he was about a billion miles away from her.

Chapter 13
ONE GREAT NIGHT

By the time I needed to go on stage to play, I'd sobered up enough to know that I owed Denny a serious apology. What I'd said to him...God, I was such a dick sometimes. But I didn't have time to make it up to him tonight. No, the remainder of tonight was for Kiera, my band, my friends, and the sea of faces that I saw in front of me.

Slinging my guitar over my chest, I approached the microphone; I almost couldn't hear myself think it was so loud in here. I held up a hand to quiet the ear-piercing shrieks. The noise settled to a dull roar, and as I swept my eyes over the crowd a profound sense of connection rippled through me. For this one moment in time, it was as if everyone here was one giant being, not multiple separate ones. We all wanted the same thing, we all needed the same thing, and the tiny differences that made us unique...didn't matter. We were one.

In an attempt to brush aside the heaviness of the moment, I smiled at the assortment of faces, at the shadows of bodies I could see hovering out the dark windows, since we were too packed to let everyone inside. "Wow...there's a lot of you here," I told the crowd. They hollered in answer, making me grin. *They really do love us.*

Removing the microphone from its stand, I stepped forward, to the edge of the stage, so I could get as close to the fans as possible. "I want to thank you all for coming, for supporting us for so long." I felt my throat closing up as I searched the crowd. Some of them, especially the ones in the front, had made it to damn-near every single show here. I wished I had more to give to them than just my voice. I wished I had a way to significantly change their lives, like they'd changed mine. "I'm gonna miss this..." I murmured, an ache in my voice.

God, Kellan, stop being so fucking melodramatic. You'll be back.

My mental pep talk amused me, and again my mood shifted. I sought out Kiera in the crowd, my vision swirling as I did. I might have sobered up, but I was nowhere near actually being sober. When I spotted my angel, I smiled. Then giggled. "I'm so wasted right now," I told the crowd. They whistled, like they loved the fact that I was fucked up. They might think differently if I couldn't actually do this. Let's hope ten thousand practices were enough to compensate for a shit-ton of alcohol.

Kiera shook her head at me while I motioned for Evan to start. *Here goes nothing.*

Surprising even myself, I got through it fine. It was great actually, one of our best shows, if not *the* best. The crowd fed us their energy, and we fed it right back to them. We played our new song —which they ate up—then we played every mega-hit we had. In fact, as I watched the fans' reaction to our setlist, I knew, if we ever actually finished setting up the soundproofing in Evan's loft, a lot of these songs should be on our demo album. Not all of them would fit though, plus there were a lot of other good songs too; deciding the final list would be really hard. Now I kind of wished I'd been more helpful with the soundproofing project, so the album would already be done, and Kiera could listen to me while we were gone. Wasted opportunity.

When we were finally done, our souls poured into all of our best songs, I felt exhausted, yet more energized than ever.

The crowd went nuts when they realized it was over—whistling and clapping their approval and appreciation. It...awed me. I raised my hand to quiet them. "The band and I would like to thank you all again. You're the best fans that we ever could have asked for and we're going to miss playing for you every weekend..."

Those words hollowed me, and I had to take a moment to compose myself. Grinning through the painful ache of change, I pointed at Matt. "Now, let's all go over to Matt's place and get royally fucked up!" This party wasn't over yet. I didn't have to say goodbye yet.

Matt frowned at me while the bar exploded in a chorus of cheers. Oops. He probably hadn't expected me to invite *everyone*, but honestly, it wouldn't be right if we didn't. This was their moment too; we wouldn't be here without them. And it would be fine. Matt overprepared for everything.

A lot of people filtered out of the bar after the show, but I stayed, so Kiera and I could go to the party together. Even though I was more or less sober, Kiera insisted on driving. I let her. Mostly because she was right—better safe than sorry. But also, because she reminded me about my uncouth comment to Denny about her not hanging out "down there." That was an argument I really couldn't win. *First place dick, right here.*

By the time we got to Matt and Griffin's, the party was at full force. We had to park down the street it was so packed, and as I took in all the cars and listened to all the noise...I was really glad I'd paid off the neighbors. It probably would have already been shut down if not for my monetary motivation. Worth every penny.

The noise intensified when I opened the front door. It washed over me like a physical thing, and I suddenly felt like we weren't at Matt's suburban utopia anymore. No, we were suddenly in the hottest nightclub in Seattle, only this one was filled to bursting with people we actually knew. Or kind of knew. Not all the faces I was spotting were familiar.

Kiera put our things in the closet, then grabbed my hand so I could lead us to the kitchen. She was going to need a drink for this. Because even with all these people, I could feel the sting of goodbye between us, and if I could feel it while I was buzzed, then she could definitely feel it completely sober. I squeezed us through the dancers in the living room to the gamers in the dining room. There was a large group playing a dice game at the table. A game I was sadly all too familiar with. A local variant of Three Man. Or as I liked to call it: Let's-Make-Sure-Kellan-Gets-Fucked-Up Man. I really wasn't sure why people, men and women alike, tended to gang up on me whenever we played drinking games. Well okay, I kind of understood why.

Matt approached Kiera and me while we were watching the game; from the curious look on Kiera's face, she'd never played this particular drinking game before. "Hey, you made it," Matt said, clapping my shoulder. "People have been asking for you."

I smiled at Matt, taking in his glazed expression. He might have been holding back at the bar, but now that work was done and he was home, caution was going out the window. Good. He needed this too. As I nodded a greeting at Rachel, attached to Matt's shoulder, Matt said, "Hey, Kiera. We got everything. What's your poison?"

I had to agree as I looked over the collection of alcohol covering his counters. He damn-near did have everything. Guess he was right about having it under control. Not that I'd actually been worried. It was Matt after all. He practically slept with a planner under his pillow. And thank God he did. One of us needed to be organized.

Rita had followed us to the party and had settled right in, making drinks in Matt's kitchen. Meeting her eye, I mouthed, *Bee*r, right as I heard Kiera tell Matt, "I'm good, really, thanks."

Matt accepted her answer with a nod, but I twisted to face her. "Uh-uh, you need a drink."

She smirked at me. "You're going to peer pressure me to drink?"

I rolled my eyes at her answer. Normally, I wouldn't have cared less if she drank at a party or not, but tonight...tonight was different. She needed to let go of the reins on her brain. We both did. Leaning in, I murmured in her ear, "I don't want you spending the entire evening thinking about me leaving." She pulled back to look at me, and the look on her face matched the feeling in my chest. "I don't want you spending our last night thinking about it...and you will, right?"

She nodded, looking pained to admit it, but it wasn't surprising. *I feel it too, Kiera.* Slipping my arms around her waist, I shoved that emotion to the back of my mind as I kissed her forehead. "I want you to loosen up and have a little fun with me. Can you do that?"

Because if you can't, then I won't be able to either. We might as well leave and go to my place, so we can sit in a dark room and spend the entire night crying in each other's arms. And I don't want to spend my last moments with you being sad. So, please, say yes to this memory I'm offering you.

Kiera's beautiful ever-changing eyes studied me for long seconds, until finally, she broke eye contact with me and turned to Matt, who was busy manhandling Rachel. She tapped his shoulder, diverting his attention, then told him, "I'll take something...sweet." Matt grinned and gave her a hug. I had to laugh at my normally reserved guitarist...and the look on Kiera's face as she gently patted his back.

"I'll hook you up, Kiera!" he exclaimed, and then he was off to make her something that I knew would be exceptionally strong.

"Thank you," I told her, kissing her neck.

She pursed her lips at me in answer, and then a scream broke out in the living room. Kiera and I angled ourselves to see that Evan had found Jenny; he'd hoisted the tiny girl onto his shoulder and was playfully smacking her ass. Which gave me a fabulous idea...

After waving a greeting to Evan, I shifted my eyes back to Kiera. She knew exactly what I was planning. "Don't even think about it, Kyle." She even stuck a finger in my chest, like that would somehow stop me. She seemed to realize that, and stepped back from me, into one of the dining room chairs. The girl there looked pretty hammered...and thoroughly finished with the game.

Grabbing Kiera's shoulders, she made her sit down. "Here, I'm done. You play."

As soon as Kiera was in the chair, Matt handed her a drink, and the girl next to her gave her the dice. And then made her drop them. They tumbled from her hand and landed on snake eyes. Oh...man. *That sucks.* That was pretty much the opposite of beginner's luck. Kiera didn't know what a pair of ones meant, but everyone else did, and the entire table groaned in sympathy for her. Matt patted her shoulder and told her he'd make another drink for her while I explained her fate.

"Snake eyes means you have to pound your drink." Her eyes widened as she absorbed that. It was really best if you rolled that when you only had a couple swigs left...and not a brand-new, super potent drink. I'd been in her shoes before...it led to bad things. I'd have to make sure she didn't play this game for too long. I wanted her buzzed, not puking.

Rita handed me my beer, and I raised it in a toast to Kiera. "Bottom's up, babe."

She shook her head, not amused. "I wasn't really playing..."

The entire table of drunken idiots started booing her. The look on her face was priceless, and I couldn't help the laugh that escaped me, but I watched her closely, looking for the *Get me out of here now* expression. She surprised me though and started chugging her fruity cocktail. When she finished it in record time, she practically got a standing ovation from the table. Some jackass made a sexual comment about how I was lucky because she was such a good sucker, and I started laughing. Until she glared at me. Then I stopped. Immediately. Oops. Sorry.

Hauling Jackass out of his seat, I stole his spot with a "My turn." If Kiera was actually going to play this game, then I'd play with her. Although, there was no way in hell I'd play with hard liquor like she was. I'd already learned that lesson.

I watched Kiera closely throughout the game. I wanted her loose and breezy, not plastered. When she giggled as she drank, I knew she was getting close. When I made a suggestive comment about our sex life, about her being drunk improving my odds, and Kiera tossed it right back at me, saying, "Since when have you ever needed help with your odds," I knew she was there. Yep, time to go. But first, I couldn't let the ball die on my side of the court. If Kiera was going to play...then let's play.

Staring her down, I murmured, "True..." I ran my teeth over my bottom lip, a move I knew from experience she found distracting. Then I lowered my voice to that seductive range that I knew she loved and started explaining just what I hoped I could get her to do to me later. "But maybe I could get you to do that one thing with your—"

She didn't even let me finish painting that glorious picture for the table. Partially standing, she snapped, "Kellan Kyle! You shut the hell up!"

That's right...I win.

Kiera's cheeks flamed as she glared at me. Amid the laughter in the room, my own included, I playfully told her, "Just saying..." Her heated eyes grew downright ferocious. God, she was cute when she was mad at me. If she didn't react like that, I wouldn't tease her half as much as I did. *I'd never tell them anything real, Kiera. And besides, I knew you'd stop me.*

Knowing I needed to simmer her down a little, I let the love I felt for her show in my face and in my voice. "You're such an adorable drunk, Kiera." *I love you so much for letting me harass you.*

I really wasn't sure how she'd react to me embarrassing her

while she was buzzing. A playful smack of reprimand, or a semi-angry stomp out of the room...making me chase her, pin her down, get her to forgive me with my undivided attention to her body. Hmmm...

I was just about to decide for her when she stood from the table and playfully motioned me over to her. She wanted to kiss me, in front of all these people... She usually objected to my very public displays of affection. She was definitely feeling no pain right now. Good. Neither was I.

Rising from my seat, I leaned over the table and tasted her; warm, soft, and sweet like the drinks she'd been sipping. Perfection. The connection instantly turned me on, and I savored the moment, even if it was punctuated with whistling and laughter.

"All right! We playing spin the bottle?"

Knowing that voice all too well, I broke apart from Kiera and glared at my bassist. As I straightened to standing, Griffin clapped me on the back with a giddy grin on his face; spin the bottle was one of his favorite party games. "No, we're not, Griffin." *There's not a chance in hell that I would let you kiss Kiera, buddy. You will die tonight if you try.*

Not intimidated by the look on my face, Griffin found an empty bottle on the table and spun it. Jackass. *Gonna test me, huh?* Crossing my arms over my chest, I stared him down. *This isn't happening, Griffin.* Well, if it landed on Kiera, it wasn't happening. I really didn't care if Griffin wanted to kiss someone else.

But then the room exploded in gut-busting laughter. Confused, I looked at the bottle to see what was so funny. And that was when I saw it...the neck of the bottle was pointed perfectly...at *me*. Well, fuck. I hadn't considered that possibility. That was a redo, right? He wouldn't...

Shit...yes, he would.

My eyes instantly snapped to him. When he looked up at me, I said, "Nuh-uh," and firmly shook my head. *No way in hell, dude.*

While the people around us died with laughter—even Kiera was clutching her stomach, her eyes watering with delight—Griffin shrugged. "Sorry, man. House rules, you play the bottle where it lies."

It felt like the entire house was suddenly in the dining room, watching us, laughing their asses off at my death sentence. Or Griffin's. I again shook my head at him. "Griff, we're not playing—"

The fucker didn't even let me finish. He grabbed my head and fucking laid one on me. Then the asshole tried to shove his tongue into my startled mouth. Oh my fucking God! Matt better have bleach, because I had an emergent need to gargle with it. I instantly shoved Griffin away from me, but the damage was done. I could still...feel him.

While I warded Griffin off with my hand, I heard a couple people falling from their chairs they were laughing so hard. They wouldn't think it was so fucking funny if it had happened to them. "Dude! What the fuck?"

Griffin gave me a confused expression as he looked me over. "Huh," he said. "Yeah, I don't get what all the fuss is about...I've had better."

Really. He was critiquing me on a kiss I didn't want? Dick. Crossing my arms over my chest, I gave him my best fuck-you eyes. He just wriggled his finger and said, "Maybe if you did this thing with your tongue..."

Asshole. But now that my moment of horror was over and I noticed the state of the room, of my friends, and of Kiera...my mood shifted to amusement. At least he'd made Kiera laugh...and I didn't think I'd ever seen her laugh quite so hard before; she had to continuously wipe the tears from her eyes. It was adorable.

I gave Griffin a light backhand across the chest, then shoved his shoulder away from me with a soft laugh. "Get the fuck out of here, Griffin."

Griffin was—of course—offended that I wasn't thanking him for his suggestion, then he planted one on Anna and made a crack about saving his skills for those who appreciated them. *Please do.* My bandmates were busting up laughing, so were their girlfriends, and so was well, everyone else. I could only close my eyes and shake my head. *Why me?*

Reopening my eyes, I smiled at Kiera, still laughing. Enjoying her joy, I grabbed my beer from the table and motioned to the drinking game we'd *actually* been playing. "Well, needless to say... I'm done."

Someone took my spot, the game resuming as the snickering died down. Walking over to Kiera, I extended my hand. "Dance with me, beautiful girl?"

Kiera sighed at me, a lovesick expression on her face that warmed my entire body, made my stomach tingle with energy. How could she still do that to me? Make me feel like I'd never even held a woman before? It was mystifying...and intoxicating.

She nodded at my suggestion, then let me pull her to her feet. We both stumbled a little; she was farther along than I'd realized. I probably should have removed her from the game sooner. Myself too. I felt pretty light, airy, and uncomplicated. But more than that, I felt electric, overly sensitive to her touch. I couldn't wait to wrap my arms around her.

I navigated us to the center of the packed living room. With the deep thump of the loud music and the sea of bodies around us, it felt like a club in here. But with Kiera's eyes locked on me as relentlessly as mine were locked on hers, it felt private too, like we were alone. I didn't really want to "dance" with her though. I wanted to *move* with her. I melded my body to hers, so every inch of us touched—chest to chest, waist to waist, hip to hip. Her arms looped around my neck, sealing us tight, while my fingers ran over her body in a loop, all the way up, all the way down. It was exquisite torture, a tease of the very best kind. But it wasn't enough.

I shifted our legs so one of mine was between hers. Kiera sucked in a shaky breath as our moves became a lot more suggestive. It ignited me, and my heart began to race as fire surged through my body. God, I loved moving with her.

We were practically simulating sex as we moved, and even half-drunk my body was responding. Resting my forehead against hers, feeling her fast breath on me, I vaguely wondered how long I could tease myself like this before I broke down and did something. I was already aching, already getting far too hard for such a public place, but damn, I didn't want it to stop. She was killing me...and I loved it.

I ran my hand up the front of her shirt, stopping right on her breast. Fuck, did she know how hot she was right now? How fast she was pushing me toward the edge of reason? Wishing there were far fewer layers between us, I ran my thumb over her rigid nipple. The soft noise she made...Jesus. I made myself smile at her, when what I really wanted to do was beg her to take me. And in a way, she did.

Her fingers reached up to clench my hair, yanking my mouth to hers. God, heaven. There was a frantic desperation to the way she kissed me, like she was about to explode if she didn't have me. It enflamed me, made my body hurt, I wanted her so much. We were both breathing so heavily, it made thinking impossible. *I need her. Now.*

I squeezed her nipple, ran my other hand down inside her jeans to feel her ass as she grinded against me, but it wasn't enough. *More.* Like she was reading my mind, Kiera pulled my head down to moan in my ear, "I want you...now."

Fuck. Me.

I pulled back to stare at her, and I knew she could see the desire on my face; I felt drunk with the need of her. Her eyes widened as she stared at me, her lips parted. I couldn't stop staring at her body, at what I wanted. Adjusting our hips, I let her feel what she was doing to me. Just lightly rubbing against her was driving me insane. I looked around, remembering where we were. We needed to get out of here.

There were several eyes staring at me as I searched for somewhere to go. Some of the eyes were amused, some were burning with interest, like if I grabbed one of them, they'd willingly come with me. I didn't want someone with us...and I didn't want to be interrupted by someone bold enough to try butting in. That meant I needed a door with a lock. And there was only one.

Untangling Kiera's fingers from my hair, I leaned down so she could hear me. "Come with me." My voice was rough, needy. So was Kiera's grip on my hand as she nodded.

I worked us through the crowd, ignoring attempts to get my attention. All I could focus on was the hallway leading to the bathroom. But even still, once we were in the hallway, past the bulk of the partiers, I pulled Kiera into me, finding her mouth again. I couldn't resist her, not even for a few more seconds. She moaned against my lips, killing me as I walked backward down the hallway. I heard laughs, amused murmurs, felt myself colliding with people, but I didn't care. Kiera was the only thought on my brain. Kiera and privacy.

I found the bathroom door. The way her mouth moved against mine was so distracting, it took me three tries to open it. Once inside, I flicked on the lights and locked the fucking door. Kiera took that brief intermission to peek at where we were. Adorable frown on her face, she looked up at me. "This is a bathroom."

She must have been expecting a bedroom. But those doors didn't lock, and I didn't entirely trust the people out there to leave us alone. I wasn't going to tell her that though. "Yeah, I know."

Needing her, I returned my mouth to hers. She instantly attacked me, clenching her fingers in my hair, pressing her body against me. The need was so intense, so focused, it almost felt like this was our first time together.

I was about to tell her how much I wanted her, but before I could make a sound, her throaty voice cut through the silence of our fast breaths. "You always make me feel so good...I'm going to make you feel good too, Kellan. I want you so much."

I felt dizzy, lightheaded. High on her. Fuck. I wasn't going to last long if she kept talking like that. But I didn't want her to stop either. I closed my eyes, letting my head drop back as her lips attached to my neck; every touch was liquid fire against my skin. "Oh God...I love it when you're like this."

That made her stop. "Like what...drunk?" I was about to tell her no, but she ran her tongue up my throat. Holy hell...

What did she ask me? "No. Confident...like you finally get it."

She pulled back to look at me, confusion in her beautiful eyes. "Get what?" Then she flicked my lip with her tongue; the world spun as need surged through me, making me ache in the best possible way.

Refocusing, because I needed her to hear this, I told her, "That I'm yours...that you can take me...anywhere, anytime, any way. That you own every piece of me." *Forever.*

As I watched, her eyes started...sizzling. "If I own you, then I want to take you...now...here. I want to make you come."

I gave her a seductive smile, but inside...I was burning. Oh... my...fuck. That was the hottest thing I'd ever heard her say. She was killing me right now. In fact, I might not actually survive this. But she wasn't stopping with words. She pushed me against the counter, rubbing her hips against mine as she yanked my mouth back to hers, claiming me. *Yes...take me.*

"God...yes. I need you, Kiera. Can you feel how much I need you?" *Can you tell I'm barely keeping it together?* She whimpered in my mouth, her fingers drifting to my jeans, tugging. *Goddamn, she wants me so much...*

Blocking out the world, I started lifting up her shirt. She gave up on my jeans and helped me, then helped me remove my shirt. The skin-on-skin contact made me delirious. But even still, I paused to touch my necklace around her throat. *You own me...do I own you too?*

I slid my hand into her bra, gently squeezing her. The moan she let out was loud, aching...needy. It was punctuated by a voice on the other side of the door. "Uh, Kellan? You in there?" Ignoring Matt's voice, I swept aside Kiera's bra to feel that glorious nipple in my mouth. She panted as she held my head to her; her hips swiveling against me bringing me to the edge of something...wonderful.

"Dude, Kellan. I know you and Kiera are in there...people saw you two head that way. Open the door."

"Goddamn it," I muttered, my body somewhat cooling. I knew Matt well enough to know that he wanted something, and he'd pound on the door every five seconds until he completely destroyed the moment to get it. Untangling Kiera from me, I unlocked the door and cracked it open. "What, Matt?" I scowled, eager for him to leave.

Kiera's head rested on my bare chest as Matt glared at me. "Are you about to have sex in my bathroom?"

Well, duh. Wasn't that painfully obvious? "Yes," I told him, closing the door.

Kiera giggled at my answer, but Matt wasn't amused. He blocked the door with his hand. "Kell, we only have one bathroom. I don't want people peeing in my kitchen sink."

With a sigh, I opened the door wider. Matt took in my state of undress, then Kiera's, then snapped his eyes to mine as his cheeks flushed a little. Shaking my head at him, I shrugged. "Bedroom or bathroom." I'd prefer the room with the lock, but I *really* didn't care anymore.

Matt's face scrunched, like he didn't understand. "Bedroom or bathroom? You pick, Matt." *Because there is no way I'm stopping...you have no idea what she just said to me. If you did, you wouldn't be bugging me, so pick a place, and do it now. Because the sex is happening.*

Matt relented with a sigh and an eye roll. "Fine, but make it quick." Way ahead of him, I slammed the door shut and locked it.

Matt added something about cleaning up, but I really wasn't listening to him anymore. Kiera was my only focus. As her mouth reattached itself to mine, I unhooked her bra. Once the material was off her, I ducked down to suck her nipple back into my mouth. She wasn't quiet when she voiced her agreement, and her fingers again tried to unbutton my jeans. She couldn't, so I helped her as I teased her about her lack of talent for stripping me while she was drunk. But then she slipped her hand into my boxers, wrapping her fingers around me, and I couldn't speak, couldn't make a sound other than a needy whimper. *God, yes...*

I pushed her against the wall, harder than I'd intended, but she groaned, "Yes," as her head thudded. Then she was stroking me, and I was ripping clothes off of her before I completely lost it. I had to remove her hand from me so I could finish undressing her. Completely bare, she ran her hands up her body like they were mine.

"Fuck," I muttered. She truly was trying to kill me.

I started shedding my clothes as quickly as I could. Once I was naked, Kiera drank me in, then said, "I want you in me."

Goddamn. She hadn't said it quietly. She'd said it firmly, like an order. And it was fucking hot.

Shit. I needed a minute to regroup. And I knew a great way to distract her. "Not yet," I said with a grin.

She actually pouted. That thrilled me. I dropped to my knees in front of her, cherishing her body with my eyes for a second, before grabbing her leg and putting it up on my shoulder. My head spun as I stared at her, ached for her, then I leaned in to taste her, and Kiera...became unglued. She sagged against the wall, letting out noises that were completely unconscious, completely uninhibited...completely free. Everything seemed to stop, everything seemed to go still, silent, except for Kiera. A part of me knew that was unnatural. We were at a party, there should be a lot of noise, but there wasn't, there was only Kiera...and that somehow felt really right.

My stomach clenched and my cock started to throb in warning as I continuously ran my tongue over her, and I suddenly realized what a horrible idea this was. I wasn't going to make it; I felt like her voice alone was going to make me come if I didn't stop. Breathless, I pulled away from her, and sought her mouth. *Calm down. Give this to her. Make it last. Think of something else...anything else. Like how fucking quiet it is. Someone turned the music off...which means...we're the entertainment now. Fuck. I don't care.*

Kiera grabbed me again, tried to lead me into her. I took her hand away before she became very unsatisfied with me. "I want you inside me...now," she panted. I still needed a second, so I pulled back, teasing her with a quick stroke of my finger. "Oh God, please...take me, Kellan."

A groaned, "Yes," escaped me as my lips found her skin again. Damn, I loved it when she begged. She was desperate for more; I was desperate for more. I started walking us backward, searching for some comfortable place to lay her down. Or stand her up. Whatever. And that was when I hit something, stumbled, and accidentally sat down on the toilet seat. Thank fuck it was closed. I had to laugh at that thought, but Kiera didn't laugh with me. No...she sank herself onto me, claiming me.

My eyes closed as her warm, wetness enveloped me, my head dropped back onto some well-placed towels behind me. "Oh God, Kiera...yes."

She started rocking her hips, slowly, teasingly, and I bit my lip at the glorious agony coursing through me. She did it again, moaning my name, and I opened my eyes to fully absorb the goddess on top of me. "You're beautiful," I told her, my hands searching her body, finally resting on her hips. *I love you so much.*

The look on her face as she bit her lip was one I knew I'd never forget. It was innocence, confidence, love, and wanton abandon, all mixed together. And then her head dropped back, and she started truly moving her hips, taking what she needed from me, vocally letting me know what I was doing to her, and all I could do was stare at her, dumbstruck and overwhelmed. She was...perfect.

"Fuck," I finally muttered, sitting up to kiss her chest.

She asked me not to swear, then she partially stood so she

could dig into me harder. It was so intense, so deep...I would do anything she asked, if she kept doing that. "I'm sorry...fuck, I'm sorry...just please, don't stop."

I couldn't contain it anymore, she was too much, this was too much, and the sounds I was starting to make were just as loud and passionate as hers. I felt the pressure building, and I knew I was right there, but Kiera was too. "Come with me," she begged, her voice strained.

And then it was happening, and I couldn't have stopped it if I wanted to. Kiera fell apart with me, holding me against her as her long cry of ecstasy vibrated around the room, mixing with my own groan. The relief, the high, the satisfaction...the love...I reveled in it as Kiera's hips gently pushed against me, prolonging the moment as she moaned my name.

God...I love this woman.

Knowing without a doubt that we were done, the people on the other side of the locked door started laughing and clapping. Kiera didn't seem to notice much as I held her to me, and I wasn't about to point it out. "I love you," she murmured in my neck.

Pure peace wrapping around me, I murmured, "I love you too." *So much.*

I could have spent the rest of the night like that, cuddling naked on top of a toilet. But eventually, she shivered, and people started knocking on the door again. With a sigh, I helped her remove herself from me. I couldn't keep the smile off my face as we got dressed. I would never be able to forget this night. It was permanently stuck in my brain. And I really hoped it would be stuck in Kiera's too. *I want her to always be that way with me. I want her to own me every night. Every day. Every second.*

When I finally opened the bathroom door and stepped into the hallway, I felt the weight of dozens of eyes on me. The unnatural silence in the house was oppressive, but it only lasted for a second, because the moment we started walking down the hallway, people started whistling and clapping. Fuck. This party was going to be over if Kiera figured out why they were cheering. But she seemed oblivious to the people smacking me on the back, to the jealousy in the guy's eyes as they nodded in approval, to the suggestive stares I was getting from women who seemed to think I'd just set up some sort of ride and they wanted a turn. No, Kiera seemed peacefully oblivious to all of it. Thank God.

But then, once we reached our dancing spot in the middle of the living room, Griffin rushed up to Kiera. If anyone could force the realization into Kiera's head, it would definitely be Griffin. She'd be mortified if she figured it out, and probably pretty upset. I'd spend the rest of the night consoling her, and I didn't want her to feel bad about what we just did. Because having her let go like that...want me like that...take me like that...damn, that was going to stay with me for the rest of my life. I didn't regret a fucking thing, and I didn't want her to either.

Griffin handed Kiera a beer; his face was so impressed and delighted, you would have thought he'd been in the room with us. "Kiera, I think I love you," he gushed. Kiera made a face at him, but she grabbed his offered beer and took a sip.

Griffin was giddy as he smacked me on the chest. "You are the luckiest fucking son of a bitch." He handed me the beer in his other hand, and his joy flipped to a frown. "I mean, I hated you before, but now, I really can't stand you."

While that comment normally would have amused me, I needed the jackass to shut up before he connected the dots for Kiera. Thankfully, she still seemed clueless as she stared at Griffin in confusion. Good. I tried pushing him away to get him to shut up, but jostling him didn't stop his mouth. "That was so hot... like, off the scales hot. You guys should make a porno...I'd totally buy it!"

Kiera sputtered the sip of beer she'd just taken, and I knew those words were penetrating her drunken haze, filling in blanks that I didn't want filled in just yet. *Goddamn it, Griffin.* Her face was starting to pale as the people around us either laughed at Griffin or nodded in agreement with him. Knowing I needed to change the mood in here quick, I shoved Griffin out of my way and hurried over to the silent stereo. I turned it up to nightclub levels again, then hopped on Matt's super-sturdy coffee table. This group needed to be entertained if they were going to forget about the bathroom, and if there was one thing on Earth I was good at, it was entertaining people.

The song playing was a good anthem type song. I started singing it to the people around me, and they started singing it right back. As a group began to form around the coffee table, making a mini stage for me, I extended my hand to Kiera so she could join me in the spotlight. She laughed as she did, and I knew she'd let Griffin's crude comment slide. I'd tell her about it later, because I didn't want her to find out from someone else, but not now. Now was just for having fun.

Chapter 14
GOODBYE

Much to my dismay, the night eventually turned into morning. Partiers started leaving, wishing me luck with a clap on the shoulder. When only a handful of people were left, Matt shut off the music. "Bed...sleep...me..." he muttered, before retreating with Rachel to his room.

Kiera yawned in my arms as we slow danced to silence. Knowing she was done, I led her to the couch. We sat for a moment, but it was pretty clear by Kiera's lethargy that she was seconds away from passing out. I laid down on the couch and Kiera climbed right on top of me, settling herself on my chest, using me as her body pillow. I couldn't stop smiling as I gently stroked her back. This was heaven. And I was really going to miss it.

I forced that awful thought from my tired brain as people collapsed in other furniture around us. A guy in the chair closest to me, leaned over and lightly punched my shoulder. "Dude... your girlfriend is seriously hot." My arms instinctively tightened around her. *I know...back off.* I must have been glaring at the guy, 'cause he raised his hands and leaned back. "Just...the bathroom thing was hot. Totally made me miss my girl..."

His thought trailed off as his expression changed. "She's not here?" I asked, curious.

He shook his head. "Nah, she went to a college back east. We're doing the whole long-distance thing." With a sigh, he let his head drop back. "It fucking sucks. Like *really* fucking sucks. I'm pretty sure she's..." His face hardened, then he shook his head. "It just sucks. I don't recommend it. We should have just broken up..." His face softened again; he looked absolutely miserable.

Ice chilled my veins listening to him. Jesus. Was this my future? I squeezed Kiera tighter, refusing to let her go. "Sorry, man."

The guy shook his head. "Yeah...anyway, your band, you're really good...good luck on the road."

His gaze took in Kiera on my chest, then his face hardened again, and he shot up off the chair like it was on fire. I had to swallow the sudden lump of anxiety in my throat as he stalked off. No...that wouldn't be us. That couldn't be us.

Someone else took lonely-guy's seat, and I silently prayed they wouldn't want to talk. But of course, they did. "Okay...what *exactly* happened in that bathroom. Like play-by-play. Details. Come on, help a brother out."

Rolling my eyes, I shook my head at him. "Nothing happened."

He gave me a *really* face. Then he sighed. "Come on...you've got to give me something. That sounded so fucking hot!"

With a laugh, I closed my eyes. "Sleeping...can't talk..."

The guy socked my shoulder, but he took the hint and left me alone.

A couple more people wanted to comment on my night after details-guy left. I was polite, but vague. Even though it had been a relatively public event, it was still none of their business. Eventually the questions and comments stopped, and I drifted off to sleep. Lonely-guy must have been stuck in my head though because the dream I had...wasn't good.

I was standing in a generic room with Kiera. Her expression was so blank, it was ice-cold. It wasn't an expression I was used to seeing on her, especially around me. The air was thick with tension, and I had no idea why. Until she spoke. "We're over, Kellan."

My heart started racing in my chest. "What do you mean?" I had to be misunderstanding her...but somehow, I knew I wasn't.

She lifted her hands to indicate the room we were in. "You're never here. And I need to be with someone who's *here*. I can't do this anymore."

My chest flared with pain; it felt like I was having a heart attack. "Kiera, please." *Don't do this.*

I tried to hold her, but she brushed off my attempt with an irritated look on her face, like she was brushing off mosquitos. "No. This isn't enough for me." Crossing her arms, she pointedly lifted her eyebrows. "*You're* not enough for me."

I woke with a start, my heart pounding, my head pounding. Goddamn it...I should have just stayed awake. *Relax, it was just a bad dream. She's still yours...none of that actually happened.* But still, the horror of what dream-Kiera had said wouldn't leave me. *You're not enough for me.*

I know...but stay anyway.

I felt Kiera stirring on my chest. My head was still replaying that moment, and a small part of me was...breaking. But I knew I couldn't blame real-Kiera for something my head made her say, so I closed my eyes, forced calm into my body and focused on what I knew was true. Right now, she loved me, and she was here, in my arms. *Enjoy it...while you have it.*

"Mornin'," I murmured, hugging her into me, savoring her.

"I'm right here, you don't have to be so noisy," she grumpily replied.

Amusement dulled the lingering pain, washing it away so that I barely felt it anymore. I *did* feel a headache pounding its way through my skull, but I welcomed that kind of pain. I'd take physical abuse over emotional abuse any day.

After making sure Kiera was okay, and not suffering too badly after her night, I decided to see what she remembered. Because she was going to need to know what had happened before my bandmates woke up. Well, before Griffin woke up.

Since teasing her was second nature, when she mentioned she was thirsty, I saw an opportunity, and asked if she wanted water from the kitchen...or the bathroom. Then I waited to see if the lightbulb clicked on. Remembering that moment, the total lack of restraint, the unbridled passion, the possessive way she took what she wanted from me...God, it turned me on just thinking about it, and I couldn't keep the devilish grin off my face. I think that finally clued her in more than anything else.

"Why do you look like...?"

She sat bolt upright on my lap, shifting all her weight onto my groin. I grunted in pain as the boys were squeezed in ways they shouldn't be squeezed this early in the morning. *Ow.* Eyes wide with alarm, Kiera practically yelled, "Did we have sex in the bathroom?"

I flinched as my head throbbed in protest. Kiera's expression matched mine; she'd also hurt herself with that volume. When my head simmered down, I cracked an eye open to see Kiera's cheeks were turning a delightful shade of red. Thoughts of her riding me, owning me, tumbled through my brain. "Oh...yeah," I drawled.

Her eyes widened again as I smiled at her. I really hoped she remembered because that...was quite a moment. She suddenly covered her mouth with her hands, and I could practically see the memories replaying in her eyes. *So, she does remember. Good.*

"Oh my God," she said, shaking her head. "Did they all hear us?"

Biting my lip, I avoided eye contact. She wasn't going to like this. "Well...we really weren't being quiet, and it is a pretty small bathroom...so..." *And the fuckers turned off the music so they could hear everything.* I knew better than to mention that though. I'd never get her to go to a party again.

Kiera groaned and dropped her head to my chest. "Oh my God."

I rubbed her back in sympathy. "Don't worry about it, Kiera. Everyone told me they thought it was hot."

She snapped her head up, her eyes narrowed. "Everyone?"

"Just the few I talked to after you passed out." Saying that made the conversation with lonely-guy try to resurface in my head, but I shoved him—and my dream—to a dusty corner. I'd rather focus on the drum beating against my brain than relive that nightmare.

Kiera didn't seem any less embarrassed as she dropped her head back to my chest and murmured, "Oh my God," again.

I tried to reassure her, let her know how much I liked her letting go like that. If she only knew how long that memory was going to stay with me, how fondly I was going to treasure it... But she was having a hard time getting past the public nature of it to feel the way I felt. Especially once she realized that Griffin wanted us to make a porno because he'd heard every moan and groan. It wouldn't surprise me in the least if he was the one who'd turned down the stereo. Asshole.

Trying to make the moment a bright spot for Kiera, I told her that at least it would be a night she wouldn't forget. She smirked at me, but that was about it. So I told her not to be embarrassed, because I wasn't. "You were hot, and every guy in that place wished they were me in that bathroom. I don't feel the least bit bad that every man was jealous. As long as you're only mine."

That finally made a genuine smile grace her lips. "I am."

"Good." *Because I don't know what I would do without you.*

Eventually Kiera and I got up off the couch. Okay, I got up while holding her and helped her to her feet. My girl was suffering pretty badly from last night. We made our way to the kitchen, shuffling around passed out partygoers scattered around the floor. I started making a pot of coffee, then filled a glass with water for Kiera; she instantly started chugging it. Leaning against the counter while I waited for the coffee, I wrapped my arms around Kiera. No matter where we physically woke up, this ritual, right here, was home to me. This might be what I missed most of all.

Matt came into the kitchen while Kiera coughed on some over-eager water consumption; he looked like death. "Hey, guys... good morning."

I threw on a bright smile. "Mornin'. How do you feel?"

I already knew the answer just by looking at him, but it was fun to hear him say it. "Peachy," he grumbled.

Amused by the look on his face, I laughed a little as I popped my thumbs through Kiera's belt buckle loops. Matt seemed peeved by my merriment. He poured himself a glass of water, then told me, "God, it's annoying how chipper you are in the morning." He paused to take a long drink. "I hope you're not like that on the road. It would really get on my nerves."

His comment made me laugh, but the sentiment behind it kind of ripped a hole through me. I didn't want to leave yet. Or maybe ever. But Matt's next words confirmed that time wasn't going to wait for me; this was happening. "Bus leaves in a few hours, so we should start getting people up...especially Griffin."

With a reluctant sigh, I nodded. We had to go. It was time.

Things were okay as we started getting ready to leave—Kiera just about killed me by accidentally saying something super suggestive to Matt; I swear to God, it sounded like she thanked him for letting us have sex in his bathroom. Poor guy had to leave the room after she said it. I was truly going to miss the embarrassing things Kiera unintentionally sputtered.

After coffee, the poker players in the dining room finally finished their game, and eventually we got the rest of the stragglers to leave Matt's house. That was right around when Evan and Jenny rejoined our group—guess they'd left the party sometime while Kiera and I were...busy.

Yes, everything was fine...until Jackass woke up.

Stumbling into the living room, he jerked his thumb toward the bathroom, where Matt was showering. "Kiera, when Matt's done, what's say you and me go suds up?" He kissed the air, like he was kissing her, and my blood started boiling. Then he took it one step further, and absolutely crossed the line. "I want to hear you moan my name like you did Kell's." This wasn't the first time Griffin had suggested sex with him to Kiera. It was going to be the last.

Just about everyone smacked him with something, but that wasn't enough for me. Maybe it was because I was still a little unsettled by my dream, maybe it was because I *really* couldn't stomach the thought of Griffin having sex with her, or maybe it was because I could feel goodbye in the air and I was dreading it, but his comment pissed me off way more than usual. Striding up to him, I grabbed a fistful of his chin-length hair and pulled his face into mine. "Knock it off, Griffin, or I'll knock it off for you."

Evan tried to get me to calm down, Anna tried to push me away, but I wasn't moving. Not until this sunk in. Kiera was mine, and he needed to back off. She didn't need to be sexually harassed by him, she didn't need him twisting a great moment for us into something embarrassing and dirty; I didn't want her to feel that way about it. I wanted her to feel confident and beautiful, like she should always feel. And dipshit wasn't helping with that.

Griffin looked stunned as he stared at me. I'd hit him before, during my darker days, but that had been quick and to the point. I'd never gotten in his face like this before, scaring the shit out of him, but a warning seemed more appropriate than just decking him. Hopefully it sank in.

But then...the dumbass started laughing. "Did you want another kiss, bro? All you had to do was ask."

The coiled spring inside me started releasing, so I let him go. He immediately doubled over in laughter. "Dude, you should have seen your face! That was awesome! I really thought you were gonna hit me."

So much for trying to be intimidating. Sometimes there was just no getting through to Griffin. Next time, maybe I'd punch him first, then intimidate him later. Annoyed, I started retreating to the kitchen for some space. Griffin's voice followed me. "Say it again, Kell! Knock it off, or I'll knock it off for you. Ah, that was classic."

Once I was in the kitchen, I inhaled a deep, cleansing breath. I shouldn't let him get to me. Especially since we were going to be damn-near inseparable for the next six months. Great.

Kiera appeared a few seconds later, a soft smile on her face. "Thanks for trying," she said, looping her arms around my waist. Her brows furrowed as she studied my face. "Are you okay? You don't usually get so physical with him."

Rubbing her arms, I considered what to tell her. *I hate this* seemed obvious. So did *I'm going to miss you*. So did *Are you sure I need to do this*? Kiera had already told me multiple times on multiple occasions that I needed to go, that it would be good for us, good for the band...good for everyone. Her continual support was one of the main reasons I was following through, but I kind of wanted her to waver...kind of wanted her to change her mind and beg me to stay. Would I stay if she asked? I honestly had no idea.

"I'm fine," I told her. "He just...he crawls under my skin sometimes. And then makes a home there."

Kiera snorted; it was adorable. "Yeah, I know the feeling..." Leaning her chin on my chest, she gazed up at me. "I really love you."

Smiling, I squeezed her tight. "I really love you too." *So much it's killing me.*

Before I was emotionally ready, we were in my car, driving to the meeting spot for the tour buses. My stomach hurt, my head hurt...my heart hurt. Why did this feel so...permanent? Like nothing would be the same after this? Like Kiera and I wouldn't be the same after this. I wanted to shake the feeling, wanted to pretend this wasn't a life-altering moment, but I just couldn't.

There was something dark in the air...and it was scaring the shit out of me.

Kiera seemed affected too. She was quiet as she sat beside me, but with every block we traveled, her frown lines deepened, and she kept rolling her eyes and shaking her head. It was almost like she was having an argument with herself. Or she was trying to convince herself that everything would be fine. That was an argument I understood since I had it constantly.

Remembering her ridiculous concerns about me—about fame and what was heading my way, in her eyes—I could easily picture just what scenario she was dreading. "It won't happen," I told her, putting my hand on her thigh.

She seemed surprised as she twisted to look at me. With a smile, I explained. "Whatever bad scenario you've created in your head, where I become a rich and famous douche and leave you high and dry...it won't happen that way."

The way she frowned let me know I'd nailed it. "I thought you said you couldn't read minds."

That remembered conversation made me laugh. "I can't...I just know how you think is all." More seriously, I spelled out her fears as I saw them. "You think you're not enough for me. You think I'll see all the hot tail in front of me and I'll dive into it without a moment's hesitation. You think I'll cheat...because I won't be able to help myself."

God, was that really how she saw me? That had been her fear once upon a time—the stumbling block that had made her choose Denny over me. That somehow, she wouldn't be enough to hold my interest long term. That we'd fizzle, and I'd seek someone else. It was such an odd worry to me. She would never lose her appeal. She would never not mean *everything*. She was the sun to me. I didn't just love her, I *needed* her. But if she really felt that way, still, then what would she do once I was gone? Especially if she was convinced that I was whoring again. *Fuck me. Why did I have to think that?*

Kiera sighed...and read my mind. "And now you're thinking

that I'll be so lonely and depressed, imagining you with every starlet wannabe out there, that I'll find comfort in another man's arms. You think I'll cheat...because I'll assume that you already are."

I almost stopped the car. Fuck. *Yes, that's exactly what I worry about.* That was why I'd left so many reminders of me scattered around her life. Why I prayed that my left-behind affection would be enough to keep her faithful to me. And how sad was that? Could we do this?

Forcing myself to keep driving, keep going, I mumbled, "Well, aren't we a pair." How fucked up were we? How could we possibly survive? *And after she leaves me, how can I live without her?*

Like she could tell I was about to lose my resolve, lose my will to test our fragile faith in each other, Kiera laid her head on my shoulder and placed a Band-aid over the ache. "I won't, Kellan. Even if I do think that about you, and I'm not saying that I will think that, but...either way, I won't...I'm yours."

Tension started melting from my body with her admission. She was flat-out saying she wouldn't cheat on me. We might not work, we might break up, but she wouldn't betray me. Hopefully, if she found herself at that kind of crossroad, she would cut me out of her life before she...moved on. That was a small comfort, and even though I knew it might not happen like that, especially if she got...swept up in something, it was still nice to hear.

Leaning my head against hers, I returned the favor. "And I won't...because I've only ever been yours." There was no need to promise her that I'd break up with her first, because there was literally no one else for me. I wouldn't ever be with another woman after Kiera. Even if we did end...I was done. I'd rather be celibate than put my heart out there again. And I didn't think I could have sex without my heart anymore. There was just no point.

We arrived at the parking lot where three huge buses were

waiting. I pulled into a spot beside Evan's car, my heart heavy as I shut off the engine. This was it. My bandmates climbed out of their vehicles with their girlfriends, all smiles and excitement. It made me feel guilty that I didn't feel the same way as them. It also worried me. Evan and Matt...they were so unfazed about leaving Jenny and Rachel. Like it didn't even occur to them that the pair of girls wouldn't be there when we got back. It wasn't even a thought in their mind, and it was *all* I could think about with Kiera. It felt ominous. I hated it.

Kiera was watching the numerous band members, and the mass of people wishing their friends and loved ones well. I could see the same moroseness on her face, and I knew her thoughts were similar to mine. It didn't make me feel any better. Needing a distraction, I pulled the keys out of the ignition, and handed them to her.

She looked confused as her fingers wrapped around them. "Take care of her for me, okay?"

Her eyes widened with—I swear to God—excitement, and I had a little trouble letting go of the keys. "You're giving me your car?" she asked, looking pleased as punch.

I immediately shook my head. "I'm just letting you borrow her. I'll want her back." Kiera's corresponding grin was a little unsettling. The Chevelle might be a muscle car...but she wasn't a toy. "Make sure you get the oil changed and fill her up with premium...and don't drive on the hills if it snows and no joy riding..." A horrible thought struck me, and I added, "And don't let Anna drive her. I've seen what she did to Denny's car." Lord help me if I came back and my baby was littered with shit. I'd definitely never leave again.

Kiera smiled at the look on my face. "I won't," she promised. "I'll keep your baby in mint condition, Kellan."

That made me smile. Deep down, I knew Kiera would treat her well. And she would treat Kiera well too. "It just seems a shame for her to sit in a driveway while you argue with Anna over who gets that P.O.S. Honda." I paused to run my fingers through

Kiera's hair, to drink her in. "I want you to be able to get to... wherever you need to go while I'm gone."

Her eyes were moist as she tucked the keys into her pocket. What felt like a lifetime of memories flashed through my mind as I stared at the keys I could no longer see. Finding the car, fixing her up, driving her home to Seattle, Kiera's face when she saw her, driving Kiera to school, fighting in the rain...stolen moments, loving moments, painful moments. There was a lot of Kiera tied up in my car now, and parting with it made the ache of parting with her even more pronounced.

Needing air, I finally said goodbye to my baby, and opened the door.

Kiera followed as I grabbed my guitar from the backseat, then my bag from the trunk. Holding Kiera's hand, I started heading over to where Matt and Evan were talking with some of the guys from Avoiding Redemption. Kiera suddenly seized up and stopped walking with me. Confused, I looked back at her.

She shook her head like she thought I was crazy. "Don't you know who they are?" She whispered that, even though we were way too far away for them to hear us.

"Yeah, they're sort of the reason we're on this tour. I was going to go say hello and thank them." By the horrified look on her face, you'd think I'd just suggested we go skinny-dipping with Griffin. "I've heard you sing their stuff. Don't you want to meet them?" I asked.

She shook her head so hard, I worried she'd hurt herself. Amused at her refusal, I started pulling her toward the band. If this was really going to be my life, then she'd need to get used to it. Might as well start now. "They're just people, Kiera. They started out as nobodies just like me." Stopping, I yanked her into my side and cocked an eyebrow at her. "And you don't seem to have a problem talking to me."

Letting out a nervous giggle, she let me lead her toward the guys. She was shaking when we stepped up to them though; even I could feel that. Wanting to relax her, I whispered in her ear,

"You're trembling just like some of my fans do...I'm a little jealous. I'll try not to be offended that I don't make you...quiver."

A loud laugh escaped her, right as the two guys from the band turned to face us. The guys gave her a funny look, and I could tell by the way she clenched my hand that she was mortified. Oops. But so cute.

Dropping my bag, I held out my hand to a member of the band that I recognized from some concert footage Matt had shown me. This was Justin, the lead singer; his signature choppy, layered blond hair and the long, scripted tattoo across his collarbones were pretty distinctive. "Kellan Kyle, D-Bag. I wanted to thank you for inviting us to this."

Justin's pale eyes seemed genuinely pleased as he shook my hand. "Yeah, man, we're honored to have you. You guys rocked the festival."

Justin's band was really good, so I sincerely appreciated that. "Thanks." Kiera was trying to hide behind my shoulder, trying to melt into the background, unnoticed. I wasn't about to let her. Like it or not, this was part of my world, and so was she. And she didn't need to be afraid of this. She should stand beside me, confident and comfortable. Looking down, I bumped her shoulder. "This is my girlfriend, Kiera." She instantly gave me evil eyes. Chuckling at the look on her face, I told Justin, "She's a huge fan of yours...more so than she is of me, I think."

I could almost see all of the blood rushing to Kiera's feet as Justin turned his full attention to her, and I knew, in her head, right now, she was murdering me. Justin had to notice that she was losing it, but he didn't make a big deal about it, just smiled politely and extended his hand to her. *Yeah, I can hang with this guy.*

As Kiera reluctantly reached for his hand, Justin said, "It's always nice to meet a fan. What's your favorite song?"

She connected with his palm and as I watched, all cognitive thought left her eyes. It was like she was mentally stuck, and could barely process what he'd asked, forget about actually answering him. Her cheeks flushed as she fumbled for words, and I had to frown at her reaction to him. *Really?*

Finally, she mumbled, "I like them all..." and I had to laugh at her adorableness. God...she killed me. She'd been shaking Justin's hand the entire time she'd been thinking of a song. She immediately dropped it when she realized that and attached herself to my side like glue. Good.

I saw Justin laugh a little, but he quickly hid it with a smile. Looking back at me, he clapped my shoulder. "Well, we're just about ready to roll. We'll see you later."

I nodded at them and watched them walk over to the first bus and get inside. Then I looked down at Kiera with an eyebrow raised. "You couldn't think of one song, could you?" She sighed and shrugged. While the embarrassment was cute, the fawning over another rock star was a little bit of an irritant, to be honest. At least I didn't have to worry about Justin; he was coming with me. "I'm not sure how I feel about another man making you so nervous," I told her. Slipping my arms around her, I added, "I want to be the one that makes you sweat."

She took my comment literally, not suggestively, as I'd meant it. "Oh my God, was I sweaty?"

Squatting down to look her in the eye, I gave her a playful, yet sort of serious scowl. She laughed, then wrapped her arms around my neck. "I am your biggest fan, Kellan Kyle." Leaning up, she gave me a soft kiss. "And don't you forget it."

Her comment warmed me, as did her mouth attaching to mine. Between our kiss, I murmured, "Well, I do aim to please the fans." Then I brushed my tongue along hers. She smacked me for my comment, and I laughed and pulled her into me. I just needed a minute to revel in her softness, her sweetness, her taste, her smell, her feel...all of it. Kiera tangled her fingers in my hair, sending bolts of electricity through my body, and our tender kiss quickly grew heated and hungry.

Just as I was wondering if I had time to lay her down on my backseat, my shoulder was tapped on. "Uh, man, it's time to go."

We broke apart and I saw Evan and Jenny standing there. Both of them looked pained, teary. Matt and Rachel were behind them, saying their tender goodbyes. Anna and Griffin were deep down each other's throats...also saying goodbye. Everyone was saying goodbye...fuck, this was it. My chest squeezed so hard, I cringed with the pain of it. Like Evan had seen it, he reached down and grabbed my bag for me, giving me more time. God, I owed him for that.

Evan gave Kiera a quick hug, then he started walking with Jenny toward bus three, our bus. Swallowing the knot of sorrow in my throat, I looked back at Kiera. Her eyes were wide, and she was trembling again. But not for Justin this time. Gently grabbing her cheeks, I gazed at her, memorizing her. *I don't want to go...but I have to.*

Her eyes were molten jade, shimmering with pain. It was almost too much to bear. "This isn't goodbye, okay. There are no goodbyes...not between us." Lowering my head, I rested my forehead against hers. "This tour is just me being gone for another show...a really long one. But when it's over, I'm coming home to you, to slip into your warm, inviting bed, like I always do..."

My throat started closing up, the ache of leaving her stealing my voice. Kiera nodded, and I swallowed through the pain, so I could tell her one last thing. One last assurance. One final plea for her to wait for me. "I'll still be with you every night, Kiera. Every night, no matter where I am, I'm crawling into bed with you. Our bed will be a lot bigger, miles wide, but it will still just be you and me inside it...okay?"

She nodded against me again, still silent, still shaking. "This doesn't have to change anything...if we don't let it. So, let's not let it, all right?" *Please...don't stop loving me. Don't forget about me. Don't let me go. Don't let us go.*

I could feel the tears down her cheeks now. My own were burning against my eyelids. "All right..." she choked out.

I pulled back to search her face. She looked...desolate. No. I didn't want to hurt her like this. "Are you okay?"

And right before my eyes, she fell apart. Choking back a sob, tears flowing freely, she shook her head, and started spouting frantic, panicked words. "No, no, I'm not okay. I've changed my mind. I don't want you to go. I don't want this. I don't want you to leave. I want you to stay here with me. I want you to give it all up and stay here with me...please."

And then she started to sob in earnest. It tore me open, seeing her pain. I never wanted to hurt her like this. I almost told her, "*Okay.*" I even inhaled a breath, prepared to do it, but as I did, I knew I couldn't. This wasn't just about us. Plus...everyone else had said goodbye without it feeling so...monumental. I wanted that for us. I wanted the comfort and safety that came from trust, and I *knew* Kiera and I would never get there if we didn't relax our hold on each other. We needed to let go, so we could be stronger, better. Even though it scared the living fuck out of me, I had to leave.

But watching her lose it...oddly enough, it was doing something else to me, besides cause me pain. In a weird way, it was also healing me. I'd been waiting for her to fall apart like she had for Denny. A dark, twisted part of me had been *wanting* it. But she'd always seemed so calm, so upbeat, so supportive. It was surprisingly nice to see the grief. To *see* the love that she had for me. She didn't want me to leave either. She *was* going to miss me.

I let out a long, relieved exhale, and I felt stress I hadn't even known I'd been carrying slide off of me. Smiling at her, I started brushing the tears away. "Good, I'm glad to hear you say that. I really thought this wasn't affecting you." I gave her two soft kisses before pulling back to gaze at her. Her sobs slowed as she locked onto my eyes. "I love you too, Kiera...so much. I'm gonna miss you...every second."

She nodded, swallowed, and then closed her eyes. She inhaled a deep breath, and I could see her trying to relax, trying to control the pain, trying to transform the misery into something positive. Watching her do it was inspiring, and I felt my own mood shifting as I studied her.

Then her eyes snapped open. "You'll be gone," she whispered, looking both surprised and saddened. *Yes...I know.* Her face looked like she meant something specific though. When she could see I didn't understand, she added, "This will be our first Christmas...together...and you'll be gone."

She looked like she was going to start breaking down again, but I saw an opportunity. With a reassuring smile, I told her, "I won't be working over the holidays. I do get some time off."

A sigh left her lips. "But who knows where you'll be. You couldn't possibly fly across the country just to spend a couple of days with me."

Really? I'd fly from one end of the earth to the other just to spend an hour *with you. Less than an hour.* "Why not? People do it all the time."

She shrugged, looking guilty for even asking for me to be inconvenienced for her. Didn't she realize it wasn't an inconvenience at all? I'd be ecstatic to meet up with her. Best day of my life. "Where will you be for Christmas?" I asked her.

Shaking her head, she shrugged again and said, "With my family in Ohio, I guess. I'll probably spend my winter break there."

Perfect. "Then I'll meet you there...in Ohio." She tried to protest, but I cut her off with a kiss. "No, I've always wanted to meet your parents, see your hometown. When I get the time off, I'll come to you." I couldn't contain my excitement as I thought about it. This was just what we needed—plans. "We'll do Christmas with your family. It'll be great, Kiera."

She sighed, then nodded, adorably biting her lip. "All right... it's a date."

I leaned down to kiss her, and I never wanted to stop. Various band members flowed past us, getting on their buses, but we ignored them. I even ignored Griffin, who had the balls to murmur, "Yes, Kellan...God, yes." That almost got me to release her, but kissing Kiera was too important. The only thing that finally did get me to stop was the bus driver yelling, "Hey! If you're supposed to be on the bus, get on now. We're leaving with or without you!"

With a sigh, I stopped kissing her. I had to swallow the lump in my throat as I forced myself to move away from her; it was surprisingly difficult to get my feet to move anywhere that wasn't toward her. Our hands moved down each other's arms, and I savored the connection right until the very end, when our fingertips brushed together. And then we were apart. Separate. The loss of her hit me like a blow to the gut, especially when she started sobbing again. God, I couldn't do this. It was too hard.

But I didn't have a choice. And if I didn't go now, I'd fuck things up for the rest of my band. I couldn't screw them over because I had attachment issues.

Adjusting my guitar on my back, I turned from her and strode purposely to the bus. This wasn't goodbye. There were no goodbyes. The driver smirked at me as he closed the door behind me. "Glad you could join us."

I know, I know. Sorry. I nodded at him, then looked for my band. The front half of the bus was a bunch of bench seats with small tables between them, and my friends were all seated at one near the back, near the tiny cubbies that were passing as beds. I tossed my guitar onto one of the bottom beds and joined the guys. Evan clapped me on the back, sympathy in his eyes. Griffin bounced up and down on the seat, like a little kid on a field trip. "Can you believe this shit, Kell?"

I gave him a brief smile in answer. I wasn't really in the mood to talk.

The windows lining the bus opened quite a bit, and band members were sticking their heads out to say goodbye to the people they were leaving behind. Evan waved at Jenny, then let me share his spot so I could say goodbye to Kiera. She was still where I'd left her, standing with Jenny, Rachel, and Anna. I gave her a small wave as I leaned on the window.

The bus driver did a quick headcount, then the bus rumbled to life. The other guys ducked back inside as the bus started moving, but I stayed put, staring at Kiera staring at me. She was crying. I fought back my own tears as I watched her. The bus started moving faster, but I still didn't sit down. I stared at Kiera, just as she stared at me, for as long as I could. Until finally we were too far away, and I couldn't see her anymore. Then I closed the window and twisted to slump into the seat. *She's gone. No... I'm gone.* But not forever. I'd be back, and she'd be waiting. She had to be. I wouldn't survive any other scenario.

Evan and Matt both had the same contemplative look on their faces as they sat there, staring at the table. I had to assume my face was the same as theirs. If it weren't for Griffin, grinning and smacking his hands on the table like he was playing the bongos, our section would have been swirling with so much melancholy, it probably would have been a physical thing, hovering in the air. Evan was right; I wasn't the only one who was going to be missing someone.

Inhaling a deep breath, I made myself relax. We needed to snap out of this funk. Matt was sitting directly across from me, chewing gum; he still had the wrapper in his hand, unconsciously playing with it as he blankly stared at nothing. I motioned for him to give it to me. He bunched his brows but handed it over. Crumpling it up, I set it on the table, then lined it up with Griffin. Evan and Matt were watching with small smiles on their faces, while Griffin obliviously watched the guys sitting across the aisle from us. I flicked the paper with my finger, nailing him right in the face. Matt and Evan instantly started laughing. Mission accomplished.

Griffin scowled as he looked over at me. He grabbed the paper from where it had landed on the table and halfheartedly chucked it at me. With a laugh, I easily batted it away. "Douchewads," he murmured. "I'm gonna go mingle." Then he got up and found a table full of new people to bug.

Matt snorted, then followed after him. While Evan relaxed back in his seat, looking a lot happier, I suddenly remembered something. I had nonstop access to Kiera resting in my pocket.

No time like the present to call her. And besides...I really wanted to make sure she was okay. Smiling, I pulled out my cell phone and called her number.

I could hear her laughing before she spoke. Good. "Hello?" she giggled.

"Hey, is it too early to miss you?" I playfully asked. Evan rolled his eyes at me, shaking his head.

Kiera's joyous laugh met my ear again. "No, it's never too early for that. I miss you too, Kellan."

Evan's face and Kiera's admittance made me laugh. "Good." A wonderful thought struck me as I pictured her grinning at me. "Is it too early for phone sex?"

Evan raised an eyebrow at me, and I bit my lip to not laugh. I knew Kiera would never agree to do that—not with where we currently were, but it did make me wonder...would she, if we were alone?

"Kellan!" she screeched, confirming my assumption.

She was so cute; I couldn't stop the laugh that came out. Especially when she started stammering, too flustered to even speak. Oh yeah, when we were alone, that was happening. I'd never had a reason to try phone sex before. There was never anyone I wanted to be with who wasn't physically in front of me before, but now...I couldn't wait to make her come just by using my voice. Just thinking about it was starting to turn me on.

"I'm just teasing, Kiera." *For the moment.* "I'm glad you're okay. I thought you might be a blubbering mess by now."

"Yeah, well, your recruits have done their job well."

She seemed a little miffed by that, but I loved it. *Thank you, Jenny.* "Good, then part one of my plan has been successful."

Her confusion was adorable. "Part one? Wait...what plan?"

"Just a little something to keep you occupied while I'm gone." *To make sure you never get the chance to forget about me.*

"Hmmm, I see," she murmured. And damn...something about the purr in her voice when she said that was really starting to light my fire, so to speak. This was going to be a painful six months. I could already tell. But no, I was going to see her for Christmas. And that wasn't all that far away.

A content sigh left me as I smiled. "I'm liking this phone idea you had. This is nice, being able to talk to you whenever I want to." This would definitely make being apart bearable.

"Yeah, see, I knew you'd like it better than handcuffs."

Well, damn. "Oh, hey now...I didn't say that," I murmured with a laugh. I couldn't stop the image that popped into my head. God, I should *not* be thinking about her chained to my bed. I did not need a stiffy while Evan was sitting right next to me. But then I heard a sound that cooled my fire...and filled me with longing. The throaty growl of a really fucking cool car. "Did you just start my baby?" I asked with a sigh. Was it wrong that I missed the Chevelle too?

Kiera laughed, amused by my obsession with my car. "Well, I do have to drive her home, so...yeah."

I immediately sat up straighter. "Well, you shouldn't drive and talk on the phone, so I'll let you go." I didn't want my baby —*or her*—injured because we were chatting, and she was distracted.

I could tell she was frowning as she murmured, "Okay...I love you."

Loving this constant connection to her, a happy sigh left me. "I love you too. I'll call you later tonight."

We said goodbye, then I disconnected and put the phone back in my pocket. Evan was looking at me funny as I did. "What?" I asked.

He twisted in his seat to face me. "That conversation reminded me of something...I think we need to talk."

Genuinely clueless, I scrunched my face trying to think about anything we would possibly need to talk about that would make him look so...annoyed. The crack about phone sex? It wasn't like I'd actually whip it out and jack-off in front of him. I had *some* class. "Okay...about what?"

Lips pursed, he lifted an eyebrow at me. "The photo."

"What pho...?" My words died as I stared at him open-mouthed. Oh...right. *That* photo. "Jenny told you?" I said, cringing.

Lips still twisted, he nodded. "Yep. Right after she did it."

Biting my lip, I searched Evan's face for signs of violence. Would he hit me for that? I probably should have cleared it with him first. No, I *definitely* should have cleared it with him first. Asking his girlfriend to take a very sexy, nearly nude photograph probably crossed about a dozen guy-code lines. Damn it. Sometimes I didn't think things through well enough.

"I..." With a long exhale, I shrugged. "I'm sorry. I should have asked you. I just...it didn't occur to me. Jenny's not...I don't see her like that. She's just...so artistic, you know? And I couldn't do it myself, and she said she'd help, and then they were throwing water on me, and it was really fucking cold, and it just didn't seem..." He was still just staring at me as I rambled. I stopped and let out another long sigh. "Fuck, man, I'm sorry." Tilting my head, I showed him my jaw. "Here...hit me. You'll feel better. Come on."

Evan started laughing, and I furrowed my brows, confused. "Dude, I'm not mad at you. If anyone could take that shot for you, it was Jenny. You made the right call."

Shaking my head, I tried to understand. "If that didn't bother you, then why...?"

His eyes narrowed. "You made her delete them all? She was really proud of those shots, and you didn't let her keep *one*? Really? It might have been your body, but it was her work, so she kind of owned it too. You should have let her keep some to put in her portfolio."

My jaw dropped as I stared at him. "I'm...sorry?"

With a grin, he shook his head. Then he punched me in the arm. "I can't believe you asked my girlfriend to take a nude photo of you. Asshole."

Seeing that he was more amused than upset, I laughed and rubbed my shoulder. "I wasn't nude, I swear."

He laughed too as he relaxed in his seat. "Yeah, I know." Twisting his head to me, he raised an eyebrow. "You'd be dead if you'd been nude." He laughed after he said it, shaking his head. "Asshole," he murmured again.

"Sorry," I repeated, still laughing.

Guess he was a *smidge* mad at me. Matt might be too, if Rachel had mentioned her part in the photography session. Damn. Guess I owed him an apology as well. And I should probably say something to Griffin for overreacting this morning. Look at me, offending people left and right. But through the sea of sorrys that I needed to make, there was one apology that was sticking out way more than the others.

Inhaling a deep breath, I pulled out my phone again...and called Denny.

It took a while for him to pick up, and when he did...he sounded half-dead. "Yeah?"

I instantly cringed. "Oh fuck...it's super early again, isn't it?"

"Hey, Kellan...yeah, it's pretty early."

"Sorry. I just...I needed to apologize for what I said...when I was wasted last night. You know, about..." *Don't make me spell it out, please.*

Denny sighed. "Yeah, I know *exactly* what you're talking about." He let out a long exhale. "It's fine. I know you weren't saying it to be...I'm fine, Kellan."

Angling my head away from Evan and the others on the bus, I said, "Yeah, okay, I just...I feel really bad. I'm sorry."

"I know you are." The line was silent for a while, then he said, "So did you leave? Are you on the road?"

I looked back at the bus full of people smiling, laughing...picking on Griffin. "Yeah, we just took off."

"Adventure awaits, huh? Well, I'm sure you'll have...fun."

The way he said it was odd, and I couldn't tell exactly what he meant by it. Because it almost sounded like he thought I was going to have fun by being bad. Being dirty. Being *me*. Well, pre-Kiera me. A part of me wanted to assure him that I wasn't going to screw around on Kiera...but that was just too weird to say. *Have no fear, Denny, I won't cheat on the woman I stole from you.* God, I was a dick. It was no great wonder that he thought that way about me. No, the only surprise here was that he still talked to me at all.

The silence between us became awkward, until finally Denny cleared his throat. "Anyway, I should try and get some more sleep. Good luck, Kellan."

An odd swell of shame washed over me. "Yeah, thanks, Denny."

I was just about to tell him goodbye when he lightly laughed. "And can you *please* learn about time zones?"

A smile broke over me, lightening my mood. "Yes...sorry."

Evan's brows were bunched again when I put my phone away. "You still talk to Denny?" he asked, seeming genuinely mystified.

With a shrug, I told him, "Yeah...kind of. It's not always easy. There's a lot of things...we just can't talk about."

Evan stared at me a moment, then nodded, clapped my shoulder, and let the conversation go. I was grateful because I suddenly felt...a little less optimistic.

Chapter 15
SHOWTIME

The bus was a cacophony of noise, but somehow, I managed to fall asleep. Saying goodbye was exhausting. When I woke up, there were a bunch of strangers at my table, playing cards.

I lifted my head from where I'd been resting against the window to look at them, and they nodded a greeting. Guess we were going to be pretty chummy on this bus. "Hey," I said stretching out the kinks. "What are we playing?"

The guy on my left immediately dealt me in. "Poker. We're playing for beds." That made me frown. Great. Looks like I was getting last choice. Oh well, didn't matter.

Names were exchanged as we started playing. Flicking my eyes around the bus, I saw my friends talking, laughing, having a good time. I took a peek outside, and all I saw were barren hills. We must have crossed over to Eastern Washington already. Then I saw a sign for a city, and I blinked in surprise. We were well into Eastern Washington, an hour or so from our destination. Damn. I'd been more tired than I'd realized.

A part of me wanted to call Kiera again, wanted to know if she was still okay. But I shouldn't. I shouldn't check up on her every five minutes. I should let her do what she needed to do, and

I should trust that what she needed to do wouldn't hurt me. Faith, right?

"You lose, man." The guy across from me—Mark—was grinning as he laid down his cards. And I could see he was right; my lone King didn't stand a chance against his three of a kind. Oops. I probably should have folded. "Poker isn't your game, is it?" he said with a laugh.

Smiling, I shook my head. "No, definitely not."

He drummed his fingers on the table for a second, then peeked back at the cubbies. "I'm gonna go stake my claim. Nice meeting you, Kellan."

Mark stood up, the other guys following as they sorted out which beds they wanted. I didn't care, so I stayed put. Griffin sat down once the table was empty. "Dude...I'm bored."

I sighed as I looked him over. Griffin needed constant entertainment, and he wasn't the kind of person who could entertain himself for long. He needed an audience. God, this was going to be such a long tour. "Sorry?" I nodded my head at the other people picking out their sleeping arrangements. "Why don't you go find somewhere to sleep."

Shaking his head, he tossed his hand toward the bunks. "I already snagged the bed in the back."

Eyebrows raised, I looked toward the back of the bus. *There's an actual bed?* I should probably get up and explore my new home. I just hadn't felt like moving yet. My body, my head, my heart, everything felt...heavy.

Griffin leaned forward, smacking the table, and I twisted back to face him. "We need to talk," he stated.

Pursing my lips, I wondered what the hell he wanted to talk about with me. Oh...maybe me manhandling him earlier. "Hey, yeah, sorry about getting in your face this morning. I'm just really sick of you trying to get into Kiera's pants."

He raised an eyebrow at me. "Why? You think she'd actually say yes?"

"No," I answered with a smile. He was the only person I was a thousand percent positive Kiera would never touch.

Griffin smirked, like he knew that. "Then why are you such a dick about it?"

I opened my mouth, then shut it. He kind of had a point... which was weird. "It bothers her, okay. But...yeah, I'm sorry for being a dick."

He waved his hand at me. "We're cool, no worries. That wasn't what I wanted to talk about anyway."

"Okay...what did you want to talk about?"

His grin grew delighted. "Groupies. What do you think it's gonna be like? Think there will be a bunch of them? Like, different ones at every show...begging us to fuck 'em?"

I sighed at him right as Evan and Matt rejoined us. "I don't know, man. I don't care."

Griffin's jaw dropped, like I'd just said I was taking a vow of chastity. Which, in a way, was exactly what I'd said. "Don't care? How can you not care?"

Now it was my turn to raise an eyebrow at him. "I'm with Kiera." *Remember? We were just talking about her?*

Griffin still looked confused though. He looked around the bus like he was expecting to see her. *I wish.* "Uh, not right now, dude."

Evan frowned at Griffin. Matt was munching on some chips, smiling as he idly watched us like we were his favorite television show. I sighed again. "What we have doesn't stop just because she's not here. I'm not dicking around on her." Did he really not get that?

Apparently, he didn't. "Why not? She'd never know."

He narrowed his eyes at Evan and Matt, like he was daring them to break our sacred bond, or some crap like that. I honestly didn't know if they would tell on me or not. Not that they'd have to; I wasn't going to cheat on Kiera. But...if *they* fooled around on *their* girlfriends...well, damn, yeah...I didn't think I'd mention it to Jenny or Rachel. It kind of sickened me to admit that, because I really liked them, but the guys were my family, and I couldn't betray their trust like that. I would most-definitely kick their asses and pretty much force them to confess though. And then I'd kick their asses again for being dumbshits. I really didn't think I'd have to worry about that though. Evan and Matt...they weren't like Griffin.

Lifting my eyebrows, I tried to get Griffin to understand. "*I* would know."

His lips twisted as he studied me. "That's just...weird. Why are you even a rock star?"

Matt sniggered while Evan rolled his eyes. I shook my head a little, then shrugged. "I like the music? I like performing? You know, it *is* possible to have fun with your pants on, Griffin." Matt choked on the chip he was eating and started cough-laughing. I supposed that was kind of a strange thing for *me* to say, and I chuckled as Matt struggled to breathe.

Griffin rolled his eyes. "Ugh...God. You guys are *so* lame. Why did you all have to get in relationships right before we hit it big?"

Evan smiled at him, amusement in his eyes. With a laugh, I told Griffin, "We haven't hit *anything*. And you can't stop yourself from falling in love. It's just not possible." Trust me, if I could have turned it off, there were multiple times when I would have done just that.

Griffin scoffed at my explanation. "Uh, sure you can. Just don't do it, simple as that." Scowl on his face, Griffin shook his head as he looked at us. "You will never see me as whipped as you guys. It's pathetic."

Matt clapped him on the shoulder. "We're not stopping *you*, dude. If you wanna be a slut, go right ahead. They're all yours."

Griffin brightened, like he just now realized what this could mean for him. "Holy shit, you're right. Since all you fuckers are doing the monogamous thing...they *are* all mine. I have no competition..." He smacked the table again. "Fuck yeah, you guys should get married. Leave all the poon to me." Matt's face went bright red; Evan just laughed. I sighed. *Trust me, Griff, that's exactly what I want to do. I just don't know if that's what Kiera wants.*

When we finally got to the venue in Spokane, I had to say...I was impressed. The place was a lot larger than I'd expected. There were a surprising number of things we had to do once we got out of the bus: directions to listen to, equipment to help with, and most surprising of all...radio interviews. I really wasn't sure why someone would want to interview us, since they didn't know us from Adam, but the tour manager had lined up something for all the bands, which was nice, so I dutifully did my part and called in so I could answer random questions about our music. It was weird, but kind of fun.

After that, all the bands went through a quick rehearsal. Matt's cheeks were pale when we stepped onto the stage to perform in front of nobody. The look on his face was understandable though, considering it was him and he pretty much hated the spotlight. The room we were in was huge; it would hold a shit-ton of people. I couldn't wait.

Before I knew it, the show was about to start, and the energy in the backstage area started making me anxious. But in a good way. I was raring to go. Fans started coming in, mixing with the artists. It kind of reminded me of being back at the bar. Everyone walking around, mingling, laughing, drinking...flirting. Girls came up to me, interest in their eyes as they asked if I was in one of the bands. I nodded politely, then asked them which band they were here to see. Not surprisingly, most of the girls were here to see Justin's band; he was the main draw on the tour.

It was kind of weird to not have anyone recognize me, but it was kind of nice too. It reminded me of when the D-Bags had first started playing in Seattle. Just an unknown band disrupting everyone's meal with some loud-ass music. Good times.

"Oh my God...are you in Avoiding Redemption?"

I stopped scanning the room to look at the shaking girl in

front of me. Her eyes were so wide as she studied me that it was almost alarming. Wanting her to relax, I smiled softly. "No...I'm with the D-Bags...we're at the bottom of the poster there." I pointed to the promo poster she was clenching for dear life.

"Oh wow..." she said, her eyes not leaving my face. "Wow... you're just...wow..."

Her reaction made a laugh escape me. If this girl were Kiera, she'd be bright red by now, trying to get away from me to hide her embarrassment. Ugh...God, I missed her—her sultry eyes undressing me, her breath on my skin, her fingertips running down my chest, her smile, her heart... I hadn't had time to call her since arriving here, and we were going to start any minute. She was working anyway. I'd have to wait until after Pete's closed to talk to her.

Trying to not let the melancholy alter my mood, I said to the girl, "Would you like me to sign that?"

She instantly shoved it in my face. "Yes..." Her voice was both a purr and a moan.

Shaking my head, I took the Sharpie from her rigid fingers, and signed my name next to the band's name. I handed the pen back to her, and she held the poster to her chest like it was her most prized possession. "D-Bags...I'll definitely remember that." Then she brightened and said, "Take a selfie with me?" Before I could even say, "Sure," she had her phone out and was leaning into my side snapping a pic. I barely had time to give her a small grin for the photo. "Thanks!" She hurried away, giggling as she stared at her phone, and I swear I heard her say, "Hot damn."

Hearing Evan's laugh behind me, I turned to see him and Matt standing there, grinning at me. "What?" I asked.

Evan shook his head. "Everywhere we go..."

Matt nodded at him. "I know, right? He's the best form of marketing we have." He frowned. "He should be wearing our band shirt, like all the time, twenty-four-seven." From the contemplative look in his pale eyes, I could tell he was actually serious about that. He wanted me to be a walking, talking billboard everywhere we went. *I don't think so.*

Not liking the idea of Matt dressing me every morning, I rolled my eyes and angled my head toward the stage. "Come on, let's go see how packed it is."

Leaving the backstage area, I started heading for the entrance to the stage. I just had to know how many people were out there...because I could hear them. Even through the noise and laughter of the people behind the scenes, I could make out the steady buzz of thousands of people talking. Evan and Matt nodded and followed me, Matt chewing on his lip. Griffin stayed behind to flirt with a group of giggling girls, his hopeful groupies. Weaving our way through various people, we eventually found the area directly behind the stage. Security was even tighter here, as was the noise. There was a huge curtain, mostly closed, blocking the entrance to the stage. Wondering if security would stop us, I slowly approached. They did glance our way, but after we flashed them our credentials, they let us pass.

Giddy, I moved the curtain aside and stepped forward onto the stairs, so I could get a good look at the crowd beyond the stage. My jaw dropped as I stared at them all. The crowd was massive, like one giant swarming mess of bodies. This place wasn't as huge as a stadium show, but it was way bigger than what we were used to. Way bigger than Pete's. God, I wished Kiera was here to see this. She'd probably freak out for me, but I wasn't scared, I was...eager. Adrenaline was already filling my stomach, and I had to force myself to not walk out there. *Is it time yet?*

From behind me, I heard a soft voice say, "Oh my God..."

I looked back to see Matt standing there, eyes locked on the crowd; he looked paler than I'd ever seen him. His panicked eyes flashed to mine. "There's so many people...how are there so many people?"

By his face, you'd think he'd never contemplated what an actual concert would look like. He'd been a wreck before

Bumbershoot, but honestly, since that had been outside, it hadn't felt like that many people. With this...the walls, the bodies trapped in front of us and around us...even I could feel the scope of it, the weight of all those eyes. I just happened to like that feeling. Unlike Matt.

Concerned, I shook my head. "Lots of bands means lots of fans...are you okay?"

He instantly shook his head. "No...no, you were right. We're not ready for this. Let's go home."

Spinning on his heel, he started speed-walking away from me. I glanced at Evan, then hurried after him. "Matt, wait!" He just shook his head and kept right on walking back to where we'd come from, back toward the waiting area, back toward the exit. Fuck. Was he really leaving?

"Shit," I muttered. Glancing around the main backstage area when we got there, I shouted for our missing bandmate; this was an *all hands on deck* moment. "Griffin!" I spotted him just as his head swung my way. He furrowed his brows, confused at the panic in my voice, and I pointed to where Matt was quickly disappearing. Griffin followed my finger, then frowned and started moving in the same direction as Evan and me.

We caught up to Matt outside in the alley next to the back entrance. He was pacing, cell phone clenched in his hand, like he was about to call for a ride. The burly guys guarding the door were watching him, but they didn't look like they were going to do anything to stop Matt from leaving the show. That wasn't their job. "Matt...?" I asked. "You okay?"

He still looked really ill, and he was shaking. "Uh-uh. I can't do this. I can't do *that*!" He pointed back at the building.

Stepping in front of him, I put my hands on his shoulders and tried to make my voice as soothing as possible. "Yes, you can. We do this all the time."

His entire body shook under my fingertips. "Not like this...I can't...I'm sorry."

I'd seen Matt get stage fright before, but *nothing* like this. It was fairly typical for Matt to be a bundle of nerves before a show, especially one at a new place, and on occasion, he did throw up before we went onstage, but he'd never flat-out *refused* to do a show before. He'd always found a way to cope and perform, usually by ignoring everyone around him. It didn't seem like that was going to work tonight though. I never got nervous about going up on stage, not anymore, and never as bad as what he was going through right now, so I really didn't know how to help him. I glanced at Evan, and he shrugged, equally unsure.

"Matt," he said, trying anyway. "It's gonna be all right. You know our songs better than all of us. I don't think you could mess up if you tried."

Matt shook his head as he turned to Evan. "I can't go out there...too many people..."

Evan shrugged again, then mouthed, *What do we do*?

Shit. What did we do? I supposed I could haul Matt over my shoulder and plop him onstage, but honestly, by the look on his face, I was pretty sure he'd just throw up all over the place if I did that. So sure, I could physically get him out there, but I couldn't force him to calm down, and that was what he needed right now —to be calmed down. Damn it...I really wished Rachel were here. I was sure she could do it. Maybe I should call her? Or maybe hearing her voice would immediately have him on a bus back home. I wasn't sure, and I didn't want to risk it. As much as a part of me loved the idea of going home, we couldn't come this far to fail without even *trying*. Matt would *never* forgive himself.

Tentatively, I looked over at Griffin, silently asking for his help, although I really wasn't sure if that was a good idea or not. Griffin *could* help...or he could make this about a thousand times worse.

Griffin glanced at my questioning face, then rolled his eyes and smacked Matt on the back of the head. "Lighten the fuck up, pansy."

Matt's freaked-out expression instantly shifted to a scowl. Griffin raised his eyebrows as Matt turned to face him. "Do you know anybody in there?" he asked. Matt shook his head and Griffin nodded. "And do you think anybody knows us?" Matt shook his head again and Griffin smiled. "Then what the fuck are you worried about? You could absolutely suck, and no one would know or care, because no one knows who the fuck we are. If you think about it, this is the one show that *shouldn't* freak you out, because it really doesn't matter." He shrugged, like it was as simple as that.

Glaring—and no longer shaking—Matt crossed his arms over his chest. "We should still care, Griffin. We should care *every* show, whether people know about us or not. We should always try to impress them."

Griffin showcased the entrance. "Then go impress them, dickwad."

Matt rolled his eyes...then stormed back inside. Griffin smirked, then shook his head. "Dude's got issues." Looking back at me, he took in my startled expression and shrugged. "You just have to know which buttons to push, Kell." He smacked my shoulder, then started following Matt back inside. I could only stare at the door, a little shocked, a little mystified. How, out of all of us, was *Griffin* the one who got through to him? Buttons indeed.

Evan laughed, then clapped my back. "Come on, let's put on a show."

I grinned, then nodded. *Yeah, let's do this.*

When we got back to the party area, Griffin was handing Matt a red Solo cup full of something that I was sure was a very strong drink. Matt started chugging it while Griffin lightly tapped him on the back in encouragement. When Matt was finished, he closed his eyes and inhaled a deep, calming breath. He wasn't great, but he was definitely better. At least, he was better until one of the crew stepped into the room and shouted, "D-Bags, you're up." Then his face went green. Uh-oh. I knew what that meant.

Matt slapped a hand over his mouth, and Griffin instantly

shouted, "Bucket!"

Someone tossed Griffin a bucket, and he handed it to Matt... right as Matt lost it. I cringed as every band member in the room let out a low, "Oooooo." Griffin lightly patted Matt's shoulder while he heaved. Tilting my head at Evan, I said, "Maybe we should do a couple of songs without him. Acoustic?"

Evan laughed. "What's the point? We're only doing three songs anyway. Let's go clean him up."

Oddly, Matt was smiling when we reached him. "Feel better?" I asked.

Handing the bucket to a grimacing crew member, he wiped his mouth and nodded. "Much. Let's go."

Griffin started laughing as Matt walked away. Looking over at the unfortunate bucket-holding crew member, he said, "When you're done rinsing that out, write *Property of Matt Hancock* on the side for me. He's gonna need it again. Like, every show." He clapped the guy on the back, then darted after Matt.

Shaking my head at the pair, I followed my friends. After letting a crew member get me ready, I followed Evan onto the stage. Our stuff was already set up, and Matt was tucked behind his guitar, finally looking content as he kept his eyes glued on his instrument. Griffin had both fists in the air in victory. Even if no one knew him, he was determined to leave an impression. As I smiled at him, I lifted a hand to the crowd. They had no fucking clue who I was, but they were still screaming at an ear-splitting level, excited for the show to start. Kicking this off was kind of fun.

Up on the stage, with all the lights blaring down on me and the rest of the room in shadow, it was harder to see just how many souls were out there, but I could still feel their presence, feel their curiosity. Shifting my focus, I examined the people in front, the ones I could see the clearest. A lot of them were girls, and they were looking at me wide-eyed with their mouths dropped open. Some were fanning their faces and giggling to their friends. I had to laugh at that.

Grabbing the microphone, I popped it off its stand and stepped closer to the edge. Squatting down a little, I stared right at a few girls who were openly fawning. "Hey. How's it going?" I casually asked.

One of them got a little weak in the knees, and her friends had to catch her. Oops. Chuckling, I straightened and addressed the entire crowd. "How's it going, Spokane?" Some bands only played on stage, but I liked a little interaction. It amused me. Plus, they really should know who they were screaming for. "My name's Kellan," I said, and I instantly heard it screamed back at me. Laughing again, I pointed at my bandmates. "That's Matt, Evan, and Griffin. We're the D-Bags...and we'd *really* like to do something for you." I'd said that low and seductive, flirty as fuck. I knew it annoyed Kiera when I did that, but I just couldn't stop myself. It was too much fun.

Amid the corresponding screams, I clearly heard a cluster of people in front yell, "Strip!"

I had to lower the mic as I paused to laugh. *So, it's going to be that kind of crowd, huh?* Griffin was starting to take off his shirt. I snapped my fingers and pointed at him to get him to stop. He smirked at me but left his clothes on. "Naughty, naughty," I told the crowd. Then I gave them a playful half-smile. "I like it."

As they screamed, I motioned behind me for Evan to start the song. When the guys started playing—when I started singing— that was when the crowd's attitude changed. They weren't just seeing us as a group of good-looking guys messing around, no, I could tell from their reaction that they were loving it, because they were loving the *music*. They were jumping up and down, a boisterous mass of enthusiasm that I could easily syphon energy from. I meandered back and forth across the stage, reaching out for the close ones, pointing out to the farthest ones, giving their energy right back to them. And even though they didn't know the words, didn't know the songs, the *feeling* was the same as when we played at Pete's. No...it was better because this was so much bigger. It electrified me. *I'm so glad I said yes.*

By the time we finished our last song—when they were firmly wrapped around my finger—I felt higher than I'd ever felt after a show. The only damper was knowing that I couldn't share the moment with Kiera. *She should be here.* That would have made this moment complete. But I could call her later. I could still share this with her a little bit, and that made it okay.

All four of us were still buzzing when we left the stage. I playfully punched Matt's arm about six times as we headed back to where the other bands were. "You were so good, man. You nailed it!" And he really had. Not that Matt wasn't always good, but I don't know, he was just on point tonight.

Matt grinned as he thanked me. "I think throwing up helped me play better."

With a laugh, I told him, "I promise I won't *ever* let you look at the crowd before a show again." No. Matt needed to be kept in the dark as long as possible pre-show if we were going to make a go of this. And it was really starting to feel like we were…

When we got back to the lounging area, the other band members started clapping. Some even whistled. It was surreal. Justin headed our way with his hands in the air. "Dudes! You guys are so fucking good! I knew you'd be perfect for this."

We were all swarmed by fans after that, wanting autographs, wanting photos, wanting to know where to buy our music. It was all so bizarre; I almost couldn't process it. *What the hell is my life right now?*

It was super-late by the time I was able to call Kiera, but I was still soaring with energy. There was no way I was sleeping any time soon. We were back on the bus, moving through the night to get us to our next show. I was stuffed into my cubby; I hadn't needed to worry about the poker game after all, since Evan had grabbed me a bottom bunk while I'd been sleeping. The cubby was slightly too small for me, and I had to bend my knees to completely fit. I was really going to miss being able to stretch out, and I suddenly wished I was a lot shorter. Staring at my phone, I listened to the people around me. Some were deeply snoring, but a lot of them were still awake too, talking to each other or to someone on a phone. I could hear Evan across the aisle from me telling Jenny that he missed her. I had the curtain on my cubby closed for privacy, and the light from my phone was bright in my hands as I pressed the button to call Kiera. She'd closed at Pete's tonight, so she *should* still be awake.

I heard the call connect, then Kiera's breathy voice was in my ear. "Hi..." Just that one word sent a pulse of energy through me.

"Hey, gorgeous. Did I wake you or are you just lying down?"

"Just crawled into my large, cold bed."

My eyes fluttered closed as the image of Kiera spread out on her mattress flooded through me. "Ah...God that sounds nice. I wish I was there with you."

I heard her let out a wistful sigh, and I knew she wanted that too. It made me feel warm all over. "You are, remember?" she said. "Our bed is just too big for me to feel you is all."

That made me smile, and a small laugh escaped me. "Yeah, that's right. Well, I'd wrap my leg around yours and bury my head in your neck if I were closer..." I sighed as a wave of homesickness tightened my chest. "I miss the smell of you..." *The feel of you, the sight of you...all of you.*

"I was going to say the exact same thing."

I laughed again, then asked her if she'd gotten any of my notes. I'd left several obvious ones behind—or had Anna leave them behind—so she should have found some of them by now. Maybe the one on Griffin's bass. Or the one with the money for the neighbors. Maybe even the one I'd tucked in the glovebox of the Chevelle. There were actually quite a few she could have found already.

Kiera admitted that she had found some, and it made me happier than I'd thought it would to hear that. *She thought of me today.* Did she think of me at midnight? I'd paused what I'd been doing and thought of her, mentally going over the letter I'd left for her, so we could share that moment together...if she'd gotten it. After another moment of chitchat about the notes, the curiosity was killing me, and I had to know if Kate had upheld her promise to me. "Did Kate give you hers?"

I cringed as I asked her that. Kiera liked romance books, so I knew she liked a little steamy talk, but maybe I'd gone too far. Although, in my humble opinion, it was classy steamy talk. I never once used the word cock. But, as sexy as it was, it had turned out really romantic too. It was actually a little sappy which was probably the real reason why I was cringing. But it was all true, and I wanted her to know what she did to me, what I felt for her. *There is no one else for me, but you.*

I could practically hear her blush when she answered me. "Um, yes, she did."

Her not immediately elaborating was killing me. "And...did you like it?"

"Yes," she breathed.

Relief coursed through me, and I started gushing as the tension released. "Good...because I meant every word. What you do to me, the way you affect me...I know you don't think you're anything special, and I think you sometimes feel like you're not attractive enough for me, but you are. My body burns for you...I can't deny that...I never could." *You're everything I could ever want. How can you not see that?*

Kiera's voice was equally relieved when she spoke. "It's the same for me, Kellan...all of it. How you affect me, how much I love you...all of it."

She didn't argue with me, didn't try to convince me I could do better—I loved that. If Kiera knew how much I loved her, and fully *accepted* it, then maybe she wouldn't replace me. Maybe I'd get to keep her. Something warm and satisfying started expanding throughout my chest, throughout my head, throughout my body...even my cramped legs felt it. Hope. That was what it was.

"Good," I told her. "I like that we feel the same. It makes me think everything is going to be fine."

But even as I said it, an errant thought flitted through my brain: *Please, God, let it be fine.*

Chapter 16
THE ROAD

Life on the road was both exhilarating and taxing. I'd never thought it was possible to be both exhausted and energized at the same time, but it really was. And it didn't take long for the constant traveling to become disorienting; it was just a few weeks into it, and already I was completely clueless about where we were. Luckily, Matt was on top of it, and he reminded me what city we were in before every show.

And the shows...they were everything I'd been hoping they would be, and so much more. Playing with the audience, goofing around with my friends, feeling the pulse of the music in my chest, in my soul...it electrified me. As much as I couldn't wait to be back home with Kiera, I never wanted it to end.

Being on the bus, however...that was quickly losing its appeal. It was monotonous, mind-numbing. Guys started shifting around, alternating buses just for new people to talk to. The four of us D-Bags usually stayed together though. We just...liked hanging out.

"So, I've got this fuck buddy back home, and she does this thing—"

Justin held up his hand, interrupting Griffin's story. "Wait. Fuck buddy? Does she know you call her that?"

Griffin swished his hand. "Yeah, she calls me that too. Anyway, she does this thing when she's riding me, like her leg is kind of here..."

He started moving into a position that I did not want stuck in my brain, so I stood up and left him to tell Justin his overly graphic story. Thankfully, he didn't have long to tell it as the bus hissed to a stop, settling into its final resting place for the show. The driver opened the doors and I immediately stepped off the bus. I needed fresh air and room to stretch. I really wished I could go for a run. I missed it.

Justin came off the bus a few seconds after me. He was laughing. Spotting me stretching out my arms, he shook his head. "That chick he's seeing sounds hot. Why is she with him again?"

I shook my head, a laugh escaping me. "No one really knows the answer to that."

Justin just shook his head again, laughing as he made his way back to his bus.

We all fell into a comfortable rhythm after that. Talking to the people we needed to talk to, setting up the equipment we needed to help with, lounging on the bus until it was time to meet with fans pre-show. It was all easy-breezy fun. Until all of a sudden, it wasn't.

"You fucking bitch!"

All of us in the backstage area twisted to look over at who had yelled that. It was Kurt, one of the guys who was usually on our bus. He was on his cell phone, his face livid as he screamed at someone on the other end. "You're such a fucking cunt! I never want to fucking see you again, you fucking whore! Go to hell!" After he said that, he threw his phone full force against the wall, breaking it.

Ice washed through me as I stared at him. We'd had multiple conversations about our girlfriends waiting for us back home, and the look on his face whenever he'd talked about his girl...it was like looking into a mirror. By the pure rage on his face now, I knew that had been her on the phone, and I knew *exactly* what she'd done to him. I wanted to go talk to him, help him in some way, but I was frozen in place, terrified of ever getting a phone call like that.

His bandmates swarmed him, but he held them off, too pissed to talk. Then his angry eyes scanned the room, and he shouted, "Who here wants to fuck me? Right now."

As I watched, four girls scattered throughout the room started making a beeline for him. He grabbed the hand of the one who reached him first and started pulling her toward a hallway. I had to swallow the panic that was suddenly blocking my throat. It was like I was inside a nightmare, only I knew I wasn't. I was awake, this was really happening. *Jesus. Please don't let that be me someday.*

"That sucks," I heard Evan say beside me. I twisted to look at him, and he nodded at where Kurt had disappeared with his... stress reliever. "He told me he just bought his girl a ring. He was gonna propose next time he saw her."

It was like I'd been socked in the gut, and I instinctively hunched over. This was too much, too similar...too close to my greatest fear. Evan put a hand on my shoulder, his brow furrowed in concern. "You okay?"

I nodded, swallowing. I couldn't let the parallel of our lives unhinge me. *Kurt's* girlfriend had cheated, not mine. Kiera and I were good. She was good. She was faithful. *She loves me. She loves me. She loves me.*

Evan clapped my shoulder and stepped away while I was trying to redirect my dark thoughts. A girl suddenly appeared in my vision. Her cheeks were flushed, her pale eyes were shining, and she was biting her lip. "Hi..." she said, staring at my mouth.

I was still a little out of it. I couldn't give her a polite smile, couldn't be professional. I was just staring at her staring at me. My response was more instinctual than a coherent thought. "Hey..."

The casualness of my answer seemed to encourage her. She sidled closer to me, pushing her side into my body. "That was kind of crazy, right?" From the look on her face, I knew what she really meant was, *Are you making that offer too? Do you want to be fucked right now?*

Seeing her looking up at me with unadulterated interest on her face was actually starting to make me nauseated. "Excuse me," I told her. I needed air. Or Kiera. Same thing. The girl frowned as I stepped away and pulled out my phone.

It was loud in here, with girls and guys laughing, flirting, but I couldn't wait another second—I needed to hear Kiera's voice. She picked up on the second ring. "Hey, you...how did you know I was missing you?" Hearing the calm love in her voice almost dropped me to my knees. *We're okay...she's still mine.*

"Guess, I'm psychic," I said with a relieved laugh. "How was your day?" *Tell me anything, tell me everything...just talk to me, please.*

Thankfully, she did. I talked to her right up until the D-Bags had to take the stage, and then I called her back the minute we were done. I just needed to hear her voice.

After the show, when we were all back on the bus, I saw Kurt sitting alone at a table, blankly staring out the window. Inhaling a deep, calming breath, I sat beside him. "Hey, man. I saw what happened. Are you all right?"

His dead eyes fixed outside, he murmured, "I don't want to talk about it."

I nodded, then got up and left him alone. If it were me, I wouldn't want to talk about it either.

Relationships seemed to fizzle left and right after Kurt's vocal breakup. Sometimes it was one of the guys yelling obscenities at his girl like Kurt had, other times it was one of the guys begging for forgiveness from his girl. Each time I saw it happen, it did something to me, terrified me to my core. And every time someone broke up, I called Kiera, just to reassure myself that we were still okay. Thank God, we still seemed to be.

Something else started happening shortly after Breakup-fest began. Girls started joining us on the bus, and the sound of people screwing started to become a regular thing. Listening to it really made me miss Kiera, and I started having—*the best*—dreams about her. More often than not, I woke up rock hard. Aching...and lonely. But I only had to wait until Christmas, then I would see her again. I couldn't fucking wait.

"You're in the D-Bags, right?"

Stirring from my thoughts, I looked over to see one of those random girls riding the bus with us. She was at the table across the aisle from mine, but the minute I made eye contact with her, she left the guy she'd been sitting with—Paul—and hopped onto my bench. Paul glared at me, like I'd somehow forced her to leave him. *That's not on me, man.* I hadn't even spoken to her yet.

Ignoring his spiteful eyes, I gave her a polite smile and subtly angled my body, so my back was against the window and my leg was farther up the bench, keeping us apart. "Yeah...Kellan, hi."

She tilted her head as she looked at me appreciatively. I couldn't imagine I looked all that great right now. There was a bathroom on the bus, and it did have a small shower, but it was the shittiest shower on Earth, and we were always being told not to use it unless we absolutely needed to. It had been a few days since I'd had a decent rinse off, and I was *really* looking forward to scrubbing the grime off of me. Thank God we were getting a hotel at this next stop. From what Justin had told me, that was a luxury that his tours didn't always have, but due to the length of this tour, the number of bands on it, and the number of repeat performances in certain cities, it was a treat that we occasionally got to partake in. And that was what it felt like every time I got to lay down in a bed—a gift.

"Kellan," the girl murmured, like she was memorizing it. "I like it, it's sexy."

I shook my head at her. "I didn't pick it, but thanks," I said with a small, amused smile. I supposed that was one tiny thing I could thank my parents for; Kellan Kyle had a certain ring to it.

Hmmm...so did Kiera Kyle. God, I loved that our initials would match...if she agreed to marry me. Would she? She hadn't found the letter in the couch yet...so we hadn't talked about it yet. I both wanted to and didn't want to.

The girl next to me got the wrong idea from my smile; she leaned forward, her hand going to my knee between us. "So... what's your story, Kellan?"

I almost sighed at her. *Not one I'm going to share with you.* I wasn't entirely sure how to get out of this conversation without making her mad. *Could you leave me alone?* seemed kind of rude. And that was when my savior sat down across from us.

Wide smile on his face, Griffin nodded his head at me. "Save your breath, cutie. He's dick-deep in some girl back home. Won't even consider cheating on her." He rolled his eyes at me, then his grin returned as he looked the girl up and down. "Me, however, I have no such restrictions. I also have a bed, right back there."

He pointed down the hallway, and the girl followed his finger. She looked back at me with a clear pout on her face. Grinning, I shrugged. "He's right. I'm not gonna sleep with you."

She sighed, then looked back at Griffin. Eyebrow raised, he splayed his fingers, waiting for her answer. She sighed again, then said, "All right...fine, let's go."

Griffin slapped the table, then swept her away to his bedroom. Thank God, potential angry confrontation averted. *Damn, I can't believe I actually owe* Griffin *one.* Who knew having him around could be helpful?

While Griffin entertained our "guest," I called Kiera. I never mentioned the girls that hovered around the bands. I didn't want her to unnecessarily worry about them, and I knew she would. But their presence was inconsequential to me—it didn't change how I felt about her, how dedicated I was to her. They could all be dancing around me naked, and I'd barely notice.

A small part of me wondered if Kiera knew about the girls though, if she'd heard anything in the background while we'd talked. If she had, and if she wondered why they were always around, she never brought it up. It made me happy that she didn't, it made me feel like she actually did trust me. And she should. Those girls...they weren't on my radar. Not even the ones who bluntly propositioned me. Kiera was the only thing in front of me, around me, behind me...she was everywhere, she was everything.

We got to our next stop early the next morning. Well, it was early for most of the guys. I'd been up for hours. Groggy and sleepy, they stumbled out of the buses and blinked at the sun like they'd never seen it before. While Griffin leaned on Matt, I noticed one of the crew escorting Griffin's "date" to a nearby cab. None of the other guys looked her way, which...kind of made me feel bad for her. But I had a feeling if I waved or acknowledged her in any way, she'd show up on our bus again, and I'd have to have that awkward conversation again. And I doubted Griffin could get me out of it twice. So, I ignored her, just like everybody else.

The tour manager, Scott, looking a little frazzled as always, was walking down the line of us, handing out hotel room keys and shouting out room assignments. When he got to us, I knew what he was going to say even before he said it. "Kyle, Wilder, you two are together, room 602. Hancock and Hancock, you two are together, room 604." Yep. That was typically how we were sorted.

He handed the four of us our key cards, while Matt grunted in annoyance. "Goddamn it," he grumbled as Scott moved down the line. "Every single fucking time..." Closing his eyes, he let out a long sigh. "I have to deal with him every single day of my life. I was kind of hoping for a day or two off on this tour."

While I smirked at the look on his face, Griffin laughed and smacked him on the back. "Sorry, cuz. You're stuck with me, twenty-four-seven."

Matt dropped his head into his hands. "Why me...?" he murmured.

Griffin poked him in the shoulder, making him look up at

him. "Because the universe wants you to stay up late watching porn with me," he stated.

Matt pursed his lips. Looking over at Evan and me, he said, "I don't care what the assignment is, I call dibs on one of you two next stop."

Evan and I glanced at each other, then started laughing. Matt flipped us off before leaving to go get his stuff.

When Evan and I got to our room, Evan immediately tossed his bag on a chair, kicked off his shoes, and collapsed onto one of the beds. He didn't move again, so I figured he was already passed out; it was really hard to get a good night's sleep in those cramped cubbies, and after so many nights of that, the body rebelled.

I debated taking a nap too, but the shower was calling me. The streaming hot water was a glorious treat, one I enjoyed for far too long. And sadly, by the time I got out of it and dried off, I was refreshed and energized. I couldn't have fallen back asleep even if I tried. Lying on the other bed, I thought over ways to kill some time. I could write out some lyrics, but honestly, I'd been doing a lot of that on the bus. I'd only brought one notebook with me, and it was already over halfway full of random poetic verses. I didn't want to read, didn't want to watch TV. There was really only one thing I wanted; it was what I always wanted.

Glancing at Evan's sleeping form, I pulled out my cell phone. I could tell he was sleeping pretty soundly, and I probably wouldn't wake him, so I called Kiera. Her voice was sleepy when she answered. "Hell...o?"

Damn. Did I mess up on the time zone change again? My eyes flicked to the clock. It was late morning here in...where the hell were we? Somewhere in Ohio, if I was remembering the last concert correctly. That made me smile, being in Kiera's home state made me feel oddly closer to her. "Sorry, did I wake you?"

"Hey...no, I was just waking up." I was about to tell her where I was, but she distracted me by saying, "I'm a little unmotivated to leave your bed."

The grin on my face was uncontainable as I pictured her spread out on my sheets. "*My* bed?"

She giggled in my ear. "I came over last night to grab your mail and go through your bills, and I just couldn't stop myself from crawling under your covers."

"Yes," I said with a soft smile. "I do seem to recall that being a problem of yours."

She laughed again, then sighed. "It smells like you here...it makes me miss you even more."

I had to close my eyes as an ache tore through me. "I miss you too." There was a moment of silence, then Kiera yawned. "You're tired," I stated.

A quiet sigh met my ear. "It's harder to sleep...knowing you're so far away." She paused and when her voice returned there was humor in it. "Our new bed is much too big. I think we should return it."

A light laugh escaped me. "Agreed. But even still...I have to thank you."

"Thank me?" she asked, sounding confused.

"For making me do this. For the gentle push. It's tiring, but it's...I don't know, it's just...it's everything I wanted it to be." The shows, the crowd, the noise, the pulse of energy...it all flashed through my mind in a microsecond, wrapping me in contentment. Then I frowned as I reconsidered. There was one missing element to my happiness. "Minus you, of course."

I could hear the smile in her voice when she responded. "Good, I'm glad. You're meant for that life, Kellan."

There was a trace of sadness in her voice, and I knew what she was thinking. *That* life...separate from hers. Like she couldn't see how she fit into my surreal chaos. Like she didn't understand that she was the framework, that everything else was molded *onto her*.

"I'm meant for you too, Kiera," I told her. "I love you...so damn much. I wish there was a better word," I said with a sigh. "Love just seems...too small. You're the most important thing in my life." *By far.*

I heard her voice catch, and it was a moment before she said anything. "Now I really wish our bed was smaller," she murmured. I smiled at her and was about to tell her I wished that too, when she started gushing. "It's the same for me, Kellan. I never knew love could be like this. It's overwhelming what I feel for you. Almost..."

"Painful?" I whispered.

"Yeah," she said with a sigh.

"I know...I feel it too." Heaven and hell, torture and bliss, one extreme followed by the other. Did everyone in love feel this way? Both completely content and utterly terrified?

Kiera was silent a moment, then she yawned again. She was more tired than she was letting on. Feeling bad that my hectic life was intruding on hers, I said, "Do you want me to sing you back to sleep?"

"I don't think I can sleep, but I would love to hear your voice."

I smiled, then started singing her a song. And because I knew she was a fan, I sang her one of Justin's songs. She laughed at first, then grew quiet as she listened. By the end of it, she was exceedingly quiet. "Kiera? Did I lose you?"

I glanced at the phone, but we were still connected. I really had sung her back to sleep. That made me deliriously happy. Grinning, I brought the phone back to my ear. "Sweet dreams, sweetheart." A swell of love and loneliness swept over me as I disconnected the call. God, I missed her.

I ended up doing laundry at a nearby laundromat while Evan slept. And because I was an awesome friend and roommate, I did his too. When he finally woke up, we debated how to spend our free time. Our show wasn't until tomorrow night, so we had the evening to ourselves. After checking in with Matt and Griffin, we decided to go exploring. Matt and Griffin joined us downstairs in the lobby, where we spotted Justin drinking alone in the hotel bar.

"Hey, Justin," I said, poking my head into the bar. "We're gonna go exploring. Want to come?"

Griffin bounced on his toes beside me. "I'm gonna find a Great Lake and skinny-dip in it, dude!"

Shaking my head, I mouthed, *No,* to Justin.

He laughed, then nodded. "Yeah, sure." Finishing his drink, he paid his tab then joined us in the lobby.

We tooled around the city for a while, checking out local shops. Matt found a vintage record store that absorbed him for a good hour. Evan found an art gallery and picked up a little something for Jenny. We came across a bakery that had these chocolate-peanut butter things called buckeyes. We ate about fifty thousand of them, and then I had them mail a bunch to Kiera's apartment. I figured she'd love a little reminder of home. And they were really fucking good. After stopping Griffin from stripping and jumping into a river—because we weren't close enough to a Great Lake—we decided to check out the local bars.

Finding one we liked, we ordered beers from the bartender, then found a table in the middle of the room where we could sit and people watch. We all relaxed into our chairs. All except for Griffin. He started rubbing his hands together as he stood before us, and there was a playful gleam in his eye that I was all too familiar with. Great. What did the jackass think up now?

Leaning over, hands on the table he said, "Let's play a game."

"Pool?" Evan asked, looking around the bar for tables.

Griffin frowned at him. "No...an interesting game."

Yeah, I'd had a feeling it wouldn't be as simple as pool. Knowing I was going to regret it, I asked, "Like what?"

Griffin's devilish grin turned toward me. "It's a little something I like to call Find-a-Skank."

Yep. Thought so. Matt, Evan, and I answered him at the same time. "No."

Griffin's mouth popped open as he finally sat down. "No? You haven't even heard the rules yet," he whined.

Shaking my head, I told him, "None of us *want* to find skanks."

He rolled his eyes at me. "Speak for yourself, dude. Finding skanks is my mission in life." Justin choked on the sip of beer he'd just taken. Griffin shook his head as he took a drink of his own beer. "It's just a game, Kell. Relax. It's not like I'm gonna force you to fuck 'em or something." He rolled his eyes again. If he kept doing that, I was going to smack him.

Before I could tell him no again, Justin tilted his head and said, "What are the rules?"

Griffin smacked the table, his grin huge. "Ah yeah, Justin wants to play! Finally, a rock star who *wants* to be a rock star." Now it was my turn to roll my eyes. Leaning in, Griffin told Justin, "It's super simple. Just talk to girls and collect things. Numbers are one point, condoms five...hotel keys are an instant win. 'Cause you're just king if that happens. At the end of the night, we add up the points. The loser gets the tab and then everybody buys the winner a shot." He looked around the table. "You guys in?"

"Whatever, Griffin," I muttered, sipping my beer.

Of course, he took that as an enthusiastic yes. "Sweet! I'm gonna start now." He immediately stood up and walked over to a table full of girls who looked around our age.

Matt shook his head at him, then looked over at me. "Do you think he'll ever learn that 'whatever' doesn't actually mean yes?"

I smiled around the beer bottle in my mouth. Shaking my head, I shrugged. "Hell...freezing..."

Ignoring Griffin's game, I spent the bulk of the night just talking and laughing with my friends. But oddly enough, as the night wore on, even though we weren't really doing anything special, our small group turned into a much larger group, full of girls and guys alike. That tended to happen when we went out. I wasn't entirely sure why, we just...attracted people.

Before I knew it, it was last call. Hearing those words made Griffin panic. He instantly appeared at our table. "Dudes! We need a winner so he can get his shots!"

Nobody but him—and maybe Justin—had truly been playing his game, but even still...I'd sensed a few things being shoved into my pockets throughout the night, and there had been a couple of brazen girls who'd walked up and boldly handed me their numbers. Because I knew it would piss off Griffin, I'd decided to play along, and I'd accepted them. Pulling out the scraps of paper I'd collected, I counted them out as I set them on the table. "I got six," I told him.

Griffin stared at my pile with a dazed look on his face. "How? How! You weren't even doing anything?"

He tossed down his pair of phone numbers. I could tell just by glancing at one of them that it was fake. The letters FU gave it away. Crossing his arms over his chest, Griffin looked at Matt, Justin, and Evan. "Please tell me one of you guys can beat him."

Matt shook his head. "I got nada."

Justin smirked. "I got three. Didn't beat him, but I beat *you*."

Griffin glared at him, then turned to Evan. "It's all on you, bro."

I watched Evan closely, curious. He looked over at me with calm brown eyes, smiled...then shook his head. "I just got one."

Matt shrugged. "Guess I lost."

Griffin ignored him; his pale, irritated eyes narrowed on me. "What the fuck? *How* the fuck? Did you cheat? Let me see those..."

He pulled out his phone, like he was going to start calling the numbers. Laughing, I grabbed the stack and crumpled them. Griffin scowled at me. "You're such a slut. You were literally just sitting there."

Matt shook his spikey head. "No, he did get up to go to the bathroom a couple times."

Evan snapped his fingers. "And he went up to the bar."

Matt nodded. "And he went over to the jukebox. That's a hot spot."

Justin started laughing, which made Matt and Evan laugh, which made me laugh. I laughed so hard tears stung my eyes. Griffin eyed us all, unamused. "I know you cheated. I'll get you next time, fucker."

He turned around and left, and I just about fell out of my chair. Matt did. "Oh God, Kell," he said, sitting back on his seat and wiping tears from his eyes. "That was awesome. I might actually enjoy that game."

Laughing at his joy, I held my beer bottle out to him, and he clinked his against mine. I might actually enjoy that game too. Just to see Griffin's head explode over and over again.

A part of me wanted to mention the game to Kiera when I called her later, but I was pretty sure she wouldn't find it as funny as we all did. She wouldn't appreciate the nature of the game, or the fact that girls slipped me phone numbers unsolicited; I was pretty sure she'd never noticed that happening at Pete's, and I didn't feel like informing her. Kiera had a bit of a jealous streak. Not that I could really complain about that; I did too.

Instead of the game, I told her about our day sightseeing in her home state. "Did you know that one of the things on Griffin's bucket list is to dip a specific part of himself into every large body of water on Earth?"

I could easily picture her cringing in disgust. "Do I want to know which body part?"

With a laugh, I told her, "It's *exactly* what you're thinking. He says water blessed by his junk will bring good luck to the world. Who knew he was such a peacekeeper." Kiera started laughing, and it was a solid minute before she could speak again.

When her giggles subsided, she told me about her day, then about what notes she'd found. We talked for hours...far later than we probably should have considering what time it was both here and there. Eventually, Kiera started yawning repeatedly. "Want me to sing you to sleep again?" I asked.

She sighed, the sound content and happy. "Yes, please."

I instantly started singing a song for her, but this time, it was one of mine. The pull of sleep started dragging me under long before the song was done, and knowing Kiera was well on her way, if not already asleep, I let myself sink into the nothingness. And it gave me the greatest sense of peace to know we were falling asleep *together*.

Chapter 17
UNEXPECTED

Days later, the guys were still cracking up about Griffin's bar game. Whenever Justin spotted him, he'd teasingly hold up three fingers. Griffin held up one in response. Then I would hold up two sets of three, and he'd flip me off with both hands. He was such a sore loser. It was a stupid game but messing with him was too much fun.

We were...somewhere in Pennsylvania now, backstage before the show, talking to fans while we waited to go onstage. There were a couple of people wearing D-Bags shirts walking around...it kind of blew me away. It wasn't like we had a CD out. Matt wanted to make an official website, but I had no idea if it was up and running or not, so I really didn't understand how anybody here knew who the hell we were. Word of mouth? Or maybe they were following the tour. Or maybe they'd just bought the shirts at the merch booth because they liked the name. That was probably it.

My gaze fell over a pair of girls nearby, sitting in folding chairs, giggling into their cups. Their eyeline was laser beam focused on my body. From behind me, I heard Matt encouragingly say, "They like you...go tell them who we are."

Twisting my head around, I frowned at him. He shrugged. "How are they going to know if we don't tell them?"

Smiling, I motioned their way. "*You* could tell them."

His blue eyes widened in apprehension, but then he grinned. "I'm not the one they're undressing." He clapped my shoulder. "Do your thing, Kell. Score us some fans."

He was snickering as he walked away. I shook my head as I watched him sit by himself, not socializing, not interacting. No, that was my job, one I typically didn't mind, but I swear to God, if Matt could pimp me out, he would. Anything to promote the band.

With a laugh, I rolled my eyes and started heading over to the girls. That was when I nearly ran into someone. "Oh, sorry," I said, taking a step back.

The girl I'd almost crashed into was biting her lip as she looked up at me. She seemed really nervous. I wished I could take the nerves out of the people who approached me. It was cute that they were so anxious, but completely unnecessary. I was just...me.

"Um, you're Kellan Kyle, right?" she said.

That surprised me. Some of the girls I met backstage knew the band's name, but most of them didn't know my name. But maybe this girl had been to Seattle and had seen me play at Pete's. I'd run into homegrown fans backstage before, although they usually didn't ask my name, they just said it, like we were friends. *Hey, Kellan, long time, no see...*

"Yeah, that's me," I said, amusement curling my lip into a half-smile.

"John and Susan's son?" she asked.

My smile instantly dropped. How the fuck did she know the name of my parents? "How do you...?" Leaning in, I examined her more closely. She was extremely attractive, but the features weren't jumping out at me. I had no memory of her. "Do I know you?"

She suddenly looked really pale. "No, no...we've never met," she said, repetitiously smoothing her honey-brown hair.

Okay, so I hadn't slept with her. Did we go to school together or something? "How do you know my parents?" I asked, narrowing my eyes as I ransacked my memories. *Who the hell is this girl?*

"I don't actually, I just know their names..." She sighed, then closed her eyes. "God, I wasn't sure how to do this, and now I feel like I'm doing it all wrong..."

"What are you talking about?" I asked, totally and thoroughly confused. Had she stalked me? That was kind of...creepy.

The girl opened her eyes and searched my face a moment before she finally spoke. "Oh God...okay. Well, first things first, my name is Hailey. Hailey Carter."

My jaw dropped as I stared at her, then my stomach followed suit. Carter. *I know that name.* That name was burned into my brain, though I never, *ever* spoke it out loud. Oh my God...no. She couldn't...she couldn't be...the world wasn't that small...

"I was wondering..." she said, still looking extremely uncomfortable. "I really want to introduce you to someone."

Oh my God...she is.

"No," I instantly told her. Like a dam had burst, anger flooded through me. *Never.*

The girl, Hailey, held up her hands. "It's not what you're probably thinking. I want to introduce you to my dad."

She reached into her bag and handed me a photo, a photo that confirmed my horrid suspicion...my terrifying fear. *I know this photo.* Mom had shown it to me before. Gavin Carter...the man who'd stolen his best friend's wife, who'd knocked her up... with me. The man I resembled so much it was undeniable that we were related. The man who'd abandoned me, fed me to the monsters who'd raised me. The man who'd given me life and then *ruined* my life. Jesus. *I can't do this right now.* Or ever.

"You see, I think my dad...is your dad too," Hailey said with a shrug.

I immediately tossed the photo at her, shaking my head as both pain and rage sizzled my stomach. "You don't know what you're talking about. *John Kyle* was my dad. He's dead, both my parents are dead. I have no family." *Dad?* No, Gavin wasn't "Dad" to me. He was *nothing* to me.

Hailey's face scrunched in a look that expressed both guilt and determination as she shoved the photo back into her bag. "I'm sorry, I know this is hard to hear...weird to hear, probably. But trust me, John Kyle wasn't your biological father. My dad... he told me what happened between him and your mom. He told me about the affair. He told me he left when your mom got pregnant. I've known all about you my entire life. I've been wanting to meet you...my entire life."

Her voice warbled with emotion, and my jaw slackened as I stared at her. And that was when what she was saying took on an entirely different meaning for me. The anger shifted into an odd, yet profound sense of wonder as I took in the unmistakable similarities. I felt like I was in some alternate reality as I scanned her face: the rare, midnight-blue eyes, the line of her jaw, the perfectly placed cheekbones, the curve of her mouth...it was all a more feminine version...of me.

"You're my...sister?" My voice hitched on the word, a word I never thought would be associated with me. A word I suddenly, *desperately* wanted to be associated with me.

Hailey smiled, and I was again struck by how much we looked alike. *How did I not see it instantly?* A fat tear rolled down her cheek as she nodded. "Yeah. Surprise."

A laugh escaped me, and then I was pulling her into me for a hug. I'd never in a million years thought I'd have family out there somewhere that *wanted* to know me. It was like a prayer I hadn't even asked for had somehow been answered. But even still, a painful sear ripped through me when her slim arms wrapped around me, and I immediately let her go. It was too much.

We stumbled apart from each other, and she had the same overwhelmed expression on her face. "I'm sorry," I said. "I lied. I do know...about him."

I couldn't even clarify who I meant, but Hailey nodded, understanding. "Do you want to meet him?"

My expression instantly hardened as the anger returned. Hailey blinked at seeing it. "No, I don't want to meet him. Ever." Her mouth popped open, and I shook my head. "I would like to know you...but not if it means knowing him too. I'd rather be strangers with you than meet that man." Just saying it made me feel like I'd been kicked in the gut, but I wasn't budging on this one. I *would* cut ties if she forced my hand. *Don't make me turn you away.*

Hailey slumped a little, but then nodded. Pulling out her phone, she shrugged. "Could I have your number? So we can keep in touch?"

My expression softened as relief filled me. "Yeah, of course." Handing her my phone, I said, "Here, put your number in. I don't know how to do it."

She lifted an eyebrow as she took it. "You don't know how to program a phone number?"

Grin on my face, I shrugged at her. "Technology isn't really my thing. Yes, I could figure it out...I just don't want to."

She laughed then shook her head and entered her number into my phone. Then she texted herself. "There, now I have yours." Handing the phone back, she said, "It's really quite simple."

"I'm sure it is," I laughed. "Want to sit?" I indicated a small couch that happened to be empty.

Hailey nodded, her smile bright and carefree. As she moved to sit, I noticed a couple of guys from the show checking her out. Paul's interested gaze was particularly troublesome. It made a surge of something dark and protective flash through me, and I had to resist the urge to shield her from his view. Or walk over there and kick his ass. Weird. I'd only ever had that instinct around Kiera. Strange how I already felt responsible for this person I'd just met.

Hailey flopped down on the couch, her dark blue eyes bright

as she looked around the casual chaos. "This is so cool," she beamed. "I can't believe my brother is a rock star."

With a laugh, I sat beside her. "I don't know if the term 'rock star' actually applies to me. We're not signed, we don't even have a recording for people to buy. We're basically a glorified garage band."

I shrugged again. Hailey shook her head. "You're not seeing what I'm seeing."

Smirking, I shook my head. She was just as ridiculous as Kiera. "So, tell me about yourself."

She bit her plump lip as she tilted her head. Guys around us were still watching her, almost as much as the girls in the room were watching me. Guess we had something in common—we both unintentionally attracted people. "Well, I'm 20, almost 21... in college. Still live at home with Dad—"

My eyes narrowed as irritation shot up my spine. *I don't want to hear about him.* Seeing my expression, Hailey quickly said, "And Riley. He's 9, almost 10."

I took a moment to process that, and when I did, I was startled. "You have a brother? *We* have a brother?"

Grinning, she nodded. "He loves music too. He would die to be here, but Dad would have a coronary. He doesn't even know I'm—"

With a frustrated sigh, I turned my head and looked away from her. She stopped speaking. *How can I talk to her when she keeps talking about him?*

"Can I ask you a question?" she said, after a long quiet moment.

Feeling wary, I slowly looked back at her. *Maybe. It depends on what you want to know.*

Hailey studied my face for a second, then said, "Why do you hate him so much?"

I dropped my head, my gaze shifting to the floor. "It's complicated. I'd rather not talk about it."

"I know he left you, and I know that must have hurt, but he really didn't have a—"

My eyes snapped to hers as rage filled my stomach. "I said I don't want to talk about it."

She swallowed, a little nervously, and I made my face relax. I didn't want to scare her; I just didn't want to hear *anything* about Gavin. I was about to ask her something that would shift the conversation when a fan approached us. "Hi, I'm sorry to interrupt, but are you with one of the bands?"

I looked up to see a girl brightly smiling at me. And trembling. I threw on a casual smile, hoping to relax her. "Yeah...I'm with the D-Bags."

She giggled. "D-Bags...got it. Can you sign this?" She handed me a poster. I signed it then returned it to her. She hugged it to her chest, then looked over at Hailey. "Could you take our picture?"

Hailey shrugged, then stood up. "Sure."

The girl passed Hailey her phone, and then took her place on the couch, snuggling into my side. I laughed at her eagerness, then smiled at the phone and waited for the photo op to be over. The girl scurried off once it was. I started apologizing to Hailey, but then I noticed three more girls with their phones out, waiting for their chance to sit with me. Maybe I shouldn't have sat on a small couch. Too inviting. Hailey laughed, but took photos for all the girls in line.

Once they were gone, I cringed and turned to her as she sat down. "Sorry. Occupational hazard."

She laughed, then pulled her phone out and leaned in to take our photo. "Guess I'll get one too." She was still laughing when she pulled away. "You're kind of a girl magnet, aren't you?"

I could only shrug at that. She laughed again, shaking her head. "My friends are going to lose their minds when they find out I have a brother closer to their age." She cringed. "I've never mentioned you to anyone, since I wasn't sure if I'd ever get to..." Shaking her head, she smiled and shrugged. "Anyway, they think Riley is adorable, and you should see the way they drool over Da..." She stopped herself from mentioning *him* again and let out a soft sigh. "Sorry. It's just..." Her eyes scanned my face. "You and Dad...the resemblance is so...surreal. It's like you're his clone or something."

Anger burned my insides, and I turned away from her again. "I'm not. Trust me." No, the only thing I was, was a mistake. That was something my parents had *never* let me forget. Growing up with *this* face had been a nightmare for me. I was fairly certain there had been several times when Dad had hit me simply because of the way I looked.

"Sorry," Hailey murmured again, sounding genuinely remorseful. "I guess it's harder than I thought...not talking about...him. Maybe I shouldn't talk about me anymore. What about you? Girlfriend? Wife?" She gasped, and I peeked back at her to see her eyes shining with delight. "Oh my God, do I have a niece or nephew somewhere?"

By her expression, it was clear that I would make her day if I said yes. I actually felt my cheeks heating as the thought of Kiera having my child flooded my mind. *God...I want that so much.* "Um, no...no kids." A soft smile lifted my lips as Kiera's hazel eyes absorbed my thoughts. "But I *do* have a girlfriend back home. She's...she's everything to me."

Hailey let out a wistful sigh, and I refocused my attention on her. She was smiling peacefully at me. "I want someone to look like that when they think about me," she said. I smirked at her, and she laughed. "She's a very lucky girl. Tell me all about her."

Because I really missed Kiera, and I wanted to talk about her, I started gushing. I didn't stop until one of the crew walked into the room and announced that we were up. "Damn...I almost forgot I was at work," I said with a laugh. Hailey laughed with me as I stood up. "Will you still be here when I get back?" I asked, hope in my voice.

She nodded, and my grin was huge when I left to go onstage. *Sister...I can't believe I have a sister.* I'd never considered that possibility before; it almost didn't seem real. *I wish someone had told me.* Of course, there were a lot of things about my life that I'd wished for, and most of them had never happened. I was used to not getting what I wanted, which was why I tried to never want anything.

The show was extra energizing for me. There was just something about knowing Hailey was listening backstage that made me pull out all the stops. It made me wish we had more than three songs to play; I'd love for her to hear a full set. When we were done and I reentered the backstage area, I immediately searched for her...but she wasn't there. The disappointment was so swift and sudden, I had to clench my stomach. *She left?* She actually left. I knew I shouldn't be surprised, all my family eventually let go of me, but yeah, I was floored. I really thought she'd stay.

Annoyed that I'd let myself want something, I grabbed a beer and started chugging it. Maybe this wouldn't hurt so much if I was trashed. I was just polishing off the drink when I felt a hand on my back. Turning, I saw Hailey standing there, a huge grin on her face. The surge of relief I felt made my eyes sting. *She didn't leave. Where was she?*

Almost like she could hear my unspoken question, she jerked her thumb at the other entrance to the backstage area. "I had to go watch you. Oh my God, Kellan. Do you know how talented you are?"

Her words, her praise, it struck me to my core. *She was watching me. She liked it.* No, by the look on her face, I'd say she *loved* it. That filled me with something...unexpectedly wonderful. And painful. And terrifying. And exhilarating.

Hailey had a million questions after that, all about the band and our music. Since that was one topic that I loved talking about, one that held nothing but joy for me, I welcomed the conversation.

She stayed backstage the rest of the night, talking to me and barely listening to the other bands' music filtering into the room.

I was a little sad when security made her leave at the end of the show. Talking to her had been…I don't know, I just felt…lighter. Less alone.

I gave her a hug before she left. It was a little lengthier than most hugs I gave to girls who weren't Kiera. I was just…reluctant to let her go. When she pulled away, there were slight tears in her eyes. "It was…really nice to finally meet you, Kellan. I hope…I hope it's not the last time I see you."

I had to swallow the lump in my throat. "It won't be. You can always come visit me." The minute I said it, uncertainty filled me. Could she? How would I explain her to people? To Kiera? How would I ever be able to talk about her?

Hailey nodded. "I'd love that."

With a wave, she left the room. As she disappeared, I felt something breaking inside me. Because I didn't know how to have a relationship with her, and I wanted one. But I could never mention her. To anyone. And I was dying to. I was dying to tell somebody that I'd just met my sister. And she was cool. And she wanted to get to know me. And I wanted to get to know her too.

But I couldn't. I couldn't tell anyone because no one knew the real story, the sordid love triangle between John, Susan, and Gavin. I didn't want to get into that, didn't want to talk about my parents, didn't want to talk about Gavin—especially that. Hailey was a separate entity to me, removed from the situation, and I wished I could present her that way. Just a girl I'd met that I really liked…but that sounded bad too. I was stuck in silence, and it killed me.

Kiera was the only one I could possibly talk to about it…but even still, when we were back in the bus, and I knew she was home, waiting for me to call her, I agonized over what to say. If I told Kiera I'd met my sister, I'd unwittingly tell her about Gavin too, about him wanting to meet me. And I knew—without a doubt in my mind—just what Kiera would say. *Oh my God, that's great, Kellan. Go meet up with him, go bond with him, go love him.*

And that was the exact opposite of what I wanted. He didn't exist to me, and I liked it that way.

So, in the end, I didn't tell Kiera anything about meeting Hailey. I couldn't. The words wouldn't even form. It was one of the most monumental moments in my life...and I glossed over it. And I felt really shitty when I hung up with her. *I should tell her.* But how?

I half expected Hailey to show up to the concert the next night, and I found myself constantly scanning the backstage area for her. A little nervously because I half expected her to bring Gavin here anyway. I had no idea what I would do if she did that—if she just showed up with him. No, I knew exactly what I would do... I'd tell security to escort him out of the building, and then I'd delete Hailey's number from my phone.

God, I hoped she didn't do that. I'd enjoyed talking to her. I wanted her in my life. *Don't make me be a dick, Hailey. Don't ruin this.*

When the D-Bags took the stage, then stepped off the stage, and she still wasn't there, I was both relieved and saddened. I'd wanted to hang out with her again, because with her living on the east coast and me being based in Seattle, it might be a long time before I saw her. And I still didn't know how to explain who she was if she did come visit me. I felt...trapped. Screwed no matter what I did, and I'd really been hoping to never feel that way again.

As I contemplated that, my phone buzzed in my pocket with a new text message. I hoped it was Kiera as I pulled it out. I kind of wanted to talk to her about this intense feeling of loss that I was having. Maybe she could help me understand it. Maybe I could even tell her the truth. Maybe I could beg her to leave Gavin out of it, out of my life. Maybe it wouldn't be the issue I was afraid it would be. Surely, Kiera would understand why I didn't want a relationship with him, and maybe she would never bring him up to me. In the end, maybe she would respect my wishes and pretend he was dead, like I did. Maybe.

But the text wasn't from Kiera. It was from Hailey, and what it said...well, I could feel the knife plunging into my back as I read it. *'Don't be mad. I gave your number to Dad. He insisted once he found out I saw you. He wants to talk to you. Please don't be mad.'*

I wasn't just mad, I was fucking livid. I was also instantly ill. *He knows how to contact me. He can reach out to me whenever he wants to. He can talk to me. Why the fuck would she give him my number?* I wanted to text her back, tell her to never contact me again, but I couldn't get my shell-shocked fingers to work, and the phone dropped from my hand.

Matt was nearby, and he bent down and picked it up. "Kell?" he said, handing it to me. "Are you okay? You look sick. Do you need my bucket?" Before I could say anything, he twisted around and shouted, "Griffin! My bucket!"

I heard Griffin tell him, "Coming!" but that was all I was aware of. *She told her dad...she told him. Fuck, fuck, fuck...*

Matt's hand went to my shoulder just as Griffin appeared and shoved Matt's bucket in my face. "You sick, bro?" he asked.

I heard my phone chime again with another text, and I shoved it into my pocket. How could I ever look at it again? Because how would I ever know if it was him messaging me? *Fuck, fuck, fuck...*

Someone shook my shoulder. "Dude, Kellan, you're freaking me out. Are you okay?" I couldn't respond, the world was narrowing, darkening. Fuck, was I about to pass out? After no response from me, I heard Matt shout, "Evan! Something's wrong with Kellan!"

I knew I needed to get my shit together before this turned into something...I did not want to explain. The chaos of the room crashed in on me as I refocused on where I was. It was an assault on the senses to snap out of it—too loud, too bright, too many fucking people. I just wanted to be alone.

Matt and Griffin were both staring at me with wide,

concerned eyes. Did I look that bad? Evan was suddenly there, spinning me to look at him. "Jesus? What happened?" he asked, and I could see fear in his eyes. *I must look like someone died.* I couldn't explain it, I couldn't tell them...I needed out of here.

Inhaling a deep breath, I drew strength from a lifetime of hiding my feelings and slapped on a breezy smile. "Sorry, man...I drank way too fucking much. I need some air." I even managed to laugh after I said it, so he wouldn't worry. So none of them would worry.

Griffin groaned, then handed the bucket to Matt. He started walking away muttering, "Lightweight."

Matt held out the bucket for me. "Do you need this?"

Shaking my head, I clapped him on the shoulder. *No, I need you to leave. I can't keep this up much longer.* I could already feel the tidal wave of my true emotions pushing against my forced calm. "I'm fine, really." My phone buzzed in my pocket again, and I almost lost it.

Matt shrugged and left, hugging his bucket to his chest. I almost sagged with relief, but Evan was still watching me. "You sure you're fine?" he asked, brows bunched.

I forced my smile wider. "Yeah, I'm just gonna step outside for a minute."

He nodded...and I fled as quickly as I could get out of there without making him suspicious.

When I got outside, I heaved myself against some nearby railing, gasping for breath. *Oh God...oh God...oh God...this can't be happening.* It was like all the pain I'd suffered throughout my brief time on this earth was piledriving into me at once. I couldn't breathe, I could barely see.

One of the security guards at the door shouted, "Hey! If you throw up, you clean it up! Fucking rock stars..."

I really wasn't sure if I was going to throw up or not. My stomach churned like it might. My head pounded, and my heart hammered. *He knows how to reach me. He wants to talk.* No. *No! He doesn't get to talk to me.* Not now, not after everything he let me go through. Everything he *forced* me to go through. The years of abuse flashed through my mind. Dad shoving me against the slider, Mom handing him the dowel in the tract, Dad smacking my thighs with it until my legs gave out and I fell to the ground. Sobbing for him to stop. Apologizing for everything I could think of. The look in his eyes as he struck me...the apathy.

All of that happened because of *him*.

My fingers tightened on the railing as pain washed over me in waves. My breath came in rapid, frantic pulls now, and my fucking phone buzzed again with another fucking message. *This can't be happening.*

No. It wasn't happening. I'd taken my life back when I'd run away, and it was *mine* now. None of *them* got to touch it, not without my permission. Fuck Gavin. He could reach out all he wanted...it didn't mean I had to answer.

I tried to calm my breathing as I straightened from the railing. *It's fine, you're fine...let it go.* I debated calling Kiera, to work through this anger and pain with her, but I knew she wouldn't understand my outright refusal to speak to him. *She'll think I'm overreacting. She'll think it's no big deal if I talk to him. She won't get it, and she won't let it go. I can't tell her about this. Ever. And that means...I'll have to hide this part of myself from her...forever.*

And realizing that tore a hole through my heart. I'd never felt quite so alone. I could feel the tears stinging my eyes, but I choked them back. *It's okay.*

No, it's not. It's not okay. I'm not okay. I was beginning to wonder if I would ever be okay.

Eventually, as I stood there, blankly staring at the dirty street, the intense pain shifted into a dull ache, and then lonely dejection. I tried to resist the emptiness, tried to stop it from infecting every cell, every molecule, but I could tell I was losing the battle. I knew if I let this melancholy get its hooks into me, I'd drown in it...and I didn't want to. There were so many good things in my life right now—my band, this tour...Kiera. I didn't want to let one excruciating sore spot ruin all the bright spots. I needed a distraction.

Inhaling a deep breath, I dug out my cell phone. Careful to not let my mind piece together any letters and form them into words, I scanned the incoming messages. Most were from Hailey...but one was from an unprogrammed phone number. *That's from him. Jesus. He really did text me. Fuck.*

My stomach knotting, I ignored Hailey, ignored Gavin, and texted Kiera. *'I miss you'.* And I did. So incredibly much.

The phone in my hand instantly started ringing, and I smiled as Kiera's name appeared on the screen. Just seeing it made the hurt evaporate, made good feelings start to return to my overcome body. Great feelings.

"Hey," I said into the phone as relief rushed through me.

"I miss you too," she said, both longing and amusement in her voice.

Suddenly feeling light as air, I smiled at the image of her in my head. "You sound...pleased. Is that because of me? Did I do something?"

She let out a soft laugh. "I just...can't get over that picture." She laughed again, and grateful for the distraction she was providing me, I laughed with her. Kiera had found Jenny's steamy photo of me a lot sooner than I'd thought she would, and as I'd predicted, she loved it. "Is there really another one?" she asked. "Because I've searched everywhere..."

Lightly laughing, I shook my head. When she'd found that one, I'd teased her that there might be more hidden about, and I *had* hidden some regular photos of us for her to find, but that was the only one of me mostly naked. Damn. Maybe I should have had Jenny print out the entire session. Too late now. Guess Evan was right—I shouldn't have made Jenny delete them all.

"You know...I just can't remember," I teased. "You'll have to keep looking." Because she still hadn't found *the* letter. And I kind of wanted her to find it.

Kiera laughed again, then she sighed. "I can't wait to see you. How are your shows going?"

A flash of pain struck me so hard, I couldn't speak for a second. *No. Don't think about that, don't think about him, don't think about Hailey. Right now is just about Kiera.* Instead of divulging the recent events that had me twisted in near-debilitating knots, I told her something that I knew she'd find entertaining. "For me, it's going great. For Matt...it's been an adjustment."

Then I started telling her about Matt and his trusty bucket. Not only did it say *Property of Matt Hancock* on the side, like Griffin had wanted, but it was also littered with band stickers, crude drawings, sentiments of encouragement, and even a couple of phone numbers from hopeful fans. Matt hadn't needed to use it again after that first time, but there was something about having it nearby that calmed him. It was kind of his lucky charm.

As Kiera was sympathetically telling me, "Oh, poor Matt!" I noticed Evan peeking his head out of the back entrance. He saw me on the phone, then mouthed, *You okay?*

Nodding, I gave him a thumbs up. Yes, with Kiera's voice in my ear, I was great. Finally.

Chapter 18
GETTING CARRIED AWAY

The next day, my phone rang and chimed so many times, I thought I might go insane. Because it wasn't Kiera who was assaulting me through that stupid device. No, whenever I glanced at my phone to see who it was, it was either Hailey or the unprogrammed number that I knew belonged to Gavin. I ignored both of them, and it chipped away at me. I'd so desperately wanted a relationship with Hailey. And I'd so desperately wanted to avoid anything that had to do with Gavin. But both desires had backfired on me, and now I was paying the price. What a fool I was for wanting something.

Instead of dwelling on Hailey and Gavin, and the agony they were bringing into my life, I focused instead on the good things that were surrounding me: my friends, the fun we were having, and my girlfriend, and how excited I was to see her on Christmas Eve. That thought became my obsession as the day wore on. One more week and she would be in my arms again.

"Hey, Kell, we're going to go find a bar. You in?"

I looked over to see Evan standing next to Matt, Griffin, and Justin. We'd just finished the show, but we had another one tomorrow, so we didn't have to leave town right away. Feeling energetically awake, I nodded. "Sounds great."

We found a bar close by that was pretty packed. The minute we stepped inside, a group of girls recognized us—or at least, they recognized Justin, the celebrity amongst us nobodies. There was a chorus of squeals, then Justin was swarmed. The half panicked, half amused look on his face was priceless. The annoyed look on Griffin's face was even better.

"Damn it, we can't play Find-a-Skank here if people know who he is. That's not fair," Griffin said with a pout.

Shrugging, I told him, "Just think of it as a challenge. If you beat him *here*, surrounded by his fans, you'll be a god."

His eyes lit up, then he smirked at me. "Dude, I'm already a god." Then he started walking deeper into the bar, starting in on his game.

I laughed as I watched him walk as far away from Justin as he could get. Matt snorted. "Good one. That should keep him occupied for most of the night." He gave me a fist bump, then started looking around for an empty table.

While I watched Justin try to disengage himself from a friendly fan, a girl stepped up to me. "Are you in Justin's band?" she asked.

Shaking my head, I politely told her, "No."

Matt cleared his throat and raised his eyebrows at me. Clearly, he wanted me to elaborate. Rolling my eyes, I told the girl, "I'm with a different band. D-Bags. We're on tour with Avoiding Redemption...tell your friends," I muttered.

I saw Matt smile, heard Evan chuckle. The girl beamed at me. "Oh...awesome. I will, for sure." She flashed a glance behind her. "Or you could? My friends and I have a table over there. You guys want to join us?"

Not wanting the girl to get the wrong idea, I shook my head and told her, "Sorry. I don't think my girlfriend would like that." That was subtle, right?

The girl's face fell. "Oh...well...it was nice meeting you." She grinned again. "D-Bags. I like it."

She walked away happy, so I figured I hadn't upset her. Matt grinned at me in approval. "Nicely done."

I glanced at Evan's amused face, then shook my head. Walking, talking billboard, right here. "Can we drink now please?"

We ended up just hanging out at the bar. The two women behind it seemed really pleased to have us there, and I don't think we got asked to pay for a single drink. That didn't sit right with me—if it were Kiera getting free drinks from strangers all night, I might have a problem with it. No, I'd definitely have a problem with it, so when last call came around, I made sure to settle our tab. And then some, since the amount she quoted me was nowhere near the amount we'd consumed.

We were all a little blitzed when we stepped out onto the sidewalk. "Where to?" Griffin asked, his face dour. He hadn't beat Justin. And he was super-pissed that *I* had beat him, beat everyone. Again.

"Back to the hotel?" I shrugged.

He glared at me. "Fuck that. You owe me a meal."

My mouth popped open. "Why do I owe you a meal?"

"Because you're still cheating," he said, his eyes narrowing. "There's no way you beat Justin on his home turf."

"I don't actually live around here," Justin murmured, amusement in his pale eyes as he watched us.

Griffin turned his annoyance on Justin. "Did you help him cheat?"

Justin just laughed. Matt was holding his stomach he was laughing so hard, and Griffin turned his face toward him. "Ah-ha! It's you! I knew it! You slipped him numbers, didn't you? Goddamn it, Matt! You're ruining the sanctity of the game."

Sanctity? Of a game designed to find easy women?

Matt didn't answer him, just hunched over, hands on his knees, struggling to breathe. Griffin took that as an affirmative. "Thought so." His eyes swung back to me. "That's why you owe me a meal. Fucking cheaters, all of you."

Laughing, I shook my head. "We didn't cheat, but whatever... I could use some food."

Griffin slapped me on the back. "Damn straight, you cheated. Now let's go get you some penance."

"But I didn't..." I was laughing too hard to keep protesting, so I didn't bother. He could think whatever the hell he wanted. At least laughing at him was a great distraction from the recent pains in my life.

It took a while to find a place to eat. Mainly because Griffin had the attention span of a two-year-old. On every street he found something new and distracting to entertain himself with. None of us were in a hurry to get anywhere, so we just followed wherever his sense of adventure took him. We finally stumbled across a hole-in-the-wall, twenty-four-hour diner. They had hash browns. I was sold.

"Here," I said, jerking Griffin toward the door.

He lost his footing and nearly smashed into it, then laughed as he opened it. The space was small—and mostly empty—but there was a round table in the back where we'd all fit. As we all sat down, everyone pulled out their phones. I pulled mine out too. It was early morning here, so it had to be just about the time Kiera got home from work. Right? Did she work today? What fucking day was it again?

Oh well. If she was asleep, I'd just leave her a message. A sexy message. Hmmm. I almost hoped she *was* asleep.

Like always, I ignored the unread messages from Hailey, the unread messages from Gavin. Seeing them sitting there unopened made a painful ache split apart my chest, but I shoved the feeling deep inside. *They don't matter*. Kiera was the only one who mattered. She was the only one I wanted to talk to right now.

Connecting the call, I brought the phone to my ear and waited for either her or her voicemail. The grin on my face when she answered betrayed my true desire. As much fun as a sexy message would be, a back-and-forth conversation with her was infinitely better.

"Hey, you," she sighed. "I've missed you all day."

I had to close my eyes as those words settled into my heart. She'd missed me, she'd thought of me. Thank God she was still thinking about me. Remembering just how often she was on my mind made a small laugh escape me. "I missed you too. Anything *note*worthy today?"

She laughed, and I knew she understood my not-so-subtle hint. "Ah, yeah, actually. The cleaning staff at school has been slacking off lately. I found at least a hundred slips of paper that the janitors missed."

My grin was huge again as I pictured her retrieving all the crap I'd stuffed in those seats. About time she'd noticed them. I was honestly surprised any of them were still there. That had been one of my more ambitious projects. And a hundred...that sounded about right. She'd gotten most of them then. Good. But still, I had to tease her. "Hmmm...just a hundred? Guess some got nabbed by your classmates." With a laugh, I added, "I hope they got the kinky ones." Let her mind spin on that. The imagined blush on her cheeks made my chest tighten with longing. God, I missed her.

Her thoughts in line with mine, she said, "I'm packing right now...I can't wait to see you next week. Is there anything you need from your place? I could grab it."

A thought instantly leapt into my head, and I knew there was just no way I couldn't say it...it would be too much fun. "I can't wait to see you either," I told her, glancing at my friends. Matt and Evan were busy texting, Griffin was showing Justin a video on his phone. Nobody was really paying me any attention. Grinning, I lowered my voice and said, "In fact, I bought this lingerie for you before I left. I tucked it away for when I got back...You could bring that."

Her reaction was exactly what I'd been hoping for. "Uh, I don't...um..."

The slightly intrigued, slightly embarrassed image of her in my head was too adorable, and I couldn't help but softly chuckle at her. "I'm kidding, Kiera. You don't have to dress sexy for me... you already are." *You're perfect, just the way you are. I don't need more; I'll never need more.*

She sighed at me, but the sound was sullen...sad. Crap. Had I hurt her feelings somehow? Made her think I was anything other than completely satisfied with her? That hadn't been my intention. At all. I wanted her to feel confident around me...I just also really liked teasing her. But surely, she had to know by now just what her body did to me. And if she ever did wear lingerie for me, Jesus...I honestly wasn't sure if I could handle that. Stimulus overload. But maybe...maybe that sigh meant something else entirely. Had something happened? Fuck. Was she about to rip out my heart?

"You okay?" I murmured, my stomach unintentionally clenching. *Are we okay? Please say we're okay.*

Her answer was immediate, an unthinking response, and it wasn't at all what I'd been expecting. "Rain says thank you...again."

Rain? Poetic Bliss Rain? Why would she be sad about Rain? Why would she even be thinking about Rain right now? "Oh. Well, tell her it was no big deal. Her band is great; they deserved the opportunity." *What's really eating at you?*

The sullenness returned as she muttered, "Yeah, and she's not one to pass up an opportunity."

The trace of sarcasm, the slight edge of bitterness and annoyance...it all clicked into place, and I suddenly understood just what was bothering her. Goddamn it. *She knows about Rain and me.* Well, of course she knows. Kiera finding out about all my dirty little escapades seemed to be the story of my life. How was she still with me?

Knowing we should probably talk about it, I made myself say, "She told you, didn't she?"

Her breath escaped her in an angry burst, and when she spoke, the edge to her voice was harder than before. "No, I overheard her and Rita comparing notes."

Well, fuck my life. Why did my past seem to run into Kiera so often? Why did girls want to talk about sleeping with me so goddamn much? And why was Kiera always in the wrong place at the wrong time so that she had to hear every fucking detail? If it were me, hearing about her, I'd go insane. Damn it. Fate was either trying to make sure she knew exactly what she was getting herself into...or fate was blatantly trying to ruin us. Either way, I just wanted fate to leave us the fuck alone.

"Oh...did you know about Rita already?" How long had she been sitting on that secret? How was she *okay* with that secret? Why did she ever touch me in the first place...?

"Yes."

Her answer was curt, like she couldn't say anymore. And she didn't have to. She knew so much. She knew *too* much. How could I fix this? Especially from *here*. A surge of agony washed through me as I struggled for something to say, *anything* that would make this better for her. Easier. There really wasn't anything for me to say, except an acknowledgement of the truth. She knew *why* I had so many...dalliances. Hopefully that would keep her near me, instead of finally pushing her away. But how long would she keep accepting me? Hopefully, for the rest of my life.

"I'm sorry, Kiera. I never wanted you to have to hear about... them. If I could stop the gossiping, you know I would." I'd give anything to erase myself from everyone's memory but hers. *Anything*.

There was guilt in her voice when she responded to me, like she hadn't meant to bring any of that up. "You don't have to apologize, Kellan. It's...water under the bridge, really."

Water under the bridge? I supposed it was, but still, if the bridge wasn't stable enough, if there were cracks in the foundation, then that torrent of water beneath the bridge was no longer insignificant. It was inevitable doom where the past would reclaim us, drown us. *Please let us be stable.*

Before I could say anything to that, Kiera lightened her voice and tried to change the subject. "What about you, what have you been up to?"

Her simple question reopened a gaping wound, and I instantly filled with pain. And guilt. *I should tell her about Hailey, about Gavin.* I opened my mouth to do it, but I couldn't make the sounds. *She won't understand. She'll poke and prod and will never leave it alone. She'll try and force something I don't want. I can't deal with this right now...*

Suddenly weary, I told her a half-truth. "Just shows and traveling. I'm so sorry I haven't had a chance to come home yet. With us on the road between shows, there just hasn't been enough time to fly back to you." And now that I was here, doing it, I could see that my original hope of seeing her on occasion wasn't as practical as I'd originally thought. It killed me that she was just out of reach. Always just out of reach. Maybe that was the true story of my life.

"I know," she sighed. "I miss you...so much."

The wistfulness in her voice broke me, but at the same time, it warmed me. It also brought an ache to the surface. A needy, physical ache, but also a lonely, emotional ache, an ache that could never be satisfied, not without her in my arms. But I wanted her to know how much I still longed for her, how profoundly I missed her.

Knowing what I wanted to confess to her made a soft, throaty laugh escape me. I glanced at the guys again before I said it, but they still weren't paying any attention to my conversation. "I miss you too," I told her in a low, seductive voice. "I have the wildest dreams about you. You would not believe the hard-ons I wake up with."

Picturing Kiera's face right now, after hearing me say that, made me lightly laugh again. But what she said in response...blew me away. "Me too," she whispered.

I couldn't contain the amused chuckle at how she'd phrased it, but the image of what she was saying...Goddamn. Just the thought of her waking up wet, aching for me, was starting to make me hard. I had to adjust the way I was sitting. *Don't go there...think of something else.*

Kiera fumbled for words. "I mean, I'm not hard, but..." She groaned, annoyed at herself. If she knew just how much she was turning me on right now, she wouldn't be nearly so embarrassed.

"Yeah, I know what you mean," I said with a smile. Not wanting her to dwell on being embarrassed, I told her a straight-up fact. "I wish I was there, to touch you when you woke up that way. I wish I could feel how much you miss me."

Her response again surprised me. "I wish you were too..." she said, her voice full of longing.

Damn. She was killing me. Letting my exhale come out husky, needy, I told her, "God, your voice...I'm hard right now, Kiera. I wish you could touch me."

"I want to..." she murmured.

I could hear the desire in her voice, the wistful wish to be satisfied. If she were open to the idea, I *could* satisfy that ache for her. Would she be open to letting go for me? I surreptitiously looked at the guys, but they were all still preoccupied. There was no reason we both needed to go to bed unfulfilled. I could please her if she let me. And I really wanted her to let me. "Oh, Kiera...I want you so bad...What do you want me to do?" *Let me know you want this.*

"Touch it. Pretend it's me."

Well, damn. I really hadn't expected her to say that, to go along with this. I glanced around the table again, but no one had noticed what I was saying. Wondering if Kiera would be able to hear it, I held the phone with my shoulder and unzipped my jacket. Hoping the guys ignored this too, I drew in a purposely noisy breath. "Oh, I'm so hard...it feels so good. What now?" I asked, genuinely curious what she would say.

"Stroke it."

Fuck. Me. I needed to stop thinking about the words she was saying. I was not in the right place to experience this *with* her, but I could definitely give the experience *to* her. I'd just have to turn her on while turning myself off. This...was going to be tricky. Letting desire leech into my voice, I breathily told her, "Kiera...God...feels so good...I wish I was wet, though, like I am when I'm inside you."

"Do you have anything that would...?"

Thrilled she was playing along, I made my voice sound strained. "Yeah...hold on." I looked around the table for something, *anything* that would make the right noise. There was a squeeze bottle of ketchup by Griffin. Perfect. Griffin was still staring at his phone, oblivious to my conversation. I quietly snapped my fingers at him, waving until he looked at me. That got everyone's attention, and now they were all looking at me. Fuck. Oh well. Kiera was into this, and there was no way I was stopping now.

Pointing at the bottle, I motioned for Griffin to pass it over. Confused look on his face, he tossed it across the table to me. God, Kiera would fucking kill me if she knew what I was doing. But if she was willing to do this with me, then I was going to give her the best orgasm I could, audience be damned, and a little realism would help set the stage for her.

I noisily squirted some ketchup into my palm, then squished it a couple times. It was pretty loud, so I was pretty sure she'd heard it. All the guys tilted their heads as they tried to figure out just what the fuck I was doing. They'd figure it out in a second.

Ignoring the eyes on me, I groaned into the phone, "Oh...God...yes, it's warm...like you. You feel so good, wrapped around me..." Every single one of my friends raised their eyebrows, but none of them said a damn word.

As I wiped the ketchup off my hand with some nearby napkins, Kiera moaned in my ear, igniting me. "Do you want to touch me, Kellan?"

Jesus...did I. Fuck. Yes. But no, I couldn't let myself get turned on. Too much. This was for her, not me. And I was determined to satisfy her. *Whatever it takes.* Closing my eyes, I crumpled some extra napkins in my hand and murmured, "Oh God, yes, please. I need to feel that warm, wet skin...I need to be inside you..." *Please do it, Kiera. I want to give this to you.* "Does it feel good?"

Her voice was a whisper. "Yes."

I had to pause and press my lips together. Goddamn. *Don't picture her touching herself. Just...don't.* Banishing the erotic image, I made my breath quicken, made my voice sound achy, needy. "Oh God, I need it harder...faster..."

Her response was perfect. "Yes. Do it, do it faster..."

"Oh God, yes...don't stop...that feels so good, please don't stop..." She moaned in my ear, and I cringed as I tried very hard not to be aroused. *Baseball, basketball...what fucking sport should I be thinking about?* I let out a low, erotic noise for Kiera, made my breaths come in short pants like I was close. "I want to come... Kiera...come with me..." *Please...let go for me.*

"Okay," she whispered. Then she said, "Harder, Kellan, I need more of you in me."

Jesus. I cracked open my eyes to see if I still had an audience. Fuck. Yep, they were all still watching me. Evan shook his head at me, his lips curled in amusement. Matt looked...oddly curious as he studied me, like I was a song he was trying to memorize. Justin was biting his lip, trying not to laugh. And Griffin...he had his head cradled in his hands as he leaned on the table; the joy on his face definitely helped turn me off. I tossed the wad of napkins in my palm at him, but he just smiled wider at me.

Ignoring them all, I reclosed my eyes. *They don't matter right now; nothing matters but Kiera.* I let out another steamy sound for her, groaning, "Yes...God, Kiera, you're so sexy, you feel so good. I'm in you...right now...can you feel me? Can you feel how deep I am?"

She moaned louder than before, and I knew she was on the brink of...something. *Don't think about it, don't think about what she's doing.* "God, Kellan, you're perfect...so perfect." *No, you're perfect.* "Yes, yes, take me..." *Anytime, anywhere, Kiera.*

There was an odd noise at our table, someone softly talking, but I ignored it. Kiera was close; I needed to give this to her. Tilting my head back, I let my breathing sound like I was about to fall over the edge. "Oh my God, Kiera, I'm almost there...come with me..." *Go over the edge for me.*

"Yes, Kellan, do it...come for me..."

I felt someone poke my shoulder, and looking over, I saw Evan pointing up at an older woman standing beside him. Our waitress. She looked unfazed by my sexy talk, or by the fact that I was panting into my phone. Actually, she looked pretty amused by the whole thing. When she saw she had my attention, she whispered, "What do you want?" Pretty nice of her to be so considerate about what I was doing. I'd have to make sure we tipped her really well.

Hating to have to interrupt Kiera's moment, I stopped intentionally breathing like a maniac, covered the bottom of the phone with my hand, and told the waitress, "I'll have a Denver omelet...thank you."

Kiera instantly yelled at me. "Kellan Kyle! Are you in a restaurant!"

Fuck. Guess I hadn't muffled the phone well enough. Damn it. Hoping humor would diffuse the bomb, I said, "Well, I wouldn't exactly call this a restaurant...greasy spoon, maybe." The waitress lightly laughed as she left our table. Evan just kept shaking his head at me.

Kiera sounded mortified. "Please tell me you are not about to be arrested for indecent exposure."

I had to laugh at that. "No, I'm not."

"You faked all that? Why would you do that to me?" She sounded stunned, and I immediately felt guilty.

With a sigh, I said, "I never expected you to go along with it and when you did, well, I wasn't about to stop you from having your moment." Lowering my voice, I told her my simple truth. "Even if I can't come right now...I want you to."

She was quiet a moment, then she said, "I may have exaggerated my part in it...but I was thinking about it."

I laughed at that. She couldn't really be mad if we were both faking, right? "Well, we'll call that a practice round then. Next time...I'll be somewhere private, and you will actually touch yourself. Deal?"

As she murmured, "Yeah," Justin leaned forward, a huge grin on his face. "Kellan, tell her hi for me."

Frowning, I shook my head at him. No, I wasn't going to let her know that he was right here listening, that they all were. She'd kill me. Unfortunately...Kiera must have heard him say that. "Oh my God, please tell me that you're sitting alone."

Well, shit. *Will I get in more trouble if I tell her the truth? Or will she appreciate the honesty?* "Um, well, no...the guys are here... and Justin. He says hey, by the way." No point in not telling her hello now. Justin lowered his head to the table as he laughed.

Kiera screeched, "Oh my God!" And then the line went dead silent.

"Hello? Kiera? Are you still there?" Lowering the phone, I saw that the call was definitely over. Damn it. With a frown, I looked over at Evan. "She hung up on me."

He started laughing so hard, his eyes watered. "You're such a dick," he said around chuckles.

I pursed my lips at him, then looked around the table; they were all dying of laughter. "I wasn't trying to be a dick. I was trying to be nice." That just made them laugh harder. Their laughter was getting to me, and I started chuckling too. "Guess I got carried away..." Maybe I should have gone somewhere else to do that. It just hadn't occurred to me at the time. Oops.

Wiping his eyes, Griffin said in a half snicker, half singsong, "Kellan Kyle, you're my hero."

That curbed my amusement some. I definitely screwed up if

Griffin *approved*. Letting out a long sigh, I shook my head and looked over at Evan. "Goddamn it. I have to call her back, right?"

Still laughing, Evan nodded, then he started pushing me out of my seat. "Beg for your life, dude...beg for your life."

Well, fuck. Hopefully she wasn't too mad...

Stepping outside, I tried to reconnect the call. I really hoped she picked up. I needed to know just how pissed she was. She answered right away, thankfully, but her tone was ice-cold. "What?" she clipped.

"I'm outside now. I'm sorry." *Don't hate me.*

I heard her inhale and exhale a calming breath. "You did all of that in front of your friends?" She sounded both mystified and irritated.

Cringing, I kept my answer short, simple, and honest. "Yeah...I'm sorry."

"They all listened to you have phone sex with me?" By her voice, it was clear that she still couldn't quite process that I'd done that. It probably wasn't a good idea to mention that it wasn't the first time the guys had overheard me doing something overly erotic like that. There *might* have been a party or two where a forward girl had dared me to fake an orgasm, and I *might* have gone through with it since, at the time, there wasn't much I wouldn't do for a forward girl. And it *might* have led to...

No, definitely not mentioning that.

"I'm sorry," I repeated. I would say it as many times as she needed to hear it. Every time we talked, if necessary.

She was quiet a moment, then she uttered, "I cannot believe you."

"I'm sorry. It won't happen again, I promise." *Please forgive me.*

She was silent again, but when she spoke, the majority of her anger seemed to be gone. "You owe me. Big time."

A smile crept over my face. "Anything you want, it's yours." *Literally anything. Just stay with me.*

She sighed. Then a small laugh escaped her. "Whore," she muttered, sounding more amused than upset.

At hearing her pet name for me, my smile widened, and I lightly laughed, relieved. "Tease," I chuckled in response. She giggled in my ear, and I caved into the desire to fully laugh with her. *God, I love this woman.*

Please let me keep her.

Chapter 19
WHAT IT FEELS LIKE TO BE WITH YOU

I woke up with a start, my heart pounding in my chest and a familiar fear coursing through my veins. Goddamn dreams. I'd kind of hoped that being on the road, being in such a strange environment, being around so many people, would squelch the nightmares, but sadly...no. Dad still tormented me whenever he could.

This last dream had been a strange mixture of pleasure and pain. I'd been lying in bed, kissing Kiera, when Dad had walked into the room and simply driven a knife into my chest. He'd never killed me in a dream before. That made it slightly easier to disassociate from it; dream-Dad typically preferred torturing me, death was far too simple.

Maybe I shouldn't have watched that horror movie with Griffin last night. Maybe this was just a regular nightmare; I honestly didn't know.

Climbing out of my cubby, I slipped on some comfortable clothes and headed to the sitting area of the bus. The bus was stopped in a parking lot; shows were much closer together here on the east coast, and we often arrived early. I waved at the driver, an older man named Samuel, then I set about my morning routine of crunches and pushups in the slim aisle. It wasn't the most ideal place to work out, but it was better than the pavement outside. Maybe I'd go for a run next though. I had time, although, there was something I wanted to do today.

I was just finishing up my pushups when someone unexpected walked out of the sleeping area. Evan. He didn't typically get up this early. Dressed in lounge pants and a holey T-shirt, he rubbed his buzz-cut head as he yawned. When he saw what I was doing, he shook his head at me. "You're insane," he muttered.

I paused an inch from the floor and looked up at him. "Matt wants a billboard, might as well give him one that looks nice." Evan chuckled while I pushed myself up, then stood up. Swishing my hand, I told him, "It's just a habit. Helps me wake up, clear my head."

He tilted his head at me as he sat down. "You need to clear your head? What about?"

I stared at him a moment, wondering if I should tell him what had been going on with me recently. *Clear my head from thinking about the daily text messages I'm receiving from the biological parent I want nothing to do with.* But no, I couldn't tell Evan that. I didn't want to get into it. With anyone. Smiling, I pointed to the back of the bus. "Griffin's habit of walking around naked for one. Did you know he was part nudist?"

Evan grimaced. "Honestly, I'm more surprised he's not a *full* nudist. Poor Matt...How has that kid kept it together all these years?"

Laughing, I sat down at the table with him. "Maybe he hasn't. Maybe that's why he's so..."

"Matt?" he said, eyebrow raised.

"Yes, exactly." We both laughed for a moment, then I lifted an eyebrow at Evan. "What are you doing up?"

He sighed. "Couldn't sleep anymore. I'm getting anxious to go home, man. I just...really miss Jenny. Like crazy miss her."

I softly smiled, thinking of Kiera. "Yeah, I know what you mean. I'm ready for a break. Although...there is something I need to take care of first. Want to come with me?"

Evan's face was instantly suspicious. "Come with you where?"

My smile turned into a wide grin. "I need to go shopping."

Evan laid his head back on the seat with a groan. "I knew you were going to say that." The look on his face made me laugh. Evan hated shopping, especially with me. He lifted his head at hearing my amusement. Frowning, he said, "Fine. But if you can't find what you're looking for in the first three stores, I'm out. You're on your own."

Laughing even more, I nodded. "We should get dressed then, so we can get started."

He groaned again, sinking his head to the table. "I hate you," he murmured, looking up at me.

I smiled at his sullenness. "You'll love me when I help you find something great for Jenny."

Lifting his head, he pursed his lips. "True. Okay, fine."

We got dressed, but it was still early, and nothing was open yet, so we took a cab to a diner to get something to eat. Evan laughed as we sat down. "What?" I asked.

He pointed to my pocket. "Your cell phone stays put, got it?"

With a laugh, I made an X over my heart. "Deal."

Almost immediately after I said that my phone buzzed and chirped with a message, and my stomach began to churn with a now-familiar ache. Knowing it was Gavin, I suppressed a sigh. Evan heard my phone and pointed at my jacket. "I'm kidding. You can get that."

I shook my head. "It's not Kiera...she wouldn't text me this early. She's at her parents' place in Ohio, waiting for me." Needing a distraction, I let out a long sigh. "I'm finally going to meet her parents. I'm not sure what they're going to think of me."

My distraction worked; Evan didn't ask who'd texted me. He smiled. "Why wouldn't they love you?"

He truly looked mystified, like he really couldn't see why I might be unappealing to them. "Well, my job for one. Her dad isn't thrilled that I'm in a band." I frowned. "He doesn't consider that a real job."

Evan swished his hand. "That's because he's never heard you. If he had, he wouldn't be so worried about it. There's no way you're not going to be successful at this, Kellan."

His praise made me feel...weird. Was everyone around me delusional? The chances of us finding "success" were a million to one. Maybe more. There were just too many people trying to make it, and I had to believe a lot of them were way more talented than me. Instead of arguing with him, I shrugged. "Well, I have a feeling he'll be even less impressed if we do make it. I don't think he trusts me."

Evan scrunched his brow. "He doesn't even know you."

I gave him a small smile. "When it comes to Kiera, I don't think he trusts anybody. From what I've pieced together, he's a bit on the overprotective side."

"Ah...I see." He pursed his lips. "You might want to sleep with one eye open then. He might try and castrate you." He started laughing after he said it.

"Thanks for *that* thought," I said with a frown. Now I really wasn't sure about this.

Evan shook his head. "Don't worry, he won't. If I know anything about girlfriends and their parents, it's that they're hoping for grandbabies one day. He won't hurt you if he thinks you might eventually give him one."

Warmth flooded through me, like it always did when I thought of Kiera pregnant. Evan watched me for a moment, then threw a crumpled napkin at me. Blinking out of my fantasy, I looked up at him. "Doesn't mean he won't kick your ass if you try to knock her up inside his house."

A small laugh escaped me. "Well then, he's gonna have to kick my ass, because it's been weeks...I'm having sex with her."

Evan laughed, then shook his head. "Yeah, we all got that from your little phone call the other day." I snickered and Evan sighed. "Her poor dad...just don't give him a heart attack, okay?

Or make him accidentally kill you. We kind of need you to come back."

With a laugh, I shook my head. "I can't guarantee you anything."

He was shaking his head at me when the waitress appeared. Before she could even ask us anything, Evan pointed at me and said, "He'll have a Denver omelet."

I had to lie down on the bench seat I was laughing so hard.

After a leisurely breakfast, Evan and I made our way to the shopping district. Evan found a necklace he liked for Jenny, and I grabbed a bottle of perfume that smelled pretty good for Anna. Buying it felt a little odd to me, and as I did, I asked Evan, "Should we get Anna something from Griffin?"

Evan thought about that for a moment. Griffin was going home, to see his family in L.A. for Christmas. As far as I knew, he hadn't invited Anna to go with him, but that wasn't all too surprising. They weren't really a couple. They just...liked having sex with each other. Was that a gift giving relationship?

Finally, Evan shook his head. "The only thing Griffin would realistically give Anna...you don't want her opening around her parents. Especially if you're trying to stop Kiera's dad from killing you. Griffin can send her something if he wants to."

I nodded and let it go. Whatever was between them, that was for them to figure out.

Evan picked up something for his family, and then for Jenny's parents, which surprised me...and inspired me. I knew just what to get for Kiera's parents, but it would have to wait until I got to the airport. That just left getting something for Kiera.

Evan sighed as we walked through another jewelry store. "You know what you're looking for, right?"

I laughed at the annoyance in his voice, then nodded. "Yes, this won't take long, I promise." I walked us to the engagement rings, and his eyebrows lifted. I stared at those sparkling diamonds for a really long time...but we weren't there yet. If she wouldn't even move in with me, then I knew she wouldn't marry me. It was too fast. And yet, it felt like I'd been waiting forever for her to be my wife. *I shouldn't have hidden that letter so well.*

I forced myself to move down the display case. And that was when I found something more in line with what I was looking for: simple matching bands. Well, the man's was simple, just a ring of silver, the woman's was lined with small diamonds. Perfect, understated beauty, just like Kiera. The rings were technically wedding bands, but that wasn't how I wanted to use them. I wanted her to know where I was in regard to our relationship, just how deeply I was committed to her...and I wanted to see if she felt the same way, if her commitment ran just as deep. *I don't want her to get tired of waiting for me. I don't want her to be worried while I'm gone. I don't want to be replaced.*

Getting the salesmen's attention, I asked to see the pair of rings. While he got them out, Evan said, "Whatcha thinking, Kellan?"

I knew what it looked like to him, and I bit my lip before answering him. "Not wedding rings...but...promise rings. I want her to know I have no intention of cheating on her. I want her to believe it."

Evan studied me a moment, then nodded. He tried to hide it, but I saw the sympathy on his face. *Yes, I know. It's a little sad that we have to physically proclaim our monogamy. But trust me, it's something we need to do. Something* I *need to do.* Evan didn't say anything else as I bought the pair of rings, and I was grateful for it.

Thinking about Kiera and Christmas and being with her family made me start thinking about mine. Not Gavin. Fuck him. But Hailey...maybe I was being too hard on her. Maybe I was overreacting. Maybe I should give her another chance. That was the whole point of Christmas, right? Forgiveness, family, acceptance? Building bonds, building memories...maybe I could still have that with her. I still *wanted* it with her.

When Evan and I got back to the buses, I pulled out my phone and nodded for him to go inside without me. He grabbed my bags for me, considerate as always, then disappeared into the bus. Curious as to what Hailey had been saying to me while I'd been ignoring her, I—very carefully—checked my messages. Scrolling through her list of texts made my chest burn, like someone was sizzling me with acid.

'I'm so sorry, please call me.' 'I know I screwed up, I'm sorry.' 'Please talk to me.' 'I don't know how to fix this, I'm sorry.' 'Please don't shut me out.'

All of those made my eyes water, made my stomach fill with pain, but it was the last one she sent me, the one I'd ignored last night, that finally broke something inside me. *'It's clear you don't want to talk to me. I won't bother you again. I'm so sorry I hurt you.'*

Before I was even conscious of doing it, I was calling her number. She picked up instantly. "Kellan, I'm so sorry."

Hearing her voice soothed the agony in my stomach. "No, I'm sorry. I shouldn't have...I should have talked to you, yelled at you, vented at you...something. I shouldn't have just ignored you. I just...couldn't deal. You shouldn't have given him my number. Why would you do that?"

Her voice hitched with pain. "I'm sorry. He cornered me once he realized what I'd done. He wasn't going to let it go...And he was so...I caved, I'm sorry." She paused to let out a long sigh. "I guess a part of me was hoping you weren't really being serious about never wanting to talk to him. I was hoping it would bring you two together, but you've been ignoring him too, so I guess...I guess I was wrong."

I had to close my eyes as the pain assaulted me. *I don't want to think about him. I don't want to talk about him.* But I had to tell her something. "I was *completely* serious. He doesn't exist to me, but you..." My voice cracked and I had to pause, had to swallow the sudden lump in my throat. "You do, and I'd like to...I want you in my life." I wasn't sure how she would fit in my world, but I knew—the second that she'd said she wouldn't bother me again—that I couldn't handle the hole of *not* having her in my life. I couldn't go back to the way I was before I'd met her. A small, childlike part of me...needed her.

A small laugh escaped her. "I'm not going anywhere, Kellan. I'm always here for you...you're family."

The grin that spread over my face at hearing that brought a lightness to my body, and I could feel the decades of despair that had formed around my heart cracking, melting. Finally, that word might mean something *positive* to me. "Thank you," I whispered. "And please...don't ever say you won't bother me again. Just... keep bothering me, okay?"

"Stubborn, huh? Yeah, I get that. Kind of a family trait."

Her words made my stomach clench, but I ignored it. This had nothing to do with *him*. "So, what have you been up to?" I asked, genuinely curious.

She went on to tell me about school, winter break, a boy she liked...and I loved hearing every word. Finally, she said, "Okay, enough about me, how is life as a rock star?" Before I could tell her anything, she changed her mind on what she wanted to hear about. "How's your girlfriend?"

The change of direction made me laugh, and smile. "God... she's great. I can't wait to see her. Just a couple more days now."

Hailey sighed, then laughed. "Don't tell your girlfriend this, but I showed the picture of you and me to my friends...there's now an official waiting list for you. And there was some serious competition for the top spot. Blood was drawn."

A laugh burst out of me, and Hailey giggled too. God, it felt great to laugh with her, like a sore muscle being massaged. "Well, sorry to burst all their bubbles, but I'm pretty sure Kiera is the one. No...I *am* sure. On my end anyway." Hopefully she felt the same.

"Good. I want an invite to the wedding."

That made me sigh, made the ache return. And not just because I wasn't sure if Kiera would say yes...but because I didn't know how to tell Kiera about Hailey. I didn't know if I even could. Not wanting to get into it with Hailey, I simply told her, "Yeah...sure." *Probably not. Definitely not. I'm so sorry.*

Silence built up as that sad fact absorbed me. In the quiet, Hailey said, "Hey, I know you don't want to be bugged or pushed—"

Knowing where she was going, I instantly cut her off. "Hailey, don't—"

Proving we really were related, she cut me off too. "I'm not going to say anything else to him about you, I promise. Our conversations are private, confidential. But that doesn't mean I can't say something to you...about him."

"I don't want to—"

"I know you don't," she said, interrupting me again. "I just... Whatever you think he is...he's not. Can you just trust that I know him in ways you don't? He's a good man, Kellan. And you're hurting him. And I don't understand why. Can you explain it to me?"

My jaw clenched tight, and words were suddenly impossible. Could I even have a relationship with her when it unintentionally brought with it so much pain? Would this ever end? Fade? Because every time she mentioned him, it was a fresh dagger in my heart. She knew him better? Well, of course she did—he hadn't abandoned *her*. He was a good man? If he was so good, then why did he leave me in hell? Why did he flush me away like I was...garbage? Good man...bullshit. Repentant, maybe. Good? No.

"I have to go," I told her, my voice brusque.

"Kellan, I..." she paused, then sighed. "Call me later?"

A small smile lifted my lips. "Yeah." Painful or not, I still needed her.

I felt...on edge after that conversation. Both happy and furious. It was difficult to maintain the two conflicting emotions, and my insides were churning as I debated how to even myself out.

"It's Kellan, right?"

I looked up to see Paul walking my way. I resisted the urge to roll my eyes. We'd talked several times. He knew my fucking name. He was the only one on the tour who seemed to openly dislike me. I really had no idea why. I'd only ever been nice to him. I was chalking it up to jealousy. Stupid, petty jealousy. A lot of girls talked to me, flirted with me, not-so-subtly came on to me, while he...struggled to make a connection.

Not giving him the satisfaction of acknowledging his belittling comment, I said, "Hey, Paul. I'm kind of in the middle of something...could I have a moment alone, please?"

Paul smirked at me as he walked closer. Paul was the type who was trying too hard in my opinion. From the disheveled hair to the ripped-up clothes, the heavy eye makeup, and his wrists and fingers covered in jewelry, he just seemed...fake. "Fight with your girlfriend? She cheat on you yet?"

His comment, and his addition of the word "yet" climbed right under my skin, and I finally settled on an emotion. Clenching my fingers around my phone, I forced myself to keep my hands at my sides, and not slug him. "Leave me the fuck alone," I told him.

He didn't like that. "What the fuck's your problem?" He'd said that louder than he needed to. He wanted attention. Wanted people to see me as the villain here. Problem was, he was making me *want* to act like the villain. His overdone face was getting more and more tempting by the second.

Goddamn it. Picking a fight with someone I had to share a bus with was not going to help the rest of this tour. Swallowing my pride, I walked around him, back toward the bus door. That finally made him happy. "That's what I thought," he muttered.

I almost stopped. I almost turned around and walked back over to him. And that was when Evan stepped out of the bus, his eyes concerned as he looked my way. He'd heard the asshole's exclamation, and he'd known I was still out here. Evan also knew the murderous look on my face—he'd seen it a time or two. His eyes flashed between me and Paul, then he started minutely shaking his head. I could practically hear his thoughts. *Don't do it, man. Just let it go.*

Closing my eyes, I kept on with my slow pace to the bus. I reopened them at the door, and looked up at Evan. "I'm going for a run now. If that fucker follows me, I *will* kill him."

Evan nodded, then clapped my shoulder. "I'll help you bury the body," he said with a smirk.

A small laugh escaped me, and I felt the tension dissolving. Evan laughed too…then he stood guard outside the bus while I got changed. Damn. I owed that man so fucking much it was ridiculous.

The next couple of days lasted *so long*, but eventually Christmas Eve rolled around, and I was on a plane, heading to Kiera. The energy coursing through me was almost too much to bear, and I found myself constantly moving. I had to be annoying the shit out of the person sitting beside me on the plane, but the older woman just smiled whenever she looked at me.

I stared out the dark window, willing time to speed up. Who knew a plane could feel so…slow.

I nearly groaned with relief when we finally touched down. It was hard to not shove everyone out of my way and burst out of the plane. It took a lot of patience, but I waited my turn. The woman beside me grinned when I handed her carry-on bag to her. Then she handed me a business card with her phone number underlined. She was gone before I could even hand it back to her. She hadn't even said a word to me the entire flight. I could easily picture Griffin standing there, shaking his head in irritation. It made me laugh.

Leaving the card on my seat, I exited the plane.

I sped-walked to the taxi line, then cursed under my breath that there was a line. A long line. A pair of women in front of me offered to split their cab with me, but I declined. *I'll wait for my own. I have somewhere to be.* I'd thought Kiera would want to meet at her parents' place, but instead she'd given me a park name and instructions on where to find her there. Something about a duck pond and a bench. I'd figure it out. I liked the idea of a moment of privacy with her before I met her family.

When I finally got a cab, I read the text to the driver, hoping he understood. Thankfully, he seemed to know where to go, so I relaxed back in the seat and watched the world go by. I debated texting Kiera that I was on my way, but I didn't. I wanted to surprise her. Even though she knew I was coming so none of this was truly a surprise. My giddy excitement to see her again made me laugh. Had I ever been this anxious for something? I didn't think so. God, I was so pathetic.

We arrived at the park near Ohio University, and I thanked and paid the driver. The cab left as I stood there absorbing the scene. It was lightly snowing, and the grass and trees were covered in a sheen of white. Everything was so damn peaceful, it calmed me. There was only one car in the parking lot, barely a hint of snow on it. I grinned as I realized that had to be Kiera's car. *She's out there somewhere, waiting for me.*

Smiling, I set off in search of my angel.

Walking down a hill toward the pond, I spotted Kiera sitting on a bench. Her back was to me, and she was looking down, but even still—my breath caught, and my heart started pounding. *God, she's beautiful. God, I've missed her.* Had she felt just a fraction of what I'd felt during these last couple of months? Had every day been a little bit of a struggle for her, like it had been for me? She told me she missed me all the time, but was the air thinner when I was gone, was the world muted, were the good times a little sad, and were the bad times especially devastating... like they were for me without her around? Did she *really* miss me? Or was that just something that was said to be comforting, and her life...it hadn't really changed all that much? She was trying to not need a man anymore after all. Maybe she didn't. Maybe she was finally okay being alone. Maybe she didn't need me. *Will she stay with me if she doesn't need me?*

Stop. Just...stop. She loves you, and she's right in front of you. That's all that matters right now.

The doubt and sadness evaporated as I let that fact settle inside me. *She's here, she's mine.* Kiera still hadn't sensed me as I continued walking down the hill. It amused me that she hadn't. Her thoughts must be a million miles away. Thoughts of me? I hoped so. I paused by a large tree at the base of the hill. I was only a few feet away from her now, but in her blind spot. There was a light post on the other side of her, and bathed in the edge of its glow, I could see her clearly. Her full lips were in a slight pout as she stared at her phone. The snow was falling on her, around her, her cheeks were rosy, her dark hair darker...she was breathtaking, and for a moment, I was struck still and silent, helpless to do anything but gaze at her.

How did someone like me end up here, with that beautiful, intoxicating, warm, wonderful woman in love with him? Why did it still feel so surreal?

Careful to not make a sound, I lowered my bag to the ground and pulled out my cell phone. Kiera was frowning. Was she upset I was late? Getting a taxi had taken a lot longer than I'd expected. I knew seeing me would make her smile. But first, I couldn't resist teasing her. It had been too long. And it was especially hard to resist considering the fact that I was *right* behind her; she really should have sensed me by now. She should have much better spatial awareness if she was going to sit in a park at night.

I stared at the phone for a moment, trying to remember what Matt had said about turning the sound off. *Was it this button?* It seemed to get quieter as I pressed it, so I had to assume that was it. I almost laughed at my own ineptitude, but that would give away my position. I quickly texted Kiera a very disappointing message. '*I'm sorry...I can't make it.*'

When I heard the message chime on her phone, I could tell I'd startled her. I had to clench my stomach to not laugh. Lifting an eyebrow, I waited for her to look around, call me on my bluff.

Come on, Kiera. You know I wouldn't miss this. You have to know I'm fucking with you.

She slumped when she read the message though. She believed me? My phone lit up with a new message—a silent one. *Ha! Take that, Matt. I did it right.* Kiera didn't notice the light from my phone. As I read her message, I saw that she really had believed me. She really had no idea I was here. '*Really? But it's Christmas...*' she'd texted.

I frowned as I looked at her. *You really can't tell I'm right here?* But clearly, she couldn't. She was starting to wipe tears from her eyes, and she was sniffling. Was she crying? For me? I bit my lip and took a step forward. I hadn't meant to make her cry. I was sure she'd look around for me, then spot me instantly, then, maybe, throw a snowball at me. But she hadn't looked for me, and I'd accidentally crushed her. But...witnessing the pain...while it made me want to run over and hold her, it was also filling me with warmth, with love, with *relief*. Maybe it was wrong, but seeing her grief made me feel...wanted. *She does miss me.* Knowing it, seeing it, made me feel buoyant, like something inside me was being patched.

Smiling, I realized I had an opportunity to make her feel just as amazing as I felt right now. I could give her a genuine surprise. A Christmas miracle, so to speak. It would just require her to feel a little worse first. But just for a second. I wouldn't let her suffer long. Hoping she didn't kill me later, I typed back, '*Yeah, I know. I tried...I'm really sorry.*' Smiling, I added another message, one I already knew the answer to. '*Are you okay? You're not crying, are you?*'

She scoffed at the phone, wiping her nose, wiping her tears. A heartbeat later, I read her response. '*No...I'm fine. I know you tried. I'm okay...really.*'

Liar, liar...but in a sweet way. She was trying to spare me guilt. I should put her out of her misery. Especially since she was starting to cry in earnest. Grinning, I typed back something that should clue her in to the fact that I was messing with her. '*You're lying.*'

A sob escaped her before her phone chimed, and I felt a stab of guilt. Was this sweet? Or was I being a dick? *I'll make it up to her if I am.*

She didn't seem to understand my clue after reading my text. Sounding a little annoyed at my presumptive message, she murmured, "Am not..."

Latching onto *that* opportunity, I instantly typed, '*Are too.*'

Kiera seemed dumbfounded by my omniscient message, and I had to bite my lip to stop from laughing. She held the phone away from her like it was alive, then she started flipping through it like she was looking to see if she'd texted that to me. *You didn't, Kiera. I heard you because I'm right behind you.* My stomach hurt from not laughing. Oh God, maybe Evan was right...I *was* a dick. She was so fucking cute though. I'd frazzled her enough that she wasn't making sense. *If you'd texted me, it would be the last message sent.* Even *I* knew that.

I heard her say, "How did you know that, Kellan?" and I had to grab my stomach.

Shaking my head, I sent her another message. '*I know that because I know everything.*' She looked genuinely alarmed now. Grinning, I immediately sent her another one. '*I also lied...turn around.*'

I stepped away from the tree as she *finally* turned around on the bench. Just as I'd predicted, the look on her face as she took me in was one of extreme joy—so much more than what she would have felt if I'd just strolled up to her and said hello. It was a little mean, sure, but now...now she knew how I felt every time I looked at her. *Every day* this *is what being with you feels like to me. Now do you understand?*

She breathed my name, and I started walking her way. That wasn't fast enough for her; she was already running toward me, slipping and sliding on the frozen ground. She collided into me, wrapping her arms around my neck. Lightly laughing, I lifted her up and spun her in a circle before returning her to the ground. She laughed as she stared at me, and I felt contently trapped by the love in her eyes. *Jesus, it's so good to see you.*

I was lowering my mouth to hers, eager to taste her again, when she pushed me back. The joy on her face shifted to annoyance. "You were kidding? You're such a jerk."

I laughed at her comment, and the cuteness of her anger. She was right, but still, I had to tease her. "I thought I was a prick?"

She shook her head at me, but then she grabbed my cheeks and pulled me into her—a silent demand to kiss her. The feel of her soft lips on mine almost made me whimper. It had been...so long. I wrapped my arms around her, holding her tight, and I finally felt whole again. Utterly complete.

"I'm sorry I'm late," I murmured.

Her hands tangled into my hair, sending fire down my body. "I'm just glad you're here," she answered.

I pulled away from her hungry lips to look at her, to let this moment fully seep in. Because it was starting to feel like a dream, and I couldn't quite banish the horrible feeling that I was about to wake up. Absorbing the feel of her, the smell of her, the heat in her eyes, the shape of her lips, I whispered, "I've missed you...so much." I didn't know how I'd have enough strength to leave her again. I couldn't think about it yet.

Smiling, she sought my lips again. "I've missed you too."

Long minutes passed as we stood there, kissing in the lightly falling snow. I could have stayed there forever, with my arms locked around her, reveling in her passion as I fed her my own, but I could feel her trembling...and not because of me.

I pushed her back during a break in our lips. "We should go. You're frozen."

Her jaw shook when she answered me. "I'm fine."

I had to smirk at that. She was far from fine. "Your teeth are chattering," I said.

She leaned up, trying to pull my head down, trying to find my lips again. "I don't care..."

Her refusal to stop kissing me was adorable, but if she got much colder, warming her up would be painful, not pleasant. With an amused laugh, I grabbed her waist and forcefully twisted her around, making her let go of me. Then I pulled her into my body, her back against my chest, and slung my arms over her, doing what I could to keep her warm. In her ear, I told her, "Well, I care."

She leaned into me, and my heart started beating faster, my body started responding. There was more than one reason why I wanted to get out of here. "Besides, I can't make love to you out here..."

She immediately stepped forward and grabbed my hand. Leading me away, she said, "You're right...it is getting pretty cold."

Looking down, I shook my head at her. And here she liked to claim that anything that had to do with sex sold *me* on an idea. *We're not so different, Kiera. You want me too. And you missed me too.* Wanting her to feel better about me teasing her earlier, I looked up at her. She was looking back at me with love and interest on her face.

My grin grew playful as she pulled me forward. "I know my trick was a little mean, but it did prove one very important thing."

She moved to walk beside me, looping her arm around mine. "Besides the fact that you haven't changed...that you're still a prick?" she asked, amusement in her voice.

With a laugh, I nodded. "Yes, aside from that." There was so much adoration on her face as she stared up at me, it again made me worry that I'd fallen asleep on that plane somehow...that this was all a fantasy. Shaking my head, I whispered, "You really did miss me." I'd meant to say it lighthearted and playful, but instead it had come out as...wonder. And that was exactly how I felt—wonderous.

How is this *my life?* Someone had missed me. Someone had cried for me. Because I hadn't been there. Mind-boggling.

Kiera stopped us. She just stared at me for a moment. The disbelief was so thick in her eyes, I had to swallow the ball of emotion forming in my throat. Somehow me trying to make light of my assholishness had morphed into me cutting open my heart, and now I was beginning to hemorrhage.

Shaking her head, she placed a hand on my cheek. "Of course I missed you. I missed you every day, every hour...practically every second."

I gave her a soft smile, then looked away. I shouldn't have let that moment get so serious. Did it make it sound like I'd doubted her? Or did it just make me sound pathetic? "Yeah, I saw that," I told her. Remembering seeing her grief for me made a swell of something dark and painful stir within me, something I thought I'd shoved down farther than I had, something I wished I could rip out of my body and be done with forever: a bitter blend of loneliness, sorrow, fear, and desperation. My voice was thick with the resurfaced emotions when I spoke again. "I just...No one's ever missed me before..." No one ever cared enough to miss me before.

Kiera's hand moved to my chin, pulling my gaze back to hers. "I miss you when you're gone. I feel like I can't breathe when you're away. I think about you so often, it borders on obsession. I love you...so much." Her eyes were intent as she studied me, like she was trying to drill the words deep into my brain, all the way into my subconscious where I wouldn't forget them...or doubt them.

Her words were everything I'd ever wanted to hear, and a swell of love shot right up my chest, into my throat, making speech impossible. Overwhelmed, I gave her a tight smile and a small nod; it was all I could do.

Chapter 20
NOTHING COMPARES

I felt completely at peace again when we arrived at Kiera's parents' place. The quaint, two-story house was completely dark. That surprised me. I'd sort of expected her dad to be awake, waiting for me. Maybe pacing the porch, shotgun in hand. But it seemed like he'd gone to bed. Maybe this wouldn't be as bad as I thought.

Kiera giggled after she shut the car off. Lifting my head from the seat, I looked over at her. She had an almost childlike giddiness about her. It was adorable. "Want to see my room?" By the look on her face, you'd think she'd just said something truly scandalous. She was so cute.

I told her I'd love to, then I grabbed my bag and we headed inside. It felt like we were breaking and entering as we stepped into the living room. Kiera even cautioned me to be quiet by placing her finger to her pursed lips. It made me want to laugh, but I did what she requested and only smiled as I shook my head at her.

Kiera pointed to an ancient couch covered in plastic. Plastic? Who actually wrapped their couch in plastic anymore? It looked extremely uncomfortable. Dashing my spirits about this trip, she whispered, "You can leave your bag here. That's where you'll be sleeping."

Frowning, I raised an eyebrow at her. *Seriously? We can't share a bed?* I could understand her dad being pissed about us having sex under his roof, but even just lying next to each other—fully clothed—was off the table? Did he think my sperm was *that* potent? And besides, didn't Evan say they probably *wanted* grandkids anyway? *Can't give you a grandkid if I can't have sex with your daughter.* Just saying.

Seeing the sullen look on my face made Kiera smile for some reason. Then she gave me a quick kiss and started unfolding the blanket and adjusting the pillow that had been left for me, making a bed. My bed. Great. Uncomfortable cubby to uncomfortable couch. Oh well. At least I was here with her. That was all I really needed. I *had* been looking forward to making love to her though...

Shaking my head, I set my bag on the ground, then slipped off my shoes and my jacket. I started sitting down, to try and get comfortable, when Kiera pulled me back to my feet. In my ear, she whispered, "You're not actually sleeping there, silly."

Understanding smacked me in the face. Was that why she'd giggled when she'd mentioned her room? She was sneaking me upstairs, like we were horny teenagers, not full-grown adults. I really was kind of a bad influence on her, not that I wanted to stop her from breaking her dad's rules. But...I also didn't want to cause a problem while I was here. I was their guest, after all. Damn it.

"Are you sure?" I asked her, glancing upstairs. "I don't want to get you in trouble." But even as I said it, I had a mischievous grin on my face. *What will you let me do to you up there?*

Nodding, she pulled me away from the couch. "Yes...you're with me."

From the sultry gleam in her eye, it was clear she meant we would be doing a lot more than sleeping in her room. *Oh, thank God.* I wasn't sure if I possessed enough willpower to lie down in a bed with her all night and not try to have sex with her. It had been too long since we'd made love. I was dying to be with her.

My smile bright, I surged forward, cupping her cheeks, and pulling her mouth to mine. We kissed the entire time we made our way to the stairs; the heat between us intensified with every step. God, I missed this fire. Nothing made me feel quite so unrestrained as kissing Kiera. Being with her...set me free.

She almost fell when we reached the stairs, and steadying her, I teased her to be quiet. She let out a soft giggle before returning her lips to mine. We somehow managed to traverse the stairs without pausing our lips for long. I was so hungry for her, I just couldn't get enough. I didn't think I'd ever get enough.

I slipped off her jacket but held it in my hands until we got to her room, then I flung it somewhere inside. Kiera closed her door, then pressed me against it. Her body tight against mine felt so fucking good, every part of me was strained, aching, needy. I hissed in a breath, then whispered, "I missed you."

Her response was an erotic moan that tore through me, flaming every nerve ending. As her lips moved with mine, her fingers tangled into my hair. Damn, I'd missed that feeling. I ran my hands down her back, pausing a moment to savor the ridge and valley of her low back, then the curve of her ass. Fuck. *I want you.*

Squatting down, I picked her up and walked her to her bed blind, since I wasn't about to stop kissing her. I stopped walking when I felt my legs hit the bedframe. Leaning over, I set her down. She instantly grabbed my head, keeping our mouths connected. It electrified me that she felt the same insatiable hunger. I felt like she was my air, and if I stopped kissing her, even for a second, I'd suffocate.

Mouths connected, hearts connected, we crawled to the middle of her bed. She relaxed onto the mattress, and I settled myself over her with a satisfied groan. Finally.

Except...

Kiera and I stopped kissing, stopped moving, stopped breathing, as we both noticed the same thing at the same time. Her bed was extremely fucking noisy. Seriously? What the hell was this thing made out of? Every aged, rusted spring in the world?

Annoyed, I propped myself up on my hands so I could test the mattress. Shoving down on it made it squeak so badly, it was almost comical. If we had sex on this thing, we might as well open the door so her dad could watch. The sound was just too blatantly obvious. Fuck my life. I tested it again, but the springs weren't relaxing. It was still way too fucking loud.

Looking down at Kiera underneath me, I watched her grimace and bite her lip. "Did your dad buy you the squeakiest bed in the world on purpose?"

She cringed, then sighed. "Yeah, probably." She squirmed beneath me, but then stopped and glanced at her door. Her face looked...resigned. Like sex was off the table now. *I don't think so.*

Smiling crookedly at her, I shook my head. "Well, your dad obviously doesn't know me very well, if he thinks that's going to be a big enough deterrent."

I stood up, then motioned for her to join me. Her expression curious, she slipped off the mattress to stand beside me. Grabbing all of her blankets, I laid them on the ground between her bed and the window. Then I grabbed her pillows, so we would be somewhat comfortable. Once I was finished, I showcased our new bed. "Your love nest awaits."

She crossed her arms over her chest, looking both amused and skeptical. I was pretty sure she wasn't thrilled about sleeping on the floor...but I also knew I could change her mind. I walked over to her, grabbed her hand, and led her to our now-quiet bed. Pulling her into my body, I murmured, "Kiera?" I placed a light kiss on her neck, under her ear; she started trembling. I kissed her a little lower. "Will you...?" Another kiss, a little lower. She tilted her head back, and I heard her breath pick up. I kissed her in a sensitive spot above her collarbone, then slowly ran my nose up her neck. Mouth hovering next to her ear, I finished my question in a low voice. "...make love to me?"

It was like I'd set a match to her. Her mouth instantly found mine, and she kissed me hard, frantic. She tugged at my clothes, wanting them off. I pulled off my shirt, tossing it somewhere behind me. Her fingers trailed over my exposed skin; everywhere she touched me burned in the best way. This was better than every erotic dream I'd had about her. No dream version of Kiera would ever truly match the love and passion of the real Kiera. And it was all for me. It still blew my mind.

Once all of our clothes were strewn about the floor, we laid down on her quilt, then brought her heavy comforter over us. Cocooned in her blankets, bathed in darkness, our fast breaths the only sound, I felt so connected to her, like she was an extension of me, like my heart was outside my body. Her legs tangled with mine, and her skin was so soft, I couldn't stop feeling every inch of her, tasting every inch of her. *I don't ever want this to end.*

Her hands glided over my body, searching, feeling. Her fingers wrapped around me, feeling how hard I was for her, how ready, and a soft, needy noise escaped me. Desire on her face, she grabbed my hips, urging me on top of her. Our eyes locked, and the depth of love I saw in hers mesmerized me. She took the moment of distraction to suck on my bottom lip, sending a shockwave of pleasure through me. Then she was nodding, begging me without words to take her.

I shifted our bodies so I could press inside her, but then I paused, absorbing the moment. Kiera's breath quickened as she anxiously waited for me to move. Feeling the ache building, I rested my forehead against hers, letting everything about her fill me: her heart, her soul, her love, her compassion. How was I so lucky? How did I get her to love me so much? Was there anything else in my life that made me feel like she did? No...nothing even came close. Not being on a stage, not being on this tour, not hanging out with my friends, not even meeting my sister, and definitely not being contacted by...

No. Stop.

But it was too late, the pain had leeched in. *He doesn't matter.* Kiera was the only thing that mattered—she would always be the only thing that mattered. Not meaning to, I vaguely confessed my swirling thoughts. "Nothing...compares to this..." And nothing ever would.

Needing to reset my mind, I finally pushed into her. The explosion of pure bliss did the trick, and I was once again, fully in the moment. I dropped my head to Kiera's shoulder as the euphoria overwhelmed me. She let out a strangled noise of restraint, trying to be silent. We slowly began to move together, but Kiera was like a coil of restless energy beneath me. I could feel her shaking, desperate to satisfy an ache she'd been holding onto for far too long. Much sooner than was typical for her, I could tell she was ready to let go but was stubbornly refusing to give in. Was she holding back for me? I didn't want her to. I wanted her to fall apart. I wanted to feel it, wanted to see it. Gently grabbing her cheek, I made her look at me. "Don't... Let go..." She shook her head, and I leaned down to whisper, "Don't worry about me...let me give this to you..."

I pushed harder against her, and she lost the battle with her body. Her back arched as her walls clenched around me. She dug her fingers into my shoulder as she struggled to not make a sound. The look on her face as she lost herself in the ecstasy of it was...unbelievable. She'd never been more beautiful. And I'd never been so turned on. I didn't want to come, didn't want this to stop, but I desperately *needed* to now. "God, Kiera...God...that was..." That was too much. *I need relief.*

I needed more. I pushed deeper into her, faster. Her mouth met mine, still eager, and I could barely contain the soft groans leaving my body. She felt...so good. Her hands pulled against my hips, urging me on. I felt lightheaded, like I was floating, and the only thing that existed anymore was pure, perfect, escalating pleasure. And then I felt it, that moment of no return. My head started lowering to her shoulder as my body clenched in preparation, but Kiera stopped my descent with a hand on my cheek. She wanted to watch, like I had watched her. I grabbed her other hand, clenching it tight, and then the release hit me.

My eyes closed as the building pressure shifted to outright bliss. I didn't want to be quiet—it was so intense—but I needed to be as silent as possible, so I bit my lip and struggled to not let it out. And that was when I felt Kiera stiffen and heard her let out a ragged exhale, coming again, prolonging the moment for me. *Fuck...yes.* Bliss slowly shifted into peace as I collapsed onto her body, satisfied in every way.

Nothing compared to making love to her...except...*being* loved by her.

Kiera and I fell asleep, lightly kissing, and even though I knew the floor would leave me sore in the morning, I'd never been happier.

I woke up to the feeling of Kiera snuggling into my body. Smiling, I tightened my arm around her waist, pulling her into me. "Mornin'," I murmured. Then I inhaled and stretched, and as predicted, every point of contact hurt. Well worth the pain though.

Especially when I felt Kiera kiss my neck. "Good morning, yourself," she told me. I felt her hovering over me, and I could almost sense her smile. "Merry Christmas, Kellan."

Opening my eyes, I drank her in. Then I reached out for that beautiful, smiling face. "Merry Christmas, Kiera." Gently wrapping my fingers around her neck, I started pulling her toward my mouth.

That was when her bedroom door opened. I froze, wondering if I was about to get my ass kicked, but then I heard Anna's voice. "Kiera? Where are you?"

Kiera sat up to look at her sister. I took the opportunity to study Kiera: the edge of the blanket clenched tight around her chest, messy hair spilling over her shoulders, a slight flush to her cheeks. Damn, she was gorgeous. Did we have time for another round?

I heard Anna giggle, then she was lying on the noisy bed,

head in her hands as she looked down at us on the floor. The expression on her face was full of amusement. As Kiera returned to my arms, Anna laughed out, "Well, I was going to wish you a Merry Christmas and ask if you wanted to head downstairs with me, but I can see that you've already unwrapped your present." Her gaze shifted to me. "Hey, Kellan, glad you finally made it."

Her comment made me laugh. "Hey, Anna. Thanks."

Kiera started covering more of my chest with the blanket, like she didn't want Anna to see even that much of me. It was cute, although, I kind of understood why she felt that way—Anna was thoroughly enjoying the view. With a sigh, Kiera asked her sister, "What time is it?"

Anna tore her gaze from my chest. "It's breakfast time... Mom's making eggs."

That made me a little sad. I wasn't ready to stop cuddling. The news freaked out Kiera though. She sat up straight, ripping most of the covers off my chest as she took them with her. "Breakfast...Is Dad up?"

Anna grinned as her view of me returned. "Yep." She pointed at me. "And he'd better get out of here before Dad realizes he's not on the couch."

Kiera instantly started pushing me, trying to shove me out of the blankets with all her might. She did remember I was naked, right? Thinking she wouldn't want me to give Anna a peep show, I fought against her. "Kiera, relax." *I'll get up when Anna leaves.*

She was too freaked out to think this through. Shaking her head, she pushed harder. "No, Anna's right, he's gonna kill you if you're up here."

I gave her an incredulous look. He might be overprotective, but I highly doubted he'd actually harm me. He wasn't like *my* dad. I already knew that much. "What's he going to do, really? Ground you?" He might be mad at her, but in the end, she was an adult. We both were. He'd get over it.

Kiera didn't see it my way. Shoving my shoulder, she nodded. "Yes, right after he castrates you."

Her words reminded me of Evan's snickered warnings. God. Fine. I didn't really want his first impression of me to be one full of anger anyway. Since Kiera didn't seem to care about my nakedness, I stopped fighting her and simply stood up. Anna had a millisecond to grin at me before Kiera slapped her hand over her eyes.

Kiera scowled at me while she tried her best to stop Anna from peeking. *Hey, you're the one who was so impatient for me to get up. I wanted to wait.* Finding my boxers, I pulled them on, then grabbed the rest of my clothes. Stepping into my jeans, I smirked and told Kiera, "Fine, I'll sneak into the hallway, so he'll think I was in the bathroom."

Kiera shook her head at me as I pulled up my jeans. "No, you should sneak out the window. Make him think you went for a walk or something."

My mouth dropped open as I zipped up my jeans. *Seriously?* That seemed a little extreme, especially considering where we were. While I gaped at Kiera, she dropped her hand from Anna's eyes. Anna frowned. Then grinned since I hadn't put on my shirt yet. Ignoring her, I pointed at the window. "We're on the second story, Kiera." Did she think I was part monkey or something?

Kiera again shook her head, wrapping the sheet tighter around her. "Please. He won't believe that you were just in the bathroom." She pointed to the window. "There's a store about a block from here that should still be open. You could pick up some milk...My mom would love you for that."

The look on her face was so endearing, and I could sense love for her parents—and their sanity—behind the request, but still...I could potentially die trying to do this. She knew that, right? Hands on my hips, I tried to pop a hole in her master plan. "My shoes and jacket are downstairs in the living room."

Already amused, Anna's grin grew wider. "No, they aren't. I put them outside when I woke up."

Kiera looked at Anna, surprised. I was just annoyed. Anna told Kiera something about having to hide a boy before while I tugged on my shirt with an irritated groan. "Damn it, I haven't snuck out of a woman's window since I was fifteen." And I'd nearly died that time too. But that one hadn't been optional. It was either death by falling or death by her husband. This situation didn't seem nearly as dire as that.

Kiera rolled her eyes at my comment. Anna laughed and said, "Kellan, I think you and I seriously need to swap some stories someday." I threw her a grin, and she winked at me. There were a lot of stories I'd never share with Anna, but I got her point—between the two of us, we'd probably done almost everything.

Whether exasperated by me or Anna's comment, Kiera was done arguing, and she started shoving me toward the window. Glumly opening it, I stuck my head out to look around. Goddamn it. It was still lightly snowing, and there was fresh snow everywhere. I was going to freeze before I slipped and died. At least there was a trellis at the edge of this decorative roofline, and I didn't have to try and dangle myself off the ledge and drop onto a bush to break my fall. Still. The trellis wasn't screaming stability to me.

Looking back at Kiera, I tried again to reason with her. "You're an adult, Kiera. He really would probably get over it quicker than you think."

"He was going to have you sleep in a tent, Kellan...in the backyard."

I started laughing...until I realized she wasn't joking. Okay... seriously overprotective then. Her dad might actually toss me out of the house if he caught me in her room, and I really wanted to stay here, wrapped up in the warmth of Kiera's family. "Fine," I said, kissing her cheek. "But you owe me, big time."

I pinched her butt before I left, and she giggled. Anna giggled too. Since I still might die, I saluted them a farewell before I ducked out the window. My feet instantly tingled with the cold as my socks soaked through. Damn it. Walking to the store with squishy feet was going to suck. Assuming I survived this of course. Careful of my footing, I stepped to the edge of the roof closest to the trellis. The top of the trellis was a little lower than the roof, so I had to squat down to reach it. *And here is where I die.*

I heard Kiera whisper, "Be careful," and I looked up at her. She looked warm and cozy as she stuck her head out the window; I was already shivering.

Anna joined Kiera at the window, and I smirked at them. Lowering my voice, I told Kiera, "You're lucky last night was completely worth this..." Even if I did die...still worth it.

Kiera's cheeks flushed with color, and Anna let out an amused laugh. I moved a hand and foot over to the trellis before my toes and fingers froze up too much and this truly was impossible. To my great relief, the trellis held my weight. I started climbing down, but Kiera's voice stopped me. "Kellan."

When I looked back up at her, she grinned. "Pick up some eggnog too."

Closing my eyes, I shook my head. Unbelievable. And yet, so adorable.

The trellis held all the way to the ground, thank God. I stepped off it and cringed. It was so fucking cold out here. I tiptoed over to the porch, looking for my shoes. I spotted them at the edge of the porch, away from any windows, and grinned—Anna had stuffed fresh socks in my boots. Damn. She was good. I switched out one sock, then shoved my foot in a boot so I could do the other side. I wrapped my jacket around me, loosely laced up my boots, then I was on the way to...somewhere. She said the store was a block away...which way though?

Containing a sigh, I randomly picked a direction. I glanced back at the house and shook my head at what I saw. Kiera's bedroom window was on the side of the house, and the footprints in the snow made it pretty damn obvious what had happened. If her dad came out here and looked, well, the jig was up. Maybe he'd appreciate the fact that I'd tried to keep him in the dark. Probably not.

Smiling, I felt for my wallet in my jeans. Still there. Then I felt for my phone in my jacket. Also still there. Pulling my phone out, I pressed the button opposite the one that had turned the sound down. From the screen it was clear that I'd—once again—hit the right button, and the volume was back on. *Look at me, becoming an expert.*

Feeling better now that I was warm and out of danger, I decided to call somebody I couldn't really call around Kiera. Not yet anyway. The phone rang a couple of times, then I heard Hailey pick up.

"Hey, Kellan! Merry Christmas!"

Her enthusiasm made my smile even wider. "Hey, Merry Christmas. I didn't wake you, did I?"

"Nope. We're all up."

That made my smile drop. *We?* Fuck. She could be sitting in the same room with...him...*right now.* No. *Don't think about it.* "Oh, well, good...I just wanted to say Merry Christmas. And I hope...you have...a good...day."

Christmas was a weird holiday for me. Not really anything...special. So, it felt a little awkward to talk about it with her. She laughed at my stunted phrasing. "You too. Are you with your girlfriend?"

Now I was the one laughing. "Yeah, we're at her parents' place. I just snuck out to go to the store." *Literally.*

"Ah, fun. Tell her hi for me, okay?"

A rush of pain struck me in the chest so hard I stumbled. *I can't. I can't talk about you without talking about* him. *And that... isn't happening. Not today. Probably not ever.* I made myself smile, so she wouldn't hear my pain, and then I lied. "Yeah, I will."

Hailey sighed. "Hey, we're about to head out, but before I go...is there anything you want me to say to...anyone?"

Her thinly veiled question made the hurt dig itself deep into my stomach. Closing my eyes, I willed the agony away. "No... there's nothing I want to say." *And there never will be. Just drop it. Please.*

She sighed again. "Okay...Merry Christmas, Kellan."

"Yeah…" I hung up the phone and shoved it back into my jacket pocket, annoyed and aching with fresh pain. Would talking to her ever get easier? No. That was just a misery I was going to have to get used to if I wanted her in my life. And I did.

I trudged along down the street, lost in dark thoughts, when I suddenly realized, I'd made a mistake with my hasty answer. I'd only been thinking about Gavin, and he was a definite no, but… there actually *was* someone else I wouldn't mind talking to.

Pulling out my phone again, I texted Hailey, '*Will you tell Riley Merry Christmas for me*?' I smiled as I thought about the fact that I had a little brother. Would I ever get to meet him? No, probably not. Not until he was an adult, like Hailey, and that felt like an eternity from now. And he was so young, so tied to Gavin, I'd barely get to talk to him until then either. That broke something inside of me.

Hailey's response was instant. '*Of course.*' She followed that with a bunch of little smiley faces.

Amused, I shook my head, then I frowned. '*When you're alone with him. I mean it.*'

I could practically hear the sigh in her response. '*Okay.*'

Inhaling a deep breath, I nodded as I put my phone away. Maybe I could somehow walk this fine line with her and keep every corner of my life in its proper place, compartmentalized into the little boxes that I was comfortable with—meaning none of them touched each other. It would just take a lot of strength on my part to juggle them all. And…potentially…a lot of lying.

That broke something inside me too.

Chapter 21
THE BEST DAY

Thankfully, I'd correctly guessed which direction the store was, and Kiera had been right about them being open. I grabbed milk for Kiera's mom, then picked up Kiera's precious eggnog. Then I hurried back, so I could see her again.

I felt a little antsy as I knocked on her dad's door. It wasn't quite nervousness, but it was fairly close. I just wanted them to like me, so they'd be okay with Kiera and I being together. Maybe even excited about it. Supportive. But I knew what I was up against. Or, more accurately, *who* I was up against. Denny. They liked Denny. They'd imagined Kiera having a life with *him*. And he was someone I would never—*could* never—measure up to. He was all light and goodness, and I was...not.

Inhaling a deep breath, I made myself relax as the front door swung open. An older man staring at me with narrowed eyes was the first thing I saw. Kiera's dad. Shit. He already looked pissed. Did he know where I was last night? Behind him, I spotted an attractive woman who was definitely an older version of Kiera. Had to be her mom. Kiera and Anna were a little in front of her. Kiera was blushing for some reason; Anna was giggling. I was curious what I'd missed, but Kiera's dad was more important at the moment.

Hoping he was still clueless about me defiling his daughter's bedroom, I tossed on a smile and extended my hand to him. "Mr. Allen, it's very nice to finally meet you. I'm Kellan Kyle."

There. That was perfectly polite, right? At least he couldn't fault me for my manners. I supposed I could thank my mom for that...she was a stickler for manners, especially around her friends. Kiera's dad didn't take my hand right away. I didn't drop it though...I wasn't giving up. Finally, he grabbed it, and shook it...for a long time. The heat of his judgment was searing into me, but I kept my expression pleasant. *I know I'm not Denny, but I'm not a threat.*

"Uh-huh," was his only verbal response to my greeting. I felt the rejection in it, and it stung, but I schooled my face. It was no great surprise that he didn't like me.

Kiera's mom let out an annoyed sound. Stepping up to the door, she put a hand on her husband's shoulder; it looked like a warning to me. "It's nice to meet you too, Kellan. Please, come in, it's freezing out there."

Kiera's dad was forcibly removed from the door, so I could enter. That made me smile. At least Kiera's mom seemed to be okay with me. One out of two wasn't so bad. Her comment about the cold made my grin turn a little devilish. Meeting Kiera's eyes, I murmured, "I know." *It's even colder without shoes and a jacket. Still worth it.*

Kiera bit her lip and looked away. So cute.

Feeling Kiera's dad burning holes into me with his eyes, I handed the bag of groceries to Kiera's mom; I couldn't help but note she had Kiera's shade of long brown hair, but her eyes were pure green, like Anna's. "Mrs. Allen, I noticed that you were low on milk, so I got you some more." As she smiled and started taking the bag from me, I looked over at Kiera and added, "I got some eggnog too just in case anyone wanted some." I smirked at Kiera before turning back to her mom.

Kiera's mom suddenly looked distracted as she blatantly

stared at my face for a second. Her hand was frozen, her fingers barely around the bag I was still extending to her. Then she blinked and shook her head, like she was forcefully changing her thoughts. Interesting. Did *all* of the Allen women find me overly attractive? That would *not* help with making Kiera's dad like me. Would *anything* help at this point?

Finally taking the bag from me, Kiera's mom politely said, "Thank you, Kellan. That was very thoughtful of you."

Whether she was just being polite or not, her comment got to me, and my gaze shifted to the floor as a strange warmth filled me. Shrugging, I told her, "It was the least I could do, since you're letting me stay for a few days." And now I really wished it had been *my* idea, so I could actually deserve her praise. Still, the unworthy compliment was nice to hear.

From beside me, I heard Kiera's dad say, "A few days?" Kiera instantly snapped at him, and he only groaned in response. Had she not mentioned that I'd be staying for a little while? Maybe I shouldn't have either. Hopefully he let me stay…

Kiera's mom eyed the two of them, then turned her attention back to me. "Why don't you take your coat off, make yourself comfortable."

Nodding, I slipped my jacket off and handed it to Kiera. She looked giddy as she took it, and I grinned at her enthusiasm. It made me feel so good to see how much she wanted me here. It made me feel perfectly relaxed. Even with her dad scowling at me. Hmmm. How the hell did I make him like me? Or at least, not hate me? What would someone like him want to talk about? Clearly, not music. Maybe food would help break the ice. I could smell coffee, bacon, and oh God…was that cinnamon rolls? Fuck, I was hungry.

We all moved to the kitchen to eat, and I sat directly across from Kiera's dad. I *would* get this man to smile at me before my time here was through. Kiera sweetly prepared some coffee for me while I debated what to say. I wasn't completely unprepared though. For the past few days, I'd quizzed everyone I could find about different sports. They'd all looked at me funny, like they thought I should already know that shit, but I'd never really paid attention. Quite the opposite...just to childishly stick it to my dad, I'd purposely ignored every single sport there was. Now I kind of regretted that decision. Because I had a theory on Mr. Allen. Denny *loved* sports, and if he'd bonded with this man... that was probably how he'd done it. I wasn't 100 percent sure, and I wasn't about to ask Denny for advice, but it seemed like a fair assumption.

Taking a chance, I asked him which Ohio baseball team was his favorite—the Cincinnati Reds or the Cleveland Indians. He almost smiled...but then he stopped himself, shrugged, then half-heartedly told me, "The Reds are all right."

I knew he was playing down his interest, so I dove into the conversation, just trying to get him to warm up to me. I used up just about every fact I knew about the team, and the game in general, but he didn't seem to notice that I didn't really have a clue, and by the time everyone was seated, and we were passing the food around the table, I actually felt like I'd made a small dent in his armor. Until he started asking me questions.

"So, Kiera tells us you are in a...band?"

The way he said it was almost a sneer. I already knew he didn't approve, so I made sure my response was extra nice. "Yes, sir," I said, smiling as I handed Kiera the plate of bacon. "We're on tour right now. Our next show is on New Year's Eve in D.C."

I glanced at Kiera and watched her slump a little. I felt the same. It was days away, but still, it was far too soon. Kiera's dad was the only one who seemed heartened by the news. "Oh, so you'll be away a lot...on this tour thing?"

Anna glared at him as she handed me the plate of cinnamon rolls. Sadness washed over me as the truth in his question struck me. "Yes," I told him. *Unfortunately*. After taking a roll, I gave the plate to Kiera. Our fingers touched and I rubbed an apology into her skin. *I would stay if I could.* She gave me a small nod, like she understood.

Kiera's dad smiled, but I wasn't claiming that one as a victory. "Oh, well, that's good that you're finding success."

I felt like frowning at him, but I merely nodded. I knew all too well that what he'd really meant was—*Thank God you won't be around my daughter all that much.* Happy news for him, an almost unbearable side effect for me.

As I finished filling my plate with food, Kiera's dad asked a question I hadn't anticipated him asking. "So, what do you boys call yourselves anyway?"

Anna laughed while I studied my plate. Fuck. I had no idea what to say. I never thought I'd be in this situation, be around someone I was trying to impress, be around someone I *wanted* to like me. When we'd named the band, we'd all been in such a different place in our lives, none of us giving a shit about what anyone thought. Well, except for Matt, who'd made us shorten the name. Now that I cared I was almost...embarrassed.

Damn it. Well, it wasn't like I could lie. Maybe he wouldn't think anything of it. Maybe he wouldn't understand the reference. Resisting a sigh, I muttered, "D-Bags."

He started coughing on his food. Fuck. He probably understood then. Leaning forward, his cheeks a little red, he said, "Excuse me?"

Extreme discomfort settled around me, suffocating me. It wasn't something I was used to feeling. Clearing my throat, I made myself look at him. "Um, the band...We're named...D-Bags. It's just...supposed to be funny." He looked anything but amused. "We might change it...if we go mainstream." That was a flat-out lie, because I already knew I wouldn't win that battle. Matt wouldn't want to do anything that could possibly disrupt our fanbase, and Griffin would chop off his left nut before he called himself anything other than a D-Bag. Good or bad, the name was ours for life.

Anna laughed while Kiera's dad scowled at me. "You better not," Anna told me. "I love that you're Douchebags."

I had to bite my lip to stop from laughing. *Not helping, Anna.* Although, it did effectively end the conversation and after a moment, peace settled around the room, and we all quietly ate our meals. And I had to say, it was so nice to have an actual, homecooked meal. It was even better watching Kiera enjoy the food. The way she was practically having an orgasm eating her cinnamon roll was turning me on. Like she knew it, she smacked my thigh under the table. *Sorry. Don't groan like that, and I won't think that way.*

Then I popped a piece in my mouth, and as I sucked the sweetness off my finger, she got the exact same look on her face before she turned away from me. *See. I'm not the only dirty one at this table, Kiera.* I softly laughed at her...then hoped there were leftovers. There were dozens of fun things I could do with them.

Kiera's dad interrupted my steamy thoughts. "Kellan...is it true what they say about rock stars?"

My stomach instantly clenched as I felt tension enter the room. I finished eating the roll in my mouth, then cautiously looked around the table. Anna and her mom both looked annoyed, Kiera looked worried. What was he really asking me? Confused and wary, I asked him for clarification. "What do you mean?"

He casually took a bite of his bacon. "You know, about the women that follow the bands around, trying to...get to know them."

I felt my stomach drop to the floor. Get to know them...he meant fuck them. Goddamn it. There was no good way for me to answer that question, which was probably why he'd asked it. *If I lie, he'll see right through me. If I tell him the truth...I'll hurt Kiera.* I heard Anna loudly drop her fork. I heard Kiera's mom ask if anyone wanted more eggs. Kiera wasn't speaking, and I couldn't look at her. I felt her discomfort though. It matched my own.

Eyes locked on her dad, I told him the truth. "Some women are like that, yes, but it's a lot less than you would probably think—"

He didn't let me finish. Waving his bacon at me, he said, "But it is true, though. You do have women trying to seduce you? To lead you away from my daughter?"

Kiera finally snapped at her dad, but I couldn't look at her. I couldn't pull my eyes from her father. He was calling me out, right now. Daring me to lie, daring me to tell the truth. Because he knew, either way, I was fucked. He'd backed me into a corner. Why? All I wanted was for him to like me. But he wasn't even going to give me a chance, because when he looked at me, he saw...what? A lowlife douche who was going to inevitably destroy his daughter. If I were him, and it were my daughter and her rock star boyfriend...would I see the same thing? Maybe.

It was that moment of empathy that made me answer him with the simple truth. "Yes," I whispered.

In my peripheral vision, I saw Kiera curl inward reflexively, like I'd struck her. I instantly wanted to take the word back, tell her it wasn't true, but fuck...it *was* true. I *did* get hit on. I *did* get propositioned. Just sitting in a fucking plane minding my own goddamn business I got handed a phone number. But it didn't mean anything. It didn't mean I was doing anything. I still couldn't look at Kiera though. I couldn't witness the pain I'd just caused her.

Anna told her dad to mind his own business, but he ignored her. Leaning forward, his hard brown eyes intense, he pointed his bacon at me and said, "Don't you think it would be better for Kiera then, if you paused the relationship while you were away... so she doesn't get hurt by your...admirers?"

Rage, pain, and disbelief exploded in my chest. Doesn't get hurt by my admirers? *Admirers*? Girls he assumed I was already fucking. Was that what he really thought of me? And...*pause*? How the fuck would we pause? How could we somehow "hold" how we felt about each other? How would it not make me sick to touch another woman? How would it not kill me...if Kiera touched another man? There wasn't a way to pause this. Did he not get the fact that she was my entire reason for being? I could barely focus my thoughts to answer him. "I never...I don't..."

Closing my eyes, I tried to control the flood of anger, pain, and...rejection. *He doesn't understand because he doesn't know me. He just sees the surface. I can't hate him for that.* Opening my eyes, I finally looked over at Kiera. Her eyes were moist, brimming with tears about to spill. *I'm so sorry for the doubt I just put in your head.*

Hating the pain on her face, I stared at her and told her father, "I love your daughter, and I'd never do anything to hurt her."

Kiera's mother came to my rescue. Stealing his plate, she roughly said, "Of course you wouldn't, dear. Martin's just being an ass."

Something silently passed between Kiera's parents, a scolding and a concession. I suddenly wanted out of the room; it felt like the walls were closing in. I'd known that having Kiera's father like me was a long shot, but what he thought of me...the look on his face, the certainty in his eyes...it was too similar to the condemnation my dad had always felt for me. I was going to lose it, and I'd rather lose it alone...but I didn't know how to leave without making a scene.

Again, Kiera's mom saved me. "Should we open presents then?"

Fixing a smile to my face, I instantly stood up. "Sounds wonderful, Mrs. Allen."

"Caroline, dear," she insisted.

"Caroline, thank you for breakfast. It was incredible." I swirled my hand around the room. "Is there a bathroom...?"

She told me sure and motioned upstairs. I excused myself, smile firmly in place, then I fled. I could feel the headache coming as my thoughts tumbled into a very dark place. Trudging up the stairs, I ignored the tense silence in my wake. Once I was in the bathroom, I clenched the sink with both hands and hunched over, finally letting the ragged breaths gush out of me. *Calm down. So, he thinks the worst of you, what's new?* Inhaling a deep breath, I lifted my eyes to the mirror. My face looked pale to me, worn. Did Kiera hate me for that confession? Or had she witnessed enough to know the women didn't matter? Would she trust me now? Would she leave me now...?

As I watched myself, I saw my eyes shimmer and redden as the rejection shifted to fear...and doubt. "Stop," I whispered. *Don't ruin this day. Don't dwell, don't think, don't feel. The only thing you have is* now, *so enjoy it.*

Shaking my head, I ran some water into the sink. Not allowing it to warm up, I splashed my face. The frigidness shocked some of the emotion out of me, snapped me back to the present. Shutting off the water, I inhaled a deep breath, held it for a few seconds, then slowly exhaled. Better. Finding a towel, I wiped off my face, then headed back downstairs. I could hear Kiera talking when I got close enough.

"I'm in love with him, Dad. Pausing...isn't an option for me."

That filled me with an unparalleled amount of warmth, and my gaze drifted to the floor. *She feels the same. She still feels the same.* Kiera sensed me in the doorway, and I heard her twist in her chair to look at me. I met her gaze, a soft smile on my face. She stood up, then walked over and cupped my cheeks. Searching my eyes, she whispered, "Not being yours isn't an option anymore."

I nodded. *Exactly, Kiera.* Leaning down, I poured my heart into a soulful kiss. *Enjoy this...while you have it.*

I let the moment fade into the back of my psyche; there wasn't anything else that I could do but let it go and try to enjoy the rest of the day. And it was enjoyable. More than enjoyable. It was damn near picture-perfect. Was this how the holiday was supposed to feel? Everyone happy, everyone smiling, everyone grateful for each other.

It was a little difficult to wrap my mind around the joy in the room as Kiera's family went about opening gifts. I'd spent every Christmas morning alone since I was 18, and I was fine with that—*happy* with that—because for all the conscious years leading up to it, I'd wished to be alone. Prayed for it. Only one time that prayer had been answered, and it had come with a steep price; I hadn't minded paying it though. Having that same contentment now—without having to pay a damn thing—I almost felt guilty as I sat beside Kiera on the couch, soaking it up like a dry, crusty, thirsty sponge.

And then Anna handed me a present from her parents. I almost didn't want to accept it...it felt like too much. Just being here, feeling the warmth in the room was enough for me. More than enough. I didn't want to be rude though, so I took it from Anna.

I just kept spinning it in my hands, amazed, mystified...overwhelmed. Kiera gently elbowed me. "Open it," she said.

I looked over at her, then her mom. "You didn't have to..."

Mrs. Allen...*Caroline*...smiled at me. "I know," she said, her deep green eyes full of warmth. And acceptance.

The sudden knot in my throat was painful. Swallowing the emotion, I opened the gift. There was a photo album inside, and it was filled with pictures. I couldn't stop grinning as I flipped through pages of Kiera, some taken recently, some adorable ones of her in her youth. She was beautiful, even back then. Young me would have been just as attracted to her as current me. There were pages of Seattle, my car resting in the driveway of my home, the stage at Pete's, the city skyline. And then there were pages of Kiera and I together. Those took my breath away. Most of them were candid shots, not taken by us. Me watching Kiera at the bar. Kiera watching me, playing with her guitar necklace, and chewing on her lip. Holding Kiera in my arms in her kitchen, softly kissing as a pot of coffee brewed behind us. The two of us cuddling on her couch, both asleep, both smiling. How did Kiera's mom get these? Who took these?

Anna giggled while Caroline answered my unasked question.

"Anna helped me put that together for you, Kellan. So you could take a piece of home with you on the road."

I was so moved...I wasn't even sure if I could speak. I needed to though. This...meant the world to me. My vision was hazy when I looked up at her. "Thank you...so much."

The thoughtfulness of the unexpected gesture reminded me that I had gifts for them. Grinning, I reached over the couch to grab my bag. "I have presents too."

Kiera smiled at me as I stood and handed presents to her family. I gave Kiera hers, and she pointed to the Christmas tree. "Don't forget yours."

She didn't need to get me anything. She'd already given me everything I could ever want. And she knew that. With a smirk, I grabbed her gift, then sat down by her. I could hear her family opening my gifts, but I was too absorbed in Kiera to watch. I wanted her to open mine, but I was a little unsure too. Would she take it the wrong way? Would it seem more desperate than heartfelt?

Kiera stared at me too, both of us watching each other instead of opening anything. "Together?" I suggested.

She nodded, and we started opening our gifts. Sort of. We were still mainly staring at each other. She laughed, then motioned at mine. "You first."

That made me frown. I wanted her to go first. Then I laughed. I could wait. Kiera's gift was more like multiple gifts—and they all cut deep into who I was as a person. There were journals for lyrics, sheets for music, a personal CD player, and a bunch of CDs with the names of all my favorite songs written on them. It blew me away that she could delve so deeply into my brain.

And then I found the photo. It was a picture of an outfit lying on her bed. An incredibly sexy outfit, that I was already picturing on her body...and then on my floor. Lingerie? She'd actually bought lingerie for me? I peeked over at her with a raised eyebrow. Did she want me to have a hard-on in front of her parents? Apparently, she did, because she pointed at something I hadn't noticed in the picture...there was a fuzzy pair of handcuffs in the top corner. Oh my fucking God...she actually bought handcuffs. Why weren't we at home?

I tucked the photo away before my thoughts turned truly indecent. *Tease*.

And that was when I spotted one more thing in the box. My smile dropped as I picked it up, and a surge of something wonderful, yet painful swept through me. It was a Hot Wheels muscle car. But it wasn't just that fact that was knotting up my insides. It was *the* Hot Wheels muscle car. The exact same one I'd had when I was little. The exact same one that my parents had thrown away. The exact same one I thought I'd never see again. I had never told Kiera that story before. How could she possibly know about this car? How could she know it would be important to me? How did she know to get this for me? I looked over at her, absolutely stunned. She'd always teased me about reading her mind, but could she read mine?

"How did you know?" I accidentally murmured. Before she could say anything, I tossed my arms around her, squeezing her tight. "Thank you, Kiera...You don't know how much I love this, all of this." Pulling back, I felt an almost unbearable joy. "How much I love you." Was it possible to die from happiness? Because I sort of felt that way.

Kiera's eyes were glossy as she nodded at me. Clenching the tiny car, I pointed at her box. "Your turn."

She exhaled a huge breath. Was she nervous? She bit her lip as she opened the present...so cute. When she saw what was inside the larger box, or the *shape* of what was inside it, she froze. My nerves spiked a little as I watched her. I knew what the ring box looked like, I knew what she was thinking, but I had no idea how she felt about it. *It's not an engagement ring...but if it was, would you want it?*

She pulled the box out and popped it open, and the sudden tension in my body started relaxing. *She opened it, that's a good sign*. When she spotted two rings inside the little box, her brows bunched. I smiled as I studied the confusion on her face. Reaching down, I grabbed my ring. "They're promise rings," I explained. Grabbing her ring, I slipped it on her right ring finger. It fit perfectly...thank God. "You wear one." I slipped mine on my right hand, and I almost sighed in relief; I'd been wanting to wear it ever since I bought it. "And I wear one." I stared at the matching rings on our fingers feeling nothing but complete and total bliss. "And we promise that no one comes between us. That we...belong to each other, and only each other."

I pulled my eyes from the hypnotic rings to look at her. Wonder on her face, a tear rolled down her cheek as she stared at me. "I love it," she whispered. She leaned over to kiss me, and I felt the truth in her words, in her lips. She *did* love it. She *did* understand. She felt the same.

Anna interrupted the moment with a wadded-up piece of wrapping paper so she could thank me for her perfume. Then Kiera's dad awkwardly cleared his throat. "Yes, thank you... Kellan." He wasn't exactly smiling, but it was close enough. This one, I *was* going to claim as a victory.

As Caroline hugged a pair of plane tickets to her chest, I looked down at Kiera's confused face. "I got them tickets to Seattle, so they could see you graduate in June."

Kiera looked shocked that I'd done that. Her adorable expression made me laugh. "Kellan...you didn't have to..."

I shrugged. "I know, but your parents should see all of your hard work pay off, and tickets are expensive, so..." It was the least I could do for them, and for her. They should be there. I had the extra money to get them there; it was as simple as that.

As Kiera cuddled into my side, I mouthed, *Thank you*, to Anna. She'd given me all the information I'd needed to get the tickets at the airport. Anna winked at me, then smiled and shook her head at Kiera and me. I supposed she was right, we *were* a little nauseating, but I didn't care; I'd never been so completely content in all my life.

Kiera let out an equally content sigh as she laced our right hands together and stared at our rings. Absentmindedly running my thumb back and forth over the wheels of the car in my other hand, I smiled as I also absorbed the vision of our joint commitment. The rings just looked so good together; I couldn't get over it.

Slightly pulling away from me, Kiera said, "When I gave you that toy, you said something. What was it?"

"It's nothing," I told her, my gaze returning to our rings. Just a dumb, stunned outburst. Obviously, Kiera couldn't know what the car meant to me. It was just a happy coincidence.

Kiera kissed my jaw. "Tell me anyway."

I looked at her, then around the room full of love, debating what to tell her. I didn't want to change the feeling in the air, and my story might. But it was a good memory for me, and she'd unknowingly made it even better. She'd...completed it. And she should know that.

Instead of plunging right into the story, I told her, "This is so nice...so peaceful. Kind of idyllic. I keep waiting for the yelling to start." I looked at her, then back at our rings. "It means so much to me that you let me...be a part of this." I returned my gaze to the warmth of her face. "I think this is my new favorite Christmas morning." No. I knew it was the best. *By far*.

Kiera smiled, then playfully poked me in the ribs. "Even though you had to climb down a trellis?" she whispered. Her smile dropped. "Even being...interrogated?"

Grinning, I nodded. "Yep...still the best." Both of those incidents seemed like such minor details now; they couldn't even touch my mood anymore.

Her eyes grew curious, and compassionate. "Before this... what was your favorite?"

Looking out over the room, I let my mind rewind to that Christmas. A Christmas I probably shouldn't remember, considering how young I was, and yet, it was a memory that was shockingly crystal clear. Parts of it, at least. "I was five. It was Christmas

Eve. My dad was angry at...something...I don't remember what, and he tossed me into a wall, broke my arm."

An odd sort of peace filled me as I thought over what had happened next. I showed Kiera the spot on my left arm, told her it had broken there; that old break was practically underneath where Denny had broken my arm. Kiera was pale when her eyes lifted from my arm to my face. She looked horrorstricken, but I felt fine. I shrugged. It was just the price I'd had to pay for one of my best memories. "They took me to the emergency room, my mom complaining the entire time that they would be late for a party. I don't know why I remember her saying that..." An odd little detail that was forever stuck in my brain. Shaking my head, I gazed at the tree. "Anyway, they checked me in, then left. I didn't see them again until Christmas night." An answered prayer.

I grinned as that moment of remembered contentment washed over me. "There was this nurse there, and I guess she felt sorry for me or something, because I was all alone on Christmas morning." I lifted the car to my vision. "She gave me a set of three Hot Wheels. A fire truck, a police car, and...a muscle car. Just like this one," I said, smiling at her.

A laugh escaped me as I remembered that one carefree morning. "I played with those cars all day..." I ran the car down her arm. "But this one was my favorite. It was the only thing I wish I'd remembered to take to L.A. when I left home. But I forgot, and my parents...tossed it."

Meeting her eyes, I told her how that Christmas had been the best one because I hadn't been home, and that the car had been the best gift because the intention behind it had been pure...no strings, no tricks. Just thoughtfulness. Swallowing the sudden knot in my throat, I searched her eyes. "I thought I'd never see anything like that car again...How did you know to get me this?"

She shook her head, her eyes shimmering with tears. "It just... seemed like you."

The emotion in her eyes made me frown. "Hey, I didn't tell you that to make you feel sorry for me." I cupped her cheek. "I'm okay, Kiera." *Perfectly okay*. Kiera nodded, but a tear spilled from her eye anyway. Brushing it away, I gave her an encouraging smile. "I just wanted to let you know what it meant to me. To...thank you for letting me have this experience with you and your family. It means more than you'll ever really understand."

She shook her head, her face still full of hurt for me. "No, I think I get it," she said, and I supposed she did. Somewhat. She gave me a light kiss, then pulled back and took a deep, cleansing breath. "I could use some eggnog. You?"

I shook my head at her, nothing but warmth in my heart. "No, I don't need anything." I already had it all.

Kiera practically fled to the kitchen, and I could tell she needed a minute to compose herself. A part of me wanted to feel bad for emotionally waterlogging her like that, but I was too at peace to feel anything but a mellow buzz of contentment. She didn't need to worry about me. Not today. Today, I was perfect.

Anna sat beside me a moment later, glee on her face. "Did you check out my month?"

When we'd first sat down, Anna had given us all a copy of the Hooters calendar she'd been photographed for earlier this summer. She'd made the cover, which was huge. Griffin was going to die when he saw it. I had a feeling Anna's calendar would be in the hands of every band member on the tour soon. It wouldn't surprise me if he started signing them for fans backstage. Autographing his conquest. Jackass.

"Not yet," I told her. I'd seen the look on Kiera's face when she'd glanced at it, the sadness, like somehow that photo had confirmed something for her. I hadn't wanted to add to whatever insecurity she'd been feeling, so I'd set it aside without looking. But now *Anna* looked insecure.

"Why not?" she asked, a slight pout on her face.

Not wanting to hurt *her* feelings now, I shrugged. "I was waiting for you. Show me."

She bounced up and down, gleeful, then she grabbed my copy of her calendar and flipped to her page. I studied it for a second, and then a small laugh escaped me. Shaking my head, I flicked a quick glance at her father. He looked happy sitting on a nearby couch, but he also looked weary, and I didn't think it was because of me at the moment. Anna wasn't wearing a bra under her thin, white tank top in the photo, and I could *just* make out a hint of...well, *everything*. Poor Martin. Maybe one of the reasons he picked on me so much was because Anna was slowly killing him. If he ever met Griffin...he would love me, I was sure.

Smiling at Anna, I told her the honest truth. "You look amazing."

"Thanks," she said with a bright grin. Leaning forward, she added, "You don't think the nipple shot is a little much?"

I could only laugh and shake my head again. I tossed a piece of wrapping paper at her in answer, and she assaulted me right back with it. We got into a playful paper fight after that, and I was suddenly struck by an overwhelming sense of...family with her. Somewhere along the line, Anna had shifted from a hot girl who wanted to screw me, to my sister. Another sister. I loved the fact that I had two now.

We played for a little while, laughing, then Anna sat back and said, "We should get everyone to play a game. I bet I could kick your ass at Monopoly."

I laughed at her assessment of my skills. "Probably. Sure, sounds like fun."

I was about to go get Kiera when Anna grabbed my right hand. She stared at my ring with a sigh. "This is nice. I saw you give Kiera hers. For a minute there, I thought you were proposing."

A smile crept onto my face. *Someday, I will.* My eyes drifted to Kiera in the kitchen. She was looking over my way, watching me, and I gave her a brief nod. *I'm still fine, Kiera, if you're still worried.* I was turning back to Anna, to tell her that maybe one day we might truly be family, when I heard something that stopped me cold. My phone had just loudly chimed with a new message...and I knew exactly who it was from. Damn it.

Ice shot up my spine as I noticed Kiera heading toward where my jacket was hung up. She looked like she was going to check it for me. She probably thought it was from one of the guys, but I knew…I just *knew*, that wasn't who was texting me.

No.

I shot up off the couch and darted over to my phone. Kiera got to it first, and she was frowning as she stared at the screen. Not a programmed number then. Shit. It was *definitely* from Gavin. Fuck…why now?

She looked like she was about to open the message, and before I was even conscious of doing it, I ripped the phone from her hands, glanced at the screen, shut off the display, then shoved the phone into my pocket. Shit. Was that suspicious? Well, of course it was, dumbass.

Kiera had a stunned expression on her face, like she couldn't believe I'd just done that, and guilt instantly flooded me. Goddamn it. What do I tell her? Not the truth, that was definitely out. *So how do I gloss over doing that?* How did I make her forget, so that she didn't ask, so that I didn't have to lie? I tried distraction, praying it would work.

Pointing over at Anna, I said, "Want to play a game? Anna thinks she can beat me at Monopoly." I laughed and shook my head, like I thought that was funny. *Like any of this is funny.*

Kiera frowned at me, but then she said, "Sure."

I almost exhaled with relief. *She's not going to ask, thank God.*

But then of course, as I was leading her away, she *did* ask. "Who was that text from?"

My heart sank, my stomach dropped, the guilt rose…and so did the bile in the back of my throat. *No one I can tell you about. And I'm so sorry for that.* Knowing I was ruining our idyllic day, I gave her a breezy smile, and then I lied through my teeth. "It was just from Griffin." Selling the lie, I leaned in and added, "Trust me, with the stuff he's been sending me lately, you don't want to see it."

Jesus. Did I seriously just ask her to trust me while I was *lying* to her? Fuck, what the hell was wrong with me? Clearly, I was *still* a horrible, horrible person. But what choice did I have? I couldn't tell her about Gavin. Not today...not ever.

And just like that, my picture-perfect day felt anything but perfect.

Chapter 22
NEWS

My remaining time with Kiera was both heaven and hell. I cherished every second we spent together as she showed me all her favorite places growing up, and I dreaded knowing that I would be leaving her again soon. But overriding all of that turmoil was a dark cloud of guilt. Every time I looked at her, I felt ashamed. Whenever she hugged me, I felt like I'd betrayed her. I knew I should tell her what was going on with me, I knew it with every fiber of my being, but still, whenever I opened my mouth—fully intent on confessing my sin—the words wouldn't form. I simply *couldn't* tell her. It killed me.

When it was finally time for me to go, when I was finally back on a plane, heading to my band, I felt...devastated. *I lied to her.* I flat-out lied to her. I hadn't said something so blatantly false since that little mix-up with her sister. Her father was right about me... I didn't deserve her.

The melancholy inside me was nearly lethal when I was finally on the ground, in a taxi, heading back to the buses. Fucking Gavin. *If he would just leave me alone, I wouldn't be in this mess.* One more pain he'd caused me. Why was he so determined to ruin every aspect of my life? Why couldn't he take the hint and leave me alone? Hailey had been about to give up on me...why couldn't he?

I wanted to toss my phone in a garbage can, maybe flush it down a toilet. But I wanted to talk to Kiera. Maybe I could talk to someone at the phone company...get the number changed. But again, I wanted to talk to Kiera. And how would I explain changing my number to her? I couldn't, not without explaining everything. I was trapped. *Once again*, I was trapped.

Wanting to change my mood, I tried to focus on something positive. Making love to Kiera Christmas Eve...Christmas morning with her family. Our secret meetups at night once Kiera's parents had gone to bed. She hadn't let me back into her bedroom, maybe too afraid of getting caught, but she'd come down to me every night, and we'd cuddled on the couch until the early hours of the morning. And I'd made love to her on that couch a couple times...like this morning, our last morning. I could still feel her lips on mine, her body under my fingers, her soft moans in my ear as I pressed into her, her whispered words of affection, the sound she made when she came...

God, I missed her. Already.

The glumness wasn't leaving me. I paid the driver once we stopped, then shuffled over to where the buses were parked. Band members were ambling around outside, greeting each other, talking about their time away. I wasn't in the mood to join the conversation, so I stuck to the outskirts and stealthily hopped onto the bus.

Evan was inside, banging a beat on the table with his fingers. He raised a hand in greeting when he saw me. I made myself smile as I returned the gesture. It was hard. After putting my bag on my bunk, I sat down beside him. I didn't feel like speaking, so I didn't say anything. Evan eyed me up and down, a playful grin on his face. When I fully met his eye, he raised an eyebrow. "So? Still in one piece?"

He pointedly looked at my lap, and a small laugh escaped me. And lightened me. Right...the castration warning. Smiling, I nodded. "Yeah, everything's still there." With a frown, I told him, "She made me climb out a window."

He started laughing. His glee made me feel even better, but my frown deepened. "It's not funny. It was a second story window."

Evan closed his eyes, laughing even harder. I briefly grinned, then frowned again as I remembered it. "I could have died. It was snowing outside."

He snorted, then laid his forehead on the table as he kept laughing. I finally fully grinned, amused by his amusement. "You're a dick," I told him, chuckling.

He just kept laughing, and I was grateful. The levity helped. A lot.

By the time Matt and Griffin stepped onto the bus, I felt more like myself. Matt and Griffin joined us at the table, and as I listened to my friends talk about their families, their girlfriends, and their time off, my contentment grew. We'd all needed that break, and even though I'd fucked up with Kiera...I was still grateful for experiencing that moment with her. I was just grateful for *her*.

As Evan and I laughed about an inane argument that had happened between Matt's dad and Griffin's dad during Christmas dinner—one involving a turkey leg, a wishbone, a slice of pecan pie, a sprig of mistletoe, and where they could all be shoved—Griffin suddenly frowned and smacked the table in front of me. "Hey, Kellan."

Grinning, I turned my head to look at him. "What?" I asked, still laughing.

Griffin's brow furrowed. "So...how was Anna?"

Surprise made me blink, made my laughter fade. Griffin *never* asked about a girl, not even Anna. "Uh...fine, I guess." She had seemed like her normal, happy self at any rate.

My answer made his frown deepen. "Did she ask about me?"

I thought about that a second, then shook my head. "No."

He seemed surprised to hear that. "Not once?"

I quickly flipped through all the moments I'd spent around Anna, but I couldn't find anything to tell him. "No...sorry?" I added, confused. It wasn't like they were actually together. What did he expect from her? Anna wasn't the pining type, even I knew that.

Griffin swished his hand, like I could have answered him either way and he wouldn't have cared. "Whatever, I was just curious."

He seemed...off though. Weird. Had Griffin actually missed someone? For a reason other than sex? That had to be a first. Wanting him to feel better somehow—also a first—I shrugged and said, "She was pretty proud of her calendar. Have you seen it yet?"

A satisfied grin melted onto his face, and I suddenly regretted asking him that. "Dude...that calendar was basically my entire fucking week." He made a jack-off motion with his hand, and I pursed my lips at him. *I understood what you meant without the visual. Thanks.*

Griffin's smile grew. "In fact..." He turned his head to Matt. "Move. I gotta take care of something."

Matt immediately stood up to let him get out; he even had his hands raised like he didn't want to accidentally touch him. After Griffin fled to the back of the bus, Matt sat back down with a scowl on his face. "How could you ask him that?" he said to me.

The disgust on his face made me laugh. "Sorry. I don't know what I was thinking." Matt rolled his eyes, then sank his head to the table, utterly defeated by his horndog cousin. Evan and I immediately started cracking up.

Damn. I'd actually missed these guys. It made coming back a little easier. Okay, a lot easier. Things were good. Really good. I couldn't let myself forget that.

Time passed, and the four of us easily fell back into our routine of organized chaos. It surprised me a little, how familiar it felt now, when just a couple of months ago it was so foreign it had felt like a dream. It was still surreal, but that surrealness was starting to feel normal. Until one evening in early January, when it suddenly felt completely *unreal* again.

"Kellan, hey, there you are."

I looked over to see Justin walking my way. The grin on his face was a mile wide. A girl was walking beside him. No...not a girl, a woman. A very sophisticated, upscale woman. She looked a little out of place in the disarray of the backstage party area, and yet, she also seemed perfectly at home here, like she belonged. Maybe more so than any of the rest of us.

Stepping up to me, Justin clapped his hands together. "I have the best news for you."

Looking between the pair, I bunched my brows in confusion. "Okay. What's up?"

Justin's grin was giddy. "We're moving your band up the lineup. You're gonna play right before us now."

My jaw dropped as that settled into my brain. "But...we were the last band to sign up..."

The woman beside him smiled warmly at me. "And you've made quite an impression. We've heard the buzz about your band all the way in L.A."

I tilted my head, even more confused. She smiled wider and held out her hand. "Lana Torres. I work for Vivasec Records. It's a pleasure to meet you."

Glancing at Justin, I took her hand. "It's nice to meet you too." What was someone from Justin's label doing here? Was that odd or normal? I had no idea.

After we separated, Lana clasped her hands together and looked me over. She had dark hair, dark skin, dark eyes, classic bone structure...she was incredibly beautiful. I hoped she didn't hit on me. Rejecting someone from the label might be...bad.

Flicking a glance at Justin, Lana murmured, "You're absolutely right. He has *exactly* the right image."

"Right image for what?" I asked.

Her grin grew. "For *everything*." She let that word hover in the air for a moment before explaining. "Vivasec is always looking for new talent to add to the label. I'm going to be joining the tour for a while, to see if anyone here fits the bill, and I will *definitely* be keeping a close eye on you, Kellan Kyle." She looked between the two of us for a moment, then gave us a polite head nod. "Have a great show."

She turned and left after that, her head high, her demeanor confident. I felt dazed when I looked over at Justin. Was I dreaming? Or did that mean...what I thought it meant? Justin bounced on his toes, then smacked my arm. "She wants you, dude. I can tell." I frowned at him, and he shook his head of messy blond hair. "Not like that, trust me. She's top-notch, total professional. And she'll only take on the best. And I'm telling you, she *wants* the D-Bags. I can feel it."

I smiled at him, trying to absorb what that might mean. A label wanted *us*? To record an album? To actually fucking record an album...oh my God. It was so dreamlike though...I couldn't fully embrace the idea. I didn't want to get too excited about it, didn't want to get my hopes up. Mine or the guys'. It was best to just let that simmer on the back burner for a while. *We'll see what happens.*

But the other news...that was definitely something I could tell the guys about.

Excusing myself, I went to go find them, to let them know we were playing right below Justin's band now. There was something about that fact that almost made this feel like *our* show. Almost.

I found Griffin first. He was on a small couch, a girl on either side of him. He was kissing one of the girls, while the other one was working her way down his neck and fondling him through his jeans. Guess he'd gotten over the sting of Anna's indifference. I thought to leave him to his playthings, but then I noticed something when the girl on his neck paused to look at me.

She...wasn't technically a *she*. I had to admit, the guy cuddling up to Griffin made a damn-fine looking woman, but there were a couple of telltale indicators that gave it away. The Adam's apple for one. The slight erection visible under the tight dress was more obvious. I shifted to take in the other girl. Same thing. Hmmm. Was Griffin trying something new? Or was he completely fucking clueless?

I shook my head with a sigh. I already knew the answer to that. And I knew Griffin would make a scene and probably hurt their feelings once he figured it out. Diplomacy was not something he possessed. *Goddamn it, Griffin. Why do you make me do this?*

Inhaling a deep breath, I stepped up to the trio. The girls paused to look at me, their eyes drinking me in with unconcealed interest. *That* wasn't going to help smooth this over with Griffin. Would he listen to me? Or would he just be pissed? Sadly, I already knew the answer to that too.

"Ladies..." I said with a polite smile. "I need to speak to my bandmate for a moment."

Griffin looked dazed as he slowly twisted his head to look up at me. Could he really not tell? Because looking at them fully, it was easy to see these two weren't truly trying to hide anything. Biting my lip, I debated if I should let them know that their little fantasy with Griffin probably wasn't going to happen. Yeah. I was sure I'd be nicer about it than Griffin. Not that he was a dick about these kinds of things, but he would definitely be surprised, and when he was surprised, he could be a little...insensitive.

Leaning forward, I softly told them, "I'm sorry, I have to be completely honest with you, you're not what he's looking for." I cringed, hoping that didn't offend them.

But all they did was sigh and frown, understanding. Griffin didn't. He looked pissed as they got off the couch and started walking away from him. Standing up, he got right in my face. "What the fuck, Kellan? What the actual fuck?"

Knowing he didn't understand, I held up my hands. "Calm down. I was doing you a favor. Those two aren't really—"

He didn't let me finish. Shoving my shoulders back, he

snipped, "Just because you're all tied down and shit, doesn't mean *I* am. Don't try and parent me, fuckwad."

Annoyed, I stepped away from him. "I'm not. Go. Have sex with them." A smirk slipped onto my face, and I couldn't help but add, "Good luck."

He gave me a derisive sniff as he tucked his hair behind his ears. "I don't need luck. Those chicks want me."

God, he was so oblivious sometimes. Well, when he finally did figure it out, I would happily let him know that I'd tried to tell him. Shaking my head, I walked away to find my bandmates that thought with their upstairs brain.

Evan and Matt were huddled together, working on a melody from what I could tell. Matt looked up when he sensed me in front of him. His face instantly lit up. "Kellan, did you hear? We got moved up the lineup. We're right under Avoiding Redemption now."

The look on his face matched the feeling in my chest. "I know, I was just coming to tell you. What the fuck, right?"

Over Matt's shoulder, I saw Paul scowling at me. His band would be the opening act now...and he didn't look pleased about that. *I didn't ask to be moved. It's not my fault, man.* Ignoring the hatred in his eyes, I looked back at Matt. "Hey, you might want to go find Griffin."

Matt's nose wrinkled as he grimaced. "Why?"

With a sigh, I said, "I think he's about to try and have sex with a couple guys."

Matt's eyes widened as his jaw dropped. Griffin liked to joke around, but ultimately, he was straight, and Matt knew that. "Is he...experimenting?" he asked.

I shook my head. "I don't think so." When Matt looked even more confused, I shrugged and explained. "They're dressed like women. I honestly don't think he knows. I tried to help him out, stop him before it got too far, but you know how he is...he just got all pissy and defiant."

Matt and Evan just stared at me for a second. Then they both started laughing. Tears in his eyes, Matt clutched his stomach. "Oh my God...I have to see this."

He shot up off the couch to go find his cousin, and I sat down beside Evan with a sigh. He was still laughing. When he could speak, he looked over at me and shook his head. "Second in the lineup...someone noticed us, man. Think this could be it? The start of something bigger?"

I opened my mouth to tell him about Lana...but I couldn't. That still seemed too...improbable. Instead, I shrugged. "Who knows. But it *is* cool..."

Evan grinned as he relaxed back in his seat. Then he laughed again. "Fucking Griffin," he murmured.

When the show started and we didn't go up first, it felt weird...like we were late for something. Matt and Griffin eventually rejoined Evan and me. Matt was clutching his bucket, but it didn't seem like he needed it. He was smiling, happy, relaxed. To my great relief, so was Griffin. He was bouncing off the walls, grinning and flashing two fingers to anyone who looked his way. I was pretty sure he was referencing our spot in the lineup...not his two almost-hookups. At least, I thought they were *almost-*hookups. I wasn't going to ask and remind him that he was mad at me.

I spotted Lana near the stage entrance when it was our turn. She nodded at me, a polite smile on her lips. I nodded back. *I hope you like it.* The crowd was massive when we got into place, and there were a surprising number of shirts and signs...for *us*. It was so weird. And incredible. We played our hearts out, I sang my heart out, and when it was over, the screaming and cheering fueled a burning fire deep inside me. *Fuck, I love this.*

Lana stopped me when I stepped off the stage. Her smile bright, she shook her head. "That was spectacular. I truly hope you can consistently recreate that kind of energy and interaction with the crowd, while still sounding just as good as you did tonight."

I nodded at her, my smile equally brilliant. "That's always our goal," I told her. Matt wouldn't put up with anything less from us, a fact I was suddenly grateful for. If we did make it, it would be because of his tenacity.

As the shows continued, it seemed like a good portion of the tour was buzzing about Lana. She was a constant presence beside the stage, absorbing every band's performance, and absorbing the crowd's reaction to every band. Some of the bands froze up, and I could tell they were playing differently under her scrutiny. Seeing the disintegration of their talent worried me, because I was pretty sure the guys hadn't heard about Lana yet...and I knew there would be a couple of issues if they did find out.

One was Matt. He was already coping with stage fright, and I really didn't know what adding *this* kind of pressure would do to him. He might soar. He might crash and burn. And if he choked and that cost us this opportunity, he would never be the same. He just wouldn't get over it—ever. I really didn't want that kind of guilt on his conscious; he was too gifted to get lost inside his own head.

The second problem, and possibly the bigger one, was Griffin. He was already a megalomaniac, and I really didn't know what this kind of *attention* would do to him. He might take it in stride, or he might try to forcefully take Matt's instrument from him, so he could selfishly try to prove he was top dog. That might lead to a very vocal fight...and a very definite rejection from the label. And the *band* would never be the same after that.

No, the *best* thing for the D-Bags right now was ignorance, so I started doing everything I could to make sure the guys had no clue Lana was here scouting for talent. Mainly, I simply never mentioned it to them, and I begged everyone who did know why she was here to not mention it to them either. I hated hiding something so important from my friends, but this secret was for their own good. And honestly, it was still a long shot. I didn't want to get their hopes up only to let them down if we failed. It would be much easier to go back home if they never knew how close we'd been.

Every band member I talked to was sympathetic to my request; they'd seen their own bands crumble under the strain. In truth, Paul was the only guy on the tour I was worried about. He would gladly spill my secret and traumatize my friends just so we would bomb. So, to head off that problem, I also asked people not to tell *him* that I was withholding information from my band. It wasn't that much of an issue because nobody on the tour had a problem with *not* talking to Paul; nobody liked him, not even his own bandmates.

But it sucked so much not talking to the guys about Lana, not talking to anyone about her. I couldn't even tell Evan. I was pretty sure it wouldn't affect his playing any, but he'd probably tell Jenny and she might tell Rachel...I couldn't risk Matt finding out, so I didn't tell anyone anything. Not even Kiera. I was sure she wouldn't tell anyone if I begged her not to, so it wasn't out of necessity that I kept it from her. No, my silence with Kiera was more from...insecurity. She was just so damn sure I could do *anything*. But if I wasn't good enough, if I screwed this up and *proved* to her that she was wrong about me...well, just the thought of her disappointment killed me a little.

Again, it was better all-around if no one I deeply cared about knew the truth. God, it was starting to feel like my entire life revolved around keeping secrets now. I fucking hated it. But I didn't have a choice.

"Are you sure you don't want to tell them?"

I looked over to see Justin's pale eyes studying my bandmates. I knew exactly what he was talking about. "Yeah, it's better if they don't know. They'll play better."

Justin tilted his head, then nodded. "Makes sense. I told my guys not to mention anything to them. They won't."

Nodding, I let out a long breath. "How much longer is Lana going to be here?"

He shrugged. "Don't know. She's looking to see who can hack it long term, so it might be a while." He paused, then asked, "Is it getting to you?"

I gave him a half-smile. "Keeping it from everyone is getting to me. I could use a break from thinking." And from Gavin's incessant interruptions. He'd texted me *five* times yesterday. And every time I saw his number on my screen, a wave of guilt hit me. *I shouldn't have lied to Kiera. I should tell her the truth. But I can't.*

Justin studied my face, and he suddenly looked worried. Did I look bad? I did feel a little...worn. All of this secrecy was starting to eat at me, slowly and surely driving me to the edge of sanity. Justin clapped my shoulder. "Yeah, you look like a man who needs to get fucked up. Good thing we're staying here tonight."

He smiled, then motioned at someone across the room. I turned to see a couple of his bandmates heading our way—Trey and Jason. "Hey, after our set we're going drinking. And by drinking, I mean we're getting Kellan shitfaced."

I frowned at him. "I said I wanted to stop thinking. That doesn't mean I want to start heaving."

Justin swished his hand at me. "You'll thank me later."

I had a feeling I wouldn't.

All of Avoiding Redemption ended up going out with us, and sadly, I did end up drinking way too much. Evan practically had to carry me to our hotel room. I was laughing as he let me fall onto the bed.

"Ev...you're the best."

Slight smile on his face, he shook his head. "And you're blitzed."

I laughed again. "That doesn't make it not true...you *are* the best."

He patted my knee. "Goodnight, Kellan."

As he got ready for bed, I stared up at the ceiling. Then I grabbed my phone and stared at the screen, debating. I looked at my messages, at the numerous ones I was careful to never read. There were more from today, I'd ignored at least three. God... Gavin was so damn persistent. Maybe I should just talk to him... get it over with. I could send him *one* message—tell him to leave me the fuck alone. I almost did it. My finger was right there. But even wasted, the thought of contacting him nauseated me. *He won't leave me alone. He'll just think I'm finally talking.*

Ignoring him, I scrolled down to Denny's name. It had been a long time since we'd talked. Since I didn't have a clue what time it was in his area, I texted him a message instead of calling him. *'Hey. How are you?'*

I waited...but he didn't respond. Maybe it was late there. Or early. I didn't even know what fucking time it was here, let alone there. Pretending he had responded, I texted, *'Things are good here. I guess. Hope you're doing all right.'* At least, that was what I meant to type. My fingers missed a few letters.

After I sent the garbled message, I wondered if I should have done that. Maybe Denny didn't really want to talk to me anymore. Maybe I was bugging him. Maybe I should just let that friendship go. But the thing was...I couldn't. He mattered to me. He probably always would.

Annoyed at myself, I texted Kiera. *'I really miss you.'* Again, my slow fingers missed some letters, and my message didn't exactly look like my thoughts. I hit send anyway.

Kiera's response was instant. *'I miss you too. Sing to me?'*

Grinning, I called her. "What do you want to hear?"

She laughed, and I closed my eyes, savoring the sound. "Mainly just your voice. Sing anything."

A low laugh escaped me, then I started singing a song that had been playing at the bar. Kiera started laughing, and I stopped singing when I realized what song was in my head. *She Hates Me*. The unedited version. Probably not what she had in mind. I was practically giggling when Evan stepped out of the bathroom. He eyed me laughing into the phone, then guessing who I was talking to, he leaned over and loudly said, "Sorry, Kiera, we got him pretty drunk."

She sighed in my ear. "That explains a lot. Was there a special occasion? Or...something else?" Her voice suddenly sounded strange, and my hazy brain couldn't place the emotion. Worry?

I shook my head. "Just got carried away...sorry."

Another wistful sound met my ear. "You don't have to apologize for letting off steam. I just...I just want you to be safe."

A sleepy smile crossed my lips, and I closed my eyes. "I'm always safe," I told her. Wrapped in her love where nothing could truly hurt me. And knowing that, feeling that, made the alcohol-induced relaxation inside me shift into something deeper, something even more peaceful. Justin was right; I'd needed this mental reprieve. "Just ask Evan," I added in a murmur.

Evan laughed on his bed, then said in a clear voice, "Yep, he's fine, Kiera. We got 'em."

Kiera laughed again, then sighed again. "Good. I'm glad he's looking out for you."

I made an agreeing sound deep in my throat. A devious thought struck me as I pictured her biting her lip, sprawled out on her comfortable bed. Grinning, I asked her a question in my low, seductive, sexy voice. "What are you wearing right now?"

I was instantly hit by one of Evan's pillows. "No!" he scolded when I looked over at him. Face stern, he pointed a finger at me. "I am tired, and I am *not* listening to that again. Say goodbye, Kellan."

Smiling at him, I brightly said, "Goodbye, Kellan."

He rolled his eyes at me, letting out a frustrated groan as he laid back down, and I started laughing again. Kiera softly laughed with me, then she said, "You should get some sleep, drunk boy. I love you...so much."

"I love you too, Kiera. Just...you." Peeking over at my annoyed bandmate, I added, "And Evan."

Evan didn't open his eyes, but he grinned.

Chapter 23
SECRETS

The tension of my many secrets crept back into me as time trudged onward. A part of me wanted to get plastered every night, just so I could let go of my demons for a while, but I knew that wasn't the right way to handle this. I just had to be patient. Once Lana left, at least *one* of my torments would be gone. The rest...I'd just have to deal with.

We were on the bus more and more lately, having left the east coast behind as the tour continued. We were ambling our way through the Midwest now. The drives were long, the views were dull...it was boring. And it allowed me far too much time to dwell. I distracted myself from thoughts I didn't want to have by flipping through the photo album of Kiera and me. Seeing her content face in those photos reminded me of simpler times. Would we ever be like that again?

"Who's the girl? She's hot."

I looked up to see a guy named Benji looking over my shoulder, staring at a photo of Kiera. His smile was a bit too pleased for my taste, but I shoved down the possessiveness stirring inside me. He was right after all. She *was* hot. "My girlfriend...Kiera."

His smile suddenly started to fade, his expression turning

dour. "She kind of reminds me of my girlfriend...well, my *ex*-girlfriend, I guess."

His eyes hardened, and I fought back the discomfort in my stomach. Benji's breakup was on the more recent side, just after the holidays. He hadn't taken the news well. It hadn't helped that she'd ditched him over a text message. She'd left him for his brother. His *twin* brother. He was all sorts of messed up.

"Sorry," I told him, not knowing what else to say.

I started to close the book, and that seemed to snap him out of his dark thoughts. Shaking his head, he told me, "Do yourself a favor...don't get attached."

He walked away, to go sit by himself at the front of the bus. The sudden lump in my throat was painful. *Too late.* I didn't think it was possible to get more attached to Kiera than I was right now. I debated calling her, to reaffirm our connection, but Matt walked by and the look on his face distracted me. He seemed introspective. That wasn't all that odd, but what he was doing was definitely curious. He was slowly pacing up and down the aisle, looking deep in thought, except whenever he got close to me. Then he would unflinchingly stare at me for a solid ten seconds before dropping his eyes to the floor.

After his third pass of staring at me without talking to me, I stuck my arm into the aisle, stopping him. When our eyes met, I said, "What?"

He sighed, looked down, then started shaking his head. "Nothing."

Bullshit. He wanted something. "Matt...what?"

He closed his eyes, and the expression on his face...it almost seemed like he wanted to make a run for it, but there was annoyance there too. What the hell? Was he mad at me or something? I couldn't think of any reason why he would be...unless...had he found out about Lana? Shit. Would he understand why I hadn't told him? Would he still perform the same, knowing she was studying him?

Matt finally sat down across from me. He seemed antsy now,

constantly moving and twitching. He looked around, like he wanted to make sure we were alone, or as alone as we could be on the bus. Then he leaned forward. "I just...had a question."

I relaxed a little. If he was curious about something, maybe he didn't know about Lana. "Okay. About what?"

He ran his hand through his short, spikey hair, and he suddenly looked like he wanted to disappear. His cheeks were even getting red. Seriously, what the hell? Shaking his head, he started to stand. "Never mind."

I grabbed his forearm, holding him in place. "Dude, just ask me." *Before your head explodes.*

He collapsed into the seat with a sigh. "Okay, it's just..." He looked around again and lowered his voice. "You remember a while back when we were at that diner..."

My brows bunched. We'd been to a lot of diners. Matt sighed when he saw that I didn't understand. "You know...that one time when you were on the phone with Kiera..."

Understanding instantly flooded me. "Right..." Narrowing my eyes, I studied Matt. Was he mad at me for that? Why hadn't he said anything before now? He didn't look mad though, and he hadn't looked mad that night. Sometimes the things I did embarrassed Matt, but he typically didn't get angry at me. He only really got angry at me when I blew off the band. I didn't want to *guess* what his problem was though. If he was mad, I needed to know. "Did that bother you? I'm sorry if—"

He cut me off. "No, no, that's not it, I just..." He paused to bite his lip. "I was wondering if you could...I wanted to try..." He exhaled in a huff, frustrated that he couldn't tell me what he wanted. I was pretty sure I finally got it though.

Giving him a soft smile, I raised an eyebrow. "You want to have phone sex with Rachel, but you're not sure what to say?"

He looked both mortified and relieved. "Yeah...I don't even know how to bring it up. Do you have any...I don't know...tips? You're just...good at that kind of stuff." He shrugged, like that was just a well-known fact.

I contained my grin. His comment was amusing, but I didn't want to make him anymore self-conscious than he already was. Looking around the bus, I searched for the one person who could make this moment an absolute nightmare for Matt. Griffin was preoccupied though, playing a violent-looking card game with a couple of guys. Perfect.

Nodding at Matt, I told him, "Step into my office." Then I tilted my head toward the back of the bus. Matt grinned, finally looking happy.

Once we were safely behind the closed door of the back bedroom, Matt seemed overly nervous again. He even started pacing again. This space was way too small for that kind of energy. I pointed at the thin mattress. "Oh my God, sit down and relax."

He cringed but sat down. "Sorry. This is weird for me."

I gave him a soft, encouraging smile. "I know. But it doesn't need to be. None of it needs to be weird. She loves you, man. And I guarantee you she misses you."

He gave me a dopey, lovesick smile, and I laughed at the look on his face. Then I clapped my hands together. "Now let's get you in her pants, figuretely speaking."

Matt groaned as he laid back on the mattress. I laughed again. Oops. Probably shouldn't tease him.

For the next several minutes, I tried to get Matt to engage in a conversation with me. It took him at least twenty minutes, but eventually he started loosening up and asking questions, and it became more of a back-and-forth discussion and less of a one-sided lecture. By the time we were finished, he looked a little more confident that he would be able to do it. I was pretty sure he could...once he got out of his own head.

"It won't be as difficult as you think, I promise. And eventually you'll get to a point where you don't give a fuck what you're saying, and then it will feel more natural." I'd never actually had phone sex before, not for real anyway, but it made sense to me. It seemed to make sense to Matt too.

"Thanks, Kell," he said, content smile on his face.

"Anytime." I shrugged.

Matt left the bedroom with a blissful smile on his face, and all I could do was shake my head. Huh. Maybe if the whole rock star thing didn't work out, I could teach a class on all things sexual. *Professor Kyle, at your service.* God...Kiera would kill me. Helping friends out was one thing, helping complete strangers, especially if a lot of them were women...no. *I think I'll stick to music.*

When I got back to the lounging area of the bus, Matt seemed a lot more relaxed. He'd even joined the card game with Griffin, and their table was loud with laughter. I pulled out my phone, wanting to talk to Kiera now.

Out of habit, I scanned my messages before calling her. Two ignored ones from Gavin. Already. One from Hailey that I'd already responded to. An older one from Denny. He'd responded the next day after I'd drunkenly texted him. His message had been polite, yet funny. *'Glad to hear it's going well. I'm good, thanks, mate. Did you drunk-text me?'*

Remembering the conversation made me laugh. My response to his text had been, *'Maaaaaybe.'*

His response had been a laughing smiley face. I took that as a good sign that he also wanted some sort of friendship with me. I debated calling him, but Kiera was on my mind. And it was probably the crack of dawn where he was anyway.

Pressing the button to connect the call, I brought the phone to my ear. The sound of it ringing made me smile. The sound of the ring stopping made me grin. "Hello?"

Closing my eyes, I savored her sexy voice. "Hey, gorgeous... Guess where I woke up today?"

"I have no idea."

The amusement in her voice made me laugh. And the fact that I also had no idea where we were. Not really. I knew where we'd been—Matt had told me at the last show—and I knew what direction we were heading, and I knew what I'd been staring at outside. From there, I took an educated guess. "Kansas...Know what's in Kansas?" I playfully asked

"No," she murmured.

"Nothing," I told her, glancing at the monotonous vastness out the window. "Miles and miles of nothing." I heard her laugh, and a sigh of longing left me. It was February now...it had been forever since I'd seen her. "God, I've missed your laugh. It's just not the same over the phone, you know." Without seeing the sparkle in her eye, the curve of her lips...without knowing I could lean over and kiss her...it was just all so...empty. Every part of me pined for her.

"I know...I've missed you too," she said.

I loved that she felt the same, that our connection was still there. And I loved the ache I heard in her voice. It reminded me of my cruel tease on Christmas Eve. *She still misses me.* Not wanting to dwell on how much I missed her, how lonely I suddenly felt, how tired the heavy, unrelenting weight of all my secrets was making me, I redirected the conversation. "So, what have you been up to lately?"

She hesitated before saying anything. Why? Was something wrong? Maybe she was just thinking of something to say. It was kind of an all-encompassing question. "Uh...just work and school. Did I tell you I started my new quarter last month? I have a poetry class now."

Hearing something new in her life brightened my mood considerably. "Really? I like poetry...It's a lot like lyric writing. Less cursing, though." I paused to laugh again, then asked her, "So what are you up to today?"

"Nothing really..."

There was sadness in the sound, wistfulness. I didn't want her to be sad. I didn't want her seeking...comfort. A soft sigh escaped me. *Please don't let her forget about me.* I forced myself to smile, so I would sound fine. "Well, I've just got endless driving in front of me...please tell me your life is more interesting than that. One of us needs a good story to tell."

"Well..." she started tentatively. "I'm on my way to have lunch with a friend."

For a second, it felt like my heart stopped. *Lunch with a friend? What the fuck does that mean?* If it was someone I knew, she'd just say their name. *Damn it, don't overreact...she has friends you don't know, friends from school. It doesn't mean they're* more than friends. *She won't hurt you. She's wearing a literal promise around her finger to not hurt you.*

I stared at the ring on my own hand, gleaming in the sunlight, and tried to draw strength from it. Showcasing my talent for hiding my emotions, I brightly told her, "Good. It's good that you're getting out, having a life." And it was. She *should* be going out—I'd purposely asked people to take her out. I'd just prefer it if she was going out with Jenny or Rachel. *Don't ask her who she's with. Trust her.*

Kiera took my words the wrong way. "Of course I still have a life. Do you think my world revolves around you?"

Her tone was heavy with sarcasm, and I knew she was teasing me for my word choice. If I'd been in a better mood, I would have laughed it off and apologized for my implication that she was somehow incomplete without me. But her words were caustically mixing with Benji's warning: *Do yourself a favor, don't get attached.*

Don't get attached...because you're replaceable. And it's inevitable. The thought was crashing around my brain so loudly, I felt like my head was splitting in two. *She doesn't need you.*

The words spilled out of me before I could stop them. "No, no, I don't think that at all." *It's my world that revolves around you, not the other way around. It's always been that way.*

"You all right?" she quietly asked.

I mentally slapped myself for letting that slip out. I wanted to sound fine, I wanted to *be* fine. I just felt so...worn. Faking it was getting harder and harder. There was too much I was juggling, too much I was hiding, too much I was...struggling with. Worrying about her, worrying about the band...worrying about

Gavin...I was being assaulted from every single fucking angle, and there was no one I could talk to about it. Not really.

The loneliness started clenching around me, suffocating and cloying, and I couldn't answer her for a long time. I forced myself to take a deep breath, to try and purge the unwanted feeling. "Yeah, I'm fine," I told her, wishing that were true.

For once, she didn't seem to believe me. "Kellan...is there something you want to tell me?"

Fuck. I should just tell her about Gavin...purge myself of the bulk of this pain, the largest of my secrets, the biggest of my sins. But telling her would open a fresh well of agony. *I can't tell her about Gavin and expect her to not do anything with that information. She'll make it worse. I'm on my own.* I knew I was taking too long to answer her again, but I didn't know what to say. I didn't want to lie again, but the truth...was out of reach.

Maybe truth-adjacent would work instead. "It's nothing, Kiera...just the stress of the road. I'm sure you can imagine what life on a bus with Griffin is like." I made myself laugh, made my voice sound lighter, happier. And then I let the fact that I hadn't entirely lied wash some peace into me.

"Okay, well...if something was going on, you know that you could tell me...right?"

I could hear the beg in her voice, the plea for me to open up. It stole some of my peace as fresh remorse rippled through me. I sighed, wishing it were as simple as she made it sound. "Yeah, I know..." The melancholy started sucking me downward, and I knew if I let it continue, I would spiral...I would tell her. I shifted my gaze to take in Matt and Griffin playing cards, having fun. Laughing. *Everything is fine. We're all fine. Relax.*

Seeing their joy made me feel better, and my voice was genuine when I told her, "But really, nothing is up, aside from the fact that I miss you like crazy."

"Yeah, me too." She sighed, then added, "Hey, I'm here at the restaurant...I need to go. I'll call you later?"

Right. The restaurant...with her friend. *Don't ask.* "Yeah, okay." Not wanting the conversation to end on a sad note, I let a dry laugh escape me. "I'll be here, on the road through nowhere, wishing Griffin didn't need to let the Hulk breathe quite so often."

The sound of her corresponding laugh was soothing. So were her words. "I love you, Kellan."

"I love you too, Kiera." More and more every second.

The call disconnected and I lowered my phone to stare at it. Was I making a mistake, withholding so much from her? Yes. I knew I was. But there wasn't another option for me. Not anymore. This burden was mine to bear, it had been since birth.

I suddenly felt exceedingly, achingly tired, exhausted down to my very core, the depths of my soul. *I don't know how to keep doing this.* And that was when my phone chimed with a message. I instinctually cringed, worried it was from Gavin. But it was Kiera's name on the screen, and seeing it brightened me.

The words were simple, but they meant everything to me. '*I love you.*'

I closed my eyes, letting that sink in, letting it erase the emotional fatigue. Then I texted her back. '*I love you too...more than anything. I can't wait to see you again...soon, hopefully.*'

'*I hope so too,*' was her response, and I inhaled a deep breath, letting peace fill me again as I put my phone away.

That was when Griffin sat down across from me. "I'm bored," he said. "Entertain me."

I looked over to see that the card game had broken up. Matt was miming playing a guitar while he animatedly talked to the group Griffin had left behind. The conversation must have switched to music, and that wasn't a compelling enough conversation for Griffin. I was barely holding on though, and I really didn't feel like entertaining him. "Do I have to?" I asked.

His grin had a familiar edge to it. "If you don't...I'll just entertain myself." He wriggled his eyebrows, and I knew I didn't want to know what he meant by that.

"Fine..." I sighed. "What did you have in mind?"

He set down an unopened bottle of Jack Daniel's. Great. Breaking the seal and opening it, he said, "Never have I ever...had sex with Kiera."

I shook my head at him. Fucking asshole. He said that obvious one just to make me drink. And he wanted to play *Never Have I Ever*? Were we teenagers? Oh well. I had nothing better to do than play a stupid drinking game with Griffin. And maybe it would get my mind off Kiera and her...friend.

As Griffin grinned at me, I grabbed the bottle and took a long draw, filling my cheeks. Since I frequently had sex with Kiera, I felt like the drink should be a big one. After I set down the bottle, Griffin grabbed it. His eyes on me the entire time, he started to make like he was going to take a drink too. What the fuck? The image of him having sex with Kiera was so disturbing, I nearly spat out the liquid in my mouth. It partially went down the wrong pipe as I harshly swallowed instead, and I started coughing. It fucking burned.

Griffin was laughing as he set down the bottle. *Dying* laughing. "Oh my God, Kellan...your face, dude."

I just about socked him, but...two could play at this game. "Never have I ever had sex with Anna," I said, then I grabbed the bottle and started swallowing a mouthful before he could stop me. He was right...the look on his face was priceless, and I felt a million times better. Maybe this was actually what I needed right now. Another mental reprieve.

Satisfied smile on my face, I set down the bottle and suggestively raised my eyebrows. Griffin was staring at me, open-mouthed. "No, you didn't." I just sat there smiling, letting his mind stew. "No, you fucking didn't!" he said again, louder. Grinning, I shrugged. His face clouded over. "When?" he demanded.

I couldn't hold onto it, and I started laughing. His pale eyes narrowed once he figured out I was just joking. He took a quick swig for his answer, then he shoved the bottle in my face, spilling some. "Take a penalty drink, fucker." I did as he commanded, and his furious eyes narrowed even more. "You fucking lie again, and you're finishing the whole fucking bottle, got it?"

With a laugh, I nodded. Oh God...sometimes Griffin was exactly the distraction I needed.

It didn't take long for me to remember why I shouldn't play that game. Especially with Griffin. The person speaking was supposed to say something they *hadn't* done, but Griffin was both competitive and a braggart. He started saying everything he *had* done, just to see if I'd done it too. Unfortunately, I had done way too many things that he'd done, and as a result, we were both plastered long before the bus stopped for the night. Thankfully, our show was the following night, and we had the evening at a hotel to crash and recover. Or try to.

I let out a loud groan after getting off the phone with Kiera. I hadn't told her about the day drinking, and I'd hid my hangover from her; I didn't want her to think getting drunk was the norm for me now. I'd just needed another break, but now I was seriously regretting it.

"Ugh, man, I feel like shit," I said, looking over at Evan on his bed. My stomach hurt, my head hurt, and my eyes felt like they weighed a thousand pounds. My only consolation was the fact that I knew Griffin felt just as crappy as I did. We'd really overdone it.

Evan looked back at me and grinned. "What did you think was gonna happen? Why would you even play that game with Griffin? Did you learn nothing from Goldschläger night?"

A brief recollection of that incident flashed through my mind. It had happened years ago, back when we'd lived in L.A., but just remembering it was enough to make me queasy. I put one hand on my stomach, the other I held in the air in warning. "Don't talk about that night. Please."

He laughed again, shaking his head. I was closing my eyes to, hopefully, pass out, when our hotel room door was suddenly—and loudly—banged on. "Kellan...Evan...Let me in!"

Evan and I exchanged glances, then I groggily got out of bed and opened the door. Griffin was standing there, pouting. He looked worse than I did...and that made me kind of happy. "I have to sleep here," he grumbled. "Matt kicked me out."

"What did you do?" Evan said with a laugh.

As I closed the door behind Griffin, he scowled at Evan. "I didn't do anything to that fucker, but he said he needed to be alone." He rolled his eyes. "I think he just wanted to jack-off in peace."

Remembering through the haze of my drunken afternoon, to the conversation I'd had earlier with Matt, I bit my lip to conceal my grin. I was pretty sure I knew why Matt had kicked him out, and in a way, Griffin was right—that was *exactly* what he was doing. *Good for you, Matt.* I knew how nervous he'd been about it, and I was pretty proud of him for trying it anyway...which meant, I had to help him out and take in Griffin. Containing my sigh, I indicated my bed. "Come on, you can sleep with me."

Looking exhausted and pained, Griffin walked over and crashed onto my mattress. Because I couldn't resist some ground rules, I told him, "You snuggle, you die."

Griffin snorted, then rolled over and cupped his junk. "Ah, come on, Kell, I know you want this. I've seen the way you look at me."

The look on his face was making my already-nauseated stomach start to churn. Grimacing, I pointed over to Evan's bed. "On second thought, sleep with him."

Curled up in his blankets, looking completely comfortable about being Griffin-free, Evan immediately tossed out, "Nope, not it."

Goddamn it. Matt owed me.

Too tired and hungover to really care, I got back into bed. Griffin, of course, called me on my bluff and slung his leg over my hip and his arm over my chest, making himself right at home against my back. "Get. Off. Me," I bit out. Evan started laughing.

"Relax, Kell," Griffin murmured. "I'm too tired to have sex with you."

Evan laughed harder. His amusement made a soft chuckle escape me, but I rolled over and shoved Griffin away on principle. Eyes closed, he stayed on his back, giggling to himself. "Never have I ever slept with Kellan Kyle," he mumbled.

I brought a hand to my stomach again as his words rekindled memories of our game. A couple guys had joined us by the end, but it had mainly been Griffin and me who had polished off that entire fucking bottle. "Stop it," I said with a pained laugh.

Griffin snorted again, then laughed himself to sleep.

I had a nightmare that night, and surprisingly, it wasn't about Griffin sleeping a foot away from me. No, it was about Kiera. I'd walked into my bedroom to find her screwing some dark-haired man who looked disturbingly like Denny. And then my dad was there, smiling at me with smug satisfaction on his face as my entire world fell apart.

When I jerked awake, I felt nauseous, but it wasn't from the alcohol this time. Careful to not disturb Griffin, I hopped out of bed and rushed to the bathroom. Closing the door behind me, I leaned over the sink and prayed I didn't lose it.

It was just a dream. A really fucked up dream. I made myself stare at the ring on my finger, made myself remember how much Kiera loved me, made myself calm down and relax. It took...a long time.

In fact, I didn't feel completely normal until I was backstage, waiting for our part of the show to start. Seeing the people, the familiar hustle and bustle of activity...it calmed me. Grounded me.

I spotted Matt by himself, staring off into space, a small smile on his lips. I took that as a promising sign that his night had gone well, but, since he was my pupil, I thought I better make sure. If the sex had gone badly, or if he'd completely chickened out, maybe I could think of another way to help him through it.

Although, I had no idea what that might entail. It wasn't like I could do it *for* him.

Matt looked up at me when he felt my presence. Smile on my face, I lifted an eyebrow. "So...how did it go?" I asked.

His cheeks filled with color, and his gaze immediately fell to the floor...but his grin was huge. "Good. It was...good." He peeked up at me. "Thank you...again."

I clapped his shoulder, happy for him. "No thanks necessary. I'm glad I could help." I paused to frown. "But you do owe me for Griffin."

Matt wrinkled his nose. "Welcome to my world. Sucks, doesn't it?"

I laughed, feeling better than I had in hours.

Matt was extra peppy during the show. He even engaged the crowd a little bit, tossing them a wave when he walked out, nodding his head at them when I introduced him. It was almost like stepping so far outside of his comfort zone like that had broken off a small chunk of his shell. And to my delight, it stayed off—over the next few weeks, he became more and more comfortable on stage.

It made me happy for more than one reason. One—he *should* relax more on stage, there was nothing for him to fear in the spotlight. And second—he was impressing the shit out of Lana. They all were. And they still had no idea.

As per usual, Lana approached me when our set was done. I liked Lana. While the reason for her presence here was knotting my stomach, as a person, she was cool, easy to talk to. And she always seemed to want to hear my thoughts after a show, so I usually took a few minutes to talk to her. And I was usually high on performance-endorphins, so I was typically a little giddy when we spoke.

"Did you hear that crowd? I think that was the loudest one yet," I told her, grinning.

She laughed, then nodded. "I agree." Smiling, she shook her head at me. "Every time you guys play, you are spot on...just incredible. So much talent. I usually have a tip or two to give the other bands, some sort of critique, but never for you four. It's like you've been doing this for twenty years."

I laughed at her comment, then leaned forward so she would hear me over the noise. "They were really good out there, weren't they?"

She got an insightful look on her face. "You're the only prospective band whose sound hasn't changed since my arrival. They have no idea I'm scouting them, do they?"

Biting my lip, I looked around, but the guys had already fled. "No. I didn't tell them who you were." I shrugged. "And I've been making sure they don't find out."

Her grin grew. "Smart. That's one of the reasons I only talk to the lead singer of the band. I want to see what he or she will do with the information. It's a skill that can't really be taught. Being the leader, you have to *know* your band. Know what to give them and know what to *keep* from them. It can be a very fine line. You're so young, and yet...you already knew exactly what to do to protect them, and you're strong enough to hide things from them, help them shine. You never cease to amaze me."

I raised an eyebrow at her. "Does that mean...?"

Her smile never changed. "It's not entirely up to me. But you definitely have my vote. You belong with Vivasec. I need to run this up the flagpole. I'll let you know what they decide. Excellent work, Kellan. You should be very proud."

She walked away and I just stood there, staring at the spot she'd been. *She said yes...Holy fuck, she said yes...* I felt like I should tell someone. Hell, I felt like I should scream it at the top of my lungs, but...it wasn't a for-sure thing yet. It could still go south, could still fall apart. I didn't want to give the guys false hope. I had to keep it inside a little longer, just in case someone higher up said no. And so, the secrets had to continue. Damn it.

Chapter 24
AM I DREAMING?

I was a ball of anxious energy waiting to hear the final word from Lana. I just wanted to either tell the guys some good news or let this whole fucking thing go so I could move on with my life. But the longer it took for Lana to get back to me, the more I started feeling something else...something darker. Rejection. Failure. It was taking so long...clearly, they were going to say no. I'd done everything I could, but it still wasn't enough. I wasn't good enough. I wasn't enough. It was such a familiar feeling, and it wrapped around me so easily, it was hard to shake. *I'm glad I didn't tell the guys, so they don't have to feel this too.*

"Dude, you okay?"

I was sitting on a couch backstage, blankly staring at a full cup of beer in my hands. I hadn't taken a sip of it yet, and I could tell from my fingers it was warm now. Shaking off my thoughts, I looked up to see Griffin staring at me, a weird mixture of concern and confusion on his face. I tossed on a smile. "Yeah, just tired...zoning."

With a nod, he relaxed back in his chair. Twirling a finger to indicate the room, he told me, "Score a chick. That'll wake you up." Twisting my lips, I lifted an eyebrow at him. He rolled his eyes. "Right...monogamy." He shook his head as he rolled his eyes...again. Then he slapped his hands on his thighs. "Well, I'm gonna score a chick. See ya."

Because I couldn't help myself, I tossed out, "Make sure it's a chick."

Griffin gave me a confused look, like he thought I was mental. I bit back a laugh. Matt had told me Griffin had never found the two guys I'd chased away from him that fateful night; he still had no idea he'd been making out with men. That was something I'd confirmed while playing that stupid drinking game with him. Griffin was utterly clueless. A fact that brought Matt an endless amount of joy; he broke down into hysterics every time he thought about it.

Smiling, feeling better, I set down my beer on a nearby table. A girl dropped down on the couch beside me. "Hi," she said, her eyes scanning my face.

"Hello," I politely returned.

She bit her lip and giggled. There was something about the gesture that really made me miss Kiera. We talked a lot, several times a day, but it just wasn't the same. It was March now, our anniversary month, and I wasn't sure if I was going to be able to see her. Our first year together...and we'd spent so much of it apart. It killed me.

I suddenly wanted to call her, talk to her until she unknowingly changed my mood, but the girl beside me suddenly became emboldened...maybe because I'd just been staring at her the entire time my mind had spun.

"Fuck it," she said, then she flung her arms around my neck and leapt onto my lap. I was so shocked I barely had time to stop her from attaching her mouth to mine.

My eyes were wide as I gently—but firmly—pushed her shoulders back. She was still straddling my lap, breathing heavier as she stared at me. She didn't seem to notice that I was completely rigid, or that I was holding her back. She strained against me, her head leaning forward, angling in, searching for me.

"Stop!" I snapped, my eyes narrowing as I pushed her further away.

That was when she seemed to wake up. Her eyes widened as she stared at me, and all the blood drained from her face. "Oh my God...I'm sorry," she said.

She seemed frozen in her embarrassment. I really wanted her off my lap, but I didn't want to make her feel any worse. I softened my expression and let out a soft laugh. "It's fine, but...could you get off me?"

She looked down, and by her expression it seemed like she hadn't even realized she was pressing herself against me. She must be very, very drunk. "Oh my God," she said again, but she finally scrambled off my lap.

I nearly sighed in relief. But then her eyes started watering, and I felt bad more than anything. Once upon a time, I wouldn't have stopped her. Maybe she should know that. Giving her an encouraging smile, I pointed to the ring on my right hand. "You're very pretty, but I'm committed to someone." My smile turned ridiculously dopey. "And I am...so in love with her."

The girl's tears dried up as she stared at my expression, then she softly smiled at me. "Lucky girl," she murmured, then she fled.

I shook my head at her hasty retreat. Then I spotted Evan across the room, staring at me. Laughing. I flipped him off. *That was not funny.* Asshole. I got off the couch and made a mental note to never sit down backstage again. Apparently, I was just too tempting.

I still attracted a swarm of girls, but they were easier to keep at bay when I was standing. I tried to keep the eye contact to a minimum as I talked to them, not wanting one of *them* to have a "Fuck it" moment. They still leaned into my side, but that was fine. Much better than them grinding their privates against me.

As I signed something for one of them, I happened to notice Lana. She was talking to Paul in a corner of the room, and he did not seem happy about what she was saying. He looked like he was pleading with her to change her mind. Fuck...she was telling him no. While I wasn't too surprised by that—his band was...okay—it was still difficult to watch someone's dream die. I wanted to give him privacy, but I was too caught up in the moment to look away.

Lana left his side, and Paul's gaze connected with mine. His eyes narrowed, and I knew he hadn't wanted me to witness that. I returned my attention to the fans around me, ignoring the hate I felt pouring from him. Lana stepped up to me next, and I felt my mouth go dry. Was this it? The moment *our* dream died.

Amusement in her eyes, Lana's gaze swept over the girls clamoring around me. In my distraction, one had attached herself to my arm. Not knowing how to shake her off while still appearing professional, I ignored the affection. Lana smiled at the group. "Excuse me, ladies. I need to speak with Kellan alone for a moment." She leaned in and winked. "I promise to give him right back."

The girls tittered as they moved a respectful distance away. Lana softly laughed, then swung her eyes up to mine. I swallowed, suddenly really nervous. Lana just smiled at me, not helping my nerves at all. Licking my lips, I asked, "Did you...hear something?"

Her dark eyes scanned my face, and her smile dropped. My stomach also dropped. *It's a no.* Then she grinned and extended her hand. "Congratulations, Kellan. They said yes."

My mouth dropped as I stared at her. *Yes?* I really hadn't been expecting that. I took her hand, but I could barely feel myself shaking it. "Yes?" I asked, stunned.

She laughed, then nodded. "Yes. I'm sorry it took so long to get back to you. I was trying to get a special deal for you, and that took a little convincing."

I tilted my head as our hands dropped. "What deal?"

Her smile brightened. "A three-record deal. Starting immediately. The second this tour is over, you'll head to L.A. and begin recording. The label wants an album as soon as possible." She winked. "I thoroughly convinced them that you…will have no limit. You *will* be our biggest artist, it's just a matter of time."

All I could do was stare at her as I was assaulted by shock, confusion, surprise…warmth. *They said yes?* Trying to wrap my head around it all, I murmured, "Three records?"

The look on my face must have been one of uncertainty. Her brows furrowed. "It's a lot to process, I know. And you don't have to say yes to this. If you think you can do better somewhere else, you're free to keep looking around. But Kellan…" She leaned in and put a hand on my shoulder. "This is a *good* deal. A once in a lifetime deal. I know I probably seem biased, but you should say yes to this."

I nodded. "Yes…I…yes, I'm saying yes," I finally said with a laugh.

She grinned. "You should talk to your band, make sure they're on board too." She pointed up. "There is a conference room upstairs. I'll have my people prepare the contracts for you, and I'll let you know when they're ready."

Overwhelmed, I just nodded again. She patted my shoulder, told me congratulations again, then walked away to get to work. I watched her leave, and as I did, my gaze fell over Paul again. His mouth was open, shocked, and I knew he understood what had just happened. Not really caring what he thought, I sought out my band. *They said yes. They fucking said yes.* I could finally let this secret out.

Evan had left the room, and Matt and Griffin weren't in here. My eager group of fans was still nearby, waiting, but I had something important I needed to do. Looking their way, I said, "Sorry," then I left to go find some D-Bags.

I ended up finding Justin first. I grabbed his shoulders as adrenaline flooded me. He blinked at me, his brows pulled together in amusement and confusion. "Dude…they said yes," I told him. He tilted his head, and I made myself calm down and explain it in a way that made sense. "We got signed."

Justin grinned, then gave me a quick hug. "I knew it! I knew she wanted you!" He smacked my shoulder when we pulled apart. "We're labelmates, man."

Laughing, I shook my head. "How the fuck is this my life?"

Justin snorted. "Kellan, I have a feeling, for you...this is just the beginning."

I rolled my eyes, then clapped him on the back. "I gotta find the guys. *Finally* fucking tell them." Getting this off my chest was going to feel so good.

Justin's grin grew; he knew this had been killing me. He pointed to the other side of the large room we were in. "I don't know where Matt and Evan are, but Griffin's over there, drinking with some girls."

"Thanks. I'm gonna go tell him."

"Congratulations, man!" he called out as I left.

The room was pretty packed, full of people and furniture. I had to weave my way around pockets of bodies. This looked like a hookup room, with flirting and making out everywhere. It didn't surprise me at all that Griffin was hanging out in here. Off to my right, I spotted the girl who'd brazenly climbed onto my lap. She was sucking on Benji's neck. I smiled at the two of them. Benji was a much better option for her tonight, and he could definitely use the pick-me-up.

I found Griffin in the far end of the room, standing near a makeshift bar. I wasn't sure where the alcohol came from—band members, the crew, or maybe even the label—but there was always something to drink backstage. And there was usually quite a variety. I grabbed an unopened bottle of beer from a cooler and popped the top off. I needed to calm down, especially if Griffin was the first person I was going to tell.

I took a long swallow from my beer as I approached him, trying to push down the giddiness. Griffin was intently staring at something in front of him as I stepped beside him, and I shifted my focus to look. There was a cute blonde on her knees on top of a table. She was clearly putting on a show for Griffin. Writhing around, touching herself, rolling her hips. I almost felt like telling her that she didn't need to try that hard. All she had to do was ask Griffin to have sex with her and he would. Gladly. One of the girl's friends whispered something to her and the blonde nodded. Then she started taking off her shirt, exposing her lacey bra. I glanced over at Griffin grinning at her, delighted, and rolled my eyes. Maybe I should tell Matt and Evan first.

Griffin finally noticed me though. He looked over at me, and then he did a double take. "You change your mind?" he asked. "'Cause I call dibs on that one." He pointed to the half-naked blonde.

I looked back at the girl. She gave Griffin a wink, then she laid back on the table. Her two friends approached her, staring at Griffin, and now me, then they started pouring alcohol on the girl and sucking it off of her. It was like witnessing one of Griffin's fantasies come to life. I laughed as I watched them. At least he'd found girls.

Leaning over, I told him, "They're all yours, remember. You can have every last one of them."

Griffin smirked at me. "Like I don't already know that," he said.

Shaking my head, I laughed again. What I wanted to tell Griffin slipped to the back of my mind as I stared at the rambunctious girls in front of me. What they were doing was distracting, true, but more than that…it was giving me a great idea. I instantly pictured lying Kiera out somewhere, filling the crevices of her body with alcohol…licking it off her skin. Jesus. That thought was doing way more for me than actually watching Griffin's future hookups doing it. I chewed on my lip as I let the fantasy carry me away. I shouldn't dwell on that back here…fans nearby might get the wrong idea. I should think of something else, anything else. What was I going to tell Griffin again?

I felt someone approaching on my right and flashed a quick

glance in their direction. Kiera and Anna. My eyes had already returned to the front before what I'd just noticed fully registered. *Kiera and Anna?* Feeling like I'd just lost my mind, I twisted to face the impossibility of my girlfriend and her sister in front of me. Was I dreaming? Kiera was staring at my crotch for some reason, but her eyes immediately shifted to my face as her cheeks filled with color. I was too floored to be too curious about her reaction. *She's here. Holy fuck, she's here. I must be dreaming.*

But then Griffin exclaimed, "Hell yeah!" and I knew it was real. She was *really* here. Griffin grabbed Anna and had his tongue down her throat before I could even wipe the shock off my face. Kiera twisted to watch Griffin sweep Anna away. When her beautiful features returned to me, I finally smiled. "You're here?" I said, stepping forward. *I'm not dreaming?*

A soft smile on her lips, she nodded. Then her hazel eyes flicked to the table, and a wave of guilt washed over me. Oh, shit. My gaze shifted back to the girls still making out with each other, oblivious to Griffin's absence. Kiera had seen me staring at them. She wouldn't understand that I hadn't really been watching *them*. She'd think I was just trying to save face if I told her the truth. So, all I could do was apologize.

Looking back at her, I cringed and shrugged. I hoped she wasn't too angry as I grabbed her hand and pulled her into me. "Sorry about that." I blindly handed my beer bottle to someone nearby, then I ran my hand through her soft, silky hair. I studied her face like I'd never seen it before, and I felt myself getting lost in her perfection. God, I'd missed her. How was she here? "Some girls will do anything to get noticed," I murmured. *But all I think about is you.*

Feeling more complete than I'd felt in weeks, I cupped her cheek. "I can't believe you're here." I flicked a glance at where we were and wondered how she'd accomplished that. Matt had told me earlier that the show was sold out, and backstage passes usually ran out long before the regular tickets. "How did you get back here?" Did she win a contest or something? How? When? *Why?*

She let out an amusing pained sound. "You would not believe what I had to do." She pursed her lips and raised an eyebrow. "Make sure you say bye to Anna...because I'm killing her when we get home."

The look on her face made me laugh, but the curiosity was killing me. Was it a contest then? Because I'd talked to some of the winners before, and the things they'd had to do...had to eat...I still couldn't believe people would do that to meet a rock star. Laughing, I told her, "Ah, I can't wait to hear this story."

Kiera bit her lip as she stepped closer to me. I instantly stopped breathing. "Maybe it could wait just a little bit?" she said, staring at my mouth.

Fuck...yes. I instantly brought my lips to hers. It was like dousing myself in fire as our mouths connected. Heavenly, wonderful, erotic fire. It was difficult to control the sudden, rampaging need coursing through me, the almost-wild desire. It had been so long...she tasted so good, felt so good...made me feel so good. Why weren't we alone? I needed to be alone with her. My hand on her cheek slid to her neck, my other hand wrapped around her waist, pulling her in closer. *More.* Her hands slid up my chest. One of them tangled in my hair, and I felt my control slipping. I wanted her. *Now.*

But before we could slip off into the darkness, my shoulder was tapped on. It was difficult to pull away from Kiera, but I made myself do it. Looking to my side, I saw Lana standing there, politely waiting for my attention. That was when I remembered that I was supposed to be doing something. Oops.

I suddenly felt extremely unprofessional as Lana's amused eyes flicked to Kiera. She probably thought I was making out with a groupie instead of rounding up the guys. I just hadn't expected Griffin's girls to distract me so much, and then I'd never even contemplated running into Kiera. All thought of my news had fled my mind long ago.

"Kellan, I'm ready for you," Lana told me.

Not wanting to admit that I hadn't even talked to the guys yet, I gave her a polite nod. "Okay, I'll need a minute, though."

Lana's eyes scanned Kiera up and down. Yep, she definitely thought Kiera was just another fan, a fan I wanted to go have sex with. Shaking her head in amusement, Lana returned her eyes to me. She didn't look upset or disappointed in any way, so maybe this was just expected behavior from a rock star. I didn't feel like explaining to Lana that I wasn't like that, and she probably wouldn't believe me anyway, so I didn't say anything.

Lana put a hand on my shoulder, then leaned forward so I could hear her better. "The conference room upstairs...when you're ready."

Polite smile on my face, I nodded at her. Lana threw another amused look Kiera's way, then turned and left.

I felt Kiera's hands slipping from my body. She had to be embarrassed about being caught like that. I wanted to apologize, but I suddenly realized...I could finally tell Kiera as well as finally tell the guys. I could get one of the weights off my chest with her. I could partially feel better whenever I talked to her. I could —*almost*—be set free.

When I turned back to face Kiera, I felt kind of...nervous. This was so monumental for me, so...unexpected. In all honesty, I was still waiting to wake up. Would telling Kiera about the record deal pop this fantasy for me, and I'd suddenly be back in my cramped cubby, wishing she was with me? Wishing I didn't have so much to hide from her. God, I didn't want to go back to that.

Kiera's expression was oddly blank as I studied her. No emotion at all. The forced lack of anything in her features was worrisome. Was she upset? Why? She usually wasn't mad when we got caught kissing. I wasn't sure what was going on with her, but I couldn't worry about it anymore. I wanted to tell her, I *needed* to tell her. I bit my lip as a weird wave of anxiety hit me. *Don't let me wake up*.

"I need to tell you something...Can we talk?"

Kiera closed her eyes, like my words had somehow either hurt or angered her. She gave me a stiff nod, then abruptly turned and started walking away. What the hell? I followed in her wake as she forcefully weaved her way through people. She definitely seemed angry now. Because of the girls I'd been watching? I thought for sure she'd let that go...the way she'd been kissing me, it sure *seemed* like she'd let that go.

When we got somewhere a little less crowded, I grabbed her elbow, stopping her. She resisted me, and I had the weirdest feeling that if I let her go...I'd never see her again. *Why is she so angry?*

Confused and a little annoyed, I searched her face for clues. She stiffened, like she wanted to pull away. I wasn't about to let her go. Not until I understood. "Hey, are you...mad at me?"

Fire was in her eyes as she raised her chin and tossed her bag off her shoulder to the ground. "No, why would I be mad?"

Exactly? *Why*? I shook my head and was about to ask her why she was acting mad, but she spoke first. "You're only about to dump me for the hot celebrity look-alike that's been stalking you for weeks. You're only about to go have sex with her on an office table. You're only about to crush me into a thousand pieces, and right after I exposed my chest to some jackass just to see you too!"

Kiera was fuming now, seething in anger, but I was so stunned, so confused, I had no idea what to respond to first. What the fuck was she talking about? Did she mean Lana? She thought that brief interaction was somehow me agreeing to go have sex with her? How the fuck did she get *there*? "Wait, you think...?" Before I could clarify my assumption, the last thing she'd said suddenly slammed into my brain, halting my train of thought. She exposed her...*what*? I had to have heard her wrong. "You did what to come see me?"

That was the wrong thing to focus on, and Kiera shoved me away from her and started storming off. I could practically see the hot, angry energy sizzling around her. Great. *Way to calm her down.* With a sigh, I swiftly grabbed her shoulders, turned her around, and backed her into a nearby wall so she couldn't run away on me. So she would *listen*. "I am not dumping you. I am not about to have sex with her. And I am not going to crush you."

I stared at her unflinchingly until her furious breaths calmed to a more normal level. Pain in her eyes, she searched my face. "Then what...is going on?"

Seeing she was more level-headed, I released her shoulders and shook my head. "Well, what I was going to tell you, before you leapt to that wild conclusion, is..." I bit my lip, excited, nervous, anxious. "We got signed." I nodded upstairs. "That's Lana. She's a rep from the record company. She's been following the tour, examining the bands...and she wants to sign us to her label." The weight of releasing that secret made me giddy. The fact that I was still here, that I hadn't woken up from some crazy dream made me damn-near delirious. I laughed, venting some of the energy, the disbelief. "We're going to have a record, Kiera, an actual, professional record...Can you believe it?"

Kiera's mouth dropped open, the green in her eyes deepening as they moistened. She looked amazed, happy, stunned...and still a little annoyed. She shoved my shoulders back, making me back up a step. "Why didn't you tell me you were being scouted, jackass!"

She started smacking my chest, her earlier anger not entirely gone. I cringed away from her strikes, but I didn't try and stop her from hitting me. I deserved a little light pummeling; I should have told her. "Because I really didn't expect much. I didn't think she'd pick us...and..." *And I didn't want you to see me fail. Your opinion is the only one that truly matters to me.*

I stopped talking and Kiera stopped hitting me. Sighing, I grabbed her hands and peeked up at her. "I didn't want to disappoint you...if she wasn't interested in us. I know you think I'm going to go all the way...I didn't want to let you down..." *No. I* couldn't *let you down. I couldn't bear it. I'd rather have you never know, then face the disappointment in your eyes.*

I looked down; it was like I could see it anyway. Hadn't I already disappointed her by not telling her in the first place? Wouldn't she be even more hurt if she knew what else I was hiding...? *No. Don't think about that. This is just about your job.*

While I struggled with my guilt and pain, Kiera wrapped her arms around me, squeezing me tight. "God, Kellan, I'd never be disappointed in you...ever." Pulling back, she cupped my cheeks and made me look at her; her eyes were even glossier. The emotion in them tore me open. "I'm so proud of you, of everything you do, and even if it ended right here, I'd be anything but disappointed in you."

I knew that wasn't entirely true, I could *easily* disappoint her if she knew I was withholding even more from her, but her words —her *pride*—struck me to my core. Pride was not something I was used to someone feeling for me. It hurt. It healed. Exhaling a long breath, I tried to let my torment go and focus on the matter at hand. My job. Lana was waiting.

Choking back the pain, I looked around us. "Well, I haven't even told the guys yet...I didn't want to jinx it, so we need to find them and get them upstairs to sign the legal stuff." Feeling better, I looked back at her with a raised eyebrow. "That's what's going down on the conference room table...not sex." My mood shifted even more and feeling playful, I grabbed her hips and pulled her into me. "But if you want to, once everyone is gone...I'd never tell you no."

I started to laugh, but she grabbed my face and gave me a fierce kiss. I wanted to let the kiss continue, wanted to cave into her arms and let the fire take over again...but I really did need to do my job. Full of reluctance, I pulled away from her and grabbed her bag from the floor. "Come on, we've got to take care of this before it's our turn onstage." Grin on my face, I extended a hand to her. "They bumped us up the lineup; we play right under Justin's band now. Pretty cool, huh?"

She leaned into my side. With a giggle and a nod, she said, "That's amazing, Kellan."

I mentally kicked myself for not mentioning that small detail to her earlier. I'd just been riding a cloud of denial lately. About a lot of things. At least one of my secrets was gone. I could almost breathe again.

Chapter 25
WHY NOW?

I searched for the guys as we walked along. If Matt wasn't feeling social, then he was usually somewhere quiet, working on music. Evan had probably joined him. And Griffin...he was having sex with Anna somewhere. No doubt in my mind.

Feeling completely at peace for once, I smiled down at Kiera walking beside me. It still blew my mind that she was here. Just when I hadn't been able to stand one more second without her... she arrived. It was the best gift I could have asked for—better than the record deal. Which reminded me...how did Kiera know about Lana?

"Hey, what did you mean when you said she's been stalking me for weeks? How did you know about that?"

Kiera looked guilty when she peeked up at me. "Uh, Rachel put up this website, and fans have posted videos of your shows. I've been watching you..."

She's been watching me? Hmmm...I like that. Just the thought of her sitting at home, watching me on stage gave me a thrill. If only it were a live feed, and I knew every time I went out there that she could see me, it would almost be like Pete's again. I really missed knowing her eyes were on me. I *preferred* having her eyes on me.

Responding to her comment, I said, "She finally got that up and running, huh? Well, that should make Matt happy." Although, he probably already knew. He'd probably told me at some point, and I'd just let it slide right out of my brain. Websites weren't really my thing. Shaking my head a little, I released Kiera's hand and slung my arm over her shoulders. "So, you've been checking up on me?" I teased.

Her voice was small when she answered me. "No..." I dropped my eyes down to hers. *Liar*. She cringed as she sighed. "Maybe...a little."

I gave her a squeeze. "And was I being good?" I playfully asked. I already knew I was...since I wasn't doing anything, but I wanted to know that Kiera knew that. Although...she'd been pretty quick to assume I was doing stuff with Lana. Had she been worrying about her?

Kiera opened and closed her mouth, making noises but no words. My brows bunched as a weird feeling started settling around me. She *had* been worrying about her. She'd thought I was messing around with Lana...she'd actually thought that. How long had she thought that? Why didn't she say anything to me before? I would have told her if she'd asked. *That* I wouldn't have lied about.

I wanted to ask her, wanted to find out why she hadn't talked to me, but before I could, Griffin and Anna came into view. They looked disheveled...and satisfied. Great. I was going to hear about this visit for weeks. As much as Griffin might experiment with other girls...and the occasional, unintentional guy...Anna was his preferred dalliance. That much was obvious. To everyone but Griffin.

I nodded a greeting to Anna; she just smiled at me as she fixed her clothes. "Kell," Griffin murmured, looking a little dazed. "How much time 'til we're up? I wanna...leave."

Grinning, I shook my head. "Sorry, you can't. We gotta go do something."

He tilted his head, looking both confused and disappointed. He wouldn't be for long. "Do what?" he whined.

Smacking his shoulder, I told him, "Sign a contract for a record deal."

He just stared at me blankly, like I'd spoken a foreign language. Letting out a laugh, I quickly explained about Lana and the label, and the killer deal she'd worked out for us, and how we needed to go upstairs to sign the paperwork. When he finally understood, his mouth dropped open. "Are you fucking serious, right now?"

I nodded. "Yeah. It's legit. We did it, man. We fucking did it."

He started jumping up and down, laughing, screaming. The joy on his face made all the stress I'd been feeling lately totally worth it. Anna screamed and celebrated with him, her exuberance matching his. She congratulated both of us, and Griffin squeezed her so hard I was sure he was hurting her. Pulling away, he twisted back to me. "Have you told Matt yet?"

I shook my head. "No, I haven't found him yet. I think he's going over music with Evan somewhere."

Griffin nodded, then he patted my shoulder. "I'm gonna go find them. We'll meet you up there, man!" And then he was gone.

A few minutes later, Kiera, Anna, and I were in the elevator on our way upstairs. Dropping Kiera's bag, I took the moment of near aloneness to wrap my arms around her. My mouth found hers, and the excitement of the moment poured into my kiss. I knew I was being a little too intense, considering Anna was watching, but Kiera didn't back down from the passionate moment. Between breaks, I murmured, "I'm sorry I didn't tell you about this earlier...but I'm glad you're here."

I could feel her lips smiling as she threaded her fingers in my hair. "I'm glad I'm here too."

She let me ravish her until the elevator stopped. I couldn't wait to get this over with...so I could be alone with her. Grabbing her bag and her hand, I playfully asked. "So, anything you've been holding off on telling me?" *Like how you got back here?*

Before she could say anything, fate decided to fuck with me. My phone started ringing and buzzing in my pocket, making all kinds of noise like the damn thing wanted Kiera to be absolutely certain she heard it. *Fuck me...why now?* I swear to God, Gavin had the worst fucking timing. And I knew that was who it was. The guys had no reason to call me right now. I'd already talked to Hailey earlier in the evening; she'd been on her way to meet up with friends for a movie. And almost everyone else I knew would have sent a text. I couldn't—and *wouldn't*—answer the phone, but would Kiera think it was weird if I ignored it? Maybe, but what other choice did I have?

Not wanting to listen to the fucking ring anymore, I grabbed my phone, silenced it, and shoved it back in my pocket. He could leave a message. One I would *never* listen to.

I felt Kiera's curious eyes on me as I purposefully ignored her, acting like nothing odd had just happened. Goddamn it. I knew I wasn't handling this right. I knew I was filling her with doubt, probably hurting her, but fuck, I couldn't handle how much acknowledging this—acknowledging *him*—would hurt *me*.

I'm so sorry, Kiera. I wish I could make you understand without actually letting you understand, but I can't. You just have to trust me.

The longer Kiera stared at me, the tenser I became. Was she going to ask again? Would I have to fucking lie to her again? I didn't want to; I still felt sickened by the last time I'd bluntly lied to her. *Don't ask. Just don't ask, then I won't have to flat-out lie to you. Please.*

Much to my relief, she didn't ask. The relief quickly shifted to guilt. And then worry. Why didn't she ask? What did that mean? Fuck. Were we okay?

I suddenly wanted to confess all my sins, but we were in the conference room now, and Lana was looking at me expectantly. I didn't have time to bear my soul to Kiera. I had a job to do. And besides...I still wasn't actually capable of telling her. I could wish it...but I couldn't say it.

PAINFUL

Kiera was unnaturally quiet as Lana explained the details of the contract to the guys. I found myself only half listening to Lana as I contemplated what Kiera was thinking. How much had I worried her? When Lana was done and the guys had all read through the contract, I made myself refocus. This was important. We all needed to be on the same page if we were going to proceed.

Glancing between Matt and Evan, I asked, "What do you guys think?" I wasn't a lawyer or anything, but the terms sounded fair to me. More than fair from other stories I'd heard. For starters, we'd get to keep control of our songs. That in and of itself was huge. We'd also have a say in what songs went on the album. Not final say, of course, but we'd at least have a voice.

Matt and Evan looked at each other. They still seemed a bit stunned and overwhelmed. By withholding this information from them, I hadn't given them a lot of time to consider. But I knew their hearts, knew their dreams. This was what they wanted for the band, and I was fairly certain this deal was the best we'd get. I wasn't worried about what Griffin thought; he'd say yes to anything that resulted in a professional album with him on the cover. But Matt and Evan...if just one of them said no, then that was it. We'd find something else, or we'd just go home and keep playing at Pete's. And I was kind of okay with that option.

Matt and Evan smiled at each other before returning their eyes to me. "Yeah, we're in," Matt said with a nod. I couldn't contain my grin. As much as going home sounded fantastic, I wanted this for them. And maybe...for myself too. Fuck. We were actually going to do this.

Lana showed us where to sign, and we all started putting pen to paper. Except Griffin. He was scowling at the paper like it had just bitten him or something. "Dude, Kell, did you read this? I don't believe this shit!"

I wanted to sigh...because I had a good idea just what he was pissed about. And I didn't want to discuss it here, in front of Kiera.

Matt laughed at Griffin's comment, murmuring, "I don't believe that you can actually read..."

Griffin glared at Matt before grabbing a paper from the stack and shoving it at me. It was exactly what I thought it was. *Goddamn it, Griffin...let it go.* "Yeah...I read it," I said, flicking a glance at Kiera.

Looking reluctant but too curious to stay silent, Kiera asked him precisely what I hoped she wouldn't. "Read what?"

Griffin shifted the paper to her while I tried to think of something that would make her feel better about this. I couldn't think of a damn thing though. It just sounded...bad.

Annoyance on his face, Griffin told her, "This says that we shouldn't have sex with all the girls hanging around, because chicks will try to screw us just to get knocked up! So we have to pay them to raise the kid! For eighteen years!"

The look of shock and disgust on his face was almost humorous. Griffin didn't often consider the consequences of his actions, and this was clearly something that had never even crossed his mind before. It was honestly sort of a miracle that he hadn't knocked someone up yet. But the way he'd phrased it, and him bringing it up here—*now*—was pissing me off. Why was tact completely beyond him?

Kiera's eyes slowly turned to me. "They gave you a pamphlet on sleeping with fans?" she asked, her voice crisp, edged with irritation.

Fucking Griffin. Shrugging, I kept my eyes on my papers. "It's just a warning..." A general, all-encompassing, doesn't-apply-to-me warning. There was also a memo about drugs and alcohol, but of course, Griffin wasn't concerned about that one. Just the sex. God forbid someone tell Griffin who he could or couldn't screw. Jackass.

Before I could say anything else, Lana intervened. "It's a standard precaution that we give to all of our rising celebrities. They will be targets to all sorts of different people, and we give them guidelines on how to best protect themselves from...being manipulated."

She paused to smile warmly at Kiera. Lana had instantly realized that Kiera was more than an eager fan the moment I'd brought her in here with me, and she'd been extremely courteous to her. I was very grateful she was taking a moment to explain this to Kiera. I felt like it had more weight coming from Lana. "It's the company's way of protecting the asset. It's a very common practice nowadays." She laughed and shrugged. "Athletes have to sit through a seminar about it. They never listen though..."

Some of the annoyance fell off Kiera's face as she absorbed that. Unfortunately, Griffin was still pissed. Throwing his pen down, he said, "Well, what's the point of being a rock star if I can't bang the groupies?"

I wanted to toss my pen at him. And maybe a bucket of cold water. Was he seriously not going to sign because of *that*? Kiera seemed incredulous too as she muttered, "I thought it was supposed to be about the music?"

I automatically cringed, because I knew what he was going to say, and I knew Kiera wouldn't like it. "No, no, I'm pretty sure it's the pussy."

Yep. Fucking Griffin.

Kiera leaned back and crossed her arms over her chest. I patted her thigh in silent apology for my bandmate, but she didn't look any less irritated. I wanted to smack Griffin for his comment, but he was too far away. Thankfully, Anna smacked him for me.

Griffin turned to glare at her as he rubbed his head. "What?" he asked, genuinely perplexed. Anna rolled her eyes and shook her head, but even still, she looked more amused than anything else.

Matt laughed. "Dude, it doesn't say you shouldn't have sex. It says you should always use protection." He rolled his eyes. "You can still sleep with them if you want, just wrap it up. And please do. The last thing the world needs is another you," he said with a smirk.

Evan let out a low laugh as Griffin turned his heated eyes on Matt. "Fuck you, man." Face softening, Griffin looked back at me. "Is that true? Do girls really do that?"

I wasn't sure why he was asking *me*. It wasn't like I had personal experience with that. But it wasn't uncommon for Griffin to come to me on the rare occasion he had a dilemma. For some reason, he valued my opinion. By the look on his face, I could tell he wanted me to deny it. He wanted reassurance for the lifestyle he loved, wanted me to say something like, "*No, the only thing girls are interested in is a few minutes with your body...don't worry about it.*" But he *did* need to worry about it, so I wasn't going to tell him that. Instead, I told him what was, most likely, the truth.

"Some," I said, squeezing Kiera's leg in another quiet apology.

Looking annoyed for a different reason, Griffin finally picked up the pen. "Well, that's fucked up," he said, signing his name.

I wanted to sigh in relief, one because he was signing it, and two because he looked like he was genuinely contemplating that warning. Maybe he'd be more careful from here on out. Maybe.

Finished with my papers, I gathered them up and handed them to Lana. She gave me a friendly smile as she tucked them away. I felt giddy now that it was over with, and eager to finally spend some time with Kiera. Leaning over, I kissed her cheek, then ran my lips along her jaw to her ear. Just that tiny tease was enough to send electricity down my body.

Gauging how much time was left in the show by the song I could hear playing below us, I told her, "I still have forty-five minutes of free time...Want to go somewhere more private?"

She nodded, and with a smile glued to my face, I stood up. "I'm gonna show her around. I'll see you guys later."

Matt and Evan gave us a knowing smile and a nod. Griffin was studying his contract like it was written in a foreign language.

Oh well. Lana and the guys could help him if he still had concerns, and honestly, I was pretty sure his largest concern had already been addressed.

Grabbing Kiera's bag and her hand, I led her back downstairs and then out the side door to the buses. I was teeming with energy when I popped the bus door open. Grinning, I told her, "Come on, let me show you where I live now."

She giggled as she followed me inside, and I was so glad she'd let that stupid conversation with Griffin go. Groupies were his issue, not mine. I hoped she genuinely understood that. Tossing her bag on an empty seat, I led her to the sleeping area of the bus. The divider curtain was closed, and when it fell back into place, the space was fairly dark, lit only by soft lights built into the floor. It wasn't uncommon for tired band members to come back to the bus after their performance, but a quick scan of the cubbies convinced me we were alone. I stopped us in front of my cubby. Maybe it was a little forward to lead her directly to my bed, but...I really fucking missed her.

I wrapped my arms around her, reveling in her warmth, in the sound of her light breath in the quiet room. Leaning my forehead against hers, I softly told her, "Welcome to my bedroom."

I could feel her breath quicken as my lips slowly started lowering to hers. "Your bedroom?" she said, her voice low, seductive...sexy as hell.

She was already igniting me, making me harden with need, but I didn't want to rush this. I missed teasing her too much. I missed the anticipation. I moved my mouth away from hers, connecting my lips to her jaw instead, and I felt a slight shudder go through her. "Mine and the other guys..." I told her. One of my hands slid down her back, over her ass, while I placed soft kisses down her neck. God, she smelled good.

She angled her head, giving me better access to her skin, and the ache inside me intensified. Slowly working my way down her throat, I said, "We're all packed into these cubbies, like sardines." At the base of her throat, I began lightly running my tongue up her neck. Damn, she tasted good. The noise she made when she dropped her head back made a surge of desire rush through me. *Fuck. I want you.*

Her hands ran over my ass and gently tugged on my jeans, subconsciously pulling me into her, telling me she wanted me too. I cupped her cheek. "It's not as spacious as your bed back home, but there's just enough room for two..."

Our faces were so close together...but I purposely kept our mouths apart. The tease was nearly excruciating, and I knew I'd need relief soon, but God...it felt so good. I sensed her minutely shift her focus to glance at the cubbies, and I pointed out the one on the bottom. "That's mine. My home away from home, where I try to get some sleep with a bunch of snoring, smelly dudes around me."

The brutal, unglamorous reality of my life made me laugh. Then I was struck by my remembered daily loneliness, and I sighed and touched her face again. Pulling back from her, I paused to absorb the beauty I had ached for so much. "Where I dream about you...where I miss you..."

My eyes misted as I stared at the depth of love in her ever-changing eyes. Being apart from her was so...hard. Harder than I'd thought it would be, and I'd anticipated it being nearly insurmountable. Maybe that was because of everything else I was going through. Maybe if all I was dealing with was homesickness it wouldn't be so bad, so devastating. I would never know for sure, because I was already so deep in my personal hell, I couldn't see a way out anymore. For a moment, as the weight became suffocating, I just wanted my old life back. *Take me home, Kiera. Free me from this agony of missing you...and hating him.*

Kiera's eyes grew glossy, matching my pain. "I miss you too, Kellan."

Then Kiera's hand threaded through my hair, and she forcefully pulled me forward, urging me toward her. Our mouths met, and the loneliness and pain instantly morphed into fiery passion. If she couldn't physically take me home, at least I could lose myself in her. Ease my pain with a glorious distraction. The quiet space around us filled with soft needy moans, as the ache of our separation overwhelmed us. Pushing Kiera back against the bed frame, I shifted her leg around my hip so I could press against her fully, show her just how much I'd missed her. Her nails scratched down my back, almost undoing me. *Fuck. Yes.*

Her fingers started tugging on my shirt, wanting it off. I pulled away to help her, tossing the fabric over my shoulder. Kiera's fingers traced the letters of her name on my chest. My skin felt electric where she touched me, and I paused a moment to savor the sensation—the connection. "I love you," I whispered.

I rocked my hips against hers, wanting to satisfy her, satisfy us. Her arms wrapped around me, pulling me closer into her. My lips found her neck, my fingers found her stomach. I bunched up her thin shirt until her bra was exposed. *That. I want that.* I swept the cup aside, then ducked down to take her nipple into my mouth. The noise Kiera made, the way she arched against me...it was like she was about to come, just from me doing this. It made me throb, needing my own release.

No. I needed hers.

Mouth never leaving her chest, I blindly unbuttoned her jeans. She moaned, "Yes," as I slid my hand inside the opening. She was clutching my shoulders, panting with need, aching for me to give this to her. My fast, frantic breaths matched hers. I needed this. I needed *her*...so much.

I was just about to touch her, feel how much she wanted me, when the room suddenly brightened. I instantly pulled my hand out of her jeans, released her nipple, and fixed her shirt. Goddamn it. My body was complaining about the change of pace; from the look on Kiera's face, her body was as well. Blocking Kiera from view, I turned around to see who the hell was here.

My stomach dropped when I saw who was holding open the curtain that separated the sleeping area from the bathroom. Paul. Fucking Paul. Of course, it would be him. That asshole was the one person I really didn't want to see Kiera like this. And from the look on his face, he'd been listening to us for a while, just waiting for his moment to spoil the mood. Fucking dick.

Paul's eyes raked over Kiera in a way that was seriously pissing me off. He knew who she was; I was constantly studying her photo on the bus. He knew what she meant to me. And he also knew he could seriously damage us with a few well-placed words. I could feel Kiera fidgeting behind me, fixing the rest of her clothes. I struggled with what to do, because what I really wanted to do was kick his ass for purposely embarrassing her. But I knew...*I knew*...Paul could make this moment so much worse than just embarrassing. I had to be calm, I had to be nice. Maybe if I was, then he would be too. *You can be jealous of me, but don't be cruel. Please.*

He was still holding up the curtain, bathing us in the light from the other room. He tried to look surprised, but the gleam of victory in his eyes gave it away. It also scared me. "Hey, sorry, Kellan...didn't mean to...interrupt." He smirked as he stepped into the room with us. "Hey, cutie, what's up?"

Fuck. The creepy way he'd said that was like a premonition of what was about to happen. He was going to start something. He was going to hurt her. I had to get him out of here. As Paul stepped closer, I felt Kiera drop her head to my shoulder, mortified. I hated that her being embarrassed was actually the *best* outcome here. I shoved Paul's shoulder, trying to hurry him along. "Yeah, well, it happens, don't worry about it."

Paul let out an amused chuckle as he let himself be pushed by me. When he was at the other curtain opening, he said, "Yeah, yeah, I'm leaving." He opened that curtain, letting a softer light reach us. Then he gave me a smile that made my blood run cold. It was a smile that clearly said, *You are so fucked*. "Damn, man, I don't know how you manage to always score with the hottest chick." His eyes slid over Kiera as my stomach started knotting. "And two in one night, bro...I wish I had that kind of stamina."

I could feel Kiera's eyes on me, but all I could do was stare at

Paul in utter disbelief. *Why would you do that to me? What the fuck did I ever do to you?* Paul gave me a satisfied sneer, then he said something that guaranteed his future fate. "Hey, sweetie, I'm available if you want to bang me next? I don't mind getting his seconds...again."

It looks like Evan will *have to help me bury your body...because I'm going to fucking kill you.*

Paul was laughing as he left. He wouldn't be laughing later when I was pummeling him. Kiera's hands dropped from my body once he was gone; I felt hope for us dropping with them. She believed him. She absolutely, 100 percent believed him. *How do I fix this?*

Closing my eyes, I swallowed the sudden lump of tension in my throat. *I don't know what to do. How do I make her believe me over him?* When he'd just wrapped up all her fears in one tidy, little sadistic present. She was just going to have to blindly trust me. Again.

Reopening my eyes, I slowly turned to face her. The rage and pain I saw on her face tore me wide open. She doesn't trust me... at all. I was about to start explaining, but she didn't even let me open my mouth. Her right hand reached out, slapping my cheek full force, her promise ring digging into my skin. The abrupt, unexpected pain sent shockwaves down my body, and all of a sudden, what I felt the most...was anger.

Mine was no match for Kiera's fury though. "You son of a bitch!" she screamed, backing away from me.

I rubbed my jaw, feeling the sting of a fresh cut over the burn of the hard contact. "Jesus, Kiera. Can I explain before you start whaling on me?"

My eyes narrowed as I glared at her. I thought she'd at least let me speak before she started assaulting me. *Guess not.* The heat in her eyes far outweighed the heat in mine. The betrayal on her face was so clear; seeing it cooled my temper. "You can explain 'scoring the hottest chick'? You can explain 'two in one night'? You can explain him 'getting your seconds...again'?"

I suddenly felt extremely exhausted. *Fuck you, Paul. Fuck you very, very much.* A weary sigh escaped me as I ran a hand down my face. "Yes, Kiera. I can explain." *If you just let me.*

She shoved a finger into my chest like she wished it was a sword. "Are you cheating on me?" she snapped.

I grabbed her hand. I tried to lace our fingers together, tried to get her to calm down, but she fought me; her rigid fingers wouldn't let me in. "No, I'm not," I told her, my voice soft. I ducked down to look her in the eye, so she could see my sincerity, but she avoided eye contact with me. This wouldn't work, not if she wouldn't even give me a chance to refute him. I tried again. "Hey, I'm not, Kiera. I've already told you that before...several times probably."

She inhaled a shaky breath, and when she spoke her voice shimmered with emotion. "Then what...was he talking about?"

I grabbed her other hand; it was tightly clenched into a fist. I tried to get her to loosen up, tried to break the walls I could see forming around her, but nothing was working. She was shutting me out, more and more with every second. Desperate, I grabbed her cheeks and forced her to look at me. Her eyes watered as she stared at me, and my heart cracked at seeing her pain. He'd slipped into her mind so easily. She was so afraid...but I could understand fear. I felt it often enough myself.

"He's lying, Kiera. He said that to get a rise out of you. He knows who you are, they all do. I flip through that photo book all the time..." I gave her a soft, reassuring smile. "They all think you're beautiful..."

I wasn't reassuring her though, and she pushed my hands off her face. The rejection stung, but I understood. She believed him, she believed I was cheating on her. She confirmed that with her next words.

"Why would *he* lie?" The inflection on the word "he" spoke volumes. She'd fully accepted that I was the one lying to her because in her mind, a stranger had no reason to lie. But she didn't know Paul. She wasn't understanding what was really going on.

I stayed away from her since she clearly wanted space. Feeling more alone than I had in weeks, I shook my head. "Because we were the last band to join the tour and we got bumped to the second in the lineup. Because Lana wanted to sign our band and not his." I paused to shrug. "Because he's a childish, immature asshole with a grudge against me, Kiera, and if making you doubt me got us fighting tonight instead of..." With another weary sigh, I tossed my hands into the air. "Because this, right here, is what he wanted...His stupid form of payback for our band being better than his." *Please believe me. I swear I'm telling you the truth.*

Her expression softened, but I could still see the pain, the doubt. "Why should I believe you?" she asked.

Her question was like having acid poured over my soul; every inch of me hurt. Could we do this? Was it even possible for us to be together? *How can I prove the unprovable to you? How do we win?* The pain, the panic, the fear—it loosened my tongue. Tossing up my hands again, I snipped, "I haven't done anything wrong! Why shouldn't you believe me?"

And that was when my phone chimed with a message. I knew exactly who it was from. Un-fucking-believable. *Goddamn it, Gavin. Why won't you just give up?* I shut my eyes, willing the universe to just go my way for once. *That's it...I'm done. Life fucking hates me, and I fucking hate it right back.* Opening my eyes, I stared at Kiera with a blank expression. It was all I could do. I had no explanations to give her, and I knew she wouldn't let this one go. *Now* I was fucked.

Anger again simmered in Kiera's eyes. "Do you need to get that?"

"No," I said, shaking my head. *Absolutely not.*

Everything about her tightened—her jaw, her eyes...her fists. "How do you know? It might be important?"

Why, why, why? Why was fate so determined to make my life

hell? I let out a slow, calming breath. "You're important...That can wait." *Forever.*

Pain flashed over her face, eradicating her anger. "What can wait?" she whispered, looking deeply afraid of my answer.

I wanted to hold her, I wanted to comfort her, I wanted to *tell her*...but telling her wasn't an option. I hated this. All of this. We'd gone through so much to be together, suffered so much pain to get to where we were, and here I was, hurting her again. I'd never wanted to hurt her again. I just wanted to love her. But my internal torment was too painful to share—sharing it would only amplify it. I knew I was being selfish, but I didn't know what else to do. I slowly stepped up to her and moved to cup her cheek, hoping she would let me. When our skin connected, I poured my heart out and prayed it was enough.

"I'm not doing anything, baby. I love you. I'm being faithful to you." I pointedly showed her my ring, my vow. "I promised...I promise."

Dropping my forehead to hers, I begged for our relationship. And for my sanity. "We don't have much time together. Please, just let this go..."

"Let what go?" she whispered, an ache in her voice.

The pain in my chest intensified, and I could feel my eyes stinging. *I can't. I can't tell you. And yes, that kills me.* Releasing a sigh of tension, I brought my lips to hers, seeking her comfort, her acceptance, even though I didn't deserve either. "I love you, Kiera...please believe in me." *Please don't leave me.*

She didn't say anything, but she kissed me back, and as our mouths moved together, I felt her body relaxing. She was letting it go. And as much as that relieved me, it hurt me too. I felt like I'd been whipped from head to toe. Maybe I was wrong...maybe this pain was greater than exposing my secret. Maybe I should tell her about Gavin. But *how*?

Chapter 26
DISTANCE

When I sensed Kiera was calmer, I broke apart from her. Quietly, I grabbed my shirt from the floor and put it back on. I indicated for her to lie down on my bed, and she crawled into my cubby. I climbed in after her, still silent as my mind spun. Her gaze took in all the things of value I kept around me—all things she and her family had given me. She fingered the toy car she'd given me for Christmas and a swell of loneliness filled me. That perfect moment was just a few months ago, but it felt like a lifetime.

There was something in the air between us now, something I hadn't felt in a really long time. Distance. There was a gap in our connection, doubt in our love for each other...and I knew it was my fault. The guilt was excruciating. *I'm ruining us.* But fixing us...that would ruin *me*.

Hating all of my options, I kissed her shoulder and told her, "I love you..." *Do you still love me? Or have I finally pushed you too far?*

Her fingers tightened on the car as her gaze slowly met mine. My heart started beating harder as I waited for her to confirm her feelings...or confirm my fears. Finally, she said, "I love you too..."

The relief was instant, and not edged with pain this time. I hadn't broken us yet. But how close was I to causing permanent damage? How much farther could I walk this line with her? Especially now when she knew I was withholding something from her. I tucked a strand of hair behind her ear, then pulled out her guitar necklace and stroked the symbolic image of me. This would eat at her now, eat at us. *I'm going to lose her if I don't tell her. I have to tell her.* Fuck.

My smile faded as words I didn't want to say bubbled to the surface. "Kiera...I should tell you something..." Just saying that much made me feel ill. *How do I get through this*? Sadly, I already knew the answer. I couldn't. I literally couldn't say another word about it. Fuck. Did I just make things worse?

But before Kiera could realize my ineptitude, she said something unexpected. "I should tell you something too..."

Ice shot through my spine as I looked up at her face. Was she keeping things from me too? What would she possibly hide from me? That...friend she went to lunch with? "Tell me what?"

She started stammering for words, then her eyes started watering. Oh my God...was *she* cheating on me? Had she found someone else? A comforting presence to hold her while I was gone? I wanted to scream at her for an answer, but I also didn't want to overreact. I had to give her the benefit of the doubt. I had to trust her, even if she didn't trust me.

"Um, well..."

Someone banged on the bus door, then I heard Evan yell, "Kell? You and Kiera in there?"

I wanted to curse his timing...I wanted to thank him for his timing. Because I really wasn't sure if I wanted to know what Kiera was keeping from me. By the guilt on her face, I already knew it was bad. But not knowing...How would I ever get that look in her eyes out of my mind now? Was this the beginning of the end for us? Just another tense, vocal, excruciating breakup on a bus that seemed to be teeming with pain? *Not us. That can't be our future. I have to be misreading her. I just have to be.*

Sighing, I leaned over and shouted, "Yeah, we're in here."

I heard Evan enter the bus, then step up to the curtain

blocking the sleeping area. I could feel his hesitation as he waited on the other side of the thick material. He awkwardly cleared his throat. "You, uh...dressed?"

The question eased some of my heartache, and a knot loosened as I laughed. "Yeah...what's up?"

Like he didn't believe me, he stayed on the other side of the curtain. "We're on in ten, so, you know, we should get ready."

Surprised, I sat up on my elbows. "Already? Damn..." I stood from the cubby as I heard Evan leaving. Looking back at Kiera, I grimaced. "I'm sorry...it's our turn."

She nodded, a trace amount of relief on her face. "I know."

I tentatively held out my hand for her. There was still so much uncertainty between us, I really wasn't sure if she'd accept it. She exhaled slowly, like she was fortifying herself. Then she stood up...and clenched my fingers tight. I'd never been so grateful for anything in my life. I kissed her hand, right over her ring. *I'm not cheating, and I have to believe that you're not either. Because I can't face a reality where that's not true.*

Her eyes studied my face, stopping on my jaw, where I could still feel the sting of a small cut. Remorse filled her features, then she leaned up and softly kissed the tender spot. Her act of contrition was healing, and I felt some of the ice in my chest melting. I gave her a silent nod, accepting her apology. Then I tilted my head toward the exit. "Come on...want to watch our show?"

The girlish grin that came over her lightened my heart even more. She loved watching us perform, and I loved performing for her. I really missed her being in the audience, her eyes tearing through me, her mind absorbing every sound, every phrase, every hidden meaning. No one listened to me quite like Kiera did. Her scrutiny had hurt in the beginning, made me want to hide, but now...it just made me love her even more. She *saw* me, the real me. And thankfully, she loved what she saw.

After Kiera told me yes, we met up with Evan outside. He smiled at Kiera, tossing an arm over her shoulders. It made me happy that my friends liked Kiera, and she liked them too. Most of them. All of us getting along made this rollercoaster we were on a lot less stressful. If that ever changed...I didn't know what I would do. But I had enough current problems without worrying over imaginary ones.

I felt more energized than usual during the show. Maybe it was because the pressure was off now that we were officially signed. Maybe it was because Kiera was here with me, watching me. Or maybe it was a combination of the two. For whatever reason, it was the best show we'd done so far. It electrified me.

The guys drifted off after our set, while I scooped Kiera into my arms, near delirious with joy that she was here. We ended up staying near the stage to watch Avoiding Redemption play, then we headed backstage where I signed a few last-minute autographs for fans. I took a little too long doing it, and Kiera was almost outed by security. Rescuing her from being evicted reminded me that she didn't have the necessary clearance to be back here in the first place. What had she said earlier? So much had happened since then, I really couldn't remember. Other than the fact that she was going to kill her sister for it.

Holding her hand as we headed for the exit, I smiled and said, "That little incident reminds me...What exactly did you do to get backstage?"

She ran a hand down her face, like she was mortified just thinking about it. "You don't want to know," she murmured.

With a laugh, I twisted around so I was walking backward, facing her. "Now I definitely want to know." Raising an eyebrow, I waited for her to tell me.

She still looked reluctant, but eventually she spilled. "I flashed the guy at the door."

I hadn't expected her to say that, although, now that she had, I seemed to recall her saying something about exposing her chest. What the fuck? Anger and shock flooded through me, stopping me in my tracks. "You what?" *She has to mean something else.*

She ran into me, not expecting me to suddenly stop. Backing up a step, she shook her head. "He wouldn't let us through until

Anna and I showed him our chests. I kept my bra on, though... Anna didn't."

I was actually seeing red as venom ripped through my veins. Apparently, Paul wasn't the only person here with a death wish. How dare someone ask her to do that. My entire body felt tight with pent-up rage. "What did he look like?" I bit out. I was already scanning the hallway, looking for the asshole. One word of a description was all I needed, and I'd be off to find the dick.

Kiera's tender fingers on my face distracted me. "Hey, it's okay. It was mortifying and humiliating, but he didn't hurt me or anything. He didn't even touch me."

Her words were calming...and confusing. It was all just so... unlike her. I exhaled a slow, steady breath, trying to quiet the anger. "Why would you do that? You could have called me...I would've let you in."

She sighed, and there was something in the sound that sparked a realization. Rubbing my cheek, she said, "I wanted to surprise you."

Maybe. But that wasn't all it was. "You thought I was sleeping with Lana. Did you want to surprise me...or catch me?"

Kiera bit her lip. She shook her head and said, "I don't know," but I saw the true answer in her eyes. *Yes.* That was exactly why she didn't call me. She thought she'd catch me in the act, confirming her suspicions.

The fury was suddenly back full force and, dropping her hand, I turned around and stormed outside. It didn't matter what I did or didn't do, because she was never going to fucking trust me. How could we possibly stay together if she didn't trust me?

The buzz of bodies around the buses was aggravating my anger. I wanted to be alone. I wanted to stew and process and try to figure out how we got past this...obstacle. But the more I thought about it, the less angry I became. Didn't I have doubts? Wasn't I constantly afraid of losing her? Could I really blame her for wondering, especially knowing that she'd seen some odd, unexplained familiarity between Lana and me? And in all fairness, I *had* been hiding Lana from her. I was *still* hiding things from her. Was this all my fucking fault? Yes. It was.

I felt a hand on my shoulder, shaking me from my dark thoughts. I looked up to see Evan watching me with concern on his face. "What's wrong?" he asked, handing me my guitar case. He flicked a glance back at the door, probably searching for Kiera. I had no idea if she had followed me or not.

I swallowed the knot in my throat as I wondered what to tell him. All I ended up saying was, "Relationships are...hard."

He sighed, then nodded. Lifting an eyebrow, he told me, "Our life is weird. And that makes it even harder. Whatever is going on, just try and remember that. It's not the two of you...it's the situation. It would test anyone's faith..." He frowned after he said it, and I suddenly wondered if he and Jenny occasionally struggled with their own doubts and fears. Oddly, I found it reassuring to know I wasn't alone. And he was right. It *was* a fucked-up life we led, but that didn't mean it had to fuck *us* up, not if I didn't let it. I couldn't blame Kiera for doubting me. She wasn't here, she didn't see. All I could do was relentlessly reassure her. Every time I talked to her, if necessary.

Smiling at Evan, I nodded. "Thanks, man."

I turned to see Kiera hesitantly approaching me. Warm smile on my face, I reached out for her hand, so she would know I wasn't angry. Evan clapped my shoulder, then left to get on the bus. Kiera seemed disheartened when she realized we weren't staying here. "Are you leaving?" she asked.

I told her that we were, and that our next stop was Reno. Matt had mentioned it earlier, and Griffin had been ecstatic. He couldn't wait to visit little Las Vegas, as he called it. Not wanting to part ways with Kiera yet, not when things still felt so...raw, I said, "You could come with me? Catch a flight home from there?"

Slinging my guitar over my shoulder, I wrapped my arms around her. She slipped hers around me, a soft smile on her face.

Then she frowned and started objecting, mainly about not wanting to lose her round-trip plane ticket. I knew she didn't have my resources, and I knew she didn't want my money, but really...in the grand scheme of things, what was more important? Time or money? It was a simple answer for me. I would happily buy her a new ticket to be with her longer. Hell, I would happily buy her ten more tickets if it meant I got to spend the night with her. Money was nothing. She was everything. *You're just going to have to let me do this for you.*

It took a little convincing, but she finally conceded when I put it as bluntly as I could. "I want some more time with you."

She let out a peaceful sigh. "All right, but only if Anna goes too. I don't want to leave her alone here."

I had to smirk at that. "I'm sure she's attached to Griffin as we speak." Again, no doubt in my mind. A fact that was confirmed when we stepped onto the bus and were greeted with the familiar sound of people screwing. I had to grin and shake my head at my eager, horny bassist. This should satisfy him for a while. Hopefully.

Kiera had an adorable, uncomfortable expression on her face when she realized what she was hearing. She was so cute. I started leading her to the table where I'd tossed her bag earlier, and as I did, my gaze washed over Paul sitting at the back of the lounging area. I narrowed my eyes at him and had to forcibly resist the urge to walk over there and beat the smirk off his face. *Later*.

Brushing aside that piece of shit annoyance, I set down my guitar and told Kiera, "I could go get my Discman, if you don't want to listen to them?"

She looked horrified by my suggestion, and she grabbed my arm so hard, her nails bit into my skin. "No!"

I started laughing as I sat beside her on the bench seat. She must not realize they were in the back. Probably because I hadn't shown her the entire bus. "It's okay," I told her. "They're probably in the back bedroom."

She frowned at me, looking a little disappointed. "There's a back bedroom?" Clearly, she was wondering why we hadn't stripped down back there. Considering what had happened, I kind of wished we had.

I made a pained face so she would understand I'd been doing her a favor. "Yeah...Griffin's kind of taken it over, though, so I figured you wouldn't want to...hang out in there." It also wasn't exclusively Griffin's love nest. I was sure she *really* wouldn't want to know that. She looked disturbed enough. And again, that knowledge might make her doubt me. Even more than she already did.

"Yeah, no thanks," she murmured.

The driver did his headcount—asking with annoyance on his face who was gettin' busy in the back—and then we were off. I kept my head down as the bus started moving and tried really hard not to listen to Anna and Griffin, but damn...those two were not quiet. The sounds coming from their room reminded me of listening to their first night together. That hadn't been a good night for me—*at all*—but the look on Griffin's face the next morning...God. Now that I wasn't upset over the memory, I could be entertained by it. Anna had nearly destroyed him. In a good way.

I was roused from my thoughts by Kiera asking me a serious question. "Are you mad at me?"

The smile on my face fell as I looked over at her. Shaking my head, I pushed a lock of hair behind her ear. "No, I'm not." I sighed as I studied her, feeling weary again. "I get it, Kiera. I get why you'd have doubts, I get why you'd question..." My gaze fell to our laced fingers. "I wish..." *I wish things were different. I wish our story was different. I wish we'd met while you were single, fell in love cleanly, and never hurt each other. I wish we trusted each other. But there's no point in wishing. We are what we are.*

Looking back up at her, I said, "It's okay, I get it, and I'm not mad." *I have no right to be. Because this is all my fault.*

She let out a slow exhale as she nodded. I wrapped my arm around her, holding her tight. It was all I could do.

Eventually Anna and Griffin finished for the night and emerged from the back. I rolled my eyes as most of the guys on the bus cheered and whistled in approval. *Don't encourage him, please.* I watched Kiera as she watched her sister, wondering what she was thinking. Was she embarrassed for her? Or was she wishing she could be like her? She shouldn't wish that...she was perfect just the way she was.

Anna and Griffin stopped at our table, plopping down after Griffin tossed aside Kiera's bag. Griffin looked...stoned. His satisfied grin took in Kiera and me, then he tilted his head toward the back. "Bedroom's free, if you want it?"

I knew Kiera wouldn't want that. Even *I* didn't want that. Not *there*. Kiera was shaking her head as I answered him. "We're good, thanks." Griffin smirked at me, like he thought I was stupid for passing up sex.

People were starting to head to their cubbies now that the entertainment was over with. I knew Kiera was getting sleepy, she'd been resting with her eyes closed on my shoulder. Looking over at her, I asked, "You want to get some sleep? You look tired."

Griffin laughed to himself, and I knew he'd somehow made my question dirty in his head. Then he made a comment about Anna's chest, and lowered his mouth to her nipple. Kiera instantly told me, "Yes...please." *Good call.*

We said our goodbyes to the insatiable pair, then headed to my "bedroom." Some of the guys we passed along the way thought the same thing as Griffin, that Kiera and I were off to have sex. They whistled and even clapped me on the shoulder. I ignored them. They could think whatever they wanted. I did, however, impale Paul with my eyes before we disappeared behind the curtain. *I'm really looking forward to kicking your ass.*

A few guys were already asleep when we got to the cubbies. I helped Kiera find a place for her shoes, then took mine off as well. We climbed into bed. After closing the privacy curtain, I emptied my pockets, shoving my wallet and phone next to my Discman on the niche built into the wall, then I pulled my thin blanket over us. We were on our sides, facing each other, but there still wasn't a whole lot of room. I knew sex was possible in the cubbies, I'd heard it happen before, but I also knew it would be a little tricky...and not what Kiera wanted. She wasn't one for an audience, and we were *not* alone.

She was so close to me though, our faces touching as we shared a pillow, and she felt so good against my body, that I couldn't resist giving her a soft kiss. When I pulled back, she leaned forward, searching for me, wanting more. I gave it to her, reveling in our connection. The soft, sweet way she was moving her mouth against mine filled me with longing. She felt like home. "I've missed this," I told her. "I've missed you."

She pulled back to study me. "I've missed you too...so much."

I could feel a good kind of tension building between us as we stared at each other. It made my heart race, made my blood surge in all the right places. But of course, the guys around me had to ruin the moment. "Less talking...more screwing."

They all laughed. I thumped the bunk above me. "Shut it, Mark." Asshole.

Kiera buried her head in my chest, embarrassed. A soft laugh escaped me as I rubbed her back. I already knew sex was off the table, but maybe I could still give her something to tide her over. It seemed a shame for her to come all this way and not be...satisfied. Putting my lips next to her ear, I whispered, "I could finish what I started earlier...if you want to—"

Not wanting to embarrass her, I didn't say it, just ran my hand over her hip, around to her ass. I wanted to pull her hips into mine, let her feel how much I wanted her. Honestly, I wanted to shift her onto her back and taste every sweet inch of her...but I knew she wouldn't be okay with that. I studied her face, waiting to see if she'd be fine with just the little bit I was offering.

She genuinely looked torn, but eventually she bit her lip and shook her head. I wasn't too surprised. Smiling at her, I brought my hand up to run the back of my fingers over her cheek. "Another time, then?"

She nodded, then pulled on my head, leading my mouth back to hers. It was...heaven.

Our languid kisses eventually slowed, then stopped. Kiera let out a long, content sigh, and I could feel her slipping, relaxing into sleep. Not tired yet, I watched her for a long time. Having her by my side again was incredible. I wished it could last longer than one night. Our earlier conversation about her plane ticket flashed through my mind, and I cautiously reached across her to grab my phone and my wallet. She'd agreed to let me buy her a ticket from Reno back to Boise, so she could still use her round-trip ticket, but that just seemed stupid. I'd rather she take a direct flight back home.

Careful to not wake her, I slipped out of bed so I could make arrangements. Surprisingly, Matt was still up when I got to the front of the bus. He was staring out the window, a peaceful smile on his face. He looked over at me when I sat down across from him. "Hey. How come you're still up?" I asked.

His grin widened. "I couldn't sleep. I just...I can't believe it. We got signed, man. It's actually happening."

My smile matched his. "Yeah, I know...it's crazy."

He tilted his head at me. "You knew we were being scouted, didn't you?" Biting my lip, I nodded. Hopefully he wasn't mad about that. He didn't appear to be. He let out a small laugh and shook his head. "And how long were you sitting on *that*?"

I cocked my head as I thought. "January?" *Early January.*

Matt laughed more, his face incredulous. "Damn, man. Why didn't you say anything?"

With a sigh, I looked out the window. "I saw what it was doing to the other bands. I didn't want you guys to...freeze up or anything." *Or ever find out about it if she said no.*

Matt was silent for a moment. I returned my gaze to him, and he softly smiled at me. "Thanks," he said. "I know that probably wasn't easy for you."

No. No, it wasn't. I didn't tell him that though, I just shrugged. Matt grinned. "We get to pick our own songs." His smile fell as he realized what that meant. "Shit...we're gonna have to go through *all* of them to figure out which ones to use. And then we need to make sure we know them forward and backward. From the contract, it's clear they want us to start right away, right after the tour. We don't have a lot of time..."

I nodded. "Yeah...I know." It was going to be a lot of work... and I already knew Matt was going to be a bit overbearing. I also knew the album was going to be amazing, mainly because of him.

I could tell Matt's mind was spinning, already stressing. Not wanting him to worry about it yet, I changed the subject. "Hey, can you help me with something?" He nodded and I showed him my phone. "I need to buy a plane ticket. I was going to call again, but I was wondering...can I just buy it on this?"

Matt started snickering at me. "Jesus, Kellan...you need to start learning this shit."

I smiled at his amusement. "Why? When I have you."

He held out his hand. "Give me your phone." He showed me where to go, then helped me through the checkout process; I had to use his email, since I didn't have one. I was grinning when we finished. Matt rolled his eyes. "It's like you're a hundred and five."

I frowned at his comment, then an idea struck me. "Can I order flowers on this too?" I had the number to a local shop, thanks to Jenny, but being able to see the arrangement I wanted would be nice.

Matt gave me a blank stare. "Dude...it's the Internet. You can do *anything* on it."

I gave the phone back to him. "Show me."

He rolled his eyes, but he helped me buy some flowers for Kiera, for our anniversary in a couple weeks. After that, he said, "I'm going to bed. You're on your own, techless."

I was laughing as he walked away, but happy. I stared at my phone a moment, then, reluctant but curious, I checked my calls and messages. As predicted, the call and text I'd ignored in front of Kiera had been from Gavin. My fingers tightened around the phone. When was he going to leave me alone? Why were months of silence not enough of a hint for him? I'd never even talked to him, and he was already fucking up my life. It needed to stop. Now.

Feeling rash, I started a message to Hailey. '*Tell Gavin that I want him to leave me the fuck alone.*'

I almost hit the send button. My finger was so close I couldn't even see the space beneath it. Changing my mind, I deleted it. Having Hailey relay messages to and from Gavin would be the same as having a direct conversation with him. And I didn't want a conversation with him. I wanted *nothing* to do with him. Tossing my phone on the table, I laid my head back on the seat. Was this nightmare ever going to end?

Snatching up my phone, I headed back to bed. I couldn't solve that problem, but at least I could fall asleep with the love of my life.

I woke up the next morning to Kiera softly kissing my chest. Smiling, I tightened my arms around her. Why couldn't every morning be like this? "Mornin'" I said, perfectly at peace.

Kiera lifted her head to look up at me. "Am I dreaming, or am I really waking up with you?"

I moved so I could see her better. "You dream about waking up with me?" That was oddly satisfying to hear.

She nodded, then she pulled back and studied my body. "You're usually naked in my dreams, though, so I must be awake."

Her comment made me laugh. Pulling her back to my chest, I said, "You're usually naked in my dreams too." I loved that we had that in common.

I started kissing her neck, but the noises coming from the guys around us quickly killed the mood. Why did this have to be a traveling day? I'd give anything to wake up with her in a hotel room. I paused to frown. "Sorry, smelly bus of boys...not exactly romantic."

With a sigh full of longing, she cupped my cheek and stroked my face with her thumb. "It's better than nothing."

I grabbed her hand, then adjusted us so we were facing each other. Kiera stared at me a moment, then said, "Hey, you mentioned that you wanted to tell me something last night... What was it?"

My eyes instantly fell from her face. Shit. Why did I have to say that? What do I tell her now? "I..." I had nothing. No words to give her that would come close to what I'd been contemplating telling her last night. My gaze slid to my phone, resting on the shelf behind Kiera. "I..."

She wanted to know about Gavin, and I knew I should clear the air between us and tell her, but fuck, just the thought was making a sickening well of acid rise up my throat. *I don't want to think about him, think about what Kiera would want us to be.* That was not my future. *He* was not my future. He was nothing. I couldn't tell her about him...but I had to tell her *something*. I didn't want to lie, not again, so I needed to tell her something true. And that was when it struck me—I actually did have something to tell her.

I almost sighed with relief. *Thank God, I have something true to tell her.* Tossing on a smile, I shrugged. "I didn't tell you the bad part about getting signed."

She looked surprised, then concerned. "What?" she asked, a strange sadness on her face.

I instantly hated myself. I shouldn't have said anything last night. I should just tell her the truth right now. But instead of owning up to my secrets, I committed to the one fact I was willing to share with her. "As soon as the tour ends in May, they want us in L.A., to record the album. In the meantime, the guys and I will be spending every free moment we have going through our songs, picking out the best ones...perfecting them. We have to be ready when we get there..."

She let out a forlorn sound. "You're basically telling me that you won't have any time to spend with me...for a while...aren't you?"

The truth of that hit me hard. Jesus. When would I see her again? I hated this already. I had to swallow back the sudden knot of sadness in my throat before I could speak. "I'm sorry...We need to do this, so I won't be able to visit, like I'd hoped. I'm sorry." *For more than you know.*

Eyes moister than before, Kiera said, "It's okay...I understand." She looked down for a moment while I wished that things were different. If only she could stay with me. Kiera's eyes suddenly flashed to mine. "Could you make it back in June?"

Knowing what she was really asking, I nodded and cupped her cheek. "I'm not missing your graduation...no matter what. I don't care if I have to walk out on a recording session...I'm not missing it, Kiera."

She smiled, sighed, and relaxed. But the sadness was still there, and I understood why; I felt it too. Being apart was so hard. Holding her close, I rubbed her back. As we laid there, I remembered the previous night's conversation that had sparked her earlier question...and I recalled that she had said she wanted to tell me something too. Not sure if I wanted to hear her answer, I whispered, "And there was something you wanted to tell me?" *Please don't let this hurt.*

She stiffened in my arms...that was not a good sign. My heart started beating harder. Maybe I shouldn't have asked. Ignorance was bliss, right? Maybe. But the ignorance was already gone and knowing there was a looming unknown between us was hell. After a long, anxious moment of deliberation, she finally sat up on her elbow and shook her head. "I love you, Kellan, and you don't have anything to worry about when it comes to me, but I don't think I can tell you just yet."

I was floored. I thought for sure she'd tell me, or maybe...at the very least, she would tell me something else that was true, like I had. But this...it had never once occurred to me that she might flat-out *refuse* to tell me. It was infuriating, frustrating beyond all comprehension. What the hell was she hiding from me?

I sat up on my elbow, matching her stance. "What? Why not?" I knew I was being a hypocrite, but goddamn it, knowing she was holding something back, something she wouldn't tell me...it fucking hurt.

Remorse was in her features, but she still shook her head. "You're just going to have to believe in me."

My mouth dropped open, ready to protest, but her words... they were too similar to what I'd told her last night, after getting that text from Gavin. *Please believe in me. Let this go...* That was what I'd asked of her, what I'd begged from her, and now she was asking the same from me. I flicked a quick glance at my phone again, and my mouth closed as everything was suddenly achingly, painfully clear. *She knows I avoided her question. She knows that phone call, that text, had nothing to do with what I just told her. She's refusing to open up to me because I'm not opening up to her. I can't ask her to tell me her secret, not without also telling her what's really going on with me. And I can't. So, I'm stuck. Trapped in this circular hell. I have to let this go...because I have to keep my secret. I won't survive anything else.*

I stared at Kiera, disheartened, drowning in guilt, regret, and remorse. Her eyes watered as she stared back at me. I could feel mine filling as I started spiraling. *I'm so, so sorry.* I swallowed the emotion choking me so I could answer her, and I knew the second I did, everything between us would change.

"Okay," I whispered. And I'd never hated myself more.

Chapter 27
MISSING YOU

The rest of Kiera's time with me was laced with sadness, but this time, I was certain the feeling wasn't because we were about to be separated again. We were keeping things from each other. Secrets. Lies. It made me sick to my stomach, and I hated feeling that way around her. I also hated the fact that after she left, for a split-second, all I felt...was relief.

The entire way back from the airport, all I could think was —*What am I doing*? Fucking up. That was what I was doing. I just didn't know how to stop. I didn't know how to get the outcome I wanted...the very best solution. All I saw in front of me was varying degrees of...shit.

"Damn, man...that was awesome."

I looked over at Griffin in the car. He still had that satisfied smile on his face. Seeing it was starting to piss me off. How did someone like *him* get to have the exact relationship he wanted? But I knew the answer to that. He didn't want anything from Anna. Just sex. So of course things with her were easy...easy and meaningless. I'd had that and it wasn't enough. I wanted more and sometimes more meant pain.

I gave him a tight smile. "Yeah...awesome."

He frowned at me. "Pissed you didn't get any?"

My smile shifted to a frown. "Not everything is about sex, Griffin."

He snorted, then shook his head. "*Right.* You still convinced that monogamy thing is worth it?"

I turned my head to look out the window. "Yes," I told him. She *was* worth it. Worth every pain, every agony, every misery. Because my life without her...*that* had been torture.

Griffin made a disbelieving sound. "You're so weird," he muttered.

I ignored him as the venue came into view. The driver pulled around back, dropping us off, and an undeniable surge of vengeance came over me. I had a score to settle. Griffin looked confused as he studied my face. "Dude, I was kidding about you being weird. Well, not really, you *are* weird, but you don't have to get all pissed about it. I don't give a fuck if your dick is tied to one chick."

Not looking at him, I shook my head. "I'm not mad at *you*."

"Who are you mad at?" he asked.

Not answering him, I started storming off to find the person who owed me a bit of blood. I felt Griffin following me, but I didn't care...as long as he didn't try to stop me. Guys loitering around the bus did a double take when they saw my face. Did I look that pissed? I felt that pissed.

Evan and Matt spotted me, and I heard Evan say, "Kell?" I ignored him, scanning for my target.

I found Paul standing alone beside Justin's bus. Perfect. He wasn't looking at me, didn't sense me coming. Because I wasn't a complete dick, I gave him a chance to defend himself. "Paul!"

His eyes swung my way when I was three long strides away from him. He smirked...and then he saw my expression. His painted eyes widened, and his hands raised. He looked like he was about to speak, but I wasn't here for words. I could feel the gathering crowd, the sizzling tension in the air...none of it mattered. Paul was about to die. One step between us had me pulling my arm back. I heard Evan shouting my name, but it was too late. I was committed. I swung, and my aim was true. Paul took the full force of my fury in the jaw. The hit knocked him to the ground. I lunged to pick him up, so I could hit him again, but hands were on me now, holding me back.

"Come on!" I yelled at him, eager to keep going.

Paul's eyes were wide as he looked up at me. His lip was split, blood dribbling down his chin. It wasn't enough for me. He'd gone too far. He spat out blood, his eyes darkening. "What the fuck?" he snipped.

I struggled against the numerous people holding me, and then Evan was in my face, pushing me back. "Calm down," he said, his dark eyes searching mine.

"You don't know what he did," I seethed.

Paul got to his feet, and the rage made me lunge for him again. I couldn't move far enough to get him. A part of me wanted to start in on the people holding me, but I knew that was just the anger wanting to be released. They didn't deserve my wrath. Paul did.

Evan studied me, then turned to Paul. "You should get out of here," he told him.

Paul glared at him, then scanned the crowd. I took a moment to look around as well. Matt and Griffin were holding me back, along with about three other people. Justin was watching with a furrowed brow, and so were several other guys that I truly admired. Seeing them watching me come unglued muted the heat in my stomach, but then I noticed that they weren't watching me...they were watching Paul.

Paul's eyes darted between them all. Even I could feel the weight of their judgement. "What?" he snapped. "The fucker just walked up and hit me! I didn't do anything!"

Justin was the one who took a step forward. "He wouldn't just hit you for no reason. What did you do?"

I started relaxing as Paul started floundering. "Are you serious? He fucking punched me. You saw that right?"

Justin crossed his arms over his chest. "Yeah. We all saw that. Now what the fuck did you do to him?"

Paul spat again; the bloody slime landed dangerously close to my boot. I jerked forward and was instantly restrained. Leaning toward Paul, I told him, "You talk to me again, you talk to my girlfriend again, and it will be the last fucking thing you do. Got it?"

He rolled his eyes, but his face was completely white. "Whatever, I don't need this shit." He started walking away, and it was really hard to let him go. I glared at him the entire time he left my sight. Nobody followed him, not even his own bandmates. Once he was gone, the arms holding me tight relaxed.

The tension started dissipating, and band members started going about their own business again. Eventually, I was alone with just my band members. And Justin. Evan was eying me with concern, Matt was studying me, like he was making sure I wasn't hurt in any way. Justin was smiling, like he was glad someone had finally hit Paul. And Griffin...was laughing.

"Damn, man...you should have taken me up on the bedroom, dude. You wouldn't be all tense and shit if you'd had a few good orgasms last night. Like me." He smirked as he raised his chin.

I stared at him for a solid five seconds...and then I started laughing. "Fuck you," I told him.

Grinning, he crouched down with his hands curled into fists. He started mock fighting with me, lightly punching my shoulder as he bobbed and weaved. "Come on, Kell, let's go. I think I can take you now."

Matt smacked his shoulder. "Dude, he would *kill* you."

Griffin looked offended. "Why do you always doubt my fighting skills? I am the shit."

Matt shook his head. "Because you can't actually learn to fight from a video game."

He pursed his lips. "Dude...I learned from kung fu movies, not video games. I'm not a complete dumbass."

Matt slung his arm over his shoulders and started pulling him away. "That is *so* debatable, cuz."

Justin and Evan eyed me after they left. Then Justin raised an eyebrow. "You gonna go after Paul again, or are you done?"

I sighed, letting the anger release from me as I did. "I'm done...sorry about that."

He grinned. "Don't be. He's pissed off everyone. You just became the tour's hero." With a laugh, he walked away...leaving me alone with Evan.

"What?" I asked, after feeling his eyes on me for several long, silent seconds.

"Feel better?" he asked, giving me a crooked grin.

A small smile touched my lips. "A little. I would've liked to hit him more than once though."

Evan nodded. "Yeah, I know." Then he clapped my shoulder. "Come on, let's go find some alcohol, then you can tell me what that fucker did."

Smiling at Evan, I nodded...and let the residual anger completely fade. Once would have to be enough. I had bigger things to worry about than Paul.

Like preparing for the album.

Now that we were officially signed, that became the band's primary focus. And as the days crept closer to my anniversary, I grew more and more annoyed. I kept trying to make plans to visit Kiera, and Matt kept blowing them up in my face. Well, Matt and the label kept blowing them up. The record kept revising the contract, and we'd all have to meet up with Lana to sign the new stuff. Then they wanted to sign off on *all* the songs before we went to L.A. to record the album. That took up the bulk of our free time. Deciding which songs, then having Lana record us performing them, then waiting for the label to approve or deny what they heard. It was...exhausting. And it was made all the more draining by Gavin, who was still refusing to respect my silence.

"Why don't you just give him a chance, Kellan? You're being

so stubborn. Just hear him out for five seconds. Five tiny, little seconds."

With a sigh, I dropped my head back, hitting the side of the bus behind me. "Hailey...I swear to God we've had this conversation three thousand times already."

"I know," she said, repeating my sigh. "But you're not seeing what I'm seeing. You're crushing him. He doesn't even look the same..."

My eyes hardened as I lifted my head. "If he was so worried about keeping in touch with me, maybe he shouldn't have left in the first place."

"Kellan...he had to..."

"I have to go," I instantly bit out. *I need this conversation to end.*

"Wait...I'm sorry. Don't hang up because you're mad at me." She paused to let out a long exhale. "Tell me about the album. How is it going picking songs?"

My face finally relaxed into a smile. *This* I could talk about. "It's taking a million fucking years," I told her, laughing. We talked for a while after that, avoiding all the sensitive subjects, and by the end of our conversation, I felt better. Worn, but better.

I tried to push aside the emotional fatigue. Today was an important day, and I didn't want to sound upset or worried or *anything* when I talked to Kiera later. It was our anniversary. One year together, officially, cleanly.

Thoughts of that night were in my head as my day trudged forward. Spotting Kiera in the crowd, thinking she was a dream, our painful conversation in the hallway...finally kissing her again. Feeling undone and whole, all at the same time. Our reunion had been much like our relationship—intoxicating and torturous. But after that night...when we'd honestly tried to be a couple, that was when my life had truly begun. God, I missed her.

It was painful to wait to call her. I'd wanted to talk to her the moment I'd woken up, and then I'd wanted to call her every hour after that. But I held off, wanting to talk to her after she got her flowers at Pete's. I wanted to hear the surprise in her voice, the happiness, the joy...the longing. I watched the clock all night, waiting for just the right time. I gave her forty-five minutes into her shift, then I called her. My smile fell when the phone rang and rang and then went to voicemail. *It is a Saturday night...maybe the bar is already slammed. Damn it. I should have called her earlier.*

"Hey, Matt's ready. He wants us to meet him in his room to go over some songs. He really wants to do Kiera's song."

Evan smiled at me, like he was happy about that. I frowned. I wasn't sure if I wanted the entire world listening to me recounting the worst night of my life. But, on the other hand, Kiera loved that song...maybe she'd like it to be on the album. "Maybe...I don't know. That one's kind of...personal."

He nodded, then tilted his head. "Are you feeling all right?"

I forced a smile to my face. "Yeah, of course. Why?"

His expression twisted into confusion as he shook his head. "I don't know, you just seem...I don't know. Off, I guess."

There was a sinking feeling in my stomach as I stared at him. I *was* off. Very, very off. Not that I could tell him that. "I'm..." My phone chirped with a message, and I automatically lifted it to look. It wasn't Kiera...it was fucking Gavin. Of course. My jaw tightened as I lowered the phone. "I'm fine."

Even I could hear the annoyance in my voice, the weariness. Evan certainly heard it. He frowned at me. "Maybe you should pass on this. Go back upstairs, lie down or something. I'll tell Matt you're sick."

I genuinely contemplated that, but I shook my head. "I'm missing my anniversary for this. I'm not going to spend tonight in bed alone when I should be spending it with Kiera." Anger ripped up my spine at the thought of wasting this evening. If I was going to sacrifice a small part of our relationship, then it had better be worth it. And besides, we had to finalize the next song tonight so we could record it with Lana tomorrow. I really didn't have a choice.

Understanding flashed through Evan's features. "Shit... right...your anniversary. I'm sorry, man. I forgot. That sucks...no wonder you look like crap."

His summation of my appearance made me frown. "Thanks?"

He laughed, then smacked the counter to get the attention of the bartender; we were hanging out at the hotel bar, killing time until Matt and Griffin were ready. It killed me that we didn't have a show tonight, but I *still* couldn't be with Kiera. Having responsibilities really fucking sucked.

Once the bartender looked our way, Evan told him, "One more round for my friend here. It's his anniversary."

The bartender nodded and turned to the minifridge to get me another bottled beer. My frown deepened. "I can't believe I'm celebrating my anniversary...with you."

Evan's face twisted into a playful scowl. "I thought I was the best?" He poked my shoulder, then he kept doing it, until finally, I smiled and batted his hand away.

"You *are* the best," I told him with a laugh. "But I can't have sex with *you*."

He laughed. "No, you can't...I'm taken."

I nearly spat out the swig of beer I'd been in the process of swallowing. As I coughed and laughed, Evan patted my back. Shaking my head at him, I tried calling Kiera again. Again, it rang and rang, then went to voicemail. *Damn it.*

I tried again before leaving the bar. Then again when we got to Matt's room. Then again while Matt was trying to convince Griffin that he would be murdered if he left the hotel to go roam the streets looking for pot. Every time I called Kiera it rang and then went to voicemail. Was the bar really that busy? Maybe she'd put her phone in the back room. She did that sometimes when she was working. I just thought tonight she might make an exception. Annoyed, I called the bar directly.

"Pete's Bar, this is Jenny."

"Hey, Jenny...it's Kellan." Evan heard me say her name and

his hand instantly shot out for the phone. I shook my head at him. He could talk to her later. He scowled at me.

"Hey, Kellan...how's it going?"

I contained a sigh. *It kind of sucks, actually.* Making myself smile, I told her, "It's good. Is Kiera there? Can I talk to her?"

Jenny sighed. "No, sorry, she's not here. She went home sick, and I don't blame her...that girl looked awful. I'm going to pop over tomorrow and make sure she's okay."

Kiera was sick, and I was stuck. Was that the universe trying to tell me something, or just crappy happenstance? "Oh...okay, thanks." If she was home but she wasn't answering her phone, she was probably sleeping. Goddamn it. Now I wanted to be there more than ever. She shouldn't have to be sick alone.

"Yep, no problem." Jenny's voice was bright and trouble-free, and for a moment, I envied her. "Hey, we got your flowers for her. They are *gorgeous*, Kellan. I put them in the back room, but I'll take them to her tomorrow. She's gonna love them."

A slight smile lifted my lips. "Thanks. Hey, you wanna talk to Evan...because he won't stop staring at me."

She laughed. "Yes, please."

I handed my phone over to Evan, and his scowl finally shifted into a smile. "Hey, Jujube," he said. "How's my sexy girl doing?" I instantly tuned him out.

Kiera was sick, and because I'd waited so long to talk to her, she probably thought I'd forgotten our anniversary. Fuck. Had she gone to bed angry? Had she gone to bed...alone?

No. Don't even contemplate that. But a part of me had to consider it...because I already knew she was keeping something from me. It killed me that I couldn't question her. It killed me that I doubted her. It killed me that I couldn't talk to her. It *all* killed me.

It took me forever to fall asleep that night, and when I did, it wasn't restful. I was absolutely miserable. Every day it felt like a little more of me was being scooped out. Gutted. I needed something to change, but I didn't know what, I didn't know how. I felt more broken than I ever had before, and that made me feel guilty. This was supposed to be the greatest experience of my life. But even this I was ruining.

The nightmare I had a few nights after my missed anniversary shouldn't have surprised me. But of course, it did. I was back on the bus, practically curled into a ball the cubby felt so small.

"Do you think any of this is going to amount to anything?" I looked over to see my father sitting on the bunk across from me, his face twisted in derision. "Getting signed, recording an album...there's only one thing that's going to come from all this. And you know it."

His finger pointed down the bus. I didn't want to look, and yet, I couldn't stop myself either. The privacy curtain was open, and I could clearly see into the lounging area. My stomach instantly clenched in revulsion as I spotted Kiera, naked, her face a picture of ecstasy as some guy plowed into her, a guy who—once again—bared a striking resemblance to Denny.

No. No, no, no...

I jerked awake, hitting my head on the bunk above me as I unintentionally sat up. Goddamn it. Falling back to my pillow, I let the pain in my throbbing skull envelope me. Feeling the ache was slowly washing away my dream, and I desperately needed that image gone from my brain. *Please, don't let that be her secret. Jesus...please.*

Hopping out of bed, I strode to the front of the bus. I needed proof that Kiera wasn't there, that none of that had actually happened. And thankfully, except for the driver behind the wheel, the front of the bus was empty. *Thank God.* She wasn't here...but...that didn't mean what I'd dreamt about wasn't happening back home. Fuck.

Needing a physical release, since my headache wasn't evaporating the dream quickly enough, I dropped to the ground and started doing pushups in the slim aisle. I didn't stop until I literally couldn't do anymore. Then I flipped over and started doing crunches. I kept going until I felt like I was going to throw up, and then I did a couple dozen more, just to drive it home. Or punish myself. I wasn't sure.

I felt minutely better after that, or at least, too worn out to care. About anything. But then I received my first text of the day. It was from Gavin. The rage and pain flooded back in, and I almost broke down. It took all my energy to bring my mood back to an even keel. And it was all for nothing, because when my last text of the day was also from Gavin, the bitter feelings rampaged through me again, and I almost threw my fucking phone against the fucking wall. It was starting to feel like I would never be truly happy again. My mind was on an endless loop of worrying about Kiera, feeling guilty about what I was keeping from her, and desperately trying *not* to think about Gavin. Any relief I found was brief. Pale. I felt lost. I felt alone. I felt like I was going insane.

But all I could do was keep moving forward, keep trying to hold it all together, and pray I was strong enough to keep everything from falling apart.

"Kell, you coming out with us? It's St. Patrick's Day, dude."

I looked over to see Griffin wearing his favorite holiday shirt —*Suck Me, I'm Irish*. Of course he'd packed it. Shaking my head, I told him, "No, I'm gonna hang here on the bus. And it's not St. Patrick's Day anymore, Griffin. It's 3 in the morning, the day *after* St. Patrick's Day." We'd had a short jaunt to the next venue, and we'd just arrived. There was no point getting a hotel at this hour, so we were all just hanging in the buses until the show tonight.

Griffin swished his hand at me. "Matt found a rave. That shit's been going all night long, so the people partying inside won't know it's tomorrow yet. It's like we're going back in time."

He grinned like this was the greatest concept ever. I shook my head again. "I'm wiped. I'm gonna sleep…have fun."

He scoffed at me, like it was an impossibility that he wouldn't. Matt and Evan waved goodbye and followed him off of the bus. Several other band members did too. I shook my head as I watched them leave. How were they not as tired as me? Probably because they didn't have as much resting on their shoulders. Still...it was good to see them taking a minute to blow off some steam. We'd all been working really hard lately. Maybe too hard. God, I was exhausted.

With a sigh, I debated lying down in my cramped cubby. I just couldn't do it. I needed to stretch out, so I headed back to Griffin's bed instead. He wasn't going to need it for several hours anyway. I passed out almost the instant I laid down, but even still, my fucking internal alarm clock woke me up just a handful of hours later.

Being sprawled out, alone in a bed, really made me miss Kiera. Was it too early to call her? I'd been so tired, I'd laid down with all my clothes on, and my phone was still in my pocket, digging into my hip. Rolling over, I pulled it out and glanced at the time. It was sort of early for Kiera, but not outrageously early. She could be up.

A wave of loneliness crashed over me, and needing to hear her voice, I decided to risk waking her. The phone rang quite a few times, and a surge of disappointment went through me. But then it stopped ringing, and I heard her weary voice say, "Hello?"

Clearly, she'd been sleeping, and I felt a little bad for waking her up, but more than that, I felt...soothed. Her voice was heaven, a momentary reprieve from the agony—as long as I didn't let myself think too much. *Please let her love be only for me. Please don't let my nightmares be true.*

Pushing aside my fears, I gave her my new typical greeting. "Happy Anniversary."

Warmth in her voice, she murmured, "You don't have to keep telling me that every time you call, Kellan."

With a sigh, I shifted on the mattress. "I know, but I still feel really bad that I missed it, that I couldn't fly out to you. A year together is a big deal, and I really wanted to see you...but stuff kept coming up..."

I'd explained about our hectic schedule-within-a-schedule before, several times, but I had to imagine she was still hurt by the news. I was. Every time I had to tell her I couldn't leave the tour, I felt a piece of my heart shredding.

Her voice was quiet and accepting when she told me it was fine, that she understood, and she'd been sick anyway, and I'd sent flowers—like somehow that was enough. It wasn't. Especially since she hadn't even gotten them until the next day. I apologized for that, again, and she told me it was okay, again. It didn't feel okay. None of this felt okay.

Feeling the melancholy seeping into me, I told her, "I'm really sorry it's turned out this way. I'll make it up to you...someday...I promise." *I'll make everything up to you. Just don't leave me.*

She didn't say anything to that. She didn't say anything for a long time. I didn't either. I didn't know what to say. The space I felt growing between us was horrifying, and I felt my eyes begin to sting as the long, silent seconds ticked by. *How do I fix us?*

Finally, Kiera broke the quiet. "I found your letter last night, the one in the couch."

I sat up on the bed as surprise and trepidation rushed through me. I'd been dealing with so much lately, I'd almost forgotten about that letter. "Oh...and?" I cringed after I asked her that. I wasn't sure if I wanted to know her answer. Had I gone too far with that letter? Pushed an idea she wasn't ready for? And fuck...there was so much unspoken crap between us now...how could she possibly embrace the idea of marriage? How *could* we get married, with so many walls in the way? *How do I break the walls, without breaking myself?*

"You really see that future for us?" she asked.

There was a trace amount of awe in her voice; hearing it calmed my nerves. "Yeah, I do, Kiera...all the time. Do...do you?" My stomach tightened again as the doubt and fear beat against my brain. *What if she says no? Does that mean we're over? I don't want us to be over.*

But she said, "Yeah," and the relief I felt was instant. And brief. "Maybe," she quickly added. "Someday."

I had no fucking clue how to process that. I hung my head as pain stung every nerve ending. *Relax. It's not a no. Take it, accept it...and leave the rest behind.*

The silence between us grew again, deafening and relentless. I felt trapped, desolate...hopeless. *I don't want to lose her...but I am. I can feel it.* Just when I was about to beg her not to leave me, she whispered, "I miss you."

I had to choke back the sudden sob in my throat, and the words flew from me all at once. "I miss you too. I know we saw each other a couple of weeks ago, but it wasn't enough, not nearly enough...I really miss you." I could feel the tears building under the stress of the torments that ceaselessly pushed against me every single second of every single fucking day. I knew I was about to lose it, and I knew she wouldn't understand why. I swallowed, trying to control it, trying to shove the misery back down deep... trying to hide.

It was too late though; Kiera had heard it. "Kellan? You...okay?"

I wanted to sigh, I wanted to scream, but I was suddenly too tired to do either. "Yeah...just exhausted. I never realized how... taxing this would be. Always on the road, always away from home, always having to deal with..." *Him.* But I couldn't tell her that, so instead I said, "People." It wasn't a lie, but it also wasn't the truth. It was that unpleasant gray area, where I always seemed to find myself these days. I was so sick of it.

Wishing she was here, wishing I could be honest, I told her, "I know it's early for you and you probably want to go back to sleep, but could you stay on the line for a bit? I'm feeling..." *So fucking overwhelmed...* I paused to swallow the pain. "I just want to listen to you breathe for a while." *Let me pretend everything is fine. Please.*

"I don't have anywhere to be but right here with you, Kellan."

The compassion in her voice was almost too much to bear, but instead of dwelling on my grief, my loneliness, I let her words relax me, soothe me. Hadn't she said I didn't have to worry about her? Hadn't she taken my promise ring, sworn her own promise in return? Hadn't she assured me she would end things before she...replaced me? If she hadn't said goodbye...then we were still good. We had to be.

I inhaled a deep breath and slowly let it go as I laid back down. Right now, she was mine and she was with me. *That* was a truth I could hold onto. "Good. I love you, Kiera. It seems like forever since I've held you, since I've made love to you." When was the last time? Over the Christmas break...at her parents' house. Just a few months ago, but it felt like years.

Kiera seemed to agree. "It has been forever, Kellan." I adjusted how I was lying, and Kiera asked, "Where are you?"

Smiling, I stretched out all my limbs; it felt so good to do that. Another small reprieve. "On the bus, in the back bedroom. All the guys are gone, so I snagged Griffin's bed." With a laugh, I told her, "I just couldn't spend another moment in that tiny bunk."

"So...you're alone? Completely alone?" She asked that so quietly, I almost didn't hear her.

"Yeah...why?" I asked, uncertainty filling my stomach. What did she need to tell me that I needed to be alone for? And why? Was it going to hurt? Did I want to know this...?

Her voice was odd when she spoke, almost strained. "I want to...Will you...?"

She couldn't continue. It didn't seem like she wanted to tell *me* something...it sounded like she wanted me to talk to *her* about something. Shit. Was she going to press me again? Would I have the strength to ask her to let it go again? "What, Kiera?" I softly asked, unsure if I should.

She let out a frustrated sigh. "I feel like we're drifting, Kellan, and I just want to feel closer to you. I—"

Her words cut straight through me, and I interrupted her.

"I'm sorry, Kiera. I feel like that's my fault." *No, it* is *my fault. I'm hurting her. I'm shoving her away. I need to stop. I need to fix this.* "I just...I...I should..." *Fuck. Say it, you coward. Tell her your secret before it rips you apart.* "We should talk about..."

Come on...tell her. It's easy, just say: My biological father found me...he won't leave me alone...he's killing me...every day he's killing me.

I wanted to say it, but the words were stuck in my throat, a hard knot that I could barely speak past. "God, this is hard..." Why was this so fucking hard? Why wouldn't the fucking words come out? *How do I get through this? How do I* rewind *this?*

Kiera's voice sounded just as pained as mine when she suddenly spoke. "No, don't, Kellan. I don't want to talk right now. I just want you to make me feel good..."

I stopped breathing for a second. Was she giving me a pass? Again? And...was she saying she wanted to...? "Kiera, are you asking me to...do you want me to make love to you?"

"Yes," she whispered, and my body instantly responded. She wanted to close our distance with sex? Would that work? I often used sex as a distraction; I knew it was a tentative solution at best. But it was far preferable to opening up, especially since I couldn't seem to do that anyway.

Her next words made me stop caring about her reasons; they made my brain shut off completely. "Make me feel it, Kellan... make me feel like your wife..."

My eyes fluttered closed as the words seared my body, seared my soul. *My wife.* I'd never heard two better sounding words in all my life. "Oh God, Kiera...I want you so much..." *I miss you so much.*

"I don't know what to do, Kellan."

The ache in her voice had me groaning, straining. Unzipping my jeans, I told her exactly what I wanted her to do. Our problems could wait...we needed this.

Chapter 28

VISITORS

I had to admit...I felt better after the sex. It did help connect us again, and while there was still way too much crap between us, the gap didn't feel quite so large as before. A bridge had been built. Now I just had to make sure I didn't accidentally burn it to the ground. I needed to see her. But the band still had so much to do...

"How many more songs do we need, Matt?" I asked, once again feeling weary to the bone.

Matt tilted his head. "Six maybe?"

Groaning in annoyance, I slumped forward in my chair. "Can you just pick them? My head hurts..."

Matt sighed as he glanced at Evan. "No. It needs to be a group decision, Kell."

I slowly shook my head. "Why did I have to write so many fucking songs...?"

Evan smiled at me. "I think the better question is, why did you have to write so many *great* songs? If you could just stop being so talented, this wouldn't be so hard."

I pursed my lips at that. "I need a break. I'm going back to the bus."

Matt studied me for a second, then nodded. "Okay, but Lana

wants to record the song tomorrow night, so we have to pick one tomorrow morning."

Running a hand down my face, I nodded. "Yeah, sure..."

We were backstage, sitting by ourselves trying to get some work done. Well, the three of us were working. Griffin had a girl on his lap, and he was paying more attention to her than us...but at least he was there. The girl tracked me with her eyes when I stood up. Hopefully she didn't leave when I did; I didn't need Griffin's pissiness right now.

"See you guys later," I said with a lift of my hand.

Matt and Evan both said bye. Griffin said, "What's going on?"

I got stopped a few times to sign things as I left. That was fine. I owed the fans a lot more than a few seconds of my time, but that was all I could give them so it would have to do. The night was almost over, but Avoiding Redemption was still playing their set. Naturally, they played more songs than anyone else. I hoped the bus was quiet. It wasn't always, since a lot of guys went back there when they were finished playing. And not all of them went back there alone. I really wasn't in the mood to listen to people having sex right now. But whatever. I had headphones.

In the parking lot, I looked around for Paul. He'd been a ghost since I'd slugged him. He wouldn't even ride our bus anymore. I was extremely grateful he wasn't going to test me on my threat. His absence was another small relief.

Hopping on my bus, I headed straight to the cubbies to lie down. Maybe I'd call Kiera. I'd talked to her earlier, before our set, but talking to her again sounded wonderful. That thought was on my mind when I stepped up to my bed...and spotted a naked woman seductively half-curled up in my blanket. For a half-second I thought it was Kiera, until the foreignness of the girl's face shattered the illusion. What the fuck was a naked stranger doing in my bed?

"Hi," she sweetly said, looking completely at ease.

A weary sigh escaped me. *I really don't need this right now.* "Hey. I think you have the wrong bed." My voice was calm, polite, but also firm. *Please leave.*

She smiled, showing a dimple in her cheek. Her eyes slowly scanned my body. "No, I think I'm in *exactly* the right place."

I looked around the cubbies, to the ones that were full. The guys there were smiling, staring at my uninvited guest. Meeting eyes with Kurt, I raised an eyebrow. "You do this?"

Grinning wider, he shook his head. "Nope. She climbed in all on her own."

Sighing again, I looked back at the girl. "Can you get out please."

She pouted as she rubbed her legs together. "Why don't you get in?"

Sitting up as much as she could in the small space, she leaned over to grab my hand. I pulled my fingers away, so she started running her hand up my jeans instead. I grabbed her hand to stop her from fondling me, and she smiled at me like she'd won.

The look on her face was pissing me off. *I just want to lie down.* I hadn't been lying about my head hurting. Tossing her hand aside, I let my anger and frustration leech out. "Get the fuck out of my bed."

A couple of the guys around us snickered. I ignored them. The girl's eyes sparkled, like she was enjoying my anger. "Fuck me, and I will."

I closed my eyes. Un-fucking-believable. Clearly, whatever I did, the girl wasn't going to take no for an answer. I didn't have the energy or patience to deal with her right now. A sudden thought occurred to me, and opening my eyes, I smiled at her. "Okay...just give me one second."

She bit her lip, looking truly excited now. I met eyes with Kurt—he looked a little surprised that I'd said yes. I smirked at him, then walked to the front of the bus. Sitting on a seat, I pulled out my phone to call the one person who could successfully empty my bed for me.

"Hey, Griffin...I need a favor."

He sounded annoyed. "Kind of in the middle of something, Kell."

I smiled into the phone. "There's a naked girl in my bed. I need you to get rid of her for me."

"Be right there." He hung up before I could even say goodbye.

He stepped onto the bus quicker than I would have thought possible. He was winded, and I knew he'd run the entire way. I held up my knuckles, and we bumped fists as he walked by me. Grin on my face, I tilted my head to listen.

"Who are you? What the hell are you doing? I'm not here for you, asshole! Put your clothes back on!" The annoyed screech in the girl's voice was very satisfying.

I heard the sounds of scuffling, then heard Griffin say, "Ow! Stop hitting me!"

There were more sounds of Griffin being assaulted, then I heard someone approaching. I twisted to see the girl, fully dressed now, storming down the aisle. Her eyes narrowed at me, her face a picture of fury.

"Jerk," she muttered, strutting past me.

I was the jerk in this situation? Really? Wow. After she left, all I heard from the back of the bus was laughter. And Griffin complaining about crazy women. He appeared a moment later, thankfully also dressed. He smirked at me as he walked by. "You're welcome," he said.

I shook my head as he left the bus, momentarily grateful that his advances hadn't been successful, and he hadn't screwed her on my bed. I'd been fairly certain of the outcome, but...you never know. Sometimes Griffin's bluntness worked.

When I returned to the sleeping area, the guys resting there were still laughing. Kurt held out his fist. "Dude...that was the best thing...I've ever seen." He was laughing so hard his eyes were watering.

I bumped fists with him, then quickly made sure the girl

hadn't left anything…or stolen anything. Thankfully, everything was as it should be. Smiling up at Kurt, I said, "Griffin does have his uses."

After taking off my boots, I laid down on my bed and pulled out my phone. Holding it in my hand, I closed my eyes. Just to rest for a second before I called Kiera. When I opened my eyes, the bus was moving. Damn it. I must have fallen asleep. A stab of guilt washed through me. We were supposed to help with the tear down. There were enough of us that it could be done minus a few slackers, but I didn't like being one of the slackers—not without good cause. I supposed needing sleep was a good cause though. Odd. The rush of performing used to keep me up for hours. I was slipping.

My phone was still clenched in my hand, and I rolled my eyes. I'd wanted to talk to Kiera before passing out. I knew it was way too early to call her, so I decided to text her instead. I noticed several missed messages, all from Gavin. Maybe I should ask Matt how to block people—there had to be a way. But Matt would want to know why, and I was too tired to think of a good lie. I'd just…keep dealing with it. At this point it didn't really matter anyway; my brain would still *feel* the messages, even if my eyes couldn't see them.

Ignoring Gavin, I texted Kiera. '*I love you. And I cannot stop thinking about the other night. You were amazing.*' Just typing that made me grin. Making love to her again, even if it was over the phone, had been *incredible*.

She didn't respond, but I wasn't surprised. It was really early. I sent another message. '*I hope you're enjoying your flowers.*' After our heated phone call, I'd called in a few favors. Okay, I'd called in a shitload of favors from just about everyone I knew back home. Well, everyone I knew whose phone number I remembered. It had taken some convincing, but I'd talked them all into finding Kiera and handing her a single rose.

"Won't she think that's creepy, Kellan?" They'd told me.

"No, she'll know it's from me," I'd replied. At least, I'd hoped she'd make that realization. And she had. Thankfully. I just didn't want her to feel distant from me again. I needed to keep me in her thoughts. I needed us to be okay.

I typed one final message before putting my phone away. '*I miss you. I love you.*'

Time trudged forward, and as March moved into April, I found myself talking to Hailey more and more. She was just the one person I didn't have to hide anything from. I could be open, honest, and uncomplicated with her. It was freeing. I even started tolerating her badgering me about Gavin better.

"Okay...you know what time it is, right?" she said.

A small laugh escaped me. "Yes. This is the part of the conversation where you tell me I'm being a stubborn idiot, and I should just talk to Gavin, right?"

She giggled in my ear. "Ding, ding. You nailed it."

I sighed. "And you already know what I'm going to say."

Now she sighed, then she lowered her voice, mimicking me. "I'll never speak to that man, stop bringing it up, Hailey."

I laughed. "Ding, ding. You also nailed it. We're getting good at this."

She laughed, then her voice grew more serious. "Hey...I know this is going to cause problems, but...Riley really wants to meet you."

A weariness settled over me. "I want to meet him too; I just don't see how. Would Gavin let him visit me with you? At a concert?" I added, cringing. They couldn't show up at home without me explaining who they were to Kiera, and that...wasn't something I was ready to do. "Or maybe you could visit me in L.A.? I'll be there for a while after the tour ends..."

I could practically hear Hailey shaking her head. "He's too young, Kellan. Dad would never let Riley go somewhere without him. Not even if he was with me. I'm sorry."

I hung my head; I'd already accepted the limitations of my

relationship with Riley. "It's okay. He won't be young forever. I'll just...catch up with him when he's older." She sighed again, and I knew what she was thinking: *Just talk to Gavin already, and then you wouldn't have to avoid your little brother.* Not wanting to get into it, I said, "Tell him hi for me though, okay? And Hails—"

She cut me off. "I know. Make sure he's alone. I will, I promise."

"Thank you. I know you don't entirely understand, but I appreciate it."

She exhaled in a huff. "That's what sisters are for, right?"

I couldn't help my grin. "Yep."

We said goodbye, and I put my phone back in my pocket, feeling lighter and a little brighter. Matt and Evan stepped off the bus then, joining me in the brilliant Texas sunshine. They both had elated looks on their faces. "What's up?" I asked, walking over to them.

Matt beamed at me. "Rachel and Jenny are coming for a visit. They're going to spend a whole week with us."

A rush of eagerness flooded my stomach. "Is Kiera coming with them?" Why hadn't she mentioned anything? And why did she sound so distracted lately? Some of the distance was creeping back into our relationship, and I didn't know why. It worried me.

Matt's face fell a little. "I don't...think so. Rachel said Jenny asked her, but she...said she couldn't right now." He cringed. "Sorry, man."

I had to swallow the knot of disappointment in my throat before I could speak. "It's fine. She probably just couldn't get the same time off work as Jenny."

Evan gave me a reassuring smile. "Yeah, that's probably why. It is spring break after all. Pete's will be packed."

I gave him a brief smile. Right. She'll be out of school for a bit...but not with me. I lifted an eyebrow at Matt. "I don't suppose this means we'll be taking a little time off from picking songs?" Maybe I could finally get away? Spend a day or two with Kiera over her break?

Matt frowned. "Kell...we're running out of time, and we still have three songs to pick. I'm sorry, man...we need you here."

Weariness crashed over me as I closed my eyes. "Yeah...okay."

I felt someone smack my shoulder, and I reopened my eyes to see Evan grinning at me. "You'll see her soon. We're getting close to the end."

Exactly. That's what I'm afraid of—the end of Kiera and me. I slapped on a smile, so he'd drop the subject. "Yeah. This will be fun. I'm glad they're coming up." Looking between the two of them, I said, "Does this mean Griffin and I have to sleep in the hallway when we're at hotels?"

Matt looked at Evan, then they both looked at me. And nodded. "Yep. That will work," Matt brightly said.

"Fuck," I muttered. This sucked already.

Matt clapped my back. "Just kidding, Kell. I'm sure one of the other guys will take you in. Griffin though...I might have to pay someone." With a sigh, he rolled his eyes.

I grinned. "We should talk to Scott, and get Griffin paired with Paul for a while..."

Matt's blue eyes sparkled with joy. "Oh, fuck yeah. God, you're brilliant."

I felt so much better after that. If anyone could punish Paul for me...it was Griffin.

Two days later, Jenny and Rachel showed up. We were at the venue, killing time around the buses when they arrived. I could hear the reunion before I could see it; Jenny squealing, Evan's booming laugh as he picked her up. Matt folding Rachel in his arms while she cried. It was sweet. It made my chest hurt. God, I missed Kiera.

Griffin frowned as the foursome started walking our way. "What's bugging you?" I asked.

His scowl deepened. "Why the fuck didn't Anna come with them?" He looked over at me with genuine confusion on his face. "Why wouldn't she want to spend a week fucking me?" By his expression, it was obvious he thought no human being would ever turn that down.

I smiled as I shrugged. "Maybe she had responsibilities she couldn't leave behind? Like a job?"

He twisted his lips at me. "Dude...it's *Anna*. She's just as irresponsible as I am." His brows furrowed. "Maybe she's just fucking someone else right now." I couldn't tell if he had a real opinion on that, besides annoyance that she was preoccupied. He turned and left before I could ask. Sometimes...it almost seemed like he cared about her. Almost.

Pushing aside that mystery, I turned to greet the friends I hadn't seen in a really long time. "Oh my God, Jenny...Rachel." I gave each one a hug in turn. It was like hugging home. "It's so good to see you." Damn, I'd really missed them.

They both grinned at me as they returned to their boyfriends. "You too, Kellan." Jenny's pale eyes studied me for a moment, and I kept my expression smooth, breezy, untroubled. Jenny was basically an extension of Kiera, and I couldn't let her see any of the turmoil I was going through.

Lifting my eyebrows suggestively, I told them, "I can empty the bus, if you guys want to be alone. There's only one real bed though, so you'll have to take turns. Or not," I added with a shrug.

Rachel's cheeks instantly flushed with color as she buried her dark head in Matt's chest. Jenny thumped me in the stomach. "Kellan! Don't be gross."

Smiling, I backed away with raised hands. "I'm not being gross. I'm trying to be helpful...offer some solutions. I'm a problem solver."

Evan laughed, while Matt shook his head and rubbed Rachel's back. Jenny sighed, then looked up at Evan. "Is he like this every day?"

Evan laughed harder and shook his head. "No, you caught him on a good day. He's usually moody and irritable." I smirked at that, then flipped him off. Evan chuckled as he looked down at Jenny. "See? Irritable."

Laughing, I socked him in the arm. "You guys are on your own then." I saluted them, then left to go find Griffin. I was laughing as I walked away. Even if Kiera couldn't come out with them, it was so good to see them.

The next several days were actually really peaceful. Having Jenny and Rachel around made it feel like we were back at Pete's everywhere we went. I didn't even mind having to share a bed with Benji when we stopped at a hotel. Anything to give my friends a little privacy.

The only thing I did mind was Kiera being so busy. Where we used to talk multiple times throughout the day, Kiera and I only seemed to talk late at night now. It freaked me out a little, but I tried really hard not to let that show. I didn't want Jenny thinking anything was wrong, because I didn't want Kiera thinking anything was wrong.

"I feel like she's pulling away from me," I said, finally confessing my fears to someone. I glanced around the bus, but no one was really paying attention to me. Rachel and Matt were having a quiet conversation. Jenny and Evan were playing cards, laughing.

Hailey sighed in my ear. "Why don't you just tell her then?" I'd recently told Hailey about the secret I was keeping from Kiera, about how I wasn't mentioning Hailey or Gavin to her. It was another thing Hailey constantly bugged me about.

I worried my lip. "I don't think *that's* why she's pulling away. Something's...going on with her."

"Have you asked her about it?" she said. From her voice, it was quite clear she wanted me to start communicating with my girlfriend. And I had. Sort of.

Remembering that dreaded conversation, when I'd asked Kiera about what she was keeping from me, made me close my eyes as pain and doubt ripped through me. *You're just going to have to believe in me. Okay.* Shaking my head, I told Hailey, "I don't want to think about it anymore. Tell me something good. Something funny."

She thought for a moment. "Hmmm...oh, I've got it."

She instantly started laughing, and I found myself chuckling too, my mood lightening. "What?"

She snorted; it was adorable. "Okay...one of my friends is seriously obsessed with you. Like, I might need to stage an intervention obsessed."

I started laughing. "What? How? Why? From that *one* picture on your phone?"

Hailey giggled. "No...from your website. Have you seen it? You're half-naked in almost every single picture. Seriously, Kellan...have you not heard of T-shirts?"

I laughed so hard I had to swipe my eyes. Jenny lifted an eyebrow at me, but I just shook my head at her. "Oh God, no...I haven't seen the website yet. Doesn't surprise me though. Matt's always been obsessed with my body."

I knew that sounded bad, and I let it sound bad. Served him right. Matt would make me walk around shirtless with D-Bags spray-painted on my chest if he could, and I was 100 percent certain he was the reason I was so exposed on our website. Hmmm...Kiera had to have noticed the same thing Hailey had, but she'd never mentioned anything about it. Was she okay with me being "sold" like that?

Hailey made a shocked noise. "Oh. Does he *want* you? Is that awkward since you're bandmates?"

My head dropped to the table as I laughed. "No...oh my God...no, he doesn't..." I couldn't even finish, I was laughing too hard. Hailey started laughing with me, once she realized she'd gotten it wrong. Matt was obviously unaware of the nature of my conversation as he chatted with Rachel, but I could easily picture the look on his face if he'd heard her say that—the half annoyed, half amused twist of his lips, the slow shake of his head, the epic eye roll. Matt was many things...but attracted to me was *not* one of them.

Hailey and I moved on to other topics after that, her school, Riley, but every so often I'd break out in a fit of giggles. *Does he want you?* That was going to entertain me for a long time.

On the last night of Jenny and Rachel's visit, we all decided to go to a club. The thumping music made me miss Kiera. I didn't feel like dancing, so I spent the bulk of the night hanging out by the bar, drinking. Girls approached me, asking me to dance, but I turned them all down. Jenny nodded her approval when she spotted me rejecting someone. I rolled my eyes at her. *Of course, I said no, Jenny. I always say no.*

For a split-second, I debated asking Jenny if she knew what was going on with Kiera. Would she tell me? I hadn't been able to flat-out ask Jenny to spy on Kiera for me, but I felt like the message had been implied. It also felt wrong. Kiera had asked for my belief in her. Going behind her back to discover the truth would only prove that I didn't believe in her...that I didn't believe in *us*. I didn't want that to be true. I wanted us to be...solid.

I had no choice but to trust Kiera and hope she wasn't doing anything that would hurt me. Maybe, like my secret, whatever she was hiding had nothing to do with our relationship. I still had no clue what that secret might be but thinking about it that way brought me comfort. I could let this go. I had to.

Right after deciding not to ask her anything, Jenny tossed her arms around my waist. "Kellan," she said, clearly drunk. "I'm so glad you're with Kiera."

"Thanks?" I said, chuckling as I gave her a brief hug.

Giggling, she let me go. "I'm just glad you fell for *her*. Because I love her. And some of those other girls you,"—she paused to use air quotes—"...dated..." She lifted an eyebrow as she continued. "They were skanky, Kellan. It would have driven me crazy to be around them all the time."

I had to laugh at her assessment of my pre-Kiera relationships. She had a point, but still, the word skanky was really funny coming from her. *Language, Jenny.* Evan came up to us while I was laughing. He eyed Jenny, stumbling a little on her feet, then me. "Do I want to know?" he asked.

Pointing at her, I laughed out, "She just called my exes skanky."

Evan smiled as he looked down at her. Jenny shrugged. "What? They were."

Wrapping an arm around her, Evan sighed and shook his head. "Jujube, I think it's time we get you to bed."

Her face lit up as she leapt into his arms. Luckily, he caught her. Her mouth was on his a second later, and I shook my head. Damn…now I really missed Kiera. I texted Matt and Griffin that Evan and I were leaving, then I stepped outside. Evan was already disappearing into a cab with Jenny, going back to the hotel. I watched them leave, then got my own cab back to the hotel. I wasn't tired yet, and I didn't want to bug Benji and his roommate yet, so I hung out at the hotel bar until it closed, then I hung out in the lobby, waiting.

When I was pretty sure Kiera would be home from work, I pulled out my phone and called her. *Please pick up.* Thankfully, she did. "Hey," she said.

I closed my eyes, savoring the sound of her voice. "Hey." Then I noticed how tired she sounded. "You worked tonight, right? Or were you sleeping? Did I wake you?"

"I was up," she said. "It's just been a long day."

She didn't elaborate, so all I said was, "Oh…"

Silence fell between us, and I hated feeling the space there again. "I miss you. I wish you'd been able to come up."

"Yeah, me too. I'm sorry about that."

"It's okay," I said, shrugging. "I understand." Not wanting to dwell on her absence, I instead said, "It's been nice having Jenny and Rachel around. Kind of feels like home again. Although, not completely like home…" It would never be completely like home until she was with me again.

Kiera sighed, and I heard wistful longing in the sound. It

made me smile. "How many times can I say I miss you before it gets annoying?" I asked.

She laughed a little. "One thousand," she firmly stated.

"Per day or in total?" I asked.

She laughed again. "Hmmm...per day."

My smile grew. "Good, then I'm nowhere near my limit. I miss you. So much. It kind of sucks actually...missing you all the time."

I'd meant that playfully, but Kiera's voice had an odd seriousness to it when she responded with, "Yeah, I know..."

Not wanting to worry about what that meant, I said, "I could distract you? Would you like me to make you feel good again?" *Like my wife?* God, I loved those words, loved that thought. *Please let us make it that far.*

Kiera giggled in my ear. "A part of me wants to say yes, the rest of me is really tired."

"Oh...another time," I murmured.

I could hear the warmth in her smile when she spoke. "Definitely. I love you."

Now I was the one with warmth in my voice. "I love you too. Goodnight, Kiera." *And I hope I get to see you soon.*

Chapter 29
SURPRISE

Things with Kiera were getting...odd. There was a strange disconnect that was happening between us, strained silences that lasted too long, uncomfortable gaps where neither person knew what to say. It had really started to kick in shortly after Jenny and Rachel returned home, and I had no idea why. I didn't know what was going on with her, and even worse, I didn't know how to talk to her about it. I felt like there was nothing I could say, because everything I asked would lead to a reciprocal question about what was going on with me. And I didn't want to talk about that, about *him*.

Gavin. He was a thorn in my side that I could never fully remove. Ignoring his calls and messages was second nature now, but every time my phone went off, I flinched. And every time I saw that fucking unprogrammed number, a small slice of my soul shriveled. I was so tired, all the time. I just felt worn. And stuck. It felt like this was going to be my life from here on out; stuck in a vicious cycle I couldn't escape from. Trapped in pain and misery and confusion...forever.

Every night as I fell asleep, I felt hope slipping from me as I spiraled into weary despondency, wondering how I could possibly keep going. But then, every morning, I somehow found it inside myself to get up, slap on a carefree smile, and keep moving, because what else could I do?

"How was your day?" I asked, trying to make my voice light and worry-free.

"Good," Kiera responded, not elaborating. "Yours?"

"Good," I answered, not knowing what else to say. The silence grew between us, and I could hear a soft sigh escape Kiera. It worried me. "I really enjoyed the other night," I told her. We'd made love over the phone again, and for a moment, everything between us had felt warm and comfortable. But unfortunately, the feeling didn't last. We were already slipping again. *Why?*

"I did too," she murmured.

There was definite happiness in the sound...but sadness too. Because she missed me? Or was it something more? *What's going on, Kiera?* Was it me? Was my absence and my avoidance finally too much for her? Was I pushing her away? I already knew that answer—I was. I should have found a way to go home already. I shouldn't have missed our anniversary. I should talk to her. *But I can't.*

"I wish I wasn't so busy. I wish I could just freeze time and come see you. I wish I could hold you. I wish..." I stopped my pointless list of impossibilities and let out a long sigh. *I wish we were like we used to be, before I came here, before the secrets seeped in.*

Kiera sighed with me. "Yeah..." was all she said in response. I wanted to ask her what she wished for, but I couldn't; a part of me was too terrified to know.

My stomach tightened and I felt my eyes stinging. "I love you, Kiera." *Please don't leave me.*

"I love you too, Kellan." I felt the sincerity in her words, and it made some of the ache leave me. *At least she truly does loves me. Is that enough?*

"I'll call you tomorrow," I told her. She told me okay, then we said our goodbyes.

I felt hollow as I stared at my phone. *I can't keep doing this. I just…can't.* I could feel the exhaustion burning my eyelids, leeching energy from my muscles, filling my body with a heaviness I could never fully escape. I felt like I couldn't breathe anymore. Not deeply. I was surviving on shallow gasps, and it wasn't enough. I *needed* Kiera. It wasn't a "want" anymore. It was much deeper and far more desperate.

My phone chimed with a message, and I closed my eyes as a wave of fatigue hit me. I checked the message, and sure enough, it was from Gavin. That made up my mind. I was going home. Matt would have to tie me down to keep me here.

As soon as Matt woke up the next day, I told him my news. As predicted, he wasn't pleased.

"What? No, you can't leave right now, Kell. We have one more new song to pick, and the label rejected our last one, so we need to find something to replace it. Now is not a good time."

I let out a long sigh. He was right on all counts. The last song was proving to be the hardest of them all, and with the label getting pickier about our deeper cuts, it was even more difficult. We'd had to replace the song before this one too. "I know, Matt. But I'm going anyway."

"Kell—"

"No! I *am* leaving. Period. I wasn't asking for permission. I was telling you a fact." His eyes narrowed, and I sighed again. "I'm going to lose her, Matt. I can feel it." My eyes and my voice grew pleading as I shrugged. "If it were Rachel, what would *you* do?"

He looked away as he thought, then finally, he sighed and nodded as he returned his eyes to mine. "Okay. One night, then we need you back."

I smiled at him, grateful that he wasn't going to turn this into a huge fight. "I know. Thank you."

Matt frowned, and when he spoke his voice was thick with sullenness. "No need to thank me, you were leaving anyway, remember?"

The look on his face made my smile grow. "I know. But still, thank you." I put my hand on his shoulder. "It's a little easier to leave knowing you understand. Somewhat."

He smirked at me, then nodded. "When are you leaving?"

I thought about that for a second. We were on our way to New Orleans—Griffin was all excited about exploring the French Quarter. Well, more accurately, he was excited to get trashed in the French Quarter. We had two shows in the city, but at different venues. Because of commitment issues with the venues, there was a day off between the two shows. I could leave after the show tonight, then come back in the morning and have plenty of time to work out a song with Matt. Maybe even record it for Lana if all went well with selecting a song. This was actually a really great time for me to leave. "I'll take a late flight back home tonight, then return in the morning...so we can work on our night off."

Matt beamed at me, finally pleased. Grinning back, I handed him my phone. "Help me buy my ticket?"

The smile immediately fell off him and he slowly shook his head. I laughed while he muttered, "A hundred and five..."

I was more energized than I'd been in a while that night, and the show was particularly good. I think Matt noticed. After the show, he smiled and nodded at me. I took that to mean, *Yeah, you're right, you need a break*. The second we were done, I left. I didn't grab a bag, didn't change my clothes...I just left. Kiera had everything I needed, and sadly, my visit wasn't going to be a long one.

A cab met me around back, and I hopped in with a huge grin on my face. I almost couldn't believe this was happening. I was going back home. *Home*. God, just the word made me feel better. I would finally see Kiera again, hold her in my arms, convince her that I loved her more than anything, that nothing was going on with me...and hope and pray that nothing was going on with her. We could reconnect, and hopefully when I left again, we'd be stronger. We'd be one again.

The plane ride was long, tiring. The two guys beside me slept the entire way, but I was too excited to sleep. I couldn't even close my eyes. I just bounced my knee and waited, waited, waited. When the plane finally started descending, I started grinning. *Almost there*.

When the plane touched down, and we rolled to our gate, I debated calling Kiera and letting her know where I was. She had no idea how close I was to her. It was easy to picture her face, picture her surprise. I imagined her leaping into my arms, kissing every inch of me. Then I imagined the look on her face as I surprised her. I pictured her hearing me knocking, her brows bunched in confusion as she swung the door open, her jaw dropping as she saw me, the excited squeal, the tears in her eyes...

I wanted that vision, so I left my phone in my pocket and decided not to call her.

I was buzzing with excitement as I got into a taxi. I gave him Kiera's address, then changed my mind and asked him to stop at a grocery store—any grocery store. I wanted to get Kiera some flowers. Even though I'd been bombarding her with roses ever since missing her on our anniversary, it just didn't feel right to show up emptyhanded. In a way, this was our anniversary 2.0. And this one, I wasn't going to screw up. Tonight was going to be perfect.

The taxi stopped in front of Kiera's apartment, and I gave the driver a huge tip for the inconvenience of having to help me run an errand. "Thank you, I appreciate it," I told him, lifting my bouquet of roses.

He nodded, smiling either at my gift for my girlfriend or the wad of cash I'd handed him. Probably the latter. As the cab drove away, I looked up at Kiera's apartment building and inhaled a deep cleansing breath. *Thank God...I'm finally close to her again*. I could finally breathe again. I smiled up at a window on her level, then I remembered something, and my gaze swept the parking lot. I felt an actual pang in my chest when I spotted my car...my baby.

Biting my lip, I flicked a glance at Kiera's level again, then back to my car. Kiera could wait another moment...I needed to say hello to my other girl first. I was grinning as I walked over to the Chevelle. Kiera had parked her next to a light, and she looked perfect—shiny, like she'd recently been washed, all the windows intact, no visible scrapes or scratches. I peeked into the windows, looking inside. Like the exterior, the interior was also perfect—no garbage, no stains, no tears. She was pristine, just as I liked her to be.

Running a hand over the roof, I sighed in contentment. God, I'd missed my car. "Hey, girl," I whispered. "Kiera taking good care of you?"

I looked around to see if I was alone, then laid my head on the roof and gave my car a brief hug. Damn. Maybe Evan was right... maybe I *was* too attached to my car. Laughing at myself, I straightened up and patted the roof. "I'll be back for you soon, girl."

I gave the Chevelle one last, long look, then turned toward the apartment building. I needed to hug the girl who could hug me back. I hummed to myself as I took the stairs to Kiera's level. The grin on my face was huge when I got to her door. I could hear talking inside, so I knew someone was up. Was that Kiera or Anna? Their voices could be eerily similar at times. But the other voice was lower, male, so even though it really sounded more like Kiera, it had to be Anna. Great. If she was on a date, I might have to take Kiera to my place. Actually, I was totally fine with that.

I raised my hand to knock but decided to try the door first. I frowned as the knob easily twisted. They shouldn't leave the door unlocked, especially this late at night. I pushed the door open, and the vague sound of the guy speaking suddenly shifted into coherent words: "Let's talk about the kiss."

The familiarity of the accented voice sent a shockwave of icy surprise through me. But when I saw who was in Kiera's apartment...it felt like someone had just pushed me off the tallest building in town and I was plummeting to my death. Denny.

Denny was *here*, talking to Kiera like he'd never left. What. The. Fuck?

My mind couldn't quite snap together the pieces of what I was seeing. Kiera, sitting on her hideous orange couch, her arms looped around my former best friend...his arms wrapped around her like she still belonged to him. Kiera smiling, laughing. Their heads close together, like they were about to kiss...or like they'd just finished kissing.

Kiss...that was what he'd said. *Let's talk about the kiss.* What kiss? *Did* he just fucking kiss her? My stomach filled with acid while my veins filled with venom. What the fuck was he even doing here? What the fuck were they doing together? Jesus fucking Christ, was *this* her secret? That Denny was back in town...and now he was kissing her? Did he come back for her? Knowing I was gone? How long had he been here? With her. Fuck.

The pair finally noticed me. They pulled away from each other, their smiles falling, their arms dropping, their eyes widening. I felt like I was going to be sick as I witnessed their stunned, guilty expressions. The only thing keeping my stomach in check, was the rage circulating throughout my body. I held onto it as tightly as I could—anything to block out the pain. *What the hell is going on here?*

"I felt bad for missing our anniversary. We had a short break in the schedule, and even though Matt's irked at me for taking off, I just had to come out and see you." I could barely speak my jaw was so tight, and my entire body was vibrating with pent-up anger. Eyes narrowed in fury, I flicked a glance between them. *Why is he here?* "I wanted to surprise you. Are you surprised...? Because I know I am."

Kiera instantly moved away from Denny. Standing, she held up her hands. "I can explain."

Really? She had an excuse for being with him? For the kiss that Denny wanted to talk about? Because they had sure looked pretty fucking cozy when I interrupted. How could she possibly explain the cuddling I *witnessed?* Overcome with the rage inside me, I slammed the door shut as I stepped closer. I pointed at them with the bouquet of flowers still in my hand. "You can explain! Explain what, exactly? The fact that he is sitting in your living room and not thousands of miles away, or the fact that you had your hands all over each other!"

I knew I was yelling, I knew I was losing it...and I didn't fucking care. They'd *kissed*, I just knew it. And a small part of me...wasn't surprised. Maybe her being with Denny was shocking, but her finding comfort in another man...no, not really. I'd almost been expecting this.

Tossing the flowers to the ground, since they weren't needed anymore, I stormed into the living room. Kiera stepped forward and put her hands on my chest, trying to stop me. Her face was pale, the green of her eyes sharp and intense. There was fear in her expression but not for herself...no, her quick glances at Denny told me what she was really afraid of—me hurting *him*. Seeing the concern made my blood boil. I pushed my body against her hands, getting closer to her. "I'm listening...start explaining!"

She swallowed...and looked for all the world like she didn't know what to say. Denny slowly rose from the couch in her silence. "Kiera...I told you to tell him..." he murmured.

My eyes snapped to the friend I'd never expected to see again, especially in my girlfriend's living room. *You were supposed to be better than me.* "Tell me what? Tell me about the kiss? Is that what I heard you say?" My focus returned to Kiera. "Is that what you need to tell me, Kiera...or is there more?" *Jesus...are you fucking him?*

Tears filled her eyes as she shook her head. "No, Kellan, he didn't kiss me."

Filling in the blanks, I pushed her shoulders back, getting her away from me. "Then you kissed him?"

She looked like she was about to break down. She looked so fucking guilty. But still, she tried to act like she was innocent. "No, Kellan, I didn't kiss anybody..."

Liar. I stepped up to her, forcing her back with my body until her legs hit the couch. Her breath was faster, but oddly, what I sensed coming from her was attraction. Really? She wanted me? Even odder...I wanted her too. It had been so long since we'd been this close, and there was desire flickering to life inside me, buried just underneath the rage. I ignored it. I didn't want to want her. Not if she was cheating on me. "But someone kissed you? Who?" *Explain that statement...if you can.*

That was when I felt a hand on my arm. "Kellan...relax, mate."

Those words sent my slim control over the edge. Twisting to Denny, I shoved him, hard. "Don't fucking call me 'mate'! Why the hell are you with *my* girl?"

Denny stumbled with the force of my push. He caught himself before falling and slowly straightened to standing. The warmth in his brown eyes vanished as he narrowed them at me. "Right...*your* girl."

Denny's dark hair was longer than before, his facial hair thicker, it made him seem older, more mature, more in control of himself, but even still, I could feel his simmering anger as he glared at me. It was nowhere near mine though. *I know I fucked you over, but that doesn't mean I'm going to sit back and let you do the same thing to me.* My fingers clenched into a fist as I stared at him. *Want to go another round, Denny? Because this time...I won't just stand there and take it. I* will *fight for her.*

Kiera suddenly grabbed my face and turned me to look at her. "A girl at school kissed me! Okay?" she said in a rush.

Her pleading eyes searched mine, and for a moment, the shock of what she'd said released some of my anger. "A girl? Really?" I looked for any sign of a lie, but I wasn't finding any. The kiss comment was about a girl? It had nothing to do with Denny?

Kiera sighed, looking weary but no longer guilty. "Yes, a girl. Denny and I haven't done anything wrong. You stepped into a situation that was easy to take out of context." She began stroking my face, and the compassion and sympathy in her eyes made a large chunk of my anger fade. "But I didn't kiss her back. I haven't kissed anyone...but you."

Is that true? I tried to find any trace of deception on her face, in her voice, but all I could sense coming from her was honesty. Was it really the truth, though? Or had she just become a better liar? But why lie to me now? I'd caught them, busted them in the act...why not just tell me what was going on? Why keep holding onto a secret unnecessarily? That seemed unfairly cruel, and I'd never known Kiera to be intentionally, blatantly cruel. Confused, sure, but not cruel. So maybe...maybe she *was* being honest. Maybe she wasn't cheating on me. *Please let that be true.*

My residual anger downshifted into irritation as I considered the fact that I might have overreacted. Giving her a crooked smile, I tried to lighten the mood. "You got kissed by a girl and I missed it?" Now that the fury was receding, that thought was a little intriguing. *I would have liked to see that.*

Kiera smiled as she lightly thumped my chest. From beside me, I heard Denny clear his throat and say, "I'll let you two work this out."

I turned my attention back to Denny. Maybe she hadn't kissed him, hadn't fucked him, but she still hadn't mentioned that he was here. How long had he been here? Why was he here? Some of the heat returned to my voice when I said, "What are you doing here?" I'd told him the truth when he was in my position...it was his turn now.

Denny sighed, then shook his head. "Look, I don't want to be involved with this. I'm here for work, nothing more. I told her to tell you way back in February that I was here, but she was scared to..." He sighed again, while I stewed over his words. *February? Fuck.* "But that's between the two of you and I don't want to be here to watch you discuss it."

I considered his words...and believed him. Kiera might have reason to lie still—if she thought the truth would end us—but Denny...he didn't have a single reason to lie to me. If he wanted Kiera back, he'd tell me, especially if telling me improved his chances of getting back together with her. He had no reason to tell me he was only here for work, other than to state a fact. And he honestly looked like he'd rather be anywhere but this living room. He didn't seem to want to fight me for her, he just wanted to be gone. I nodded at him, accepting his answer.

He brushed past me, his dark eyes never leaving mine. Once he was well clear of me, his gaze shifted to Kiera. "Thanks for listening, Kiera. I'll call you tomorrow."

Those words made a pang of something dark, painful, and spiteful rip through me. *Call you tomorrow*? *Seriously*? Denny glanced at me a final time before grabbing his jacket and leaving. I glared at him the entire time. While I appreciated his honesty, that comment was hitting every last nerve I had. What the hell was going on here? Why hadn't either of them told me about it?

The anger reignited as I turned back around to face Kiera. "He'll call you tomorrow? What? Are you guys...buddies now?" I'd dealt with their phone friendship. That had seemed relatively safe, but this...

Kiera's face was soft, calm as she shook her head. Her hand was on my chest, and her fingers trailed down my stomach. My muscles tightened as her hand drifted lower. I tried to push back the electric sensation of her touching me, tried to block the desire that was resurfacing. It was nearly impossible to not be turned on by her; even angry, a part of me would always want her.

"Yes, we are," she said. "And I'm sorry I didn't tell you he was here. I didn't know how you'd react."

They were *friends* now? In-person, let's-hang-out *friends*? The word seemed foreign to me when put in context with Kiera. I didn't think I could ever be just friends with her. No, I knew I couldn't. I'd never been able to be just friends with her when we *were* friends; that was the bulk of our problem in the beginning. Was it possible for them though? To be just friends in person? I wasn't sure. I remembered too clearly how hard it was for Kiera to leave him.

My jaw tightened as I stared her down. "You didn't know

how I'd react, or how you'd react?" I touched her chest, and as I did, anger—and wanton need—rushed through me. "Maybe you thought you'd start back up again." I leaned into her, furious but aching with hunger. Our lips close, but still too far away, I spilled my darkest fear to her. "Maybe you were hoping for it to start back up again?"

She shoved against my chest, trying to get me to back up, but my body was so rigidly tight, she ended up pushing herself down onto the couch. My eyes narrowed as I watched her, my breath fast as anger and desire waged war within me, each battling for control. Kiera looked up at me, and I saw lust in her eyes as she studied my reaction. It electrified me, and I felt myself hardening as I stared at her.

Running her tongue over her bottom lip, she told me, "Nothing happened, Kellan, and I didn't want anything to happen. Denny and I are just friends...I promise."

God, I wanted to believe her. I wanted to forget all of this and make love to her, but fuck...the pain was starting to seep in, stimulated by my fear of losing her. I held onto the anger...the anger kept the agony away. Kiera was looking up at me with hooded eyes. The desire helped block the pain too. I let the ache of wanting her fill me, latched onto it like a lifeline. Leaning down, I pulled her to her feet. Our bodies instinctively melded together, every section of her front touching mine. It sent bolts of lightning through me, quickened my heartbeat, made my body surge with white-hot need. One of my hands drifted over to cup her ass, pulling her into me. I wanted more. So much more. But how could I go there...if she wasn't telling the truth?

My lips lowered to hover over hers. It was so hard not to kiss her, but I forced myself to say the words that were holding me back. "Don't lie to me, Kiera." I couldn't cave if she was lying. I'd never survive that kind of betrayal. *You promised.*

She shook her head, her breath fast against me. "I'm not, Kellan...I swear. I never touched him like that. I gave him a hug because he's sad his girlfriend is stuck back in Australia, but there's never been more than friendship between us while you've been gone...I promise."

Her words were everything I wanted to hear, but still, fear made me balk, made me doubt. It was too easy to picture them together. It was too easy to remember. Kiera pressed harder against me. Her hands lifted to my chest, filling me with fire. And pain. I lowered my forehead to hers, torn, confused, angry... needy. "Kiera...don't, don't lie to me...please." I could hear the odd ache in my voice as desperation filled me. It was half anguish, half lust. I needed her...but I also needed her words to be true. I couldn't handle her cheating on me. Not now, not after we'd pledged ourselves to be faithful to one another. *Let it be true, Kiera...and if it's not...just kill me.*

Kiera let out a throaty moan as I placed a hand on her waist. My fingers on her ass instinctively squeezed as the hunger of wanting her intensified. Resisting her was painful...but taking her could be too.

"I'm not, Kellan..." Her hands ran up my chest, her fingers stroking my neck before tangling into my hair. I suppressed a groan at how good it felt. Kiera's voice was full of matching need when she spoke again. "Please...believe me..."

God, I wanted to believe her. God, I *wanted* her. Her fast breath was driving me insane. Her mouth so close to mine was excruciating torture. My body was throbbing, my heart was aching. *She's swearing her faithfulness, she's asking me to believe in her. It must be true. It has to be true.* My hand on her side slid up her chest, over her breast. I couldn't contain the groan that time.

Kiera sucked in a sharp breath; her arms squeezed me tight. "Kellan, please...take me..."

Her begging was my undoing. I simply couldn't resist her anymore. My mouth found hers before I was even aware of doing it. The sensation, the satisfaction, it was beyond all expectation. There was a frantic desperation to the way our mouths moved together—the way we attacked each other. I couldn't get enough of her. I knew I should be gentler, softer, more romantic...but I couldn't calm down. I just fucking needed her so goddamn much. And Kiera seemed to need me too. She met every forceful kiss, her body clamping around me, her fingers tightening in my hair.

Slightly bending, I ran my hands down her thighs and picked her up. Her legs instantly cinched around me. I turned us around, trying to make it to her bedroom. It was difficult. My mind was too hazy to remember the layout of her apartment, and I couldn't stop kissing her to look properly. When Kiera started grinding against me, sending shockwaves of pleasure through me, I stumbled against the wall. Fuck. Could I just take her here? "God, I want you so bad..." I groaned.

"I want you too," she moaned back.

I found her room, set her down, and shoved the door shut. The second the door was closed, I pulled at her clothes while she pulled on mine. The need grew painful as more of her skin was exposed, as more of mine was freed. I felt incoherent, drunk on her nearness. When the last pieces of our clothing were finally gone, I pushed her onto the bed, moving over the top of her as she laid back. I paused for just a second, trying to slow down, but Kiera whimpered beneath me. "Yes, take me..."

I let the madness fully take me over and drove into her, hard, owning her. She moved against me just as intensely, the cries leaving her only filled with ecstasy. It was so hard, deep, fast...it didn't take long to feel the build-up cresting. I didn't try to resist it. I wanted this too much, wanted her too much. Kiera's legs around me tightened as a loud moan left her. Feeling her climax sent me over the edge. My body tightened as the euphoria exploded through me. I rode out the sensation with Kiera...it felt like it lasted forever.

Worn, I sagged against Kiera when the bliss ebbed. My breath was still fast, my heart was still racing, and I was slightly sweaty. Kiera too. She held me tight to her as she panted in my ear. A flash of guilt went through me. That hadn't been the anniversary greeting I'd wanted to give her. That hadn't been making love at all. That had been flat-out, lust-filled fucking. But also love-filled. Maybe that brought it a step up from fucking, a step down from tender love making. A passionate, fiery, much-needed in between. I hoped Kiera felt the same, but even still, I felt the need to apologize.

I shifted to her side. Her hand was over her eyes as she struggled to breathe normally. "I'm sorry," I told her. "That's not how I wanted our first time after so long to be..." I'd pictured romance, gentleness, hours of teasing and tasting, not...that. I shifted to my back and stared up at the ceiling, disappointed at myself. And the situation. Tonight hadn't at all gone as I'd expected, and I wasn't sure what to feel right now. A little lingering anger, more than a little bit of sadness, a large dose of happiness, and even some relief. *At least I know what she's been hiding now. I just wish she'd told me earlier. I wish I hadn't found out that way.*

Kiera twisted to face me. After a long, silent moment, she asked, "Do you believe me? About Denny?"

That was the real question, wasn't it? Did I believe her? Did I believe that she didn't want him anymore? That all this time nothing had happened between them? That she'd merely been comforting a friend earlier? There were several times in her relationship with Denny when I could have sworn there was more friendship-love than romantic-love between them. Even Kiera not wanting to let him go at the end...now that I was looking at it through the lens of time and experience, that choice seemed fueled by friendship too. Thinking rationally and not fearfully, it was easy to picture the two of them as friends. I didn't like it...but I could see it.

My gaze swung down to hers. "Yeah, I believe you."

She gave me a soft smile as she nodded, then she leaned over to gently kiss me. "I'm glad you're here. I've missed you..."

A genuine smile broke over my face; it significantly improved my mood. "I've missed you too...if you couldn't tell." With a small laugh, I indicated my spent body. I supposed I could partially blame my eagerness on being apart from her for so long.

Kiera adorably bit her lip as she examined my bare skin. The cute expression on her face made my heart swell. God, I'd missed her. Thank God, she hadn't cheated on me. Now that I knew her secret...and knew how much it hurt to be blindsided... maybe it was time to tell her mine. Because it was driving us apart. I knew it. And I didn't want to go through that kind of anger and pain with her again. Somehow...I had to find the courage to tell her about Gavin. Staying silent was no longer an option. Hopefully she wouldn't be too upset with me. And hopefully she'd respect my wishes to *never* accept him into my life.

Leaning forward, Kiera gave me a quick kiss. "I'm gonna brush my teeth and get ready for bed. I'll be right back." She sat up, a slight frown on her face. "You won't leave, right?"

Knowing she was worried that I was still mad, I smiled and shook my head. "I'll be here, Kiera." *Struggling to find the words to finally tell you what's going on with me.*

She grinned, then stood up and put on her pajamas. I watched her the entire time she got ready, the entire time she left, but my mind was spinning, and my stomach was churning. I didn't want to tell her. I wanted to take this secret to my grave. But I didn't want to lose her, so it was time for me to fucking man up.

With a sigh, I sat up. I glanced at the clothes tossed around her floor. I wanted to be dressed for this, since it was an important conversation—a fucking monumental conversation—but I really didn't want to put on my grimy concert/travel clothes. Then I remembered my drawer here, and I grinned again. Fresh clothes. That was just what I needed to...barely make it through this conversation.

Rolling my eyes at myself, I walked over to her dresser. *Stop being so fucking melodramatic. It's not like you're going to tell her you slipped up and cheated on her.* This wouldn't even really hurt her, just me. It shouldn't be so difficult. It shouldn't, but fuck...it was. My stomach was dangerously close to emptying.

Annoyed at myself, I yanked open my dresser drawer. My hand paused over the opening as I stared at something inside that didn't belong. A brown paper bag. Weird. Had Kiera left me a surprise? Like the ones I'd left for her? I looked over to the open door, a small grin on my face. I could hear Kiera in the bathroom, hear the water running; she was probably brushing her teeth. Smiling wider, I picked up the bag. *I wonder what she left for me?* Opening the bag, I peeked inside, then frowned. *What...are these?* Reaching in, I pulled out a plastic stick looking thing. Once it was in the light coming from the hallway, it was easy to tell what it was. The giant word staring at me gave it away too: *Pregnant*. It was a pregnancy test, and the result screen was saying...yes.

My mouth popped open as my churning stomach settled. I pulled out a few more sticks, and in one way or another, they all said the same thing...pregnant. My heart started beating faster. *Oh my God...Kiera is pregnant. We're gonna have a baby.* I was just about to run to the bathroom to sweep her into my arms and kiss every inch of her when it suddenly dawned on me...if she was pregnant...it wasn't mine.

My hand tightened around the bag as rage and disbelief flooded every cell in my body. Before tonight, I hadn't had sex with Kiera since December. I'd just seen her naked. Her body was flat, perfect...she couldn't be that far along. It wasn't mine. It wasn't fucking mine. She lied to me? She fucking lied to me?

Tears stung my eyes as I felt my entire world crumbling to pieces. Everything we'd had, everything we'd shared, every dream I'd ever wanted...gone. Confirmed by a dozen different tests. She *had* fucked him. And Denny had finally gotten what he'd always wanted: Kiera, pregnant with his child. They'd both lied to me... and I'd fucking believed them. Jesus Christ...she had his child inside of her. I was gonna be sick. I needed out of here. There was no fucking reason to stay now.

Chapter 30
IT'S OVER

Shoving the bag back into the drawer, I put on my dirty clothes strewn about the floor. I didn't want to be clean. I didn't need to be clean. I needed to be gone. Kiera was still in the bathroom when I walked into the hallway. The door was closed, but even still, I didn't look her way. I didn't think I'd ever be able to look at her again. Bile rose up my throat. How could she?

Needing an outlet for my rage, I yanked her bedroom door shut, slamming it hard against the frame. The sound was satisfying, but it did nothing to diminish my anger. Turning away from Kiera, away from our life together, I stormed down the hall. I needed my keys. I needed to get to the door. Once I was gone, then I could fall apart. Or start tearing shit apart. I wasn't sure which way my emotions were going to lead me. And I didn't care.

I wasn't two steps from the bedroom when I heard Kiera's voice. "Kellan? What are you doing?"

She seemed genuinely stunned. Fucking bitch. *Like I would stay? What the hell did you think was going to happen here?* My hands curled into fists as the boiling heat inside me begged to be set free. I pushed down the fury and, ignoring her question, I kept walking down the hallway; I didn't owe her an explanation. I didn't owe her anything anymore. *How could you?*

I spotted her school bag resting on the card table and praying my keys were inside, I headed over to it. My fingers found the cool metal, and I clenched my hand around them, then shoved them in my jacket pocket. I never should have given her these. I never should have given her *me*. I should have run, fled from her like my life depended on it...because it was starting to feel like it did. How could I have been so stupid?

Pent-up rage swirled through my soul as I shifted to the door. I needed to hit something. I needed to scream. I needed to throw up. *His baby is growing inside her.* Fuck. Me.

Kiera beat me to the door. She stood in front of it, blocking it with her body. "Are you leaving?"

I couldn't look at her, couldn't focus on her body. I wanted her gone. I wanted her out of the way. But even still...I didn't want to hurt her, so I knew I couldn't touch her. I was too fucking angry to touch her right now. I would *not* be gentle, and I was not about to let myself become my father. I would *not* be that monster, no matter how much she fucking pushed me. So I just stood there, staring through her body, ignoring her, willing her to move and leave me alone. *Let me go.*

Instead of granting my silent request, Kiera pressed herself into the door. "Why? Because of Denny? I already told you nothing—"

Another refusal was too much to bear, and my eyes involuntarily snapped to hers. She stopped speaking as she took the full force of the fury in my glare. "Nothing? You must think I'm an idiot." I certainly felt like one. *How the fuck did I ever believe her?* "I may not be as 'brilliant' as Denny, but I'm not stupid, Kiera." *I can do simple math. I know the baby isn't mine. I know you fucked him. You left me the proof, you fucking bitch. So just stop denying it and let me go.*

Needing relief, needing escape, I accepted the fact that I was going to have to forcibly remove her from my path. Careful to not hurt her, I grabbed her arm and tugged. "Now get out of my way!"

She resisted my pull. Shaking her head, she snapped, "Not until you talk to me. Why are you so pissed?"

My jaw dropped like she'd struck me. Seriously? She was still going to play the innocent card? "Are you fucking kidding me?" Stepping back, I ran my hands through my hair in frustration; I wanted to rip it out in frustration. *Just let me leave. Why won't you ever let me leave*? Did she enjoy tearing my heart out? Maybe I was wrong about her not being cruel. This felt pretty fucking cruel.

She took a tentative step forward, away from the door. "Okay, I should have told you about Denny, I know that, but we didn't do anything!"

My eyes slammed shut as her words sizzled my brain. Didn't do anything? They didn't fucking do anything? They made a fucking baby! They fucked me over. They both fucking lied. They did...*everything*.

I felt myself shaking, I felt my control slipping. I couldn't stay here much longer, not without escalating this in a way I didn't want it to escalate. *Let me fucking leave, bitch*! Barely holding the reins on my fury, I kept my eyes closed and tried to speak calmly, rationally. "I need to get away from you. Please move, so I don't do something really stupid."

Instead of respecting my wishes...she did the exact opposite. She grabbed my fucking face, shocking me into opening my eyes and looking at her. I instantly batted her hands away and shoved her back, into the door. My breath was heavy, and my fingers dug into her skin as I stared at her. *Calm down. Get out of here, then lose it*.

Kiera shook her head. "No, talk to me!"

Talk to her? Why? There was no point, not anymore. The damage was already done. Forcing myself to back down, I shook my head and took a step away from her. Maybe if I stood here long enough, silently stewing, she'd finally give up and leave me the fuck alone. But of course...she didn't.

She shoved her hands into my chest and fucking yelled at me.

"You son of a bitch! No, you don't get to run away from me. You're always trying to run away from me!" She shoved me again, pushing me back a step as her sudden anger took me by surprise. "But not this time. This time...you will talk to me! We talk things out, remember!"

No, we don't...not anymore. Seeing an opportunity, I shoved her hands off of me and lunged for the doorknob. I had the knob twisted, the door partially cracked open, escape finally showing itself, but then Kiera fucking body slammed the door shut with her shoulder. Fucking bitch. Glaring at her, I snapped, "I've got nothing to say to you. Get out of my way!"

Her eyes glistened with tears. Even furious at her, it tore something inside of me. "Nothing to say? After everything you've done to me?"

For a moment, all my anger shifted into utter shock and disbelief. *Everything...I've done...to her?* What the fuck was she talking about? All I had ever done was love her. Wholly. Completely. *Faithfully*. "Me? What I've done to you?" My jaw tightened as the anger slammed back into me. How dare she try and make this about me. I never betrayed her. Ever. I stepped into her body, pressing her against the door. "You're fucking your ex and I'm the bad guy? Is that how you want to play this, Kiera?"

She shoved me away from her with all her might, catching me off guard again. My hand slipped from the doorknob as I stumbled back, and she instantly shifted over to block it. Fists clenched, fury in her eyes, she shook her head. "I...am...not... sleeping with Denny! And, yes, you—"

I was so sick of hearing her deny it. *I saw, Kiera. I saw*! Not letting her finish her lies, I reached down, grabbed her waist, pulled her into me, away from the door, then lifted her up and physically removed her from my exit. Once she was clear of my escape, I finally again cracked open the door. She instantly grabbed one of my arms with both hands and tugged, stopping me. *Goddamn it, just let me leave*.

Barely able to keep restraining myself, I snapped my eyes to hers. "Let me go, Kiera. I'm done. I don't want to be here anymore." *I can't look at you anymore.*

Heavy tears in her eyes, she spat out, "You weren't done with me ten minutes ago, when you were screwing my brains out!"

I felt like she'd struck me again, and I flinched as pain ripped through me. How could she let me do that? How could she ask for that? Beg for that? How could she kill me like that? Why was she still acting so fucking innocent? "That...was a mistake." All of this was a mistake. Fuck. My entire fucking life was a mistake. Why did I expect this to be any different? How could she do this to me?

She swallowed several times before speaking. I needed to leave. I could feel the anger shifting to despair. I didn't want to feel despair. "You said you believed me," she finally whispered.

Right. *Because I did believe you, Kiera. You fooled me. You genuinely fooled me.* I could feel the tears burning my eyes, I sniffed them back as I shook my head. "And you said you wouldn't lie to me. Goodbye, Kiera."

Her mouth dropped open, and her fingers released my arm, freeing me. Tears fell from her eyes onto her cheeks, and the despair inside me cracked wide open. Agony flashed through my body, mixing with the anger...the hopelessness. *I don't want this. All I ever wanted was you.*

"You said there weren't any goodbyes between us..." she murmured, looking stunned.

How could she still be stunned? How could she cheat on me? How could she ruin us? My eyes closed as my head dropped. All my dreams were gone, all the things I'd stupidly let myself want were over. What was the point now? True, there weren't supposed to be any goodbyes between us. Because we were supposed to be forever. She was supposed to be my wife. She was supposed to have *my* child. Not his.

As I lifted my head to face her one final time, a tear rolled down my cheek; I felt the burn of it, like acid, all the way through my soul. "I said a lot of things that weren't true..." *I told myself you loved me. I told myself you'd be faithful to me. I told myself we'd be together forever.* I was so wrong.

Her breath became frantic, like she was hyperventilating. "Are you breaking up with me?" she whispered.

Her question tore me apart. *No...you broke up with me, the instant you fucked him. This...this is just a formality.* Another tear fell from me as I searched her face, looking for a way out of this hell. But there wasn't one. She was having his baby. She'd slammed the door on us, and I still didn't know why she wouldn't tell me. *Don't I deserve the truth?* It killed me that she wouldn't be honest with me right now. How could I be so wrong about her? It seemed so...hard to believe. So unlike her. Maybe I was wrong. Maybe she...

My eyes drifted down her body to her stomach. Her flat, perfect stomach. The pregnancy tests swam in my vision, choking me with the hard, painful truth. No. I wasn't wrong. She just didn't want to admit she'd failed me. Well, she didn't have to admit it for it to be true. We were over. There was no saving us now.

I lifted my eyes to hers, took a deep, calming breath...and then ripped my own heart out. "Yes, I am." I could barely speak the words, and after I did, I knew I couldn't say anything else.

Kiera started sobbing as she stared at me, still looking absolutely shocked. I couldn't take it, couldn't handle witnessing her pain. Not when this was all her fault. *I didn't break us...you did. Don't cry for me now...now that it's too late.* Turning from her, I fled. I didn't stop moving until I was in my car, didn't let myself think or feel until I'd started my car. It wasn't until I was pulling onto the street that it hit me. And when it did, it was like getting smacked with a wrecking ball—there was nothing of me left.

I managed to pull my car to the curb, managed to put it in park. And then I let out all the anger and pain I'd been holding onto. I yelled until my throat ached, sobbed until my eyes were dry, slammed the steering wheel so hard I nearly broke it. Tossing open the door, I started pacing the street. My hands were in my hair, yanking. My breaths were fast, my heart was pounding...and my stomach was rising. How could she do this to me? How the fuck could she do this to me? *She's having his baby.*

Knowing I was about to lose it, I stumbled to the sidewalk, sank to my knees, and let myself throw up the bile in my empty stomach on a nearby berm. *She's pregnant. She's fucking pregnant. Jesus...I can't do this. I can't deal with this. Haven't I suffered enough for one lifetime?* Why did the universe hate me so fucking much? Why was I so fucking unlovable?

Wiping my mouth, I sat back on my heels. *What do I do now? How the fuck do I keep going? Where do I go?*

Home. It was the only place I could think of.

Pushing myself to my feet, I forced myself back into the car... and tried to ignore the fact that it smelled like her. Goddamn it. Everything was going to remind me of her again, and this time it was going to hurt so much more, because this time...I had too much history to pull from. We'd had a year of being together, and it had been really fucking good. Or at least...I'd thought so. *I guess she didn't agree. I guess she needed more.* Why was I never enough for her?

Lying my head back, I tried to take some deep, calming breaths. I needed to redirect my thoughts, focus on something besides the utter agony of losing her. And that was when I found it...my armor. My head snapped up as I wrapped myself in emotions I was extremely comfortable with: anger, hate, rage. That fucking, betraying bitch. I was better off without her.

Holding tight to the fury, I sped home. The growl of my car matched my mood, and I was reluctant to shut off the engine when I got to my driveway. I would hang out here for a few hours, then go to the airport and rejoin the guys...and never come back to this fucking city again. The guys and I would go to L.A. to record the album, and I would just fucking stay there. I'd stay in L.A., I'd focus on work, and I'd forget all about that two-timing bitch. *You can have her, Denny. Fuck. You lied to me too... you deserve each other.*

Shutting off the car, I ripped my keys out of the ignition. I'd have to have someone bring my car to me. Hire someone. Or maybe Evan would do it for me. Whatever. It didn't fucking matter how, as long as she got to me. My car, my baby...the only "girl" I could count on.

I stroked the steering wheel, silently apologizing for beating the shit out of her again, then I opened the door and got out. My house seemed to mock me as I stepped up to it, and I could almost see my dad in the doorway, smirking at me. "Told you it wouldn't last." I opened my mouth to tell him to fuck off, then shut it. He wasn't actually here. I didn't need to add insanity to my list of problems.

Unlocking my front door, I debated torching the place when I left. That sounded really cathartic. And hazardous for my too-close neighbors. I'd sell it instead...then torch the money. That would work too. *Fuck all of you*.

I slammed my door once I was inside, then debated doing it again. I wanted to hit something, release the rage inside me, but I knew releasing it would let all the other feelings slip inside, and I didn't want to feel them. I had to let this anger simmer, fester, boil. I didn't think I could even drink this away, but I headed to the kitchen anyway. I paced in front of my fridge, flicking glances at the cupboard that held my alcohol. I could drown myself into oblivion, or I could accidentally dull my armor and allow myself to slip into despair. It could go either way, and that fear kept me from trying. All I wanted to feel was hate.

Going back to the entryway, I tossed my keys on the half-moon table and hung up my jacket. I stared at my jacket pocket, at my phone resting inside it. Maybe I should call someone. Evan? He was too far away to help me. Jenny? She was too close to Kiera —I'd just end up yelling at her, and she didn't deserve that. Denny? Denny I wouldn't mind yelling at. Why the fuck didn't he just tell me? Why the fuck didn't he ever mention he was back? I really thought... I know I screwed him over, and he had every right to treat me like shit, but I really thought he was a better person than this. I thought he was better than me. *Guess not.*

Twisting away from my phone, I ran my hands through my hair. I needed to do something; I just had no idea what. I should leave. I should change my flight and go back now. So I could be pissed on the airplane? Assuming I could even get a flight this late? No, I was fucking stuck here, in this fucking hell, until the world fucking opened up again. Why did I even come home?

And that was when there was a soft knock on my door. Who the actual fuck was here at this hour? Stepping over to the door, I cracked it open...and was met with Kiera's fucking face. Goddamn it. She could never just leave me alone. *What more do you want from me? I already gave you absolutely everything.* Rolling my eyes, I slammed the door in her face. *I'm not playing by your rules anymore. This is my house, and you're no longer welcome.*

As I walked away from the door, I instantly realized I should have locked it. Kiera stepped inside, slamming the door behind her. I flinched at the unexpected sound, then turned to face her. *Bitch. You have no right to be here. None.*

I ran my hand through my hair with an annoyed sigh. "I'm not doing this, Kiera. I'm not having this conversation again... we're over." I was so pissed those words didn't even faze me anymore. Almost.

Holding onto the heat in my stomach, I turned away from her. She grabbed my arm. "No, we're not, Kellan! Not until you tell me the truth."

Truth? Everything about that word set me off. "You first!" I snapped, turning to face her.

With a sigh, she released my arm and tossed her hands into the air. "I did! I told you the truth about Denny. Nothing happened! Goddamn it, why don't you believe that anymore? Or did you ever really believe me? Was that a lie just to have sex with me one last time?"

Shock and disgust flooded through me. She actually thought

I would do that? "You think I knew that I was going to break up with you before I slept with you? You think I'd even touch you if I knew what I know now!" My eyes flashed to her stomach as rage boiled inside me. How the fuck could she accuse me of that after what *she* did?

Her cheeks flushed with embarrassment...or anger. "And what the hell do you think you know!"

I backed away from her, disbelieving her absolute refusal to tell me her real secret. "You still can't be honest, can you?" *Fine. Then I'll be honest for you...bitch.* "I saw, Kiera. I saw the tests...the positive tests." Hurt tried to find a way through my cracks; I forced it down as I took a step toward her. "You shoved them in *my* drawer, with *my* clothes, just so I'd find them! Did you really think I'd stick around once I did?"

Her jaw dropped and her face paled. *Yeah...got you. Tests don't lie...just you.* She took a step back. "What are you talking about?" she asked.

Oh my fucking God. Still? Still, she was going to refuse to admit that she... "I know you're fucking pregnant, Kiera, so stop acting like you're fucking innocent!"

She stared at me, stunned silent for a second, then she had the nerve to start shaking her head. Defiant to the very fucking end. I didn't let her speak. "Don't even try to deny it now. Not now, now that you know I know. Admit it, Kiera. Admit the truth... for once in your life."

It had taken her so long to be honest with me, to admit she loved me, and now...now I wasn't sure if *that* was even true. If she loved me, how could she do this to me? She lied about Denny being in town, and she was lying about this too. She'd fucked him...and now I was fucked. The cracks in my armor started widening, allowing more and more acidic pain to seep inside, and I felt my expression shift from rage to grief. Holding onto the anger was getting harder and harder the longer she stayed here, tormenting me.

Kiera helped restoke the angry flame though. She shook her head, still fucking denying it. "Kellan, no, Denny and I didn't—"

Her hands reached out for me, like she wanted to fucking hold me, and I shoved her away. She didn't get to touch me anymore. Not after letting him... Not after repeatedly denying the truth. Whatever lie she thought she was going to sell me right now, it wouldn't work. Because I'd already caught her in a lie tonight. She knew it, I knew it. And she couldn't deny *that* one... because I'd been there when *he* had left her apartment earlier.

"Don't, Kiera. Don't give me another half-truth. You lied about Denny being here!" She started shaking her head, and I spat out, "No, Kiera, a lie of omission is still a lie!" Leaning forward, I whispered, "You should know that better than anyone." Our lie, our secret...most of the time, especially in the beginning, it hadn't been a straight-up, bold-faced denial to Denny, to our friends. We'd simply...never mentioned it.

Her face fell. She looked completely defeated, but still, she tried to lie. "I've only been with you..."

Unbelievable. Un-fucking-believable. "Until today, we haven't had sex since December..." My eyes purposely lowered to her stomach—the proof of her deception. "And I intimately know that you're not showing yet, so you're not four or five months along." My eyes snapped up to hers, the hate inside me re-hardening my shell. "I'm not stupid, Kiera...I know the kid isn't mine." *Just stop lying. Please...just fucking stop.*

After a rough swallow, she opened her mouth. Anticipating another denial, my rage steamrolled right over her. I got in her face, and let the hatred spill out of me in an unexpected way. "If you're still going to try denying that you slept with Denny, then go ahead, Kiera...tell me the only thing you can. Tell me you were raped. I dare you."

I almost couldn't believe I said it, and a part of me wanted to take it back, but...fuck...when was she going to be fucking honest with me? And really, if she was still going to deny the truth, then what else could she say to explain being pregnant? An odd sense of understanding flashed through me then. Was this how my father felt when he'd confronted my mother? His unrelenting hatred toward me was not something I could ever forgive him for, but with how I felt right now, now that I was in his shoes...I almost felt sympathy for him. Almost.

I never in a million years thought Kiera would have something in common with my mother. That she would do to me what Mom had done to Dad. It sickened me. *I can't handle this.*

Kiera's jaw dropped as I unflinchingly stared at her. I saw the anger building in her eyes, and from her expression, I knew what she was going to do. I did nothing to stop her, did nothing to defend myself. I welcomed the pain. *Go ahead...hit me. You'll only prove how like them you are.* Her hand started moving toward my face, but then...she stopped herself. Her fingers dropped from the air. In defeat. Because she was lying about Denny, and we both knew it.

My lips twitched into a smirk. That was the closest to an admission that I was going to get from her, and I would take it. Shaking my head, I told her, "You can leave now."

Tears burned in her eyes again. "You're so wrong..."

Not wanting to watch her pain again, not wanting to hear her lies again, I turned around and walked away from her. Even still, I couldn't help but toss out a sarcastic, "Am I?"

The bitch started following me, and I cursed myself for antagonizing her. I should have left it alone. "Yes, you are completely off on this one," she snipped. "I didn't sleep with Denny. I didn't sleep with anyone. I'm not the one who—"

She stopped talking when she heard an annoying, frustrating, ill-timed chirp coming from my jacket pocket—from the phone in my jacket pocket. Her eyes narrowed in anger at me, then she dashed for the phone.

Our conversation dropped from my mind the second I realized what she was going to do. Jesus fucking Christ...no. If she responded to him, if she engaged him, he'd never fucking leave me alone. I couldn't handle that future. I could barely handle the present. "Kiera, no!" I'd never felt more desperate as I yelled at her.

She didn't care though, and she didn't stop. She grabbed the phone out of my pocket and was reading the message before I could get near her. Hearing her say Gavin's words out loud hit me like a two-by-four to the stomach. "Call me. I need to see you."

Her voice seethed with anger, but I was too shocked, stunned, and sickened to say anything. *Call me...I need to see you.* I'd done so much to never see his words, to never let my eyes read his messages, and here she was, ruining all of that, ripping down my walls like she'd ripped apart my heart. Goddamn it. Why the fuck was she being so cruel? She was right. I was wrong...about *her*.

Hoping beyond hope that she'd stop hurting me, that she wouldn't fucking respond to him, I held out my hand for the phone; my fingers were shaking. "Please, give it back, Kiera." *Please. This isn't about us.*

Her fingers clenched around the phone, and she held it tight to her body. Face red with anger, she shook her head. "No, no, I think I'll text the hussy back."

Fuck...no. She looked down and started typing something, and my body reacted out of pure, fear-based, survival-mode instinct. Rushing over to her, I simultaneously grabbed the phone with one hand and shoved her with the other. I ended up pushing her into the coat hooks along the wall, and her face flashed with pain. I hadn't meant to hurt her, and a stab of guilt went through me. It was quickly replaced by a tidal wave of relief. She hadn't completed the message. Gavin wouldn't get his hopes up. And maybe one day he'd actually leave me the fuck alone.

Betrayal on her face, tears in her eyes, Kiera shook her head. "Who's the liar now, Kellan?"

I knew what it looked like, I knew what she thought, but she was wrong, and our lies were *not* comparable. I shook my head at her. "This is different. This isn't about you and me."

Her hands went to her hips, her stance demanding. "Then tell me the truth. What are you hiding?"

A brief second of panic went through me as I contemplated how to tell her. But then, as my eyes drifted to her stomach, I remembered...I didn't have to tell her anything. Not anymore. We weren't together anymore, and she was still fucking lying to me. My jaw tightening, I snapped, "It doesn't concern you and I don't have to tell you anything anymore."

The tears poured down her cheeks now and seeing them still sent a crack of pain through me. She tossed her hands into the air, like she was giving up. "Fine, keep your fucking secrets, Kellan." The swear was jarring coming from her, but I didn't let it—or her tears—weaken my resolve. She didn't get to know about Gavin. Not anymore. She didn't get to know *anything* about me anymore.

Kiera twisted to the front door, finally fucking leaving. She opened it, then paused. Half turning her head to me, she said, "And just so you know, I'm not pregnant, asshole. Anna is. Griffin knocked her up in Boise and she's freaking out about it." Then she stepped outside and slammed the door shut behind her.

All the air left me in a rush, and I couldn't fucking breathe. Anna was pregnant? *Anna*? That thought had never once occurred to me, but it made perfect fucking sense. It matched all of Kiera's objections, it fit the timeline, it completely evaporated all of the cruelty that had seemed so incomprehensible coming from Kiera. It completely altered our fight, completely changed the narrative. It made me seem completely...

Oh my fucking god...I was wrong. I was fucking wrong, and I just...

I just ruined *everything*.

My phone dropped from my fingers, and I almost fell to my knees and started sobbing as the truth pummeled me to pieces. She wasn't pregnant, she hadn't lied, Denny hadn't lied. She'd been telling me the truth from the beginning, and I'd refused to listen. I'd shoved her away from me and now...

Panic made me toss open the door. She wasn't gone yet. I could fix this. Somehow, I could fucking fix this. Running outside, I instantly spotted her walking across the street. She was walking? Why the fuck was she walking? How did she even get here? I didn't have time to worry about it. She was leaving. I couldn't let her leave. Not with us broken like this.

"Kiera, wait! Stop!" She didn't listen to me, just kept storming away from me. I didn't blame her. I was such a dick. I ran to catch up to her. She was on the sidewalk, on the other side of the street. I grabbed her arm, making her stop and face me.

Her eyes were pure fury as she took in my stunned expression. "Anna? Anna's pregnant?"

She ripped her arm away from me and raised her chin. The heat from her expression immediately took all the chill out of the air around us. "Yes," she bit out.

The one clipped word felt like a strike. Goddamn it. God-fucking-damn it. What did I do to us? I tried to touch her arm again, pull her into me, but she moved away. "Why didn't you tell me?" I whispered, heartbroken for us. She had to have known for a while. Why would she keep that a secret from me?

She sighed, and I saw some of her anger shift to conflict, confusion. "Anna made me promise not to say anything." Her head dropped, along with her voice. "She's not sure if she's going...to keep it."

Not going to keep it? Did she mean...? Was Anna going to...? Fuck. It was her choice, of course, she could do what she felt she needed to do, but the baby was part Griffin...and Anna and Griffin, they were both so important to me. They were family. I *wanted* this baby to happen. For the two of them...and for me. Maybe that was selfish of me to want that, but I did. Maybe it was because the situation hit way too close to home. My mother could have easily made that choice with me. In fact, there were days when I'd been shocked that she hadn't. I think the only reason she'd kept me, was the vague hope that Gavin would change his mind and come back to her. But he hadn't, and I'd paid the price for it. Daily.

Needing to know Anna's intentions, I cautiously asked, "She's not...she's not going to...?"

I couldn't even say it, but Kiera understood my question. She shook her head. "No, she's going through with the pregnancy, she's just not sure about...adoption." Kiera sighed, and I saw the pain and sadness in her. She wanted this baby too. She'd been helping Anna deal with this all alone, and it had clearly been eating at her. I wanted to hold her, but I knew she wouldn't let me yet. How badly had I messed us up? *You broke up with her, dickwad. It's pretty fucking bad*.

I let out a long exhale as I absorbed Kiera's answer. "Oh, good, I'd hate for..."

I still couldn't say it. I just kept picturing my mom and my dad and Gavin and myself, and the whole fucked-up mess of my existence. But Mom had kept me, and Anna was keeping her baby too, and that was good. At least the child would have a chance, like me. Maybe a better chance than me. But not with adoption. Sure, that would have been an improvement in my case, but Anna and Griffin...they weren't my parents. They could do this. We would all help them. They wouldn't be alone. We would all love that baby...so much.

Fuck. I almost couldn't believe one of us was going to be a father. And of course, it would be the most irresponsible one of us. Rolling my eyes, I muttered, "Damn, Griffin...I'm gonna kill him..."

Kiera, done with her part of the conversation, started walking away from me. I rushed forward and grabbed her arm, stopping her again. "Wait...please." She was slow to look back at me. *How can I fix this*? I tried simple, honest remorse. "I'm sorry, Kiera... please don't walk away."

Heat in her eyes, she removed my hand from her arm. "You basically called me a whore and said you never wanted to see me again. Why shouldn't I walk away?"

I hung my head as shame struck me. I should have at least *tried* to listen to her. "I didn't know." Knowing that was a pale excuse, I peeked up at her. "I thought…Seeing Denny here…and then…those tests…" The pain of betrayal was still inside me, even though I knew I was wrong about her. I closed my eyes. "I just thought…I thought what happened to my dad was happening to me. I thought you had another man's baby in you. I was just…angry. I've never felt that ill…" I made myself open my eyes and look at her. "I'm so sorry that I didn't believe you."

She nodded, her face looking accepting, like she understood, and I nearly crumpled in relief. Maybe there was still hope for us. God, I wanted that to be true. I moved to hug her…but she pushed me away. Some of my hope died as I gave her a questioning look. She narrowed her eyes at me; they were still holding a huge well of anger. Lifting her right hand, she pointedly showed me the ring on her finger.

"I kept my promise…I was faithful." She jerked her thumb back toward my house…back toward my phone. "Were you?"

Fuck. I chewed on my lip as I looked back at the house. I didn't know how to explain without…explaining. And I still, even now, didn't want to tell her. Not completely. A part of me desperately wanted to hide. Looking back at her, my eyes fixated on her ring, then down to mine. How could I *not* tell her after everything I'd just accused her of? Goddamn it. "Kiera…it's not what you think." *Can we leave it at that?*

But of course, she wasn't going to accept a non-answer anymore. No more half-truths from me either. She grabbed my cheek, making me lift my gaze. "I don't know what to think because you won't talk to me. What does that text mean?" There was heat in her voice still. And pain. So much pain. *She thinks you're having an affair…just fucking tell her.*

How?

I started to panic as I felt the walls closing in on me. There was nowhere left to run, nowhere left to hide, and that was all I wanted to do. *I don't want to deal with this. I don't want to talk about this. Just accept that I'm not doing anything. Just let me sweep this under the rug again.* "I can't...I don't think I can..." I couldn't even tell her that I couldn't fucking talk about it. I felt like I couldn't breathe. How did she expect me to get the words out when all I wanted to do was run? *Let me go so I can run.*

She shook her head, fury in her eyes. "You have to tell me now, Kellan, because this is tearing us apart."

I know. I'm sorry.

Kiera pointed at the stop sign at the end of the street. "Tell me now...or I keep walking and we really do end this."

The panic and fear shifted to desolation at the thought of her being gone. *I can't go on without you.* My eyes stung as the agony welled inside me. Shaking my head, I pleaded with her to stay. "Please, don't leave me." *But don't make me talk either.*

She lifted her eyebrows, waiting. She wasn't going to cave, and she wasn't bluffing. If I didn't open up to her right now, she was going to leave me. I was going to lose her. *I don't want to lose her.* Gavin wasn't worth losing her. I had to find the courage. I had to rip off the Band-aid.

I tried to swallow the knot in my throat, tried to scrub away the pain in my eyes. It wasn't working. I felt like I was breaking apart. "Ugh. Goddamn it..." Why was everything so fucking hard? Closing my eyes, I inhaled a few deep breaths. This wasn't optional anymore. It just...was. Resisting was getting me nowhere; it was just digging a deeper hole. I felt empty inside when I opened my eyes and looked at her. There was concern on her face. And fear.

"Okay, I'll tell you." I glanced around the street; the openness was suffocating. "But not here, all right...let's go back inside..."

She released a tension-filled breath, and I grabbed her hand. She let me take it, let me lead her back to the house. Where I was about to crack myself wide open.

Chapter 31
TIME FOR PAIN

I indicated for Kiera to sit when we got back inside the house. She did as I asked, silently sitting down on the couch in the living room. I knew I couldn't join her. I couldn't calmly sit beside her while I did this. There was too much...energy inside me. Too much anxiety. I felt sweaty, and sick, and would have given anything to not be here. But I didn't have a choice anymore. Losing Kiera wasn't an option. Not if I could do something to stop it. Even if that something was extremely difficult.

I paced in front of her, occasionally wiping my clammy palms on my jeans as my heart raced inside my chest. I could see Kiera's nerves increasing as she watched me, and I knew I was making this harder for her. She had to think I was lying, she had to think I was hiding an affair. I wished I could calm down, for her sake, but fuck...this was killing me.

My mouth felt glued shut, and I didn't know how to start the conversation. *So, I ran into my sister who gave all my information to my father who now stalks me daily.* Sounded so easy to say...but it wasn't.

Kiera seemed to sense that I was incapable of beginning this conversation. "Who was that on the phone?" she softly asked.

Her words stopped me cold. Feeling a headache coming, I

pinched the bridge of my nose. "Ugh, I can't...start there, Kiera." I needed to ease into this. I needed...distance from the immediate answer.

Kiera nodded and waited. I stood in front of her for a second, feeling the heaviness of weariness settle around me. God, I was so used to feeling that way now...exhausted to the core. I ran a hand down my face, wishing I remembered what it felt like to be unburdened. Shaking my head, I started at the beginning. "Back in December, a girl came up to me backstage."

All of the blood drained from Kiera's face. I knew what she was thinking, and I knew I shouldn't have said it that way, but it was the only way I could begin. Gently. Softly. I hated seeing Kiera's pain, so I made myself continue. She wouldn't hurt for long. But I would. "She told me..."

My throat went dry, and I swallowed to relieve the ache. Kiera's expression changed during my pause, like she'd just realized the truth. Seeing it filled me with hope. Maybe I wouldn't have to say it, maybe she'd just know. But then she said, "She told you that you have a child...right? Sometime in your life, you weren't safe...and now, somewhere out there, you've got a kid."

My hope vanished as she got it wrong. She still thought this was about sex. About a woman I'd been with, either past or present. But it wasn't. Not at all. It was so much worse. For me, at least. I'd almost prefer it if this had been about a child. But then I saw the sadness on Kiera's face, the despair in her eyes as a tear rolled down her cheek. For her, a child with another woman was the nightmare. Did she want to be the first to have my kid? The only one to have my children? I wanted that too, and she could still have that...if she didn't leave me.

Squatting in front of her, I cupped her cheek and assuaged her fears. "No, Kiera...that's not it at all." With a sigh, I rested my head against hers. "There isn't a miniature version of me out there anywhere, Kiera...okay?"

She swiped her fingers under her eyes, looking more confused than ever. "Then what is it, Kellan? Because I really don't understand."

I hated this, hated the pain I was causing her, hated the pain I was causing myself. I sat back on my heels with my head down. "I know you don't. And I know it seems like I'm hiding an affair..." I looked up at her, hoping against hope that she could just see the answer—the *right* answer. *You know me better than anyone. Please. See the truth.* "Do you really not see, knowing what you know about me, what might make me...lie to you?"

She flinched at hearing me admit that I'd lied. More tears streamed down her face and the guilt inside me grew exponentially. I wanted to apologize for ever lying to her, but an apology wasn't what she wanted to hear. She wanted an explanation. She wanted the truth.

She shook her head at me, still not having a clue, and I let out a heavy sigh. There was no easy way out for me. I was just going to have to tell her. I closed my eyes and prayed for strength. "She told me that she wanted me to meet...her father."

Just saying it tore me open, and I could feel the tears springing to life as I looked up at Kiera. She still seemed confused. "Father? That's...odd."

No. The way I phrased it was odd. Again, I was being a coward, trying to tell her without actually telling her. Annoyed at myself, I gave her a sad, sarcastic smile. "Yeah, well, she seems to think that...he might be my father too." *And he is. Fuck me...he is.*

I could see Kiera's confusion slowly shifting to realization. But because I'd said it so weirdly, it took her a few seconds to get there. "Your father too? So, she's your...? Wait, your father? Your biological father? Is he? Is she...your sister?"

Every word, every question...it was a sword through the gut. I wanted to walk away, no, I wanted to *run* away, anything to stop talking about this, but I knew I had to stay. She needed to understand, so she didn't leave me. "Yes, she showed me an old picture of him and even if the resemblance didn't make it painfully obvious…I'd seen the same picture before. Mom showed it to me once…"

My eyes filled to the brim as the memory of that moment seared me. Mom, drunk, screaming at me as she held the photo an inch from my face, telling me who he was and how I'd messed up their relationship by having the audacity to be conceived. "You ruin everything!" she'd yelled at me. And she was right. I did ruin everything. But I wasn't alone in that first one. Gavin started this. Gavin left her because of me. Gavin left *me*.

I swallowed back the pain as I held Kiera's gaze. "And I can't, Kiera, I just can't see him…I can't do it." I *won't* do it.

Kiera just looked at me for a moment, shocked, but then she leaned forward and cupped my cheeks. I felt trapped as I stared at her, and I had to resist the urge to scramble away from her. I knew where this was going, I knew what she was going to want from me. It was the entire reason I didn't tell her in the first place.

"Why didn't you ever say anything to me?" she asked, looking hurt. And confused.

I hated her pain, but it was *nothing* compared to mine. I shook my head. "I know you. You'd want me to meet with him. You'd want me to have some…bonding family moment with him…and I…I can't, Kiera."

She sighed as she stroked my cheek, and I felt the request coming. It made my heart race. "He's your family, Kellan…"

I jumped to my feet, finally moving away from her. *Family*? Bullshit. "No, no, he's nothing to me!" I ran my hands through my hair as I looked around, looked for escape. There was none. Everywhere I turned I saw my parents. And Gavin. And a lifetime of pain. "He left me. He took off and abandoned me. He let me grow up with…*those*…people."

Every hit started replaying in my mind. Every word of derision. Every glance of contempt. Every bitter, spiteful comment, every moment when they'd shoved me away from them, every time when I'd stupidly tried to get them to love me…and failed miserably. And Jesus Christ…I *still* wanted them to love me. How fucked up was that? That after everything, I still wished for that? And it was all Gavin's fault. "He wanted nothing to do with me... so I want nothing to do with him..."

My voice cracked. My entire body was shaking, and I couldn't stop it. I felt like I was vibrating apart, repeatedly ripping into small pieces. I didn't want to be here, but there was nowhere for me to go—no relief from the pain.

Kiera stood up. She stepped into my body, ran her hand up my chest, to the tightness of my jaw. I couldn't look at her, I couldn't look anywhere. The past wasn't leaving me; I felt like I was drowning in it. When Kiera spoke, her voice was soft, like she wanted to be soothing, but what she said was anything but soothing. "He didn't know what situation he was leaving you in. How could he? Maybe he thought he was doing you a favor by stepping away, by not permanently breaking up the family he'd already...damaged."

A word she'd used burned through my fog of pain. My eyes locked on hers. "A favor? My dad used to whip me with his belt when he got angry. He'd hit me so hard that I had to sleep on my stomach for days afterward. And I learned early on that running away from him would only make it worse when he did catch me. So, I had to stand there, like a dog, and let him beat me. How is that...a favor?"

I hadn't meant to confess that, and the tears in my eyes grew heavy as I took in Kiera's horrified expression. She swallowed back her emotion so she could speak, and once she did, I instantly wished she hadn't. "He didn't know...Maybe you should see him so you can tell him, so you can finally talk about this stuff with someone."

I didn't need her implying that I was broken again. I wasn't. Needing movement, I brushed past her. "I don't need to talk about it, Kiera. I'm fine." I started pacing, started embracing the anger I felt brewing. "And I don't need to see him...ever. Besides, I do have family. I have one aunt who despises me as much as my mom did. But I don't care. I don't need them. I'm fine on my own." I strongly suspected Mom had told her sister the lie, that I was the result of her being raped, and that was why my aunt hated me. I wasn't sure...I'd never asked her, and I was never *going* to ask her. Because none of it fucking mattered.

Kiera stepped in front of me, halting my movement and calling me on my bluff. "That's just it, you aren't on your own anymore. You have family members out there that want to get to know you." I tried to look away, but she followed me, reinserting herself in my eyeline. "You have a sister, Kellan...don't you want to know her?"

That eased some of my anger. Yes, I did want to know her. And Riley. Looking over Kiera's shoulder, I told her that my family was bigger than she knew. "Hailey told me I have a brother too..." A brother I'd yet to talk to directly. I hated that I hadn't.

There was happiness in Kiera's voice when she said, "Hailey? Is that your sister?"

I nodded, then looked down at her. "I gave her my cell number once she told me who she was, and we've kept in contact." Remembering our conversations made me smile, made me laugh a little. "She's pretty funny. Pretty smart too. We've been talking a lot lately...she's a good kid."

Kiera's eyes widened. "That's who Jenny saw you talking to on the phone when she was visiting Evan? Your sister, right?"

Confused, I shook my head. "Jenny? In Texas?" Glancing away, I tried to remember Jenny's visit. I supposed I had been on the phone with Hailey a few times while she'd been there, but why would Kiera ask Jenny about that? Why would me on the phone seem weird to her? Unless...

My eyes returned to Kiera. "Is that why you thought I was cheating on you? Because Jenny saw me laughing on the phone with someone else?"

She looked remorseful, but she nodded. Pointing to my jacket, to where I'd returned my phone after picking it up off the floor, she frowned and said, "Plus all of the mysterious texts you wouldn't let me see. You have to admit that was kind of suspicious."

I saw the flash of pain on her face, heard it in her voice. I'd purposely shut her out, and she knew it. She'd known it for a while, she just hadn't known why. She'd thought the worst, and I couldn't blame her. I had thought the worst about her too. I softly grabbed her cheeks. "I'm sorry...I never meant for any of this to hurt you. I just wasn't ready..." I dropped my gaze as that damn guilt returned. "I wanted to tell you, so many times...but I couldn't make myself say the words." I lifted my eyes to hers and shrugged. "It was like, if I told you...it was real...and I wanted to pretend that it wasn't." Grief washed through me, and I closed my eyes. "I just wanted to ignore it—ignore him—but Hailey gave him my number, and he texts me every day... every goddamn day..." He was so fucking relentless. I couldn't take it.

Releasing her face, I tried to stave off the headache I felt returning. "Every day he sends me messages, and every day I ignore him." I lifted my head to the ceiling, feeling more worn than ever. "And I'm getting so tired of it all...I just want him to leave me alone."

Looking at her again, I sighed. "I even thought about changing my number, so he wouldn't have it anymore, but...I wanted to still be able to talk to you. And I couldn't exactly tell you why I wanted to change it without...telling you why I wanted to change it. So, I get painful texts every day that I try to forget about." *And fail to forget about.*

I could feel the emotion rising, starting to choke me again, and I scrubbed my eyes, trying to get rid of the pain. Kiera gently rubbed my shoulder. "This is killing you, Kellan, don't you see that?"

I gave her a darkly amused smile. I doubted I was actually dying because of this. Just emotionally dying...but that was different. That was survivable. This just...sucked. Kiera shook her head as she examined me. "No, it is. It's eating at you...I can see it now.

Have you talked with anyone about this? The guys? Evan? Have you been dealing with this alone...all this time?"

Of course, I've been dealing with it alone. Alone is my default setting. I fell onto the couch, too tired to keep standing. "Who would I tell, Kiera? Everyone thinks my dad died with my mom." I looked up at her and shrugged. "You're the only one I've ever been able to tell about my dad...not being my real dad. I just can't get the words out around other people. Just you..." I supposed Hailey knew that much, but she knew nothing about the abuse—I'd never given her a real reason why I didn't want to see Gavin. Kiera was the only one who knew all my dark corners. And still I'd kept quiet. It just...hurt too much.

Kiera sat beside me on the couch. Putting a hand on my knee, she called me out on the thought I'd just had. "But your real dad contacting you...? You had to keep that from me?"

I could hear the sadness in her voice, and I looked away from her. "I didn't want to, and I did try to tell you a couple of times..." My eyes returned to hers. "It was just too hard...too fresh." My gaze drifted to the floor. "I'm sorry if I hurt you..."

She grabbed my head and pulled me into her body. I reveled in the warmth I didn't deserve. *I should have told her.* "It's okay," she whispered. "I get it."

Letting out a relieved exhale, I wrapped my arms around her. In a soft voice, she asked, "Christmas Day...was that text really from Griffin?"

I stiffened as I realized she'd known I'd been lying. Fuck. Pulling back, guilt in my heart, pain in my eyes, I shook my head. "No...that was from him." I cupped her cheek, hoping she could forgive me for this too. "I'm so sorry I lied...I just didn't want you to ask...I wasn't ready."

Tears rolled down her cheeks, killing me, but she nodded. "All those texts...?"

Knowing what she was asking, I quickly told her, "Were from him, I promise." Needing her, I gave her a gentle kiss. Her lips softened the ache around my heart, made my confession easier to bear. "They were all from him. I'll let you look at them if you want, if you don't believe me, but that's all I've been hiding...I promise." I kissed her again. "I promise..."

She kissed me back, then whispered, "I believe you."

My fingers shifted to her neck as our mouths moved together. The intoxication of touching her again was chipping away at the pain. But not quickly enough. I still felt rubbed raw. I needed more. I needed to stop thinking, stop feeling. I needed her to distract me. Would she do that for me? Were we...okay enough for that? I needed her so much right now, needed to know if she could be on the same page as me. I deepened the kiss, experimenting with her forgiveness.

She pulled away, but I saw passion in her eyes, not rejection. The way she searched my face though...I wasn't sure what she saw, but it was enough to make her concerned. "You need to see him, Kellan. You need to put this chapter behind you, so you can move forward."

Annoyance shot up my spine. Shaking my head, I tried to find her lips again. The only thing I needed was for us to stop talking about it. She knew everything, knew all my secrets...that was how I was putting the past behind me.

I almost reconnected with her lips, but she firmly held me back. "You need to," she said again.

The annoyance shifted to anger, and I compressed my lips tight so that I didn't say something rash. I inhaled a deep breath, but it did nothing to calm me. Shaking my head again, I told her, "This is exactly why I didn't want to tell you." All those other reasons applied too, but *this* was the biggest reason I held back. I knew she wouldn't let it go.

She opened her mouth to say something, but I shook my head again and cut her off. "No, you can save all of your logical reasons and philosophical viewpoints. I will never see that man. Got it?" *I don't give a shit if it doesn't make any sense to you. It's what I want.*

Not allowing her time to try and debate with me, since her

opinion was irrelevant, I shot up off the couch and headed for the stairs. If she couldn't be on board with this...I wasn't sure what that meant for us. *Just let me have this, please.*

Kiera didn't follow me as I headed for my room, and I was grateful for the space. I just needed a minute to calm the fuck down. I paced near my bed, my hands clenching and unclenching. I really wanted to hit something, but what I really wanted to hit—*who* I really wanted to hit—wasn't here. Kiera was wrong. I didn't need to see him. What I needed was to *never* see him. Or hear from him. I needed to go back to that time when I had no idea where he was or if he was even alive. The ignorance had been bliss. I didn't think about him, and he didn't think about me. It had been a mutual agreement, one I was more than happy to keep honoring, but for some reason, that fucker got it into his head that I owed him something. But I didn't owe him a fucking thing. If anything, he owed me, but all I wanted from him was for him to be gone.

Collapsing onto my bed, I dropped my head into my hands. Why couldn't he just leave me the fuck alone? What had changed for him? No. It didn't matter what had changed. He gave up his right to know me the minute he left me.

He left me. He hadn't even waited for me to be born, he just...left me. He let them smack me around, tear me down... torture me...for years. He could have saved me, but he didn't. He didn't even try. He just...stopped thinking about me. Stopped caring. Or more accurately, he never *started* caring. I was nothing in his eyes. He'd let me become...nothing.

Lifting my head, I stared at a patched hole in my wall—an outlet for my rage back when I first saw this place, when I saw how my parents had tried to erase me. They'd never cared either. I remembered the day I'd called them after I'd run away, the day I'd let them know I was still alive...months after I'd left home.

Dad answered the phone. "Yes?"

"Hey...it's me." Silence met my ear. *"Kellan,"* I added, feeling like I needed to explain.

"Yes," he said, his voice apathetic. "What do you want?"

"I just...I wanted to let you know...I'm okay."

"All right," he answered, still sounding almost...bored. I wished he would yell at me, call me names...that would have hurt so much less than his disinterest.

My throat tightened up, but I managed to tell him, *"I'm living in L.A. This is my number if you want to reach me..."* He was quiet after I rattled off the number, and I had no idea if he'd written it down. *"Is Mom there?"* I asked, my voice cracking just as much as my heart.

"She's busy."

"Can I talk to her?" I hated that I was pleading. I really hated that he didn't care if I was pleading.

I heard him let out an annoyed sigh, then heard him say to her, *"Kellan wants to talk to you."* There was a brief pause, then his voice returned to me. *"She says she's busy...just like I told you she was."*

The rejection stung. It still fucking stung. *"Just...let her know I'm fine."*

"Yeah. You coming back?" It didn't sound like he cared either way. It was more like he needed to ask so he would know how to plan.

"No." The word felt bitter in my mouth. Cold and unfeeling, just like them. Dad didn't care about that either.

"Okay," he stated.

I felt Kiera's presence in the doorway as that remembered word echoed in my brain. *Okay.* It was okay that I was gone, and it was okay that I was never coming back. It was all just...okay. That was the last conversation I'd ever had with them. Eight months later, they were both dead, and I'd done what I'd said I wouldn't do—I'd come back. I still wasn't entirely sure why.

"Can I come in?" Kiera softly asked.

Making myself disengage from the past, I inhaled a deep breath and looked over to see her leaning against the doorframe. I nodded at her, then returned my eyes to the damaged wall. It felt like looking inside myself. Sure, it was patched-up, fixed to the best of my ability, but it would never look the same. The scar would always be there.

Kiera sat beside me on the bed, then she gently laid her head on my shoulder. I just sat there for a moment, wallowing in the pain of regret and abandonment. Then I let it go. With a weary sigh, I laid my head against Kiera's, choosing to absorb her warmth instead of my pain.

"I'm sorry if that was harsh, Kiera. I'm just...don't push me on this one, okay?" *Please*.

I felt my stomach clenching, tensing for another fight I didn't want to have, but Kiera surprised me. Nodding against my shoulder, she said, "All right, Kellan." I nearly sagged with relief. *Thank God...she's going to let it go.*

We sat there in silence for a long time, resting against each other, recovering from the emotional onslaught. Then finally, Kiera placed her hand over my heart and quietly asked, "How long do you have? Until you have to go back?"

I let out a haggard sigh. *Not long enough*. "I have a flight in the morning, well, in a few hours."

Her fingers clutched at my shirt, like she wanted to hold me here. "I wish you didn't have to go..."

The hope her words gave me hurt so much. I was sure I'd lost her, sure I'd finally shoved her away from me, and even though she'd given me an ultimatum and I'd chosen her over my secret, I still wasn't sure if she wanted...this. I lifted my head from hers and she looked up at me. I couldn't keep the fear from my expression, couldn't stop the ice from flooding my veins. Were we okay? Shaking my head, I whispered the question that could potentially undo me. "Do you still want to be with me?"

She seemed surprised that I would ask that. She shouldn't be. I had broken up with her after all. It wasn't right for me to assume anything about us. Pulling back further, she searched my face. "Of course," she told me. Her hand went to my cheek as my fear started evaporating. "I'm in love with you. Of course, I still want to be with you."

The relief was overwhelming and exhausting. *Thank God*. I looked down at the floor as I remembered all of the horrible things I'd said to her. She deserved so much better than me. Sometimes, I felt like I was holding her back. She should have stayed with Denny. He never would have assumed the worst about her and then not let her explain. He never would have dared her to say she was raped. He was a good guy, easy to get along with. I wasn't so easy. I could be...challenging. I knew that.

"I know I'm not the easiest person to love," I told her. "I thought maybe you'd had enough..." *And I won't blame you if you change your mind right now. You* should *go. You're better off without me.*

Kiera grabbed my chin and made me look at her. Her smile was warm, loving, but it was the compassion in her eyes that struck me. "Loving you, Kellan, is so easy, it's effortless." I smiled at her sentiment. *I hope that's true*. Her smile fell as she stared at me. She sighed, then said, "Trusting you...that's the hard part."

God. Truer words had never been spoken. My gaze drifted to the floor. Was there any hope for us? Feeling broken, I told her, "We messed up, didn't we?"

"What do you mean?" she asked.

I peeked up at her; there was fear on her face. It matched how I felt. I shrugged. "How we got together, the lies, the betrayals... we doomed ourselves before we even started." I felt the despair welling inside as I shook my head. "We love each other so much... and we don't trust each other at all." Push come to shove, we'd both feared the worst about each other, we'd both *believed* the worst about each other. It was so possible that we might hurt each other that it made the thought of us staying together seem... impossible. *Where do we go from here?*

Kiera didn't object to my statement. She couldn't. She knew it was true. Her eyes watered as she stared at me, as she contemplated the hopelessness of our future. Her breath became so fast it was erratic. She tossed her arms around me and squeezed with everything inside her. Panic in her voice, she squeaked out, "Don't leave me."

I wrapped my arms around her, her stress and my pain cinching around me tight. *I can't leave you. Not again. I'm not strong enough.* "I won't," I told her. "I'm yours, Kiera, for as long as you want me." I would never end it with her again. Even if... even if she did cheat on me. Next time, if there was a next time, it would be her choice to end things.

Pulling away, she cupped my cheek and frantically searched my eyes; I could feel them growing heavy with tears. "Forever, I want you forever," she stated.

A tear rolled down my cheek as I stared at her. "I want that too, Kiera." *It's all I've ever wanted.*

She touched her lips to mine, wanting me, needing me. I tried to push out the desolation as I let my love for her consume me. She hadn't betrayed me. I hadn't betrayed her. Our fear of hurting, our fear of pain, that was what made us doubt, and the doubt was what made us not trust each other. But we could work on that. *God, please let us be able to work on that.* I needed her.

Kiera's fingers tugged at the hem of my shirt, lifting it. I paused from her lips to pull it off. Her hands drifted down my stomach to my jeans. While I moved my mouth softly against hers, she unbuttoned my jeans, then carefully unzipped them. I kicked off my boots, then sat up a little, so I could take off the rest of my clothes. Kiera's fingers explored my bare skin while I removed her shirt, her pants, and every last obstacle between us.

When she was as bare as me, I laid her back onto my bed, cherishing every touch. I'd been so sure this would never happen again—could never happen again. My gaze swept down her body, lingering on her flat, empty stomach. I wanted to fill it, wanted to give her my child, but we weren't there yet. Not nearly there yet.

Kiera's hand went to my cheek, bringing my gaze back to her face. There was so much love in her eyes, it tore at me. There was so much compassion in her eyes, it shattered me. I could see what she wanted for me, what she wanted for us...and it restored my hope. Faith. That was how we'd get through this.

Her other hand gently pushed on my hip, urging me on top of her. Our eyes never leaving the others', I settled over her, then slowly slid inside her. The euphoria stole my breath, but it paled compared to the...connection I felt with her. All my life, I'd been looking for *this*. This feeling of belonging, of being wanted, being needed...being loved. And she was giving me that feeling so intensely right now that it hurt...in the best way.

The feeling only grew as we began to move together. It was almost too much to bear, but I didn't shy away from it. I let it overwhelm me. I embraced it, embraced her love for me... accepted it. I searched her face, her glorious eyes filled with tears of love—for me. "I love you, Kellan...only you."

I closed my eyes, letting the words wash over me. Opening them, I told her, "And I only love you...I will only ever love you."

I lowered my mouth to hers, kissing her as slowly as I was moving inside her. The restraint was difficult, but it made me feel so...in tune with her, like we were one. The connection lasted for so long, it felt so good; I never wanted to stop making love to her. This was what I wanted. This was how tonight was supposed to go...before it all fell apart. Before we put it all back together.

Kiera grabbed my hand, squeezing me tight, and I could tell she was getting close. I was too; I could feel the need to find relief building, the urge to release the pressure, satisfy the ache. Instead of quickening the pace, I slowed down...and *everything* amplified. The sensation, the connection, the love...everything. Kiera started shaking beneath me. She was running out of time. I was too. I grabbed her cheek. Sucking in a quick breath, I kissed her, then hurriedly told her, "I love you. God, I love you so much..."

It was all I had time to say. My body shuddered with the intensity of my climax. Kiera came a second after me, her body tightening around me as she rode out the bliss, mumbled words about loving me more than anything escaping from her lips.

A part of me wanted to keep going even though it was over,

but I was so tired, so completely and utterly spent, I just couldn't. I slumped against her body for a second, catching my breath, then I shifted to her side and pulled her into my body. I never wanted to let her go again.

I kissed her hair, grateful for that moment, grateful for this one, grateful for all the future ones we might still get to share. If we could start being honest with each other. Brutally honest. "I promise I won't keep anything from you again," I pledged.

She stared at me a second, her gaze warm and peaceful, her eyes shimmering, then she nodded and softly kissed me. "And I promise that I won't keep anything from you either."

I nodded, accepting her promise, then I squeezed her tight. *Never again*.

Chapter 32
TRYING AGAIN

Kiera drifted off to sleep, but I stayed awake, holding her, stroking her soft skin. I didn't have much time with her, and I didn't want to waste a second of it sleeping. But so much had happened in so little time that I was definitely drained. I was certain the second I was on that plane back to the guys, I would pass out. But for now...I would fight it. Anything to stay with her.

But time was against me, and eventually the clock on my nightstand told me I needed to get up, needed to start getting ready. I did *not* want to...but I owed Matt. And Kiera and I were fine. I could go back and stop worrying, stop stressing, stop causing myself pain. Things would be better now, and that made it a little easier to leave.

And besides, I'd be back. Maybe after the tour ended. Definitely for her graduation. And after she graduated...the world would be wide open for her. Maybe she could come to me then. I couldn't think of a single reason why she couldn't.

With that wonderful thought in my brain, I carefully slipped out of bed. I took a nice, long shower, letting the emotional weariness of the last several hours rinse off of me. Kiera was still zonked when I was done, her bare body sprawled across my bed, under my sheets. I really liked the visual of her draped over my mattress, but I let her sleep and got dressed in some fresh clothes. And then, because I loved her and I *was* going to miss her, I shoved one final note into the pocket of one of her jeans. *Remember today, that I love you.*

I felt like skipping when I went downstairs. Everything just seemed…better. The house was brighter, the air crisper, the day more hopeful. It was like I'd rebooted myself, and everything was running a little smoother now. I loved it.

Humming to myself, I started a pot of coffee. God, I missed having a daily cup of good coffee. Bus coffee and diner coffee just didn't cut it. Kiera was still asleep when the pot finished brewing. Usually, the smell woke her up. Not today though. She was just as drained as me. I drank a quick cup, then grabbed my jacket. My time here was almost over, and I needed to say goodbye to Kiera. For now.

I prepped a cup of coffee for Kiera, since the least I could do was leave her with a treat. Careful to not spill it, I headed upstairs. Wondering if the smell would wake her up now, I squatted by the bed and held it toward her. I grinned as she started stirring. It still worked.

Her eyes slowly opened, then they found me. Ignoring the coffee in my hand, she reached out for me. "Hey," she said, propping up on her elbow to lean over and kiss me.

"Mornin'," I told her.

She giggled at my greeting, then grabbed the coffee cup I was still offering. "You are a godsend," she said, taking a sip.

I laughed softly as I ran a hand through her hair. "You and coffee…"

An intoxicating pink blush ran over her skin. God, I'd missed that too. "What time is your flight?" she asked, glancing at the clock.

Her calm eyes, more brown than green today, returned to me, and my smile widened. She was so beautiful. And still mine. "I have to go soon."

Her eyes widened with alarm, and she sat all the way up, spilling her drink. "Well, I'll get ready. I'll come with you."

Taking her coffee before she burned herself, I set it on the nightstand. Shaking my head, I told her, "No, I want you to stay here and relax." She frowned, but I smiled. "Every separation between us seems to be long and dramatic, like we're never going to see each other again." I paused to run my knuckle down her cheek. "It's like we're...savoring every moment because we both think it might be the last."

She clamped down on her bottom lip and nodded, like she'd had that thought too. My smile grew. "So, let's break out of that cycle." I inhaled a deep breath. "Goodbye, sweetheart. I have to go to work." That was how normal people said goodbye, right?

Kiera grinned. With a small shrug she said, "See ya."

I laughed at her super-casual response, then shook my head at how adorable she was. Leaning forward, I gave her a kiss. "Keep the bed warm for me," I murmured. She laughed as I pulled away. "I'll call you when I land," I told her.

She was nodding when my phone suddenly chimed in my pocket. It was a relief that I didn't have to worry about her hearing it anymore, but it was still annoying to have to hear it. Gavin was never going to give up. Kiera raised a questioning eyebrow as she looked at my pocket. I rolled my eyes and sighed. Pulling out my phone, I glanced at the screen and saw that my assumption was correct. It was Gavin. "That would be my father with his morning message." I raised an eyebrow at her. "There will be an afternoon and an evening one, I'm sure." Probably more. And a few phone calls.

I instantly hit the button that darkened the screen. Kiera frowned as she watched me. "Don't you even read them?"

Sniffing, I shoved the phone back in my pocket. "No. I never read them, and I never respond." I lowered my head as guilt resurfaced. I'd almost forgotten that I'd accidentally hurt her last night when I'd...panicked. "That's why I freaked out when you were going to. I don't want him to be...encouraged." I looked up at her. "I want him to stop."

I thought she might argue again, but surprising me once more, she simply nodded in acceptance. "What does your sister think about you ignoring him?" she asked, then she cringed, like she hadn't meant to ask that.

With a sigh, I moved to sit beside her on the bed. "She thinks I'm being stubborn. She doesn't understand why I'm hurting him by refusing to..." My thought trailed off as I grabbed my phone again. "She asks me to give him a chance, every time I talk to her." A fact that was incredibly frustrating. She wasn't going to leave me alone either. Hailey telling me that stubbornness ran in the family was apparently an understatement.

While I mused on that, I heard Kiera murmur, "Wise girl."

I lifted an eyebrow in annoyance, but Kiera didn't press the issue. Instead, she held out her hand. "Can I read it?" she asked. My eyes involuntarily narrowed as something dark stirred inside me. Seeing my expression, Kiera quickly added, "I won't respond. But I feel like someone should at least read them."

Maybe. Maybe not. I wasn't sure that I owed Gavin anything, but...I did owe Kiera something. And as long as she promised not to talk back to him, I didn't really see the harm in letting her read them. It wouldn't change the fact that *I* wasn't going to read them. My stomach still twisted into knots, though, as I slowly handed her the phone.

She smiled as she took it. Then she held it in her palm and exaggerated the fact that she wasn't going to type anything. I appreciated that. To avoid accidentally seeing what she was reading, I studied her face while she studied my phone. The emotions I saw there were almost as bad as reading the texts though. Her face scrunched in pain, her eyes watered, and she bit her lip like she was trying to hold back a sob. What the hell was he saying to make her look like that?

When a tear finally fell onto her cheek, I couldn't take the curiosity anymore. "What...what did he say?" I asked. Then I instantly wished I hadn't. *It doesn't matter. I don't care.* Except...I did care. Too much. Way too much. Maybe that was the real reason why I'd allowed his messages to continue. Why I'd never deleted them.

Kiera sighed, shook her head, and handed me the phone. I put it away without looking at it, and Kiera's sad eyes lifted to my face. "He just wants a chance to explain. He wants to get to know you." Her hand came up to gently rest on my cheek. "He regrets leaving you, Kellan."

The sudden assault on my heart was too much. I nodded as my eyes began stinging. Her words kept repeating in my brain. *He wants to explain, wants to get to know you...he regrets leaving you.* Well, we all had regrets. That was just life. It didn't mean anything. I tried to swallow back the ache, but it wouldn't leave me. I swallowed multiple times, then finally stood up, needing movement. "I should get going." I should stop thinking, stop feeling...stop resisting? Could I do that?

I was lost in that thought—in the thought of actually talking to Gavin—when I heard Kiera call my name. "Kellan." I stopped in the doorway to look back at her. She was lying down on my bed again, looking completely comfortable wrapped in my sheets. I smiled, staring at her perfect beauty.

"I just wanted to wish you luck on the end of your tour, and tell you..." She paused to chew on her lip. It was adorable, sensual, playful, and seeing it made my smile grow. God, I was lucky. Giggling, she finished with, "I'll be here when you get back."

She indicated the room with her eyes, and my small grin turned into a massive one. I took a step back into the room, toward her. "You're moving back in with me?"

Giggling more, she nodded and sat up, wrapping her arms around her knees. She looked so damn beautiful, and what she'd just said...fuck...it was *everything* to me. But how could she tell me that right before I had to leave? *As if I can leave now.* No, that statement needed to be celebrated.

Shaking my head at her, I tore off my jacket. She suddenly looked confused as she watched me strip off my shirt and unbutton my jeans. "What are you doing? I thought you had to go?"

Smiling at her, I crawled over the bed, making her lie back down. "I've got five minutes," I said. And there was no way on Earth I *wasn't* going to try to make love to her after hearing her say that. She'd literally have to hose me down to turn me off. And I had a feeling she wouldn't.

She giggled as I kissed her. "Five?" she murmured as my hand traveled up her thigh.

Kicking off my boots, I told her, "Okay, fifteen then." Standing up, I stripped off the rest of my pesky clothes, then darted under the sheet with her. She giggled when we collided, but she stopped when my hungry mouth found hers.

Celebrating her momentous news took way longer than fifteen minutes…and I didn't fucking care. I'd miss the damn flight for this. For her. For *us*. Finally…I'd be able to come home to her again. I couldn't fucking wait.

After calling a cab, I gave Kiera one last, long goodbye kiss. We were both grinning when I left, and I took that as a really good sign. I just about missed the flight, but the girl at the gate let me through at the last possible second. By the way she was looking at me, I had a feeling it was my face that had gotten me through the door, but that was okay. Whatever it took to keep Matt off my back.

As predicted, I fell asleep on the plane. I think I was falling asleep before the plane even started moving. I sort of remembered them going through the safety speech, but that was about it. Next thing I knew, an older woman beside me was gently tapping my shoulder. "We're here," she said, her dark eyes warm as she gazed at me.

Lifting my head, I looked over to see people standing up,

beginning to exit. "Oh...thanks," I told her. "Guess I was more tired than I thought. Hope I didn't snore."

She bit her lip as she drank me in. "Nope...not at all." She studied me for a second longer, then shook her head and muttered something that sounded like, "If I were ten years younger..."

I smiled to myself at her comment, then pulled out my phone. Seeing a missed call and a voicemail from Kiera made my grin grow. I listened to the message as I followed the woman off the plane. Kiera was concerned about me telling Griffin he was about to be a father. Or more accurately, *Anna* was the one concerned about it. That made me frown as I stepped into the airport. Griffin as a dad. Jesus. But that was assuming Anna kept the baby...and let Griffin anywhere near it.

I almost wanted to call Anna directly, try and plead Griffin's case for him, but it wasn't my place. And there wasn't anything I could say that Anna didn't already know. She knew exactly who Griffin was and how he would be with a child. It was...difficult to picture. He was just so fucking irresponsible. And he abhorred commitment. The band was just about the only thing he'd ever put an ounce of effort into, and sometimes even that felt...like he'd grow tired of it and walk away one day. But a baby...there was no walking away from that. Or at least, he shouldn't walk away from that. I knew what *I* wanted Anna to do, but I had no idea what she actually *should* do.

Pressing the button to call Kiera, I brought the phone to my ear. I laughed a little when she answered. "Hey, I just landed. Miss me already?"

Her voice low and seductive, she said, "Always."

I smiled at the sentiment, feeling full of warmth and peace, then I asked about her message. "You said your sister was freaking out?"

Kiera sighed. "Yeah, she's just afraid of Griffin finding out... before she's ready to tell him."

A weary sigh escaped me. Fucking Griffin. "I wouldn't...

that's not my secret to share." And I really hoped it wasn't a secret that I would have to carry to my grave. *She should tell him. Either way, Anna should tell him.*

Kiera's response gave me some hope. "Well, I think she will tell him, and I think she's going to keep it...or her, I should say, since Anna is convinced she's having a girl."

That made me grin. With a soft laugh, I told her, "Let's hope so. I think a baby girl to dote on is just what Griffin needs." Maybe he'd learn a thing or two, start seeing women as more than just receptacles for his junk. Maybe.

Kiera suddenly asked a question that surprised me. "Would you want a baby girl one day?"

I smiled again as I thought about that. God, Kiera pregnant with my child...holding a miniature version of her in my arms... what a great image. "Yeah...a girl, or a boy, would be fine, but... yeah, I do want kids." *With you. And only you.*

She laughed a little, then whispered, "Me too." The sound was full of longing, and hearing it made my smile widen. It was so nice to be on the same page again.

A warm silence fell between us, then Kiera sighed. "I should go...are we good?"

Her comment made me laugh. "I didn't convince you of that before I left? Really? You...sounded convinced." I paused, smiling as I pictured her flushed face, then I said, "Yeah, Kiera...I think we're better than we've ever been, actually."

"Even with Denny being back in town?"

I tried to find some part of me that was still worried about him, but it just...wasn't there. If she hadn't done anything with him during our darkest moment, when she'd been pretty sure I'd been cheating on her, then I just couldn't picture her doing anything with him *now*. We were too...as Evan had once said —solid.

A soft, content sigh escaped me. "Yeah, even with Denny in town. I don't know, Kiera, but Denny just doesn't worry me anymore. Maybe...maybe I really do trust you."

She exhaled in relief. "Oh, I'm so glad to hear you say that, Kellan, because there really is nothing there. No one...no one compares to you, Kellan. No one even comes close."

I had to close my eyes as a rush of desire—and love—went through me. "God, you're making me wish we were back in my bed when you say stuff like that." Kiera let out an adorable giggle, and I softly laughed. "I feel the same way, Kiera. No one comes close to you in my eyes...no one."

"I love you. I'll see you in a few weeks."

I smiled, excited and impatient to see her again. "Okay, I love you too."

Shoving my phone back in my pocket, I took a minute to cherish the happiness inside me, to wrap myself around the multiple wonderful futures that were now possible for Kiera and me. Living with her again, marrying her, having children with her...I felt like I could do anything with her firmly beside me, and when I heard my phone chirp with another message—a message that I just knew was from Gavin—it barely even fazed me. With Kiera in on the secret, supporting me through the pain, ignoring him was so much easier. *I should have told her from the beginning*.

Knowing that dwelling on regret would get me nowhere, I started heading for the taxi line so I could get back to the guys... where another man with unknown regrets was waiting in oblivious bliss. What the fuck was I going to do about Griffin? What was I going to say around him? Not mentioning this was going to be harder than I thought, because I really wanted to fucking yell at him. And then have Matt yell at him. But I couldn't. This was between him and Anna, and I had to stay out of their way. But that didn't mean I couldn't occasionally smack Griffin upside the head for no apparent reason.

I texted Matt that I was here, then asked him to remind me of the name of the hotel so I could give it to the taxi driver. Matt's response was instant. As I held my phone, I debated calling Denny. I probably owed him an apology. Or did I? It wasn't like he'd felt the need to tell me he was in town. Was that because

Kiera had asked him not to tell me? Or because he hadn't wanted me to know? Or maybe it was just because we really hadn't talked all that much since I'd left. With the tour, and Gavin, and the record deal, and the oddness with Kiera...I just hadn't had time for Denny. I felt kind of bad about that.

Shaking my head, I typed him a brief message. '*I'm sorry I yelled at you.*'

His response was surprisingly quick. '*I'm sorry I didn't tell you I was here. I wasn't trying to hide anything from you.*'

I bit my lip, wondering if that was true. But it was Denny...it had to be true. '*Kiera asked you not to tell me, didn't she?*'

His response was simple. '*Yes.*' Then he added, '*She was worried you'd leave the tour.*'

I frowned as I debated that. Would I have left? If she'd told me in the beginning? Fuck...maybe. Shaking my head, I told him, '*She might have been right.*'

Denny didn't respond for a while. I was starting to put my phone back in my pocket when he finally did. '*You don't have to worry about me. I don't want her.*'

His brutal honesty was surprisingly refreshing. '*I know. I'm glad you're happy.*'

His response again took some time. '*Thanks. But I think you missed the obvious follow-up to my statement.*'

I tilted my head, confused. '*And what's that?*'

'*She doesn't want me either, mate. She loves you. I think she always has.*'

I had to close my eyes at that. Jesus Christ. This was why I would never measure up to Denny. He was just...a thousand times a better person than I would ever be. I didn't even know what to say to that. Denny seemed to sense that I was speechless. His next text effectively ended the conversation. '*I hope the rest of your tour is good. See ya around, mate.*'

'*Thanks. See ya.*'

Shoving the phone into my pocket, I shook my head in disbelief. Why the fuck was he so good to me? I stewed on that the entire car ride to the hotel, and when I got there, I still had no idea. Denny was just...a remarkable person.

My friends were hanging out in the hotel bar when I walked inside; I could hear them from the lobby. Justin and the rest of Avoiding Redemption were with them. Evan noticed me first and raised a hand in greeting. I nodded at him as I approached their boisterous section. Everyone turned to look at me then, saying hello in one way or another. Except for Griffin. He had his head on the table, and he looked a little green. He was staring up at me, but he wasn't saying anything, and he wasn't moving; if it weren't for the occasional eye movement as he scanned me, I might have thought he was dead. I could only assume he went out last night and had thoroughly overdone it.

Because I was in a really good mood, because I couldn't resist fucking with him, and because Griffin deserved a few consequences, I smacked the table in front of him, hard. "How's it going, Griffin?" I said, loudly, brightly.

He cringed and groaned. "Fuck...off," he murmured. The guys around me snickered as Griffin weakly lifted his head. "I hate New Orleans," he pouted.

Matt clapped his back. "That's not what you said last night. I'm pretty sure you said you were moving here."

Evan nodded. "Yep. You said you were grabbing Anna, and the two of you were gonna live together here, right above a bar." I raised an eyebrow at hearing that, and Evan gave me a small nod that clearly said: *I know, right?*

Griffin snorted, then grimaced. "There's no fucking way I would say that. I'm not living *anywhere* with a chick."

I opened my mouth, desperate to tell him what I knew, then I silently pressed my lips together. It wasn't for me to say. And it might not change anything anyway. Matt grinned at him. "It's not that you *won't* live with a chick, Griffin, it's that a chick won't live with *you*. And as your roommate, I totally understand why."

Griffin slowly twisted to face him. "Matty, you keep acting

like you hate living with me, but then you never move out. So, I think I'm not as bad as you say I am."

Matt rolled his eyes. "I just can't afford to live without you. It's not a choice, I'm stuck with you...there's a difference."

"Maybe you're the one who should move in with a chick then," Griffin murmured, annoyed.

Seeing an opportunity, I shrugged and said, "He might be on to something, Matt. Kiera just decided to move in with me. *You* could live with Anna?"

Evan smiled at me, happy for my news. Matt smirked. Seeing the breadcrumbs I'd laid out for him, he looked over at Griffin and suggestively raised his eyebrows. "Great idea, Kellan. *I'll* live with Anna."

Even though he looked like he was going to puke, Griffin's cheeks flooded with color. "You fucking touch her, and I will fucking kill you."

Whoa. That sounded like a genuine threat, not just his typical competitive jealousy. Griffin had an odd look on his face, like he wasn't sure why he'd said that, or more accurately, why he'd *meant* it. Matt glanced up at me with a knowing smile, then he tilted his head at Griffin. "Why? You got a problem with Anna and me being together?"

Griffin's jaw dropped. "Well, yeah," he said with a shrug.

Matt lifted an eyebrow. "Why? You're not exclusive. What's it matter?"

We all leaned forward a little, waiting for him to say it—for him to finally admit that he actually had feelings for her, something beyond lust. But Griffin seemed perplexed by Matt's question. He also seemed sickened, and I didn't think it was the hangover making him look that way anymore. "Dude..." He seemed lost for a valid reason, until one suddenly struck him, and he smiled. "Because you'd be cheating on Rachel. And me and Rach are tight. You fuck her over, I'll fuck you up."

He smirked, like he was sure that completely ended the argument. I rolled my eyes. Really? He was going to make this about

Rachel? As Griffin had told us before, back when he'd complained about us not being "true" rock stars who banged groupies left and right, he didn't care if we cheated on our girlfriends. He thought monogamy was lame.

Matt stared at him a moment, stunned by his choice of a rebuttal, then he started laughing. "You and Rachel are...*tight*? Since when?"

Griffin frowned. "Since always. She's practically family, right? I mean, since you're my family, and you fuck Rachel, then she's like my...fuck-family." He nodded after he said it. "And that's a sacred bond. You don't mess with fuck-family...which means you can't mess with Anna." He grinned, looking very pleased with himself.

The guys listening all started laughing. God...fucking Griffin. Matt was just staring at Griffin and slowly shaking his head. Looking up at me, he mouthed, *Fuck-family?* I laughed at the look on his face, and I laughed at Griffin's absolute refusal to admit he cared about Anna. God, what was he going to do when she told him she was pregnant? That thought sobered me a little. If she wanted to keep it, raise the baby with him, and he pushed her away...I really wasn't sure how I'd handle that.

But that was a problem for a later day. Right now, we had work to do.

Matt was still laughing at Griffin's twisted but almost sensical logic. I clapped his shoulder. "You ready to finish this, Matt?"

He looked up at me, and I could tell he knew exactly what I meant. "Absolutely," he said, a bright smile on his face.

I nodded at him, then Evan, then Griffin. "All right...let's get to work."

Chapter 33
HOME AGAIN

It took two more weeks, but we finally had all the songs picked and approved. Everyone was so relieved to be done with that part of it; I swear, doing all that was going to be harder than actually making the album. Lana was thrilled with our selections. I was thrilled with the fact that the label was letting us go home right after the tour, and we wouldn't be starting on the album until a few days after Kiera's birthday. I was damn-near giddy to be able to spend it with her.

Surprising the hell out of me, all of Avoiding Redemption decided to join us in Seattle when we went home. They said they wanted to see Pete's.

"It's just a bar, man. I really don't get why you'd want to go all the way up there just to see it."

Justin glanced at his band where we were gathered backstage. Smiling, he shook his shaggy head. "It's not just a bar, it's where the D-Bags got their start. And that means it's gonna be important one day. I want to see it before it gets all...touristy."

I just pursed my lips and stared at him. Seriously, why was everyone I met so insistent that the D-Bags were gonna be bigger than the Beatles or something? That wasn't how life worked. Not for me. If we were lucky, we'd get *one* song on the radio. Hopefully it wouldn't be so overplayed that people started hating us. I'd like to be able to do this for a little bit longer.

Rolling my eyes, I shook my head at him. Justin laughed at the look on my face, but from his expression, it was clear he thought he was right, and I was being the ridiculous one. For a rock star, he sure was delusional.

When I called Kiera later and told her Justin's plan to come up and spend some time with us, she was just as mystified as me. But whatever, Justin could do what he wanted, and showing him and the guys Pete's actually sounded like a lot of fun. I was ready for the tour to be over with.

The last show, however, was surprisingly emotional for me. We were in Miami, and as I stared out over the screaming crowd, I felt my throat getting tight. This tour had been emotionally and physically exhausting, but in a weird way, I was going to miss it.

"Hey, Miami! How's it going?" I paused to let the screaming die down. Smiling, I met eyes with some of the fans in front. A couple of girls started fanning themselves, making me laugh a little. "Since this is our last stop, I just wanted to say...this has been the greatest experience of our lives." I indicated the guys behind me. Glancing back, I saw them smiling and nodding. Even Matt was grinning as he scanned the massive crowd. He looked so much calmer now than he had in the beginning; it was great to see.

Turning back to the fans, I said, "I want to thank you all for being a part of it, for supporting all these great bands tonight. On behalf of everyone, we all really appreciate it." With a laugh, I pointed at the audience and added, "And I fully expect to see all of you at our next show." *Whenever the hell that might be.*

The crowd started screaming again, like every single one of them was on board for that idea. My grin was huge as I motioned for Evan to start the song. Who knows, maybe some of the people here might actually take me up on that and start following us around. That would be a win-win. There was something really satisfying about how symbiotic the relationship was between the fans and the bands. It appealed to every part of me.

We nailed the show, and I left the stage on an exquisite high. Not even the fact that the tour was over could get me down. After the concert was completely finished, we all helped tear down the show, then congregated outside by the buses. It was weird to not have another concert to travel to, and for a moment, I felt a little lost as I looked over the group of guys I'd bonded with over the last several months.

My friends and I started saying goodbye. I was a little choked up as I said farewell to all the guys I'd gotten to know during the super-long tour: Kurt, Benji, my bunkmate Mark, and so many others. Most of us had exchanged phone numbers during the tour, so I knew I'd talk to them again, but still...it was oddly difficult to say goodbye. We'd gone through a lot together, ups and downs.

Then I spotted the one person I was genuinely happy to leave behind: Paul. He'd been shockingly absent in my life after I'd threatened him, but he still sneered at me when he caught me looking his way. Shaking my head, I turned away from him; I really hoped I never became that jaded.

After our long goodbyes, the guys started piling back on the buses. All except us and the members of Avoiding Redemption. We were staying in Miami, for the night at least. Matt had our group booked on a flight home tomorrow. Justin said one of his guys had booked a similar flight. The buses were headed back to Seattle, back to where they'd begun the journey, to drop off the rock stars and all their equipment. We could have stayed on them, of course, but the trek home would take forever that way, and we just didn't have that kind of time.

We were due in L.A. on Monday, where all our stuff would be waiting for us. Lana had retrieved our equipment right after our set, and all of our personal belongings—even Matt's security bucket had been packed up to come with us. Matt had been a little leery about letting our things be taken unsupervised by someone in the band. So as a show of good faith, I'd let them take my prized guitar too. Seeing that I was okay with it had made Matt more okay with it too. And now I seriously hoped everything made it there unscathed; the only thing I'd kept with me, the only thing I hadn't risked losing, was the Hot Wheels car Kiera had given me for Christmas. It was safely tucked in my pocket.

But I was sure everything would be fine—Lana knew what she was doing. And she assured us that she would be closely monitoring our equipment's progress as it sped its way to Los Angeles, to a massive house the label had available for visiting artists. From what she'd told us, the house was *extremely* nice. Griffin couldn't wait. I couldn't wait to walk into Pete's again. And see my girl again.

It felt like it took forever to get back to Seattle, and it was early evening by the time we landed. There was a restless air of excitement in the cab as we made our way to Pete's. Kiera and Jenny were already there, working. Rachel was joining us there when she got off work. Anna...I really had no idea if she'd be there or not, if tonight was the night she'd finally tell Griffin he was a father. I kept glancing at him in the cab. Was this when his life completely changed? I supposed it already had changed, he just wasn't aware of it yet.

He was the first one out of the cab when we got to the bar. I paid the driver while Matt followed Griffin. Evan was waiting for me, and I couldn't stop grinning when I turned around to face the front of the bar. Smiling himself, Evan looked over at me. "Damn, I've really missed this place," he said.

I nodded as we started walking toward the doors. "Yeah, me too. As fun as the tour was, I think *this* might be my favorite part."

Evan tilted his head at me, lifting his newly pierced eyebrow. "Better than that one time Griffin got trapped in the hotel elevator, but we got the door open just far enough that we were able to spritz him with some random kid's juice box?"

Evan caught the closing bar door and we walked through, laughing as we remembered that day. Griffin had been so pissed, especially when Matt had run to the hotel café and purchased a bunch more of the juice boxes. Ah...good times.

I let the past slide off me as the present assaulted me. Everyone in the bar was cheering, clapping, whistling...it was so weird. I acknowledged the affection with a small nod and a lift of my hand. My gaze swept the room before settling on Kiera, standing at the far end of the bar with Kate; Jenny was already leaping into Evan's arms. Bright grin on my face, I started striding over to my girl. She met me halfway, and then I was grabbing her face, pulling her mouth to mine.

I reveled in the kiss, feeling her, tasting her. Kiera didn't usually let me get so passionate in such a public place, but when she ran her hands up to tangle her fingers in my hair, I figured she wasn't really worried about it right now. I let myself get lost in the moment as our mouths moved together, but eventually, I wanted so much more, and my fingers slid down her body to squeeze her ass.

That was when she pulled away from me. Breathing heavier, she gave me a reproachful look. I shrugged at her in apology. *Give me an inch, Kiera, and I'll take it. Every time.* Forgiving my wandering hands, she laughed and gave me a soft, innocent kiss.

"You're here," she sighed.

"There was nowhere else I wanted to be," I told her.

She shook her head and smiled. As we broke apart, I was swarmed by friends from the bar wanting to congratulate me. People wanted to know how it was on the road, wanted to hear funny stories. I told them the few I could think of off the top of my head, and they laughed, making me laugh, and it suddenly felt like I'd never been gone. Until Sam tried to kill me.

"Damn, man, it's good to see you," he said, wrapping his mammoth arms around me and squeezing so hard I swear something popped.

"Jesus, Sam," I said when I could breathe. "Don't break me."

He smirked at me, and I crooked a grin. "I never would have left if I'd realized just how much you love me."

He smacked the back of my head. "Jackass," he muttered.

I laughed at the look on his face, then I noticed that Justin and his band had arrived. Grinning, I made my way over to him. "Hey, man," I said, extending my hand. "Good timing, we just got here."

Justin briefly shook my hand before looking around at my old stomping grounds. "This place is cool...I like it."

"Yeah, this place is great." Better than great. This place was *home*.

I indicated the band's regular table, and we both sat down to start people watching. Everything here was so damn familiar—the wall of guitars behind the stage, the glowing neon signs in the windows, the worn floors, the chip in the table where Griffin had damaged it, my friends lounging around, relaxing, talking, laughing, Jenny giggling at Evan, Kiera at the bar, smiling at me as she grabbed me a drink...Rita undressing me with her eyes. Seeing all the things I was used to filled me with peace. There was really only one thing that was slightly different here...and it made a weird sort of sadness wash through me. The instruments resting on the stage. I was so used to seeing our shit there, but the bright Poetic Bliss logo on the drum set, and the electric blue, neon pink, and deep purple guitars loudly proclaimed the stage as being someone else's. I once thought we'd come back here after the tour ended, reclaim our weekly gig, but now...I wasn't so sure. Like it or not, things were different.

But not completely different.

Kiera stopped at the table, Kate in tow. Kate was blatantly staring at Justin. She only flicked a cursory glance at me when I said hello. Kiera handed me a bottle of beer with a wink. I grinned at her as Kate nervously held a tray holding a pitcher of beer and glasses for all the guys. Justin looked up at Kiera, gave her a smile, then slid his eyes to Kate; they stayed on Kate. Interesting.

Kiera lifted a hand toward her friend and coworker. "Hey, Justin. This is Kate. She's helping me tonight." I raised my eyebrows as I watched Kiera interact with Justin. She talked to him smoothly, easily, just as she would with me or the other D-Bags. It was nice to see her more comfortable in her own skin. Because it was truly remarkable skin, and she should be comfortable in it.

Kate awkwardly put down the tray and lifted her hand in a small wave. "Hi...I just...love your music."

Her cheeks flushed with color, and I shook my head in amusement. Justin went on to thank her, but I tuned them out as Kiera sat down on my lap. Ah...heaven. Wrapping my arms around her, I smiled and said, "Thanks for the beer."

She gave me a soft kiss. "Just doing my job."

Grabbing her hips, I pulled her into me, rubbing her against me. "*This* is your job?" I suggestively asked.

She laughed, then tucked a loose strand of dark hair behind her ear. Leaning forward, she quietly said, "Only when *you're* the customer."

I chuckled at her answer then kissed her neck. "Well, I like it, so I'll just have to make sure I'm your *only* customer from now on."

The look on her face when she pulled back was adoring. "You are...my only."

Damn. My heart swelled, squeezed, and did this weird fluttery thing. Soft smile on my face, I looked down as I let the content feeling overwhelm me. Kiera kissed my cheek, then stood up to take care of the other customers that she actually did have, but her words stuck with me. *My only*.

As much fun as it was to hang out with Justin and the guys, I was ready to go home with Kiera...to *our* home. Just the thought made me grin. But she couldn't leave yet, so I made the most of my time—laughing, drinking, and eventually, dancing. Since Kiera was the only one I wanted to dance with, I twirled her around the edge of the crowd whenever she had a break between customers.

I was just pulling her tight to me when Griffin suddenly approached us. Looking forlorn, he tapped Kiera's shoulder. Her expression when she looked over at him was priceless; it was almost like she thought he was going to ask for a turn. I didn't think that was it though.

"Hey, where's your sister?" he asked.

Kiera bit her lip while I tried really hard not to frown. Anna wasn't here, and I hadn't asked Kiera, but I had the feeling Anna wasn't coming. She was still avoiding Griffin, still avoiding the hard conversation she obviously didn't want to have with him. I could understand wanting to hide, but I also knew from experience that she couldn't hide forever—the truth *was* going to come out.

I watched Kiera closely, wondering what she was going to tell him...and not tell him. Kiera saw my expression, saw me raise an eyebrow in question. She looked torn, but eventually she shrugged and said, "Sorry, she had to go back east for a few days to see our parents."

Griffin frowned, looking truly disappointed. "Really? Now?" He shook his head, and I couldn't help but feel a little bad for him; it was odd to feel that way. "I told her we were coming up this weekend. She couldn't wait?"

Kiera sighed, and I could see how much she hated this. Even though Griffin wasn't her favorite person, she still wanted him to know. I did too. Jackass or not, he deserved the truth. "Sorry, family thing."

Griffin rolled his eyes, annoyed, and Kiera frowned. "Well, I'm sure you could find someone else to...hang out with this weekend."

I pursed my lips as I watched Kiera. Anna and Griffin's relationship was an odd one to her. I think Kiera wanted Griffin to love Anna like the rest of us loved our girlfriends—heart and soul, wholly and completely...faithfully. But that wasn't what they had, and I wasn't sure if they ever would have a relationship like that. It just didn't seem to interest them. Either one of them. Although, I had seen...*something* from Griffin on occasion, so I wasn't entirely throwing in the towel yet.

Griffin still had that disappointed, disgruntled look on his face. He shrugged. "Yeah, sure...but Anna's the best, though. She knows just what I like." His eyes scanned the bar, his frown deepening. "These girls, they're all too...giddy. It can be annoying...sometimes."

My jaw almost dropped. Giddy was Griffin's favorite type of girl. Or at least, it had been. I had to wonder if Kiera had caught the significance of what he'd just said. But then Kiera said something that blew my fucking mind. "You could hang out with Kellan and me?"

My eyes instantly snapped to hers. *Why the fuck would you ask him to hang out with us? I just spent six fucking months with him. I need a break.* Kiera looked chagrined as she bit her lip, and I instantly realized she hadn't meant to say that. Every so often, things just came out of her mouth with no thought behind them. It was something we had in common since my tongue loosened on me sometimes too. Usually just when I was pissed though. Kiera could do it on a whim.

I was still giving Kiera a questioning, admonishing look when I heard Griffin say, "Nah, no thanks." Then he suddenly smacked me on the chest. "I'd rather be alone than hang out with this jackoff."

Genuinely confused, I looked over at Griffin. "What did I do to you?" He was the one who was constantly being irritating. I think he'd been smacked by everyone on the tour at one point or another. And as for picking on him...well, that was typically Matt, not me. I was an innocent bystander. Usually.

Griffin narrowed his eyes at me, clearly disagreeing with my assessment of our relationship. "Jersey...those two hot girls?"

Oh my God...I knew exactly what he was talking about now. *Jesus, Griffin*...He still had no clue. And he still hadn't forgotten about it. That was so fucking long ago. I bit my lip, trying not to laugh. "Uh, Griff...I was doing you a favor." *You just don't realize it.*

"Save it, man." He poked me in the chest. "You were just jealous 'cause you were doing the monogamous thing. Whatever. You didn't need to cock block me! And right when things were getting interesting!"

I could barely contain my laughter now; a small chuckle escaped me. "Griffin..."

Griffin shook his head and walked away. At least he wasn't truly furious anymore, but still...God...dumbass. Letting the laughter bubble out of me, I finally told him what he should have realized all along. "I tried to tell you...those weren't girls, dude."

He raised his middle finger into the air, not looking at me. Oh God...he didn't believe me. I had a feeling he never would. I laughed harder, then looked down at Kiera; she was smiling and laughing too. "Maybe I should have just let him figure it out for himself?" I told her. *Next time, I will.*

Kiera laughed with me for a moment. I wrapped my arms around her waist, and she wrapped hers around my neck. "Monogamous thing?" she said, tilting her head.

Grinning, I rested my head against hers. "Yeah, see, I told you I was being good."

She giggled, then gave me a soft kiss. "I know you were." Looking amused and astonished, she shook her head. "Who knew I'd ever find a conversation with Griffin comforting?"

"Life's little mysteries," I told her.

Kiera threaded her fingers through my hair, gazing at me with love in her eyes while I gazed at her. Then her expression changed, and she suddenly looked a little...nervous. I bunched my brows in confusion as I studied her odd reaction. After clearing her throat, she glanced around the bar and said, "Um, Kellan, since we're doing the honesty-at-all-costs policy, I have something to confess."

I wasn't sure why she looked so worried, but she was giving

me an opportunity to tease her, and I was going to take it. "Rob a bank while I was gone?"

She smirked, then shook her head. "No."

A better idea popped into my head, and I leaned in, eyebrow raised. "A sex shop?"

Her cheeks flushed with color as she looked away and murmured, "No, I didn't rob anyone." She laughed as she looked back at me. I was still grinning, because I was still imagining her wading through a sea of erotic toys. She knew it too. Her cheeks were bright red now as she smacked my chest. "Stop picturing me...where you're picturing me."

I laughed, then kissed her cheek. So adorable. "Okay, what is it?"

The expression on her face changed again, turned far more serious than it should have. She bit her lip, nervous again. "Okay, it's going to make you mad, but hear me out before you start yelling."

I was confused for half a second. *Why would I yell at you*? I was certain she hadn't cheated on me, and she wouldn't cheat on me, so I honestly couldn't think of anything that would make me yell at her anymore. And then I was struck cold with icy realization. Shit. No, there actually *was* one thing that she might do that would definitely make me mad. She wouldn't. It *had* to be something else. "What did you do?" I tentatively asked.

She swallowed, then started tracing my tattoo. Normally, I loved that, but right now, it kind of felt like a warning: *Remember you love me*. "I invited your dad and his family to my graduation party at Pete's."

God-fucking-damn it. I knew it. Anger flooded me, along with a good dose of fear and a slice of betrayal. She had no right to do that. Before I could stop myself, I shoved her away from me. "You what? Kiera, I told you I didn't want any contact with him. Why would you do that?" It was the entire reason I hadn't told her from the beginning. Although, my original worry had been about her bugging me to contact him. Her contacting him *directly* had never even occurred to me.

Kiera sighed as she stepped up to me. "Because you need them, Kellan."

Bullshit. I didn't need anything from them. Or at least, anything from *him*. Shaking my head, I started to tell her that, but she cut me off. "No, you don't believe that you do...but you do, Kellan." She rested her hand on my chest; it calmed me a little. So did her words. "I've heard you talk about your sister. You care about her. And your brother? You've never even met him...Don't you want to?"

Yes. That was truly my only regret about the situation. I'd have to wait so long to meet Riley. Or, I would have, if Kiera hadn't done this. I gave her a slight nod, conceding her point. She smiled at me, then said, "And your dad...how do you know what you'll feel toward him, if you never give him a chance?" She brought her other hand to my cheek, stroked my skin with her thumb. "You could be missing out on something really good... because you're scared."

Or avoiding something really bad... I didn't need more pain in my life. I just needed *her*. I looked down. "Kiera..." *Don't make me do this.*

She lifted my head, returning my gaze to hers. "I saw you on Christmas morning, Kellan. You wanted that bond, that family bond...and you can have it. You just have to be brave." Her smile grew wider as she studied me. "You are a smart, handsome, rock star with a girlfriend who adores you. You have nothing to fear...ever."

She was repeating my sentiment of encouragement back to me, and I couldn't help but grin at her. Maybe she was right. Maybe I'd been holding so tightly to my rage out of fear. Maybe it wouldn't be so bad to have a...to have a family of my own. One that wanted me. I wasn't sure if Gavin wanted me, I wasn't entirely sure why he'd disappeared, but Hailey and Riley...I could have them in my life, and that, I *did* want.

Letting go of my annoyance at her, I shook my head. "When did you get so wise?" I asked.

With an adorable smirk on her face, she shrugged. "I am a college graduate, you know."

I gave her look right back to her. "Not yet."

Laughing, she slung her arms around me again. "Close enough."

Curious, I asked her how she got Gavin's number. She gave me a blank look, like she was stunned I'd ask her that. "Are you kidding, that number's been burned into my brain since December."

Cringing, I stared at the floor. Right. When I'd flat-out lied to her. "Yeah, sorry about that."

She gave me a soft, forgiving kiss. "It's okay...I get it now." I was so grateful that she did.

Kiera eventually had to get back to work. She pulled me up to the bar with her though, like she was reluctant to be too far away from me. I loved that she felt that way; I didn't want to be far from her either. Once we got to the bar, Kiera frowned and glanced back at the dancefloor. Rita had abandoned her post ages ago and was currently dirty dancing with Justin. Or trying to. Justin kept pushing her away, but she just kept right on returning to him. I felt bad for the guy; I knew from experience just how persistent Rita could be. I wasn't about to rescue him though. I'd just end up taking his place.

Kiera looked back at me with a smirk on her lips. "Want to fill in for Rita?"

She didn't have to ask me twice. I'd been wanting to sling drinks back here for a while, but with Rita always there, it hadn't really been an option...until now. Before Kiera could tell me she was just joking, I hopped onto the bar and swung my legs around to the other side. Once there, I tied an apron around my waist and started thinking through all the drinks I knew; my knowledge base wasn't all that large, since I typically just ordered beer. Whatever. I'd just make shit up if I didn't know it. Looking at the eager crowd of women waiting for me, I had a feeling they wouldn't mind.

Kiera gave me an adoring smile as she returned to her duties. I grinned as I started in on mine. "Ladies, what can I get for you?"

They started giving me every dirty drink name in the book: Sex on the Beach, Slippery Nipple, Screaming Orgasm, Fuck Me Hard. I laughed as I shook my head, then started making...something for them.

I was thoroughly enjoying myself when I noticed someone stepping into the bar. Denny. Seeing him made my stomach drop a little. God, I'd been such a dick to him. Again. True, I'd already apologized to him, but it was still bugging me. Seeing him in person made me want to apologize again. Before the night was through, I had to talk to him.

Surprisingly, Denny didn't walk into the bar alone. A cute blonde was holding his hand. Knowing what I knew about him, I had to assume that she was his girlfriend, Abby. I seemed to recall Kiera saying something about her being stuck in Australia. Guess she finally made it over here. Good. Denny deserved to be with the woman he loved. And honestly, that made me feel even better about him being here in Seattle. I finally trusted Kiera and Denny, but that didn't mean I suddenly liked it now. It just...was what it was.

Kiera had spotted Denny too, and she motioned for him to sit in her section. I watched his progress, wondering how long I should wait to talk to him. Maybe he should have a drink first. Maybe *I* should have another drink first. From the corner of my eye, I saw Kiera approaching the bar. I pulled my eyes from Denny to look over at her. Adorable smile on her face, she leaned over the bar to me. Grinning crookedly, I leaned toward her. Her eyes began scanning my body, and I smiled, waiting for her to reach my face again. I'd really missed her drinking me in.

When our eyes met, I nodded over her shoulder at Denny. "I should go say hi. The last time we saw each other I wasn't exactly...nice."

Kiera's face matched mine for a moment as we both remembered me yelling at him. At least I hadn't punched him. Kiera looked back at Denny. "Yeah, I should talk to him too. I haven't had a chance to meet Abby yet."

Like he knew we were talking about him, Denny glanced up at us and frowned. He partially stood, like he wanted to talk to us too. I was just about to head over there when someone pinched my ass. Startled, I stepped away from my attacker—Rita. She instantly moved forward and wrapped her arms around my waist. "I knew I'd get you back behind this bar again, sweetheart," she cooed.

Annoyance ran up my spine. I should have been watching her more carefully while I worked. Rita was never one to be subtle about her interest in me. I shouldn't have ever had sex with her. Willing or not, she was married, and I should have respected that. Hell, I should have respected *myself*.

I tried to disengage from her, but every time I moved one hand away, she'd just move it back when I grabbed her other one. Kiera was giggling as she watched my futile attempt at freedom. It filled me with relief that she wasn't upset, but I frowned at her on principle. *It's not funny*. Rita laid her head on my chest, perfectly at home curled up to my body, and I let out a long sigh. Damn it. *Now what do I do?*

Kiera gave me a look that spoke volumes—*You only have yourself to blame. I know, Kiera...I know*. I smiled at the look on Kiera's face, grateful that she wasn't jealous. Or needlessly worried. Maybe she was genuinely starting to trust me too. And she should. Especially with Rita. But with everyone else too. Kiera was it for me. My body, my soul, were hers. And Rita needed to finally understand that.

Knowing I'd need to be a little more forceful than I was currently being, I grabbed Rita's shoulders and pushed her away from me. Her eyes flashed open in surprise; I generally wasn't rough or dismissive with her. Honestly, I'd tolerated her relentless flirting for far too long, and this wasn't entirely her fault. I made my voice gentle, but firm. "I know we had a thing once, but that was years ago, and I've moved on. We've both moved on." I pointedly looked at her wedding ring. It was a different husband now than when we'd been together, which meant a new opportunity for her to be faithful. And she should be faithful...or she shouldn't be married. "But I'm with Kiera now, and your constant flirting isn't appropriate. Neither is your gossiping about things we did together. I would appreciate it if, in the future, both of those things would stop...please."

She only stared at me, stunned, and I suddenly realized we should have had this conversation ages ago. I hopped over the bar, then untied my apron and handed it to her. "Thank you, Rita, it was fun." *But it's definitely over*. She pouted as she took my apron, but she didn't object. Thank God.

Soft smile on her face, Kiera took my hand and started leading us toward Denny. But Denny had already decided to approach us, and the two of them almost collided. Denny and Kiera both laughed in a similar, friendly way. I waited for the jealousy to hit me...but it didn't, and its absence made me smile.

Grinning brightly, Denny looped an arm around his girlfriend's waist and said, "Kiera, Kellan, this is my girlfriend, Abby."

Abby extended her hand to Kiera first; she didn't look at all fazed by the fact that Kiera had once been very important to her boyfriend. It delighted me that Denny had found someone who was that secure in their relationship. I doubted Abby would ever cheat on him. And thinking that made me feel even worse. Kiera cheated on him because of me. Because I hadn't been able to live up to my promise. Because I basically sucked as a human being.

In a pleasant, accented voice, Abby said, "Hello Kiera, it's nice to finally meet you." From what I could tell, there was nothing but genuine warmth behind the sentiment. God...she was just as remarkably forgiving as Denny.

Kiera seemed amazed by that too as she subtly examined Denny's girlfriend. I found it amusing that Denny's current flame was so different appearance-wise than his old flame: long blonde hair, pale gray eyes, and way more self-esteem. I also found it amusing that I'd always pictured him with a blonde, and here he was, finally dating a blonde.

"You too, Abby. Denny talks about you all the time," Kiera said, smiling at her. That statement made me happier than it should, and I couldn't stop my grin.

When the two girls broke apart, I extended my hand to Abby. "It's nice to meet you, Abby." I felt myself tensing a little as she turned to fully appraise me. I didn't want her to gawk at me, or be flustered by me, or have any reaction to me that would take away from her relationship with Denny. But her eyes only briefly scanned my face. Seeing the disinterest made me relax. Good. *Denny deserves someone who doesn't give a shit what I look like.*

She demurely took my hand, glancing back at Denny while she did, like she was making sure touching me wouldn't hurt him. I kind of loved that she did that. He was first in her heart. They were solid. Denny gave her a small nod as he smiled at her, completely unworried, and I loved that too. Maybe Denny finally trusted me too. No...it was Abby he trusted. And that was okay. I wouldn't blame him if he never trusted me again.

Abby's eyes returned to me, and her smile widened, showing twin dimples. "It's nice to meet you too, Kellan. Denny says... good things about you."

What? She could have slapped me, and I would have been less surprised. Completely floored, I stared at Denny in shock. "You do? Why? I was an asshole to you..."

Denny's gaze drifted to the floor, and I swear I saw guilt on his face. When he looked back at me, I was sure I saw guilt. Why the fuck would he feel guilt toward *me*? "And I nearly killed you." He paused to sigh and run a hand through his hair. "In the end... whose crime was greater?"

Mine. By a longshot. The only reason he'd even come unglued in the first place was because of me. How could he blame himself for something *I'd* done to him? I was so...annoyed, I had to look away from him. Not only had I caused him pain, I'd caused him remorse too. I'd destroyed a part of him, a part of his innocence. I'd...changed him...and I would never forgive myself for that.

I felt Kiera's hand on my stomach, giving me comfort, strength. I looked at her face, saw the matching guilt in her eyes, then returned my attention to Denny. "I still took something that wasn't mine. Even if you feel guilty for the fight..." *and you shouldn't*, "...you really shouldn't ever talk to me again."

My gaze sank to the floor as worthlessness filled me. *This isn't even what I wanted to apologize to him about.* I had so much to apologize to him for it was...overwhelming. How had I screwed someone over so badly?

An odd sound made me snap my eyes up. Denny was...laughing. And smiling. Holding Abby tight to him, he shook his head and said, "You should see the looks on your faces right now."

I glanced at Kiera; she had the same guilty, confused look on her face. Denny laughed a little harder, and we returned our eyes to him. He clapped my shoulder, shaking his head as he told me, "Look, I know your life was hard, and I realize that Kiera must have been a...salve...for you." He pointedly raised his eyebrows. "I get it. I didn't like it, but I get it."

Salve? Yes...she was. In every way she'd opened me, cleaned me, healed me. Resisting that kind of love hadn't been possible for me. Not when I'd gone my entire life without it. A small smile graced my lips as I looked at him. At least he understood why I'd betrayed him.

Denny turned his gaze to Kiera. "And you..." He paused, bit his lip, then sighed. "I know I put my job first." Kiera shook her head, but Denny didn't let her speak. "No, I did, Kiera. I was coming to Seattle, with or without you. I was going to Tucson, with or without you. And, I may have panicked and rushed back to Seattle when I thought I'd lost you, but...my head was still on my job...not you. And I'm so sorry for that. And I don't blame you anymore for falling for someone who gave you the attention you wanted, the attention you deserved."

My eyes drifted to Kiera. I'd never thought about it that way. Not really. I'd always placed the blame on my inability to leave her alone or on her inability to be alone. I'd never let myself blame Denny. I wasn't sure that I ever could blame him, but hearing him admit to having a small part in it, it took some of the sting out of the guilt. Not a lot—it still wasn't his fault—but some.

Tears in her eyes, Kiera nodded at him, accepting his apology. Our group grew silent as the past crashed around us. Abby was the one who broke the stillness. "Oh my God, will the three of you just hug already?"

And we did. And it was extremely...healing.

Chapter 34
HAPPY BIRTHDAY

Some guys had stolen Denny and Abby's seats, so I invited them to sit at the band's table with us. On the way, I apologized to Denny—again—for being an ass when I'd caught him with Kiera. Since I'd already apologized, he brushed it off with a joke about him being used to me being an ass. I had to laugh at that. Yes, I supposed he *had* gotten used to me being a jerk. Hopefully my days of snapping at him were over.

Denny and Abby left the bar long before me, and then, at the tail end of the night, my friends left too. Since I wasn't going anywhere without Kiera, I stayed until her shift was over, and we walked out of Pete's hand-in-hand. I was so happy to be going home with her, I hummed a D-Bags song the entire way to my car.

My car...in my joy to reconnect with Kiera, I'd almost forgotten that I'd be reconnecting with my other baby too. Running my hand over the hood made me grin; there was a fresh coat of polish on her. Turning to Kiera, I told her, "Thanks for not wrecking her."

Soft smile on her face, she kissed my jaw. "I know what she means to you...I was good to her." She started walking around to the other side of the car. "I only got her up over a hundred that one time."

Icy dread flashed through me as my eyes darted over my baby. She was joking, right? I glanced up to see Kiera shake her head at me, amused, as she got into the car. Frowning at her comment, I got behind the wheel. "Not funny," I told her.

She grinned at me, then leaned over to kiss me. I pulled away before she could, and she pouted. Smiling, I told her, "Happy birthday, Kiera."

She looked confused for a second, like she'd forgotten the date had changed during her shift, then she gave me a beautiful grin. "Thank you, you're the first one to say it."

I smirked at her as I leaned forward. "I know, I planned it that way." My mouth met hers, soft, teasing. I slid my tongue along her lip, then angled our connection so I could feel more of her. I didn't think I'd ever get enough of her. Need surged through me as our mouths moved together, as her tongue touched mine. Kiera groaned, sending an ache straight through me. It had been too long since we'd last made love. I *needed* her.

Just as I was debating lying her down on the seat, Kiera pulled away. Her eyes were hooded with desire as she examined my face. "Take me home, Kellan." Leaning forward, she breathed soft, wonderful words into my ear. "Take me to our home."

Her words just about undid me, and a needy groan escaped me. *Our* home. God... I closed my eyes and chewed on my bottom lip as desire and happiness pummeled me. It was so overwhelming, I stopped breathing.

I heard Kiera say, "Kellan? Are...you okay?" I cracked an eye open to look at her.

Grinning, my lip still firmly under my teeth, I nodded. "Yeah, I just needed a minute." Or a lifetime. Those words were *everything* to me. *She* was everything to me.

I got her home in record time. Her mouth was on mine the second we were out of the car. I unlocked the front door and opened it blind. I pulled her inside and stripped off my jacket. I tossed it in the general direction of the coat hooks and heard it hit the floor. Whatever. I didn't fucking care. I kicked the door closed, then grabbed Kiera's thighs and lifted her into my arms. As I kissed her neck, I said, "Hmmm, which room should we christen first?"

She giggled at me, and her answer was humorous. "We've never done much in the laundry room?"

Fine with me. I instantly started walking us that way and she laughed and squirmed against me. "I was joking! Bed, Kellan..." She paused to cup my cheek before kissing me again. "I want to explore you in a bed."

Adoration swept through me as I gazed at her. And a little disbelief that she was mine, that I got to keep her, got to live with her, got to have a life with her. It blew my mind. Changing our direction, I carried her upstairs. As I set her down by our bedroom, I noticed something odd—her old bedroom with Denny was wide open. After I'd shut the door to that room, so very long ago, I hadn't opened it again. I couldn't. I'd needed those ghosts to be cut off. Seeing it open now was jarring, and a little painful.

Kiera started pulling me toward that room, like she wanted to show it to me. I didn't want to see it; I'd seen enough of it for a lifetime. But this was clearly important to her, so I let her lead me. Maybe facing this demon head-on was something we both needed. But then I saw the room, saw what she'd done to the room, and once again, I was blown away.

Everything of Joey's was gone—the bed, the dresser, the nightstand—everything. And in its place were things that turned the room into a living space, not a bedroom. Kiera's old futon was folded into a couch, there was a bookcase crammed full of all my notebooks, my old guitar was hanging on the wall...it was like a shrine to my job, a dedicated space for me to work, to create. I'd never once imagined turning this room into something productive. I hadn't been able to get past the pain, the guilt. I'd been holding onto it so tightly. Letting some of it go sounded really...refreshing.

"Is this for me?" I asked, touched beyond words that she would do something like this for me.

She put her hands on my chest as I twisted to hold her. Nodding, she said, "Yeah, since you don't need to have a roommate anymore, I thought I would give you a better use for the spare room." Leaning forward, she kissed my jaw. "It's all for you, for your art."

There wasn't one part of that sentiment that I didn't absolutely love, and she was right, with her beside me, I would never need a roommate again. Just when I was going to tell her how much I loved it, Kiera frowned, and jerked her thumb over her shoulder. "Except the closet. I needed somewhere to put my clothes."

I laughed at her comment, then squeezed her tight. "It's perfect, thank you." It was such a thoughtful gift...but it reminded me that it wasn't her turn for gifts. It also reminded me that I hadn't had time to go shopping before coming home. I really hated being empty-handed on her birthday. Pulling back from her, I frowned. "Wait, it's your birthday. Shouldn't I be doing something for you?"

I hoped she wasn't upset that I didn't have a present for her, but she only smiled at me. "Well, we missed celebrating your birthday last month, so you can think of this as a belated birthday present." I was about to object, but she bit her lip and nodded at our bedroom door. "But there is one thing you can do for me."

She started pulling me toward our room, and the smile on my face was unstoppable. Was she seriously asking for sex as a present? That seemed a little unfair, since it would be just as much a present for me, but I wasn't about to say no. I would just have to make sure it was the best sex she'd ever had. Slowly raking my eyes over her body, I suggestively said, "Yeah? And that would be...?"

Instead of answering me, she closed the door behind us, then backed me into it and trapped me there with her body. The sensuousness of the movement, the way her curves pressed against me, it instantly ignited me. My breath hitched, and my jaw dropped as desire flooded me. God, she felt so good. She ran her nose along my jaw, sending bolts of electricity through me. I grabbed her hips, pulling her into me. The ache I had for her was already painful. If she kept teasing me, I wasn't going to be able to give her the best night of her life...or at least, it wouldn't be a very long night. But damn, I didn't want her to stop.

I instantly realized, as her tongue flicked my upper lip, as her lips trailed along my jaw, as she lightly licked the inner curve of my ear, that I never should have taught her how to tease. She was entirely too fucking good at it. And while I loved teasing her, being teased was excruciating torture; I felt like I was about to fall apart. And then she whispered something...that just about made me come.

"I put some handcuffs under your pillow...if you want to use them on me."

She pulled back to look at me, her expression a mixture of innocence and desire, and I had to mentally force my body to calm the fuck down. Jesus. She was so hot. But it was more than just that. What she was offering me was way outside of her comfort zone. I knew that. But she trusted me to give this to her, to make it an experience that she'd look back on fondly, and that warmed me. Her trust meant absolutely everything to me. I would never betray it, and I hoped she knew that.

I was almost overwhelmed by the connection I felt to her. It was so odd to me, how I'd once needed sex to feel this way, but now...just staring at her, just thinking about her was enough. Giving her a soft kiss, I murmured my affection. "I love you, Kiera. Happy birthday."

She nodded, then her eager mouth found my lips. We undressed each other, our mouths hardly pausing. When we were both bare, Kiera pulled me over to the bed, then darted her hand under the pillow and showed me the aforementioned cuffs. I smiled when I saw they were very cheap novelty cuffs. They clicked closed, but they didn't lock in any secure way; she'd be able to escape whenever she wanted to. I'd just have to make sure she didn't want to.

A soft chuckle escaped me as I took them from her. "Are you sure?" I asked.

Her cheeks were flushed, but she bit her lip and nodded. My eyes traveled over her face as I trailed my fingers down her arm; she shivered under my touch. Her lips parted as her eyes stayed locked on mine. Intently staring at her, I slipped one cuff around her wrist, gently closing it. A soft gasp escaped her, and my body surged with need. Damn... Still intently watching her face, I took the other cuff...and closed it around my own wrist.

Her brows bunched as she looked down at what I'd just done. "I'm no expert, but I don't think this is how it's supposed to go," she said, a little breathless.

My grin widened as I studied her. "If you're going to be locked to anything, I want it to be me."

She gave me a soft smile, then shook her head as she looped her free arm around my neck. "You're absolutely ridiculous," she told me, interlacing the fingers of our locked hands.

I nodded as I bent to find her lips. "I know."

She laughed as she sat down on the bed. I laughed as I had no choice but to follow her. Our bodies collided, and we stretched out in my bed—in *our* bed. With one pair of hands locked together, I could only explore her with the other. It was a fun challenge, one that eventually led to her begging me to take her. I kissed her as I pressed inside her, and she moaned in my mouth. Her locked hand jerked away from me, like she wanted to hold me, and I ripped the stupid thing off so she could. Her arms wrapped around me as our pace quickened. Her breath was fast in my ear, and I knew she was close. Then I felt her stiffen, and her fingers raked down my back. Fuck, I loved that. I was coming a second after her, groaning as the waves of bliss washed over me.

Kiera's arms and legs were firmly wrapped around me as she

recovered. "I think we cheated," she murmured, briefly lifting her freed wrist.

A soft laugh escaped me as I kissed her collarbone. "I don't fucking care," I muttered.

She smirked at me, then grinned and shook her head. "I love you," she told me.

Moving to her side, I pulled her to my chest. "I love you too," I said, nestling into her warm, wonderful skin.

I held her for a long while, absorbing her love for me as she stroked my back, threaded her fingers through my hair. I was blissfully content. But then she started kissing me, first my shoulder, then my neck, and the fire returned. Her lips met mine, hungry for more. I kissed her until the kiss grew heated, until our breaths were heavy, until her fingers were repeatedly clenching my skin, until mine were clenching her hips. Then I reached over and grabbed the discarded handcuffs. "Okay, now I want to tie you to something," I said.

She giggled as I re-cuffed one of her wrists. "Kellan...?"

I looped the other end around a post of my headboard, then gently brought her other wrist up and trapped her. She smiled at me, still giggling. "Kellan?" she said again.

Grinning, I shook my head at her. "What?" I said, kissing her neck. My lips traveled down to her chest, my tongue swirling over her nipple before I pulled it into my mouth. I saw her close her eyes as I peeked up. "It was your birthday request, if I remember correctly."

She bit her lip as she gently pulled against the post and my grin grew. Oh yeah...this was going to be so much fun.

I ran my lips up to the base of her throat, then very gently, traced her throat with the tip of my tongue. She was panting long before I got to her jaw. Smiling, I kissed along her jaw until I got to her ear. She squirmed when I sucked on her earlobe, pulling harder against the post. "Careful," I whispered in her ear. "You'll break them."

"I don't care," she murmured.

"I do," I said, sucking her bottom lip into my mouth. "It won't be a proper present if you break them."

She started to smile at me, but I ran my hands down her body and the smile quickly turned into her moaning my name. Her eyes were closed as I traveled south again, her lips parted, her breath fast. God, she was beautiful. I didn't think I'd ever fully understand how I got so lucky. My mouth traveled down her abdomen, my hands sliding down her hips. I heard her breath stop when I started leaving soft kisses along the curve of her hip. It started again when I reached her inner thigh, and it was much faster than before.

I shifted her leg so I could taste her, but I paused to look up at her before I did. She was clearly struggling not to free herself so she could grab me. The forced restraint was intoxicating to watch. I ran my tongue over her, gently, teasingly, and she just about came unglued, crying out, bucking against me. It turned me on so much I reconsidered my stance on being teased versus teasing—both were exquisite torture. And I loved it.

It was a good forty minutes later before I let myself fully push inside her again, driving into her with a focused purpose, rather than just briefly slipping inside to prolong the tease. She didn't last long once I was no longer holding back, and honestly, neither did I. We finished at almost the same time, the sound of our much-needed releases echoing around the room.

"Happy birthday," I murmured, breathless as I shifted to her side.

She gave me an exhausted giggle, then tugged on the cuffs. "Can I take these off now?"

Leaning over, I softly kissed her neck. "No," I muttered.

She lifted an amused eyebrow at me, then she released herself. I shook my head at her. "Didn't I say no?"

She flexed her fingers, which made me wonder if she'd gone a little numb. Oops. Maybe I shouldn't have teased her for quite so long. She didn't look upset though. Grinning crookedly at me, she sat up on an elbow and leaned over me. "You did, but it's my birthday, so I make the rules."

Smiling at her, I placed my hand behind her neck and pulled her toward me. "Yes, ma'am," I murmured before our mouths met. *Whatever you want...it's yours. I'm yours. Forever.*

Kiera was all smiles the next morning. I was too. Teasing her had to be my all-time favorite pastime. Satisfying her was a close second. I wrapped my arms around her waist as the coffee brewed. "So, what would you like to do for your birthday?"

Tilting her head, she chewed on her lip, then glanced up at our bedroom. My smiled widened as I inferred her wish. "Really? Again?" Shaking my head, I said, "I truly have corrupted you."

She giggled, then gave me a soft kiss. "I don't care what we do. I just want to be with you." Her lips twisted into a frown. "Before you have to leave again."

I sighed as I squeezed her. "Yeah...but that's not today. We have some time."

And I would spend every second of it locked to her if she wanted me to. In fact, I would spend the rest of my life locked to her if she wanted me to. Which got me thinking...I wanted her to marry me. Not later in some distant future, but now. I didn't see any reason for us to put it off. My feelings for her weren't going to change, and I was pretty confident that her feelings for me weren't going to change either. There was no reason for us not to do it, but still, the thought of asking her made me nervous, anxious.

I stewed over how to ask her the entire weekend. We ended up celebrating not only her birthday, but all of the little occasions we'd missed while I'd been gone. We had champagne and strawberries for our anniversary, a box of chocolates for Valentine's Day, green beer for St. Patrick's Day, cake for her birthday, pie for mine, hardboiled eggs for Easter, and we even celebrated Thanksgiving...with a feather. It was all sort of ridiculous...and I loved every second. But it didn't get me any closer to a solution, and by the time Monday rolled around and I needed to leave, I still hadn't asked her.

Lana arrived with a limo to pick us up at the bar, and after saying goodbye to everyone, my friends and I piled into it and headed to the airport.

Griffin downed the free champagne while I chewed on my lip. "Something bugging you, Kell?" I looked over to see Evan studying me. He raised his pierced eyebrow. "You're gonna see her soon, you know? Her graduation isn't that far away."

I rolled my eyes at the fact that I'd gotten to the point where my friends thought every goodbye with Kiera was going to leave me huddled in a corner, sobbing. "No, that's not it. I wanted to do something before I left, and I kind of...couldn't figure out how to do it."

Griffin spat out the champagne in his mouth. "Oh my God... there was a sex thing you couldn't figure out how to do? What was it?"

He leaned forward, genuinely intrigued. I gave him a blank look. "I know I've told you this before, but not everything revolves around sex."

He smirked at me, then he dropped his gaze to my crotch and said, "Oh...I get it. That sucks."

I narrowed my eyes at him. I knew I was going to regret it, but I had to ask. "What sucks?"

He shrugged. "Obviously, you couldn't get it up. So that sucks for you. And I guess for Kiera. I've heard that can happen though, as you get older. Maybe you were just dehydrated." He held out a bottle of champagne for me. "You should drink more."

There were so many things wrong with everything he just said, and for the millionth time, I couldn't believe he was about to be a dad. I closed my eyes and inhaled a deep, cleansing breath. I heard someone smack Griffin, and I was immensely grateful. Opening my eyes, I saw him rubbing his arm and glaring at Matt.

"What? I can't offer advice? The dude clearly needs help. Some friend you are, Matty."

Shaking my head, I turned to look at Evan. He cringed in apology. "I'm fine," I told him, closing the door on our conversation. I returned my gaze to Griffin. "And everything works *just fine*. But thanks for the advice...dipshit."

Griffin grinned, nodded, then told me, "That's what I'm here for, dude."

It was only then that I remembered Lana was in the car with us. She was biting her lip, staring out the window, obviously struggling not to laugh. So much for sounding like professionals. I sighed and rolled my eyes. Jesus fucking Christ. Why me?

Matt sympathetically patted my knee. "I know," he said. "Trust me...I know."

That made me laugh, and then I couldn't stop laughing. And then everyone was laughing. Oh well. I was sure it wouldn't be the last time Griffin got everything wrong...at my expense.

Once we were in L.A., Lana had another limo waiting to take us to the house where we'd be staying while recording the album. It was all so surreal. I almost couldn't wrap my mind around what was happening. Surely, this was just some long, elaborate dream, and any minute I was going to wake up. Because there was no way this was actually my life.

Looking outside at the palm trees and sunshine reminded me of when I used to live here. It felt so long ago, but really, it was just under five years ago. I remembered it all—arriving in L.A. and getting a crappy apartment with Evan, getting a job at a coffee shop so I could somewhat afford the crappy apartment with Evan, meeting Matt and Griffin, inviting them into the band, practicing in Matt's friend's garage, getting our first gig, getting multiple gigs, actually making a living off it...

And now look at us...riding in a fucking limo on our way to a mansion in the hills. What the actual fuck?

Evan and Matt had the exact same stunned expression on their faces. Griffin took it all in like he owned the city, and he was simply surveying his territory. Lana smiled as she watched me. "Better get used to this," she said. "Because this is just the beginning for you."

Knowing that she also thought we were going to be huge made me smirk and shake my head. Everyone *was* delusional. I didn't bother arguing with her though; only time would tell which one of us was right. We approached a gate with an actual freaking guard who had to let us inside the neighborhood. It felt like we were in another world as I studied the houses we drove past. Jesus. My childhood home in West Seattle had been pretty nice, but it was nothing compared to these homes. Or would palaces be more accurate?

Evan whistled as he looked around. "Damn...think any celebrities live here?"

Lana smiled at him. "Several," she answered.

We all looked at each other, then Evan, Matt, and I twisted in unison to look at Griffin. Matt pointed at him. "No streaking, no doorbell ditch, no flaming sacks of—"

Griffin made a disgusted sound as he cut Matt off. "How childish do you think I am?" Matt pursed his lips at him, and Griffin rolled his eyes. "Fine. I'll be the perfect, boring neighbor. They won't even know I'm here."

I almost believed him, until he smirked and looked out the window. Great.

We finally arrived at the house owned by the label, and my mouth popped open when I stepped out of the limo. Like all the other houses we'd seen, it was massive. It was also swarming with people. I hadn't expected that, but I supposed it made sense that we wouldn't be the only people using the house right now. Lana explained that any artist signed with the label was free to use the house and free to invite guests. That made me deliriously happy. *That means Kiera can be here.*

Lana led us past people in swim trunks and barely-there bikinis. Griffin bit his knuckle as a girl in a thong winked at him; it was like this place was his personal paradise. There were even more people inside the house, and a sinking feeling started to fill me. Would there be *any* privacy here? True, I didn't like to be alone, and I preferred a little company, but I also liked being able to recharge at times. Lana led us up some stairs, the windows there showcasing an impressive view of the pool in the back. She explained the history of the house as she walked, but nobody was really listening to her; we were all too busy absorbing the opulence.

When we got to the second floor, Lana led us to a common area with a huge TV and a slider to a deck. I was a little relieved after seeing the space; it was much quieter here than down below. In fact, nobody was even up here, and that gave me hope that privacy would indeed be possible.

Lana pointed behind her to several sets of doors. "These are your bedrooms; your things have already been placed inside."

That surprised me. I hadn't expected for us to get our own bedrooms. We all thanked her, then started opening up doors. Choosing the door closest to me, the first door along the wall, I opened it and stepped inside. I grinned at seeing my bag and guitar case on the bed. I ran my hand over the case, then popped it open to make sure my guitar was okay. Thankfully, it was exactly how I'd left it; even my photo of Kiera and me was still there.

My smile grew wider as I examined the luxurious bedroom. It was huge, almost like a small apartment, with its own bathroom and its own shower. It was furnished with expensive looking pieces: a massive bed, a stately dresser, twin nightstands, a chair for lounging, a giant TV bolted to the wall, and a freaking chandelier hanging from the ceiling. It was a little lavish for my taste, but it was quiet, and it was private. This place would be perfect for Kiera and me. Now, I just needed to get her here.

Chapter 35
FEAR AND HOPE

A few weeks later, we were all back in Seattle for Kiera's graduation. She was getting ready for the ceremony, and I was droning on about how recording the album was going, but my mind was a million miles away. I'd been avoiding even thinking about it, but now that the moment was here—now that it was *today*—it was all I could think about.

Gavin would be at Kiera's party. I was going to finally meet him. I was also going to be sick. Would Kiera understand if I bailed on the party and went home instead? Probably. But knowing her, she'd just try again. Maybe she'd cuff *me* to the bed and then invite him over while I was stuck; she'd need much sturdier cuffs for that to work.

Damn it. She wanted me to be brave, she wanted me to face this. I might as well get this shit over with so I could move forward...with her. And besides, Hailey was going to be there, and I'd finally get to meet Riley. That made it...almost worth it.

Kiera was debating her outfit, holding up a very sensible choice: black slacks and a gray button-up. Anna instantly voiced her opinion from the doorway. "No, not that one." Stepping inside our bedroom, she handed Kiera something. "Here, wear this. Lord knows I won't be wearing it for a while."

Her words made my gaze drift to her protruding stomach. The outfit she was wearing was somehow still clingy and provocative, showing off her chest just as much as her growing baby. It was still shocking to see Anna pregnant; every time I saw her, I felt like doing a double take. But knowing she was still getting used to the idea, I only gave her encouraging smiles. She could do this. I was sure she could. Griffin, on the other hand...

Thinking about my bandmate almost made my smile falter. He'd been contemplating flying up today for Kiera's party. Of course, he'd also been contemplating skipping it so he could stay at his dream mansion filled with almost-naked women. I honestly had no idea which way his libido would take him. The rest of us had left L.A. yesterday, and I'd almost—*almost*—told Griffin he needed to come with us. But he would have demanded to know why, and I couldn't tell him why...so I hadn't told him anything. He better fucking show up. I was tired of him not knowing.

Because I didn't know for sure if he was coming, I hadn't mentioned anything to Kiera. I also hadn't told her about Evan and Matt being in town. One, because my thoughts had been completely scattered lately, thanks to Gavin's impending arrival, and two, because it was entirely possible the guys would get preoccupied with their girlfriends and forget all about Kiera's party. I know if our roles were reversed, and I had Kiera's naked body wrapped around mine...I would forget about a party for one of their girlfriends. Hell...I forgot about *everything* when I was wrapped in Kiera's arms; I wouldn't blame them in the slightest if they didn't show up.

Kiera unfolded what Anna had handed her, and I smiled when I saw what it was: an extremely short, extremely tight, little black dress. When Kiera held it up to herself, my grin grew. The neckline was also extremely low. If Kiera actually wore that today, I might be walking around a little uncomfortable. That was fine with me...because I *really* wanted to see her in it.

"That...is perfect," I told her, my eyes locked on her chest. I was pretty sure she wouldn't be able to wear a bra with it. I was also sure I could easily pull it down and suck her nipple into my mouth. Later. Obviously.

Anna told her sister she would be beautiful, and I had to agree. With or without the dress—she'd be absolutely stunning. She couldn't help it.

Kiera's dad stepped up to stand beside Anna. I'd offered my home to Kiera's parents, and they were staying in the spare room, sleeping on Kiera's super-uncomfortable futon. I kind of felt bad about that—maybe I should have bought them a hotel room. But Kiera had seemed to really like the idea of them being here with us; overprotective or not, she missed them.

Martin frowned slightly at the dress Kiera was holding but then he managed to flip it into a smile. He told her she was beautiful and that he was proud of her, and I loved seeing the warmth in his eyes. He might not like me, but he loved Kiera, without a doubt, and I respected the hell out of him for that. *He's what a parent should be.* And, of course, that thought made me think of Gavin again. Goddamn it. *I don't want to see him.* I was still avoiding his texts, but they'd eased up considerably once Kiera had given him the invite. No...he didn't need to keep bugging me now that he knew he was getting his way and we were meeting. Fuck.

Shaking my head out of those thoughts, I focused on Kiera thanking her dad for his kind words. Kiera's parents had flown in yesterday too, but they'd landed a few hours after me. Knowing when they'd come in—since I'd purchased their tickets—I'd taken full advantage of our brief time alone together. Damn. She should have been wearing that dress yesterday. Oh well...we were pretty good at being quiet when we needed to be.

Kiera looked uncomfortable for a moment, then she laughed. "Can I...change now?" Her question was clearly directed only at Martin and Anna. It made me happy that she hadn't included me in her dismissal. Good. After all this time, she should be able to change in front of me without any hesitation or need to coverup. Even if I *was* blatantly staring at her body...daydreaming about all the things I could do to it. And there were so many things I could do...

Lost in those delicious thoughts, I vaguely heard Anna say something about food. *Hmmm...food...I wonder if we still have that bottle of Hershey's syrup?* Hearing my name being said interrupted my dirty little fantasy.

"Kellan, son, you want to give me a hand with...something?"

I had to grin at Martin's clumsy attempt to protect his daughter's virtue by getting me out of the room. He had to know that ship had sailed long ago. Ah, denial. That was something I could understand. And...did he just call me son? Damn. That was pretty huge of him, so of course I needed to be respectful and comply.

My smile was bright as I stood up. Maybe there was still a chance for him to like me. "Sure, no problem," I peppily told him.

I kissed Kiera's head before leaving, and she thanked me for being nice to her dad. Martin clapped me on the shoulder as we left, and damn if it didn't feel like acceptance. Then he started talking about baseball. Shit. I'd already exhausted all my facts the last time we'd talked about this. I had a feeling, if I was truly going to bond with the man, then I'd need to actually start watching baseball. For Kiera, I'd happily make that sacrifice.

I made small talk with Martin and Caroline while Anna had a snack and Kiera got ready. I was talking to Caroline about our house in L.A., when I noticed Kiera entering the living room. "It's really nice, like one of those houses you'd see in a..." My voice trailed off mid-sentence as I stared at Kiera. My jaw dropped open, and I just couldn't seem to close it. The dress fit her perfectly, highlighting her body in a way that made me ache. She'd curled her deep brown hair and left it loose around her shoulders; there was a perfectly twisted lock resting near her collarbone that I was dying to wrap around my finger. Her ever-changing eyes were a deep green today, made even more striking by the darkness of the dress—and the depth of love I saw in them.

God, she was just…so…fucking…beautiful. Stunning. Breathtaking. Glorious. And *mine*.

Kiera smiled at me, her brows bunched as she tried to understand my expression. Blinking out of my overwhelmed state, I slapped on a smile and stood up. "You look amazing," I told her.

As I wrapped my arms around Kiera, I noticed her mother appraising me. Her face was contemplative, but also…approving, like seeing what her daughter did to me affirmed something for her. I just hoped Martin hadn't noticed. He might not appreciate me practically drooling over his daughter.

Kiera stepped back from me, her expression unsure. "You don't think it's too short?" she asked, pulling down the bottom.

The more she tugged at the bottom, the farther the cleavage line plunged. I stopped her hands so she wouldn't accidentally expose herself and gave her a soft smile. "No, not at all." She looked fantastic, and she had nothing to worry about wearing this. Sure, it was a smidge on the too-short side, but as long as she didn't flagrantly bend over with her legs locked, she'd be fine. Hmmm, what a great visual though.

From behind me, I heard her dad say, "Well, actually…"

Anna steamrolled right over him as she stepped into the room. "Shush, Dad, she looks great!" Anna beamed at her sister, then indicated the dress. "I hope you went commando, and if you did, just remember to squat to pick things up, not bend over. That's very important." She winked after she said it.

Kiera turned bright red, and I had to press my lips together to not laugh…or picture her without any underwear on. I managed to not laugh. I failed to hold back the erotic image. *Jesus, Anna… why did you have to put that in my brain?* And just when I was making some headway with her parents. Hopefully they didn't notice how much I loved the idea.

Everyone in the room reprimanded Anna at the exact same time. Everyone except me. I gave her a discreet, appreciative grin… because I was really enjoying the new-and-improved visual she'd just given me. Jesus. Now I really wanted to skip this party. *Goddamn it, Anna. I'm trying to be good today.*

Kiera was a bundle of nerves as I drove her to school, anxious about being the center of attention, even if it was just for a split-second. Wanting her to be as calm as possible for as long as possible, I walked with her to where she was supposed to go. She leaned into my side, grateful. "I love how you take care of me," she said.

Peeking down at her, I asked, "You don't think I'm...clingy? Always needing to be near you?" Even I felt clingy sometimes. I couldn't help it. She was my happy place.

Kiera let out a soft laugh as she looked up at me. "No...I think you got that part just right."

That made me smile. It also reminded me that I couldn't be that way with her as much as I wanted or for as long as I wanted. This visit was going to be a short one. Far too short. I was flying back to L.A. on Monday.

A group of people loitering in the hallway made me come to a stop. Candy and her friends. Once upon a time, I could barely remember Candy's name, but after she and her friends had tried to convince Kiera that I'd cheated on her—making up some bullshit story and using my tattoo as proof—everything about Candy was burned into my brain. And not in a good way. She'd gone too fucking far.

I'd confronted Candy about the lie before leaving for the tour, ages ago now. I'd told her in no uncertain terms to back the fuck off and leave Kiera alone. I'd also found out where they'd spotted my tattoo. One of them had seen me exercising —shirtless—at the park. Them twisting that little-known knowledge into a fake story to hurt Kiera still pissed me off. But Kiera hadn't mentioned Candy again, so I felt like she'd taken my warning to heart. I might have scared her a little with my intensity. I didn't want to scare her now, or encourage her, so I kept my expression as blank as possible as she turned to face us. That became a little more difficult when I saw she was very pregnant. Thank all the fucking stars in the world that it wasn't mine.

Candy looked really surprised when she saw us. She said something to her friends, then started walking our way. Kiera sighed, not looking forward to talking to her. She didn't need to worry; I would put Candy in her place, if needed. Hopefully, I wouldn't need to.

There was a confusing amount of solemnness on Candy's face when she stopped in front of us. Her eyes lowered to the floor, almost remorsefully. "Hey, I just wanted to apologize...for all the crap I used to give to you about Kellan."

I was stunned to hear her say that. Candy had never seemed like the apologetic type to me. Or ever truly interested in me. She was just...possessive, like Joey had been. She looked up at Kiera, then me. "I guess I wanted attention." Her gaze drifted back to her shoes. "I was pretty ignored in my high school and being with you gave me a certain amount of...clout...here." She looked back up at me. "Sorry. That was pretty shallow of me."

Any lingering anger I had toward her disappeared at hearing her apology, at seeing the sadness on her face, the guilt. I kind of felt bad for her. She still shouldn't have tried to fuck up my relationship, but...I could understand wanting to be noticed, wanting to feel connected to people. It was fairly similar to what I'd done. I'd had sex with whoever I could to feel like I belonged. Candy had sex with *me* to feel like she belonged, or more accurately, she'd had sex with my *fame* to feel like she belonged. It had little to do with me, as a person. It was a good thing for both of us that *that* cycle was over with. It wasn't healthy.

Not wanting her to feel guilty about using me, I smiled and told her, "It doesn't matter." My eyes drifted to her stomach, then to Kiera. *We've both moved on.* "We're not those people anymore, Candy. Don't worry about it," I finished, looking back at her.

Candy looked thoughtful for a moment, then nodded and walked away. As she left, I hoped that she truly cared about whoever had fathered her baby. I felt like I understood her a little better now, and I genuinely hoped she was happy.

Not long after that meeting, Kiera was practically tackled by a perky blonde. The girl pulled on her so hard, her hand was yanked away from mine. Seeing someone who obviously adored Kiera made me grin. At least not every girl here had treated her like Candy. Not that they all would...it wasn't like I'd slept with *everyone* at the school.

"Kiera, can you believe it! We did it!" She had a cute Southern accent, and she beamed at Kiera. Then her sparkling blue eyes shifted to me. She studied me for a second, then gave me a polite smile. "You must be the boyfriend?"

I extended my hand with a nod. "Kellan."

As we shook hands, she tilted her head toward Kiera. "Now I can see why you're straight. I think he'd make anybody reconsider their orientation."

Hearing her say that filled in so many puzzle pieces for me. This had to be the girl who had kissed Kiera. She'd told me her name in a later conversation...Cheyenne. They'd had the same class, and then they'd been study partners, and then Cheyenne had taken a chance and kissed her. I knew it should have made me mad—someone kissing my girl at least deserved a scolding—but damn if the image didn't turn me on.

Kiera could tell I knew from the look on my face. She rolled her eyes at me, then shoved my shoulder. "Why don't you go have a seat with my parents?"

I couldn't help but tease her. "You sure? Are you...good... here?" *Because if there's a problem, I could stay. And watch.*

Even though I was making it sound like I'd be okay with it, I already knew I wouldn't be—I didn't share anymore, not even with girls. Still, there was something primal and appealing about two girls making out, and I could *not* stop picturing it. And leaving all the potential jealousy out of it...it was pretty fucking hot.

Kiera forcefully turned me around and pushed me away. I

left...but I thought about it the entire time I walked away, and I gave Kiera a purposefully devilish grin before I disappeared around the corner. Then I shook my head at myself and let the erotic imagery go. I wanted Kiera's lips to *only* be on mine anyway. Her kissing me was my favorite fantasy...my only fantasy.

Kiera was way more relaxed once the ceremony was over. I, however, was way more freaked out. I felt like hyperventilating as I drove us all to the bar. *I'm not ready. I can't do this.* When I parked the car and pulled the key out of the ignition, I felt an impending sense of doom settling over me. It was painful, like a vise around my chest, slowly squeezing the life out of me. *I really can't do this.*

Anna and her parents got out of the car, breezy smiles on their faces as they greeted other people coming to the party. My eyes locked onto the reflection of the bar in my rearview mirror, and I couldn't look away. I felt trapped, cornered, and the urge to run was steadily increasing, second by second. I wasn't sure if I could actually, physically make myself walk into the bar. Was he here? Was he waiting? Fuck.

Kiera was still in the car, lingering with me since I hadn't moved. I heard her unbuckle her belt and open the door. "Coming?" she asked.

Fuck. *No...I can't.* "I'll be there in a sec." Would she understand if I left? Would she be mad? Hurt? I should go inside, for her sake, but fuck...the last place I wanted to be was the bar. I felt like I'd been dumped in a pool of concrete, and it was slowly hardening around me, freezing me, suffocating me. I had to move, but I had no choice but to stay.

Kiera closed her door and moved closer to me. "Hey, you okay?" she tenderly asked.

I forced myself to look at her, and I felt the panic rising as I did. "I don't think I can do this, Kiera." Now...or ever.

Her face filled with so much compassion, it made my chest

hurt. Her eyes never wavering from mine, she placed a hand on my cheek and confidently said, "Yes, you can. You can do anything."

I could tell she meant it. I could tell she truly believed it...but it wasn't true. I wasn't as perfect as she thought I was. And there were a lot of things I simply could *not* do. This was one of those things.

I shook my head to object, and she leaned forward to kiss me. I couldn't react, the panic and fear were holding me hostage. There was so much tension in my body, I thought I might explode if I didn't do something. I just couldn't make myself do either option—stay or go, they both seemed impossible.

But then Kiera lightly ran her tongue along my lip and something else started to break through the conflict within me. A trickle of desire began melting the ice. My jaw dropped, my mouth relaxing, and Kiera sucked on my bottom lip. My eyes fluttered closed as I absorbed the sensation, the flash of white-hot need. She dipped her tongue inside my mouth, and I shuddered as I shifted to find her lips. *More.*

Our mouths moved together, and all the anxiety inside me evaporated in the sudden heat. I couldn't even remember what I'd been worried about. She was my only thought. My hand went to her cheek, pulling her into me, deepening our connection. Her hand went to my chest, and she gently, but firmly pushed me away from her. I stared at her through a fog of desire, and she bit her lip as she studied my face. *I want you.*

She tilted her head toward somewhere outside. "Come on, people are waiting for us. Let's go say hello."

It took a second to release the rampant desire running through me. Once my head was clearer, I was floored by what she'd just done to me. And a little proud. Even though I wanted to grin at her for successfully distracting me, I put on a playful frown. "You turned me on...that's cheating."

She laughed as she got out of the car. When I got out as well, she shook her head at me. "When do I ever not turn you on?"

My smile broke free. *Exactly, Kiera. It's about time you owned that fact.* Closing my door, I told her, "Well, finally, you understand the problem that has plagued me from day one."

She held out her hand for me, and I eagerly joined her. "Yes, I do," she murmured. Then she leaned up and nibbled on my ear. Jesus. Did she want me to be rock hard when I walked in there? I guess she did, because right after that, she added, "And I'll fix your little problem later, I promise."

Damn. This girl was going to be my undoing. And I couldn't think of a better way to go.

Not caring about anything but taking her home, I grinned and pulled her toward the bar. "Let's get this over with then."

I felt so much better, but even still, I held my breath as we stepped through the doors. Not spotting anyone unexpected made a surge of relief go through me. *He's not here. Thank God.* Kiera was bombarded by friends who wanted to congratulate her. Her cheeks flushed, but she took their praise in stride. It filled me with an odd sense of pride and bliss to see her growth, to see the connections she'd made without me. She wanted to be a well-rounded person, with joys and interests that didn't solely rely on me, on my presence...and I wanted that for her too. Our tendency toward dependency wasn't healthy. We should be just as strong apart as we were together.

Even still...I wanted her to join me. We could make it apart—I *knew* we could now—but she was my best friend, my lover, my soulmate. She enriched me, and I wanted to share every moment of my upcoming future with her. I wanted her by my side. I wanted her to be my wife. I didn't want to wait anymore.

I fantasized about marrying Kiera while I talked to Troy at the bar. By the way he was flirtatiously tilting his dirty-blond head, softly smiling as he openly admired me, I thought maybe I shouldn't fantasize about Kiera while talking to him. I knew he had a thing for me, and I didn't want to lead him on. As he made a tray of sodas for me, Jenny stepped up to my side.

"Hey," I said to her. "Where's Evan? I figured you two would arrive together." With a grin, I added, "If you bothered to get out of bed to join us at all, that is."

Troy smiled at my suggestive remark, his light brown eyes amused. Jenny rolled her eyes and thumped my chest. "You're just as bad as Griffin sometimes, you know that, right?"

I gave her a playful look of mock indignation, and I heard Troy laugh...then sigh.

Jenny laughed too, then said, "Evan will be here soon. He and Matt went to the airport to get...you know who."

My jaw dropped. "He's coming?" I really thought he might pick the bikinis.

Jenny pursed her lips and nodded. As one, we both looked back at Anna. Griffin was going to find out he was a father-to-be today. I was relieved, but I was nervous. I inhaled a deep breath, then muttered, "I hope Griffin doesn't make me kill him."

"You and me both, Kellan," Jenny said. She sighed, then her mood brightened. "Hey, did Kiera tell you about the book she's writing about you?"

My brows knitted in confusion as I flicked a glance at Kiera talking to her family. "About *me*?" Why would she write a book about me?

When I looked back at Jenny, she was nodding and smiling. "About how the two of you got together. She's really enjoying writing it. It's what she's meant to do...I can tell." Her face scrunched as she examined me. "How do you feel about that?"

I bit my lip as I looked back at Kiera. A book about *us*. About us having an affair...fuck. That would be...painful. But maybe cathartic too. There had been so many times during that mess when I'd wondered just what she'd been thinking. I wasn't sure if I could handle reading her thoughts about the *whole* thing, but I knew...no matter what...if this was what she wanted, I would support her through it.

Grinning, I looked back at Jenny. "I couldn't be prouder of her."

Smiling, Jenny slowly shook her head at me. "You know...if

you'd been *this* guy all those years ago, I might have actually said yes to you."

I laughed at her comment. "Yeah. Thing is..." My eyes drifted back to Kiera. "Without her...I never would have become this guy." And I never would have known how it felt to be *this* happy.

Jenny let out a long, sappy sigh that clearly said: *That's so romantic*. Troy sighed in the exact same way. Knowing I was being nauseating, I rolled my eyes and grabbed the tray from Troy. "You're both ridiculous," I said, glancing between them.

Jenny just laughed as I walked away. Troy sighed again.

My friends arrived at the bar not too much later. Griffin entered with as much noise as he could, smacking open both doors so everyone would look at him. Evan was next. He instantly spotted Jenny and they reunited with gusto, like they hadn't seen each other in years. Matt shook his head at the eager pair in the exact same amused way that I did. *And Evan says I've developed a flair for the dramatic. Not the only one, buddy.*

Matt and Rachel stepped inside, holding hands, while Griffin scanned the bar, probably searching for Anna. I walked over to them, giving Anna a moment to compose herself; she had to be freaking out. "Hey, guys...thanks for coming," I said, my smile suggestive. Jenny smirked at me, since she knew what I meant by that. The guys just shrugged.

"Of course, wouldn't miss it," Matt said, clapping me on the shoulder.

Hoping Anna was ready, I motioned toward our table. When I twisted to look, I saw that Anna was still there, but I wasn't sure if it was by her choice or not. She was rigidly standing beside the table, and Kiera was physically holding her in place. Anna was so pale as we approached, I worried she might faint.

Griffin grinned when he spotted Anna, and I knew from the look on his face...he hadn't realized she was pregnant yet. Fucking idiot. It couldn't be more obvious. Maybe he just hadn't looked at her body yet. Kiera let Anna go as Griffin stepped up to her. Anna started shaking, but she didn't leave.

I'd never seen Griffin be so completely clueless. Instead of saying anything, instead of asking her anything, he just grabbed her face and started kissing her. Anna moaned a little, and I took the moment of distraction to glance at Evan and Matt, slightly in front of me. Both of them had wide eyes as they stared at Anna's stomach. They knew. But of course, once again, it was exceedingly obvious.

Kiera waved a greeting to them when their stares turned to her, then she rolled her eyes and nodded, answering their unasked questions: *Yes, Anna is pregnant...yes, Griffin is about to be a dad.* I'd never seen my friends look so stunned. Their mouths popped open in utter disbelief. I knew the feeling. It *still* shocked me.

Griffin finally noticed something was different about Anna when he hugged her. But even then...he didn't seem to understand. His brows furrowed in confusion. "Uh, Anna?" He took a step back and poked her in the stomach. "What happened to you?" I wanted to roll my eyes. *Jesus, Griffin. Really?*

Anna seemed to feel the same way. She batted his hand away and scowled at him. "You happened to me...ass hat."

He still seemed confused. Matt smacked Griffin over the head, annoyance clear on his face. "Dude, I told you to wrap it up! Don't you ever listen to me?" he snapped.

Griffin twisted to sneer at him. "What the fuck are you talking about?"

Oh my fucking God, how did he still not get it? I was about to say something, but Kiera's dad beat me to it. Stepping up to Griffin, he poked him in the shoulder. Griffin's scowl turned his way, and Martin calmly but firmly told him, "You will watch your language around my daughter, especially when she's carrying your child."

He pointedly raised an eyebrow at Griffin. Griffin still looked like he didn't understand, but then, *finally*, the pieces clicked together. And when they did, he looked absolutely horrified. His eyes snapped to Anna's stomach. "You're pregnant?" By the way he'd said it, you'd think she had a bomb strapped to her. I contained a sigh. I knew he'd react this way. So had Anna...it was why she hadn't told him.

Anna merely smirked at his comment though. Rolling her eyes, she said, "God, I hope our daughter somehow gets Kiera's smarts...otherwise she's doomed."

In the span of three seconds, something happened with Griffin that I *never* would have expected. His face morphed into an expression I'd never seen on him before. It was soft, warm, almost...fond. "Daughter? We're gonna have a girl?" he asked, his eyes shifting to Anna's face, a small, accepting smile on his lips.

Anna's eyes watered as she also saw the genuine tender emotion. She shook her head. "I don't know yet. I just feel like...I feel like we made a girl."

Griffin moved his hand to her stomach. It was like he'd suddenly become an entirely different person as he ran his thumb over where his child was resting, and in that instant...I could see it. I could see him as a father. I could see him caring for someone other than himself. And even weirder...I could see him being *really* good at it. Seeing it gave me hope. And damn if it didn't make me love him.

Thank you for showing me I was wrong, Griffin. Thank you for not being a douche. Maybe now I won't have to kill you.

I smiled when I heard Griffin murmur, "A girl...I'm gonna have a little girl?"

Anna's response made my eyes snap to her. "I don't know if I'm keeping her." Really? Was she still considering adoption? Couldn't she see how much he wanted this? I'd really thought his acceptance would change her mind.

Kiera's mom stepped forward, but Martin held her back. Everyone but Kiera looked stunned by Anna's statement, but no one was more stunned than Griffin. His gaze instantly returned to Anna's tear-streaked face. "What? You can't give away my kid," he said, a surprising amount of anger in his voice.

There was panic on Griffin's face as he started searching the bar for something...for me. His eyes locked on mine, and they were wide with fear; I'd never seen him look this way either, like something he cherished was about to be stolen from him. "She can't do that, right, Kell? Don't I have a say?"

I'd never wished more desperately to have an answer for him, but I had no fucking clue. I didn't have any experience with this. I could tell he wanted comfort, but I didn't have any to give him. I floundered for something to say, but thankfully, I didn't have time to speak. Anna touched his cheek, returning his eyes to hers. Griffin trembled as she said, "I won't...if you want to keep her...if you want to do this with me...I won't give her up."

I noticed Kiera holding her breath, noticed her parents clenching their hands together, but I instantly felt relaxed. I'd already seen Griffin's truest, deepest desire—it had been written all over his face. I already knew what his decision would be, and I was smiling long before he finally said it. "Can we name her after my grandma?"

Anna started sobbing, and I saw the relief on her face as she hugged him. She wanted this baby too. She'd just been too scared, too worried, to admit it. But now, God, I'd never seen them look so happy. Evan and Matt glanced back at me, also smiling, also looking relieved. And excited. I was too, but as happy as I was about this, I still couldn't believe that *Griffin* was going to be the first one of us to have a child. Maybe it really shouldn't surprise me though. He *was* the most reckless one of us. He was going to need our help through this.

Matt confirmed that for me when I heard him lean down and tell Rachel, "One of us should probably tell her that Grandma's name was Myrtle."

Yes, he might be a good father, but Griffin was going to need a shit-ton of help to be a good parent. God help us all.

Chapter 36
MOVING FORWARD

I laughed at Matt's comment and Griffin's name choice. Evan twisted around to look at me. Shaking his head, he said, "Griffin is seriously going to be a dad? That's one of the signs of the apocalypse, right?"

Jenny, beside him, laughed, and I nodded in agreement. "Yep. Our fate has been sealed."

Evan laughed as I glanced at Anna and Griffin kissing. They seemed blissful, and I really hoped it lasted. But I had to wonder what this meant for them as a couple. Were they *together* now?

Returning my eyes to Evan, I said, "You know Griffin raising a child means we'll *all* be raising a child, right? We might need to intervene on occasion."

Evan nodded as he looked over at Anna and Griffin. "Yeah... we'll have Matt draw up a schedule, so one of us can always be within earshot."

I laughed at his comment. "That's an excellent plan."

Matt and Rachel had moved over to congratulate Anna and Griffin. Evan clapped my shoulder, then he and Jenny moved over with them. I could feel someone staring at me, and my eyes drifted over to Kiera. The look on her face was...odd. She was pale, her eyes were wide open, and her jaw was dropped in stunned surprise. My brow furrowed as I studied her expression. Why did she look like she'd just seen a ghost?

And that was when I remembered what was going on today. The monumental moment that I was not prepared for. All the blood drained from my face; I felt like all of it was draining from my entire body and something else was keeping me alive. Barely. I could feel the weight of eyes on my back, stares burning into me. My heart started racing. *No. I change my mind. I don't want to do this.*

I closed my eyes, willing them to leave...ordering myself not to turn and look. *If I don't look, he'll go away. It will be like this never happened.*

I felt someone cupping my cheeks. Kiera. "Kellan...it's time." Her voice was soft, encouraging, but it wasn't helping. My heart thundered in my chest. I felt faint.

Eyes firmly closed, I shook my head. "I can't, Kiera." Hating how weak I was, I grimaced as I cracked an eye open. "Ask them to come back later...I just can't right now."

Like she knew what I actually meant was I couldn't *ever*, Kiera shook her head and soothingly rubbed my cheeks. "You can do this, Kellan...I know you can."

She wants me to be strong. Brave. I can be brave. I let out a long, shaking exhale. Feeling anything but brave, I slowly twisted my head. Seeing Gavin in person was like a sock to the gut; it physically pushed me back a step, made tremors ripple through my body. Reaching down, I clenched Kiera's hand like a lifeline. Gavin was older than in his picture, but still, exactly the same. He was tall, lean but muscular, with thick sandy-brown hair, a strong jaw, and the familiar, almost unreal deep-blue eyes. Looking at him was like looking into my future...and I hated it. Because looking like him had been the root of most of my problems as a child. Because he *left* me.

He lifted a hand to wave at me. Like we were friends. Like we were *family*.

We're not. He didn't want me.

I don't want to know him. I don't want to need *him. This hurts too much...I can't...*

Fear and panic slammed into me so hard, I started violently shaking, like I was freezing, and I couldn't get warm. My gaze snapped to Kiera's, and I started begging for my sanity. "I can't...I can't do this...please, let's just go." *Don't make me do this.* I grabbed her arms, desperate to run. "I'll go anywhere you want to go. Let's just sneak out the back, and we can do anything you want to do..."

More words left my mouth, but they were incoherent to my brain. All I could think about was the fact that he was staring at me. He was here. And he was staring at me.

I. Can. Not. Do. This.

Kiera inhaled a deep breath and patiently waited for my words to run dry. I felt like I'd run a marathon once they had. Every part of me was exhausted. Every part of me ached. Absorbing the love in her tranquil eyes, I tried to calm my breathing, tried to squelch my fears. I only partly succeeded. "I'm scared," I finally whispered, and I felt a tiny amount of relief in the confession.

Kiera nodded, her eyes moist with sympathy. "I know...but I'm here, and I'll help you. Besides, what's the worst thing that could happen?"

I swallowed the lump in my throat. "*I could care.*" I wasn't sure if I'd said that out loud or not. If I had, Kiera's expression didn't change. I closed my eyes, gathering strength, then I nodded.

If I was going to get through this, I couldn't let fear and panic be my driving force. That would have me running out the door, not finally confronting him. There was only one thing that would help me confront him, and maybe Kiera was right...maybe it was time that I did exactly that: confront the son of a bitch.

Hardening my core, I let a lifetime of abuse stoke my anger, my armor. Twisting to face him, I gripped Kiera tight. Her fingers in mine gave me strength, and I sucked it up like I was dying from the lack of it. I started walking toward Gavin, letting my rage flare. Every step, I let myself get more and more angry until I was so furious I could barely see.

I was almost in his face when I finally stopped. He didn't react to my nearness, except to smile softly at me. "Hello, son," he whispered.

Son? I almost decked him for saying that. I think I would have if Kiera hadn't been holding my hand. I squeezed her fingers, hard. I gave Gavin a curt nod, since I couldn't speak yet, my throat was cinched tight. Then I waited for him to start the conversation. *What was so important that you had to hound me every day for six fucking months*? I glared as I waited, but he didn't say anything, he just kept fucking staring at me. *Now you have nothing to say? Really?* Fucking asshole.

That was when I felt a hand on my arm. I looked down to see Hailey giving me a cautious half-smile, and the raging anger inside me started diminishing. I'd been so focused on Gavin, I hadn't even noticed Hailey and Riley yet. Suddenly realizing how hard I was holding Kiera's hand, I made myself relax and back up a step.

Hailey put her hand on our little brother's shoulder. The tension dissolved in me as I looked at him. His hair was just a smidge darker than mine, but he had it in a messy shag that was a pretty fair imitation of mine. I had to wonder if that was intentional. His eyes were lighter, more of a spring-day blue than deep-lake blue. But his face...

It was like looking into the past, and I was instantly reminded of myself at his age...if I could see myself without the emotional scars that had hovered around me. Because I didn't see any trauma in the openness of Riley's expression, didn't see any sign of needing to be rescued in the innocence of his eyes. Looking at him choked me up. He was what I could have been...if life had given me a chance.

Hailey introduced us, and Riley—looking awestruck—extended his hand to me. "Wow, I watched some of your shows online. You're...really good. I just started playing the guitar, but I hope I'm as good as you someday." God, even his voice sounded like mine had, although, his lacked the edge of sarcasm, sadness, and fear.

Riley gave me a smile that matched the awe in his voice, and I laughed a little. He shouldn't idolize me...but it was sweet that he did. Scuffing his messy hair, I told him, "Maybe I can teach you a thing or two one day."

I heard Gavin making an emotional noise as he cleared his throat, and I peeked up at him. The look on his face was heavy with relief and regret. I felt trapped by his expression, and I couldn't look away from him. Now that the anger was gone, the pain was starting to return. And so was the desire to run.

Hailey said something to Riley about giving us a minute, then she pulled him away. I felt Kiera's hand in mine slipping, like she was going to leave too, and I instantly gripped her tight; I needed her here, I needed her strength. I felt like mine had completely left me.

Kiera put her hand on my arm, silently telling me that she wasn't going anywhere. Gavin looked pained as he started talking. "Look, I know you're mad at me...for walking out on you, and I don't blame you, but I was young and foolish, and I hope you can give me a chance to make—"

Every word out of his mouth rekindled the anger inside me. And the fact that—like Riley—his voice also sounded like mine. Holding onto the fire in my stomach, I cut him off with a question. "Do you know what they did to me?"

He looked genuinely confused as he furrowed his brow. "Who? Your parents?"

The word *parents* coming from him made a flash of rage go through me. Assholes was more appropriate. I gave him a stiff nod in answer, then asked him the only question that truly mattered to me. "Did you know what they would do...how they would raise me...when you left? Did you know what sort of people they were?" *If you did...just leave now. Because there will never be anything between us.*

He still looked confused. "John and Susan? What are you talking about?" His eyes narrowed as he studied me, and I couldn't tell if he was genuinely baffled, or if he just didn't want to admit it, admit he knew exactly what kind of hell he was leaving me in.

Hearing my parents' names from his lips was like a slap to the face, and I instinctively cringed. Needing an answer, I stepped toward him again, getting in his face again. My body coiled with tension as I clarified my question for him. "Did you know that you left me with people who would viciously abuse me...day in, day out?" Riley's innocence flashed in my mind. *That could have been me. You stole that from me. But did you do it on purpose?* Voice shaking with pain, I spit out, "Did...you...know?"

All the blood drained from his face, and he was suddenly sickeningly pale. His dark blue eyes filled with tears as he studied me, as he absorbed the fact that I wasn't joking, I wasn't exaggerating. My life had been shit. Complete and utter shit.

"Kellan...no...I had no idea. I thought..." He paused to swallow, and I swear he looked like he was about to be sick. Seeing that reaction softened me more than his words. It truly seemed like he didn't know. "I thought I was leaving you to a happy home, happier than I could have given you back then."

He reached out to touch my arm, and it was only then that I realized I was shaking. "I know you won't understand, but I was a mess back then. I didn't know what I was doing. I got caught up in something with your mother that...was a horrible mistake," he said with a sigh. Eyes widening, he quickly added, "Not that you were a mistake, just, the situation..."

The guilt on his face, the lingering revulsion in his expression as he realized what my childhood had been like, it...melted me. With a sigh, I looked at Kiera. I'd always told her our stories were similar. If I could erase what I knew about my parents, if I could put myself in Gavin's shoes...if I'd gotten Kiera pregnant...would

I leave so she and Denny could stay together and raise the baby in peace? I honestly wasn't sure what I would have done, but with how many times I'd tried to leave Kiera...I could see myself walking away. Walking away to save their relationship, to give my child the best chance at life, since Denny was by-far a better person than me...

No matter how much it cost me, killed me...I might have made the same choice and walked away. And if Gavin had misjudged his friend, if he'd felt the same way about John Kyle as I do about Denny? If his past had been wholly similar to mine... then I couldn't really blame him for leaving. If he was truly clueless, then maybe he was also blameless.

Still looking at Kiera, I told Gavin, "Yeah, I think I get that part." Kiera's eyes moistened as she stared at me, and I knew she could see the truth in my eyes. The guilt as I remembered what we'd done, as I contemplated abandoning my child. I was so grateful I'd never had to make that choice, that I didn't have to live with Gavin's regrets.

The empathy I felt sucked all the anger out of my body, filled it with acceptance. I nodded at Gavin as I stepped back, letting him know that I understood. He smiled at me, looking relieved. Then he said something that blew my mind.

"I tried to see you once, you know. When you were about Riley's age."

My jaw dropped as I stared at him. *He did*? "No, Mom never mentioned that you..." *Why hadn't he?*

Gavin's eyes lowered. "Yeah, she told me that you didn't know about me, that you believed John was your father." He glanced up to look me in the eye. "Was that true?"

That fucking bitch. Of course she wouldn't let me meet my father. Of course she wouldn't let me know that he thought about me...cared about me. Of course she would hurt Gavin by hurting *me*. I shook my head. "No, I've always known that I was a bastard child."

Gavin flinched, and his face filled with anger. "She convinced me that I'd hurt you by showing up in your life. That it was better if I stayed away...so I did."

He looked like he was beating himself up as he shook his head. His turmoil was as painful as his words. "She was manipulating me because I'd hurt her. I never should have listened to her. I should have tried harder to see you...I'm so sorry."

I could tell from the way he said that, that he meant he was sorry for all of it—for misjudging them, for leaving me with them, for not rescuing me. I had to turn away and close my eyes as the waves of pain crashed over me. My life could have been so different. All this time I'd hated him as much as my parents, on the rare occasions that I'd even let myself think about him. Most of the time I'd simply ignored the fact that he existed, that he'd ever existed. Because I'd felt so invisible to him. But I wasn't.

"I never knew you even thought about me," I whispered, my voice shaky.

He put his hand on my arm again. "Of course I did. What father could forget about his son, his firstborn?"

I looked back at him, hopeful, but still full of disbelief. Being wanted was too surreal...my go-to response was to reject the feeling. Gavin sighed as he looked at me. "I stayed away for the wrong reasons, thinking I was protecting you by letting you believe the lie, even after their deaths." His voice failed him and seeing him struggle broke something inside me—the final wall keeping him back. Clearing his throat, he said, "But I'm here now, and I'd like to get to know you."

Gavin slapped on a carefree smile. He extended his hand to me and casually said, "Hello. My name is Gavin Carter, and I'm your father."

The way he said it amused me. Grinning, I dropped Kiera's hand to grab his as I played along. "I'm Kellan Kyle...and I guess I'm your son."

Gavin laughed as we shook hands; the warm sound soothed a long-buried ache inside me, and I felt something...mending. "It's nice to finally meet you, Kellan."

I nodded. "Yeah...you too." And surprisingly...I meant that.

In a gesture of warmth, Gavin folded his other hand on top of ours. "I don't want to push you, but you have a home with us in Pennsylvania, Kellan. Whenever you're ready, you're always welcome there."

Welcome...it was such a foreign concept to me, something the child inside me yearned for. My immediate instinct was to reject it, to hide myself, protect myself. I knew I couldn't keep doing that though. I would have lost Kiera completely if I hadn't let her in. She'd taught me that I had to let myself be vulnerable if I ever wanted...*more* from life. And I did. Desperately. So, I nodded at him. *When I'm ready*.

Gavin clapped my shoulder. "Can I buy you a beer?" he asked.

I looked down at Kiera, wondering if she'd be okay with me separating myself from her party for a moment. She beamed at me, wetness on her cheeks and hope on her face. I knew her answer before she nodded. She wanted this for me. I'd known all along she'd wanted this for me. She kissed my cheek, then left us to our bonding.

I walked with Gavin the short distance up to the bar. Gavin ordered beers from Troy, who stared at us openmouthed, like he couldn't believe there were two of us now. I suppressed a smile as he handed us each a bottle. Troy had to see the family resemblance. It made me wonder if other people in the bar were noticing it too, but oddly...I didn't care. After going through that gut-wrenching experience with Gavin, telling the world he was my natural father suddenly seemed...easy.

Gavin smiled at me as he sat on a bar stool. He tilted his head toward where Kiera had disappeared. "Your girlfriend is very nice. She was quite kind to me. I hope you're not angry about what she did."

I glanced back at her; she was talking to Denny, back by her family. "Honestly...I was furious at first." I looked over at him and shrugged. "I'd worked so hard to ignore you, and she just went and...ruined it." I grinned as I shook my head. "She's always been able to wreck me."

Gavin chuckled. "The good ones always do."

I wondered briefly if he considered my mother to be one of the "good ones," but knowing what I knew about her, I figured probably not. *He must mean Hailey and Riley's mom.* Hailey had told me that her mother had died several years ago, when Riley was just a toddler. It didn't feel right to ask Gavin about it yet, so instead, I apologized for something that I genuinely felt bad about.

"Hey...I'm sorry I ignored you for so long. I should have...if I'd just...responded...maybe this wouldn't have been so hard."

Gavin looked at me a moment, then nodded. "And I'm sorry I...hounded you. I probably should have stopped after the first month or so."

I laughed as I remembered his relentlessness. "Well, Hailey did say stubbornness ran in the family, so..."

Gavin laughed at that, then he held his beer bottle out to mine. "To being stubborn," he said.

I clinked his bottle with mine as I laughed. And it felt...great.

We took a drink after the laughter died, then Gavin sighed. "Kellan...I'm so sorry about what happened to you, about what they did to you. You have to believe me, I didn't know. If I had known, if I'd even suspected what they were doing...I would have gotten you out of there so fast. Even if I had to steal you, I would have gotten you out of there. I'm so sorry..."

His eyes were brimming again, and I couldn't bear to look. My throat had closed tight on me; I couldn't even swallow. Staring at the bar, I nodded. It was too late for it to make a difference, of course, but fuck...it was so nice to hear that he *would* have rescued me.

He patted my back, and I finally looked up at him. "For what it's worth," he said, "you've handled your life extremely well. I'm so impressed by you."

Jesus. I had to look away again. Was he trying to kill me? I found myself shaking my head, murmuring, "You don't even know me. How can you be impressed by me?"

He sighed softly, and I looked over to see him smiling. "Riley shows me everything he can find on you. Your talent, your presence on stage, your success...it's clear you've managed to ground yourself somehow. I was impressed just watching you perform, but now that I *know* what you've gone through to get where you are...it just makes your journey all the more...inspiring."

My mouth popped open at that. *Inspiring*? That didn't sound right at all. Needing the world to start making sense again, I shook my head and tried to lighten the mood. "You sound just as ridiculous as Kiera."

He grinned. "Maybe wise is the better word."

I laughed at that, then rolled my eyes. "Maybe," I muttered.

I spent the rest of the night talking to Gavin, Hailey, and Riley. It made me feel a little guilty that I wasn't spending more time with Kiera's family, but Kiera never once seemed upset with me, as she flitted between groups, spending time with everyone who was celebrating with her.

Eventually, the bar turned into a raucous, rowdy place. Poetic Bliss had a show tonight, and they were already a couple of songs into their set. Conversations were much harder now. I'd talked Sam into letting Riley hang out in the bar, even though he was underage, and he and Hailey both looked like they wanted to close the place down. Gavin looked exhausted though. He was on East Coast time, and it was much later for him than me. Plus, today had been draining.

After gathering his children, he told me, "It was so nice finally meeting you, Kellan. I hope we can see each other again soon?" By the way he raised his eyebrow, I could tell he wanted an invitation. And I wanted to give him one.

"Want to...have breakfast tomorrow?"

I was actually a little nervous waiting for his response...I had no idea why. He instantly grinned and nodded. "That would be wonderful."

He reached out and hugged me then, and I instinctively stiffened. It was weird to have him hug me. The feeling faded, and I wanted to hug him back, but he was already gone. I settled for hugging Hailey instead. And then I gave Riley a one-armed squeeze. I grinned uncontrollably as they left the bar.

Kiera came up to me a second later. "Did your dad just leave?"

Wrapping my arms around her, I nodded. "Yeah, but we're meeting for breakfast tomorrow."

She grinned as she laced her arms around my neck. "Good, I'm glad." Tilting her head, she bit her lip for a moment. "How are you?" she finally asked.

I inhaled a deep breath, taking stock of my emotions. All I felt was...relief. And happiness. So much happiness. "I'm great, Kiera. Better than great." My smile faded as I stared at her. "Thank you. I never would have done that without you. I never would have let myself..." I paused to swallow the sudden lump in my throat. "You were right...I needed that."

Her glorious hazel eyes grew glossy as she nodded. "Still...I'm sorry it hurt you."

I gave her a soft smile. "Sometimes healing hurts."

Her face filled with love and compassion as she nodded again. Shaking her head, she leaned up to kiss me. "God, I love you," she murmured in my ear as she hugged me.

Closing my eyes, I hugged her back. "I love you too." *Always and forever.*

Kiera and I listened to the rest of Poetic Bliss's set, saying goodbye to friends and family as they left. Eventually, the show was done, and most of the people here for Kiera's party had left the bar. Even though the music had stopped, Kiera and I were slow dancing near the stage. I couldn't stop staring at her, couldn't stop being amazed by her. What would I be without her? I didn't even want to picture it.

Because I didn't want to be without her anymore. Not for a single day, and definitely not for months on the road again. And that was where my life was heading. Lana had already confirmed that for me when we'd started recording. Once the album was ready, the label wanted us to hit the ground running with another tour. There wouldn't be much of a pause for us, or much time for Kiera and me...if she stayed here.

Tilting my head, I began the conversation that I hoped would end with our lives completely changing. "So, graduate...what's next?"

She inhaled a deep, cleansing breath then gave me a radiant smile. "Anything...everything."

Everything. I loved the sound of that. I leaned down to kiss her. My hand curled around her neck, and I savored the moment for a minute before I pulled away. Resting my head against hers, I said, "I have to go back soon, to finish the album."

She seemed sad to be reminded of that fact. Her hand shifted to stroke my cheek as she sighed. "I know," she whispered.

"And after that...will be another tour...to promote the album." My smile felt sad to me; I didn't want to go without her again.

Kiera kissed the corner of my mouth, brightening my smile. "It will be okay," she said. "We'll find a way to stay close, just like we have the past few weeks."

I nodded. I knew we could keep going as we had been, and we would be fine—strong and secure—but I missed her. I wanted more. As Kiera laid her head against my chest, I debated how to ask for what I wanted. Kissing her head, I decided to just say it. "Come with me."

Kiera looked confused as she pulled back. "What? Go with you...where?" She looked at the front doors, like she thought I wanted to take her somewhere right now.

A soft chuckle escaped me. Tucking a lock of hair behind her ear, I murmured, "So cute..."

She frowned as she peeked up at me. The annoyance on her face amused me even more. "Come on tour with me. Hell, come to L.A. with me." *Right now, the day I leave, just come with me.*

A look of surprise flashed over her face, like she hadn't realized she could live there with me. But then she seemed sad, like she wanted to, but something was holding her back. She shook her head. "But my..." She stopped talking and her expression shifted into surprise again, like she'd suddenly remembered her major obligation here was over with.

Seeing that she'd grasped her newfound freedom made me smile. "You're done with school now. You can do whatever you want."

She frowned. "Shouldn't I have higher aspirations than being a groupie?"

I laughed at her word choice. "You're not a groupie if I invite you to come with us." Ducking down, I met her eye. "When are you ever going to have another chance like this, Kiera? You have the rest of your life to find a job...or never find one. That would be fine with me."

She pursed her lips. "My parents will be so proud."

True. They probably would hate the life I was suggesting. I was almost certain they'd get over it though. Eventually. I shrugged. "Blame it on me. They hate me, anyway."

Grinning, she shook her head. "They don't hate you...that much."

Maybe not hate, but they definitely didn't trust me. With time, I could win them over. Maybe. I gave Kiera a kiss, then sighed. "I don't care what you do, Kiera, I just want you with me." Remembering what Jenny had told me earlier, I saw a convincing argument that I could use. "And besides, don't you want to be a writer? Aren't you writing a book about us, about our life together?"

She raised an eyebrow, surprised that I knew that. With a grin, I shrugged again. "Jenny mentioned it...and I'd love to read it, when you're done."

She paused, biting her lip and wrinkling her nose. I knew why she looked that way. I knew exactly how her book would affect me. I still wanted to read it though. I still wanted to see how she saw me, no matter how much it hurt. Finally, she nodded. "When it's ready."

Happy that she'd agreed, I dipped her. She laughed when I pulled her back up. "Well, writing is something that can be done anywhere, and to be the best writer you can be, you'll need to do a lot of research. What better research could you have than traveling across the nation with me...and Griffin?"

She cringed at that thought, but then laughed. Squeezing her, I rested my head against hers again. "You could come back as often as you wanted, Kiera, to visit Anna...your friends, but I'd like us to do this together this time." *I really want this. Please say yes.*

Her arms tightened around my neck. Giving me a soft kiss, she said, "Okay, let's do it."

My smile was exuberant. She was going to be with me. I couldn't think of anything better. Except...that wasn't entirely true. What I'd wanted to ask her ever since her birthday suddenly leapt into my brain. I hadn't thought of a clever way to do it yet, but now...I saw an opportunity that was playful, sneaky, and amusing. But sweet too. Hopefully she'd forgive me for misleading her.

"There's only one problem, though." I said, shifting my grin into a frown.

She instantly copied my expression. "What's that?"

I exaggerated a sigh as I hung my head. "They don't let girlfriends tour on the bus with the band anymore..." *And by "they" I mean* me. *I want my* wife *to join me.*

"Oh..." she said. Her body sagged as disappointment filled her. She really did want to come with me. It thrilled me that she did.

My heart started racing at what I was about to say, and I was a little mystified that I was actually nervous. We'd already talked about getting married one day. She'd already told me she wanted that. We just hadn't talked about when. We hadn't talked about *now*. And that was what I wanted more than anything. I wanted to leave this bar married to her. It was my only wish. My nerves bubbled into soft chuckles, and Kiera instantly looked suspicious; my mischievous grin probably didn't help with that.

Giving her a casual shrug, I said, "They only let the wives come with." *So, marry me?*

Her jaw dropped open in a really satisfying way. So adorable. Smirking, I closed her mouth. "Wife?" she whispered, and I could tell she was wondering if I was sneakily proposing to her. *Yes, I am...and more. I want to marry you* right now.

Smiling, I ran my finger along her jaw. Sure, the situation I'd presented was a joke, but the request behind it was very much real. I wanted her to be my wife. I'd wanted it for a while now. I dropped the teasing lilt in my voice, so she would know I was being absolutely serious. "We've gone about as slow as I can go, Kiera. I love you. I'm sure that I want my life to always have you in it." I shrugged as I stared at her. "Are you sure about me?"

She instantly nodded. "Yes, I'm sure," she said, no doubt in her voice.

Grinning, I kissed her. *She said yes—to us, to this*. I didn't think she completely understood what I wanted, but she had no doubts about us anymore, so I couldn't think of one reason why we couldn't skip everything and just get married. She would understand my true desire soon enough. Because I was marrying her tonight. Nothing had ever felt more right. Hopefully, she felt the same.

Kiera wanted to kiss me longer, but I pulled back. Removing her hands from around my neck, I grabbed her right one. I pulled off her promise ring and placed it on her left ring finger. Then I repeated the movement with my ring and my left ring finger. And damn if it didn't feel natural to have that ring on my left hand. I'd never felt so complete. Until I absorbed the matching ring on Kiera's left hand. *Now* I'd never felt so complete.

Holding her left hand with mine, I brightly told her, "There, now we're married."

There were tears in her eyes as she shook her head at me. "I'm pretty sure it doesn't work like that, Kellan."

"Semantics," I said. Smiling at her, I placed her left hand on my heart, and my left hand on her heart. "We're married...you're my wife." I nodded at her, holding eye contact, desperately hoping she would understand, hoping she would agree. What could a legal document give us that we didn't already have? How could the way we felt about each other, the depth of love we had for each other, be anything other than a husband-and-wife bond? What more did we need than this?

Marry me, right now, right here. Be my wife.

Tears streaming down her face now, Kiera nodded and said, "And you're my husband..."

Relief flooded me. *She understands. She agrees. She* married *me. She just fucking married me!* Grabbing her face, I ended our simple, heartfelt wedding with a kiss that left me reeling. We were both laughing and crying when I finally broke apart from her. I suddenly wanted witnesses, I wanted someone to know. That was when Kiera waved someone over. I wasn't sure who was still here. When I saw it was Denny and Abby, I grinned. It should be them.

Abby's gray eyes watered when Kiera showed her our rings and told her we'd just gotten married. Denny briefly smirked and then shook his head, knowing full-well what we'd done was in no way legally binding. But I didn't care about it being legal right now. That wasn't the important part. It was *emotionally* binding, and that was all I really needed. The rest could be worked out later; I was just too impatient to wait that long.

Content smile on his face, Denny gave me a hug. "Congratulations, mate. I'm glad I could be here for it," he said, clapping me on the back and chuckling.

His support filled me with a tremendous amount of warmth. My eyes drifted to the floor as I laughed too. "Yeah, me too. It seems appropriate," I said, looking back up at him.

Denny nodded, then he hugged Kiera. She was crying so hard Abby had to hand her a napkin. She better stop it, or I was gonna lose it. The lump in my throat already made it difficult to swallow properly.

Denny whispered something to Kiera that I couldn't hear, then he pulled back and said, "But I'm happy that you did," so I figured it was something about our slim odds during our...rough patch. I felt pretty positive that those days were long behind us.

Beaming, Kiera told him, "Thank you...so much."

She started sobbing again, so I wrapped her in my arms and tried my best to lighten the mood. "Should we go home and celebrate?" I asked her, suggestively raising my eyebrows.

Kiera and Abby laughed. Denny shook his head again, but he was smiling. Kiera also shook her head. "No...we're going to go rent the best hotel room in the city." I lifted an eyebrow in surprise, and she giggled. "I am not spending my wedding night in the room right next door to my parents."

I laughed at her comment, and at the fact that she'd said it right next to Denny. And she hadn't felt bad about it. Neither had he...and neither had I. We'd all moved on, and we were all okay. I was so grateful for that. I started pulling Kiera away, so we could go start our life together, when another sudden thought struck me. Pausing, I looked back at Denny. He and Abby were slow dancing now. "I could probably scrounge up a couple of rings if you guys want to get married too?" I told him.

Kiera thumped my chest, but Denny laughed, amused. Abby raised an eyebrow. "Oh, no, I'm not getting married in a bar. I'm getting the whole shebang." Denny looked over at her, and she stared him down. He just smiled and hugged her. Smart man.

Looking at them made me laugh. Hell, everything was making me laugh. I'd just had the greatest day of my life, and I'd ended it by marrying the greatest person in my life. Everything seemed possible now—even the outrageous notion that my band might actually become something one day. But ultimately, that didn't matter. The only thing that mattered to me was the woman standing by my side.

My wife. My life. *Damn, how in the hell did I get so lucky?*

Acknowledgments

This one is for the fans, for everyone who begged me for more Kellan Kyle. You kept him in my thoughts, and as it turned out—I couldn't let him go either! A huge thank you to Lori and Becky for reading through the story for me and giving me the go-ahead. And an extra thank you to Lori for all the last-minute help—you're a lifesaver! Thank you, Madison Seidler, for fitting me into your busy editing schedule. Thank you, Hang Le, for another breathtaking cover (and for putting up with all my notes about shirtless guys). Thank you, HMG Formatting, for holding my hand and helping me through the conversion process. Thank you, Kim Loraine and Audibly Addicted, for helping me bring the audiobook to life. And thank you, Lysa Lessieur of Pegasus Designs, for making my website pretty. You guys are amazing, and I'm so happy and thankful for all your help!

A huge thank you to Tina Gephart for always checking on me and for always being there when I need some help. You're a doll! Thank you, K.A. Linde, for always being ready with rapid-fire answers whenever I toss random questions your way. You are still the world's greatest multitasker. Thank you, Wendy, Diksha, Amy, Jennifer, Charleen, Bel, Nicky, Mandee, Kathy, and everyone at Pete's, for always being so excited and supportive. It means a lot. Truly.

To all my readers—you guys are the absolute best! I hope you enjoy being in Kellan's head as much as I do. I had so much fun writing this book, and I sincerely hope you enjoy reading it. Hanging out with the boys again was such a blessing, and I'm so grateful that I'm still able to do this after all these years. And just in case you're wondering, yes, I *am* working on writing *Reckless* through Kellan's point of view. I'm not going to rush it, so it might take some time. Thank you in advance for being patient with me!

And lastly, thank you to my friends and family. I couldn't do this without your never-ending love and support. I love you all!

About the Author

S.C. Stephens is a bestselling author who enjoys spending every free moment creating stories that are packed with emotion and heavy on romance. Her debut novel, *Thoughtless*, an angst-filled love story featuring insurmountable passion and the unforgettable Kellan Kyle, took the world of romance by storm in 2009. Stephens has been writing nonstop ever since.

In addition to writing, Stephens enjoys spending lazy afternoons in the sun reading fabulous novels, loading up her iPod with writer's block–reducing music, heading out to the movies, and spending quality time with her friends and family. She currently resides in the beautiful Pacific Northwest with her two equally beautiful children.

You can learn more at:

AuthorSCStephens.com
Twitter @SC_Stephens_
Facebook.com/SCStephensAuthor
Instagram sc_stephens_